William Maxwell

THE CHÂTEAU

William Maxwell was born in 1908, in Lincoln, Illinois. When he was fourteen his family moved to Chicago and he continued his education there and at the University of Illinois. After a year of graduate work at Harvard he went back to Urbana and taught freshman composition, and then turned to writing. He has published six novels, three collections of short fiction, an autobiographical memoir, a collection of literary essays and reviews, and a book for children. For forty years he was a fiction editor at *The New Yorker*. From 1969 to 1972 he was president of the National Institute of Arts and Letters. He has received the Brandeis Creative Arts Award Medal and, for his novel *So Long, See You Tomorrow*, the American Book Award and the Howells Medal of the American Academy of Arts and Letters. He lives with his wife in New York City.

VINTAGE

INTERNATIONAL

ALSO BY WILLIAM MAXWELL

All the Days and Nights (1995)

Billie Dyer and Other Stories (1992)

The Outermost Dream (1989)

So Long, See You Tomorrow (1980)

Over by the River and Other Stories (1977)

Ancestors (1971)

The Old Man at the Railroad Crossing and Other Tales (1966)

Stories (1956)
(with Jean Stafford, John Cheever, and Daniel Fuchs)

Time Will Darken It (1948)

The Heavenly Tenants (1946)

The Folded Leaf (1945)

They Came Like Swallows (1937)

Bright Center of Heaven (1934)

THE CHÂTEAU

William Maxwell

THE CHÂTEAU

Vintage International

Vintage Books

A Division of Random House, Inc.

New York

First Vintage International Edition, November 1995

Copyright © 1961 by William Maxwell

All rights reserved under International and Pan-American
Copyright Conventions. Published in the United States by
Vintage Books, a division of Random House, Inc., New York,
and simultaneously in Canada by Random House of Canada
Limited, Toronto. Originally published in the United States
in hardcover by Alfred A. Knopf, Inc., New York, in 1961.

Acknowledgment for the epigraphs is made to Alfred A. Knopf, Inc.,
for the quotation from *A World of Love* by Elizabeth Bowen and to
W. W. Norton & Company, Inc., for the quotations from
The Letters of Rainer Maria Rilke 1892–1910.

Library of Congress Cataloging-in-Publication Data
Maxwell, William, 1908–
The château / William Maxwell.
p. cm. — (First Vintage international edition)
ISBN 0-679-76156-X
I. Title. II. Series.
PS3525.A9464C5 1995
813'.54—dc20 95-14183
CIP

Author photograph © Dorothy Alexander

Manufactured in the United States of America
10 9 8 7 6 5 4 3 2

For
{
E. B.

E. C.

M. O'D.

F. S.

W. S.
}

"... wherever one looks twice there is some mystery."
ELIZABETH BOWEN,
A World of Love

"And there stand those stupid languages, helpless as two bridges that go over the same river side by side but are separated from each other by an abyss. It is a mere bagatelle, an accident, and yet it separates. . . ."
RAINER MARIA RILKE,
letter to his wife, September 2, 1902, from Paris

"... a chestnut that we find, a stone, a shell in the gravel, everything speaks as though it had been in the wilderness and had meditated and fasted. And we have almost nothing to do but listen. . . ."
RILKE,
letter to his friend Arthur Holitscher, December 13, 1905, from Meudon-Val-Fleury

Part I

Leo and Virgo

Chapter 1

THE BIG OCEAN LINER, snow white, with two red and black slanting funnels, lay at anchor, attracting sea gulls. The sea was calm, the lens of the sky was set at infinity. The coastline— low green hills and the dim outlines of stone houses lying in pockets of mist—was in three pale French colors, a brocade borrowed from some museum. The pink was daybreak. So beautiful, and no one to see it.

And on C Deck: Something had happened but what he did not know, and it might be years before he found out, and then it might be too late to do anything about it. . . . Something was wrong, but it was more than the mechanism of dreaming could cope with. His eyelids opened and he saw that he was on shipboard, and what was wrong was that he was not being lifted by the berth under him or cradled unpleasantly from side to side. He listened. The ship's engines had stopped. The straining and creaking of the plywood walls had given way to an immense silence. He sat up and looked through the porthole and there it was, across the open water, a fact, in plain sight, a real place, a part of him because he could say he had seen it. The pink light was spreading, in the sky and on the water. Cherbourg was hidden behind a long stone breakwater—an abstraction. He put his head clear out into the beautiful morning and smelled land.

His lungs expanding took in the air of creation, of the beginning of everything.

He drew his head back in and turned to look at the other berth. How still she was, in her nest of covers. Lost to the world.

He put his head out again and watched a fishing boat with a red sail come slowly around the end of a rocky promontory. He studied the stone houses. They were more distinct now. The mist was rising. Who lives in those houses, he thought, whose hand is at the tiller of that little boat, I have no way of knowing, now or ever. . . .

He felt a weight on his heart, he felt like sighing, he felt wide open and vulnerable to the gulls' cree-cree-creeing and the light on the water and the brightness in the air.

The light splintered and the hills and houses were rainbow-edged, as though a prism had been placed in front of his eyes. The prism was tears. Some anonymous ancestor, preserved in his bloodstream or assigned to cramped quarters somewhere in the accumulation of inherited identities that went by his name, had suddenly taken over; somebody looking out of the porthole of a ship on a July morning and recognizing certain characteristic features of his homeland, of a place that is Europe and not America, wept at all he did not know he remembered.

THE CABIN STEWARD knocking on their door woke her.

"Thank you," he called. Then to his wife: "We're in France. Come look. You can see houses." He was half dressed and shaving.

They stood at the porthole talking excitedly, but what they saw now was not quite what he had seen. The mist was gone. The sky was growing much brighter. And they had been noticed; two tenders were already on their way out to the liner, bringing more gulls, hundreds of them.

"So beautiful!" she said.

"You should have seen it a few minutes ago."

"I wish you'd wakened me."

"I thought you needed the sleep," he said.

Though they had the same coloring and were sometimes mistaken for brother and sister, the resemblance was entirely a matter of expression. There was nothing out of the ordinary about his features, nothing ordinary about hers. Because she came of a family that seemed to produce handsomeness no matter what hereditary strains it was crossed with, the turn of the forehead, the coloring, the carving of the eyelids, the fine bones, the beautiful carriage could all be accounted for by people with long memories. But it was the eyes that you noticed. They were dark brown, and widely spaced, and very large, and full of light, the way children's eyes are, the eyebrows naturally arched, the upper eyelids wide but not heavy, not weighted, the whites a blue white. If all her other features had been bad, she still would have seemed beautiful because of them. They were the eyes of someone of another Age, their expression now gentle and direct, now remote, so far from calculating, and yet intelligent, perceptive, pessimistic, without guile, and without coquetry.

"I don't remember it at all," she said.

"You probably landed at Le Havre."

"I mean I don't remember seeing France for the first time."

"It could have been night," he said, knowing that it bothered her not to be able to remember things.

Mr. and Mrs. Harold Rhodes, the tags on their luggage read.

A few minutes later, hearing the sound of chains, he went to the porthole again. The tenders were alongside, and the gulls came in closer and closer on the air above the tenders and then drifted down like snow. He heard shouting and snatches of conversation. French it had to be, but it was slurred and unintelligible. A round face appeared, filling the porthole: a man in a blue beret. The eyes stared solemnly, unblinking, without recog-

nition as the face on the magic-lantern slide moved slowly to
the left and out of sight.

✤ ✤
✤

ON SHORE, in the customs shed at seven thirty, they waited
their turn under the letter R. She had on a wheat-colored traveling suit and the short black cloth coat that was fashionable that
year and black gloves but no hat. He was wearing a wrinkled
seersucker suit, a white broadcloth shirt, a foulard tie, and
dusty white shoes. He needed a haircut. The gray felt hat he
held in his hand was worn and sweat-stained, and in some mysterious way it looked like him. One would have said that, day in
and day out, the hat was cheerful, truthful, even-tempered,
anxious to do what is right.

How she looked was, Barbara Rhodes sincerely thought, not
very important to her. She did not look like the person she felt
herself to be. It was important to him. He would not have fallen
in love with and married a plain girl. To do that you have to be
reasonably well satisfied with your own appearance or else have
no choice.

He was thin, flat-chested, narrow-faced, pale from lack of
sleep, and tense in his movements. A whole generation of loud,
confident Middle-Western voices saying: *Harold, sit up straight
. . . Harold, hold your shoulders back . . . Harold, you need
a haircut, you look like a violinist* had had no effect whatever.
Confidence had slipped through his fingers. He had failed to be
like other people.

On the counter in front of them were two large suitcases,
three smaller ones, a dressing case, and a huge plaid dufflebag.

"Are you sure everything is unlocked?" she asked.

Once more he made all the catches fly open. The seven pieces
of luggage represented a triumph of packing on her part and the
full weight of a moral compromise: it was in his nature to pro-

6

vide against every conceivable situation and want, and she, who had totally escaped from the tyranny of objects when he married her, caught the disease from him.

They stood and waited while a female customs inspector went through the two battered suitcases of an elderly Frenchwoman. Everything the inspector opened or unfolded was worn, shabby, mended, and embarrassingly personal, and the old woman's face cried out that this was no way to treat someone who was coming home, but the customs inspector did not hear, did not believe her, did not care. There was the book of regulations, which one learned, and then one applied the regulations. Her spinsterish face darkened by suspicion, by anger, by the authority that had been vested in her, she searched and searched.

"What shall I tell her if she asks me about the nylon stockings?" Barbara Rhodes said.

"She probably won't say anything about them," he answered. "If she does, tell her they're yours."

"Nobody has twelve pairs of unused nylon stockings. She'll think I'm crazy."

"Well, then, tell her the truth—tell her they're to give to the chambermaid in hotels in place of a tip."

"But then we'll have to pay duty on them!"

He didn't answer. A boy of sixteen or seventeen was plucking at his coat sleeve and saying: "Taxi? Taxi?"

"No," he said firmly. "We don't want a taxi. One thing at a time, for God's sake."

The wind was off the harbor and the air was fresh and stimulating. The confusion in the tin-roofed customs shed had an element of social excitement in it, as if this were the big affair of the season which everybody had been looking forward to, and to which everybody had been asked. More often than not, people seemed pleased to have some responsible party pawing through their luggage. In the early spring of 1948 it had seemed to be a question of how long Europe would be here—that is, in a way that was recognizable and worth coming over to see. Before the Italian elections the eastbound boats were half empty. After the elections, which turned out so much better than anybody expected, it took wire-pulling of a sustained and anxious sort to get passage on any eastbound boat of no matter what size or kind or degree of comfort. But they had made it. They were here.

"Taxi?"

"I wish I hadn't brought them now," she whispered.

Tired of hearing the word "taxi," he turned and drove the boy away. Turning back to her, he said: "I think it would probably look better if we talked out loud. . . . What has she got against that poor woman?"

"Nothing. What makes you think exactly the same thing wouldn't be happening if the shoe were on the other foot?"

"Yes?" he said, surprised and pleased by this idea.

He deferred to her judgments about people, which were not infallible—sometimes instead of seeing people she saw through them. But he knew that his own judgment was never to be trusted. He persisted in thinking that all people are thin-skinned, even though it had been demonstrated to him time and time again that they are not.

In the end, the female customs inspector made angry chalk marks on the two cheap suitcases. The old woman's guilt was not proved, but that was not to say that she was innocent; nobody is innocent.

When their turn came, the inspector was a man, quick and pleasant with them, and the inspection was cursory. The question of how many pairs of stockings a woman travels with didn't come up. They were the last ones through the customs. When they got outside, Harold looked around for a taxi, saw that there weren't any, and remembered with a pang of remorse the boy who had plucked at his coat sleeve. He looked for the boy, and didn't see him either. A hundred yards from the tin customs shed, the boat train stood ready to depart for Paris; but they weren't going to Paris.

I: *Leo and Virgo*

Two dubious characters in dark-blue denim—two comedians —saw them standing helplessly beside their monumental pile of luggage and took them in charge, made telephone calls (they said), received messages (perhaps) from the taxi stand at the railroad station, and helped them pass the time by alternately raising and discouraging their hopes. It was over an hour before a taxi finally drew up and stopped beside the pile of luggage, and Harold was not at all sure it hadn't arrived by accident. Tired and bewildered, he paid the two comedians what they asked, exorbitant though it seemed.

The taxi ride was through miles of ruined buildings, and at the railway station they discovered that there was no provision in the timetables of the S.N.C.F. for a train journey due south from Cherbourg to Mont-Saint-Michel. The best the station agent could offer was a local at noon that would take them southeast to Carentan. At Carentan they would have to change trains. They would have to change again at Coutances, and at Pontorson. At Pontorson there would be a bus that would take them the remaining five miles to Mont-Saint-Michel.

They checked their luggage at the station and went for a walk. Most of the buildings they saw were ugly and pockmarked by shellfire, but Cherbourg was French, it had sidewalk cafés, and the signs on the awnings read *Volailles & Gibier* and *Spontex* and *Tabac* and *Charcuterie*, and they looked at it as carefully as they would have looked at Paris. They had coffee at a sidewalk café. They inquired in half a dozen likely places and in none of them was there a public toilet. The people they asked could not even tell them where to go to find one. He went into a stationery store and bought a tiny pocket dictionary, to make sure they were using the right word; also a little notebook, to keep a record of their expenses in. Two blocks farther on, they came to a school and stood looking at the children in the schoolyard, so pale and thin-legged in their black smocks. Was it the war? If they had come to Europe before the war, would the children have had rosy cheeks?

He looked at his wrist watch and said: "I think we'd better not walk too far. We might not be able to find our way back to the station."

She saw a traveling iron in a shop window and they went in and bought it. They tried once more—they tried a tearoom with faded chintz curtains and little round tables. The woman at the cashier's desk got up and ushered Barbara to a lavatory in the rear. When they were out on the sidewalk again, she said: "You should have seen what I just saw!"

"What was it like?"

"It was filthy. And instead of a toilet there was a stinking hole in the floor. I couldn't believe it."

"I guess if you are a stranger, and homeless, you aren't supposed to go to the bathroom in France. Are you all right?"

"Yes, I'm perfectly all right. But it's so shocking. When you think that women with high heels have to go in there and stand or squat on two wooden boards. . . ."

They stopped to look in the window of a bookstore. It was full of copies of "Gone With the Wind" in French.

THE LOCAL TRAIN was three coaches long. At the last minute, driven by his suspicions, he stepped out onto the platform, looked at the coach they were in, and saw the number 3. They were in third class, with second-class tickets. The fat, good-natured old robber who had charged them five hundred francs for putting them and their luggage in the wrong car was no-where in sight, and so he moved the luggage himself. His head felt hollow from lack of sleep, and at the same time he was excited, and so full of nervous energy that nothing required any exertion.

The train began to move. Cherbourg was left behind.

The coach was not divided into compartments but open, like

an American railway car. Looking out of the train window, they saw that the sky was now overcast. They saw hedgerows enclosing triangular meadows and orchards that were continually at a slant and spinning with the speed of the train. House after house had been shelled, had no windows or roof, had been abandoned; and then suddenly a village seemed to be intact. They saw poppies growing wild on the railroad embankment and could hardly believe their eyes. That wonderful intense color! They were so glad they had seen them. They saw a few more. Then they saw red poppies growing all through a field of wheat—or was it rye? They saw (as if seeing were an art and the end that everything is working toward) a barn with a sign painted on it: *Rasurel*.

Their eyes met, searching for some relief from looking so intently at the outside world. "We're in France," he said, and let his hand rest lightly in hers. The train came to a stop. They looked for the name on the station: *Valognes*. They saw flower beds along the station platform. Blue pansies. "*Pensées*," it said in the pocket dictionary. They saw a big blond man with blue eyes and bright pink cheeks. They saw a nice motherly woman. They saw a building with a sign on it: *Café de la Gare*. The station was new. In a moment this tiny world-in-itself was left behind. He looked at his watch.

"What time do we change?" she asked, smothering a yawn.

"At two. It's now seventeen minutes of one."

"We'd better not fall asleep."

He felt his right side and was reassured; his wallet and their passports were in his inside coat pocket, making a considerable bulge. "Is it the way you remembered it?" he asked anxiously. "I know there weren't any ruined buildings, but otherwise?"

"Yes. Except that we were in a car."

That other time, she was with her father and mother and two brothers. They went to England first. They saw Anne Hathaway's cottage, and Arlington Row in Bibury, and Oxford, and Tintern Abbey. And because she was sick in bed with a cold, they left her alone in the hotel in London while they went sight-seeing, and she had a wonderful afternoon. The chambermaid brought her hot lemonade with whisky in it, and it was the first time she had ever had any whisky, and the chambermaid took a liking for her and gave her a gold locket, which she still had, at home in her blue leather jewel case.

After England, they crossed the Channel and spent two weeks in Paris, and then they drove to Concarneau, which they loved. In her snapshot album there was a picture of them all, walking along a battlement at Carcassonne. That was in 1933. The hem of her skirt came halfway to her ankles, and she was twelve years old.

"What is Cinzano?" she asked.

"An apéritif. Or else it's an automobile."

. . . five, six, seven. Knowing that nothing had been left behind, he nevertheless could not keep from insanely counting the luggage. He looked out of the train window and saw roads (leading where?) and fields. He saw more poppies, more orchards, a church steeple in the distance, a big white house. Could it be a château?

The yawn was contagious, as usual.

"Where do you suppose the Boultons are now?"

"Southampton," he said. "Or they might even be home. They didn't have far to go."

"It was funny our not speaking until the last day—"

"The last afternoon."

"And then discovering that we liked them so much. If only we'd discovered them sooner." Another yawn.

"I have their address, if we should go to England."

"But we're not."

She yawned again and again, helplessly.

They no longer had to look at each hedgerow, orchard, field, burning poppy, stone house, barn, steeple. The landscape, like any landscape seen from a train window, was repetitious. Just when he thought he had it all by heart, he saw one of Van Gogh's little bridges.

Her chin sank and sank. He drew her over against him and put her head on his shoulder, without waking her. His eyes met the blue eyes of the priest across the aisle. The priest smiled. He asked the priest, in French, to tell him when they got to Carentan, and the priest promised to. Miles inland, with his eyes closed, he saw the gulls gliding and smelled salt water.

His eyelids felt gritty. He roused himself and then dozed off again, not daring to fall sound asleep because they had to change trains. He tried willing himself to stay awake, and when that didn't work, he tried various experiments, such as opening his eyes and shutting them for a few seconds and then opening them again immediately. The conductor came through the car examining tickets, and promised to tell him when the train got to Carentan. Though the conductor seemed to understand his French, how can you be sure, speaking in a foreign language, that people really have understood you? . . . The conductor did come to tell them, when the train was slowing down, on the outskirts of Carentan, but by that time the luggage was in a pile blocking the front of the coach, and they were standing beside it, ready to alight.

What should have been a station platform was, instead, a long, long rock pile. Looking up and down it as the train drew to a stop he saw that one of his fears, at least, was justified: there were no porters. He jumped down and she handed him the lighter suitcases, but the two big ones she could not even lift. The other passengers tried to get by her, and then turned and went toward the other end of the coach—all except a red-headed man, who saw that they were in trouble and without saying a word took over, just as Harold was about to climb back on the train.

What a nice, kind, *human* face . . .

All around them, people were stepping from rock to rock, or leaping, and it was less like changing trains than like a catastrophe of some kind—like a shipwreck. The red-haired man swung the dufflebag down expertly and then jumped down from the train himself and hurried off before they could thank him. Until that moment it had not occurred to Harold to wonder how much time they would have between trains.

He stopped a man with a light straw suitcase. "Le train à Coutances?"

"Voie D!" the man shouted over his shoulder, and when they didn't understand, he pointed to the entrance to an underpass, far down the rock pile. "De ce côté-là."

"Oh my God!"

"Why aren't there any porters?" she asked, looking around. "There were porters in Cherbourg."

"I don't know!" he said, exasperated at her for being logical when they were faced with a crisis and action was what was called for. "We'll have to do it in stages." He picked up the big brown suitcase, and then, to balance it, two smaller ones. "You stay here and watch the rest of the luggage until I get back."

"Who is going to watch those?" she demanded, pointing at the suitcases he had just picked up. "What if somebody takes them while you are coming back for more?"

"We'll just have to hope they don't."

"I'm coming with you." She picked up two more suitcases.

"No, don't!" he exclaimed, furious at not being allowed to manage the crisis in his own way. "They're too heavy for you!"

"So are those too heavy for you."

Leaving the big white suitcase and the dufflebag (two thousand cigarettes, safety matches, soap, sanitary napkins, Kleenex, razor blades, cold cream, cleaning fluid, lighter fluid, shoe polish, tea bags, penicillin, powdered coffee, cube sugar, etc.—a four months' supply of all the things they had been told they couldn't get in Europe so soon after the war) behind and unguarded, they stumbled along in the wake of the other passengers, some of whom were now running, and reached the underpass at last, and went down into it and then up another long flight of steps onto Track D, where their train was waiting.

"How *can* they expect people to do this?" she exclaimed indignantly.

Track D was an ordinary station platform, not another rock pile, and all up and down the train the doors of compartments were slamming shut. "It's like a bad dream," he said.

He left her standing with the luggage beside a second-class carriage and ran back down into the underpass, his footsteps echoing against the cold concrete walls. When he emerged onto Track A again, the train from Cherbourg was gone. Far down the deserted rock pile he saw the big white suitcase and the dufflebag; they hadn't been stolen. From that moment it was not merely France he loved.

He swung the dufflebag onto his shoulder and picked up the suitcase. It weighed a ton. The traveling iron, he thought. And Christ knows what else . . . His heart was pounding, and he had a stitch in his side. As he staggered up the steps of the underpass out onto Track D again, he saw that she was the only person left on the platform, beside the last open compartment door.

"Hurry!" she called. (As if he weren't!)

He thought surely the train would start without them, not realizing that it was full of ardent excitable people who would have thrown themselves in front of the engine if it had. They leaned out of all the windows all up and down the train, shouting encouragement to the American tourists, shouting to the conductor and the brakeman that Monsieur was here, finally, but still had to get the luggage on.

When the luggage had been stowed away in the overhead racks, they sat trembling and exhausted and knee to knee with six people who did not speak a word of English but whom they could not under the circumstances regard as strangers. A well-dressed woman with a little boy smiled at them over the child's

15

head, and they loved her. They loved her little boy, too. Looking out of the train window, they saw the same triangular meadows and orchards as before, the same tall hedgerows, and poppies without number growing in the wheat.

"It was very nice of that man to hand the suitcases down to you," she said.

"Wasn't it."

"I don't know what we'd have done without him."

"I don't either."

"What an experience."

Conscious that by speaking English to each other they were separating themselves from the other people in the compartment, and not wanting to be separated from them, they lapsed into silence. He made himself stop counting the luggage. After a time, the man directly across from them—a farmer or a laborer, judging by his clothes and his big, misshapen, callused hands— took down a small cardboard suitcase. They saw that it contained a change of underwear, a clean shirt, a clean pair of socks, a loaf of bread, a sausage, and a bottle of red wine that had already been uncorked. The sausage was offered politely around the compartment and politely refused. With dignity the man began to eat his lunch.

"What time is it?" Barbara asked.

Harold showed her his watch. If only there were porters in the station in Coutances . . . He looked searchingly at the other faces in the compartment. He was in love with them all.

There were no porters in the railway station at Coutances, and the crisis had to be gone through all over again, but nothing is ever as bad the second time. The station platform was not torn up, and he did not wait for somebody to see that they were in difficulty; instead, he turned and asked for help and got it. As he shook hands with one person after another, looking into their intelligent French eyes and thanking them with all his heart, he began to feel as if an unlimited amount of kindness had been deposited somewhere to his account and he had only to draw on it. Coupled with this daring idea was an even more dangerous one: he was becoming convinced by what had happened to them that in France things are different, and people more the way one would like them to be.

At Pontorson he saw a baggage truck and helped himself to it, thinking that this time he had surely gone too far and an indignant station agent would come running out and make a scene. No one paid any attention to him. The bus parked in front of the station said *Le Mont-Saint-Michel* over the windshield but it was empty, and they discovered from a timetable posted on the wall nearby that it did not leave for an hour and a half. He looked at her drawn, white face and then walked out into the middle of the station plaza in search of a taxi. The square was deserted. For a moment he did not know what to do. Then he saw a bus approaching and hailed it. The bus came to a stop in front of him, and he saw the letters *St. Servan–St. Malo* and that there were no passengers.

"Nous cherchons un hôtel," he said when the driver put his head close to the open window. "Nous avons beaucoup de baggages, et il n'y a pas de taxi. . . . Ma femme est malade," he lied, out of desperation, and then corrected it in favor of the truth. "Elle est très fatiguée. Nous désirons—"

The door swung open invitingly and he hopped in. The big bus made a complete turn in the middle of the square and came to a stop in front of the pile of luggage. He jumped out and ran into the station and found Barbara, and they got in the bus, which went racing through the very narrow, curving streets, at what seemed like sixty miles an hour, and stopped in front of a small hotel. The driver refused to take any money, shook hands, and drove on.

Harold took the precaution of looking the hotel up in the Guide Michelin. "Simple mais assez confortable," it said. He stuffed the Michelin back in his raincoat pocket.

The hotel was old and dark and it smelled of roasting coffee beans. The concierge led them up a flight of stairs and around a corner, to a room with windows looking out on the street. The room was vast. So was the double bed. So was the adjoining bathroom. There was no difficulty about hot water. The concierge took their passports and went off down the hall.

"Whenever I close my eyes I see houses without any roofs," he said.

"So do I."

"And church steeples." He loosened his tie and sat down to take off his shoes. "And Cinzano signs."

The automatic images fell on top of one another, as though they were being dealt like playing cards.

"There's something queer about this bed," she said. "Feel it."

"I don't have to. I can see from here. I don't think we'll have any trouble sleeping, though."

"No."

"The way I feel, I could sleep hanging from a hook."

While she was undressing, he went into the bathroom and turned on both faucets. Above the sound of the plunging water, he heard her saying something to him from the adjoining room. What she said was, she was glad they hadn't gone on to Mont-Saint-Michel.

"I am too," he called back. "I don't think I could bear it. If I saw something beautiful right now, I'd burst into tears. The only thing in the world that appeals to me is a hot bath."

The waitress was at the foot of the stairs when they came down, an hour later. "Vous désirez un apéritif, monsieur-dame?"

She hadn't the slightest objection to their sitting at one of the tables outdoors, in front of the hotel, and before they settled down, he raced back upstairs and got the camera and took Barbara's picture. He managed to get in also the furled blue and white striped umbrella, the portable green fence with geraniums and salvia growing in flower boxes along the top and bottom, and the blue morning-glories climbing on strings beside the hotel door.

"Quel apéritif?" demanded the waitress, when the camera had

been put away. Finding that they didn't know, because they had had no experience in the matter, she took it upon herself to begin their education. She returned with two glasses and six bottles on a big painted tin tray, and let them try one apéritif after another, and, when they had made their decision, urged them to have the seven-course dinner rather than the five; the seven-course dinner began with écrevisses.

"Ecrevisses" turned out to be tiny crawfish, fried, with tartar sauce. There were only two other guests in the dining room, a man and a woman who spoke in such low tones and were so absorbed in each other that it was quite clear to anyone who had ever seen a French movie that they were lovers.

As the waitress changed their plates for the fourth time, Barbara said: "Wonderful food!" The color had come back into her face.

"Wonderful wine," Harold said, and asked the waitress what it was that they were drinking. The wine was Algerian and had no name, so he couldn't write it down in his little notebook.

When they went up to their room, the images started coming once more. Their eyelids ached. They felt strung on wires.

The street outside their window was as quiet as a cemetery. They undressed and sank sighing into the enormous bed, so like a mother to them in their need of rest.

AFTER TEN O'CLOCK there was no sound in the little hotel, and no traffic in the street. The night trucks passed by a different route.

At midnight it rained. Between three and four in the morning, the sky cleared and there were stars. The wind was off the sea. The air was fresh. A night bird sang.

The sleepers knew nothing whatever about any of this. One minute they were dropping off to sleep and the next they heard shouting and opened their eyes to broad daylight. When they sat up in bed they saw that the street was full of people, walking or riding bicycles. The women all wore shapeless long black cotton dresses. An old woman went by, leading her cow. Chickens and geese. Goats. The shops were all open. A man with a vegetable cart was shouting that his string beans were tender and his melons ripe.

"It's like being in the front row at the theater," she said. "How do you feel?"

"Wonderful."

"So do I. Do you think if I pressed this button anything would happen?"

"You mean like breakfast?"

She nodded.

"Try it," he said with a yawn.

Five minutes later there was a knock at the door and the waitress came in with a breakfast tray. "Bonjour, monsieur-dame."

"Bonjour, mademoiselle," he said.

"Avez-vous bien dormi?"

"Oui, merci. Très bien. Et vous?"

"Moi aussi."

"Little goat, bleat. Little table, appear," Harold said as the door closed after her. "Have some coffee."

After breakfast, they got up and dressed. She packed while he was downstairs paying the bill. The concierge called a taxi for them.

"I hate to leave that little hotel," she said, looking back through the rear window as they drove off.

"I didn't mean for the taxi to come quite so soon," he said. "I was hoping we could explore the village first."

But he was relieved that they were on their way again. Six days on shipboard had made him hungry for movement. They rode through the flat countryside with their faces pressed to the car windows.

"Just look at that woodpile!"

"Look how the orchard is laid out."

"Never mind the orchard, look at the house!"

"Look at the vegetable garden."

Look, look. . . .

Though they thought they knew what to expect, at their first glimpse of the medieval abbey they both cried out in surprise. Rising above the salt marshes and the sand flats, it hung, dreamlike, mysterious, ethereal. "Le Mont-Saint-Michel," the driver said respectfully. As the taxi brought them nearer, it changed; the various parts dissolved their connection with one another in order to form new connections. The last connection of all was with the twentieth century. There were nine chartered sight-seeing buses outside the medieval walls, and the approach to the abbey was lined on both sides of the street with hotels, restaurants, and souvenir shops.

The concierge of the Hôtel Mère Poulard was not put out with them for arriving a day late. Their room was one flight up, and they tried not to see the curtains, which were a large-patterned design of flowers in the most frightful colors. Without even opening their suitcases, they started up the winding street of stairs. Mermaid voices sang to them from the doorways of the open-fronted shops ("Monsieur-dame . . . monsieur-dame . . .") and it was hard not to stop and look at everything, because everything was for sale. He bought two tickets for the conducted tour of the abbey, and they stood a little to one side, waiting for the tour to begin.

"Did you ask for a guide who speaks English?"

He shook his head.

"Why not?"

"I don't think there are any," he said, arguing by analogy from the fact that there were no porters in the railway stations.

"The other time, we always had a guide who spoke English."

"I know, but that was before the war."

"You could ask them if there is one."

But he was reluctant to ask. Instead, he studied the uniformed guides, trying to make out from their faces if they spoke English. At last he went up to the ticket booth and the ticket seller informed him disapprovingly—rather as if he had asked if the abbey was for sale—that the guides spoke only French.

It was their first conducted tour and they tried very hard to understand what the guide said, but names, dates, and facts ran together, and sometimes they had to fall back on enjoying what their eyes saw as they went from room to room. What they saw —stone carvings, stone pillars, vaulting, and archways—seemed softened, simplified, and eroded not only by time but also by the thousands and thousands of human eyes that had looked at it. But in the end, reality failed them. They felt that some substitution had been effected, and that this was not the real abbey. Or if it was, then something was gone from it, something that made all the difference, and they were looking at the empty shell.

They stood in front of the huge fireplace in the foyer of their hotel and watched the famous omelets being made. With their own omelet they had a green salad and a bottle of white wine, which was half a bottle too much. Half drunk, they staggered upstairs to their room and fell asleep in the room with the frightful curtains, to the sound of the omelet whisk. When they woke, the afternoon was half gone. Lying in one another's arms, dreamy and drained, they heard a strange new sound, and sat up and saw through the open casements the sea come rushing in. Within twenty minutes all the surrounding land but the causeway by which they had come from Pontorson was under water. They waited for that too to be covered, but this wonderful natural effect, so often described by earlier travelers, the tide at Mont-Saint-Michel, had been tampered with. The island was not an island any more; the water did not cover the tops of the sight-seeing buses; it did not even cover their hubcaps.

But another tide rising made them turn away from the window. All afternoon, while they were making love and afterward, whether they were awake or asleep, the omelet whisk kept beating and the human tide came and went under their window: tourists from Belgium, tourists from Denmark and Sweden and Switzerland, tourists from Holland, Breton tourists in embroidered velvet costumes, tourists from all over France.

In the evening, they dressed and went downstairs. The omelet cook was again making omelets in front of the roaring wood fire. Harold found out from the concierge that there was no provision in the timetable of the S.N.C.F. for a quick, easy journey by train from Mont-Saint-Michel to Cap Finisterre. They would have to go to Brest, which they had no desire to see, changing trains a number of times along the way. At Brest they could take a bus or a local train to Concarneau.

They stepped out of the hotel into a surprising silence. The cobblestone street was empty. The chartered buses were all gone.

Turning their back on the street of stairs, they followed the upward-winding dirt paths, and discovered the little gardens, here, there, and everywhere. They stood looking down on the salt marshes and the sandbars. Above them the medieval abbey hung dreamlike and in the sky, and that was where they were also, they realized with surprise. The swallows did not try to sell them anything, and the sea air made them excited. Time had gone off with the sight-seeing buses, and they were free to look to their heart's content. Stone towers, slate roofs, half-timbered houses, cliffs of cut stone, thin Gothic windows and crenelated walls and flying buttresses, the rock cliffs dropping sheer into the sea and the wet sand mirroring the sky, cloud pinnacles that were changing color with the coming on of night, and the beautiful past, that cannot quite bear to go but stands here (as it does everywhere, but here especially) saying *Good-by, good-by. . . .*

SHORTLY BEFORE NOON the next day, they returned to Pontorson by bus, left their luggage at the hotel, where their old room was happily waiting for them, and went off sight-seeing. The bus driver was demonically possessed. Dogs, chickens, old people, and children scattered at the sound of his horn. The people who got on at villages and crossroads kept the bus waiting while they delivered involved messages to the driver or greeted those who were getting off. Bicycles accumulated on the roof of the bus. Passengers stood jammed together in the aisles. On a cool, cloudy, Wednesday afternoon, the whole countryside had left home and was out enjoying the pleasures of travel.

St. Malo was disappointing. Each time they came to a gateway in the ramparts of the old town, they stopped and looked in. The view was always the same: a street of brand-new boxlike houses that were made of stone and would last forever. They took a motor launch across the harbor to Dinard, which seemed to be made up entirely of hotels and boarding houses, all shabby and in need of paint. The tide was far out, the sky was a leaden gray, the wind was raw. At Concarneau it would be colder still.

They bought postcards to prove to themselves later that they had actually been to Dinard, and tried to keep warm by walking. They soon gave up and took the launch back across the harbor. Something that should have happened had not happened; they had been told that Dinard was charming, and they had not been charmed by it, through no fault of theirs. And St. Malo was completely gone. There was nothing left that anybody would want to see. The excursion had not been a success. And yet, in a way, it had; they'd had a nice day. They'd enjoyed the bus ride and the boat ride and the people. They'd enjoyed just being in France.

They had the seven-course dinner again, and, lying in bed that night, they heard singing in the street below their window. (Who could it be? So sad . . .)

In the morning they explored the village. They read the inscriptions in the little cemetery and, in an atmosphere of extreme cordiality, cashed a traveler's check at the mairie. They stared in shop windows. A fire broke out that was like a fire in a dream. Smoke came pouring out of a building; shopkeepers stood in their doorways watching and made comments about it, but did not try to help the two firemen who came running with a hose cart and began to unreel the hose and attach it to a hydrant in a manhole. Though they couldn't have been quicker or more serious about their work, after twenty minutes the hose was still limp. The whole village could have gone up in flames, and for some strange reason it didn't. The smoke subsided, and the shopkeepers withdrew into their shops. Barbara saw a cowhide purse with a shoulder strap in the window of a leather shop, and when they reappeared a few minutes later, she was wearing the purse and he was writing "purse—1850 fr." in his financial diary.

They went back to the hotel and the waitress drew them into the dining room, where she had arranged on an oak sideboard specimens of woodcarving, the hobby of her brother, who had been wounded in the war and could not do steady work. The rich Americans admired but did not buy his chef-d'œuvre, the art-nouveau book ends. Instead, trying not to see the disappointment in her eyes, they took the miniature sabots (500 fr.), which would do nicely for a present when they got back home and meanwhile take up very little room in their luggage. The concierge inquired about their morning and they told him about the fire. A sliding panel in the wall at the foot of the stairs slid open. The cook and the kitchenmaid were also interested.

Upstairs in their room, he said: "I don't suppose we ought to stay here when there are a thousand places in France that are more interesting."

"I could stay here the rest of my life," Barbara said.

They did nothing about leaving. They squandered the whole rest of the day, walking and looking at things. As for their journey to Brittany, they would do better to go inland, the concierge said; at Rennes, for example, they could get an express train from Paris that would take them straight through to Brest.

The next morning, they closed their suitcases regretfully and paid the bill (surprisingly large) and said good-by to the waitress, the chambermaid, the cook, and the kitchenmaid, all of whom they had grown fond of. Their luggage went by pushcart to the railway station, and they followed on foot, with the concierge. Out of affection and because he was sorry to see them go, the concierge was keeping them company as long as possible, and where else would they find a concierge like him?

When they got off the train in Rennes, the weather had grown colder. There was no train for Brest until the next day, and so they walked half a block to the Hôtel du Guesclin et Terminus. Rennes was an ugly industrial city, and they wished they were in Pontorson. An obliging waiter in the restaurant where they ate dinner gave Barbara the recipe for Palourdes farcies. "Clams, onions, garlic, parsley," Harold wrote in his financial diary. It was raining when they woke the next morning. Their hotel room was small and cramped and a peculiar shape. Only a blind person could have hung those curtains with that wallpaper. They could hardly move for their luggage, which they hated the sight of. What pleasure could they possibly have at the seashore in this weather? They decided to go farther inland, to Le Mans, in the hope that it would be warmer. When they got there, they could decide whether to take the train to Brest or one going in the opposite direction, to Paris. But they had not planned to be in Paris until September, and perhaps they would like Le Mans enough to stay there a week. They had arranged to spend the two weeks after that as paying guests at a château in Touraine.

Late that same afternoon, pale and tired after two train journeys—Le Mans was hideous—they stood in the lobby of the Hôtel Univers in Tours, watching the profile of the concierge, who was telephoning for them and committed heart and soul to their cause. With the door of the phone booth closed, they couldn't hear what he said to the long-distance operator, but they could tell instantly by the way he shed his mask of indifference that he was talking to someone at the château. They watched his eyes, his expression, his sallow French face, for clues.

The call was brief. The concierge put the receiver back on its hook and, turning, pushed open the glass door. "I talked to Mme Viénot herself," he said. "It's all right for you to come."

"Thank God," Harold said. "Now we can relax."

Taking Barbara's arm above the elbow, he guided her across the lobby to the street door. Outside, a white-gloved policeman directed the flow of Saturday-afternoon bicycle traffic around the orange and green flower beds in the middle of a busy intersection.

"I think I've seen that building before," she said, meaning the Hôtel de Ville, directly across the street. He consulted a green Michelin guide to the château country that he had bought in the railway station in Le Mans. The Hôtel de Ville was not starred, and the tricolor flags that hung in clusters along the façade, between caryatids, were old and faded. This was true everywhere they went, and it had begun to trouble him. In the paintings they were always vivid and fresh. Was something not here that used to be here and everywhere in France? Had they come too late?

The cathedral (**) and the Place Plumereau (*) and the Maison de Tristan (*) all appeared to be at a considerable distance, and since it was late in the afternoon and they did not want to walk far, they decided in favor of the leafy avenue de Grammont, which was wide enough to accommodate not only an inner avenue of trees but also a double row of wooden booths hemmed in by traffic and the streetcar tracks. Unable to stop looking, they stared at the patrons of sidewalk cafés and stood in front of shop windows. What were "rillettes de Tours"? Should they buy a jar?

Eventually they crossed over into the middle of the street and moved from booth to booth, conscientiously examining pots and pans, pink rayon underwear, dress materials, sweaters, scarves, suspenders, aprons, packets of pins and needles, buttons, thread, women's hats, men's haberdashery, knitted bathing suits, toys, stationery, romantic and erotic novels, candy, shoes, fake jewelry, machine-made objets d'art, the dreadful dead-end of the Industrial Revolution, all so discouraging to the acquisitive eye that cannot keep from looking, so exhausting to the snobbish mind that, like a machine itself, rejects and rejects and rejects and rejects.

With their heads aching from all they had looked at, they found their way back to the hotel. Tours was very old, and they had expected to like it very much. They had not expected it to be a big modern commercial city, and they were disappointed. But that evening they were given a second chance. They went for a walk after dinner and came upon a street fair all lit up with festoons of electric lights and ready to do business with the wide-eyed and the young, who for one reason and another (the evening was chilly, the franc not yet stabilized) had stayed away. There was only a handful of people walking up and down the dirt avenues, and they didn't seem eager to part with their money. The ticking lotto wheels stopped time after time on the lucky number, the roulette paid double, but no one carried off a sexy lamp, a genuine oriental rug, a kewpie doll. In this twilight of innocence, nobody believed enough in his own future to patronize the fortunetelling machine. No sportif character drew a bead on the plastic ducks in the shooting gallery. The festooned light bulbs were noticeably small and dim. With no takers, the familiar enticements were revealed in the light of their true age—tired, old, worn out at last.

"It makes me feel bad," Harold said. He loved carnivals. "They can't keep going much longer, if it's always like this."

He stepped up to a booth, bought two tickets for the little racing cars that bump, and entered the sum of twenty francs in his financial diary. Only one other car had somebody in it—a young man and his girl. When Harold and Barbara bumped into them, the young man wheeled around and came at them again with so much momentum that it made their heads jerk. He was smiling unpleasantly. It crossed Harold's mind that there was something here that was not like the French movies—that they had been bumped too hard because they were Americans. He saw the young man preparing to come at them again, and steered his own car in such a way that they couldn't be reached. But unless you did bump somebody, the little cars were not exciting. And all the empty ones, evoking a gaiety that ought to have been here and wasn't, reminded them of their isolation as tourists in a country they could look at but never really know, the way they knew America. They bought a bag of white taffy, which turned out to be inedible, and then stood looking at the merry-go-round, the Ferris wheel, the flying swings, the whip—all of them empty and revolving inanely up, down, and around. The carnival occupied a good-sized city block, and in its own blighted way it was beautiful.

He said soberly: "It's as if the secret of perpetual motion that my Grandmother Mitchell was always talking about had been discovered at last, and nobody cared."

But somebody did care, somebody was enjoying himself—a little French boy, wide awake and on his own at an hour when, in America at least, it is generally agreed that children should be asleep in their beds. Since he did not have to pay for his pleasure, they assumed that he was the child of one of the concessionaires. They tried to make friends with him and failed: he had no need of friends. Liberty was what he cared about—Liberty and Vertigo. He climbed on the merry-go-round and in a moment or two the baroque animals began to move with a slow, dreamlike, plunging gait. The little boy sat astride a unicorn. He rose in the stirrups and reached out with a long pole for the stuffed rabbit that dangled just out of reach. Time after time, trying valiantly, he was swept by it.

"I'd take *him*," Barbara said wistfully.

"So would I, but he's not to be had, for love or money."

The merry-go-round went faster and faster, the calliope

29

showed to what extremes music can go, and eventually, in accordance with the mysterious law that says: *Whatever you want with your whole heart and soul you can have*, the stuffed rabbit was swept from its hook (the little boy received a prize—a genuine ruby ring—and ran off in search of something new) and the Americans turned away, still childless.

She asked for a five-franc piece to put in the fortunetelling machine. The machine whirred initially and produced through a slot a small piece of cardboard that read: "En apparence tout va bien pour vous, mais ne soyez pas trop confiant; l'adversité est en train de venir. Les morts, les séparations, sont indiqués. Dans les procès vous seriez en perte. La maladie est sérieuse." She turned and discovered the little French boy at her elbow. Curiosity had fetched him. She showed him the fortune and he read it. His brown eyes looked up at her seriously, as if trying to decide what effect these deaths, separations, and lawsuits would have on her character. She asked him if he would like to keep it and he shook his head. She tucked the cardboard in her purse.

"C'est votre frère?" the little boy asked, indicating Harold.

"Non," she said, smiling, "il est mon mari."

His glance shifted to the bag of candy. When she put it into his hands, he said politely that he couldn't accept it. But he did, with urging. He took it and thanked her and then ran off. They stood watching while a bearded man, the keeper of a roulette wheel, detained him. The little boy listened intently (to what? a joke? a riddle?) and then he suddenly realized what was happening to him and escaped.

"I think he all but fell in love with you," Harold said. "If he'd been a little older or a little younger, he would have."

"He fell in love with the candy," Barbara said.

They made one more circuit of the fair. The carnival people had lost the look of wickedness. Their talent for not putting down roots anywhere, and for not giving the right change, and for sleeping with one eye open, their sexual promiscuity, their tattooed hearts, flowers, mermaids, anchors, and mottoes, their devout belief that all life is meaningless—all this had not been enough to sustain them in the face of too much history. They were discouraged and ill-fed and worried, like everybody else.

He bought some cotton candy. Barbara took two or three licks and then handed it to him. Pink, oversweet, and hairy, *it* hadn't changed; it was just the way he remembered it from his childhood. Wisps clung to his cheeks. He couldn't finish it. He got out his handkerchief and wiped his chin. "Shall we go?" he asked.

They started walking toward the exit. The whole failing enterprise was as elegiac as a summer resort out of season. They looked around one last time for the little French boy but he had vanished. As they passed the gypsy fortuneteller's tent, Harold felt a slight pressure on his coat sleeve. "All right," he said. "If you want to."

"Just this once," she said apologetically.

He disliked having his fortune told.

The gypsy fortuneteller sat darning her stocking by the light of a kerosene lamp. It turned out that she had lived in Chicago and spoke English. She asked Barbara for the date of her birth and then, nodding, said "Virgo." She looked inquiringly at Harold. "Scorpio," he said.

The gypsy fortuneteller looked in her crystal ball and saw that he was lying. He was Leo. Raising her eyes, she saw that he had kept his hands in his pockets.

She passed her thin brown hand over the crystal ball twice and saw that there was a shadow across their lives but it was not permanent, like the shadows she was used to finding. No blackened chimneys, no years and years of wandering, no loved one vanished forever into a barbed-wire enclosure, no savings stolen, no letters returned unopened and stamped *Whereabouts Un-*

known. Whatever the trouble was, in five or six years it would clear up.

She took Barbara Rhodes's hand and opened the fingers (beautiful hand) and in the lines of the palm discovered a sea voyage, a visitor, popularity and entertainment, malice she didn't expect, and a triumph that was sure to come true.

Chapter 2

THE AMERICANS were last in line at the gate, because of their
luggage, and as the line moved forward, he picked up a big
suitcase in each hand and wondered which of the half-dozen
women in black waiting outside the barrier would turn out to
be Mme Viénot. And why was there no car?

The station agent took their tickets gravely from between
Harold's teeth, and as he walked through the gate he saw that
the street was empty. He went back for the dufflebag and another suitcase. When the luggage was all outside they stood and
waited.

The sign on the roof of the tiny two-room station said:
Brenodville-sur-Euphrone. The station itself had as yet no
doors, windows, or clock, and it smelled of damp plaster. The
station platform was cluttered with bags of cement and piled
yellow bricks. Facing the new station, on the other side of the
tracks, was a wooden shelter with a bench and three travel
posters: the Côte D'Azur (a sailboat) and Burgundy (a glass of
red wine) and Auvergne (a rocky gorge). Back of the shelter a
farmyard, with the upper story of the barn full of cordwood
and the lower story stuffed with hay, served as a poster for
Touraine.

They waited for five minutes by his wrist watch, and then he
went back inside and consulted the station agent, who said that

the Château Beaumesnil was only two and a half kilometers out-side the village and they could easily walk there. But not with the luggage, Harold pointed out. No, the station agent agreed, not with their luggage.

There was no telephone in the station and so, leaving the dufflebag and the suitcases on the sidewalk where they could keep an eye on them, they walked across the cobblestone street to the café. He explained their situation to the four men sitting at a table on the café terrace, and learned that there was no telephone here either. One of the men called out to the proprietress, who appeared from within, and said that if Mon-sieur would walk in to the village, he would find several shops open, and from one of these he could telephone to the château.

Standing on the sidewalk beside the luggage, Barbara followed Harold with her eyes until the street curved off to the left and he disappeared between two slate-roofed stone houses. He was gone for a long, long time. Just as she was beginning to wonder if she would ever see him again, she heard the rattle of an ap-proaching vehicle—a noisy old truck that wheezed and shook and, to her surprise, turned into the station platform at the last minute and drew to a stop beside her. The cab door swung open and Harold hopped out.

In the driver's seat was a middle-aged man who looked like a farmer and had beautiful blue eyes.

"I was beginning to worry about you," she said.

"This is M. Fleury. What a time I've had!"

Sitting in the back of the truck, on the two largest suitcases, they were driven through the village and out into open country. The grain was turning yellow in the fields, and they saw poppies growing along the roadside. The dirt road was rough and full of potholes, and they had to keep turning their faces away to keep from breathing in the dust.

"This is too far to walk even without the luggage," he said.

"I'll have to wash my hair," she said. "But it's beautiful, isn't it?"

I: *Leo and Virgo*

Before long they had a glimpse of the château, across the fields. The trees hid it from view. Then they turned in, between two gate posts, and drove up a long curving cinder drive, and saw the house again, much closer now. It was of white lime-stone, with tall French windows and a steep slate roof. Across the front was a raised terrace with a low box hedge and a stone balustrade. To the right of the house there was an enormous Lebanon cedar, whose branches fell like dark-green waves, and a high brick wall with ornamental iron gates. To their eyes, accustomed to foundation planting and wisteria or rose trellises, the façade looked a little bare and new. The truck went through the gate and into a courtyard and stopped. For a moment they were aware of how much racket the engine made, and then M. Fleury turned the ignition off to save gasoline, and after that it was the silence they heard. They sat waiting with their eyes on the house and finally a door burst open and a small, thin, black-haired woman came hurrying out. She stopped a few feet from the truck and nodded bleakly to M. Fleury, who touched his beret but said nothing. We must look very strange sitting in the back of the truck with our luggage crammed in around us, Harold thought. But on the other hand, it was rather strange that there was no one at the station to meet them.

They had no way of knowing who the woman was, but she must know who they were, and so they waited uneasily for her to speak. Her eyes moved from them to the fresh Cunard Line stickers on their suitcases. "Yes?" she said coldly in English. "You wanted something?"

"Mme Viénot?" Barbara asked timidly.

The woman clapped her hand to her forehead. "Mme Rhodes! Do forgive me! I thought— Oh how extraordinary! I thought you were middle-aged!"

This idea fortunately struck all three of them as comical. Harold jumped down from the truck and then turned and helped Barbara down. Mme Viénot shook hands with them and, still amazed, still amused at her extraordinary mistake, said: "I

cannot imagine what you must think of me. . . . We were just
starting to go to the station to meet you. M. Carrère very kindly
offered his car. The Bentley would have been more comfortable,
perhaps, but you seem to have managed very well by yourselves." She smiled at the camion.

"We thought of telephoning," Barbara said, "but there was no
telephone in the station, and at the Café de la Gare they told
us—"

"We can't use the telephone after eleven o'clock on Sundays,"
Mme Viénot interrupted. "The service is cut off. So even if you
had tried to reach us by telephone, you couldn't have." She was
still smiling, but they saw that she was taking them in—their
faces, their American clothes, the gray dust they were powdered
with as a result of their ride in the open truck.

"The stationmaster said we could walk," Barbara said, "but
we had the suitcases, so I stayed with them, at the station, and
my husband walked into the village and found a store that was
open, a fruit and vegetable store. And a very nice woman—"

"Mme Michot. She's a great gossip and takes a keen interest
in my guests. I cannot imagine why."

"—told us that M. Fleury had a truck," Barbara finished.

Mme Viénot turned and called out to a servant girl who was
watching them from a first-floor window to come and take the
suitcases that the two men were lifting from the back of the
truck. "So you found M. Fleury and he brought you here. . . .
M. Fleury is an old friend of our family. You couldn't have come
under better auspices."

Harold tried to prevent the servant girl from carrying the two
heaviest suitcases, but she resisted so stubbornly that he let go
of the handles and stepped back and with a troubled expression
on his face watched her stagger off to the house. They were
much too heavy for her, but probably in an old country like
France, with its own ideas of chivalry and of the physical
strength and usefulness of women, that didn't matter as much as
who should and who shouldn't be carrying suitcases.

"You are tired from your journey?" Mme Viénot asked.

"Oh, no," Barbara said. "It was beautiful all the way."

She looked around at the courtyard and then through the open gateway at the patchwork of small green and yellow fields in the distance. Taking her courage in both hands, she murmured: "Si jolie!"

"You think so?" Mme Viénot murmured politely, but in English. A man might perhaps not have noticed it. Barbara's next remark was in English. When Harold started to pay M. Fleury, Mme Viénot exclaimed: "Oh dear, I'm afraid you don't understand our currency, M. Rhodes. That's much too much. You will embarrass M. Fleury. Here, let me do it." She took the bank notes out of his hands and settled with M. Fleury herself.

M. Fleury shook hands all around, and smiled at the Americans with his gentian-blue eyes as they tried to convey their gratitude. They were reluctant to let him go. In a country where, contrary to what they had been told, no one seemed to speak English, he had understood their French. He had been their friend, for nearly an hour. Instinct told them they were not going to manage half so well without him.

The engine had to be cranked five or six times before it caught, and M. Fleury ran around to the driver's seat and adjusted the spark.

"I never hear the sound of a motor in the courtyard without feeling afraid," Mme Viénot said.

They looked at her inquiringly.

"I think the Germans have come back."

"They were here in this house?" Barbara asked.

"We had them all through the war."

The Americans turned and looked up at the blank windows. The war had left no trace that a stranger could see. The courtyard and the white château were at that moment as peaceful and still as a landscape in a mirror.

"It looks as if it had never been any other way than the way it is now," Harold said.

37

"The officers were quartered in the house, and the soldiers in the outbuildings. I cannot say that we enjoyed them, but they were correct. 'Kein Barbar,' they kept telling us—'We are not barbarians.' And fancy, they expected my girls to dance with them!"

Mme Viénot waited rather longer than necessary for the irony to be appreciated, and then with a hissing intake of breath she said: "It's exciting to be in the clutches of the tiger . . . and to know that you are quite helpless."

The truck started up with a roar, and shot through the gateway. They stood watching until it disappeared from sight. The silence flooded back into the courtyard.

"So delicious, your arriving with M. Fleury," Mme Viénot said.

He searched through his coat pockets for a pencil and the little notebook, wherein the crises were all recorded: "Rennes départ 7ʰ50 Le Mans 10ʰ20, départ 11ʰ02," etc. Also the money paid out for laundry, hotel rooms, meals in restaurants, and conducted tours. This was a mistake, he thought. We shouldn't have come here. . . . He wrote: "100 fr transportation Brenodville-sur-Euphrone to chateau" and put the pencil and notebook back in his breast pocket.

Mme Viénot was looking at him with her head cocked to one side, frankly amused. "I wonder what it was that made me decide you were middle-aged," she said. "Why, you're *babies!*"

He started to shoulder the dufflebag and she said: "Don't bother with the luggage. Thérèse will see to it." Linking her arm cozily through Barbara's, she led them into the house by the back door and along a passageway to the stairs.

When they reached the second-floor landing, the Americans glanced expectantly down a long hallway that went right through the center of the house, and then saw that Mme Viénot had continued on up the stairs. She threw open the door on the left in the square hall at the head of the stairs and said: "My daughter's room. I think you'll find it comfortable."

I: *Leo and Virgo*

Harold waited for Barbara to exclaim "How lovely!" and instead she drew off her black suede gloves. He went to the window and looked out. Their room was on the front of the château and overlooked the park. The ceiling sloped down on that side, because of the roof. The wallpaper was black and white on a particularly beautiful shade of dark red, and not like any wallpaper he had ever seen.

"Sabine is in Paris now," Mme Viénot said. "She's an artist. She does fashion drawings for the magazine *La Femme Elégante*. You are familiar with it? . . . It's like your *Vogue* and *Harper's Bazaar*, I believe. . . . We dine at one thirty on Sunday. That won't hurry you?"

Barbara shook her head.

"If you want anything, call me," Mme Viénot said, and closed the door behind her.

There was a light knock almost immediately, and thinking that Mme Viénot had come back to tell them something, Barbara called "Come in," but it was not Mme Viénot, it was the blond servant girl with the two heaviest suitcases. As she set them down in the middle of the room, Barbara said "Merci," and the girl smiled at her. She came back three more times, with the rest of the luggage, and the last time, just before she turned away, she allowed her gaze to linger on the two Americans for a second. She seemed to be expecting them to understand something, and to be slightly at a loss when they didn't.

"Should we have tipped her?" Barbara asked, when they were alone again.

"I don't think so. The *service* is probably *compris*," Harold said, partly because he was never willing to believe that the simplest explanation is the right one, and partly because he was confused in his mind about the ethics of tipping and felt that, fundamentally, it was impolite. If he were a servant, he would resent it; and refuse the tip to show that he was not a servant. So he alternated: he didn't tip when he should have and then, worried by this, he overtipped the next time.

"I should have told her that we have some nylon stockings for her," Barbara said.

"Or if it isn't, I'll do something about it when we leave," he said. "It's too bad, though, about M. Fleury. After those robbers in Cherbourg it would have been a pleasure to overtip him—if four hundred francs was overtipping, which I doubt. She was probably worrying about herself, not us." Trying one key after another from Barbara's key ring with the rabbit's foot attached to it, he found the one that opened the big brown suitcase. "What about the others?" he asked, snapping the catches.

"Maybe we'll run into him in the village," Barbara said. "Just that one and the dufflebag." She took the combs out of her hair, which then fell to her shoulders. "The rest can wait."

He carried the dufflebag into the bathroom, and she changed from her suit into a wool dressing gown, and then began transferring the contents of the large brown suitcase, a pile at a time, to the beds, the round table in the center of the room, and the armoire. She was pleased with their room. After the violent curtains and queer shapes of the hotel rooms of the past week, here was a place they could settle down in peacefully and happily. An infallible taste had been at work, and the result was like a wax impression of one of those days when she woke lighthearted, knowing that this was going to be a good day all day long—that whatever she had to do would be done quickly and easily; that the telephone wouldn't ring and ring; that dishes wouldn't slip through her nerveless hands and break; that it wouldn't be necessary to search through the accumulation of unanswered letters for some reassurance that wasn't there, or to ask Harold if he loved her.

Standing in the bathroom door, with his shirt unbuttoned and his necktie trailing from one hand, he surveyed the red room and then said: "It couldn't be handsomer."

"It's cold," she said. "I noticed it downstairs. The whole house is cold."

He glanced at the fireplace. The ornamental brass shield over

the opening was held in place with screws and it looked permanent. There was no basket of wood and kindling on the hearth.
In her mind the present often extended its sphere of influence
until it obscured the past and denied that there was going to be
any future. When she was cold, when she was sad, she was convinced that she would always be sad or cold and there was no
use doing anything about it; all the sweaters and coats and
eiderdown comforters and optimism in the world would not
help, and all she wanted him to do was agree that they would
not help. Unfortunately, she could not get him to agree. It was
a basic difference of opinion. He always tried to do something.
His nature required that there be something practical you could
do, even though he knew by experience that it took some small
act of magic, some demonstration of confidence or proof of
love, to make her take heart, to make her feel warm again.

"Why don't you take a hot bath? You've got time if you
hurry," he said, and turned to the bookcase. Because there
were times when he was too tired, or just couldn't produce any
proof of love, or when he felt a deep disinclination to play the
magician. At other times, nothing was too much trouble or exhausted his strength and patience.

His finger, in the pursuit of titles, stopped at Shaw and Wells,
in English; at Charles Morgan and Elizabeth Goudge, in French,
and so inconsistent from the point of view of literary taste with
the first two; at *La Mare au Diable*, which he had read in high
school and could no longer remember anything about; at *Le
Grand Meaulnes*, which he remembered hazily. The letters of
Mme de Sevigné (in three small volumes) he had always meant
to read some time. The *Fables* of La Fontaine, and the *Contes*,
which were said to be indecent. A book of children's songs, with
illustrations by Boutet de Monvel. A book of the religious
meditations of someone that he, raised a Presbyterian, had never
heard of. He said: "Say, whose books *are* these, do you suppose?"
and she answered from the bathroom in a shocked voice: "Why,
there's no hot water!"

41

"Let it run," he called back.

"There's no water to let run."

He went into the bathroom and tried both faucets of the immense tub. Nothing came out of them, not even air.

"It's the war," he said.

"I don't see how we can stay here two weeks without a bath," Barbara said.

He moved over to the washstand. There the cold-water faucet worked splendidly but not the faucet marked *chaud*.

"She said in her letter 'a room with a bath.' If this is what she means, I don't think it was at all honest of her."

"Mmmm."

"And I don't see any toilet."

They looked all around the room, slowly and carefully. There was one door they hadn't opened. He opened it confidently, and they found themselves staring into a shallow clothes closet with three wire coat hangers on the metal rod. They both laughed.

"In a house this size there's bound to be a toilet somewhere," he said, by no means convinced that this was true.

They washed simultaneously at the washbowl, and then he put on a clean shirt and went out into the hall. He listened at the head of the stairs. The house was steeped in silence. He put his head close to the paneling of the door directly opposite theirs, heard nothing, and placed his hand on the knob. The door swung open cautiously upon a small lumber room under the eaves. In the dim light he made out discarded furniture, books, boxes, pictures, china, bedclothes, luggage, a rowing machine, a tin bidet, a large steel engraving of the courtyard and Grand Staircase of the château of Blois. He closed the door softly, struck with how little difference there is in the things people all over the world cannot bring themselves to throw away.

The remaining door of the third-floor hall revealed a corridor, two steps down and uncarpeted. The fresh paint and clean wallpaper ended here, and it seemed unlikely that their toilet would be in this wing of the house, which had an air of disuse, of decay, of being a place that outsiders should not wander into. The four dirty bull's-eye windows looked out on the back wing of the château. There were doors all along the corridor, but spaced too far apart to suggest the object of his search, and at the end the corridor branched right and left, with more doors that it might be embarrassing to open at this moment. He opened one of them and saw a brass bed, made up, a painted dresser, a commode, a rag rug on the painted floor, a single straight chair. He had ended up in the servants' quarters.

Retracing his steps, he listened again at the head of the stairs. The house was as still as houses only are on Sunday. When he opened the door of their room, Barbara had changed back into her traveling suit and was standing in front of the low dresser. "I couldn't find it," he said.

"Probably it's on the second floor." She leaned toward the mirror. She was having difficulty with the clasp of her pearls. "But it's funny she didn't tell us."

"She has dyed hair," he said.

"Sh-h-h!"

"What for?"

"There may be someone in the room across the hall."

"I looked. It's full of old junk."

She stared at him in the mirror. "Weren't you afraid there'd be somebody there?"

"Yes," he said. "But how else was I going to find it?"

"I don't believe that she was about to go to the station to meet us."

"Do you think she forgot all about us?"

"I don't know."

He put on a coat and tie and stood waiting for her.

"I'm afraid to go downstairs," she said.

"Why?"

"We'll have to speak French and she'll know right away that Muriel helped me with those letters. She'll think I was trying to deceive her."

"They don't expect Americans to speak idiomatic French," he said. "And besides, she was trying to overcharge us."

"You go down."

"Without you? Don't be silly. The important thing is you got her to figure the price by the week instead of by the day. She probably respects you more for it than she would have if we—"

"Do you think if we asked for some wood for the fireplace—"

"I don't know," he said doubtfully. "Probably there isn't any wood."

"But we're right next door to a forest."

"I know. But if there's no hot water and no toilet— Anyway, we're in France. We're living the way the French do. This is what goes on behind the high garden walls."

"I don't trust her," Barbara said.

"Fortunately, we don't have to trust her. Come on, let's go."

Chapter 3

As they descended the stairs, they listened for the sound of voices, and heard the birds outside. The second-floor hall was deserted. In the lower hall, at the foot of the stairs, they were confronted with two single and two double curtained French doors. One of the single doors led to the passageway through which Mme Viénot had brought them into the front part of the house. He opened one of the double doors, and they saw a big oval dining table. The table was set, the lights in the crystal chandelier were turned on, the wine and water carafes were filled. "At least we're not late for dinner," he said, and pulled the door to.

The other single door opened into a corner room, a family parlor. Two large portraits in oil of the epoque of Louis XV; a radio; a divan with a row of pillows; a fireplace with a Franklin stove in front of it; a huge, old-fashioned, square, concert-grand piano littered with family photographs. In the center of the room, a round table and four straight chairs. The windows looked out on the courtyard and on the park in front of the château.

He crossed the room to examine the photographs. "Mme Viénot has changed surprisingly little in the last quarter of a century," he said. His eyes lingered for a moment on the photograph of a thin, solemn schoolboy in the clothes of a generation ago. "Dead," he said softly. "The pride of the family finished off at the age of twelve or thirteen."

"How do you know that?" Barbara asked from the doorway.

"There are no pictures of him as a grown man."

As he deferred to her judgment of people, so she deferred to his imagination about them, which was more concrete than hers, but again not infallible. (Maurice Bonenfant died at the age of twenty-seven, by his own hand.)

They went back into the hall and tried again. This time when the door swung open, they heard voices. The doorway was masked by a folding screen, and there was just time as they emerged from behind it to be aware that they were in a long pink and white room. Mme Viénot rose to greet them, and then led them around the circle of chairs.

"My mother, Mme Bonenfant . . ." (a very old woman)

"Mme Carrère . . ." (a woman of fifty)

"M. Carrère . . ." (a tall, stoop-shouldered man, who was slightly older)

"And M. Gagny . . . who is from Canada . . ." (a young man, very handsome, with prematurely gray hair and black eyebrows)

When the introductions had been accomplished, the old woman indicated with a smile and a slight gesture that Barbara was to take the empty chair beside her, and Harold sat down next to Mme Viénot.

Perceiving that their arrival had produced an awkward silence, he leaned forward in his chair and dealt with it himself. He began to tell them about his search through the village for the house of M. Fleury. "Je ne comprends pas les directions que Mme Michot m'a données, et par consequence il me faut demander à tout le monde: 'Où est la maison de M. Fleury—du côté de là, ou du côté de là?' On m'a dirigé encore . . . et encore je ne comprends pas. Alors . . . je demande ma question à un petit garçon, qui me prendre par la main et me conduire

chez M. Fleury, tout près de la bureau de poste. . . . Je dis
'merci' et je frappe à la porte. La porte ouvre un très peu.
C'est Mme Fleury qui l'ouvre. Je commence à expliquer, et elle
ferme la porte dans ma figure."

He saw that the tall middle-aged man was amused, and
breathed easier.

"Le garçon frappe à la porte," he continued, "et la porte
ouvre un peu. C'est le fils de M. Fleury, cette fois. Il écoute. Il
ne ferme pas la porte. . . . Quand j'ai fini, il me dit 'Un instant!
Attendez, monsieur! . . . J'attends, naturellement. J'attends et
j'attends. . . . La porte ouvre. C'est M. Fleury lui-même, les
pieds en bas, pas de souliers. . . . J'explique que madame et
les baggages sont à la gare et que nous désirons aller au château.
. . . Il entends. Il est très sympathique, M. Fleury, très gentil.
Il envoie son fils en avant pour prendre le clef du garage où le
camion repose. Le garage est fermé parce que c'est dimanche.
. . . Et puis, nous commençons. M. Fleury—" He paused, unable to remember the word for "pump," and realized that he was
out in deep water. "—M. Fleury pompe l'air dans les tires, et
moi, je lève quelques sacs de grain qui sont dans le derrière du
camion. Le camion est plus vieil que le Treaty de Versailles.
. . . Plusier années plus vieil. Et le fils de M. Fleury versait un
litre de petrol dans le tank, que est empty, et l'eau dans le radiator. . . ."

Out of the corner of his eyes, he saw Mme Viénot nervously
unfolding her hands. Was the story going on too long? He tried
to hurry it up, and when he couldn't think of the French word
he fell back on the English, which he hopefully pronounced
as if it were French. Sometimes it was. The camion that antedated
the Treaty of Versailles shuddered and shook and came to life,
and the company burst out laughing. Harold sat back in his
chair. He had pulled it off, and he felt flooded with pleasure.

There was a pause, less awkward than before. Mme Bonenfant confided to Barbara that she was eighty-three and a great-
grandmother.

Mme Viénot said to Harold: "M. Gagny has just been telling us why General de Gaulle is not held in greater esteem in London."

"So many noble qualities," M. Carrère said in French, "so many of the elements of true greatness—all tied to that unfortunate personality. My older brother went to school with him, and even then his weaknesses—especially his vanity—were apparent.

The conversation shifted to the Mass they had just come from. It had a special interest in that the priest, who was saying his first Mass, was a boy from the village. Mme Viénot explained parenthetically to the Americans that, since the war, young men of aristocratic family, really quite a number of them, were turning to the priesthood or joining holy orders. It was a new thing, a genuine religious awakening. There had been nothing like it in France for more than two generations.

The Americans were conscious of the fact that the gray-haired young man could have talked to them in English and, instead, continued to speak to the others in French. The rather cool manner in which he acknowledged the introduction implied that he felt no responsibility for or interest in Americans.

Harold looked around at the room. It was a long rectangle, with a fireplace at either end. The curtains and the silk upholstery were a clear silvery pink. The period furniture was light and graceful and painted a flat white, like the molding and the fireplaces, which were identical. So were the two horizontal mirrors over the Adam mantelpieces. In the center of the room, four fluted columns and a sculptured plant stand served as a reminder that in France neo-classicism is not a term of reproach. Along one side of the room, a series of French doors opened onto the terrace and made the drawing room well lighted even on a gray day. The circle of chairs where they were sitting now was in front of one of the fireplaces. At the other end of the room, in front of the other fireplace, there were two small sofas and some chairs that were not arranged for conversation. In its proportions and its use of color and the taste with which it was furnished, it was unlike any drawing room he had ever seen. The more he looked at it, the more strange and beautiful it became.

The sermon had exceeded the expectations of the company, and they continued to talk about it complacently until the servant girl opened the hall doors and removed the folding screen. The women rose and started toward the dining room. M. Carrère had to be helped from his chair, and then, leaning on his cane, he made his way into the hall. Harold, lightheaded with the success of his story, waited for the Canadian to precede him through the doorway. The Canadian stopped too, and when Harold said: "After you," he changed. Right in front of Harold's eyes he stopped being a facsimile of a Frenchman and became exactly like an American. With his hand on Harold's shoulder, he said: "Go on, go on," goodnaturedly, and propelled him through the door ahead of him.

In the dining room Harold found himself seated between Mme Carrère and old Mme Bonenfant. Mme Carrère was served before him, and he watched her out of the corner of his eye, and was relieved to see that there was no difference; table manners were the same here as at home. But his initial attempts to make conversation met with failure. Mme Carrère seemed to be a taciturn woman, and something told him that any attempt to be friendly with her might be regarded as being over-friendly. Mme Bonenfant either did not understand or was simply not interested in his description of the terraced gardens of Mont-Saint-Michel.

George Ireland, the American boy who had spent the previous summer at the château and was indirectly responsible for their being here now had said that it was one of his duties to keep Mme Bonenfant's water glass filled. Harold saw that there was a carafe of water in front of him and that her glass was empty.

Though she allowed him to fill it again and again during dinner, she addressed her remarks to M. Carrère.

As the soup gave way to the fish and the fish in turn to the entree, the talk ranged broadly over national and international politics, life in Paris before the war, travel in Spain and Italy, the volcanic formations of Ischia, the national characteristics of the Swiss. In his effort to follow what was being said around the table, Harold forgot to eat, and this slowed up the service. He left his knife and fork on his plate and, too late, saw them being carried out to the pantry. A clean knife and fork were brought to him with the next course. Mme Viénot interrupted the flow of wit and anecdote to inquire if he understood what was being said.

"I understand part of it," he said eagerly.

A bleak expression crossed her face. Instead of smiling or saying something reassuring to him, she looked down at her plate. He glanced across the table at Barbara and saw, with surprise, that she was her natural self.

After the dessert course, Mme Viénot pushed her chair back and they all rose from the table at once. Mme Carrère, passing the sideboard, lifted the lid of a faïence soup tureen and took out a box of Belgian sugar. The Canadian kept his sugar in a red lacquer cabinet in the drawing room, and Mme Viénot hers and her mother's in the writing desk in the petit salon. Harold excused himself and went upstairs to their room. Strewing the contents of the dufflebag over the bathroom floor, he finally came upon the boxes of cube sugar they had brought with them from America. When he walked into the drawing room, the servant girl had brought the silver coffee service and Mme Viénot was measuring powdered coffee into little white coffee cups.

The Canadian lit a High Life cigarette. Harold, conscious of the fact that their ten cartons had to last them through four months, thought it might be a good idea to wait until he and

Barbara were alone to smoke, but she was looking at him expectantly, and so he took a pack from his coat pocket, ripped the cellophane off, and offered the cigarettes to her and then around the circle. They were refused politely until he came to Mme Viénot, who took one, as if she was not quite sure what it might be for but was always willing to try something new.

"I think the church is in Chartres," Barbara said, and he knew that she had been talking about the little church at the end of the carline. There were two things that she remembered particularly from that earlier trip to France and that she wanted to see again. One was a church, a beautiful little church at the end of a streetcar line, and the other was a white château with a green lawn in front of it. She had no idea where either of them was.

"You don't mean the cathedral?" Mme Viénot asked.

"Oh, no," Barbara said.

Though there were matches on the table beside her, Mme Viénot waited for Harold to return and light her cigarette. Her hand touched his as she bent over the lighted match, and this contact—not accidental, he was sure—startled him. What was it? Was she curious? Was she trying to find out whether his marriage was really pink and happy or blue like most marriages?

"There is no tram line at Chartres," she said, blowing a cloud of smoke through her nostrils. "I ought to know the château, but I'm afraid I don't. There are so many."

And what about M. Viénot, he wondered. Where was he? Was he dead? Why had his name not come up in the conversation before or during dinner?

"It was like a castle in a fairy tale," Barbara said.

"Cheverny has a large lawn in front of it. Have you been there?" Mme Viénot asked. Barbara shook her head.

"I have a brochure with some pictures of châteaux. Perhaps you will recognize the one you are looking for. . . . You are going to be in France how long?"

"Until the beginning of August," Barbara said. "And then we're going to Switzerland and Austria. We're going to Salzburg for the Festival."

"And then to Venice," Harold said, "and down through Italy as far as Florence—"

"You have a great deal in store for you," Mme Viénot said. "Venice is enchanting. You will adore Venice."

"—and back through the Italian and French Rivieras to Paris, and then home."

"It is better not to try to see too much," Mme Viénot said. "The place one stays in for a week or ten days is likely to be the place one remembers. And how long do you have? . . . Ah, I envy you. One of the most disagreeable things about the Occupation was that we were not permitted to travel."

"The luggage is something of a problem," he said.

"What you do not need you can leave here," she said.

Tempting though this was, if they left their luggage at the château they would have to come back for it. "Thank you. I will remember if we . . ." He managed not to commit them to anything.

The Canadian was talking about the Count of Paris, and it occurred to Harold that for the first time in his life he was in the presence of royalists. His defense of democracy was extremely oblique; he said: "Is the Count of Paris an intelligent man?"—having read somewhere that he was not.

"Unfortunately, no," Mme Viénot said, and smiled. "Such an amusing story is going the round. It seems his wife was quite ill, and the doctors said she must have a transfusion—you say 'transfusion' in English?—or she would die. But the Count wouldn't give his consent. He kept them waiting for two whole days while he searched through the Almanach de Gotha."

"It was a question of blue blood?"

She nodded. "He could not find anyone with a sufficient number of royal quarterings in his coat of arms. In the end he had to compromise, I believe, and take what he could get." She took a sip of coffee and then said: "Something similar happened in our family recently. My niece has just had her first child, and two days after it was born, she commenced hemorrhaging. They couldn't find her husband—he was playing golf—so the doctor went ahead and arranged for a transfusion, without his consent —and when Eugène walked in and saw this strange man—he was a very common person—sitting beside his wife's bed, he was most upset."

"The blood from a transfusion only lasts forty-eight hours," Harold said, in his own peculiar way every bit as much of a snob as the Count of Paris.

"My niece's husband did not know that," Mme Viénot said. "And he did not want his children to have this person's blood in their veins. My sister and the doctor had a very difficult time with him."

On the other side of the circle of chairs, M. Carrère said that he didn't like Germans, to Mme Bonenfant, who was not defending them.

Mme Viénot took his empty cup and put it on the tray. Turning back to Harold and Barbara, she said: "France was not ready for the war, and when the Germans came we could do nothing. It was like a nightmare. . . . Now, of course, we are living in another; we are deathly afraid of war between your country and the Union of Soviet Republics. You think it will happen soon? . . . I blame your President Roosevelt. He didn't understand the Russian temperament and so he was taken in by promises that mean nothing. The Slav is not like other Europeans. . . . Some years ago I became acquainted with a Russian woman. She was delightful to be with. She was responsive and intelligent. She had all the qualities one looks for in a friend. And yet, as time went on, I realized that I did not really know her. I was always conscious of something held back."

She was looking directly at Harold's face but he was not sure she even saw him. He studied her, while she took a sip of coffee, trying to see her as her friend the Russian woman saw her—the pale-blue eyes, the too-black hair, the rouged cheeks. She must be somewhere in Proust, he thought.

"Never trust a Slav," she said solemnly.

And what about the variations, he wondered. There must be variations, such as never trust an Englishman; never trust a Swede. And maybe even never trust an American?

"Are French people always kind and helpful to foreigners?" he asked. "Because that has been our experience so far."

"I can't say that they are, always," Mme Viénot said. She put her cup and saucer on the tray. "You have perhaps been fortunate."

She got up and moved away, leaving him with the feeling that he had said something untactful. His own cup was empty, but he continued to hold it, though the table was within reach.

M. Gagny was talking about the British royal family. He knew the Duke of Connaught, he said, and he had danced with the Princess Elizabeth, but he was partial to the Princess Margaret Rose.

Mme Viénot sat down beside her mother, patted her dry mottled hand, and smiled at her and then around at the company, lightly and publicly admitting her fondness.

M. Carrère explained to Barbara that he could speak English, but that it tired him, and he preferred his native tongue. Mme Carrère's English was better than his, but on the other hand he talked and she didn't. Mme Bonenfant did not know English at all, though she spoke German. And the Canadian was so conspicuously bilingual that his presence in the circle of chairs was a reproach rather than a help to the Americans. Harold told himself that it was foolish—that it was senseless, in fact—to make the effort, but nevertheless he couldn't help feeling that he must live up to his success before dinner or he would surrender too much ground. A remark, a question addressed directly to him, he understood sufficiently to answer, but then the conversation became general again and he was lost. He sat balancing the empty cup and saucer in his two hands, looked at whoever was speaking, and tried to catch from the others' faces whether the remark was serious or amusing, so that he could smile at the right time. This tightrope performance and fatigue (they had got up early to catch the train, and it had already been a long day) combined to deprive him of the last hope of understanding what was said.

Watching him, Barbara saw the glazed look she knew so well —the film that came over his eyes whenever he was bored or ill-at-ease. As she got ready to deliver him from his misery, it occurred to her suddenly how odd it was that neither of them had ever stopped to think what it might be like staying with a French family, or that there might be more to it than an opportunity to improve their French.

"COULD YOU UNDERSTAND THEM?" he asked, as soon as they were behind the closed door of their room.

She nodded.

"I couldn't."

"But you talked. I was afraid to open my mouth."

This made him feel better.

"There's a toilet on this floor, at the far end of the attic corridor. I asked Mme Bonenfant."

"Behind one of the doors I was afraid to open," he said, nodding.

"But it's out of order. It's going to be fixed in a day or two. Meanwhile, we're to use the toilet on the second floor.

They undressed and got into their damp beds and talked drowsily for a few minutes—about the house, about the other guests, about the food, which was the best they had had in France—and then fell into a deep sleep. When they woke, the afternoon was gone and it was raining softly. He got into her bed, and she put her head in the hollow of his shoulder.

"I wish this room was all there was," he said, "and we lived in it. I wish it was ours."

"You wouldn't get tired of the red wallpaper?"

"No."

"Neither would I. Or of anything else," she said.

"It's not like any room that I've ever seen."

"It's very French."

"What is?" he asked.

"Everything. . . . Why isn't she here?"

"Who?"

"The French girl. If this was my room, I'd be living in it."

"She's probably having a much better time in Paris," he said, and looked at his wrist watch. "Come on," he said, tossing the cover back. "We're late."

After dinner, Mme Viénot led her guests into the family parlor across the hall. The coffee that Harold was waiting for did not appear. He and Barbara smoked one cigarette, to be sociable, and then wandered outside. It had stopped raining. They walked up and down the gravel terrace, admiring the house and the old trees and the view, which was gilded with the evening light. They were happy to be by themselves, and pleased with the way they had managed things—for they might, at this very moment, have been walking the streets of Le Mans, or freezing to death at the seashore, and instead they were here. They would be able to include this interesting place among the places they had seen and could tell people about when they got home.

From the terrace they went directly to their room, their beautiful red room, whose history they had no way of knowing.

The village of Brenodville was very old and had interesting historical associations. The château did not, if by history you mean kings and queens and their awful favorites, battles and treaties, ruinous entertainments, genius harbored, the rise and fall of ambitious men. Its history was merely the history of the family that had lived in it tenaciously, generation after generation. The old wing, the carriage house, the stables, and the brick courtyard dated from the seventeenth century. Around the year 1900, the property figured in still another last will and testament, duly signed and sealed. Beaumesnil passed from the dead hands of a rich, elderly, unmarried sportsman, who seldom used it, into the living, eager hands of a nephew who had been sufficiently attentive and who, just to make things doubly sure, had been named after him. Almost the first thing M. Jules Bonenfant did with the fortune he had inherited was to build against the old house a new wing, larger and more formal in design. From this time on, instead of facing the carp pond and the forest, the château faced the patchwork of small fields and the River Loire, which was too far away to figure in the view. For a number of years, the third-floor room on the left at the head of the stairs remained empty and unused. Moonlight came and went. Occasionally a freakish draft blew down the chimney, redistributing the dust. A gray squirrel got in, also by way of the chimney, and died here, while mud wasps beat against the windowpanes. The newspapers of 1906 did not penetrate this far and so the wasps never learned that a Captain Alfred Dreyfus had been decorated with the Légion d'Honneur, in public, in the courtyard of the artillery pavilion at St. Cyr. In September of that same year, Mme. Bonenfant stood on the second-floor landing and directed the village paperhanger, with his scissors, paste, steel measuring tape, and trestle, up the final flight of stairs and through the door on the left. When the room was finished, Mlle Toinette was parted from a tearful governess and found herself in possession of a large bedroom that was directly over her mother's and the same size and shape. The only difference was that the ceiling sloped down on one side and there was one window instead of two. With different wallpaper and different furniture, the room was now her younger daughter's. So much for its history. Now what about the two people who are asleep in it? Who are they? What is their history?

Well, where to begin is the question. The summer he spent in bed with rheumatic fever on an upstairs sleeping porch? Or the street he lived on—those big, nondescript, tree-shaded, Middle Western white houses, beautiful in the fall when the leaves turned, or at dusk with the downstairs lights turned on, or in winter when the snow covered up whatever was shabby and ugly? Should we begin with the tree house in the back yard or with the boy he was envious of, who always had money for ice-cream cones because his mother was dead and the middle-aged aunt and uncle he lived with felt they had no other way to make it up to him? Given his last name, Rhodes, and the time and place he grew up in, it was inevitable that when he started to go to school he should be called Dusty. Some jokes never lose their freshness.

It helps, of course, to know what happened when they were choosing up sides and he stood waiting for his name to be called. And about the moment when he emerged into the public eye for the first time, at the age of six, in a surgical-cotton wig, knee britches, buckles on his shoes, and with seven other costumed children danced the minuet in the school auditorium.

The sum total of his memories is who he is, naturally. Also the child his mother went in to cover on her rounds, the last thing at night before she went to bed—the little boy with his own way of sleeping, his arm around some doll or stuffed animal, and his own way of recognizing her presence through layers and layers of sleep. Also the little boy with a new navy-blue suit on Easter Sunday, and a cowlick that would not stay down. Then there is that period when he was having his teeth straightened, when he corresponded with postage-stamp companies. The obedient, sensible, courteous ten-year-old? Or the moody boy in his teens, who ate them out of house and home and had to be sent from the table for talking back to his father? Take your choice, or take both of them. His mother's eyes, the Rhodes nose and mouth and chin; the Rhodes stubbornness, his mother said. This book belongs to Harold Rhodes, Eighth Grade, Room 207, Central School. . . . And whatever became of those boards for stretching muskrat skins on, the skins he was going to sell and make a fortune from? Or his magic lantern and his postcard projector? Or his building blocks, his Boy Scout knife, his school report cards? And that medicine-stained copy of *Mr. Midshipman Easy?* And the Oz books? Somewhere, all these unclaimed shreds of his personality, since matter is never entirely lost but merely changes its form.

As a boy of thirteen he was called up on the stage of the Majestic Theater by a vaudeville magician, and did exactly what the magician told him (under his breath) to do; even though the magician told him out loud not to do it, and so made a monkey of him, and the audience rocked with perfectly kind laughter. Since then he hasn't learned a thing. The same audience would rock with the same laughter if he were called up on the stage of the Majestic Theater tomorrow. Fortunately it has been torn down to make a parking lot.

In college he was responsive, with a light in his eye; he was a pleasure to lecture to; but callow, getting by on enthusiasm because it came more natural to him than thinking, and worried about his grades, and about the future, and because, though he tried and tried, he could not break himself of a shameful habit. If he had taken biology it would have been made clear to him that he too was an animal, but he took botany instead.

But who is he? which animal?

A commuter, standing on the station platform, with now the *Times* and now the *Tribune* under his arm, waiting for the 8:17 express. A liberal Democrat, believing idealistically in the cause of labor but knowing few laborers, and a member in good standing of the money-loving class he was born into, though, as it happens, money slips through his fingers. A spendthrift, with small sums, cautious with large ones. Who is he? Raskolnikov—that's who he is.

Surely not?

Yes. Also Mr. Micawber. And St. Francis. And Savonarola. He's no one person, he's an uncountable committee of people who meet and operate under the handy fiction of his name. The minutes of the last meeting are never read, because it's still going on. The committee arrives at important conclusions which it cannot remember, and makes sensible decisions it cannot possibly keep. For that you need a policeman. The committee members know each other, but not always by their right names. The bachelor who has sat reading in the same white leatherette chair by the same lamp with the same cigarette box within reach on the same round table for so long now that change is no longer possible to him—that Harold Rhodes of course knows the bridegroom with a white carnation in his buttonhole, sipping a glass of champagne, smiling, accepting congratulations, aware of the good wishes of everybody and also of a nagging doubt in the back of his mind. Just as they both know the head of the family, the born father, with the Sunday paper scattered around him on the living-room rug, smiling benignly at no children after three years of marriage. And the child of seven (in some ways the most mature of all these facets of his personality) who is being taken, with his hand in his father's much bigger hand, to see his mother in the hospital on a day that, as it turned out, she was much too sick to see anyone.

What does he—what do all these people do for a living?

Does it matter?

Certainly.

After two false starts he now has a job with a future. He is working for an engraving firm owned by a friend of his father.

What did he do, where was he, during the war?

He wasn't in the war . . . 4F. He has to be away from Barbara, traveling, several times a year, but the rest of the time he can be home, where he wants to be. His hours are long, but he has already had two raises, and now this four months' leave of absence, proof that his work is valued.

And who is she? whom did he marry?

Somebody who matches him, the curves and hollows of her nature fitting into all the curves and hollows of his nature as, in bed, her straight back and soft thighs fit inside the curve of his breast and belly and hips and bent legs. Somebody who looks enough like him that they are mistaken occasionally for brother and sister, and who keeps him warm at night, taking the place of the doll that he used to sleep with his arm around: Barbara Scully. Barbara S. Rhodes, when she writes a check.

And what was her childhood like?

Well, where to begin is again the question. At the seashore? Or should we take up, one after another, the dogs, the nurse-maids? Or the time she broke her arm? She was seven when that happened. Or the period when she cared about nothing but horses? Or that brief, heartbreaking, first falling in love? Or the piles of clothes on the bed, on the chairs in her room, all with name tapes sewed on them, and the suitcases waiting to be filled?

Or should we open that old exercise book that by some accident has survived?

"One day our mother gave the children a party.

There were fourteen merry girls and boys at the party.

They played games and raced about the lawn with Rover.

But John fell from a tree and broke his arm.

Mother sent a boy to bring the doctor.

The doctor set the arm and said that it would soon be better.

Was not John a brave boy to bear the pain as he did."

Three times 269 is not 627, of course; and neither does 854 minus 536 equal 316. But it is true that there are seven days in the week, and that all the children must learn their lessons. Also that it is never the raveled sleeve of just one day's care that sleep knits up. She should have been at home nursing her baby, and instead here they both are in Europe. And every month contains doomed days, such sad sighs, the rain that does not rain, and blood that is the color of bitter disappointment when it finally flows. This is the lesson she is now learning.

The shadow that showed up in the crystal ball?

Right. And all the years he was growing up, he would have liked to be somebody else—an athlete, broad-shouldered, blond, unworried, and popular. Even now he avoids his reflection in mirrors and wants to be liked by everybody. Not loved; just liked. On meeting someone who interests him he goes toward that person unhesitatingly, as if this were the one moment they would ever have together, their one chance of knowing each other. He is curious and at the same time he is tactful. He lets the other person know, by the way he listens, by the sympathetic look in his brown eyes, that he wants to know everything; and at the same time the other person has the reassuring suspicion that Harold Rhodes will not ask questions it would be embarrassing to have to answer. He tries to attach people to him, not so that he can use them or so that they will add to his importance but only because he wants them to be a part of his life. The landscape must have figures in it. And it never seems to occur to him that there is a limit to the number of close friendships anyone can decently and faithfully accommodate.

If wherever you go you are always looking for eyes that meet your eyes, hands that do not avoid touching or being touched by you, then you must have more than two eyes and two hands; you must be a kind of monster. If, on meeting someone who interests you, you go toward them unhesitatingly as if this is the only moment you will ever have for knowing each other, then you must learn to deal with second meetings that aren't always successful, and third meetings that are even less satisfactory. If on your desk there are too many unanswered letters, the only thing to do is to write to someone who hasn't written to you lately. And if sometimes, hanging by your knees head down from a swinging trapeze high under the canvas tent, you find too many aerial artists are coming toward you at a given moment and you have to choose one and let the others drop, you can at least try not to see their eyes accusing you of an inhuman betrayal you did not mean and cannot avoid. Harold Rhodes isn't a monster, he doesn't try to escape the second meetings, he answers some of the letters, and he spends a great deal of time, patience, and energy inducing performers with hurt feelings to climb the rope ladder again and fling themselves across the intervening void. Some of them do and some of them don't.

That's all very interesting, but just exactly what are these two people doing in Europe?

They're tourists.

Obviously. But it's too soon after the war. Traveling will be much pleasanter and easier five years from now. The soldiers have not all gone home yet. People are poor and discouraged. Europe isn't ready for tourists. Couldn't they wait?

No, they couldn't. The nail doesn't choose the time or the circumstances in which it is drawn to the magnet.

They would have done better to do a little reading before they came, so they would know what to look for. And they could at least have brushed up on their French.

They could have, but they didn't. They just came. They are the first wave. As Mme Viénot perceived, they are unworldly, and inexperienced. But they are not totally so; there are certain areas where they cannot be fooled or taken advantage of. But there is, in their faces, something immature, reluctant—

You mean they are Americans.

No, I mean all those acts of imagination by which the cupboard is again and again proved to be not bare. And putting so much faith in fortunetelling. Playing cards, colored stones, bamboo sticks, birthday-cracker mottoes, palmistry, the signs of the zodiac, the first star—she trusts them all, but only with a partial trust. Each new prognostication takes precedence over the former ones, and when the cards are not accommodating, she reshuffles them and tells herself a new fortune. Her right hand lies open now, relaxed on the pillow, her palm ready and waiting for a fortuneteller who can walk through locked doors and see in the dark.

Unaccustomed to sleeping in separate beds, they toss and turn and are cold and have tiring dreams that they would not have had if their two bodies were touching. But they won't be here long, or anywhere else. Ten days in Paris after they leave here. A night in Lausanne. Six days in Salzburg. Four days in Venice. Four more days in Florence. Ten days in Rome, a night in Pisa, two days in San Remo . . . No place can hold them.

And it is something that they are turned towards each other in their sleep. It means that day in and day out they are companionable and happy with one another; that they have identical (or almost) tastes and pleasures; and that when they diverge it is likely to be in their attitude toward the world outside their marriage. For example, he thinks he does not believe in God, she thinks she does. If she is more cautious about people than he is, conceivably this is because in some final way she needs them more. He needs only her. Parted from her in a crowd he becomes anxious, and in dreams he wanders through huge houses calling her name.

Chapter 4

WHAT TIME IS BREAKFAST?" he asked, rising up from his bed. She did not know. They had forgotten to ask about breakfast. They saw that it was a dark, rainy Monday morning. They washed in ice-cold water, dressed, and went downstairs. He peered around the folding screen, half expecting the household to be assembled in the drawing room, waiting for them. The beautiful pink and white room was deserted, and the rugs were rolled up, the chairs pushed together. In the dining room, the table was set for five instead of seven, and their new places were pointed out to them by their napkin rings. Talking in subdued tones, they discovered the china pitcher of coffee under a quilted cozy, and, under a large quilted pad, slices of bread that were hard as a rock and burned black around the edges from being toasted over a gas burner. The dining-room windows offered a prospect of wet gravel, long grass bent over by the weight of the rain, and dripping pine branches. The coffee was tepid.

"I think it would have been better if we hadn't got her to lower the price," he said suddenly.

"Did she say anything about it?"

He shook his head. "The amount she asked was not exorbitant."

"It was high. Muriel said it was high. She lived in France for twenty years. She ought to know."

"That was before the war. In the total expenses of the summer, it wouldn't have made any difference, one way or the other."

"She said it was not right, and that it was a matter of principle."

"Muriel, you mean? I know, but the first two or three days after we got off the boat, I consistently undertipped people, because I didn't know what the right amount was, and I didn't want us to look like rich Americans throwing our money around, and in every case they were so nice about it."

"How do you know you undertipped them?"

"By the way they acted when I gave them more."

"Mme Viénot has a romantic idea of herself," Barbara said. "The way she flirts with you, for instance . . ."

He took the green Michelin guide to the château country from his coat pocket and put it beside his plate. After a week of sight-seeing, any other way of passing the time seemed unnatural.

"You're sure she was flirting with me?"

"Certainly. But it's a game. She's attempting to produce, with your help, the person she sees herself as—the worldly, fascinating adventuress, the heroine of *Gone with the Wind*."

He filled their cups again and offered her the burned bread, which she refused. Then he opened the guidebook and began to turn the pages as he ate. Programmes de voyage . . . Un peu d'histoire . . . wars and maps . . . medieval cooking utensils . . . The fat round towers of Chaumont, and Amboise as it was in the sixteenth century.

"How old do you think Gagny is?" Barbara said.

"I don't know. He varies so. Somewhere between twenty-three and thirty-five."

More maps. Visit rapide . . . Visite du Château . . .

"Why isn't he married?"

"People don't have to get married," he said. "Sometimes they just—"

Rain blew against the windowpanes, so hard that they both turned and looked.

"Besides, he's in the diplomatic service," Harold said. "He can't just marry any pretty girl he feels like marrying. He needs a countess or somebody like that, and I suppose they won't have him because he isn't rich."

"How do you know he isn't rich?"

"If he were rich he wouldn't *be* here. He'd be somewhere where the sun is shining."

Behind his back a voice said: "Good morning!" and Mme Viénot swept into the dining room, wearing a dark-red housecoat, with her head tied up in a red and green Liberty scarf. She sat down at the head of the table. "You slept well? . . . I'm so glad. You must have been very tired after your journey." She placed her box of sugar directly in front of her, so there could be no possible misunderstanding, and then said: "What a pity it is raining again! M. Gagny is very discouraged about the weather, which I must say is not what we are accustomed to in July."

"Is it bad for the grain?" Harold asked.

Mme Viénot lifted the quilted pad and considered the burned bread with a grimace of disapproval. "Not at this time of year. But my gardener is worried about the hay." She peered into the china pitcher and her eyebrows rose in disbelief. "Perhaps it is only a shower. I hope so." She picked up the plate of toast and pushed her chair back. "The cook, poor dear, forgot to moisten the bread. I don't care for it when it is hard like this. Taking the pitcher also with her, she went out to the kitchen.

"We shouldn't have had a second cup," Barbara whispered.

"I think it was all right," he said.

"But she looked—"

"I know. I saw it. Coffee is rationed, but surely that wasn't coffee. . . . There wasn't enough for the others, in any case."

"You won't forget to speak to her about the beds, will you?" Barbara said. "I wrote her that we wanted a room with a *grand lit,* and if she didn't have anything but twin beds, it was up to her to tell us. And she didn't."

"No," he agreed, shifting in his chair, the uneasy male caught between two females.

"And the bicycles . . . You don't think she overheard what we were saying?"

"It wouldn't matter, unless she was standing out in the hall the whole time."

"She could have been."

They sat in wary silence until the pantry door opened.

"We must plan some excursions for you," Mme Viénot said. "You are in the center of one of the most interesting parts of France. The king used to come here with the court, for the hunting. They each had their own château and it was marvelous."

"We want to see Azay-le-Rideau," he said, "and Chinon, and Chenonceau—"

"Chinon is a ruin," Mme Viénot said disapprovingly. "Unless you have some particular reason for going there—" She surveyed the table and then got up again and pried open the door of the sideboard with her table knife. They heard a faint exclamation and then: "Within twenty-four hours after I open a jar of *confitures* it is half gone.

"Do have some," she said as she sat down again. "It is plum."

They both refused.

"Chenonceau is ravishing," Mme Viénot said, and helped herself sparingly to the jam. "It belonged to Diane de Poitiers. She was the king's mistress. She adored Chenonceau, and Catherine de Médicis took it away from her and gave her Chaumont instead."

He asked the reason for this exchange.

"She was jealous," Mme Viénot explained, with a shrug.

"But couldn't the king stop her?"

"He was killed in a tournament."

"Are the châteaux within walking distance?" Barbara asked.

"Alas, no," Mme Viénot said.

"But we can bicycle to some of them?" he asked.

In one of the two polite letters that arrived before they left New York, Mme Viénot had assured them that bicycles would be waiting for them when they arrived. Now she filled their cups and then her own and said plaintively: "I inquired about bicycles for you in the village, and it appears there aren't any. Perhaps you can arrange to rent them in Blois. Or in Tours. Tours is a dear old city—you know it?"

"We were there overnight," Barbara said.

"You saw the cathedral?"

Barbara shook her head.

"You must see the cathedral," Mme Viénot said. "The old part of the city was badly damaged during the war. Whole blocks went down between the center of town and the river. So shocking, isn't it?"

The servant girl appeared with a plate of fresh toast that had not been burned and the china pitcher, now full of steaming hot coffee. Mme Viénot remarked in French to the surrounding air that someone in the house was extremely fond of *confitures*, and with a sullen look Thérèse withdrew to the kitchen.

"Now, with the rubble cleared away," Mme Viénot said cheerfully: "you can have no idea what it was like. . . . The planes were American."

For a whole minute nobody said anything. Then Harold said: "Riding on the train we saw a great deal of rebuilding. Everywhere, in fact."

"Our own people raised the money for the new bridge at Tours," Mme Viénot said. "Naturally we are very proud of it. They are of stone, the new buildings?"

He nodded. "There's one thing, though, I kept noticing, and that is that the openings—the windows and doors—were all the same size. Do they have to do that? The new buildings look like barracks."

"In Tours all the new buildings are of stone. It would have

been cheaper to use wood, but that would have meant sacrificing the style of the locality, which is very beautiful," Mme Viénot said firmly, and so prevented him from pursuing a subject that, he now perceived, might well be painful to her. Probably it wasn't possible to rebuild, exactly as they were before, houses that had been built hundreds of years ago, and added onto and changed continually ever since.

He said: "Is there a taxi in the village?"

"There is one," Mme Viénot said. "A woman has it, and I'm afraid you will find her expensive. I'm sorry we haven't a car to offer you. We sold our Citroën after the war, thinking we could get a new one immediately, and it was a dreadful mistake. You can take the train, you know."

"From Brenodville?"

She nodded. Rearranging her sleeves so they wouldn't trail across her plate, she said: "I used to go to parties at Chaumont before the war. The Princesse de Broglie owned it then. She married the Infant Louis-Ferdinand, of Spain, and he was not always nice to her." She looked expectantly at them and seemed to be waiting for some response, some comment or anecdote about a royal person they knew who was also inconsiderate. "The Princesse was a very beautiful woman, and immensely rich. She was of the Say family—they manufacture sugar— and she wanted a title. So she married the Prince de Broglie, and he died. And then in her old age she married the Infant, and mothered him, and gave parties to which everyone went, and kept an elephant. The bridge at Chaumont is still down, but there is a ferry, I am told. I must find out for you how often it goes back and forth. . . . The Germans blew up all the bridges across the Loire, and for a while it was most inconvenient."

"How do we get to Chenonceau?" Harold asked.

"You take a train to Amboise, and from there you take a taxi. It's about twelve kilometers."

"And there are lots of trains?"

"There are two," Mme Viénot said. "One in the morning and one at night. I'll get a schedule for you. Before the war, the mayor of Brenodville was a member of the Chamber of Deputies and we had excellent service; all the fast trains between Paris and Nantes stopped here. . . . Amboise is also worth seeing. Léonard de Vinci is buried there. And during the seventeenth century, there was an uprising—it was the time of the Huguenot wars—and a great many men were put to death. They say that Marie Stuart and the young king used to dine out on the battlements at Amboise, in order to watch the hangings."

"What about buses?"

"I don't think you'll find the bus at all convenient," Mme Viénot said. "You have to walk a mile and a half to the highway where it passes, and usually it is quite crowded." Then as the silence in the dining room became prolonged: "I've been meaning to ask you about young George Ireland. We grew very fond of him while he was here, and he was a great favorite in the village. What is he doing now?"

"George is in school," Harold said.

"But now, this summer?"

"He's working. He's selling little dolls. He showed them to us the last time we were at the Irelands' for dinner. A man and a woman this high . . . You wind them up and they dance around and around."

"How amusing," Mme Viénot said. "He sells them on the street corner?"

"To tobacco stores, I believe."

"And is he successful?"

"Very. He's on his way to becoming a millionaire."

Mme Viénot nodded approvingly. "When he arrived, he didn't know a word of French, and it was rather difficult at first. But he spoke fluently by the end of the summer. We also discovered that he was fond of chocolate. He used to ride into the village after dinner and spend untold sums on candy and sweetmeats. And he was rather careless with my bicyclette. I had to have it repaired after he left. But he is a dear, of course. That reminds me—I haven't answered his mother's letter. I must write her today, and thank her for sending me two such charming clients.

It was most kind of her. I gather that she knows France well?"

Harold nodded.

"Such an amusing thing happened—I must tell you. My younger daughter became engaged last summer, and before she had quite made up her mind, George came to me and said that Sabine must wait until he could marry her. Fancy his thinking she would have him? I thought it was very fresh—a fifteen-year-old boy!"

"He speaks of you all—and of the place—with great affection," Harold said.

"It was a responsibility," Mme Viénot said. There are so many kinds of trouble a boy of that age can get into. You're quite sure you won't have anything more? Some bread, perhaps? Some more coffee?" She rolled her napkin and thrust it through the silver ring in front of her, and pushed her chair back from the table. "When George left, he kissed me and said: 'You have been like a mother to me!' I thought it sweet of him—to say that. And I really did feel like his mother."

As they were moving toward the door, he said hurriedly: "We've been meaning to ask you— Is there some way we could have hot water?"

"In your room? But of course! Thérèse will bring it to you. When would you like it? In the evening, perhaps?"

"At seven o'clock," Barbara said.

"I could come and get it myself," he said. "Or would that upset them?"

"Oh, dear no!" Mme Viénot exclaimed. "I'm afraid that wouldn't do. They'd never understand in the kitchen. You must tell Maman about the *poupées*. She will be enchanted."

"Porc-épic is French for porcupine," he announced. He was stretched out on the chaise longue, in the darkest corner of their room, reading the green Michelin guide to the château country. "The porcupine with a crown above it is the attribute—emblem, I guess it means—of Louis XII. The emblem of François premier is the salamander. The swan with an arrow sticking through its breast is the emblem of Louise of Savoy, mother of François premier. And it's also the emblem of Claude de France, his wife. Did you know we have a coat of arms in our family?"

"No," Barbara said. "You never told me." She had covered the towel racks in the bathroom with damp stockings and lingerie, and was now sitting at the kidney-shaped desk, with her fur coat over her shoulders and the windows wide open because it was no colder outside than it was in, writing notes to people who had sent presents to the boat. There were letters and postcards he should have been writing but fortunately there was only one pen.

"The ermine is Anne of Brittany and Claude de France," he said, turning back to the guidebook.

"Why does she have two emblems?"

"Who?"

"Claude de France. You said—"

"So she does . . . Ummm. It doesn't say. But it gives the genealogy of the Valois kings, the Valois-Orléans, the Valois-Angoulême, and the Bourbons through Louis XIV. . . . Charles V, 1364–1380, married Jeanne de Bourbon. Charles VI, 1380–1422, married Isabeau de Bavière. Charles VII—"

"Couldn't you just read it to yourself and tell me about it afterward?"

"All right," he said. "But it's very interesting. Charles VIII and Louis XII both married Anne of Brittany."

"The salamander?"

"No, the ermine. I promise not to bother you any more." But he did, almost immediately. "Listen to this, I just want to read you the beginning paragraph. It's practically a prose poem."

"Is it long?"

" 'Between Gien and Angers, the banks of the Loire and the

73

affluent valleys of the great river present an incomparable ensemble of magnificent monuments.' That's very good, don't you think? Don't you think it has sweep to it? 'The châteaux, by their number, their importance, and their interest appear in the foreground. Crammed with art and history, they occupy the choicest sites in a region that has a privileged light—' "

"It looks like just any gray day to me," she said, glancing out at the sky.

"Maybe the light is privileged and maybe it isn't. The point is you'd never find an expression like that in an American guidebook. . . . 'The landscapes of the Loire, in lines simple and calm'—that's very French—' owe their seductiveness to the light that bathes them, wide sky of a light blue, long perspectives of a current that is sometimes sluggish, tranquil streams with delicate reflections, sunny hillsides with promising vineyards, fresh valleys, laughing flower-filled villages, peaceful visions. A landscape that is measured, that charms by its sweetness and its distinction—' "

He yawned. The guidebook slipped through his fingers and joined the pocket dictionary on the rug. After a minute or two, he got up and stood at the window. The heavy shutters opened in, and the black-out paper was crinkled and torn and beginning to come loose. Three years after the liberation of France, it was still there. No one in a burst of happiness and confidence in the future had ripped it off. Germans, he thought, standing where he stood now, with their elbows on the sill. Looking off toward the river that was there but could not be seen. Lathering their cheeks in front of the shaving stand . . . Did Mme Bonenfant and Mme Viénot eat with their unwelcome guests, or in the kitchen, or where?

It had stopped raining but the air was saturated with moisture and the trees dripped. In the park in front of the château, the gardener and his wife and boy were pulling the haystacks apart with their forks and spreading the hay around them on the wet ground. He was tempted to go down and offer his services. But if they wouldn't understand in the kitchen, no doubt they wouldn't understand outdoors either.

"What time is it?" Barbara asked.

"Quarter of eleven. How time flies, doesn't it. Are you warm enough?"

"Mmmm."

"It's like living at the bottom of the sea."

He left the window and stood behind her, reading as she wrote. She had started a letter to her mother and father. The quick familiar handwriting moved across the page, listing the places they had been to, describing the château and the country-side and the terribly interesting French family they were now staying with. The letter seemed to him slightly stepped up, the pleasures exaggerated, as if she were trying to conceal from them (or possibly from herself) the fact that they were not as happy in their present surroundings as they had been in the Hôtel Ouest et Montgomery in Pontorson.

He moved on to the big round table in the center of the room. Among the litter of postcards, postage stamps, and souvenirs, a book caught his eye. Mme Viénot had come upon him in the drawing room after breakfast, and had made a face at the book he was looking at—corrections, additions, and objections to the recently issued grammar of the French Academy—and had said, with a smile: "I don't really think you are ready for that kind of hair-splitting." Taking the book out of his hands, she had given him this one instead. It was a history of the château of Blois. He opened it in the middle, read a paragraph, and then retired to the chaise longue.

Barbara finished her letter, folded it, and brought it to him to read. "Is it all right?"

"Mmmm," he said.

"Should I do it over?"

"No," he said. "It's a very nice letter. Why should you do it over? It will make them very happy."

"You don't like it."

"Yes, I do. It's a fine letter." The insincerity in his voice was so marked that he even heard it himself.

"There isn't a thing wrong with that letter," he said, earnestly this time. "There's no point in writing it over." But she had already torn it in half, and she went on tearing it in smaller pieces, which she dropped in the wastebasket.

"I didn't mean for you to do that!" he exclaimed. "Really, I didn't!" And a voice in his head that sounded suspiciously like the voice of Truth asked if that wasn't exactly what he had wanted her to do. . . . But why, he wondered. What difference did it make to him what she wrote to her father and mother? . . . No difference. It was just that they were shut up together in a cold house, and it was raining.

She sat down at the desk and took a blank sheet of paper and began over again. Ashamed of his petty interfering, he watched her a moment and then retrieved the pocket dictionary from the rug and placed it on the chaise longue beside his knees. While he was trying to untangle the personal and political differences of Henri III and the Duc de Guise, he raised his eyes from the print and observed Barbara's face, bent over her letter. Her face, on every troubled occasion, was his compass, his Pole Star, the white pebbles shining in the moonlight by which Hop-O'-My-Thumb found his way home. When she was happy she was beautiful, but the beauty came and went; it was at the mercy of her feelings. When she was unhappy she could be so plain it was frightening.

After a short while—hardly five minutes—she pushed the letter aside and said, quite cheerfully: "It's stopped raining. Should we go for a walk?"

They went downstairs and through the drawing room and outdoors without seeing anyone. Something kept them from quite liking the front of the house, which was asymmetrical and bare to the point of harshness. They looked into the courtyard at the carriage house, the stables, the high brick wall, and windows they had now looked out of. They followed the cinder drive around the other end of the house. Climbing roses and English ivy struggled for possession of the back wing, which had a much less steeply sloping roof and low dormers instead of bull's-eyes.

The drive took them on up a slope, between two rain-stained statues, and past a pond that had been drained, and finally to another iron gate. Peering through the bars, they saw that there was no trace of a road on the other side. Nothing but the forest. They tried the gate; it was locked. They turned and looked back, and had an uncomfortable feeling that eyes were watching them from the house.

On the way down again, they stopped and looked at the statues. They looked again at the clock that straddled the roof tree of the back wing. It had stopped at quarter of twelve. But quarter of twelve how long ago? And why was there no water in the pond? Seen from the rear, the whole place cried out that there had once been money and the money was gone, frittered away.

They noticed a gap in the hedge, and, walking through it, found themselves in a huge garden where fruit trees, rose trees, flowers, and vegetables were mingled in a way that surprised and delighted them. So did the scarecrow, which was dressed in striped morning trousers and a blue cotton smock. Under the straw hat the stuffed head had sly features painted on it. They saw old Mme Bonenfant at the far end of the garden, and walked slowly toward her. By the time they arrived at the sweet-pea trench her basket was full. She laid her garden shears across the long green stems and took the Americans on a tour of the garden, pointing out the espaliered fruit trees and telling them the French names of flowers. She did not understand their schoolroom French. They felt shy with her. But the tour did not last very long, and they understood that she was being kind, that she wanted them to feel at home. Leading them to some big fat bushes that were swathed in burlap against the birds, she told them to help themselves to the currants and gooseberries, and then she went on down the garden path to the house.

A few minutes later they left the garden themselves and followed the cinder drive down to the public road, where they turned left, in the opposite direction from the village. The road led them past fields on one side and the forest on the other. They came to a farmhouse and an excitable dog, detecting an odor that was not French, barked furiously at them; then to an opening in the forest, where a wagon track wound in through tall oak trees and out of sight. They left the road and followed the wagon track. The tree trunks were green with moss and there was no underbrush, which made the forest look unreal. The ground under their feet was covered with delicate ferns. Barbara kept stooping to gather acorns. These had a high polish and a beautiful shape and were smaller than the acorns she was accustomed to. Her pockets were soon full of them.

"We don't have to stay," she said, turning and looking at him.

"No," he agreed doubtfully. He was relieved, now she had given voice to his own uneasiness. But at the same time, how could they leave? "Of course we don't," he said. "Not if we don't want to."

"But we said we'd stay two weeks. What if she's counting on that, and has turned other people away?"

"I know."

"So in a way, we're bound to do what we said we'd do."

"We could tell her, I guess," he said. "The trouble is, we'll never have anywhere else as good a chance to learn to speak French."

"That's true."

"And later we may be glad we stuck it out. We may find when we get to Paris that it is possible to talk to people in a way that we haven't been able to, so far."

"So let's stay," she said.

"We'll try it for a few days, and then if it doesn't work, we can leave."

There seemed to be no end to the forest. After a short while they turned back, not because they were afraid of getting lost—there was only one road—but the way swimmers confronted with the immensity of the ocean swim out a little way and then, though they could easily swim farther, give way to a nameless fear and turn and head for the shore.

As they came back up the cinder drive, they saw the Canadian pacing the terrace in front of the château and staring up at the sky. The clouds had coalesced for the first time in several days, and the sun was trying to break through.

Away from the French, he seemed perfectly friendly, and willing to acknowledge the fact that Canada is right next to the United States.

"I congratulate you," he said, smiling.

"On what?" Harold asked.

"On the way you made your escape last night, after dinner. The evenings are very long."

"Then we ought to have stayed?" Barbara said.

"You have established a precedent. From now on, they expect you to be independent."

"But we didn't mean to," Harold said, "and if it was really impolite—"

"Oh, yes," Gagny said, smiling. "I quite understood, and the others did too. There was no comment."

"Are *you* expected to remain with them after dinner?" Harold persisted.

"As Americans you are in an enviable position," Gagny said, ignoring the question. Still smiling, he held the door open for them to pass into the drawing room, where Mme Carrère, with tortoise-shell glasses on, sat reading a letter. In her lap were half a dozen more. Mme Viénot was also reading a letter. Mme Bonenfant was reading *Le Figaro*, without glasses.

"Sabine has seen the King of Persia," Mme Viénot announced. And then, turning the page: "There is to be an illumination on Bastille Day. . . . I inquired about ration stamps for you in the village, M. Rhodes, and it seems you must go to Blois and apply for the stamps in person. I'm going there tomorrow afternoon. I could take you to the ration bureau."

"Oh, fine," he said.

"I'm sorry to put you to this trouble, but I do need the stamps."

On the way upstairs, Barbara said: "Do you think we ought to write to the Guaranty Trust Company and have our mail forwarded here?"

"I don't know," he said. "I can't decide."

The first thing they saw when they walked into their room was the big bouquet of pink and white sweet peas on their table. "Aren't they lovely!" Barbara exclaimed, and as she put her face down to smell the flowers, he said: "Let's wait. We've only been gone ten days, and that way there'll be more when we do get it."

"Think of her climbing all the way up here to bring them to us," Barbara said, and then, as she began to brush her hair: "I'm glad we decided to stay."

M. Carrère had breakfast in his room and came downstairs for the first time shortly before lunch. He walked with a cane, and Mme Carrère had to help him into his chair, but once seated he ignored his physical infirmity and so compelled the others to ignore it also. Mme Viénot explained privately to the Americans that he was recovering from a very serious operation. His convalescence was fulfilling the doctors' best hopes. He had gained weight, his appetite was improved, each day he seemed a little stronger. In her voice there was a note of wonder. So many quiet country places he could have gone to, she seemed to be saying, and he had come to her, instead.

He was not like anybody they had ever seen before. Though he seemed a kind man, there was an authority in his manner that kind men do not usually have. His face was long and equine. His eyes were set deep in his head. His hands were extraordinary. You could imagine him playing the cello or praying in the desert. When he smiled he looked like an expert old circus clown. He did not appear to want the attention of everybody when he spoke, and yet he invariably had it, Harold noticed. If he was aware of the dreary fact that there are few people who are not ready to take advantage of natural kindness in the eminent and the well-to-do, it did not bother him. The overlapping folds of his eyelids made his expression permanently humorous, and his judicious statements issued from a wide, sensual, shocking red mouth.

M. Carrère's great-grandfather, Mme Viénot said, had financed the building of the first French railway. M. Carrère himself was of an order of men that was becoming extremely rare in France today. His influence was felt, his taste and opinions were deferred to everywhere, and yet he was so simple, so sincere. To know him informally like this, to have the benefit of his conversation, was a great privilege.

She did not say—she did not have to say—that it was a privilege they were ill-equipped to enjoy.

Mme Carrère, quiet in her dress and in her manner, with black eyes and a Spanish complexion and neat gray hair parted in the middle, looked as if she were now ready for the hard, sharp pencil of Ingres—to whom, it turned out, her great-grandparents had sat for their portrait. She sat in a small armchair, erect but not stiff or uneasy, and for the most part she listened, but occasionally she added a remark when she was amused or interested by something. To Harold Rhodes' eyes, she had the look of a woman who did not need to like or be liked by other people. She was neither friendly nor unfriendly, and when her eyes came to rest on him for a second, what he read in them was that chance had brought them all together at the château, and if she ever met up with him elsewhere or even heard his name mentioned, it would again be the work of chance.

Unable to say the things he wanted to say, because he did not know how to say them in French, able to understand only a minute part of what the others said, deprived of the view from the train window and the conducted tour of the remnants of history, he sat and watched how the humorous expression around M. Carrère's eyes deepened and became genuine amusement when Mme Bonenfant brought forth a *mot*, or observed Mme Carrère's cordiality to Mme Viénot and her mother, not with the loving eye of a tourist but the glazed eye of a fish out of water.

He thought of poor George Ireland, stranded in this very room and only fifteen years old. If I could lie down on the floor I'd probably understand every word they're saying, he thought. Or if I could take off my shoes.

M. Carrère made a point of conversing with the Americans at the lunch table. They were delighted with his explanation of the phrase "entre la poire et le fromage" and so was Mme Viénot, who said: "I hope you will remember what M. Carrère has just said, because it is the very perfection of French prose style. It should be written down and preserved for posterity."

M. Carrère had recently paid a visit to his son, who was living in New York. He had seen the skyscrapers, and also Chicago and the Grand Canyon, on his way to the West Coast. "I could converse with people vis-à-vis but not when the conversation became general, and so I missed a great deal that would have been of interest to me. I found America fascinating," he added, looking at Harold and Barbara as if it had all been the work of their hands. "I particularly liked the 'ut doaks that are served everywhere in your country." They looked blank and he repeated the word, and then repeated it again impatiently: "'ut doaks, 'ut doaks—le saucisson entre les deux pièces de pain."

"Oh, you mean hot dogs!" Barbara said, and laughed.

M. Carrère was not accustomed to being laughed at. The resemblance to a clown was accidental. "'ut doaks," he said defensively, and subsided. The others sat silent, the luncheon table under a momentary pall. Then the conversation was resumed in M. Carrère's native tongue.

Chapter 5

THE BENTLEY was waiting in front of the house when they got up from the table and went across the hall for their coffee. As the last empty cup was returned to the silver tray, Mme Carrère rose. Ignoring the state of the weather, which they could all see through the drawing-room windows, she helped M. Carrère on with his coat, placed a lilac-colored shawl about his shoulders, and handed him his hat, his pigskin gloves. Outside, the Alsatian chauffeur held the car door open for them, and then arranged a fur robe about M. Carrère's long, thin legs. With a wistful look on their faces, the Americans watched the car go down the drive.

As they turned away from the window, Mme Viénot said: "I have an errand to do this afternoon, in the next village. It would make a pleasant walk if you care to come."

Off they went immediately, with the Canadian. Mme Viénot led them through the gap in the hedge and down the long straight path that bisected the potager. Over their heads storm clouds were racing across the sky, threatening to release a fresh downpour at any moment. She stopped to give instructions to the gardener, who was on his hands and knees among the cabbages, and the walk was suspended a second time when they encountered a white hen that had got through the high wire netting that enclosed the chicken yard. It darted this way and that when they tried to capture it. With his arms spread wide, Gagny ran at the silly creature. "Like the Foreign Office, she can't bear to commit herself," he said. "Steady . . . steady, now . . . Oh, blast!"

When the hen had been put back in the chicken yard, where she wouldn't offer a temptation to foxes, they resumed their walk. The path led past an empty potting shed with several broken panes of glass, past the gardener's hideous stucco villa, and then, skirting a dry fountain, they arrived at a gate in the fence that marked the boundary of Mme Bonenfant's property. On the other side, the path joined a rough wagon road that led them through a farm, and the farm provoked Mme Viénot to open envy. "It is better kept than my garden!" she exclaimed mournfully.

"In Normandy," Harold said, "in the fields that we saw from the train window, there were often poppies growing. It was so beautiful!"

"They are a pest," Mme Viénot said. "We have them here, too. They are a sign of improper cultivation. You do not have them in the fields in America? . . . I am amazed. I thought they were everywhere."

He decided that this was the right moment to bring up the subject of the double bed in their room.

"We never dreamed that it would take so long to recover from the Occupation," she said, as if she knew exactly what he was on the point of saying, and intended to forestall him. "It is not at all the way it was after the Guerre de Quatorze. But this summer, for the first time, we are more hopeful. Things that haven't been in the shops for years one can now buy. There is more food. And the farmers, who are not given to exaggeration, say that our wheat crop is remarkable."

"Does that mean there will be white bread?" he asked.

"I presume that it does," Mme Viénot said. "You dislike our dark bread? Coming from a country where you have everything in such abundance, you no doubt find it unpalatable."

Ashamed of the abundance when his natural preference was to be neither better nor worse off than other people, he said untruthfully: "No, I like it. We both do. But it seemed a pity to be in France and not be able to have croissants and brioches."

They had come to a fork in the road. Taking the road that led off to the right, she continued: "Of course, your government has been most generous," and let him agree to this by his silence before she went on to say, in a very different tone of voice: "You knew that in order to get wheat from America, we have had to promise to buy your wheat for the next ten years—even though we normally produce more wheat than we need? One doesn't expect to get something for nothing. That isn't the way the world is run. But I must say you drive a hard bargain."

And at that moment Hector Gagny, walking a few feet behind them, with Barbara, said: "We're terribly restricted, you know. Thirty-five pounds is all we can take out of England for travel in a whole year, and the exchange is less advantageous than it is with your dollars."

What it is like, Harold thought, is being so stinking rich that there is no hope of having any friends.

Walking along the country road in silence, he wondered uneasily about all the people they had encountered during their first week in France. So courteous, so civilized, so pleasant; so pleased that he liked their country, that he liked talking to them. But what would it have been like if they'd come earlier—say, after the last excitement of the liberation of Paris had died down, and before the Marshall Plan had been announced? Would France have been as pleasant a place to travel in? Would the French have smiled at them on the street and in train corridors and in shops and restaurants and everywhere? And would they have been as helpful about handing the suitcases down to him out of train windows? In his need, he summoned the driver of the empty St. Malo–St. Servan bus who was so kind to them, the waitress in the hotel in Pontorson, the laborer who had offered to share his bottle of wine in the train compartment, the nice woman with the little boy, the little boy in the carnival, M. Fleury and his son—and they stood by him. One and all they assured Harold Rhodes solemnly in their clear, beautiful, French voices that he was not mistaken, that he had not been taken in, that the kindness he had met with everywhere was genuine, that he had a right to his vision.

"Americans love your country," he said, turning to look directly at the Frenchwoman who was walking beside him. "They always have."

"I am happy to hear it," Mme Viénot said.

"The wheat is paid for by taxation. *I* am taxed for it. And everybody assumes that it comes to you as a gift. But there are certain extremely powerful lobbying interests that operate through Congress, and the State Department does things that Americans in general sometimes do not approve of or even know about. With Argentina, and also with Franco—"

"Entendu!" Mme Viénot exclaimed. "It is the same with us. The same everywhere. Only in politics is there no progress. Not the slightest. Whatever we do as individuals, the government undoes. If France had no government at all, it would do much better. No one has faith in the government any more."

"There is nothing that can be done about it?"

"Nothing," she said firmly. "It has been this way since 1870."

As they walked along side by side, his rancor—for he had felt personally attacked—gradually faded away, and they became once more two people, not two nationalities, out walking. Everything he saw when he raised his eyes from the dirt road pleased him. The poppy-infested fields through which they were now passing were by Renoir, and the distant blue hills by Cézanne. That the landscape of France had produced its painters seemed less likely than that the painters were somehow responsible for the landscape.

The road brought them to a village of ten or twelve houses, built of stone, with slate roofs, and in the manner of the early Gauguin. He asked if the village had a name.

"Coulanges," Mme Viénot said. "It is very old. The priest at Coulanges has supernatural powers. He is able to find water with a forked stick."

"A peach wand?"

"How did you know?" Mme Viénot asked.

He explained that in America there were people who could find water that way, though he had never actually seen anyone do it.

"It is extraordinary to watch," she said. "One sees the point of the stick bending. I cannot do it myself. They say that the priest at Coulanges is also able to find other things—but that is perhaps an exaggeration."

A mile beyond the village, they left the wagon road and followed a path that cut diagonally through a meadow, bringing them to a narrow footbridge across a little stream. On the other side was an old mill, very picturesque and half covered with climbing blush roses. The sky that was reflected in the millpond was a gun-metal gray. A screen of tall poplars completed the picturesque effect, which suggested no special painter but rather the anonymous style of department-store lithographs and colored etchings.

"It's charming, isn't it?" Mme Viénot said.

"Is it still used as a mill?" Harold asked.

"Indeed yes. The miller kept us in flour all through the war. He has a kind of laying mash that is excellent for my hens. I have to come and speak to him myself, though. Otherwise, he isn't interested."

When she left them, they stood watching some white ducks swimming on the surface of the millpond.

The Canadian said, after quite some time: "Why did you come here?" It was not an accusation, though it sounded like one, but the preface to a complaint.

"We wanted to see the châteaux," Barbara said. "And also—"

"Mmmm," Gagny interrupted. "I'd heard about this place, and I thought it would be nice to come here, but I might as well have stayed in London. There hasn't been one hour of hot sunshine in the last five days."

"We were hoping to rent bicycles," Barbara said. "She wrote

us that it had been arranged, and then this morning at breakfast she—"

"There are no bicycles for rent," Gagny said indignantly.

"I know there aren't any in the village," Barbara said. "But in Blois?"

He shook his head.

"Then I guess we'll have to go by train," she said.

"It's no use trying to get around by train. It will take you all day to visit one château."

"But she said—"

"If you want to see the châteaux, you need a car," he said, looking much more cheerful now that his discouragement was shared.

They saw Mme Viénot beckoning to them from the door of the mill.

"If this weather keeps up," Gagny said as they started toward her, "I'm going to pack my things and run up to Paris. I've told her that I might. I have friends in Paris that I can stay with, and Wednesday is Bastille Day. It ought to be rather lively."

"I've just had a triumph," Mme Viénot said. "The miller has agreed to let me have two sacks of white flour." The Americans looked at her in surprise, and she said innocently: "I'm not sure that it is legal for him to sell it to me, but he is very attached to our family. I'm to send my gardener around for it early tomorrow morning, before anyone is on the road."

Instead of turning back the way they had come, she led them across another footbridge and they found themselves on a public road. Walking four abreast, they reached the crest of a long ridge and had a superb view of the valley of the Loire.

Turning to Barbara, Mme Viénot said: "When did you come out?"

"Come out?" Barbara repeated blankly.

"Perhaps I am using the wrong expression," Mme Viénot said. "I am quite out of the habit of thinking in English. Here, when a young girl reaches a certain age and is ready to be introduced to society—"

"We use the same expression. I just didn't understand what you meant. . . . I didn't come out."

"It is not necessary in America, then?"

"Not in the West. It depends on the place, and the circumstances. I went to college, and then I worked for two years, and then I got married."

"And you liked working? So does Sabine. I must show you some of her drawings. She's quite talented, I think. When you go to Paris, you must call on her at *La Femme Elégante*. She will be very pleased to meet two of my guests, and you can ask her about things to see and do in Paris. There is a little bistro that she goes to for lunch—no doubt she will take you there. The clientele is not very distinguished, but the food is excellent, and most reasonable, and you will not always want to be dining at Maxim's."

Harold opened his mouth to speak and then closed it; Mme Viénot's smile made it clear that her remark was intended as a pleasantry.

"I think I told you that my daughter became engaged last summer? After some months, she asked to be released from her engagement. She and her fiancé had known each other since they were children, but she decided that she could not be happy with him. It has left her rather melancholy. All her friends are married now and beginning to have families. Also, it seems her job with *La Femme Elégante* will terminate the first of August. The daughter of one of the editors of the American *Vogue* is coming over to learn the milieu, and a place has to be made for her."

"But that doesn't seem fair!" Barbara exclaimed.

Mme Viénot shrugged. "Perhaps they will find something else for her to do. I hope so."

The road led them away from the river, through fields and

vineyards and then along a high wall, to an ornamental iron gate, where the Bentley was waiting. The gatehouse was just inside, and Mme Viénot roused the gatekeeper, who came out with her. His beret was pulled down so as to completely cover his thick gray hair, and he carried himself like a soldier, but his face was pinched and anxious, and he obviously did not want to admit them. Mme Viénot was pleasant but firm. As they talked she indicated now the lane, grown over with grass, that led past the gatehouse and into the estate, now the car that must be allowed to drive up the lane. In the end her insistence prevailed. He went into the gatehouse and came out again with his bunch of heavy keys and opened the gates for the Bentley to drive through.

The party on foot walked in front of the car, which proceeded at a funeral pace. Ahead of them, against the sky, was the blackened shell of a big country house with the chimneys still standing.

It looks like a poster urging people to buy war bonds, Harold thought, and wondered if the planes were American. It turned out that the house had been destroyed in the twenties by a fire of unknown origin. At the edge of what had once been an English garden, the chauffeur stopped the car, and M. and Mme Carrère got out and proceeded with the others along a path that led to a small family chapel. Inside, the light came through stained-glass windows that looked as if they had been taken from a Methodist church in Wisconsin or Indiana. The chapel contained four tombs, each supporting a stone effigy.

With a hissing intake of breath Mme Viénot said: "Ravissant!"

"Ravissant!" said M. and Mme Carrère and Hector Gagny, after her.

Harold was looking at a vase of crepe-paper flowers in a niche and said nothing. The chapel is surely nineteenth-century Gothic, he thought. How can they pretend to like it?

The effigies were genuine. Guarded by little stone dogs and

gentle lap lions, they maintained, even with their hands folded in prayer, a lifelike self-assertiveness. Looking down at one of them—at the low forehead, the blunt nose, the broad, brutal face—he said: "These were very different people."

"They were Normans," Mme Viénot said. "They fought their way up the rivers and burned the towns and villages and then settled down and became French. He's very beautiful, isn't he? But not very intelligent. He was a crusader."

There was no plaque telling which of the seven great waves of religious hysteria and tourism had picked the blunt-nosed man up and carried him all the way across Europe and set him down in Asia Minor, under the walls of Antioch or Jerusalem. But his dust was here, not in the desert of Lebanon; he had survived, in any case; the tourist had got home.

"What I brought you here to see," Mme Viénot said, "is the *prieuré* on the other side of the garden. I don't know the word in English."

"Priory," Barbara said.

"The same word. How interesting!"

While they were in the chapel, it had commenced to sprinkle. They hurried along a garden path. The garden still had a few flowers in it, self-sown, among the weeds and grass. Except for the vaulting of the porch roof, the priory looked from the outside like an ordinary farm building. The entrance was in the rear, down a flight of stone steps that M. Carrère did not attempt. He stood under the shelter of the porch, leaning on his cane, looking ill and gray. When they were around the corner of the building, Harold asked Mme Carrère if the expedition had been too much for him and she said curtly that it had not. Her manner made it as clear as words would have that, though he had the privilege of listening to M. Carrère's conversation, he did not know him, and Mme Carrère did see that he had, therefore, any reason to be interested in the state of her husband's health. He colored.

The key that Mme Viénot had obtained from the gatekeeper they did not need after all. The padlock was hanging open. The two young men put their weight against the door and it gave way. When their eyes grew accustomed to the feeble light, they could make out a dirt floor, simple carving on the capitals of the thick stone pillars, and cross-vaulting.

Barbara was enchanted.

"It is considered a jewel of eleventh-century architecture," Mme Viénot said. "There is a story— It seems that one of the dukes was ill and afraid he would die, and he made a vow that if he recovered from his sickness he would build a prieuré in honor of the Virgin. And he did recover. But he forgot all about the prieuré and thought of nothing but his hawks and his hounds and hunting, until the Virgin appeared in a dream to someone in the neighborhood and reminded him, and then he had to keep his promise."

The interior of the building was all one room, and not very large, and empty except for an object that Harold took for a medieval battering ram until Mme Viénot explained that it was a wine press.

"In America," he said, "this building would have been taken apart stone by stone and shipped to Detroit, for Henry Ford's museum."

"Yes?" Mme Viénot said. "Over here, we have so many old buildings. The museums are crammed. And so things are left where they happen to be."

He examined the stone capitals and walked all around the wine press. "What became of the nuns?" he asked suddenly.

"They went away," Mme Viénot said. "The building hasn't been lived in since the time of the Revolution."

What the nuns didn't take away with them other hands had. *If you are interested in those poor dead women*, the dirt floor of the priory said—*in their tapestries, tables, chairs, lectuaries, cooking utensils, altar images, authenticated and unauthenticated*

visions, their needlework, feuds, and forbidden pets, go to the
public library and read about them. There's nothing here, and
hasn't been, for a hundred and fifty years.

⚜ ⚜
⚜

ON THE WAY HOME the walking party was caught in a heavy
shower and drenched to the skin.

Dressing hurriedly for dinner, Barbara said: "It's so like her:
'Thérèse will bring you a can—what time would you like it?'
and then when seven o'clock comes, there isn't a sign of hot
water."

"Do you want me to go down and see about it?"

"No, you'd better not."

"Maybe she does it on purpose," he said.

"No, she's just terribly vague, I've decided. She only half
listens to what people are saying. I wouldn't mind if we were on
a camping trip, but to be expected to dress for dinner, to have
everything so formal, and not even be able to take a bath! Do
you want to button me up in back? . . . I've never seen anyone look as vague as she does sometimes. As if her whole life had
been passed in a dream. Her eyelids come down over her eyes
and she looks at us as if she couldn't imagine who we were or
what we were doing here."

"M. Carrère likes Americans, but Mme Carrère doesn't. I
don't think she likes much of anybody."

"She likes the Canadian."

"Does she?"

"She laughs at his jokes."

"I don't think Gagny's French is as good as he thinks it is. It's
an exaggeration of the way the others speak. Almost a parody."

"M. Carrère speaks beautiful French."

"He speaks French the way an American speaks English. It

just comes out of him easily and naturally. Gagny shrugs his shoulders and draws down the corners of his mouth and says 'mais oui' all the time, and it's as if he had picked up the mannerisms of half a dozen different people—which I guess you can't help doing if the language isn't your own. At least, I find myself beginning to do it."

"But it *is* his language. He's bilingual."

"French-Canadian isn't the same as French." He pulled his tie through and drew the knot snugly against his collar. "While you are trying to make the proper sounds and remember which nouns are masculine and which feminine, the imitation somehow unconsciously— M. Carrère's *English* is something else again. His pronunciation is so wide of the mark that sometimes I can't figure out what on earth he's talking about. " 'ut doaks, 'ut doaks!" And so impatient with us for not understanding."

"I shouldn't have laughed at him," Barbara said sadly. "I was sorry afterward. Because our pronunciation must sound just as comic to the French, and they never laugh at us."

⚜ ⚜
⚜

At dinner, Mme Viénot's navy-blue silk dress was held together at the throat by a diamond pin, which M. Carrère admired. He had a passion for the jewelry of the Second Empire, he said. And Mme Carrère remarked dryly that there was only one thing she would do differently if she had her life to live over again. She let her husband explain. In the spring of 1940, as they were preparing to escape from Paris by car, she had entrusted her jewel case to a friend, and the friend had handed it over to the Nazis. The few pieces that she had now were in no way comparable to what had been lost forever. Even so, Barbara had to make an effort to keep from looking at the emerald solitaire that Mme Carrère wore next to her plain gold wedding ring, and she was sorry that she had listened to Harold when he suggested that she leave everything but a string of cultured pearls in the bank at home.

Having established a precedent, the Americans were concerned to live it down. They remained in the petit salon with the others, after dinner. The company sat, the women with sweaters and coats thrown over their shoulders, facing the empty Franklin stove. Observing that Gagny smoked one cigarette and then no more, the Americans, not wanting to be responsible for filling the room with smoke, denied the impulse each time it recurred, and sometimes found to their surprise that they had a lighted cigarette in their hand.

While Hector Gagny and M. Carrère were solemnly discussing the underlying causes of the defeat of 1940, the present weakened condition of France, and the dangers that a reawakened Germany would present to Europe and the rest of the world, a quite different conversation was taking place in the mirror over the mantelpiece. Harold Rhodes's reflection, leaning forward in his chair, said to Mme Viénot's reflection: "I am not accustomed to bargaining. It makes me uneasy. But we have a friend who lived in France for years, and she said—"

"Where in France?" Mme Viénot's reflection interrupted.

"In Paris. They had an apartment overlooking the Parc Monceau."

"The Monceau quarter is charming. Gounod lived there. And Chopin."

"She said it was a matter of principle, and that in traveling we must keep our eyes open and not be above bargaining or people would take advantage of us . . . of our inexperience. It was she who told us to ask you to figure the price by the week instead of by the day, but if I had it to do over again, I wouldn't listen to her. I'd just pay you what you asked for, and let it go at that."

Instead of giving him the reassurance he wanted, Mme Viénot's reflection leaned back among the sofa pillows, with her hand to her cheek. It would have been better, he realized, not to have brought the matter up at all. It was not necessary to bring it up. It had been settled before they ever left America. In his embarrassment he turned for help to the photograph of the schoolboy on the piano. "What I am trying to say, I guess, is that it's one thing to live up to your principles, and quite another thing to live up to somebody else's idea of what those principles should be."

"My likeness is here among the others," the boy in the photograph said, "but in their minds I am dead. They have let me die."

"The house is cold and damp and depressing," Barbara Rhodes's reflection said to the reflection of M. Carrère. "Why must we all sit with sweaters and coats over our shoulders? Why isn't there a fire in that stove? I don't see why we all don't get pneumonia."

"People born to great wealth—"

All the other reflections stopped talking in order to hear what M. Carrère's reflection was about to say.

"—are also born to a certain kind of human deprivation, and soon learn to accept it. For example, those letters that arrive daily, even in this remote country house—letters from my lawyer, from my financial advisors, from bankers and brokers and churchmen and politicians and the heads of charitable organizations, all read and acknowledged by Mme Carrère, lest they tire me (which indeed they would). The expressions of personal attachment, of concern for my health, are judged according to their sincerity, in most instances not great, and a few are read aloud to me, lest I think that no one cares. I am accustomed to the fact that in every letter, sooner of later, self-interest shows through. I do not really mind, any more. Music is my delight. When I want companionship, I go to the Musée des Arts Décoratifs and look at the porcelains and the period furniture."

"I used to have a friend—" Mme Bonenfant's reflection said. "She has been dead for twenty years: Mme Noë—"

"Mme Noë?" M. Carrère interrupted. "I knew her also. That is, I was taken to see her as a young man."

"Mme Noë was fond of saying, and of writing in letters and on the flyleaf of books: 'Life is something more than we believe it to be.' "

"Since my illness," M. Carrère said, "I have become aware for the first time of innumerable—reconciliations, I suppose one would call them, that go on around us all the time without our noticing it. Again and again, Mme Carrère hands me something just as I am on the point of asking for it. And in her dreams she is sometimes a party to financial transactions that I am positive I have not told her about. . . . But it is strange that you should speak of Mme Noë. I was thinking about her this very afternoon as I stood looking at that grass-choked garden and that house gutted by fire. She was quite old when I was taken to see her. And she asked me all sorts of questions about myself that no one had ever asked me before, and that I went on answering for days afterward."

"She had that effect on everyone," Mme Bonenfant said.

"I remember that she led me to a vase of flowers and we talked."

"And what did you say?" Barbara Rhodes asked.

"I said something that pleased her," M. Carrère said, "but what it was I can no longer remember. All I know is that it was not at all like the sort of thing I usually said. And when she left me to speak to someone else, I did not have the feeling that I was being abandoned. Or that she would ever confuse me afterward with anyone else. . . . She is an important figure in the memoirs of a dozen great men, and reading about her the same question always occurs to me. What manner of woman she was really, if you made no claim on her, if you asked for nothing (as she asked for nothing) but merely sat, silent, content merely to be there beside her, and let her talk or not talk, as she felt like doing, all through a summer afternoon, none of them seem to know."

"She was frail," Mme Bonenfant said. "She was worn out by ill-health, by the demands, the endless claims upon her time and energy—"

"Which she must have encouraged," M. Carrère said.

"No doubt," Mme Bonenfant said. "By temperament she was

not merely kind, she was angelic, but there was also irony. Once or twice, toward the end of her life, she talked to me about herself. It seems she suffered always from the fear that, wanting only to help people, she nevertheless unwittingly brought serious harm to them. This may have been true but I do not know a single instance of it. For my own part, I am quite content to believe that life is nothing more than our vision of it—of what we believe it to be. Tacitus says that the phoenix appears from time to time in Egypt, that it is a fact well verified. Herodotus tells the same story, but skeptically."

"At the Council of Nicaea," M. Carrère said, "three hundred and eighteen bishops took their places on their thrones. But when they rose as their names were called, it appeared that they were three hundred and nineteen. They were never able to make the number come out right; whenever they approached the last one, he immediately turned into the likeness of his neighbor."

"Before Harold and I were married," Barbara said, "a woman in a nightclub read our palms, and she said Leo and Virgo should never marry. Their horoscopes are in conflict. If they love each other and are happy it is a mistake. . . . That's why he doesn't like fortunetellers. I don't think our marriage is a mistake, but on the other hand, sometimes I lie awake between three and four in the morning, planning dinner parties and solving riddles and worrying about curtains that don't hang straight in the dark, and about my clothes and my hair, and about whether I have been unintentionally the cause of hurt feelings. And about Harold, sound asleep beside me and sharing not only the same bed but some of my worst faults. . . . Does anybody know the answer to the riddle that begins: 'If three people are in a room and two of them have a white mark on their forehead—' "

"The answer to the riddle of why I am not married," Hector Gagny said, "is that I am. And my wife hates me."

"So did the woman I gave my jewel case to," Mme Carrère said. "But I didn't know it."

"She has all but ruined my career," Gagny said. "She is beautiful and willful and perverse, and in her own way quite wonderful. But she makes no concessions to the company she finds herself in, and I sit frozen with fear of what may come out of her mouth."

"Do not despair," Mme Bonenfant said. "Be patient. Your wife, M. Gagny, may only be acting the way she does out of the fear that you do not love her."

"In the beginning we seemed to be happy, and only after a while did it become apparent that there were things that were not right. And that they were not ever going to be right. I began to see that behind the fascination of her mind, her temperament, there was some force at work that was not on my side, and bent on destroying both of us. But what is it? Why is she like that?"

"Though there was only two years difference in our ages," Mme Viénot said, "my mother held me responsible for my brother's safety when we were children. I used to have nightmares in which something happened to him or was about to happen to him. When we played together, I never let go of his hand."

"Maurice was delicate," Mme Bonenfant said.

"He cried easily," Mme Viénot said. "He was always getting his feelings hurt. My daughter Sabine is very like him in appearance. I only hope that her life is not as unhappy as his."

"I see that you haven't forgiven me," the boy in the photograph said. "I failed to distinguish myself in my studies but I made three friendships that were a credit to me, and I died bravely. It took me almost an hour to kill myself. . . . Now I am an effect of memory. When you have completely forgotten me, I assume that I will pass on to other places."

"They say that people who talk about committing suicide never actually do it," Mme Viénot said. "Maurice was the exception. When his body was brought home for burial we were warned that it would be better not to open the coffin."

"It was an accident," Mme Bonenfant said.

"And M. Viénot?" Harold Rhodes asked the boy in the photograph. "Why does nobody speak of him? His name is never mentioned."

"Do not interrupt," the boy in the photograph said. "They are speaking of me—of what happened to me."

AT QUARTER OF ELEVEN, when the Americans went upstairs, they found a large copper can in their bathroom. The temperature of the water in the can was just barely warm to the touch.

Lying awake in the dark, she heard the other bed creak.

"Are you awake?" she whispered, when he turned again.

He was awake.

"We don't have to stay," she said, in a small, sad voice.

"If it's no good I think we could tell her that we're not happy and just leave." He sat up and rearranged the too-fat pillows and then said: "It's funny how it comes and goes. I have periods of clarity and then absolute blankness. And my mind gets so tired I don't care any more what they're saying." The bed creaked as he turned over again. He tried to go to sleep but he had talked himself wide awake. "Good night. I love you," he said. But it didn't work. This declaration, which on innumerable occasions had put his mind at rest, had no effect because she was not in his arms.

"It isn't simply the language," he said, after several minutes of absolute silence. "Though that's part of it. There's a kind of constraint over the conversation, over everything. I think they all feel it. I think it's the house."

"I know it's the house," she said. "Go to sleep."

Five minutes later, the bed creaked one last time. "Do I imagine it," he asked, "or is it true that when they speak of the Nazis—downstairs, I mean—the very next sentence is invariably some quite disconnected remark about Americans?"

Chapter 6

THE VILLAGE OF BRENODVILLE was too small and unremarkable to be mentioned in guidebooks, and derived its identity from the fact that it was not some other village—not Onzain or Chouzy or Chailles or Chaumont. It had two principal streets, the Grande Rue and the avenue Gambetta, and they formed the letter T. The avenue Gambetta went from the Place de l'Eglise to the railway station. The post office, the church, the mairie, and the cemetery were all on the Grande Rue. So was the house of M. Fleury. It ought to have given some sign of recognition, but it didn't; it was as silent, blank, secretive, and closed to strangers as every other house up and down the village street. While they stood looking at it, Mme Viénot came out of the post office and caught them red-handed.

"You are about to pay a call on M. Fleury?"

"We weren't even sure this was where he lived," Harold said, blushing. "The houses are all alike."

"That is the house of M. Fleury. You didn't make a mistake," Mme Viénot said. "I think it is unlikely that you will find him at home at this hour, but you can try."

After an awkward moment, during which they did not explain why they wanted to pay a call on M. Fleury, she got on her bicycle and pedaled off down the street. Watching the figure on the bicycle get smaller and smaller, he said: "She's going to be soaked on the way home. Look at the sky."

"A hundred francs was probably enough," Barbara said. "In a place as small as this."

"It would reflect on her, in any case," he said.

"And if he isn't there, we'd have to explain to his wife."

"Let's skip it."

They bought stamps at the post office, and wondered, too late, if the postmistress could read the postcards they had just mailed to America. The woman who sold them a sack of plums to eat in their room may have been, as Mme Viénot said, a great gossip, but she did not gossip with them. They tried unsuccessfully to see through, over, or around several garden gates. With the houses that were directly on the street, shutters or lace curtains discouraged curiosity. They stood in the vestibule of the little church and peered in. Here there was no barrier but their own Protestant ignorance.

The Grande Rue was stopped by a little river that was a yard wide. Wild flags grew along the water's edge. A footbridge connected an old house on this side with its orchard on the other. They decided that the wooden shelter on the river bank was where the women brought their linen to be washed in running water.

"I don't suppose you could have a washing machine if you wanted to," he said.

"No, but you'd have other things," she said. "You'd live in a different way. You wouldn't want a washing machine."

The sky had turned a greenish black while they were standing there, and now a wind sprang up. Out over the meadows a great abstract drama was taking place. In the direction of Pontlevoy and Montrichard and Aignan, the bodies and souls of the unsaved fell under the sway of the powers of darkness, the portions of light in them were lost, and the world became that much poorer. In the direction of Herbault and St. Amand and Selommes, all glorious spirits assembled, the God of Light himself appeared, accompanied by the aeons and the perfected just ones. The angels supporting the world let go of their burden and everything fell in ruins. A tremendous conflagration consumed meadows and orchard, and on the very brink of the little river, a perfect separation of the powers of light and darkness took place. The kingdom of light was brought into a condition of completeness, all the grass bent the same way. Darkness should, from this time on, have been powerless.

"We'd better start home," Barbara said.

On the outskirts of the village they had to take shelter in a doorway. The rain came down in front of their faces like a curtain. At times they couldn't even see through it. Then the sky began to grow lighter and the rain slackened.

"If we had a car," he said, "it would be entirely different. We wouldn't feel cooped up. The house is damp and cold. The books accumulate on the table in our room and I read a few sentences and my mind gets tired of translating and having to look up words and begins to wander."

"A lot of it's our fault," she said, "for not speaking French."

"And part of it isn't our fault. It wasn't like this anywhere else. With time hanging heavy on our hands, we always seem to be hurrying, always about to be late to lunch or dinner. We ask for a double bed and nothing is done about it, and she says nothing *can* be done about it because of the lamp. What actually has the lamp got to do with it? We didn't ask for a lamp. Nothing is done about anything we ask for in the way of comfort or convenience. And neither is it refused. The hot water arrives while we're at dinner. The cook's bicycle is too frail for us to borrow, and we can't borrow hers because it has just been repaired. The buses and trains run at the wrong time, the taxi is expensive. George Ireland showed me a snapshot of the horse hitched up to a dog cart, but that was last summer. Now the horse is old and needed in the garden. When I try to find her to ask her about some arrangement, she's never anywhere. I don't even know where her room is."

"Did you hear her say 'I like your American custom of not shaking hands in the morning'?"

"They shake hands at *breakfast?*"

"Apparently."

"The cozy atmosphere of the breakfast table is a fabrication that we are supposed to accept and even contribute to," he went on, "as the other guests politely accept and support the fiction that Mme Viénot and her mother are the very cream of French society and lost nothing of importance when they lost their money."

"Perhaps they *are* the cream of French society," Barbara said.

"From the way Mme Viénot kowtows to Mme Carrère, I would say no. Mme Viénot is a social climber and a snob. And that's another thing. Yesterday evening before dinner, Mme Carrère asked the Canadian to call on them. In Paris."

"And did he accept?"

"He behaved like a spaniel that has just been petted on the head."

"Probably if you were French the Carrères would be very useful people to know."

"I found myself wondering whether—before they go on Monday—they would invite *us* to call on them," he said.

"Do you want to see the Carrères in Paris?"

"I don't care one way or the other."

"Our French isn't good enough," she said. "Besides, I don't think they do that sort of thing over here. It isn't reasonable to expect it of them."

"Who said anything about being reasonable? He gave Gagny his card, and I want him to do the same thing to us. And it isn't enough that he should invite us to call on him at his office. I want us to be invited to their home."

"We have nothing to say to them here. What point is there in carrying it any farther?"

"No point," he said. "There's no excuse for our ever seeing them again, except curiosity."

They saw that they were being stared at by a little boy in the open doorway of the house across the street.

"If they did ask us, would you go?"

"No," he said.

"It would be interesting to see their apartment," she said, and so, incriminating herself, sharing in his dubious desires, made him feel better about having them.

"They give me the creeps," he said. "Mme Carrère especially."

"What did she say that hurt your feelings?"

"Nothing."

"It isn't raining so hard," Barbara said.

He stepped out of the shelter of the doorway with his palm extended to the rain.

"We might as well be starting back or we'll be late again," he said.

He took off his coat and put it around her shoulders. As they went off down the street, she tried not to listen to what he was saying. In the mood he was in, he exaggerated, and his exaggerations gave rise to further exaggerations, and helplessly, without wanting to, analyzing and explaining and comparing one thing with another that had no relation to it, he got farther and farther from the truth.

They stopped to look at a pink oleander in a huge tub. The blossoms smelled like sugar and water.

"As soon as we're outside," he said, "in the garden or stopping to pick wildflowers along the road or like now—the moment we're off somewhere by ourselves, everything opens up like a fan. And as soon as we're indoors with them, it closes."

"We could go to Paris," she said.

"With the Canadian?"

"If you like."

"And be there for Bastille Day? That's a wonderful idea. We could run up to Paris and come back after two or three days."

"Or not come back," she said.

At lunch Mme Viénot said: "We should leave the house by two o'clock."

But when two o'clock came, they were on the terrace, leaning against the stone balustrade, and she had not appeared.

"I'd go look for her," he said, "if it weren't so much like looking for a needle in a haystack."

"Don't talk so loud," Barbara said, glancing up at an open window directly above them.

"I'm not talking loud. I'm practically whispering."

"Your voice carries."

He noticed that she was wearing a cotton dress and said: "Are you going to be warm enough?"

"I meant to bring a sweater."

He jumped down and started across the terrace, and she called after him: "The cardigan."

He pushed the door open and saw a small elderly woman standing in an attitude of dramatic indecision beside the white columns that divided the drawing room in half. She was wearing a tailored suit with a high-necked silk blouse. A lorgnette hung by a black ribbon from her collar. Her hair was mouse-colored. Like the old ladies of his childhood she wore no rouge or lipstick. She saw him at the same moment that he saw her, and advanced to meet him, as if his sudden appearance had resolved the question that was troubling her.

"Straus-Muguet," she said.

He put out his hand and she took it. To his surprise, she knew his name. She had heard that he was staying in the house, and she had been hoping to meet him. "J'adore la jeunesse," she said.

He was not all that young; he was thirty-four; but there was no one else in the room that this remark could apply to, and so he was forced to conclude that she meant him. He looked into her eyes and found himself in another climate, the one he had been searching for, where the sun shines the whole day long, the prevailing wind is from the South, and the natives are friendly.

She was not from the village, he decided on the way upstairs. She was a lady, but a lady whose life had been lived in the country; a character out of Chekhov or Turgenev. Probably she belonged in one of the big country houses in the neighborhood and was a family friend—a lifelong friend of old Mme Bonenfant, who had come to call, to spend the afternoon in quiet reminiscences over their embroidery or their knitting, with tea and cake at the proper time, and, at parting, the brief exchange of confidences, the words of reassurance and continuing affection that would make it seem worth while, for both of them, to go on a little longer.

When he came back with the sweater, the drawing room was empty and Mme Viénot and the Canadian were standing on the terrace with Barbara. Walking at a good pace they covered the two kilometers to the concrete highway that followed the river all the way into Blois. The bus came almost immediately and was crammed with people.

"I'm afraid we won't get seats," Mme Viénot said. "But it's only a ten-minute ride."

There was hardly room to breathe inside the bus, and all the windows were closed. Harold stood with his arm around Barbara's waist, and craned his neck. His efforts to see out were defeated everywhere by heads, necks, and shoulders. It took him some time to determine which of the passengers was responsible for the suffocating animal odor that filled the whole bus. It was twenty-five minutes before they saw the outskirts of Blois.

Threading her way boldly between cyclists, Mme Viénot led them down the rue Denis Papin (inventor of the principle of the steam engine), through the Place Victor Hugo, up a long ramp, and then through a stone archway into the courtyard of the château, the glory of Blois. They saw the octagonal staircase, the chapel, and a splendid view, all without having to purchase tickets of admission. Then they followed her back down the ramp, through the crowded narrow streets, to a charcuterie, where she bought blood sausage, and then into the bicycle shop next door, where they saw a number of bicycles, none of which were for rent. They saw the courtyard of the ancient Hôtel d'Alluye, built by the treasurer of François premier, but did not quite manage to escape out onto the sidewalk before the concierge appeared. While Harold stood wondering if they should be there at all and if the concierge would be as unpleasant as she looked, Hector Gagny extracted fifty francs from his wallet and the threat was disposed of. Climbing a street of stairs, they saw the cathedral. There they separated. Gagny went off in search of a parfumerie, and Mme Viénot took the Americans to the door of the ration bureau and then departed herself to do some more shopping. They stood in line under a sign—*Personnes Isolées*—that had for them a poignancy it didn't have for those who were more at home in the French language. They could not get ration coupons because Harold had not thought to bring their passports.

When they emerged from the building, they saw that it was at one end of a long terrace planted in flower beds, with a view over the lower part of the city. Leaning against a stone balustrade, with his guidebook open in front of him, he started to read about the terrace where they now were.

"What's that?" Barbara asked.

He looked up. At the far end of the terrace a crowd had gathered. The singing came from that direction. They listened intently. It sounded like children's voices.

"It's probably something to do with Bastille Day," he said, and stuffed the guidebook in his raincoat pocket, and they hurried off down the gravel paths.

❧ ❧
❧

FOR TOURISTS who fall in love with the country they are traveling in, charms of great potency are always at work. If there is a gala performance at the Opéra, they get the last two tickets. Someone runs calling and gesturing the whole length of the train to find them and return the purse that was left on a bench on the station platform. And again and again they are drawn, as if by wires, to the scene that they will never be able to forget as long as they live.

At first the Americans stood politely on the outskirts of the crowd, thinking that they had no right to be here. But then they worked their way in gradually, until at last they were clear inside.

The children, dressed all in white, had no leader, and did not need one. They had been preparing for this occasion for years. Their voices were very high, pure, on pitch, thoroughly drilled, and happy. Music heard in the open air is not like music in a concert hall. It was as if the singing came from one's own heart.

Remember what the lark sounds like, said the stones of the Bishop's Palace. *Try for perfection. . . .*

Try for joy, said the moss-stained fountain.

Do not be afraid to mark the contrasts if it is necessary, said the faded tricolor. *But do not let one voice dominate. . . . Remember that you are French. Remember that in no other country in the world do children have songs that are as beautiful and gay and unfading as these. . . .*

The exact sound of joy is what you must aim for. . . .

. . . of a pure conscience . . .

. . . of an enthusiastic heart . . .

"Oh, oh, oh," Harold exclaimed under his breath, as if he had just received a fatal wound.

Full of delight but still exact and careful and like one proud voice the children sang: "Qui n'avait jam-jam-jamais navigué!"

He looked at Barbara. They shook their heads in wonder.

"They must be very old songs," he whispered.

Turning, he studied the adults, dressed in somber colors and shabby suits, but attentive, critical, some of them probably with ears only for the singing of a particular child. They appeared to take the songs for granted. This is what it means to be French, he thought. It belongs with the red-white-and-blue flags and the careful enunciation and the look of intelligence in every eye and the red poppies growing in the wheat. These songs are their birthright, instead of "London Bridge Is Falling Down. . . ."

The children finished singing and marched off two by two, and the crowd parted to let in some little boys, who performed a ferocious staff dance in which nobody got hurt; and then six miniature couples, who marched into the open space and formed a circle. The boys had on straw hats, blue smocks, and trousers that were too large for them. The little girls wore white caps and skirts that dragged the ground and in some instances had to be held up with a safety pin. At a signal from an emaciated man with a violin, the gavotte began. In the patterns of movement, and quite apart from the grave self-conscious children who danced, there was a gallantry that was explicitly sexual, an invitation now mocked, now welcomed openly. But because they were only eight-year-olds, the invitation to love was like a melody transposed from its original key and only half recognizable. Suddenly he turned and worked his way blindly toward the outer edge of the crowd. Barbara followed him out into the open, where a group of fifteen-year-old girls in diaphanous costumes waited to go on. If the sight of a foreigner wiping his eyes with his handkerchief interested them, they did not show it. They stretched and bent over, practicing, or examined the blackened soles of their feet, or walked about in twos and threes. He saw that Barbara was looking at him anxiously and tried to explain and found he could not speak. Again he had to take his handkerchief out.

"There's Mme Viénot," Barbara said.

Turning, he saw her hurrying toward them between the flower beds. Ignoring his condition, she said: "M. and Mme Carrère are waiting in the pâtisserie," and hurried them off down the gravel path.

The pastry shop was down below, in the rue de Commerce, and it was crowded and noisy. Cutting her way through clots of people, squeezing between tables, frustrating waitresses with trays, Mme Viénot arrived at the large round table in the rear of the establishment where M. and Mme Carrère and Mme Bonenfant were waiting, their serenity in marked contrast to the general noise and confusion. Mme Carrère invited Harold and Barbara to sit down, and then she allowed her eyes to roam over the room, as if something were about to happen of so important a nature that talk was not necessary. Mme Bonenfant asked if they had found Blois a beautiful city and was pleased when he said that they preferred Brenodville. The village was charming, she agreed; very old, and just the way a village should be; she herself had great affection for it. Mme Viénot went off in search of M. Gagny, and for the next ten minutes M. Carrère devoted himself to the task of capturing a busboy and ordering a carafe of "fresh" water. Human chatter hung in the air like mist over a pond.

They saw that Mme Viénot had returned, with the Canadian. She stopped to confer with the proprietress and he came straight back to their table. He had found the parfumerie, he explained as he sat down, but it did not have the kind of perfume his mother had asked him to get for her. The proprietress of the pâtisserie nodded, shrugged, and seemed in no way concerned about what Mme Viénot was saying to her. Arriving at the table in the rear, Mme Viénot said: "She's going to send someone to take our order." She sat down, glanced at her watch nervously, and said: "The Brenodville bus leaves at seven minutes to six and it is now after five," and then explained to the Americans that the pâtisserie was well known.

The water arrived, was tested, was found to be both cool and fresh. They sat sipping it until a waitress came to find out what they wanted. This required a good five minutes of animated conversation to decide. The names meant nothing to Barbara and Harold, and since they could not decide for themselves, Mme Carrère acted for them; Mme Rhodes should have *demi-chocolat et demi-vanille* and M. Rhodes chocolat-praliné. The ices arrived, and with them a plate of pâtisseries—cream puffs in the shape of a cornucopia, strawberry tarts, little cakes that were rectangular, diamond-shaped, or in layers, with a soft filling of chocolate, or with almond paste or whipped cream. The enthusiasm of the Americans was gratifying to the French, who agreed among themselves that the pâtisseries, though naturally not what they had been before the war, were acceptable. "If you consider that they have not been made with white flour," M. Carrère said, "and that the ices have to be flavored with saccharine . . ."

Harold was conscious of a genuine cordiality in the faces around the table. They were being taken in, it seemed; he and Barbara were being initiated into the true religion of France.

The *addition*, on a plate, was placed in front of M. Carrère, who motioned to Harold to put his wallet away. In America, he said, he had been treated everywhere with such extraordinary kindness. He was grateful for this opportunity of paying it back.

There was a crowd waiting in the rue Denis Papin for the bus, but they managed to get seats. Six o'clock came and nothing happened; the driver was outside stowing bicycles away on the roof. More people kept boarding the bus until the aisle was blocked. Sitting beside Barbara, with his hand in hers, Harold saw Gagny get up and give his seat to a colored nun, but it did not occur to him to follow this example, and he was hardly aware of when the bus started at last. The children's voices, high, clear, and only half human, took him far outside his ordinary self. He felt as if he were floating on the end of a long kite string, the other end of which was held by the hand that was, in actuality, touching his hand. He did not remember anything of the ride home.

❧ ❧
❧

WHEN THE HOUSEHOLD ASSEMBLED before dinner, Harold saw that the elderly woman who had introduced herself to him earlier in the afternoon was still here, and he was pleased for her sake that she had been asked to stay and eat with them. In that first glimpse of her, standing beside the white columns in the drawing room, she had seemed uneasy and as if she was not sure of her welcome. He sat down beside her now, ready to take up where they had left off. She leaned toward him and confessed that it was the regret of her life that she had never learned English. She had a nephew—or a godson, he couldn't make out which —living in America, she said, and she longed to go there. Harold began to talk to her about New York City, in French, and after a minute or two she shook her head. He smiled and sat back in his chair. Her answering smile said that though they were prevented from conversing, they needn't let that stand in the way of their being friends. He turned his head and listened to what Mme Bonenfant was saying to M. Carrère.

" . . . To them the entry into Paris was a perfectly agreeable occasion, and they insisted on showing us snapshots. They could see no reason why we shouldn't enjoy looking at them."

"The attitude is characteristic," M. Carrère said. "And extraordinary, if you think how often their own country has been invaded. . . . I had an experience . . ."

In his mind Harold still heard the children's voices. Mme Viénot addressed a remark to him, which had to be repeated before he could answer it. He noticed that Mme Straus-Muguet was wearing a little heart encrusted with tiny diamonds, on a fine gold chain. So appropriate for her.

M. Carrère's experience was that a Nazi colonel had sent for him, knowing that he was ill and would have to get up out of bed to come, and had then kept him waiting for over an hour in his presence while he engaged in chit-chat with another officer. But then he committed an error; he remarked on the general lack of cultivation of the French people and the fact that so few of them knew German. With one sentence, in the very best *hoch Deutsch*, M. Carrère had reduced him to confusion.

"I have a friend," Mme Viénot said, "who had a little dog she was very fond of. And the German officers who were quartered in her house were correct in every way, and most courteous to her, until the day they left, when one of them picked the little dog up right in front of her eyes and hurled it against the marble floor, killing it instantly."

It's their subject, Harold thought. This is what they are talking about, everywhere. This is what I would be talking about if I were a Frenchman.

Mme Straus-Muguet described how, standing at the window of her apartment overlooking the Etoile, peering through the slits of the iron shutter, with the tears running down her face, she had watched the parade that she thought would never end. "Quelle horreur!" she exclaimed with a shiver, and Harold checked off the first of a whole series of mistaken ideas about her. She was not a character out of Turgenev or Chekhov. Her life had not been passed in isolation in the country but at the center of things, in Paris. She had been present, she said—General Weygand had invited her to accompany him to the ceremony at the Invalides, when the bronze sarcophagus of Napoléon II, which the Nazis had taken from its crypt in Vienna, was placed beside the red porphyry tomb of his father, Napoléon Ier.

The room was silent, the faces reflecting each in its own way the harsh wisdom of history.

Since she was a friend of General Weygand, it was not likely that she was socially unsure in the present company, Harold said to himself. He must have been mistaken. He turned to Mme Viénot and explained that they were thinking of going up to Paris with M. Gagny in the morning, and would probably return on Friday. To his surprise, this plan met with her enthusiastic approval. He asked if they should pack their clothes, books, and whatever they were not taking with them, so that the suitcases could be removed from their room during the three days they would be gone.

"That won't be necessary," Mme Viénot said, and he took this to mean that they would not be charged during their absence, and was relieved that this delicate matter had been settled without his having to go into it. For the first time, he found himself liking her.

She offered to telephone the hotel where they were planning to stay, and make a reservation for them. As she went toward the hall, M. Carrère called out the telephone number. The hotel was around the corner from their old house, he said, and he knew it well. During the war it had been occupied by German officers.

Mme Bonenfant reminded Barbara that there was to be an illumination on the night of July 14, and Harold took out his financial notebook and wrote down the route that Mme Carrère advised them to follow: if they began with the Place de la Concorde and the Madeleine, and then went on to the Place de l'Opéra, and then to the Place du Théâtre Français and the Comédie Française, with its lovely lamps, and then to the Louvre, and finally Notre Dame reflected in the river, they would see all the great monuments, the city at its most ravishing.

They got up and went in to dinner, and something that Mme Straus-Muguet said during the first course made Harold realize at last that she was not a caller but a paying guest like them. He looked across the table at her, at the winking reflections of the little diamond-encrusted heart, and thought what a pity it was that she should have come to stay at the château just as they were leaving.

When the company left the dining room, Mme Straus-Muguet excused herself and went upstairs and brought back down with her a box of *diamonoes*. She asked Harold if he knew this delightful game and he shook his head.

"I take it with me everywhere I go," she said.

Mme Bonenfant removed the cover from the little round table in the center of the petit salon, and the ivory counters were dumped onto the green felt center. While Mme Straus-Muguet was explaining the rules of the game to Barbara, Mme Viénot captured M. Carrère and then indicated the place beside her on the sofa where Harold was to sit.

The Canadian, Mme Carrère, Mme Bonenfant, Barbara, and Mme Straus-Muguet sat down at the table and commenced playing. The game, a marriage of dominoes and anagrams, was agreeable and rather noisy. M. Carrère excused himself and went upstairs to read in bed.

Mme Viénot, reclining against the sofa cushions with her hand to her temple, defended the art of conversation. "The young people of today are very different from my generation," she said, setting Harold a theme to develop, a subject to embroider, as inclination or experience prompted. "They are serious-minded and idealistic, and concerned about the future. My daughter's husband works until eleven or twelve every night at his office in the Ministry and Suzanne sits at home and knits for the children. At their age, my life was made up entirely of parties and balls. Nobody thought about the future. We were having too good a time."

She sat up and rearranged the pillows. Her face was now disturbingly close to his. He shifted his position.

"My nephew maintains that we were a perverted generation," Mme Viénot said cheerfully, "and I dare say he is right. All we cared about was excitement. . . ."

Though he was prevented from going toward the gaiety in the center of the room, he was aware that Mme Carrère had come out of her shell at last and, pleased with the extent of Barbara's vocabulary, was coaching her.

"I'm no good at anything that has to do with words," the Canadian said mournfully. "When something funny happens to me, I never can put it in a letter. I have to save it all up until I go home."

Mme Bonenfant was slower still, and kept the others waiting, and had to be shown where her pieces would fit into the meandering diagram. Mme Straus-Muguet was quick as lightning, and when Barbara completed a word, she complimented her, seized her hand, called her "chérie," taught her an idiom to go with the word, and put down a counter of her own—all in thirty seconds.

"Mme Carrère loves words," Barbara said later as she was transferring four white shirts from the armoire to an open suitcase. "Any kind of abstraction. Anything sufficiently intellectual that she can apply her mind to it. When we started to play that game she became a different person."

"I saw that she was. Gagny asked us to have lunch with him on Thursday at a bistro he goes to. He said it was quite near our hotel."

"Did you say we would?"

He shook his head. "I left it up in the air. I wasn't sure that was what we'd most want to be doing."

"Did you enjoy your conversation with Mme Viénot?"

"It was interesting. I had a different feeling about the house tonight. And the people. I'm glad we decided not to leave."

"So am I."

"All in all, it's been a nice day."

"Very."

He pulled the covers back and jumped into bed.

"They seemed very pleased with us when I said we were thinking of going up to Paris. . . . As if we were precocious children who had suddenly grasped an idea that they would have supposed was too old for us."

"I expect they'd all like to be going up to Paris in the morning," Barbara said.

"Or as if we had found the answer to a riddle. Or managed to bring a long-drawn-out parlor game to an end."

Chapter 7

THE CANADIAN did not appear at breakfast, and Mme Viénot did not offer any explanation of why he was not coming, but neither did she appear to be surprised, so he must have spoken to her. Either his threats had been idle and he had no friends in Paris who were waiting for him with open arms, or else he was avoiding a long train journey in their company. If he was, they did not really care. They were too lighthearted, as they sipped at their peculiar coffee and concealed the taste of the bread with marmalade, to care about anything but their own plans. They were starting on a train journey across an entirely new part of France. They were going to have to speak French with all kinds of strangers, some of whom might temporarily become their friends. They were going to change trains in Orléans, and at the end of their journey was Paris on Bastille Day. They could hardly believe their good fortune.

The taxi was old, and the woman who sat behind the wheel looked like a man disguised as a woman. Mme Viénot stood in the open doorway and waved to them until they were out of sight around the corner of the house. As the taxi turned into the public road, they looked back but they could not see the house from here. He felt the bulge in his inside coat pocket: passports, wallet, traveler's checks. He covered Barbara's gloved hand with his bare hand, and leaned back in the seat. "This is more like it," he said.

❧ ❧
❧

"Just where is the Hôtel Vouillemont?" Harold said when they were out in the street in front of the Gare d'Austerlitz.

Barbara didn't know.

He managed to keep from saying: "How can you not know where it is when you spent two whole weeks there?" by saying instead: "I should have asked Mme Viénot." But she was aware of his suppressed impatience with her, and sorry that she couldn't produce this one piece of helpful information for him when he, who had never been to Europe before, had got them in and out of so many hotels and railroad stations. Actually she could have found it all by herself, simply by retracing her steps. It was the only way she ever found her way back to some place she didn't know the location of. Back through three years of being married to him, and two years of working in New York, to the day she graduated from college, and from there back to the day she sat watching her mother and Mrs. Evans sewing name tapes on the piles of new clothes that were going off with her to boarding school, and then back to the time when the walls of her room were covered with pictures of horses, and so finally to the moment when they were leaving the Hôtel Vouillemont to go to the boat train—which was, after all, only what other people do, she thought; only they do it in their minds, in large jumps, and she had to do it literally.

She tried, anyway. She thought very carefully and then said: "I think it's not far from the Louvre."

They went into the Métro station, and there he found an electrified map and began to study it.

Also, she thought, when she was here before, it was with her father, who had an acutely developed sense of geography and never got lost in strange cities, any more than in the woods. Instead of trying to figure out for themselves where they were, they always stood and waited for him to make up his mind which was north, south, east, and west. As soon as he had arrived at the points of the compass, he started off and they followed, talking among themselves and embroidering on old jokes and keeping an eye on him without difficulty even in crowds because he was half a head taller than anybody else.

Harold pushed a button, lights flashed, and he announced: "We change trains at Bastille."

With a sense that they were journeying through history, they climbed the steps to the platform. They were delighted with the beautiful little toy train, all windows and bright colors and so different from the subway in New York. They changed at Bastille and got off at Louvre and came up out onto the sidewalk. The big forbidding gray building on their left was the Louvre, Barbara was positive, but there was no dancing in the street in front of it. A short distance away, they saw another building with a sign *Louvre* on it, but that turned out to be a department store. It was closed. All the shops were closed. Paris was as empty and quiet as New York on a Sunday morning. They listened. No sound of distant music came from the side streets. Neither did a taxi. Their suitcases grew heavier with each block, and at the first sidewalk café they sat down to rest. A waiter appeared, and Harold ordered two glasses of red wine. When he had drunk his, he got up and went inside. The interior of the café was gloomy and ill-lit, and he was glad he had left Barbara outside. It was clearly a tough joint. He asked if he could see the telephone directory and discovered that there was more than one, and that they were compiled according to principles he didn't understand, and in that poor light the Hôtel Vouillemont did not seem to be listed in any of them. So he appealed to the kindness of Madame la Patronne, who left the bar untended and came over to the shelf of telephone books and looked with him.

"The Hôtel Vouillemont?" she called out, to the three men who were standing at the bar.

"In the rue Boissy d'Anglas," Harold said.

"The rue Boissy d'Anglas . . ."

"The rue Boissy d'Anglas?"

"The rue Boissy d'Anglas."

One of them remembered suddenly; it was in the sixteenth arrondissement.

"No, you are thinking of the rue Boissière," the waiter said. "I used to help my cousin deliver packages for a shop in the sixteenth arrondissement, and I know the quarter well. There is no Hôtel Vouillemont."

The three men left their drinks and came over and started thumbing through the telephone directories. The waiter joined them. "Ah!" he exclaimed. "Here it is. The Hôtel Vouillemont . . . It's in the rue Boissy d'Anglas."

"And where is that?" Harold asked.

The waiter peered at the directory and said: "The eighth arrondissement. You got off too soon. You should have descended at Concorde."

"Is that far from here?"

They all five assured him that he could walk there.

"But with suitcases?"

"In that case," Madame said, "you would do well to return to the Métro station."

He shook hands all around, hesitated, and then took a chance. It didn't work; they thanked him politely but declined the invitation to have a glass of wine with him. So his instinct must have been wrong.

"Is there any way that one can call a taxi?" he asked.

The waiter went to the door with him and showed him which direction they must go to find a taxi stand. Harold shook hands with him again, and then turned to Barbara. "We should have descended at Concorde," he said, and picked up the suitcases. "It's miles from here."

I: *Leo and Virgo*

The taxi driver knew exactly where the Hôtel Vouillemont was, and so they could sit back and not worry. They peered through the dirty windows at Paris. The unfamiliar streets had familiar names—the rue Jean-Jacques Rousseau; the rue Marengo. They caught a glimpse down a long avenue of the familiar façade of the Opéra. The arcades of the rue de Rivoli were deserted, and so were the public gardens on the other side of the street. So was the Place de la Concorde. The sky over the fountains and the Egyptian obelisk was cold and gray. The driver pointed out the American Embassy to them, and then they were in a dark, narrow street. The taxi stopped.

"He's made a mistake," Barbara said. "This isn't it."

"It says 'Hôtel Vouillemont' on the brass plate," Harold said, reaching for his wallet. And then, though he disliked arguments, he got into one with the taxi driver. Mme Viénot had said he must refuse to pay more than the amount on the meter. The driver showed him a chart and explained that it was the amount on the chart he must pay, not the amount on the meter. Harold suggested that they go inside and settle the matter there. The driver got out and followed him into the hotel, but declined to help with the suitcases. To Harold's surprise, the concierge sided with the driver, against Mme Viénot.

Still not sure they hadn't cheated him, he paid the driver what it said on the chart and turned back to the concierge's desk. If it turned out that the concierge was dishonest, he was not going to like staying at the Hôtel Vouillemont. He studied the man's face, and the face declined to say whether the person it belonged to was honest or dishonest.

While he was registering, Barbara stood looking around her at the lobby. She could not even say, as people so often do of some place they knew as a child, that it was much smaller than she remembered, because she didn't remember a thing she saw. She wondered if, all these years, she could have misremembered the name of the hotel they stayed in. It was not until they were in the elevator, with their suitcases, that she knew suddenly that they were in the right hotel after all. She remembered the glass elevator. No other hotel in the world had one like it. It was right out in the center of the lobby, and it had a red plush sofa you could sit down on. As they rose through the ceiling, the past was for a moment superimposed on the present, and she had a wonderful feeling of lightness—as if she were rising through water up to the surface and sunshine and air.

Their room was warm, and when they turned on the faucets in the bathroom, hot water came gushing out of the faucet marked *chaud*. They filled the tub to the brim and had a bath, and dressed, and went off down the street to have lunch at a restaurant that Barbara remembered the name of: Tante Louise. Like the glass elevator, the restaurant hadn't changed. After lunch they strolled. Harold stopped at a kiosk and bought a map-book of Paris by arrondissements, so that he wouldn't ever again be caught not knowing where he was and how to get to where he wanted to go. They looked in the windows of the shops in the rue St. Honoré, full of beautiful gloves and scarves, and purses that probably cost a fortune.

They were in Paris at last, and aware that they should have been happy, but there was no indication anywhere that Paris was happy. No dancing in the streets, no singing, no decorations, no flags, even. They discovered the Madeleine and the American Express and Maxim's, none of which gave off any effervescence of gaiety, and finally, toward the end of the afternoon, they gave up searching for Paris on Bastille Day, since it appeared to be only an idea in their minds, and went back to their hotel.

That evening, before it was quite dark, they set off to see the illuminations. They were encouraged when they saw that the streets had begun to fill up with people. They went first to the Place de la Concorde, and admired the light-soaked fountains and the flood-lighted twin buildings. With lights trained on it, the Madeleine, at the end of the rue Royale, no longer looked quite so gloomy and Roman. They were about to start off on the route that Mme Carrère had recommended, when a skyrocket exploded and long yellow ribbons of light fell down the sky. So, instead, they joined the throngs of people hurrying toward the river. For half an hour they stood in the middle of the Pont de la Concorde, looking now at the fireworks and now at the up-raised, expectant French faces all around them. Bouquet after bouquet of colored lights exploded in the sky and in the black water. They decided that, rather than retrace their steps, they would reverse the directions Mme Carrère had given them. This turned out to be a mistake. They rushed here and there, got lost, doubled back on their route, and wasted a good deal of time changing trains in the Métro. And they never did see the lighted lamps of the Comédie Française.

At one o'clock, exhaustion claimed them. They were lost again, and a long way from home. They asked directions of a gendarme, who hurried them into a Métro station just in time to catch the last train back to Concorde.

⚜ ⚜
⚜

THE ADDRESS of the editorial officers of *La Femme Elégante* turned out to be a courtyard, and the entrance was up a short flight of steps. They gave the receptionist their name and, as they waited for Sabine Viénot to appear, Harold's eyes roamed around the small foyer, trying to make out something, anything, from the little he saw—nobly proportioned doors with heavy molding painted dove gray, nondescript lighting fixtures, and dove-gray carpet. When Mme Viénot spoke of her daughter's career, her tone of voice suggested that she was at the forefront of her profession. But then she had showed them some of her daughter's work—thumbnail sketches of dress patterns buried in the back of the magazine. The girl who came through the doorway and shook hands with them was very slight and pale and young, with observant blue eyes and brown hair and a high, domed forehead, like the French queens in the *Petit Larousse.*

Harold started to explain who they were and she said that she knew; her mother had written to her about them. "You can speak English if you prefer," she said. "I speak it badly but— They are all well in the country?"

Barbara nodded.

"I'm afraid you haven't had very nice weather. It has been cold and rainy here, also. You arrived in Paris when?"

"Yesterday," Barbara said.

"But we didn't see any dancing in the streets," Harold said. "Last night at midnight we saw a crowd of people singing and marching in the square in front of Notre Dame, but they were Communists, I think. Anyway, there was no dancing.

"In Montmartre you would have seen it, perhaps," the French girl said. "Or the Place Pigalle."

They couldn't think what to say next.

"Mother has written how much she enjoyed having you with her," the French girl said.

"We are returning to Brenodville tomorrow," Harold said, "and your mother asked us to let you know the train we are taking. She thought you might also be intending to—"

"I may be going down to the country tomorrow," the French girl said thoughtfully. "I don't know yet."

"We're taking the four o'clock train," he said. "Your mother suggested that we might all three take one taxi from Blois."

"That is very kind of you. Perhaps I could telephone you tomorrow morning. You are staying where?"

"It's quite near here, actually." He tore a leaf out of his financial diary, wrote down the name of their hotel, and held it out to her. She glanced at the slip of paper but did not take it from him. They shook hands, and then she was gone.

Standing on the sidewalk, waiting for the flow of traffic to stop so they could cross over, he said: "I thought at first she was like her mother—like what Mme Viénot was at that age. But she isn't."

"Not at all," Barbara said.

"Her voice made me realize that she wasn't."

"She has a lovely voice—so light. And silvery."

"She has a charming voice. Something of the French intonation carries over into her English, of course. But it's more than that, I think. It's an amused voice. It has a slight suggestion of humor, at no one's expense. As if she had learned to see things with a clarity that—that was often in excess of whatever need there was for seeing things clearly. And the residue had turned into something like amusement."

"But she didn't ask us to lunch."

"I know."

They went to the Guaranty Trust Company and were directed to the little upstairs room where their mail was handed to them.

"So what do we do now?" Barbara asked when they were outside again.

He looked at his watch. They had spent a considerable part of their first twenty-four hours in Paris walking the streets. He was dog-tired, his feet hurt, and Notre Dame in daylight faced the wrong way. For the moment, they were satiated with looking, and ready to be with someone they knew, it didn't matter how slightly, so long as they could talk about what they had seen, ask questions, and feel that they were a part of the intense sociability that they were aware of everywhere around them. Paris on the day after Bastille Day was not a deserted city. Also the sun was shining, and it was warm; it was like summer, and that lifted their spirits.

He said: "What about having lunch with Gagny at that bistro he told us about?"

"But we don't know where it is."

"Rue de Castellane." He consulted the plan of Paris by arrondissements. "It's somewhere behind the Madeleine . . . L17." He turned the pages. "Here it is. See?"

She pretended to look at the place he pointed out to her on the map, and then said: "If you're sure it's not too far."

The rue de Castellane proved to be farther than it appeared to be on the map, and when they got there, they found two, possibly three, eating places that answered to Gagny's description. Also, they were not very clear in their minds about the distinction between a bistro and a restaurant. They walked back and forth, peering at the curtained windows and trying to decide. They took a chance on one, the smallest. Gagny had said that it was a hangout of doubtful characters, and that there was sometimes brawling. The bistro was very quiet, and it looked respectable. They were shown to the last free table. Harold ordered an apéritif, and they settled down to read their mail from home, unaware that they were attracting a certain amount of attention from the men who were standing at the bar. Thugs and thieves do not, of course, wear funny hats or emblems in their buttonholes, like Lions and Elks, and some types of human behavior have to be explained before they are at all noticeable. The bistro was what Hector Gagny had said it was. In her letter about him, the cousin of the Canadian Ambassador failed to inform Mme Viénot of something that she happened to know, and that he didn't know she knew. It was in his folder in the Embassy files: he had a taste for low company. He enjoyed watching heated arguments, stage after stage of intricate insult, so stylized and at the same time so personal, all leading up to the point where the angry arguers could have exchanged blows— and never did. He also enjoyed being the unengaged spectator to situations in which the active participants must feel one another out. His eyes darting back and forth between their eyes, he measured accurately the risk taken, and then calculated enviously the chance of success.

In places the police knew about, Gagny never disguised his

education, or pretended to be anything but an observer. He sat, well dressed, well bred, quiet, and conspicuous, with his glass of wine in front of him, until the *type* who had been eying him for some time disengaged himself from the others and wandered over and was invited to sit down at his table.

"We're terribly restricted, you know," Gagny would tell the character with franc notes to be converted into dollars or, if worst came to worst, pounds sterling. "I mean to say, thirty-five pounds is all we're allowed to take out of England." Or, as he handed the pornographic postcards back to their owner: "Why do the men all have their shoes and socks on?" The *type*, a cigarette hanging from his lips and sometimes a question hanging in his eyes, would begin to talk. After a moment or two, Gagny would interrupt him politely in order to signal to the waiter to bring another glass.

In exchange for the glimpses of high life that he offered casually, not too much or too many at a time, he himself was permitted glimpses into the long corridor leading down, where crimes are committed for not very much money, or out of boredom, or because the line between feeling and action has become blurred; where the gendarme is the common enemy, and nobody knows the answer to a simple question, and danger is ever-present, the oxygen in the wine-smelling, smoke-filled air.

Only in France did Gagny allow himself this sort of diversion. In London it was not safe. He might be followed. His name was in the telephone directory. And he might have the bad luck to run into some acquaintance who also had a taste for low company.

Also, it was a matter of the Latin sensibility as compared with Anglo-Saxon. Oftener than not in Paris the *type* proved to be gentle, amiable, confused and more than willing (though the occasion for this had never presented itself) to pass over into the world of commonplace respectability. His education may have been sordid, pragmatic, and one-sided, but at least it had taught him how to stay alive, and he had a story to tell, invariably. Gagny had a story to tell, too, but he refrained from telling it. The *types* understood this. They were responsive, they understood many things—states of feeling, human needs, gradations of pleasure, complexities of motive—that people of good breeding unfortunately do not.

The sense of unreality—the dreadful recognition that he belonged not to the white race but to the pink or gray—that often came over him at official functions, among people of the highest importance and social distinction, he never experienced in any place where there was sawdust on the floor. He enjoyed the tribute that was paid to his social superiority (sometimes it only lasted a second, but it was there, nevertheless—a flicker of incredulity that he should be talking to them) and also their moment of vanity, encouraged by his lack of condescension. Though their fingernails were dirty and their clothes had been bought and worn by somebody else, they thought well of themselves; they were not apologetic. As a rule they understood perfectly what he wanted of them, and when he had checked the *addition* and put the change in his pocket notebook, they clapped him on the shoulder, smiling at his way of doing business, and went back to theirs. Now and then, misunderstanding, they offered him their friendship—were ready to throw in their lot, such as it was, with his, whatever that might prove to be. And when this offer was not accepted, they became surly or abusive, and it was a problem to get rid of them.

The Americans passed their letters back and forth, and when they were all read, Harold glanced at his watch again and said: "It looks as if he isn't coming."

Before he could catch the eye of the waitress, they saw Gagny, and saw that he had already seen them, but it was a very different Gagny from the one they had known in the country—erect and handsome and as wildly happy as if he had just succeeded in extricating himself from a long-standing love affair with a woman ten years older than he, and very demanding, given to emotional scenes, threats, tears, accusations that could only be answered in bed. He was delighted that they had kept their engagement with him. He had checked in at his hotel, he said, and come straight here, hoping to find them. They had been missed, he told them cheerfully. Mme Viénot and Mme Carrère had agreed that the house was not the same without the Americans. Then, seeing the look of surprise on their faces, he said: "You can believe me. I never make anything up." He surveyed the bar, in one fleeting glance, and for this afternoon renounced its interesting possibilities.

The waitress came and stood beside the table.

"Let me order for you," Gagny said, "since I know the place. And this is *my* lunch."

"Oh no it's not!" Harold cried.

"Oh yes it is!"

By the time the pâté arrived, they were all three talking at once, exchanging confidences, asking questions, being funny. The Americans found it a great relief to confide to someone their feelings about staying at the château, and who was in a better position to understand what they meant than someone who had seen them floundering? But if they had only known what he was really like . . .

He kept saying "Well exactly!" and they kept saying "I know. I know." They talked steadily through course after course. They finished the carafe of red wine and Gagny ordered a second, and cognac after that. The bistro was empty when they finally pushed their chairs back from the table. In spite of the adverse exchange, Gagny seized the check and would not hear of any other arrangement.

The sun was shining in the street outside. Gagny had an errand to do in the rue St. Honoré, and they walked with him as far as the rue Boissy d'Anglas. He was their favorite friend, and they felt sure that he was just as fond of them, but when the moment came for exchanging addresses, they were all three silent.

Standing on the street corner, Gagny smiled at the blue sky and then at them, and said: "You don't happen to know where Guerlain is, by any chance?"

"Just one moment," Harold said, "I'll look it up." He brought out his plan of Paris and began thumbing the pages. " 'Théâtres et spectacles . . . cabarets artistiques . . . cinémas . . .' "

"You won't find it in there," Gagny said.

" 'Cultes,' " Harold read. " 'Eglises Catholiques . . . Chapelles Catholiques Etrangères . . . Rite Melchite Grec' . . . Certainly it's in here. 'Eglises Luthériennes . . . Eglises réformées de France . . . Eglises protestantes étrangères . . . Science Chrétienne . . . Eglise Adventiste . . . Eglises Baptistes . . . Eglises Orthodoxes . . . Culte Israélite, Synagogues . . . Culte Mahométan, Mosquée . . . Facultés, Ecoles Supérieures . . .' "

Barbara put a restraining hand on his arm, and he looked up and saw that Gagny was ten feet away, in lively conversation with an English couple—friends, obviously—who had just arrived in Paris, by car, they said, from the south of France. They were very brown.

After a few minutes they said good-by and went off down the street. Gagny rejoined Harold and Barbara and said with a note of pure wonder in his voice: "They had beautiful weather the whole time they were on the Riviera."

"We came up out of the Métro," Harold said earnestly, all that wine having caught up with him at last, "and there it was right in front of us, with searchlights trained on the flying buttresses, and it was facing the *opposite* direction from Cleopatra's Needle and the Place de la Concorde."

"You're sure about that?" Gagny said, looking at him affectionately.

"Positive," Harold said.

"Well, old chap, all I can say is, there's something wrong somewhere."

"*Terribly* wrong," Harold said.

"I'd love to help you straighten it out," Gagny said. "But not this afternoon. I've got to buy perfume for my mother. Cheerio."

THEY SPENT all Friday morning at the Louvre and had lunch sitting on the sidewalk looking at the Comédie Française, but it was broad daylight and the lamps were not lighted; it was impossible to imagine what they were like at night. By not doing what they were told to do they had missed their one chance of having this beautiful experience. There was not going to be another illumination the whole rest of the summer.

They went back to the Louvre, and barely left time to check out of their hotel and get to the station. Sabine Viénot had not called, and they did not see her on the station platform. On the train they amused themselves by filling two pages of the financial diary with a list of things they would like to steal from the Louvre. Harold began with a Romanesque statue of the Queen of Sheba, and then took *The Lacemaker* by Vermeer, and *Lot and His Daughters* by Lucas van Leyden, and some panels by Giotto. Barbara took a fragment of a Greek statue—the lower half of a woman's body—and a section of the frieze of the Parthenon, and a Bronzino portrait. He took a Velasquez, a Goya, a Murillo, some Fra Angelico panels, La Belle Ferronière, and a fragment of a horse's head. She took two Rembrandts, a Goya, an El Greco crucifixion, and a Bruegel winter scene. . . . And so on and so on, as the shadows outside the train window grew longer and longer. When the compartment began to seem oppressive, they stood in the crowded corridor for a while. They saw a church spire that was like the little church in Brenodville, and here and there on the line of hills a big country house half hidden by trees, and sometimes they saw the sky reflected in a river. When they grew tired of standing, they ground out their cigarettes and went back into their compartment and read. From time to time they raised their eyes to observe the other passengers or the sunset.

Mme Viénot had said that she was expecting some relatives on Friday, and would Harold look around for them when he got off the train? But there was no one in the railway station in Blois who appeared uncertain about where he was going or to be looking for two Americans. The taxi brought them by a back road through the forest instead of by the highway along the river, and this reminded Harold of something. "We thought they would come from the direction of the highway," Mme. Bonenfant had said, "and they came through the forest instead." He turned and looked back. There were no Germans in the forest now, but would it ever be free of them? Was that why the gate was kept locked?

It was just getting dark when they turned into the drive and saw the lights of the house. Leaving their suitcases in the hall, they walked past the screen and into the drawing room. Mme Viénot and her mother and M. and Mme Carrère and Mme Straus-Muguet were all sitting around the little table in front of the fireplace. Seeing their faces light up with pleasure and expectancy, Harold thought: Why, it's almost as if we had come home. . . .

"We've been waiting dinner for you," Mme Viénot said as she shook hands with them. "How did you like Paris?"

"Did anyone ever not like Paris?" Harold said.

"And you were comfortable at the Vouillemont?"

He laughed. "Once we found it, we were comfortable," he said.

"And the weather?"

"The weather was beautiful."

"Sabine telephoned this evening," Mme Viénot said, on the way into the dining room. "She tried to reach you, it seems, after you had gone. I'm afraid she does not have a very exact idea of time."

"But she wasn't on the train with us? We looked for her—"

"She is coming next week end instead," Mme Viénot said as he drew her chair out for her. "I hope you didn't give yourself any anxiety on her account?"

He shook his head.

"She enjoyed meeting you," Mme Viénot said.

"We enjoyed meeting her," he said, and then, since she seemed to be waiting for something more: "She's charming."

Mme Viénot smiled and unfolded her napkin.

He noticed that there were two people handing the soup plates around the table—Thérèse and a boy of seventeen or eighteen, in a white coat, with thick glasses and slicked-down hair. His large hands were very clean but looked like raw meat. He served unskillfully, in an agony of shyness, and Harold wondered if Mme Viénot had added a farm boy to her staff.

As always, he could speak better when he was sure he had an audience. ". . . There we were in the Métro," he said, "with no idea of what station to get off at, or what arrondissement our hotel was in."

"I should have told you," Mme Viénot said. "I'm so sorry. And this time you didn't have M. Fleury to take you there."

"Barbara thought it was somewhere near the Louvre—"

"Oh dear no! You should have descended at Concorde."

"So we discovered. But we got off at the Louvre, instead, and walked two or three blocks until we came to a sidewalk café, and the waiter showed me where the telephone books were, but there were so many and I couldn't make head nor tail of them, so he and the proprietress and everybody there dropped what they were doing and thumbed through telephone directories and finally the waiter found it."

"I should have thought anyone could have told you where it is," M. Carrère said. "It is very well known."

"*They* didn't know about it. . . . I tried to buy them all a drink before I left—they had been so kind—and they refused. Was that wrong? In America it would not have been wrong."

"Not at all," Mme Viénot said. "Another time just say: 'I insist that you have a glass of wine with me,' and the offer will be accepted. But it wasn't at all necessary."

"I wish I'd known that."

"They were no doubt happy to have been of assistance to you. And you found your hotel?"

"We took a taxi," he said. "And the fares have gone up. They have a chart they show you. I remembered that you had said not to pay more than the amount on the meter, and when the driver got angry I made him come into the hotel with me and the concierge straightened it out. After that, whenever we took a taxi I was careful to ask the driver if I had given him enough."

"But they will cheat you!" Mme Viénot exclaimed.

"They didn't. I knew from the chart what it *should* be, and added the tip, and they none of them asked for more."

"Perhaps they found you sympathetic," Mme Bonenfant said.

"It was pleasanter than arguing."

He saw that Mme Straus-Muguet was looking at him and he said to her with his eyes: *I was afraid you wouldn't be here when we got back.* . . .

Mme Viénot lifted her spoon to her lips and then exclaimed. Turning to Barbara, she said: "My cook gave notice while you were gone. The new cook, poor dear, is very nervous. Last night there was too much salt in everything, so I spoke to her about it, and tonight there is no salt whatever in the soup. Do I dare speak to her again?" She turned to M. Carrère, who said, his clown's eyes crinkling: "In your place I don't think I should. It might bring on something worse."

"I hope you will be patient with her," Mme Viénot said. "She has a sister living in the village, whom she wanted to be near. The boy is her son. He has had no experience but she begged me to take him on so that he can learn the métier and they can hire themselves out as a couple. . . . Tell us what happened to you in Paris."

"We spent all our time walking the streets," Barbara said, "and looking in shop windows."

"They are extraordinary, aren't they?" Mme Carrère agreed. "Quite like the way they were before the war."

"And we had lunch with M. Gagny," Harold said.

"Yes? You saw M. Gagny?" Mme Viénot said, and Mme Carrère asked if they had followed her directions on the night of the illumination. Harold hesitated, and then, not wanting to spoil her pleasure, said that they had. He had a feeling that she knew he was not telling the truth. She did not attempt to catch him out, but the interest went out of her face.

As he and Barbara were undressing for bed, they remarked upon a curious fact. They had hoped before they came here that a stay at the château would make them better able to deal with what they found in Paris, and instead a stay of three days in Paris had made them able, really for the first time, to deal with life in the château. Neither of them mentioned their reluctance to leave Paris, that afternoon, or the fact that their room, after the comforts of the hotel, seemed cold and cheerless. Thérèse had again forgotten to bring them a can of hot water; the fan of experience was already beginning to close, and in Paris it had opened all the way.

Chapter 8

THEY SPENT Saturday morning in their room. Barbara filled the washbasin with cold water and while she washed and rinsed and washed again, Harold sat on the edge of the tub and told her about the murder of the Duc de Guise, in the château of Blois, in the year 1588.

"He got in, and then he found he couldn't get out. . . . He was warned on the Grand Staircase, but by that time it was too late; there were guards posted everywhere. He asked for the Queen, who could have saved him, and she didn't come. He sent his servant for a handkerchief, as a test, and the servant didn't come back. . . . Are you listening to me?" he demanded above the sound of the soapy water being sucked down the drain.

"Yes, but I've got to change the water in the sink."

"You don't have to make so much noise. . . . Everywhere he looked, people avoided meeting his eyes. He had just come from the bed of one of the Queen's ladies-in-waiting."

"Which queen was this?"

"Not Queen Victoria. Catherine de Médicis, I think. Anyway, it was two days before Christmas. And he was cold and hungry. He stood in front of the fireplace, warming himself and eating some dried prunes, I guess it was. It's hard to make out, from that little dictionary. The council of state convened, and they told him the King had sent for him. So he left the room—"

At this point Barbara left the bathroom and went to the armoire. Harold followed her. "The eight hired assassins in the next room bowed to him," he said, helping himself to a piece of candy from the box on the table. "I suppose it comes from living in the same house with *her,* but somebody's been at the chocolates while we were away."

"Oh, I don't think so," Barbara said, and closed the doors of the armoire and went back to the bathroom with a nightgown and a slip, which she added to the laundry in the washbasin.

"Want to bet?"

"It doesn't matter if they did."

"I know it doesn't. But I don't think it was Thérèse, even so."

"Who else could have?"

"Somebody that likes chocolate. . . . He got as far as the door to the King's dressing room, and saw that there were more of them, at the end of the narrow passageway, waiting for him with drawn swords in their hands."

"Poor man!"

"Mmm. Poor man, indeed—he was responsible for the Massacre of St. Bartholomew. It took forty men to do him in. He was huge and very powerful. And when it was all over, the King bent down cautiously and slapped his face."

"After he was *dead?*"

"Yes. Then he went and told his mother. What people!"

"If you knew what it is like to wash silk in cold water!" Barbara said indignantly.

"Why do you do it, then? I could go down and ask them for a can of hot water?"

There was no answer.

He wandered back into the bedroom, and stood looking around the room, seeing it with the eyes of the person who took the chocolates. Not Mme Bonenfant. The flowers hadn't been changed. And anyway, she wouldn't. Not the houseboy, in all probability. He was new, and he had no reason to be in this part of the house. Mme Viénot? Who else? If they were curious about her, why shouldn't she be curious about them?

She had stood in the doorway waving to them until the taxi disappeared around the corner of the house. And then what happened? Was she relieved? Was she happy to see them go? He put himself in her shoes and decided that he would have been relieved for a minute or two, and then he would have begun to worry. He would have been afraid that they would find in Paris what they were looking for—they were tourists, after all —and not come back. He had offered to have the luggage packed so that it could be removed from their room, and if she remembered that, she would surely think they had planned not to come back, and that in a day or so she would get a letter saying they'd changed their plans again, and would she send their luggage, which was all packed and ready, to the Hôtel Vouillemont. . . . Only the luggage was not packed, of course. And what she must have seen when she threw open the door of the room was that they had left everything—clothes, books, all their possessions, scattered over the room. There was a half-finished letter on the desk, and the box of Swiss chocolates open on the table. The room must have looked as if they had left it to go for a walk.

He stood reading the letter, which had lain on the pad of the writing desk since last Tuesday. It was to Edith Ireland, of all people. Barbara was thanking her for the book and the bottle of champagne she had sent to the boat. Barbara's handwriting was very dashing, and not very legible, because of a tendency to abbreviate and leave off parts of letters, but if you were patient you could get the hang of it, and no doubt Mme Viénot had.

On the table, beside a pile of guidebooks, were three pages— also in Barbara's handwriting—of a diary she was keeping. The entries covered the period from July 11, when they came to the château from Tours, through July 13, the day before they went up to Paris. He turned away from the table, relieved and grinning.

She had a façade that she retired behind when she was with strangers—the image of an unworldly, well-bred, charming-looking, gentle young woman. The image was not even false to her character; it merely left out half of it. Who could possibly have any reason to say anything rude or unkind to anyone so shy and unsure of herself? Nobody ever did.

It was the façade that was keeping the diary.

❧ ❧
❧

WHEN THEY WENT down to lunch they learned that Mme Viénot's relatives had arrived sometime during the morning. The dining-room table was larger by two leaves to accommodate them and there were three empty chairs. Two of them were soon filled, by a middle-aged woman and a young man. The cook's son brought two more soup plates, and Mme Viénot said: "How do you find Maman? Doesn't she look well?"

"She is more beautiful than ever," the young man said, his face totally without expression, as if it had been carved out of a piece of wood and could not change.

"The weather has been most discouraging here," Mme Viénot said.

"In Paris it is the same. Rain day after day," the young man said. "One hears everywhere that it is the atomic bomb that is responsible. I myself think it is by analogy with the political climate, which is damp, cold, unhopeful. . . . Alix said to tell you that she is giving Annette her bottle. She will be down presently."

"Perhaps she can manage some slight adjustment of the baby's schedule which will permit her to come to meals at the usual time," Mme Viénot said. "It is not merely the empty chair. It upsets the service. . . . Your father and mother are well?"

"My father is having trouble with his eyes. It is not cataracts, though it seems that the difficulty may be progressive. It is a question of the arteries not carrying enough food to the optic nerve. Maman is well—at least, well enough to go to weddings. There has been a succession of them. My cousin Suzanne, in Brittany. And Philippe Soulès. You remember that de Cléry girl everyone thought was a mental defective? She has turned out to be the clever one of the family. They are going to live with his parents, it seems. And my Uncle Eugène, for the third time. Or is it the fourth? And Simone Valéry. Maman has been thinking of taking a job. She has been approached by Jacques Fath. She has just about decided to say no. It is rather an amusing idea, and if she could come and go as she pleased—but it seems they would expect her to keep regular hours, and she is quite incapable of that. Besides, she has set her heart on a trip to Venice. In August."

"The Biennale?"

"No, another wedding. I have not seen Jean-Claude. I read about him in *Figaro*. And Georges Dunois had lunch with him last Wednesday in London. Georges asked me to pay you his devoted respects. He said Jean-Claude has aged."

"The responsibility is, of course, very great," Mme Viénot said modestly, and then turning to Barbara: "We are discussing my son-in-law, who is in the government."

"He now looks twenty-two or three, Georges said."

"Suzanne writes that he is being sent to Oran, on an important mission, the details of which she is not free to disclose."

"Naturally."

"She is expecting another child in November."

"She is my favorite of the entire family, and I am not sure I would recognize her if I saw her. I never see her, not even at those functions where one would have supposed her husband's career might be affected by her absence. Proving that the Ministry is helpless without him."

"She is absorbed in her family duties," Mme Viénot said.

"So one is told. As for Jean-Claude, one hears everywhere

that he is immensely valued, successful, happy, and— Ah, there you are."

The young woman who sat down in the chair next to Barbara was very fair, and her blue eyes had a look of childlike sweetness and innocence. She acknowledged the introductions in the most charming French accent Harold had ever heard, and then said: "I did not expect to be down for another quarter of an hour, but she went right off to sleep. She was exhausted by the trip, and so many new sensations."

Harold decided that he liked her, and that he didn't like the man, who seemed to have a whole repertoire of manners—one (serious, intellectual) for M. Carrère; another (simpering, mock-gallant) for Mme Viénot; another (devoted, simple, respectful) for Mme Bonenfant; and still another for Barbara, whose hand he had raised to his lips. Harold was put off by the hand-kissing (though Barbara was not; she did not, in fact, turn a hair; where had she learned that?) and by the limp handshake when he and the young Frenchman were introduced and the look of complete indifference now when their eyes met across the table.

⚜ ⚜
⚜

AT TWO O'CLOCK, when they came downstairs from their room, Mme Straus-Muguet was waiting for them in the second-floor hall at the turn of the stairs. Speaking slowly and distinctly, the way people do when they are trying to impress careful instructions on the wandering minds of children, she asked if they would do an errand for her. She had overheard them telling Mme Viénot that they were going to Blois this afternoon. On a scrap of paper she had written the name of a confiserie and she wanted them to get some candy for her, a particular kind, a delicious bonbon that was made only at this shop in Blois. She gave Barbara the colored tinsel wrapper it came in, to show the

143

confiseur, and a hundred-franc note. They were to get eight pieces of candy—six for her and two for themselves.

This time the bus was not crowded. They found seats together and all the way into town sat looking out of the window at scenery that was simple and calm, as Harold's guidebook said —long perspectives of the river, with here and there a hill, some sheep, a house, two trees, women and children wading, and then the same hill (or so it seemed), the same sheep, the same house, the same two trees, like a repeating motif in wallpaper. It was a landscape, one would have said, in which no human being had ever raised his voice. They went straight to the ration bureau and stood in line at the high counter, with their green passports ready, and were quite unprepared for the unpleasant scene that took place there. A grim-faced, gray-haired woman took their passports, examined them efficiently, and then returned them to Harold with ration stamps for bread, sugar, etc. She also said something to him in very rapid French that he did not understand. Speaking as good French as he knew how to speak, he asked her if she would please repeat what she had said, and she shrieked furiously at him in English: "They're for ten days only!"

They stood staring at each other, her face livid with anger and his very pale. Then he said mildly: "If you ever come to America, you will find that you are sometimes obliged to ask the same question two or three times." And because this remark was so mild, or perhaps because it was so illogical (the woman behind the counter had no intention ever of setting foot out of France, and if by any stretch of the imagination she did, it would not be to go to a country that so threatened the peace of the world), there was no more shouting. He went on looking directly into her eyes until she looked away.

Outside, standing on the steps of the building, he said: "Was it because we are taking food out of the mouths of starving Frenchmen?"

"Possibly," Barbara said.

"But we haven't seen anybody who looked starving. And they *want* American tourists. The French government is anxious to have them come."

"I know. But she isn't the French government."

"Maybe she hates men." His voice was unsteady and he felt weak in the knees. "Or it could be, I suppose, that her whole life has been dreadful. But the way she spoke to us was so—"

"It's something that happens to women sometimes," Barbara said. "An anger that comes over them suddenly, and that they feel no part in."

"But why?"

She had no answer.

If it is true that nothing exists without its opposite, then the thing they had just been exposed to was merely the opposite of the amiability and kindness they had encountered everywhere in France. Also, the gypsy fortuneteller had promised Barbara malice she didn't expect.

Facing the ration bureau was a small open-air market, and they wandered through it slowly, looking at straw hats, cotton dresses, tennis sneakers, and cheap cooking utensils. They were unable to get the incident out of their minds, though they stopped talking about it. The day was blighted.

From the market they made their way down into the lower part of the city, and found Mme Straus's candy shop. They also spent some time in the shop next door, where they bought an intermediate French grammar, two books on gardening, and postcards. Then they walked along the street, dividing their attention between the people on the sidewalk and the contents of shop windows, until they arrived at the ramp that led up to the château.

They stood in the courtyard, looking at the octagonal staircase and comparing what the Michelin said with the actuality in front of them. Because it was getting late and they weren't sure they wanted to join a conducted tour—they were, in fact, rather tired of conducted tours—they walked in the opposite direction from the sign that said *guide du château*, and toward the wing of Gaston d'Orléans. Harold put his hand out and tried a doorknob. It turned and the door swung open. They walked in and up a flight of marble stairs, admiring the balustrades and the ceiling, and at the head of the stairs they came upon two large tapestries dealing with the Battle of Dunkerque—a previous battle, in the seventeenth century, judging by the costumes and theatrical-looking implements of war. The doors leading out of this room were all locked, and so they made their way down the stairs again, trying other doors, until they were out in the courtyard once more. They were just in time to see two busloads of tourists from the American Express stream out of the wing of Louis XII and crowd into the tiny blue and gold chapel. The tourists were with a guide and the guide was speaking English.

Standing under an arcade, surrounded by their countrymen, Barbara and Harold learned about the strange life of Charles d'Orléans, who was a poet and at fifteen married his cousin, the daughter of Charles VI. She had already been married to Richard II of England, when she was seven years old. The new marriage did not last long. She died in childbirth, and the poet remarried, lost the battle of Agincourt, and was imprisoned for twenty-five years, after which, a widower of fifty, he again married—this time a girl of fourteen—and surrounded himself with a little court of artists and writers, and at seventy-one had at last, by his third wife, the son he had waited more than fifty years for.

"I see what you mean about having a guide who speaks English," Harold said as they followed the crowd back across the courtyard and up a flight of steps to the Hall of State. They were waiting to learn about that, too, when the guide came over to them and asked Harold to step outside for a moment, with Madame.

He was about thirty years old, with large dark intelligent eyes, regular features, a narrow face cleanly cut, and dark skin.

I: *Leo and Virgo*

An aristocratic survival from the time of François premier, Harold thought as they followed the guide across the big room, with the other tourists looking at them with more interest than they had shown toward the Hall of State. He did not know precisely what to expect, or why the guide had singled them out, but whatever he wanted or wanted to know, Harold was ready to oblige him with, since the guide was not only a gentleman but obviously a far from ordinary man.

Though the guide made his living taking American tourists through historical monuments, he did not understand Americans the way he understood history. If you are as openhanded as they mostly are, you cannot help rejoicing in small accidental economies, being pleased when the bus conductor fails to collect your fare, etc., and it doesn't at all mean that you are trying to take advantage of anybody. The guide asked them if they were members of his party, and Harold said no, and the guide said would they leave the château immediately by that little door right down there?

The whole conversation took place in English, and so Harold had no trouble understanding what the guide said, but for a few seconds he went right on looking at the Frenchman's face. The expression in the gray eyes was contempt.

Blushing and angry, with the guide and with himself (for he had had in his wallet the means of erasing this embarrassment as completely as if it had never happened), he made his way down the ramp with Barbara, past the château gift shop, and into the street.

It was too soon for the bus, and so they turned in at the pâtisserie, and ordered tea and cakes, and found that they had no appetite for them when they came. They got up and left, and a few minutes later had a third contretemps. The bus driver, misunderstanding Harold's "deux" for "douze," gave him the wrong change and would not rectify his mistake or let them get on the bus until everybody else had got on. So they had to stand, after being first in line at the bus stop.

"So far," he said, peering through the window at the river, "we've had very few experiences like what happened this afternoon, and they were really the result of growing confidence. We were attempting to behave as if we were at home."

Out of consideration for his feelings, Barbara did not point out that this was only partly true; at home he was neither as friendly nor as trusting as he was here, and he did not expect strangers to be that way with him. She herself did not mind what had happened half as much as she minded having to come down to dinner in a dress that she had already worn three times.

⚜ ⚜
⚜

MME STRAUS-MUGUET was waiting for them on the stairs. She praised them for carrying out her errand so successfully, in a city they did not know well, and invited them to take an apéritif with her before lunch on Sunday morning. She seemed subdued, and as if during their absence in Paris she had suffered a setback of some kind—a letter containing bad news that her mind kept returning to, or unkindness where she least expected it.

Feeling tired and bruised by their own series of setbacks, they hurried on up the stairs, conscious that the house was cold and there would not be any hot water to wash in and they would have to spend still another evening trying to understand people who could speak English but preferred to speak French.

From the conversation at the lunch table, Harold had pieced together certain facts about Mme Viénot's relatives. The blonde young woman with the charming low voice and the beautiful accent was Mme Viénot's niece, and the young man was her husband. Listening and waiting, he eventually found out their names: M. and Mme de Boisgaillard. And they had brought with them not only their own three-months-old baby but Mme de Boisgaillard's sister's two children, who were too young to come to the table, and a nursemaid. But when they sat down to dinner he still did not know who the middle-aged woman directly across from him was. There was something that separated her from everybody else at the table. Studying her, he saw that she wore no jewelry of any kind, and her blue dress was so plain and inexpensive-looking that he wasn't absolutely sure that it wasn't a uniform—in which case, she was the children's nurse. Or perhaps M. de Boisgaillard's mother, he decided; a woman alone in the world, and except for her claim on her son, without resources. Now that he was married, the claim was, of course, much slighter, and so she was obliged to be grateful that she was here at all. No one spoke to her. Thinking that it might ease her shyness, her feeling of being (as he was) excluded from the conversation, he smiled directly at her. The response was polite and impersonal, and he decided that, as so often was the case with him, she was past rescuing.

He listened to the pitch, the intonations, of Mme de Boisgaillard's voice as if he were hearing a new kind of music, and decided that there were as many different ways of speaking French as there were French people. Because of her voice he would have trusted absolutely anything she said. But he trusted her anyway, because of the naturalness and simplicity of her manner. Looking at her, he felt he knew her very well, without knowing anything at all about her. It was as if they had played together as children. Her husband's voice was rather high, thin, and reedy. It was also the voice of someone who knows exactly what to respect and what to be contemptuous of. So strange that two such different people should have married . . .

Mme de Boisgaillard spoke English fluently. In an undertone, with a delicate smile, she supplied Barbara, who sat next to her, with the word or phrase that would limit the context of an otherwise puzzling statement or explain the point of an amusing remark. Harold clutched at these straws eagerly. When Mme Viénot translated for them, it was usually some word that he knew already, and so she was never the slightest help. He watched M. de Boisgaillard until their eyes met across the table.

The young Frenchman immediately looked away, and Harold was careful not to look at him again.

Mme Viénot was eager to learn whether her nephew thought the Schumann cabinet would jump during September. The young man and M. Carrère both thought it would—not because of a crisis, easy though it was to find one, but because of political squabbles that were of no importance except to the people directly involved.

"Why would they wait until September?" Harold asked. "Why not in August?"

"Because August is the month when Parliament takes its annual vacation," Mme Viénot said. "No government has ever been known to jump at this time of year. They always wait until September."

The joke was thoroughly enjoyed, and Mme Straus-Muguet nodded approvingly at Harold for having made it possible.

After the dessert course, napkins were folded in such a way as to conceal week-old wine stains and then inserted in their identifying rings.

Barbara saw that Mme Straus was aware that she had been looking at her, and said: "I have been admiring your little diamond heart."

"You like it?" Mme Straus said. From her tone of voice one would almost have supposed that she was about to undo the clasp of the fine gold chain and present the little heart, chain and all, to the young woman at the far end of the table. However, her hands remained in her lap, and she said: "It was given to me by a friend, long long ago," leaving them to decide for themselves whether the fiery little object was the souvenir of a romantic attachment. Mme Viénot gave her a glance of frank disbelief and pushed her chair back from the table.

The ladies left the dining room in the order of their age. Harold started to follow M. Carrère out of the room and to his surprise felt a hand on his sleeve, detaining him. M. de Boisgaillard drew him over to the other side of the room and asked him,

in French, how he liked it at the château. Harold started to answer tactfully and saw that the face now looking down into his
expected a truthful answer, was really interested, and would
know if he was not candid; so he was, and the Frenchman laughed
and suggested that they walk outside in the garden.

He opened one of the dining-room windows and stepped out,
and Harold followed him around the corner of the house and
through the gap in the hedge and into the potager. With a light
rain—it was hardly more than a mist—falling on their shoulders,
they walked up and down the gravel paths. The Frenchman
asked how rich the ordinary man in America was. How many
cars were there in the whole country? Did American women
really rule the roost? And did they love their husbands or just
love what they could get out of them? Was it true that everybody had running water and electricity? But not true that
everybody owned their own house and every house had a dish-
washer and a washing machine? Did Harold have any explanation to offer of how, in a country made up of such different
racial strains, every man should be so passionately interested in
machinery? Was it the culture or was it something that stemmed
from the early days of the country—from its colonial period?
How was America going to solve the Negro problem? Was it
true that all Negroes were innately musical? And were they
friendly with the white people who exploited them or did they
hate them one and all? And how did the white people feel about
Negroes? What did Americans think of Einstein? of Freud? of
Stalin? of Churchill? of de Gaulle? Did they feel any guilt on
account of Hiroshima? Did they like or dislike the French?
Had he read the Kinsey Report, and was it true that virtually
every American male had had some homosexual experience?
And so on and so on.

The less equipped you are to answer such questions, the more
flattering it is to be asked them, but to answer even superficially
in a foreign language you need more than a tourist's vocabulary.

"You don't speak German?"

Harold shook his head. They stood looking at each other help-lessly.

"You don't speak *any* English?" Harold said.

"Pas un mot."

A few minutes later, as they were walking and talking again, the Frenchman forgot and shifted to German anyway, and Harold stopped him, and they went on trying to talk to each other in French. Very often Harold's answer did not get put into the right words or else in his excitement he did not pro-nounce them well enough for them to be understood, the ap-proximation being some other word entirely, and the two men stopped and stared at each other. Then they tried once more, and impasses that seemed hopeless were bridged after all; or if this didn't happen, the subject was abandoned in favor of a new subject.

It began to rain in earnest, and they turned up their coat col-lars and went on walking and talking.

"Shall we go in?" the Frenchman asked, a moment later.

As they went back through the gap in the hedge, Harold said to himself that it was a different house they were returning to. By the addition of a man of the family it had changed; it had stopped being matriarchal and formal and cold, and become solid and hospitable and human, like other houses.

At the door of the petit salon, they separated. Harold took in the room at a glance. M. Carrère sat looking quite forlorn, the one man among so many women. And did he imagine it or was Mme Viénot put out with them? There was an empty chair beside Mme de Boisgaillard and he sat down in it and tried once more to follow the conversation. He learned that the woman he had taken for the children's nurse or possibly M. de Bois-gaillard's mother was Mme de Boisgaillard's mother instead; which meant that she was Mme Viénot's sister and had a perfect right to be here. What he had failed to perceive, like the six blind men and the elephant, was that she was deaf and so could not take part in general conversation. During dinner she did not even try, but now if someone spoke directly to her she adjusted the pointer of the little black box that she held to her ear as if it were a miniature radio, and seemed to understand.

When the others retired to their rooms at eleven o'clock, Eugène de Boisgaillard swept the Americans ahead of him, through a doorway and down a second-floor hall they had not been in before, and they found themselves in a bedroom with a dressing room off it. They stood looking down at the baby, who was fast asleep on her stomach but escaped entirely from the covers, at right angles to the crib, with her knees tucked under her, her feet crossed like hands, her rump in the air.

Her mother straightened her around and covered her, and then they tiptoed back into the larger room and began to talk. Mme de Boisgaillard translated and summarized quickly and accurately, leaving them free to go on to the next thing they wanted to say.

Unlike M. Carrère, Eugène de Boisgaillard did not hate all Germans. His political views were Liberal and democratic. He was also as curious as a cat. He wanted to know how long Harold and Barbara had been married, and how they had met one another, and what part of America they grew up in. He asked their first names and then what their friends called them. He asked them to call him by his first name. And then the questions began again, as if the first thing in the morning he and they were starting out for the opposite ends of the earth and there was only tonight for them to get to know each other. Once, when a question was so personal that Harold thought he must have misunderstood, he turned to Mme de Boisgaillard and she smiled and shook her head ruefully and said: "I hope you do not mind. That is the way he is. When I think he cannot possibly have said what I think I have heard him say, I know that is just what he did say."

At her husband's suggestion, she left them and went downstairs to see what there was in the larder, and they were surprised to discover that without her they couldn't talk to each other.

They waited awkwardly until she came into the room carrying a tray with a big bowl of sour cream and four smaller bowls, a sugar bowl, and spoons.

Eugène de Boisgaillard pointed to the empty fireplace and said: "No andirons. Does the one in your room work?"

Harold explained that it had a shield over it.

"During the Occupation the Germans let the forests be depleted—intentionally—and so one is allowed to cut only so much wood," Mme de Boisgaillard said, "and if they used it now there would not be enough for the winter. Poor Tante! She drives herself so hard. . . . The thing I always forget is what a beautiful smell this house has. It may be the box hedge, though Mummy says it is the furniture polish, but it doesn't smell like any other house in the world."

"Have your shoes begun to mildew?" Eugène de Boisgaillard said.

Barbara shook her head.

"They will," he said.

"You will drive them away," Mme de Boisgaillard said, "and then we won't have anyone our age to talk to."

"We will go after them," Eugéne de Boisgaillard said, "talking every step of the way. The baby's sugar ration," he said, saluting the sugar bowl.

Sweetened with sugar, the half-solidified sour cream was delicious.

"Have you enjoyed knowing M. Carrère?" Eugène asked.

Harold said that M. Carrère seemed to be a very kind man.

"He's also very rich," Eugène said. "Everything he touches turns into more money, more gilt-edged stock certificates. He is a problem to the Bank of France. Toinette has a special tone of voice in speaking of him—have you noticed? Where does she place him, I wonder? On some secondary level. Not with Périclès, or Beethoven. Not with Louis XIV. With Saint-Simon, perhaps . . . In the past year I have learned how to interpret the public face. It has been very useful. The public face is much more ponderous and explicit than the private face and it asks only one question: 'What is it you want?' And whatever you want is unfortunately just the thing it isn't convenient for you to be given. . . . Do you get on well with your parents, Harold?"

He listened attentively to Alix's translation of the answer to this question and then said: "My father is very conservative. He has never in his whole life gone to the polls and voted."

"Why not?" Barbara asked.

"His not voting is an act of protest against the Revolution."

"You don't mean the Revolution of 1789?"

"Yes. He does not approve of it."

Tears of amusement ran down Harold's cheeks and he reached for his handkerchief and wiped them away.

"What does your father do?" Barbara asked.

"He collects porcelain. That's all he has done his whole life."

In a moment Harold had to get his handkerchief out again as Eugène launched forth on the official and unofficial behavior of his superior, the Minister of Planning and External Affairs.

At one o'clock the Americans stood up to go, and, still talking, Eugène and Alix accompanied them down the upstairs hall until they were in their own part of the house. Whispering and tittering like naughty children, they said good night. Was Mme Viénot awake, Harold wondered. Could she hear them? Did she disapprove of such goings on?

Eugène said that he had one last question to ask.

"Don't," Alix whispered.

"Why not? Why shouldn't I ask them? . . . Is there a double bed in your room?"

Harold shook his head.

"I knew it!" Eugène said. "I told Alix that there wouldn't be. Don't you find it strange—don't you think it is *extraordinary* that all the double beds in the house are occupied by single women?"

They said good night all over again, and the Americans crept up the stairs, which, even so, creaked frightfully. When Barbara fell asleep, Harold wrapped the covers around her snugly and moved over into his own damp bed and lay awake for some time, thinking. What had happened this evening was so different from anything else that had happened to them so far on their trip, and he felt that a part of him that had been left behind in America, without his realizing it, had now caught up with him. He thought with wonder how far off he could be about people. For Eugène was totally unlike what he had seemed at first to be. He was not cold and insincere but amusing and unpredictable, and masculine, and direct, and intelligent, and like a wonderful older brother. Knowing him was reason enough for them to come back time after time, through the years, to France. . . .

Chapter 9

AT BREAKFAST the next morning, Mme Viénot's manner with the Americans did not convey approval or disapproval. She urged on them a specialty of the countryside—bread with meat drippings poured over it—and then, folding her napkin, excused herself to go and dress for church. Harold asked if they could go to church also, and she said: "Certainly."

At ten thirty the dog cart appeared in front of the house, with the gardener in the driver's seat and his white plow horse hitched to the traces. It had been arranged that Barbara should go to church in the cart with Mme Straus-Muguet and Alix and Eugène; that Mme Bonenfant should ride in the Bentley with M. and Mme Carrère; that Harold and Mme Viénot should bicycle. She rode her own, he was given the cook's, which got out of his control, in spite of Mme Viénot's repeated warnings. Unaccustomed to bicycles without brakes, he came sailing into the village a good two minutes ahead of her.

They were in plenty of time for Mass, but instead of going directly to the little church she went to Mme Michot's, where she stood gazing at the fruit and vegetables, her expression a mixture of disdain and disbelief, as if Mme Michot were trying to introduce her to persons whose social status was not at all what they pretended. Madame Michot's tomatoes were inferior and her plums were too dear. In the end she bought two lemons, half a pound of dried figs, and some white raisins that were un-accountably cheap.

As they came out of the little shop, she explained that she had one more errand; her seamstress was making her a green silk dress that was to have the New Look, and it had been promised for today.

At the seamstress's house, Mme Viénot knocked and waited. She knocked again. She stood in the street and called. She stopped and questioned a little girl, who told her reluctantly where the seamstress had said she could be found. Mme Viénot looked at her wrist watch. "I really don't see why she couldn't have been home!" she exclaimed. "We are already quite late for church, and it means going clear to the other side of the village."

Once more they got on their bicycles. As they were riding side by side over the bumpy cobblestones, she remarked that the village was older than it looked. "There is a legend—whether it is true I cannot say—that Jeanne d'Arc, traveling toward Chinon with her escort of three or four soldiers, arrived at Brenodville at nightfall and was denied a lodging by the monks."

"Why?"

"Because of her sex, no doubt."

"Where did she go?" Harold asked.

"She slept in a farmhouse, I believe."

He looked around for Gothic stonework and found, here and there, high up out of harm's way, a small gargoyle at the end of a waterspout, a weathered stone pinnacle, a carved lintel, or some other piece of medieval decoration, proving that the story was at least possible. The houses themselves—sour, secretive, commonplace-looking—said that if Jeanne d'Arc were to come again in the middle of the twentieth century, she would get the same inhospitable reception, and not merely from the monks but from everybody.

The house where the little girl had said the seamstress said she could be found was locked and shuttered, and no one came to the door. At five minutes of twelve, they arrived at the vestibule of the church. Mme Viénot genuflected in the aisle outside the family pew and then moved in and knelt beside her mother. Harold followed her. Half kneeling and half sitting, he tried not to look so much like a Protestant. The drama on the altar was reaching its climax. A little silver bell tinkled. The congregation spoke. (Was it Latin? Was it French?) Mme Viénot struck her flat chest three times and seemed to be asking for something from the depths of her heart, but though he listened intently, he could not hear what it was; it was lost in the asking of other low voices all around them. The bell tinkled again and again, insistently. There was a moment of hushed expectation and then the congregation rose from their knees with a roaring sound that nobody paid any attention to, filled the aisle, streamed out of the chill of the little church into the more surprising chill of a cold gray July day, and, pleased that an essential act was done, broke out into smiles and conversation.

Harold waited beside the two bicycles while Mme Viénot went into the stationer's for her mother's *Figaro*. He looked around for Mme Straus-Muguet, not sure whether she had meant them to meet her here in the village after church or where. And if he saw her beckoning to him, how would he escape from Mme Viénot? Mme Straus was nowhere in sight now, and he had made two trips downstairs after breakfast without encountering her.

When Mme Viénot took a long, thin, empty wine bottle out of her saddlebag and went into still another shop, he followed her out of curiosity and was introduced to M. Canourgue, whose stock was entirely out of sight, under a wooden counter or in the adjoining room. She counted out more ration coupons, and explained that Harold was American and a friend of M. Georges who was so fond of chocolates. The wine bottle went into the back room and came back full of olive oil. Mme Viénot bought sardines, and this and that. When they were outside in the street again, Harold saw that the canvas saddlebag of her bicycle was crammed, and so he took the bottle from her and placed it carefully on its side in his saddle bag, which was empty.

As they rode home, he asked where she had learned English and she said: "From my governess . . . And in England."

Her education had been rounded off with a year in London, during which she had lived with a private family. She admired the British, she said, but did not particularly like them. "They dress so badly, in those ill-fitting suits," she said. He waited, hoping that she would say that she liked Americans, but she didn't.

They dismounted in the courtyard and wheeled their bicycles into the kitchen entry, where Mme Viénot let out a cry of distress. He saw that she was looking at his saddlebag, and said: "What's the matter?" She pointed to the wine bottle lying on its side. "The cork has come out," she said, in the voice of doom.

He started to apologize, and then realized that she wasn't paying any attention to what he said. She had picked up the bottle and was examining the outside, turning it around slowly. It was dry. They examined the saddlebag. Not a drop of oil had been spilled! He learned a new French phrase—"une espèce de miracle"—and used it frequently in conversation from that time on.

Mme Straus-Muguet was in the drawing room, with M. and Mme Carrère and Mme Bonenfant and Barbara and Alix and Eugène. They had all been invited to take an apéritif with her on Sunday morning. An unopened bottle of Martinique rum stood on the little round table. Thérèse brought liqueur glasses and the corkscrew. The rum loosened tongues, smoothed away differences of background, of age, of temperament, of nationality. The conversation became animated; their eyes grew bright. Thérèse removed the screen, and they all rose and, still talking, floated on a wave of intense cordiality through the hall and into the dining room, where the long-promised poulet awaited them. As Harold unfolded his clean napkin, he decided that life in the country was not so bad, after all.

I: *Leo and Virgo*

The gaiety did not quite last out the meal. The nine people around the table sank back, one after another, into their ordinary selves. There had been no real, or at least no lasting, change but merely a sleight-of-hand demonstration. As some people know how to make three balls appear and disappear and a whole flock of doves fly out of an opera hat, Mme Straus-Muguet knew how to lift a dead social weight. Out of the most unpromising elements she had just now constructed an edifice of gaiety, an atmosphere of concert pitch. Shreds of her triumph lasted until teatime, when Mme Viénot surrendered the silver teapot to her, and she presided—modestly, but also as if she were accustomed to having this compliment paid her.

Sitting with the others, in the circle of chairs at one end of the drawing room, Barbara listened to what Alix and Eugène were saying to each other. His train left at six, and there were last-minute instructions and reminders, of a kind that she was familiar with, and that made her feel she knew them intimately merely because the French girl was saying just what she herself might have said in these circumstances.

"You know where the bread coupons are?"

"You put them in the desk, didn't you?"

"Yes. You'll have to go and get new ones when they expire. Do you think you will remember to?"

"If I don't, my stomach will remind me."

"I have arranged with Mme Emile to buy ice for you, and butter once a week. And if you want to ask someone to dinner, Françoise will come and cook it for you. She will be there Fridays, to clean the apartment and change the linen on your bed. Can you remember to leave a note for the laundress? I meant to do it and forgot. She is to wash your dressing gown. Is it late?"

"There is plenty of time," Eugène said, glancing at his wrist watch.

"If it should turn hot, leave the awning down at our window and close the shutters, and it will be cool when you come home at night. It might be better to leave all the shutters closed—but then it will be gloomy. Whatever you think best. And if you are too tired after work to write to me, it will be all right. I will write to you every day. . . ."

A few minutes more passed, and then he stood up and started around the circle, shaking hands and saying good-by. His manner with M. and Mme Carrère was simply that of a man of breeding. And yet beneath the confident surface there was something a little queer, Harold thought, watching them. Was Eugène trying to convey to them that his father would not have permitted them to be introduced to him?

When he arrived at Harold and Barbara, he smiled, and Harold said as they shook hands: "We'll see you on Friday."

Eugène nodded, turned away, and then turned back to them and said: "You are coming up to Paris—"

"Next Sunday."

"Good. We will all be taking the train together. That is what I had hoped. And where will you stay?"

Harold told him.

"Why do you spend money for a hotel," Eugène said, "when there is room in my mother-in-law's apartment?"

Harold hesitated, and Eugène went on: "I won't be able to spend as much time with you as I'd like, but it will be a pleasure for me, having you and Barbara there when I come home at night."

"But it will make trouble for you."

"It will be no trouble to anyone."

Harold looked at Barbara inquiringly, and misinterpreted her answering look.

"In that case—" he began, and before he could finish his sentence she said: "Can we let you know later?"

"When I come down next week end," Eugène said, and bent down to kiss Mme Bonenfant's frail hand.

Harold thought a slight shadow had passed over his face when they did not accept his invitation, and then he decided that this was not so. The relations between them were such that there was no possibility of hurt feelings or any misunderstanding.

Later, Barbara said that she would have been delighted to accept the invitation except for one thing: it should have come from Alix's mother. "Or at least he should have made it clear that Mme Cestre had been consulted before he invited us. And also, perhaps we ought to be a little more cautious; we ought to know a little more what we're getting into."

"Eugène enjoyed talking to you so much," Alix said, in the petit salon after dinner. "It was a great pleasure to him to find you here. He learned many things about America which interested him."

"The things he wanted to know about, most of the time I couldn't tell him," Harold said. "Partly because nobody knows the answer to some of his questions, and partly because I didn't know the right words to explain in French the way things are. Also, there are lots of things I should know that I don't. Sometimes we couldn't understand each other at all, and when I was ready to give up he would insist that I go on. And eventually, out of my floundering, he seemed to understand what it was I was trying to say. I've never had an experience quite like it."

"Eugène is very intuitive. . . . I have been telling him that he ought to learn English, and until now he hasn't cared to take the trouble. But it distressed him that I could speak to you in your language, badly though I do it, and he—"

"Your English is excellent."

"I am out of the habit. I make mistakes in grammar. Eugène has decided to go to the Berlitz School and learn English, so that when you come back to France he will be able to talk to you. So you see, you have accomplished something which I try to do and couldn't."

She turned away in order to repeat to her mother a remark of M. Carrère's that had pleased the company. Mme Cestre's face lit up. She was reminded of an observation of her husband's that in turn pleased M. Carrère. Alix waited until she saw that this conversation was proceeding without her help and then she turned back to Harold. "Eugène was so excited to learn that you have been married three years. We thought you were on your wedding journey."

"How long have you been married?"

"A little over a year. Eugène thought that in marriage, after a while, people changed. He thought they grew less fond of one another, and that there was no way of avoiding it. When he saw you and your wife together, the way you are with each other, it made him more hopeful."

"Where did you meet?" Harold said, to change the subject. He was perfectly willing to discuss most subjects but not this, because of a superstitious fear that his words would come back to him under ironical circumstances.

"When the Germans came," she said, "my father was in the South, and we were separated from him for some time. We were here with my grandmother. But as soon as we were able, we joined my father in Aix-en-Provence, and it was there that I met Eugène. He was different from the boys I knew. I thought he was very handsome and intelligent, and I enjoyed talking to him. At that time he was thinking of taking holy orders. I felt I could say anything to him—that he was like my brother."

"That's what he seems like to me," Harold said. "Like a wonderful older brother, though actually he is younger than I am."

"Do you have any brothers and sisters?"

"One brother," he said. "When we were growing up, we couldn't be left together in the back seat of the car, because we always ended up fighting. But now we get along all right."

"It never occurred to me that Eugène would want me to love him," she said. "When he asked me to marry him, I was surprised. I was not sure I would marry. I don't know why, exactly. It just didn't seem like something that would happen to me. . . . As a child I always played by myself."

"So did I," Harold said.

"I lived in a world of my own imagination. . . . When I grew older I began to notice the people around me. I saw that there were two kinds—the bright and the stupid—and I decided that I would choose the bright ones for my friends. Later on, I was disappointed in them. Clever people are not always kind. Sometimes they are quite cruel. And the stupid ones very often are kind."

"Then what did you do?"

"I had to choose my friends all over again. . . . I have a sister. The two small children we brought with us are hers. She is two years younger than I, and for a long time I was hardly aware of her. One day she asked me who is my best friend, and I named some girl, and she began to cry. She said: '*You* are *my* best friend.' I felt very bad. After that we became very close to each other."

Mme Viénot addressed a question to her, and Alix turned her head to answer. If I only had a tape recording of the way she says "father," "brother," and "other," Harold thought, smiling to himself. When she turned back to him, he said: "It must have been very difficult—the Occupation, I mean."

"We lived on turnips for weeks at a time. I cannot endure the sight of one now."

She saw that her grandmother was watching them and said in French: "I have been telling Harold how we lived on turnips during the Occupation." It was the first time she had used his Christian name, and he was pleased.

Mme Bonenfant had an interesting observation to make: perpetual hunger makes the middle-aged and the elderly grow thinner, as one would expect, but the young become quite plump.

Was that why she thought she would never marry, he wondered.

"The greatest hardship was not being allowed to write letters," Alix said.

"The Germans didn't allow it?"

"Only postcards. Printed postcards with blanks that you filled in. Five or six sentences. You could say that so-and-so had died, or was sick. That kind of thing. We used to make up names of people that didn't exist, and we managed to convey all sorts of information that the Germans didn't recognize, just by filling in the blanks."

"Did my niece tell you that during the Occupation she and my sister hid a girl in their apartment in Paris?" Mme Viénot said. "The Gestapo was looking for her."

"She was a school friend," Alix explained. "I knew she was in the Résistance, and one day she telephoned me and asked if she could spend the night with me. I told her that it wasn't convenient—that I had asked another girl to stay with me that night. And after she had hung up, I realized what she was trying to tell me."

"How did you manage to reach her again?"

"I sent word, through a little boy in the house where she lived. She came the next night, and stayed four months with us."

"I was in and out of the apartment all the time," Mme Viénot said, "and never suspected anything. I saw the girl occasionally and thought she had come to see Alix."

"We didn't dare tell anyone," Alix said, "for her sake."

"After the war was over, my sister told me what had been going on right under my nose," Mme Viénot said. "But it was very dangerous for them, you know. It might have cost them their lives."

Mme Cestre raised her hearing aid to her ear, and Alix leaned toward her mother and explained what they were talking about.

"She was rather imprudent," Mme Cestre said mildly.

"She went out at night sometimes," Alix said. "And she told several people where she was hiding. She enjoyed the danger of their knowing."

"Were many people you know involved in the Résistance?" Harold asked.

"In almost every French family something like that was going on," Mme Viénot said.

A silence fell over the room. When the conversation was resumed, Harold said: "There is something I have been wanting to ask you: when people do something kind, what do you say to them?"

" 'Merci,' " Alix said.

"I know, but I don't mean that. I mean when you are really grateful."

" 'Merci beaucoup.' Or 'Merci bien.' "

"But if it is something really kind, and you want them to know that you—"

"It is the same."

"There are no other words?"

"No."

"In English there are different ways of saying that you are deeply grateful."

"In French we use the same words."

"How do people know, then, that you appreciate what they have done for you?"

"By the way you say it—by your expression, the intonation of your voice."

"But that makes it so much more difficult!" he exclaimed.

"It is a question of sincerity," she said, smiling at him as if she had just offered him the passkey to all those gates he kept trying to see over.

Chapter 10

O N MONDAY MORNING the Bentley appeared in front of the
château for the last time. The chauffeur carried the luggage out, and then a huge bouquet of delphiniums wrapped in
damp newspaper, which he placed on the floor of the back seat.
Mme Viénot, Mme Bonenfant, Harold, Barbara, and Alix accompanied M. and Mme Carrère out to the car. Harold watched
carefully while Mme Carrère was thanking Mme Viénot for the
flowers and the quart of country cream she held in her hand.
They did not embrace each other, but then Mme Carrère was
not given to effusiveness. The fact that she didn't speak of seeing
Mme Viénot again in Paris might mean merely that it wasn't
necessary to speak of it. One thing he felt sure of—there was not
one stalk of delphinium left in the garden.

The necessary handshaking was accomplished, and Mme Carrère got into the back seat of the car. M. Carrère put his hand
in his pocket and drew out his card, which he handed Harold.
It was a business card, but on the back he had written the address and telephone number of the apartment in the rue du
faubourg St. Honoré. As Harold tucked the card in his wallet,
he felt stripped and exposed, a small boy in the presence of
his benign, all-knowing father. If they found themselves in
any kind of difficulty, M. Carrère said, they were to feel free

to call on him for help. What he seemed to be saying (so kind was the expression in the expert old clown's eyes, so comprehending and tolerant his smile) was that human thought is by no means as private as it seems, and all you need in order to read somebody else's mind is the willingness to read your own. With his legend intact and his lilac-colored shawl around his shoulders, he leaned forward one last time and waved, through the car window.

Waving, Harold said: "I hope the drive isn't too much for him."

"They are going to stop somewhere for lunch and a rest," Mme Viénot said. Already, though the car had not yet turned into the public road, she seemed different, less conventional, lighter, happier. "They are both very dear people," she said, but he could not see that she was sorry to have them go.

"We are thinking of going to Chaumont this afternoon," he said.

"And you'd like me to arrange about the taxi? Good. I'll tell her to come at two."

"Alix is coming with us," he went on, and then, spurred by his polite upbringing: "We hope you will come too." He did not at all want her to come; it would be much pleasanter with just the three of them. But in the world of his childhood nobody had ever said that pleasure takes precedence over not hurting people's feelings, even when there is a very good chance that they don't have any feelings. "If the idea appeals to you," he said, hoping to hear that it didn't. "Perhaps it would only be boring, since you have seen the château so many times."

"I would enjoy going," Mme Viénot said. "And perhaps the taxi could bring us home by way of Onzain? I have an errand there, and it is not far out of the way."

But if Mme Viénot was coming to Chaumont with them, what about poor Mme Straus-Muguet? Wouldn't she feel left out?

"And will you please invite Mme Straus-Muguet for us," he said.

"Oh, that won't be necessary," Mme Viénot exclaimed. "It is

very nice of you to think of it, but I'm sure she doesn't expect to be asked, and it will make five in the taxi."

When he insisted, she agreed reluctantly to convey the invitation, and a few minutes later, meeting him on the stairs, she reported that it had been accepted.

The taxi came promptly at two, and all five of them crowded into it, and still apologizing cheerfully to one another for taking up too much space they arrived at a point directly across the river from Chaumont, which was as far as they could go by car. The ferry was loading on the opposite shore, and Alix and Mme Viénot did not agree about where it would land. After they had scrambled down the steep sandbank to the water's edge, they saw some hikers and cyclists waiting a hundred yards upstream, at the exact spot where Mme Viénot had said the ferry would come. She and Harold began to help Mme Straus-Muguet up the bank again. The two girls took off their shoes and waded into the water. The sound of their voices and their laughter made him turn and look back. Alix tucked the hem of her skirt under her belt. Then the two girls waded in deeper and deeper, with their dresses pulled up and their white thighs showing.

There are certain scenes that (far more than artifacts dug up out of the ground or prehistoric cave paintings, which have a confusing freshness and newness) serve to remind us of how old the human race is, and of the beautiful, touching sameness of most human occasions. Anything that is not anonymous is all a dream. And who we are, and whether our parents embraced life or were disappointed by it, and what will become of our children couldn't be less important. Nobody asks the name of the athlete tying his sandal on the curved side of the Greek vase or whether the lonely traveler on the Chinese scroll arrived at the inn before dark.

He realized with a pang that he had lost Barbara. He was up here on the bank helping an old woman to keep her balance instead of down there with his shoes and stockings off, and so he had lost her. She had turned into a French girl, a stranger to him.

The girls' way was blocked by a clump of cattails. They stopped and considered what to do. Then, taking each other by the hand, they started slowly out into still deeper water. . . . The water was too deep. They could not get around the cattails without swimming, and so they turned back and went the rest of the way on dry land.

The ferryboat coming toward them from the opposite shore was long and narrow, and the gunwales were low in the water. When it was about fifty yards from the bank, the ferryman turned off the outboard motor, which was on the end of a long pole, and lifted it out of the water. The boat drifted in slowly. Harold did not see how it could possibly hold all the people who were now waiting to cross over—hollow-cheeked, pale, undernourished hikers and cyclists, dressed for *le sport*, in shorts and open-collared shirts, with their sleeves rolled up. The slightest wind would have blown them away like dandelion fluff.

They pulled the prow of the boat up onto the mud bank and took the bicycles carefully from the hands of the ferryman. When the passengers had jumped ashore, the hikers and cyclists stood aside politely while the party from the château went on board. Mme Viénot and Mme Straus-Muguet sat in the stern, in the only seat there was. Barbara and Alix perched on the side of the boat, next to them. Harold stood among the other passengers. Under the ferryman's direction a dozen bicycles were placed in precarious balance. The boat settled lower and lower as more people, more bicycles with loaded saddle bags came on board. There were no oars, and the ferryman, on whom all their lives depended, was a sixteen-year-old boy with patches on his pants. He pushed his way excitedly past wire wheels and bare legs, shouting directions. When everybody was on board, he shoved the boat away from the shore with his foot, all but fell in, ran to the stern, making the boat rock wildly, and lowered the outboard motor. The motor caught, and they turned around slowly and headed for the other shore.

"This boat is not safe!" Mme Viénot told the ferryman, and when he didn't pay any attention to her she said to Barbara: "I shall complain to the mayor of Brenodville about it. . . . The current is very treacherous in the middle of the river."

Mme Straus-Muguet took Barbara's hand and confessed that she could not swim.

"Harold is a very good swimmer," Barbara said.

"M. Rhodes will swim to Mme Straus and support her if the boat capsizes," Mme Viénot decided.

"Très bien," Mme Straus-Muguet said, and called their attention to the scenery.

Harold's mind ran off an unpleasant two-second movie in which he saw himself in the water, supporting an aged woman whose life was nearly finished, while Barbara, encumbered by her clothes, with no one to help her, drowned before his eyes.

Out in the middle of the river there was a wind, and the gray clouds directly over their heads looked threatening. Mme Straus-Muguet was reminded of the big painting in the Louvre of Dante and Virgil crossing the River Styx. She was so gallant and humorous, in circumstances a woman of her age could hardly have expected to find herself in and few would have agreed to, that she became a kind of heroine in the eyes of everyone. The cyclists turned and watched her, admiring her courage.

The shore they had left receded farther and farther. They were in the main current of the river for what seemed a long long time, and then slowly the opposite shore began to draw nearer. They could pick out details of houses and see the people on the bank. As Harold stepped onto the sand he felt the triumph and elation of a survivor. The ferryboat had not sunk after all, and he and everybody in it were braver than they had supposed.

The climb from the water's edge up the cliff was clearly too much for a woman in the neighborhood of seventy. Mme Straus-Muguet took Harold's arm and clung to it. With now Alix and now Barbara on her other side supporting her, she pressed on, through sand, up steep paths and uneven stone stairways, stopping again and again to exclaim to herself how difficult it was, to catch her breath, to rest. Her face grew flushed and then it became gray, but she would not hear of their turning back. When they were on level ground at last and saw the towers and drawbridge of the château, she stopped once more and exclaimed, but this time it was pleasure that moved her. "You do not need to worry any more about me," she said. "I am quite recovered."

While they were waiting for the guide, she bought and presented to Harold and Barbara a set of miniature postcards of the rooms they were about to see. She called Barbara's attention to the tapestries in the Salon du Concert before the guide had a chance to speak of them. Confronted with a glass case containing portrait medallions by the celebrated Italian artist Nini, she said that she had a passion for bas-relief and could happily spend the rest of her life studying this collection. They were shown the dressing table of Catherine de Médicis, and Mme Straus insisted on climbing the steep stone staircase to the tower where the Queen had learned from her astrologer the somber fate in store for her three sons who would sit on the throne of France: one dead of a fever, within a year of his coronation, one the victim of melancholy, and one of the assassin's dagger. As Mme Straus listened to this story, her sensitive face reflected the surprise and then the consternation of Catherine de Médicis, whose feelings she, a mother, could well appreciate, though they were separated by four centuries. Mme Viénot congratulated the guide on his diction and his knowledge of history, and Mme Straus-Muguet congratulated him on the view up and down the river. She was reluctant to leave the stables where the elephant had been housed, but perfectly willing to return to the river bank and for the second time in one day risk death by drowning.

The taxi was where they had left it. It had waited all afternoon for them, time in Brenodville being far less dear than gasoline. Mme Viénot's errand took them a considerable distance out of their way but gave them an opportunity to see the villages of

Chouzy and Onzain. The grain merchant at Onzain was away, and his wife refused to let Mme Viénot have the laying mash she had come for. They rode home with two large sacks of inferior horse feed tied across the front and back of the taxi.

That evening before dinner, Harold heard a knock and went to the door. Mme Straus entered breathing harshly from the stairs. "What a charming room!" she exclaimed.

She was leaving tomorrow morning, to go and stay with friends at Chaumont, and she wanted to give them her address and telephone number in Paris. "When you come," she said, squeezing Barbara's hand, "we will have lunch together, and afterward take a drive through the city. It will be my great pleasure to show it to you."

She had brought with her two books—two thin volumes of poetry, which they were to read and return to her when they met again—and also some letters. They lay mysteriously in her lap while she told them about the convent in Auteuil where she now lived. She was most fortunate that the sisters had taken her in; the waiting list was long. And the serenity was so good for her.

She looked down at the letters in her lap. They were from Mme Marguerite Mailly, of the Comédie Française, whose Phèdre and Andromaque were among the great performances of the French theater. Mme Straus considered these letters her most priceless possession, and took them with her wherever she went. Mme Mailly's son, such a gifted and handsome boy, so intelligent, was only eighteen when his plane was shot down at the very beginning of the war.

"I too lost a son in this way," Mme Straus said.

"Your son was killed in the war?" Harold asked.

"He died in an airplane accident in the thirties," Mme Straus-Muguet said. The look in her eyes as she told them this was not tragic but speculative, and he saw that she was considering their chaise longue. Because she knew only too well the dangers of giving way to immoderate grief, she had been able, she said, to lead her friend gently and gradually to an attitude of acceptance. She opened her lorgnette and, peering through it, read excerpts from the actress's letters, in which Mme Mailly thanked her dear friend for pointing out to her the one true source of consolation.

Harold read the inscription on the flyleaf of one of the books (the handwriting was bold and enormous) and then several of the poems. They seemed to be love poems—incestuous love sonnets to the actress's dead son, whose somewhat girlish countenance served as a frontispiece. But when would he ever have time to read them?

"I'm afraid something might happen to them while they're in our possession," he said. "I really don't think we ought to keep them."

But Mme Straus was insistent. They were to keep the two volumes of poetry until they saw her again.

The next morning, standing in the foyer, with her suitcases around her on the black and white marble floor, she kept the taxi waiting while she thanked Mme Viénot elaborately for her hospitality. When she turned and put out her hand, Harold bent down and kissed her on the cheek. Her response was pure pleasure. She dropped her little black traveling bag, raised her veil, said: "You have made it possible for me to do what I have been longing to do," and with her hands on both his shoulders kissed him first on one cheek and then on the other.

"Voilà l'amour," Mme Viénot said, smiling wickedly. The remark was ignored.

Mme Straus kissed Barbara and then, looking into their eyes affectionately, said: "Thank you, my dear children, for not allowing the barrier of age to come between us!"

Then she got into the taxi and drove off to stay with her friends at Chaumont. In order that her friends here should not be totally without resource during her absence, she was leaving behind the box of *diamonoes*.

THAT AFTERNOON, Barbara and Harold and Alix took the bus into Blois. The Americans were paying still another visit to the château; Harold wanted to see with his own eyes the rooms through which the Duc de Guise had moved on the way to his death. They suggested that Alix come with them, but she had errands to do, and she wanted to pay a visit to the nuns at the nursery school where she had worked during the early part of the war. They would gladly have given up the château for the nursery school if she had asked them to go with her, but she didn't ask them, and she refused gently to meet them for tea at the pâtisserie. They did not see her again until they met at the end of the afternoon. She was pushing a second-hand baby carriage along the sidewalk and they saw that she was radiantly happy.

"It is a very good carriage," she said, "and it was cheap. Eugène will be very pleased with me."

The baby carriage was hoisted on top of the bus, and they took turns pushing it home from the highway. Alix pointed out the house of Thérèse's family, and in a field Harold saw a horse-drawn reaper. "Why, I haven't seen one of those since I was a child!" he said excitedly, and then proceeded to describe to Alix the elaborate machine that had taken its place.

It was a nice evening, and they were enjoying the walk. "I hope you will decide to stay in our apartment," Alix said suddenly. "It would be so pleasant for Eugène. It would mean company for him."

They did not have to answer because at that moment they were passing a farmhouse and she saw a little boy by the wood-shed and spoke to him. He was learning to ride a bicycle that was too big for him. She left the baby carriage in the middle of the road and went over to give him some pointers.

When they got home, the Americans went straight to their room, intending to rest before dinner. Harold had just got into bed and pulled the covers up when they heard a knock. Barbara slipped on her dressing gown, and before she got to the door it opened. Though one says the nail is drawn to the magnet, if you look very closely you see that the magnet is also drawn to the nail. Mme Viénot had come to tell them about her visit to the mayor of Brenodville.

". . . I said that the ferry at Chaumont was extremely dangerous, and that some day, unless something was done about it, a number of people would lose their lives. . . . You won't believe what he said. The whole history of modern France is in this one remark. He said"—her eyes shone with amusement—"he said: 'I know but it's at Chaumont.' . . . How was your afternoon?"

She sat down on the edge of Harold's bed, keeping him a prisoner there; he was stark naked under the covers.

Since she did not seem concerned by the fact that his shoulders and arms were bare, he did his best to forget this, and she went on talking cozily and cheerfully, as if their intimacy were long established and a source of mutual pleasure. He realized that, with reservations and at arm's length, he really did like her. She was intelligent and amusing, and her pale-blue eyes saw either everything or nothing. Her day was full of small but nevertheless remarkable triumphs. In spite of rationing and shortages of almost everything you could think of, the food was always interesting. Though the house was cold, it was also immaculately clean. And there were never any awkward pauses in the conversations that took place in front of the empty Franklin stove or around the dining-room table.

She told them how she had searched for and finally found the wallpaper for this room; and about the picturesque fishing villages and fiords of Ile d'Yeu, where, in happier circumstances, the family always went in August, for the sea air and the bathing; and about the year that Eugène and Alix had spent in Marseilles. Rather than be a fonctionnaire in Paris, Eugène chose to work as a day laborer, carrying mortar and rubble, in Marseilles. They lived in the slums, and their evenings were spent among working people, whom he hoped to educate so that France would have a future and not, like Italy, merely a past. He was not the only young man of aristocratic family to dedicate himself to the poor in this way; there were others; there was, in fact, a movement, which was now losing its impetus because the church had not encouraged it. Eugène should perhaps have taken holy orders, as he once thought seriously of doing. It was in his temperament to go the whole way, to go to extremes, to become a saint. Shortly before the baby was born, they came back to Paris. Alix did not want their child to grow up in such sordid surroundings. He was not very happy in his job at the Ministry of Planning and External Affairs, and Mme Viénot could not help thinking that both of them were less happy than they had been before, but the decision was, of course, the only right one. And after all, if one applied oneself, and had the temperament for it, one could do very well in the government. Her son-in-law, for instance— "I hope you didn't repeat to M. Carrère what I said about his being talked about as the future Minister of Finance?"

Harold shook his head.

"I'm afraid it was not very discreet of me," she said. "Jean-Claude is quite different from the rest of his family, who are charming but hors de siècle."

"Does that mean 'old-fashioned'?"

"They are gypsies."

"Real gypsies? The kind that travel around in wagons?"

"Oh mercy no, they are perfectly respectable, and of a very old family, but— How shall I put it? They are unconventional. They come to meals when they feel like it, wear strange clothes, stay up all night practicing the flute, and say whatever comes into their minds. . . . Is there a word for that in English?"

"Bohemian," Barbara said.

"Yes," Mme Viénot said, nodding. "But not from the country of Bohemia. His mother is so amusing, so unlike anyone else. Sometimes she will eat nothing but cucumbers for weeks at a time. And Jean-Claude's father blames every evil under the sun on the first Duke of Marlborough—with perhaps some justice but not a great deal. There are too many villains of our own époque, alas. . . . I am keeping you from resting?"

Reassured, she stayed so long that they were all three late for dinner. The box of *diamonoes* remained unopened on Mme Viénot's desk in the petit salon, and the evening was given over, as before, to the game of conversation.

❧ ❧
❧

ON WEDNESDAY MORNING the cook prepared a picnic lunch and the Americans took the train to Amboise. There was a new bridge across the river at Amboise, and so they did not have to risk their lives. After they had seen the château they went and peered into the little chapel where Leonardo da Vinci either was or was not buried.

Down below in the village, Harold saw a row of ancient taxis near the Hôtel Lion d'Or, and arranged with the driver of the newest one to take them to Chenonceau, twelve kilometers away. After they had eaten their lunch on the river bank, they went back to where the row of taxis had been and, mysteriously, there was only one and it was not their taxi, but the man Harold had talked to was sitting in the driver's seat and seemed to be waiting for them. It was a wood-burning taxi, and for the first few blocks they kept looking out of the back window at the trail of black smoke they were leaving in their wake.

Crossing a bridge on the narrow dirt road to Chenonceau, they passed a hiker with a heavy rucksack on his back. The driver informed them that the hiker was a compatriot of theirs, and Harold told him to stop until the hiker had caught up with them. He was Danish, not American, but on finding out that he was going to the château, Harold invited him into the car anyway. He spoke English well and French about the way they did.

The taxi let them out at an ornamental iron gate some distance from the château itself. They stayed together as far as the draw-bridge, and then suddenly the Dane was no longer with them or in fact anywhere. Half an hour later, when they emerged from the château with a dozen other sight-seers, they saw him stand-ing under a tree that was far enough away from the path so that they did not have to join him if they did not care to. The three of them studied the château from all sides and found the place where they could get the best view of the inverted castle in the river. The formal gardens of Catherine de Médicis and Diane de Poitiers were both planted in potatoes. A small bronze sign said that the gardens had been ruined by the inundation of May 1940, and since the river flowing under the château at that moment was only a few inches deep, they took this to be a reference to the Germans, though as a matter of fact it was not. They rode back to Amboise in the wood-burning taxi and, sitting on the bank of the Loire, Harold and Barbara shared what was left of their lunch and a bottle of red wine with the Dane, who pro-duced some tomatoes for them out of his rucksack and told them the story of his life. His name was Nils Jensen, he was nineteen years old, and he had cut himself off from his inheritance. It had been expected that he would go into the family business in Copenhagen and instead he was studying medicine. He wanted to become a psychiatrist. He could only bring a small amount of money out of Denmark, and so he was hiking through France. Harold saw in his eyes that there was something he wanted them to know about him that he could not say—that he was well bred and a gentleman. He did not need to say it, but he was a gentleman who had been living largely on tomatoes and he badly needed a bath and clean clothes.

He had not yet decided where he was going to spend the night; he might stay here; but if he went on to Blois he would be taking the same train they were taking. He had not yet seen the château of Amboise, and so they said good-by, provisionally. The Americans went halfway across the bridge and down a flight of stairs to a little island in the middle of the river, and there they walked up and down in a leafy glade, searching for just some small trace of the Visigoths and the Franks who, around the year 500 A.D., met here and celebrated a peace treaty, the terms of which neither army found it convenient to honor.

At the railroad station, Harold and Barbara looked around for Nils Jensen, and Harold considered buying third-class tickets, in case he turned up later, but in the end decided that he was not coming and they might as well be comfortable. When the train drew in, there he was. He appeared right out of the ground, with a second-class ticket in his hand—bought, it was clear, so that he could ride with them.

The god of love could be better represented than by a little boy blindfolded and with a bow and arrow. Why not a member of the Actors' Equity, with his shirt cuffs turned back, an impressive diamond ring on one finger, his long black hair heavily pomaded, his magic made possible by a trunkful of accessories and a stooge somewhere in the audience. Think of a card—any card. There is no card you can think of that the foxy vaudeville magician doesn't have up his sleeve or in a false pocket of his long coattails.

The train carried them past Monteux, past Chaumont on the other side of the river. There was so much that had to be said in this short time, and so much that their middle-class upbringing prevented them from saying or even knowing they felt. The Americans did not even tell Nils Jensen—except with their eyes, their smiles—how much they liked being with him and everything about him. Nils Jensen did not say: "Oh I don't know which of you I'm in love with—I love you both! And I've looked everywhere, I've looked so long for somebody I could be happy with. . . ." Nevertheless, they all three used every minute that they had together. The train, which could not be stopped, could not be made to go slower, carried them past Onzain and Chouzy. At Brenodville they shook hands, and Angle A and Angle B got out and then stood on the brick platform waving until the train took Angle C (as talented and idealistic and tactful and congenial a friend as they were ever likely to have) away from them, with nothing to complete this triangle ever again but an address in Copenhagen that must have been incorrectly copied, since a letter sent there was never replied to.

Walking through the village, with the shadows stretching clear across the road in front of them, they saw windows and doors that were wide open, they heard voices, they met people who smiled and spoke to them. They thought for a moment that the man returning from the fields with his horse and his dog was one of the men who were sitting on the café terrace the day they arrived, and then decided that he wasn't. Coming to an open gate, they stopped and looked in. There was no one around and so they stood there studying the courtyard with its well, its neat woodpile, its bicycle, its two-wheeled cart, its tin-roofed porch, its clematis and roses growing in tubs, its dog and cat and chickens and patient old farm horse, its feeding trough and watering trough, so like an illustration in a beginning French grammar: *A* is for *Auge*, *B* is for *Bicyclette*, *C* is for *Cheval*, etc.

When they were on the outskirts of the village, they saw Mme Viénot's gardener coming toward them in the cart and assumed he had business in the village. He stopped when he was abreast of them, and waited. They stood looking up at him and he told them to get in. Mme Viénot had sent him, thinking that they would be tired after their long day's excursion. They *were* tired, and grateful that she had thought of them.

In the beautiful calm evening light, driving so slowly between fields that had just been cut, they learned that the white horse was named Pompon, and that he was thirty years old. The gardener explained that it was his little boy who had taken Harold by the hand and led him to the house of M. Fleury. They found it easy to talk to him. He was simple and direct, and so were the words he used, and so was the look in his eyes. They felt he liked them, and they wished they could know him better.

On the table in their room, propped against the vase of flowers, was a letter from Mme Straus-Muguet. The handwriting was so eccentric and the syntax so full of flourishes that Harold took it downstairs and asked Alix to translate it for them. Mme Straus was inviting them to take tea with her at the house of her friends, who would be happy to meet two such charming Americans.

He watched Alix's face as she read the protestations of affection at the close of the letter.

"Why do you smile?"

She refused to explain. "You would only think me uncharitable," she said. "As in fact I am."

He was quite sure that she wasn't uncharitable, so there must be something about Mme Straus that gave rise to that doubtful smile. But what? Though he again urged her to tell him, she would not. The most she would say was that Mme Straus was "roulante."

He went back upstairs and consulted the dictionary. "Roulante" meant "rolling." It also meant a "side-splitting, killing (sight, joke)."

Reluctantly, he admitted to himself, for the first time, that there was something theatrical and exaggerated about Mme Straus's manner and conversation. But there was still a great gap between that and "side-splitting." Did Alix see something he didn't see? Probably she felt that as Americans they had a right to their own feelings about people, and did not want to spoil their friendship with Mme Straus. But in a way she *had* spoiled it, since it is always upsetting to discover that people you like do not think very much of each other.

When he showed Barbara the page of the dictionary, it turned out that she too had reservations about Mme Straus. "The thing is, she might become something of a burden if she attached herself to us while we're in Paris. We'll only be there for ten days. And I wouldn't like to hurt her feelings."

Though they did not speak of it, they themselves were suffering from hurt feelings; they did not understand why Alix would not spend more time with them. For reasons they could not make out, she was simply inaccessible. They knew that she slept late, and she was, of course, occupied with the baby, and perhaps with her sister's children. But on the other hand, she had brought a nursemaid with her, so perhaps it wasn't the children who were keeping her from them. Perhaps she didn't want to see any more of them. . . . But if that were true, they would have felt it in her manner. When they met at mealtime, she was always pleased to see them, always acted as if their friendship was real and permanent, and she made the lunch and dinner table conversation much more enjoyable by the care she took of them. But why didn't she want to go anywhere with them? Why did she never seek out their company at odd times of the day?

She was uneasy about Eugène—that much she did share with them. She had hoped that he would write and there had been no letter. Harold suggested that he might be too busy to write, since the government had jumped after all, without waiting this time for the August vacation to be over. He asked if the crisis would affect Eugène's position, and she said that, actually, Eugène had two positions in the Ministry of Planning and External Affairs, neither of which would suffer any change under a different cabinet, since they were not that important.

The dining-room table was now the smallest the Americans had seen it and, raising her hearing aid to her ear, Mme Cestre took part in the conversation.

Alix explained that her mother's health was delicate; she was a prey to mysterious diseases that the doctors could neither cure nor account for. There would be an outbreak of blisters on the ends of her fingers, and then it would go away as suddenly as it had come. She had attacks of dizziness, when the floor seemed to come up and strike her foot. She could not stand to be in the sun for more than a few minutes. Alix herself thought sometimes that it was because her mother was so good and kind—really much kinder than anybody else. Beggars, old women selling limp, tarnished roses, old men with a handful of pencils had only to look at her and she would open her purse. She could not bear the sight of human misery.

Leaning toward her mother, Alix said: "I have been telling Barbara and Harold how selfish you are."

Mme Cestre raised the hearing aid to her ear and adjusted the little pointer. The jovial remark was repeated and she smiled benignly at her daughter.

When she entered the conversation, it was always abruptly, on a new note, since she had no idea what they were talking about. She broke in upon Mme Bonenfant's observation that there was no one in Rome in August—that it was quite deserted, that the season there had always been from November through Lent— with the observation that cats are indifferent to their own reflection in a mirror.

"Dogs often fail to recognize themselves," she said, as they all stared at her in surprise. "Children are pleased. The wicked see what other people see . . . and the mirror sees nothing at all."

Or when Alix was talking about the end of the war, and how she and Sabine suddenly decided that they wanted to be in Paris for the Liberation and so got on their bicycles and rode there, only to be sent back to the country because there wasn't enough food, Mme Cestre remarked to Barbara: "My husband used to do the packing always. I did it once when we were first married, but he had been a bachelor too long, and no one could fold coatsleeves properly but him. . . . It is quite true that when I did it they were wrinkled."

It was hard not to feel that this note of irrelevance must be part of her character, but once she was oriented in the conversation, Mme Cestre's remarks were always pertinent to it, and interesting. Her English was better than Alix's or than Mme Viénot's, and without any trace of a French accent.

Sometimes she would sit with her hearing aid on her lap, content with her own thoughts and the perpetual silence that her deafness created around her. But then she would raise the hearing aid to her ear and prepare to re-enter the conversation.

"Did Alix tell you that I am writing a book?" she said to her sister as they were waiting for Thérèse and the boy to clear the table for the next course.

"I didn't know you were, Maman," Alix said.

"I thought I had told you. It is in the form of a diary, and it consists largely of aphorisms."

"You are taking La Rochefoucauld as your model," Mme Bonenfant said approvingly.

"Yes and no," Mme Cestre said. "I have a title for it: 'How to Be a Successful Mother-in-Law.' . . . The relationship is never an easy one, and a treatise on the subject would be useful, and perhaps sell thousands of copies. I shall ask Eugène to criticize it when I am finished, and perhaps do a short preface, if he has the time. I find I have a good deal to say. . . ."

"My sister also has a talent for drawing," Mme Viénot said. "She does faces that are really quite good likenesses, and at the same time there is an element of caricature that is rather cruel. I do not understand it. It is utterly at variance with her nature. Once she showed me a drawing she had done of me and I burst into tears."

⚜ ⚜
⚜

THURSDAY WAS A NICE DAY. The sun shone, it was warm, and Harold and Barbara spent the entire afternoon on the bank of the river, in their bathing suits. When they got home they found a scene out of *Anna Karenina*. Mme Bonenfant, Mme Viénot, Mme Cestre, and Thérèse were sitting under the Lebanon cedar, to the right of the terrace, with their chairs facing an enormous burlap bag, which they kept reaching into. They were shelling peas for canning.

Alix was in the courtyard, making some repairs on her bicycle. She had had a letter from Eugène. "He sends affectionate greetings to you both," she said. "He is coming down to the country tomorrow night. And Mummy asked me to tell you, for her, that it would give her great pleasure if you would stay in the apartment while you are in Paris."

This time the invitation was accepted.

After dinner, Mme Viénot opened the desk in the petit salon and took out a packet of letters, written to her mother at the château. She translated passages from them and read other passages in French, with the pride of a conscientious historian. Most of the letters were about the last week before the liberation of the city. The inhabitants of Paris, forbidden to leave their houses, had kept in active communication with one another by telephone.

"But couldn't the Germans prevent it?" Harold asked.

"Not without shutting off the service entirely, which they didn't dare to do. We knew everything that was happening," Mme Viénot said. "When the American forces reached the southwestern limits of the city, the church bells began to toll, one after another, on the Left Bank, as each section of the city was delivered from the Germans, and finally the deep bell of Notre Dame. In the midst of the street fighting I left the apartment, to perform an errand, and found myself stranded in a doorway of a house, with bullets whistling through the air around me." In the letter describing this, she neither minimized the danger nor pretended that she had been involved in an act of heroism. The errand was a visit, quite essential, to her dressmaker in the rue du Mont-Thabor.

⚜ ⚜
⚜

On Friday afternoon, Mme Viénot rode with Harold and Barbara in their taxi to Blois, where they parted. She went off down the street with an armful of clothes for the cleaner's, and they got on a sight-seeing bus. They chose the tour that consisted of Chambord, Cheverny, and Chaumont instead of the tour of Azay-le-Rideau, Ussé, and Chinon, because Barbara, looking through the prospectus, thought she recognized in Cheverny the white château with the green lawn in front of it. Cheverny did have a green lawn in front of it but it was not at all like a fairy-tale castle, and Chambord was too big. It reminded them of Grand Central Station. Since they had already seen Chaumont, they got the driver to let them out at the castle gates, and stood looking around for a taxi that would take them to the house of Mme Straus-Muguet's friends. It turned out that there were no taxis. The proprietor of the restaurant across the road did not know where the house was, and it was rather late to be having tea, so instead they sat for a whole hour on the river bank, feeling as if they had broken through into some other existence. They watched the sun's red reflection on the water, the bathers, the children building sand castles, the goats cropping and straying, and the next two trips of the ferryboat; and then it was time for them to cross over, themselves, and take the train home.

Though they were very late, dinner was later still. They sat in the drawing room waiting for Eugène and Sabine to arrive.

When they met again at the château, Harold's manner with Mme Viénot's daughter was cautious. He was not at all sure she liked him. He and Eugène shook hands, and there was a flicker of recognition in the Frenchman's eyes that had in it also a slight suggestion of apology: at the end of a long day and a long journey, Harold must not expect too much of him. Tomorrow they would talk.

As Sabine started toward the stairs with her light suitcase, Mme Viénot said: "The Allégrets are giving a large dinner party tomorrow night. I accepted for you." Then, turning to Harold and Barbara: "My daughter is very popular. Whenever she is expected, the telephone rings incessantly. . . . You are included in the invitation, but you don't have to go if you don't want to."

"Are Alix and Eugène going?" he asked.

"Yes."

He and Barbara looked at each other, and then Barbara said: "Are you sure it is all right for us to go?"

"Quite sure," Mme Viénot said. "The Allégrets are a very old family. They are half Scottish. They are descended from the Duke of Berwick, who was a natural son of the English King James II, and followed him into exile, and became a marshal of France under Louis XIV."

During dinner, Eugène entertained them with a full account of the fall of the Schumann government. Day after day the party leaders met behind closed doors, and afterward they posed for the photographers on the steps of the Palais Bourbon, knowing that the photographers knew there was nothing of the slightest importance in the brief cases they held so importantly. What made this crisis different from the preceding ones was that no party was willing to accept the portfolios of Finance and Economics, and so it was quite impossible to form a government.

"But won't they have to do something?" Harold asked.

"Eventually," Mme Vienot said, "but not right away. For a while, the administrative branches of the government can and will go right on functioning."

"In my office," Eugène said, "letters are opened and read, and copies of the letters are circulated, but the letters are not answered, because an answer would involve a decision, and all decisions, even those of no consequence, are postponed, or better still, referred to the proper authority, who, unfortunately, has no authority. I have been working until ten or eleven o'clock every night on a report that will never be looked at, since the man who ordered it is now out of office."

At that moment, as if the house wanted to point out that there is no crisis that cannot give way to an even worse situation, the lights went off. They sat in total darkness until the pantry door opened and Thérèse's sullen peasant face appeared, lighted from below by two candles, which she placed on the dining-room table. She then lit the candles in the wall sconces and in a moment the room was ablaze with soft light. Looking at one face after another, Harold thought: This is the way it must have been in the old days, when Mme Viénot and Mme Cestre were still young, and they gave dinner parties, and the money wasn't gone, and the pond had water in it, and everybody agreed that France had the strongest army in Europe. . . . In the light of the still candle flames, everyone was beautiful, even Mme Viénot. As her upper eyelids descended, he saw that that characteristic blind look was almost (though not quite) the look of someone who is looking into the face of love.

At the end of dinner she pushed her chair back and, with a silver candlestick in her hand, she led them across the hall and into the petit salon, where they went on talking about the Occupation. It was the one subject they never came to the end of. They only put it aside temporarily at eleven o'clock, when, each person having been provided with his own candle, they went up the stairs, throwing long shadows before and behind them.

Chapter 11

"Avez-vous bien dormi?" Harold asked, and Eugene held up his hand as if, right there at the breakfast table, with his hair uncombed and his eyes puffy with sleep, he intended to perform a parlor trick for them. Looking at Barbara, he said: "You don't lahv your hus-band, do you?" and to Harold's astonishment she said: "No."

He blushed.

"I mean yes, I do love him," Barbara said." I didn't understand your question. Why, you're speaking *English!*"

Delighted with the success of his firecracker, Eugène sat down and began to eat his breakfast. He had enrolled at the Berlitz. He had had five lessons. His teacher was pleased with his progress. Still in a good humor, he went upstairs to shave and dress.

Thérèse brought the two heaviest of the Americans' suitcases down from the third floor, and then the dufflebag, and put them in the dog cart. Mme Viénot had pointed out that the trip up to Paris would be less strenuous if they checked some of their luggage instead of taking it all in the compartment with them. Harold and the gardener waited until Eugène came out of the house and climbed up on the seat beside them. Then the gardener spoke to his horse gently, in a coaxing voice, as if to a child, and they drove off to the village. At the station, Eugène took care of the forms that had to be filled out, and bought the railroad tickets with the money Harold handed him, but he was withdrawn and silent. Either his mood had changed since breakfast or he did not feel like talking in front of the gardener. When they got back to the château, Harold went upstairs first, and then, finding that Barbara was washing out stockings in the bathroom and didn't need him for anything, he went back downstairs and settled himself in the drawing room with a book. No one ever used the front door—they always came and went by the doors that opened onto the terrace—and so he would see anybody who passed through the downstairs. When Eugène did not reappear, Harold concluded that he was with Alix and the baby in the back wing of the house, where it did not seem proper to go in search of him, since he had been separated from his family for five days.

It was not a very pleasant day and there was some perverse influence at work. The village electrician could not find the short circuit, which must be somewhere inside the walls, and he said that the whole house needed rewiring. And Alix, who was never angry at anyone, was angry at her aunt. She wanted to have a picnic with Sabine and the Americans on the bank of the river, and Mme Viénot said that it wasn't convenient, that it would make extra work in the kitchen. This was clearly not true. They ate lunch in the dining room as usual, and at two thirty they set out on their bicycles, with their bathing suits and towels and four big, thick ham sandwiches that they did not want and that Mme Viénot had made, herself.

The sunshine was pale and watery and without warmth. They hid the bicycles in a little grove between the highway and the river, and then withdrew farther into the trees and changed into their bathing suits. When Barbara and Harold came out, they saw Alix and Sabine down by the water. Eugène was standing some distance away from them, fully dressed, and looking as if he were not part of this expedition.

"Aren't you going in?" Harold called, and, getting no answer, he turned to Alix and said: "Isn't he going in swimming with us?"

She shook her head. "He doesn't feel like swimming."

"Why not?"

"He says the water is dirty."

Then why did he bring his bathing suit if he didn't feel like swimming in dirty water, Harold wondered. Didn't he know the river would be dirty?

The water was also lukewarm and the current sluggish. And instead of the sandy bottom that Harold expected, they walked in soft oozing mud halfway up to their knees, and had to wade quite far out before they could swim. Alix had a rubber ball, and they stood far apart in the shallow water and threw it back and forth. Harold was self-conscious with Sabine. They had not spoken a word to each other since she arrived. The ball passed between the four of them now. They did not smile. It felt like a scene from the Odyssey. When the rubber ball came to him, sometimes, aware of what a personal act it was, he threw it to Sabine. Sometimes she sent it spinning across the water to him. But more often she threw it to one of the two girls. He didn't dislike or distrust her but he couldn't imagine what she was really like, and her gray wool bathing suit troubled him. It was the cut and the color of the bathing suits that are handed out with a locker key and a towel in public bathhouses, and he wondered if she was comparing it with Barbara's, and her life with what she imagined Barbara's life to be like.

From down river, behind a grove of trees, they heard some boys splashing and shouting. On the other bank, sheep appeared over the brow of the green hill, cropping as they came. Farther down the river, out of sight, was Chaumont, with its towers and its drawbridge. Then Amboise, and back from the river, on a river of its own, Chenonceau. Much farther still were those other châteaux that he knew only by their pictures in the guidebook—Villandry and Luynes and Langeais and Azay-le-Rideau and Ussé and Chinon. And no more time left to see them.

They stopped throwing the ball, and he waded in deeper and started swimming. The current in the channel was swifter but it did not seem very strong, even so, and he wanted to swim to the other bank, but he heard voices calling—"Come back!" (Barbara's voice) and "Come back, it's dangerous!" (Alix's voice) and so, reluctantly, rather than cause a fuss, he turned around. "People have drowned near here," Alix said as he stood up, dripping, and walked toward them. "And there is quicksand on the other bank."

They wiped their feet on the grass and then, using their towels, managed to get the mud off. Near the highway, two girls with bicycles and knapsacks were putting up a small tent for the night. Eugène stood watching them. The bathers went into the grove to dress and came out and sat on the ground and dutifully, without appetite, ate the thick ham sandwiches. Alix called to Eugène to come and join them and he replied that he was not hungry.

"Why is Eugène moody?" Sabine asked.

"He is upset because he has to wear a tweed coat to the Allégrets' party," Alix said.

"But so do I!" Harold exclaimed.

"No one expects you to have a dinner coat," she said gently. "It is quite all right. If Eugène had known, he could have brought his dinner coat down with him. That is why he is angry. He thinks I shouldn't have accepted without consulting him. Also, he is angry that there aren't enough bicycles."

"Aren't there?" Sabine asked.

"There are now," Alix said. "Eugène went and borrowed two from the gardener. But it annoys him that he should have to do that—that there aren't bicycles enough to go round."

She herself had long since reverted to her usual cheerful, sweet-tempered self.

Harold went into the trees and brought out the bicycles and they started home, the three girls pedaling side by side, since the highway was empty. After a quarter of a mile, Harold slowed down until Eugène drew abreast of him, and they rode along in what he tried to feel was a comfortable silence. The afternoon had been a disappointment to him, and not at all what he expected, but perhaps, now that they were alone, Eugène would open up—would tell him why he was in such an unsociable mood. For it couldn't be the coat or the bicycles. Something more serious must have happened. Something about his job, perhaps.

Eugène began to sing quietly, under his breath, and Harold rode a little closer to the other bicycle, listening. It was not an old song, judging by the words, but in the tune there was a slight echo of the thing that had moved him so, that day in Blois. When Eugène finished, Harold said: "What's the name of that song you were singing?"

"It's just a song," Eugène said, with his eyes on the road, and pure, glittering, personal dislike emanating from him like an aura.

The painful discovery that someone you like very much does not like you is one of the innumerable tricks the vaudeville magician has up his sleeve. Think of a card, any card: now you see it, now you don't . . . .

Struggling with the downward drag of hurt feelings, as old and familiar to him as the knowledge of his name, Harold kept even with the other bicycle for a short distance, as if nothing had happened, and then, looking straight ahead of him, he pedaled faster and moved ahead slowly until he was riding beside the three girls.

The bicycles were brought out of the kitchen entry at six o'clock, and just as they were starting off, Mme Viénot appeared with three roses from the garden. Alix pinned her rose to the shoulder of her dress, and so did Sabine, but Barbara fastened hers in her hair.

"How pretty you look!" Mme Viénot said, her satisfied glance taking in all three of them.

With Eugène leading and Harold bringing up the rear, and the girls being careful that their skirts did not brush against the greasy chain or the wire wheels, they filed out of the courtyard and then plunged directly into the woods behind it. There were a number of paths, and Eugène chose one. The others followed him, still pushing their bicycles because the path was too sandy to ride on. After a quarter of a mile they emerged from the premature twilight of the woods into the open country and full daylight. Eugène took off his sport coat, folded it, and put it in the handlebar basket. Then he got on his bicycle and rode off down a dirt road that was not directly accessible to the château. Harold disposed of his coat in the same way. At first they rode single file, because of the deep ruts in the road, but before long they came to a concrete highway, and the three girls fanned out so that they could ride together. The two men continued to ride apart. Sometimes they all had to get off and push their bicycles uphill as the road led them up over the top of a long arc. At the crest, the land fell away in a panorama—terraced vineyards, the river valley, more hills, and little roads winding off into he wondered where—and they mounted their bicycles and went sailing downhill with the wind rushing past their ears.

"Isn't this a lovely way to go to a party?" Barbara said as Harold overtook her. "It's so unlike anything we're used to, I feel as if I'm dreaming it."

"Are you getting tired?" Alix called to them, over her shoulder.

"Oh no!" Barbara said.

"How far is it?" Harold asked.

"About five miles," Alix said.

"Such a beautiful evening," he said.

"Coming home there will be a moon," Alix said.

Just when the ride was beginning to seem rather long, they left the highway and took a narrow lane that was again loose sand and that forced them to dismount for a few yards. Pushing their bicycles, they crossed a small footbridge and started up a steep hill. When they got to the top, they had arrived. The Americans saw a big country house of gray stone with castellated trimming and lancet windows and a sweep of lawn in front of it. The guests—girls in long dresses, young men in dinner jackets—were standing about in clusters near a flight of stone steps that led up to the open front door.

The party from the château left their bicycles under a grape arbor at the side of the house. The two men put on their coats, and felt their ties. The girls straightened their short skirts, tucked in stray wisps of hair, looked at their faces in pocket mirrors and exclaimed, powdered their noses, put on white gloves. In front of the house, Alix and Eugène and Sabine were surrounded by people they knew, and Harold and Barbara were left stranded. It was a party of the very young, they perceived; most of the guests were not more than eighteen or nineteen. How *could* Mme Viénot have let them in for such an evening!

"I foresee one of the longest evenings of my entire life," Harold said out of the corner of his mouth.

Just when he was sure that Alix had abandoned them permanently, she came back and led them from group to group. The boys, thin and coltlike, raised Barbara's hand two thirds of the way to their lips, without enthusiasm or gallantry. The gesture was not at all like hand-kissing in the movies, but was, instead, abrupt, mechanical: they *pretended* to kiss her hand.

Alix was called away, and the Americans found themselves stranded again but inside the party this time, not outside. They struck up a conversation in French with a dark-haired girl who was studying music; then another conversation, in English, with a girl who said that she wanted to visit America. They talked about America, about New York. Alix returned, bringing a blond young man who was very tall and thin. An old and very dear friend of hers and Eugène's, she said. He bowed, started to say something, and was called away to answer a question, and didn't return. Then Alix too left them.

Barbara began to talk to another young man. Harold turned and gave his attention to the view—an immense sweep of marsh-land, the valley of the Cher, now autumn-colored with the setting sun. He looked back at the house, which was Victorian Gothic, and nothing like as handsome as Beaumesnil. It was, in fact, a perfectly awful house. And he was the oldest person he could see anywhere.

Once when he was a small child, he had had an experience like this. He must have been about six years old, and he was visiting his Aunt Mildred, who took him with her on a hay-ride party. But that time he was the youngest; he was the only child in a party of grownups; and so he opened his mouth and cried. But it didn't change anything. The hay-ride party went on and on and on, and his aunt was provoked at him for crying in front of everybody.

There was a sudden movement into the house, and he looked around for Alix and Sabine, without being able to find them. And then he saw Barbara coming toward him, against the flow of people up the stone steps to the front door. With her was a young man whom he liked on sight.

"I am Jean Allégret," the young man said as they shook hands. "Your wife tells me you are going to Salzburg for the Festival. I was stationed there at the end of the war. It is a beautiful city, but sad. It was a Nazi headquarters. Don't be surprised if— You are to sit with me at dinner." Taking Harold by the arm, he led him toward the stone steps.

As they passed into the house, Harold looked around for Bar-bara, who had already disappeared in the crowd. He caught a glimpse of rooms opening one out of another; of large and small paintings on the walls, in heavy gilt frames; of brocade armchairs, thick rugs, and little tables loaded with *objets*. The house had a rather stiff formality that he did not care for. In the dining room, the guests were reading the place cards at a huge oval table set for thirty places. Jean Allégret led him to a small table in an alcove, and then left him and returned a moment later, bringing a tall pretty blonde girl in a white tulle evening dress. She looks like a Persian kitten, Harold thought as he acknowledged the introduction. The girl also spoke English. Jean Allégret held her chair out for her and they sat down.

"In America," Harold said as he unfolded his napkin, "this would be called 'the children's table.' "

"I saw a great deal of the Americans during the war," Jean Allégret said. "Your humor is different from ours. It is three-quarters fantasy. Our fantasy is nearly always serious. I understand Americans very well. . . ."

Harold was searching for Barbara at the big table. When he found her, he saw that she was listening attentively, with her head slightly bowed, to the very handsome young man on her right. He felt a twinge of jealousy.

"—but children," Jean Allégret was saying. "I never once found an American who knew or cared what they were fighting about. And yet they fought very well. . . . What you are doing in Germany now is all wrong, you know. You make friends with them. And you will bring another war down on us, just as Woodrow Wilson did."

"Where did you get that idea?" Harold asked, smiling at him.

"It is not an idea, it is a fact. He is responsible for all the mischief that followed the Treaty of Versailles."

"That is in your history books?"

"Certainly."

"In our history books," Harold said cheerfully, "Clemenceau and Lloyd George are the villains, and Wilson foresaw everything." He began to eat his soup.

"He was a very vicious man," Jean Allégret said.

"Wilson? Oh, get along with you."

"Well, perhaps not vicious, but he didn't understand European politics, and he was thoroughly wrong in his attitude toward the German people. My family has a house in the north of France, near St. Amand-les-Eaux. It was destroyed in 1870, and rebuilt exactly the way it was before. My grandfather devoted his life to restoring it. In 1914 it was destroyed again, burned to the ground, and my father rebuilt it so that it was more beautiful than before. Thanks to the Americans, I am now living in a farmhouse nearby, because there is no roof on the house my father built. I manage the farms, and when it is again possible, I will rebuild the house for the third time. My life will be an exact repetition of my father's and my grandfather's."

"Does it have to be?" Harold asked, raising his spoon to his lips.

"What do you mean?"

"Why not try something else? Let the house go."

"You are joking."

"No. Everyone has dozens of lives to choose from. Pick another."

"I am the eldest son. And if the house is destroyed a fourth time, I will expect my son to rebuild it. But if the Americans were not such children, it wouldn't have to be rebuilt."

"We didn't take part in the war of 1870," Harold said mildly. "And we didn't start either of the last two wars."

The Frenchman pounced: "But you came in too late. And you ruined the peace by your softness—by your idealism. And now, as the result of your quarrel with the Russians, you are going to turn France into a battlefield once more. Which is very convenient for you but hard on us."

Harold studied the blue eyes that were looking so intently into his. Their expression was simple and cordial. In America, he thought, such an argument was always quite different. By this time, heat would have crept into it. The accusations would have become personal.

"What would you have us do?" he asked, leaning forward. "Stay out of it next time?"

"I would have you take a realistic attitude, and recognize that harshness is the only thing the German people understand."

"And hunger."

"No. They will go right back and do it over again."

Harold glanced at the girl who was sitting between them, to see whose side she was on. Her face did not reveal what she was thinking. She took a sip of wine and looked at the two men as if they were part of the table decorations.

Caught between the disparity of his own feelings—for he felt a liking for Jean Allégret as a man and anger at his ideas—Harold was silent. No matter what I say, he thought, it will sound priggish. And if I don't say anything, I will seem to be agreeing.

"It is true," he said at last, "it is true that we understand machinery better than we understand European politics. And I do not love what I know of the German mentality. But I have to assume that they are human—that the Germans are human to this extent that they sleep with their wives"—was this going too far?—"and love their children, and want to work, at such times as they are not trying to conquer the world, and are sometimes discouraged, and don't like growing old, and are afraid of dying. I assume that the Japanese sleep with their wives, the Russians love their children and the taste of life, and are sometimes discouraged, don't like growing old, and are afraid of—"

"You don't think that your niggers are human," Jean Allégret said triumphantly.

"Why not? Why do you say that?"

"Because of the way you treat them. I have seen it, in Normandy. You manage them very well."

"We do not manage them at all. They manage us. They are a wonderful people. They have the virtues—the sensibility, the patience, the emotional richness—we lack. And if the distinction between the two races becomes blurred, as it has in Martinique, and they become one race, then America will be saved."

"They are animals," the Frenchman said. "And you treat them like animals."

The girl stirred, as if she were about to say something. Both men turned toward her expectantly.

"I prefer a nigger to a Jew," she said.

At the end of the meal, the guests at the large table pushed their chairs back. Barbara Rhodes, turning away from the young man who had bored her so with his handsome empty face, his shallow eyes that did not have the thing she looked for in people's eyes but only vanity, glanced toward the little table in the alcove. She saw Harold rise, still talking (what could they have found to talk about so animatedly all through dinner?) and draw the little table toward him so that the girl could get up. . . . *Oh no!* she cried as the table started to tilt alarmingly. She saw the Frenchman with a quick movement try to stop it but he was on the wrong side of the table and it was too late. There was an appalling crash.

"Une table pliante," a voice said coolly beside her.

Unable to go on looking, she turned away, but not before she had seen the red stain, like blood, on the beautiful Aubusson carpet, and Harold, pale as death, standing with his hands at his side, looking at what he had done.

"These ideas of yours are foolish and will not work," Jean Allegret said an hour later.

"Perhaps not," Harold said.

They were sitting on a bench on the lawn, facing the lighted windows but in the dark. On another bench, directly in front of them, Barbara and Sabine and another girl whose name Harold didn't know were sitting and talking quietly. There were five or six more people here and there, on the steps, in chairs, or on other benches, talking and watching the moon rise. The others were inside, in the library, dancing to the music of a portable record player.

"Perhaps they *are* foolish," he said, "but I prefer them, for my own sake. If it is foolish to think that all men are brothers, it is at least more civilized—and more agreeable—than thinking that all men—you and I, for instance—are enemies, waiting for a chance to run a bayonet through each other's back."

The wine had made him garrulous and extravagant in speech; also, he had done much less than the usual amount of talking since they had landed in France, and it gave him the feeling of being in arrears, of having a great deal backed up that he urgently needed to say.

"If it is really a question of that," he went on, "then I will get up and turn around and—since I like you too much to put a bayonet in your back—offer you my back instead. Hoping that you won't call my bluff, you understand. Or that something will distract your attention long enough for me to—"

"Very dear, your theories. Very gentle and sweet and impossible to put into practice. Nevertheless, you interest me. You are not the American type. I didn't know there were Americans like that."

"But that's what I keep telling you. Exactly what I am *is* the American type."

"You have got everything all wrong, but your ideas interest me."

"They are not my ideas. I have not said one original thing all evening."

"I like you," Jean Allégret said. "And if it were possible, if there was the slightest chance of changing human nature for the better, I would be on your side. But it does not change. Force is what counts. Idealism cannot survive a firing squad. . . . But in another way, another world, maybe, what you say is true. And in spite of all I have said, I believe it too. I am an artist. I paint."

"Seriously?"

"Excuse me," the Frenchman said. "I neglect my duties as a host. I will be back in a moment." He got up and went across the lawn and into the house.

The moon was above the marshes now, round and yellow and enormous. The whole sky was gilded by it. The house was no longer ugly. By this light you could see what the Victorian architect had had in mind. Harold stood behind Barbara, with his hand on her shoulder, listening to the girls' conversation. Then, drawn by curiosity, he went up the steps and into the house, as far as the drawing-room door. The fruitwood furniture was of a kind he had little taste for, but around the room were portraits and ivory miniatures he would have liked to look at. But would it (since the French were said to be so reluctant to ask people into their homes) be considered an act of rudeness for him to go around looking at things all by himself?

He turned back toward the front door and met Jean Allégret in the hall. "Oh there you are," the Frenchman said. "I was looking for you."

They went and sat down where they had been before, but turned the bench around so that they could watch the moon rising through the night sky.

"I do not like the painting of our time," Jean Allégret said. "It is sterile and it has nothing to do with life. What I paint is action. I stand and watch a man cutting a tree down, a farmer in the field, and I love the way he swings the ax blade, I see every motion, and it's that motion that interests me—not color or design. It's life I want to paint."

"You are painting now?"

"I have not painted since the war. I am rebuilding what was destroyed, you understand. I cannot do that and also paint. The

painting is my personal life, which has to give way to the responsibilities I have inherited."

"You are not married?"

The Frenchman shook his head. "When the house is rebuilt and
the farms are under cultivation again, then I will find a wife who
understands what I expect of her, and there will be children."

"And she must expect nothing of you? There can be no
alteration of your ideas to fit hers?"

"None whatever. I do not approve of American ideas of how
to treat women. They are gallant only on the surface. You lose
control over your women. And you have no authority over your
children or your home. You continually divorce and remarry
and make a further mess of it."

"Modern marriage is very complicated."

"It need not be."

Harold saw Eugène stop in front of Barbara and say something. After a moment he walked away. He did not appear to
be having a good time. The tweed coat, Harold thought.

Turning to Jean Allégret, he said: "You do not know my
name, do you?"

The Frenchman shook his head.

"Very good," Harold said. "I have a suggestion to make. Suppose I do not tell you my name. Some day you may find that
you cannot go on carrying the burden of family responsibilities, or that you were wrong in laying aside your personal life.
And you may have to drop everything and start searching for
what you once had. Or for something. Everybody at one time or
another has to go on a search, and if I do not tell you my name,
or where I live, then you will have an object to search for, an
excuse. America is a large country, it may take years and years
to find me, but while you are searching you will be discovering
all sorts of things, you will be talking to people, having experiences, and even if you never find me— You don't like my idea?"

"It's completely impractical. Romantic and charming and
impractical—a thoroughly American idea."

"I suppose it is," Harold said. He took his financial diary out of his pocket and wrote his name and forwarding address in Paris and their address in America. Then he tore the page out and handed it to the Frenchman, and went over to the bench where the three girls were sitting. They looked up as he approached.

"Do you want to come and join us?" he asked.

"Are you having a pleasant conversation?" Barbara asked.

"Very."

"Then I think I'll stay here. We're talking about America."

"When you come back to Paris in September," Jean Allégret said as Harold sat down, "I'd like very much to have you come and stay with me in the country. At my own place, I mean. This is my uncle's house, you understand."

Harold noticed that he had said "you," not "you and your wife."

"We'd like to very much," he said.

"We could have some shooting. It's very primitive, you understand. Not like this. But I think you will find it interesting. Actually," Jean Allégret said, his voice changing to accommodate a note of insincerity, "I am young to have taken on so large a responsibility. I'm only twenty-seven, you know." Behind the insincerity was the perfectly sincere image that he projected on the screen of his self-approval—of the man who lays aside his youth prematurely.

Like those people who, weeping at the grave of a friend, have no choice but to dramatize the occasion, Harold thought, and search around in their mind for a living friend to write to, describing how they stood at the grave, weeping, etc. The grief is no less real for requiring an audience. What the person doubts and seeks confirmation of is his own reality.

"There are six farms to manage," the Frenchman went on, "and I am—in spite of my lack of experience—in the position of a father to the village. They wanted to make me mayor. They bring all their problems to me, even their marital problems. I am also working with the boys. . . . The whole life of the community was destroyed, and slowly, a little at a time, I am helping them rebuild it. But it means that I have very little time to myself, and no time for painting. If the Communists take over, I will be the first to be shot, in our village."

"Are there many?"

"Five or six."

"And you know who they are?"

"Certainly. They have nothing against me personally, but if I am successful I will defeat their plans, and so I will be the first person taken out and shot. But you must come and see my village. . . . I want to give you my address, before I forget it."

Harold produced the financial diary again and while the Frenchman was writing, he sat looking at the dancers framed by the lighted windows. He still felt amazed and numb when he thought of what happened in the dining room, but most of the time he didn't think about it. A curtain had come down over his embarrassment. After a startled glance at the wreckage of the children's table, the guests had politely turned away and filed from the room as if nothing had happened. Jean Allégret went to the kitchen and came back with a damp cloth and scrubbed at the wine stain in the rug. Harold started to pick up the broken glass and found himself gently pushed out of the dining room. The sliding doors closed behind him. In a few minutes, Jean Allégret reappeared and brushed his apology aside—it was nothing, it was all the fault of the table pliante—and took him by the arm and led him outdoors and they went on talking.

Now, when the financial diary and the pencil had been returned to him, Harold said: "Would you take me inside and show me the house? I didn't want to walk around by myself looking at things. Just the two rooms they're dancing in."

To his surprise, the Frenchman stood up and said stiffly: "I will speak to my uncle."

"If it means that, never mind. I don't want to bother anyone.
I just thought you could take me around and tell me about the
portraits, but it isn't in the least important."

"I will speak to my uncle. It is his house."

Twice in one evening, Harold thought with despair. For it
was perfectly clear from the gravity with which his request
had been received that it was not the light thing he had thought
it was.

Jean Allégret conducted him up the steps and into the hall
and said: "Wait here." Then he turned and went back down
the steps. Watching through the open doorway, Harold saw him
approach a tall elderly man who was standing with a group of
people in the moonlight. He bent his head down attentively
while Jean Allégret spoke to him. Then, instead of turning and
coming toward the house, they left the group and walked up
and down, talking earnestly. A minute passed, and then another,
and another. Harold began to feel more and more conspicuous,
standing in the lighted hall as on a stage, in plain sight of everyone on the terrace. He had already been *in* those two rooms.
The others were dancing there now. And he could have looked
at the pictures, the tapestries, the marble statuary, by himself,
if he hadn't been afraid that it would be bad-mannered. And in
America people were always pleased when you asked to see
their house.

Uncle and nephew made one more complete turn around the
terrace, still talking, and apparently arrived at a decision, for
they turned suddenly and came toward the house. Jean Allégret
introduced Harold to his uncle and then left them together.
M. Allégret spoke no English. He was about sixty, taller than
Harold, dignified, and soft-spoken. For a minute or two he went
on making polite conversation. Then he said abruptly, as if in
reply to something Harold had just said: "Vous prenez un
intérêt aux maisons?"

"Je prends un intérêt dans cette maison. Mais—"

"Alors." Turning, M. Allégret led him over to a lithograph

hanging on the wall beside the door into the salon. "Voici un tableau d'une chasse à courre qui a eu lieu ici en mille neuf cent sept," he said. "La clef indique l'identité des personnes. Voici le Kaiser, et auprès de lui est le Prince Philippe zu Eulenberg . . . le Prince Frédéric-Guillaume . . . la Princesse Sophie de Württemberg, portant l'amazone noire, et le roi d'Angleterre . . . Mon père et ma mère . . . le Prince Charles de Saxe . . . avec leurs chasseurs et leurs laquais. Le tableau a été peint de mémoire, naturellement. Ces bois de cerf que vous voyez le long du mur. . . ."

⚜ ⚜
⚜

AT ELEVEN O'CLOCK Alix came toward the circle in the library, where Harold and four or five young men were talking about French school life, and said: "Eugène thinks it is time we went home."

Harold shook hands around the circle and then sought out Jean Allégret.

"We have to go," he said, "and I wanted to be sure I said good night to all your cousins. Would you take me around to them? I am not sure which—"

This request presented no difficulties. Barbara and Harold said good night to Mme Allégret, to various rather plain young girls, and to M. Allégret, who came out of the house with them. The others were waiting with the bicycles, under the grape arbor. Jean Allégret and his uncle conducted the party from the château along the driveway as far as the place where it dropped steeply downhill, and there they said good night. Harold and Jean Allégret shook hands warmly, one last time. Calling good night, good night, they coasted down the hill, through the dark tunnel of branches, with the dim carbide bicycle lamps barely showing the curves in the road, and emerged suddenly into bright moonlight. Dismounting at a sandy patch before the bridge, Harold risked saying to Eugène: "Did you have a pleasant evening?"

"No. They were too young. There was no one there who was very interesting." His voice in the moonlight was not unfriendly, but neither was it encouraging.

Out on the main road, Harold pedaled beside Barbara, whose lamp was brighter than his. "Wasn't it awful about the folding table?" he said.

"It wasn't your fault."

"I felt terrible about it, but they were so kind. They just closed the doors on it, and it was exactly as if it had never happened. But I keep thinking about the broken china and glasses that can never be replaced probably. And that stain on the carpet."

"What were you talking about?"

"I don't remember. Why?"

"I just wondered."

"They attacked poor dead Woodrow Wilson. And then they started on the Jews and Negroes. I thought France was the one country where Negroes were accepted socially. They sounded just like Southerners. What was it like at dinner?"

"All right. I didn't like the boy I sat next to."

"He was very handsome."

"He is coming to America on business, and he thought we could be useful to him. I didn't like him at all."

"And Alix's friend, who sat on the other side of you?"

"He was nice, but he was talking to Alix."

"I had a lovely time. And I saw the house. Jean Allégret's uncle showed me all through the downstairs, as far as the kitchen, and then he took me upstairs, through all the bedrooms, which were wonderful. It was like a museum. And in a dressing room I saw the family tree, painted on wood. It was interminable. It must have gone back at least to Charlemagne. And then we went outside and saw the family chapel. Jean Allégret wants us to come and stay with him up near the Belgian border. . . . Did you have a nice evening? Afterward, I mean?"

"All except for one thing. I think I hurt Eugène's feelings. He came and asked me to dance with him and I refused. I was interested in what Sabine was saying, and I didn't feel like dancing at the moment, and I'm afraid he was offended."

"He probably understood. . . . They don't use the chapel as a chapel any more. They keep wine in it."

"And I don't think Sabine had a very good time," Barbara said. "She sat with Alix or me all evening, and the boys didn't ask her to dance. I don't understand it. She's very pretty, and Mme Viénot said that she was so popular and had so many invitations."

"The money," he said.

"What money?"

They were overtaking Alix, and so he did not answer. The winding road was almost white, the distant hills were silver, and they could see as well as in daylight. They rode now in single file, now all together.

"Think of going five miles to a party on bicycles," Barbara said to Harold, "and coming home in the moonlight!"

In a high, thin, eerie voice, Sabine began to sing: "Au clair de la lune, mon ami Pierrot, prête-moi ta plume pour écrire un mot . . ." The tune was not the one the Americans knew, and they drew as near to her as their bicycles permitted. After that she sang "Cadet Rouselle a trois maisons qui n'ont ni poutres ni chevrons . . ." and they were so taken with the three houses that had no rafters, the three suits, the three hats, the three big dogs, the three beautiful cats, that they begged her to sing it again. Instead she told them a ghost story.

In a village near here, she said, but a long time ago, there was a schoolmaster who drove himself into a frenzy trying to teach reading and writing and the catechism to boys who wanted to be out working in the fields with their fathers. He had a birch cane, which he used frequently, and an expression which he used still more. Whenever any boy didn't know his lesson, the schoolmaster would say: "One dies as one is born. There is never any improvement." Then he'd reach for his birch rod.

One rainy autumn evening when he got home, he discovered that he had left his examination books at the school. And though he could have waited until next day to correct them, he was so anxious to find what mistakes his pupils had made that he went back that night, after his supper. A waning moon sailed through black clouds, and the wind whipped his cloak up into the air, and the familiar landscape looked different, as everything does on a windy autumn night. And when he opened the door of the schoolhouse, he saw that one of the pupils was still there, sitting on his bench. "Don't you even know enough to go home?" he shouted. "One dies as one is born." And the boy said, in a voice that chilled the schoolmaster's blood: "I was never born, and therefore I cannot die." With that he vanished.

Now I know what she's like, Harold thought. This is her element—telling ghost stories. And this filtered moonlight. All this silveriness.

The supernatural shouldn't be understood too well; it should have gaps in it for you to think about afterward. . . . What he missed because he didn't know the words or because their bicycles swerved, drawing them apart for a moment, merely added to the effect.

The next day, the schoolmaster was very nervous when he came to teach the class. He looked at each face carefully, and saw with relief only the usual ones. But one thing was not usual. André, who had never in his life recited, knew his whole day's lesson without a fault. Growing suspicious, the schoolmaster stopped calling on him. Even then the hand waved in the air, so anxious was he to recite. That evening, the schoolmaster walked home the long way round, and stopped at André's house, and learned that he was sick in bed. So then he knew.

After that, somebody always knew his lesson, and it wasn't long before the boys caught on. One at a time they played hookey, knowing that whatever it was—a ghost, a fairy, an uneasy spirit—would come to school that day looking exactly like them, and recite and recite. The schoolmaster grew thin. He began to make mistakes in arithmetic and to misspell words. He would start to say: "One dies as one is—" and then be afraid to finish. Finally, unable to stand the strain any more, he went to the curé one morning before school and told him his troubles. The curé reached for his hat and coat, and filled a small bottle with holy water from the font. "There is only one way that a person can be born," he said, "and that is in Jésus-Christ. When the possessed boy—because it can only be a case of possession—stands up to recite, I will baptize him." And that's what happened. The schoolmaster called on one boy who didn't know his lesson after another, until he came to Joseph, who was a great doltish boy with arms as long as an ape's. And when Joseph began to name the kings of France without a single mistake, the curé said: "In nomine patris et filii et spiritus sanctus," and uncorked the vial of holy water and flung it all in his face. The boy looked surprised and went on reciting. When he had finished, he sat down. There was no change in his appearance. The schoolmaster and the curé rushed off to Joseph's house and it was as they feared: Joseph was not there. "Isn't he at school?" his mother asked, in alarm.

"Yes, yes," the curé said, "he's at school," and they left without explaining.

As they were going through the wood, the curé said: "There is only one thing you can do. You must adopt this orphaned spirit, give him your name, and make him your legal heir." When they came out of the wood they went to the mairie and began to fill out the necessary adoption papers, which took all the rest of the day. When they finished, the maire took them, looked at them blankly, and handed them back. There was no writing on the documents they had spent so much time filling out.

So when the class opened the next day, the boys saw to their surprise that the schoolteacher was not at his desk in the front of the room but sitting on the bench that was always reserved for dunces. They were afraid to titter because of his birch rod, and when he saw their eyes go to it he got up and broke the rod over his knee. Then they sat there and waited. Finally one of the boys summoned enough courage to ask: "What are we waiting for?" "For the schoolmaster," the man said. "I have tried very hard to teach you, but I had a harsh unloving father and I never learned how to be a father to anybody else, and so you boys learn nothing from me. But I have learned something from the spirit that takes your place on the days when you are absent, and I know that he should be teaching you, and I am waiting now in the hope that he will come and teach us all."

After a time, Joseph left his seat and went to the desk and in a voice of the utmost sweetness began to conduct the lesson.

"Are you the spirit?" the boys asked.

"No, I am Joseph," he said.

"Then how is it you know the lesson?"

"I learned it last night. It took me a long time and it was very hard, but now I know it."

The next day, the same thing happened, only it was André who went to the front of the class. And right straight through the room, they took turns, each day a different boy, until it was the schoolmaster's turn. Looking very pale, he stood in front of them once more, and they waited, expecting him to say: "One dies as one is born." Instead, he began to hear the lesson, which they all knew. "But are you really the schoolmaster, or are you the spirit that takes our place?" they asked. "I am the schoolmaster," the man said sadly. "One dies as one is born, and I was born a man. But through the grace of Heaven, one is— one can hope to be of the company of spirits." That was the last time they ever heard him utter this familiar expression, though he stayed at his desk and taught them patiently, in a voice of the utmost gentleness and reasonableness, from that time on.

❧ ❧
❧

IF THE RIDE TO THE PARTY SEEMED LONG, the ride home was too brief. Harold found himself pushing his bicycle into the darkness of the woods behind Beaumesnil long before he expected to. The courtyard, like everywhere else, was flooded with moonlight. There was a lighted kerosene lamp on the kitchen table. All the rest of the château was either white in the moonlight or in total shadow.

They piled their bicycles in a heap in the kitchen entry. Alix lit the other lamps that had been left for them. In a procession, they went through the pantry and the dining room to the stairs and parted in the second-floor hallway. They were relaxed and sleepy and easy with each other; even Eugène. It was as if they had come home from any number of parties in just this way ("Good night") and were all one family ("Good night, Barbara") and knew each other's secrets ("Good night, good night") and took for granted the affection that could be heard in their voices. ("It was lovely, wasn't it? . . . I hope you sleep well. . . . Good night. . . .")

Chapter 12

O N Sunday morning, Harold sat tense and ready, his week-old, wine-stained, really horrible-looking napkin rolled and inserted in its ivory ring. He refused another cup of coffee and pretended to be following the history of the Allégret family that Mme Viénot was telling with so much pleasure. He was waiting for her to leave the table. When she pushed her chair back, he got up also and followed her out into the hall.

"If it would be convenient," he began, "if there is time before church, that is, could we—"

"Yes, of course," Mme Viénot said, as if she were grateful to him for reminding her of something she should have thought of, herself. She led the way through the pink and white drawing room to a room beyond it, a study, which Harold had not been in before. Composed and businesslike, she indicated a chair for him and sat down at the flat-topped mahogany desk in the center of the room. To be embarrassed by a situation one has deliber-ately contrived to bring about in one's own interests is not real-istic; is not intelligent; in short, is not French. As Mme Viénot opened a drawer and drew out a blank sheet of paper, she saw that his eyes were focused on the wall directly behind her and said: "That is a picture of Beaumesnil as it was when my father inherited it. As you see, it was a small country house. I find it rather charming. Even though the artist was not very talented. As a painting it is rather sentimental. . . . I spoke to my cook about the pommes de terre frites."

He looked blank.

"You remember that Mme Rhodes asked for the recipe—and it was as I suspected. She is unwilling to divulge her secret. They are so peculiar in this respect."

"It doesn't matter," he said.

"I'm sorry. I would have liked to have got it for her. You came here on the eleventh—"

He nodded.

"—and today is Sunday the twenty-fifth. That makes two full weeks—"

His eyes opened wide. So they were being charged, after all, for the three days they were in Paris.

"—and one day," Mme Viénot concluded.

They had arrived at one o'clock; they would be leaving for the train at three thirty this afternoon. The extra day was two and a half hours long.

A moment later, Mme Viénot interrupted her writing to say: "I did not think it proper to allow M. Carrère to pay for the ices and the pâtisseries that afternoon in Blois. Your share of the *addition* came to a hundred and eighty francs." The amount was written down, while he tried to reconcile M. Carrère's pleasant gesture toward America with the fact that he had afterward allowed the cost of the gesture to be deducted from his bill and added onto theirs. Only in dreams are such contradictions reconciled; in real life, fortunately, it isn't necessary. Nothing was deducted for the ten or eleven meals they had not taken at the château, or for the taxi ride to Blois that Mme Viénot had shared with them. The taxi to and from the ferry, the day they went to Chaumont, was six hundred francs. He had not intended that Mme Viénot, Mme Straus-Muguet, and Alix should have to pay a share of this amount; he would not have allowed it. Apparently it was, as Alix said, a question of sincerity. But *had* M. Carrère allowed her to deduct their ices and pastry from his bill? It did not seem at all like him. And had Mme Straus-Muguet been charged for her share of the taxi to and from the ferry at Chaumont?

The sense of outrage, clotted in his breast, moved him to fight back, and the form his attack took was characteristic. In one of her letters she had written them that the *service* was included. He offered her now a chance to go the whole hog.

"What about the cook and Thérèse and Albert?"

"I shall give them something," Mme Viénot said.

But will she, he wondered.

The sheet of paper that she handed across the desk read:

Note de Semaine de M. Harold Rhodes
  2 semaines
  + 1 jour   32,100 f
  5 téléphones   100 f
  Goûter à Blois   180 f
  Laundry   125 f
                 payé le 24 Juillet 48
  Château Beaumesnil
  Brenodville s/Euphrone

With the pen that she offered to him he wrote the date and his signature on four American Express traveler's checks—a fifty, two twenty-fives, and a ten—and handed them to her as he wrote.

"Will you also give me a statement that you have cashed these four checks?"

"Is that necessary?" Mme Viénot asked.

"For the customs," he said. "The amount we brought in is declared in our passports, and the checks have to be accounted for when we leave."

"I have been advised not to put down the money I receive from my clients, when I make out my tax statement," Mme Viénot said. "If they do not ask to see the statement when you go through customs, I would appreciate your not showing it."

He agreed to this arrangement.

She opened a little metal box and produced four hundred-franc notes, a fifty, a twenty-five, and two tens, and gave them to him. He folded the huge paper currency and put it in his coat pocket. With the traveler's checks neatly arranged in front of her, she said: "It has been a great pleasure having you. . . . I hope that when you come again it will be as friends."

He said nothing. He had paid the full amount, which was perhaps reasonable, since he had not asked outright if they would be charged for the three days they were in Paris. If she had really felt kindly toward them, or had the slightest impulse toward generosity or fairness, she could have made some slight adjustment. She hadn't, and he was therefore not obliged to pretend now.

His eyes met hers in a direct glance and she looked away. She picked up the checks and put them down again, and then said: "There is something I have wanted to tell you, something I would like to explain. But perhaps you guessed— We have not always lived like this."

"I understand that."

"There has been a *drame* in our family. Two years ago, my husband—"

She stopped talking. Her eyes were filled with tears. He leaned forward in his chair, saw that it was too late for him to say anything, and then sat back and waited for the storm of weeping to pass. He could not any more help being moved, as he watched her, than if she had proved in a thousand ways that she was their friend. Whatever the trouble was, it had been real.

⚜ ⚜
⚜

FIVE MINUTES LATER he closed the door of their third-floor room and said: "I almost solved the mystery."

"What mystery?" Barbara asked.

"I almost found out about M. Viénot. She started to tell me, when I finished paying her—"

"Did she charge us for the full two weeks?"

"How did you know that? And then she started to tell me about *him*."

"What happened to him?"

"I don't know," he said. "I didn't let her tell me."

"But *why*, if she wanted to tell you?"

"She broke down. She cried."

"Mme Viénot?"

He heard the sound of wheels and went to the window. The dog cart had come to a stop in front of the château, and the gardener was helping Mme Bonenfant up into the seat beside him. She sat, dressed for church, with her prayerbook in her hand.

Harold turned away from the window and said: "I could feel something. She changed, suddenly. She started searching for her handkerchief. And from the way she looked at me, I had a feeling she was asking me to deliver her from the situation she had got herself into. So I told her she didn't need to tell me about it. I said I was interested in people, that I observed them, but that I never asked questions."

"But are you sure she changed her mind about telling you?"

"Not at all sure. She may have been play-acting. I may have given her the wrong cue, for all I know. But she didn't cry on purpose. That much I'm sure of."

Leaning on his elbows, he looked out at the park. The hay stacks were gone, and the place had taken on a certain formality. He saw how noble the old trees were that lined the drive all the way out to the road. The horse restlessly moved forward a few paces and had to be checked by the gardener, who sat holding the reins. Mme Bonenfant arranged her skirt and then, looking up at the house, she called impatiently.

From somewhere a voice—light, unhurried, affectionate,

silvery—answered: "Oui, Grand'maman. A l'instant. Je viens, je viens . . ."

"What an idiotic thing to do," Barbara said. "Now we'll never know what happened to him."

"Yes we will," he said. "Somebody will tell us. Sooner or later somebody always does."

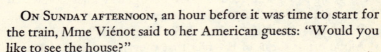

ON SUNDAY AFTERNOON, an hour before it was time to start for the train, Mme Viénot said to her American guests: "Would you like to see the house?"

Alix and Mme Bonenfant went with them. The tour began on the second floor at the head of the stairs, with Mme Bonenfant's bedroom, which was directly under theirs. The counterpane on the huge bed was of Persian embroidery on a white background. The chair covers were of the same rich material. They were reminded of the bedchamber of Henri IV at Cheverny. The bedroom at Beaumesnil smelled of camphor and old age, and the walls were covered with family photographs. As they were leaving the room, Harold glanced over at the bedside table and saw that the schoolboy whose photograph was on the piano in the petit salon had not been finished off at the age of twelve; here he was, in the uniform of the French army.

They saw the two rooms that had been occupied by M. and Mme Carrère and that would have been theirs, Mme Viénot said, if they had come when they originally planned. And at the end of the hall, they were shown into Mme Cestre's room, on which her contradictory character had failed to leave any impression whatever. The curtains, the bedspread were green and white chintz that had some distant connection with water lilies.

Mme Viénot's room, directly across the hall from her mother's but around a corner, where they had never thought to search for her, was much smaller, and furnished simply and apparently without much thought. It was dominated not by the bed but by the writing desk.

Mme Viénot opened a desk drawer and took out some post-cards. "I think you have no picture of Beaumesnil," she said.

"We took some pictures with our camera," Barbara said, "but they may not turn out. We're not very good at taking pictures."

"You may choose the one you like best," Mme Viénot said.

They looked through the cards and took one and handed the others to Mme Viénot, who gave them to her mother as they were going along the second-floor passageway that connected the two parts of the house. Mme Bonenfant gave the cards back to Barbara, saying: "Keep them. Keep all of them."

Alix did not speak of the fact that they had already seen her room. It almost seemed that the room itself, as they stood in the doorway looking in, was denying that that illicit evening had ever taken place. They passed on to the bare, badly furnished room that had been Mme Straus-Muguet's. It was so much less comfortable than their own third-floor room or than any of the rooms they had just seen that Harold wondered if a deliberate slight had been involved. As Mme Viénot closed the door she said dryly: "It seems Mme Straus saw your room and she has asked for it when she comes back in August. I do not think I can see my way clear to letting her have it."

But why did Mme Viénot not want her to have their room, he wondered. Unless Mme Straus was unwilling to pay what they had paid, or perhaps was unable to pay that much. And if that was so, should they allow her to entertain them in Paris?

In this back wing of the house there was a box-stair leading up to a loft that had once been used as a granary. It still smelled of the dust of grain that had been stored there, though it was empty now, except for a few old-fashioned dolls (whose dolls, he wondered; how long ago had their place been usurped by children?) and, in the center of the high dim room, the wooden works of the outdoor clock.

They were quite beyond repair, Mme Viénot said, but the

wooden cogwheels had turned, the clock had kept time, as recently as her girlhood. The pineapple-shaped weights were huge, and a hole had had to be cut in the floor for them to rise and descend through. Standing in this loft, Harold had the feeling that they had penetrated into the secret center of the house, and that there were no more mysteries to uncover.

⚜ ⚜
⚜

As ALWAYS at the end of a visit, there was first too much time and then suddenly there was not enough and they were obliged to hurry. Alix and Eugène had already started out for the village on foot. The gardener's bicycles having been returned to him, again there weren't enough to go round. The Americans took one last survey of the red room, free of litter now, the armoire and the closet empty, the postcards, guidebooks, and souvenirs all packed, the history of the château of Blois and the illustrated pamphlet returned to their place downstairs. The dying sweet peas in their square vase on the table in the center of the room said: *It is time to go. . . .*

"Where will we find another room like this?" he said, and closed the door gently on that freakish collection of books, on the tarnished mirrors, the fireplace that could not be used, the bathtub into which water did not flow, the map of Ile d'Yeu, the miniatures, the red and black and white wallpaper, the now familiar view, through that always open window, of the bottom of the sea. As he started down, he thought: *We will never come here again. . . .*

Mme Viénot was waiting for them at the foot of the stairs, and they followed her along the back passageway by which they had first entered the house, around a corner, and then another corner. A door opened silently, on the right, and Harold found himself face to face with a maniacal old woman, who clawed at his coat pocket and for a second scared him out of his wits. It was the cook. He was seeing the cook at last, and she had put something in his pocket. Too astonished to speak, he pressed a five-hundred-franc note into her hand, and she withdrew behind the door. He glanced ahead of him and saw Mme Viénot's skirt disappearing around the next corner. He was more than half convinced that she had seen—that she had eyes in the back of her head. She must, in any case, have sensed that something strange was going on. But when he caught up with her in the courtyard, she made no reference to what had happened in the corridor and, blushing from the sense of complicity in a deception he did not understand, he also avoided any mention of it.

Mme Bonenfant and Mme Cestre were waiting outside with the two children, whom the Americans had scarcely laid eyes on, and Alix's baby in her stroller. The Americans shook hands with their hostess, with Mme Bonenfant, with Mme Cestre. They disposed of the dressing case and the two small suitcases among the three of them. Sabine kissed her mother and grandmother, and then, mounting their bicycles, waving and calling good-by, they rode out of the courtyard, past the Lebanon cedar that was two hundred years old, and down the cinder drive.

Harold did not dare look at the piece of paper until they had turned into the road and there was no possibility of his being seen from the house. He let Barbara and Sabine draw ahead and then, balancing a suitcase with one hand, he put his other into his pocket. By all the rules of narration it should have been a communication from M. Viénot, a prisoner somewhere in the attic, crying out for help through his only friend, the cook. It was, instead, a recipe for French-fried potatoes, and with it, on another piece of paper three inches square, a note:

Si, par hasard, M. et Mme Rhodes connaissaient quelqu'un desirant du personnel français mon fils et moi partirions très volontiers à l'Etranger. Voici mon addresse Mme Foëcy à St. Claude de Diray Indre-et-Loire. . . .

So he was not so far off, after all. It was the cook who wanted them to rescue her, from Mme Viénot and the unhappy country of France.

❖ ❖
❖

In all the fields between the château and the village, the grain had been cut and stacked. The scythe and the blades of the reaper had spared only those poppies that grew along the road, among the weeds and the wildflowers. The *bluets* had just come into flower.

"My sister was married at Beaumesnil," Sabine said, "and because of the Occupation we couldn't have the kind of flowers that are usual at weddings, so, half an hour before the ceremony, the bridesmaids went out and picked their own bouquets, at the side of the road."

"It sounds charming," Barbara said.

"It was." Sabine swerved to avoid a rut. "There were some people from the village present, and they thought that if my sister had field flowers for her wedding it must be the fashion. Since that time, whenever there is a wedding in Brenodville the bride carries such a bouquet."

The note of condescension he heard in her voice was unconscious, Harold decided, and had nothing to do with the fact that she belonged to one social class and the village to another but was simply the smiling condescension of the adult for the child. He kept turning to look back at the château, so white against the dark woods. Since he couldn't do what he would have liked to do, which was to fold it up and stuff it in the suitcase and take it away with him, he tried to commit it to memory.

Then they were at the outskirts of Brenodville, and it looked as if the whole village had come out to meet them and escort them to their train. Actually, as he instantly realized, it was simply that it was Sunday afternoon. The people they met spoke to Sabine and sometimes nodded to the Americans. They cannot not know who we are, he thought, and at that moment someone spoke to him—a middle-aged man in a dark-blue Sunday suit, with his two children walking in front of him and his wife at his side. Surprised and pleased, Harold answered: "Bonjour, monsieur!" and when they were past, he turned to Sabine and asked: "Who is that?"

"That was M. Fleury."

He looked back over his shoulder to see if their old friend had stopped and was waiting for him to ride back, but M. Fleury had kept on walking.

"Have I got time to ride back and speak to him?" he said.

"You did speak to him," Barbara said.

"But I didn't recognize him. He looked so different."

The girls were talking and didn't hear him.

Riding past the cemetery, he took one last look at the monuments, which were surely made of papier-mâché, and at the graves decorated with a garish mixture of real and everlasting wreaths and flowers. As for the village itself, in two weeks' time they had come to know every doorway, every courtyard, every purple clematis, climbing rose, and blue morning-glory vine between here and the little river.

In the cobblestone square in front of the mairie they turned left, into a street that led them downhill in the direction of the railway station, and soon overtook Eugène, striding along by himself, with his coat on one arm and in the other his light suitcase. Alix was not with him. Harold looked around for her and saw that she wasn't anywhere. He slowed down, ready to ride beside Eugène. Receiving no encouragement, he rode on.

"What do we do with the bicycles?" he asked, when the two girls caught up with him.

"Someone will call for them," Sabine said.

On the station platform, he saw their two big suitcases and the dufflebag, checked through to Paris. The smaller suitcases they could manage easily with Eugène's help, even though they had to change trains at Blois. Traveling with French people, there would be no problems. He wouldn't have to ask the same question four different times so that he would have four answers to compare.

Eugène arrived, and drew Sabine aside, and stood talking to her farther down the platform, where they were out of earshot. Harold turned to Barbara and said in a low voice: "Where is Alix?"

"I don't know," she answered.

"Something must have happened."

"Sh-h-h."

"It's very queer," he said. "She didn't say good-by. There is only one direct way home—the way we came—and we didn't meet her, so she must have wanted to avoid us."

"Possibly."

"Do you think they quarreled?"

"Something has happened."

"Do you think it has anything to do with us?"

"What could it have to do with us?"

"I don't know," he said.

When Sabine came and joined them on the station platform, he thought: Now she will explain, and everything will be all right again. . . . But her explanation—"Alix has gone home. She said to say good-by to you"—only deepened his sense of something being held back.

The station was surrounded by vacant land, and the old station still existed, but in the form of a low mound covered with weeds. Harold kept looking off in the direction of the château, thinking that he might see Alix; that she might suddenly appear in the space between two buildings. She didn't appear. Eugène remained standing where he was. The bell started to ring, though there was no train as far as the eye could see down the perfectly straight tracks in the direction of Blois, Orléans, and Paris or in the direction of Tours, Angers, and Nantes. The ringing filled the air with intimations of crisis. The four men seated on the terrace of the Café de la Gare paid no attention to it, which meant that they were either stone deaf or long accustomed to this frightful sound.

After five minutes the station agent appeared. He walked the length of the brick platform and, cranking solemnly, looking neither at the avenue Gambetta on his right nor at the bed of blue pansies on his left, let down the striped gates and closed the street to traffic.

A black poodle leaning out of the window of the house next to the café waited hopefully for something to happen, with its paws crossed in an attitude that was half human. The woolly head turned, betraying a French love of excitement, and the poodle watched the street that led toward the river. The bell went on ringing but with less and less conviction, like a man giving perfectly good advice that he knows from past experience will not be followed. Just when it seemed that nothing was ever going to happen, there was a falsetto cry and the four men on the terrace turned their heads in time to see the train from Tours rush past the café and come to a sudden stop between the railway station and the travel posters. Carriage doors flew open and passengers started descending. They reached up for suitcases that were handed down to them by strangers. They shouted messages to relatives who were going on to Blois, remembered a parcel left on the overhead rack, were alarmed, were reassured (the parcel was on the platform), held small children up to say good-by, or hurried to be first in line at the gate.

Eugène found a third-class compartment that was empty, and they got in, and he pulled the door to from the inside. Harold let the glass down and kept his head out, with all the other heads, until the train had carried them past the place where they had waited for the bus. Having seen the last of the country he wanted especially to remember, he sat down. Barbara and Sabine were talking about their schools. He waited to see what Eugène would do. Eugène had a book in his coat pocket, and he took it out and read until the train drew into the station at Blois.

Eugène made his way along the crowded cement platform, and Harold followed at his heels, and the two girls tagged along after him, as relaxed as if they were shopping. Suddenly they came upon a group of ten or twelve of the guests at the Allégrets' party. Their youth, their good looks, their expensive clothes and new English luggage made them very noticeable in the drab crowd. Harold would have stopped but Eugène kept on going. Several of them nodded or smiled at Harold, whose eyes, as he spoke to them, were searching for Jean Allégret. He was there too, a little apart from the others. Harold started to put the suitcase down and shake hands with him, and then realized that he had just that second received all that was coming to him from Jean Allégret—a quick, cold nod.

Fortunately, the suitcases were still in his hands and he could keep on walking. He remembered but did not resort to a trick he had learned in high school: when you made the mistake of waving to somebody you did not know or, as it sometimes happened, somebody you knew all right but who for some unknown reason didn't seem to know you, the gesture, caught in time, could be diverted; the direction of the hand could be changed so that what began as a friendly greeting ended as smoothing the hair on the side of your head. Bewildered, he took his stand beside Eugène, a hundred feet further along the platform.

In giving him the money to buy Sabine's ticket, Mme Viénot had explained that third class was just as comfortable as second and only half as expensive. The second part of this statement was true, the first was not. He didn't look forward to a four-hour ride, on a hot July night, on wooden slats.

Just before the train drew in, the announcer's voice, coming over the loud-speaker system, filled the station with the sound of rising panic, as if he were announcing not the arrival of the Paris express, stopping at Orléans, etc., etc., but something cataclysmic—the fall of France, the immanent collision of the earth and a neighboring planet. When the train drew to a stop, they were looking into an empty compartment. Again Eugène closed the door from the inside, to discourage other passengers from crowding in. Just before the train started, the door was wrenched open and a thin, pale young man—Eugène and Alix's friend—looked in. Behind him, milling about in confusion, was the house party. Surely *they're* not traveling third class, Harold thought.

Eugène told them there was room for four in the compartment. After a hurried consultation, they decided that they did not want to be separated. Leaning out of the window, Harold saw them mount the step of a third-class carriage farther along the train. Were they all as poor as church mice, he wondered. The question could not be asked, and so he would never know the answer.

As the train carried them north through the evening light, Sabine and Barbara and Harold whiled away a few miles of the journey by writing down the names of their favorite books. *A Passage to India,* he wrote on the back of the envelope that Sabine handed to him. Barbara took the envelope and wrote *Fear and Trembling.* He gave Sabine the financial diary and on a blank page she wrote *Le Silence de la Mer,* while he looked over her shoulder. "Vercors," she wrote. And then, "un petit livre poétique." Barbara wrote *Journey to the End of the Night* on the back of the envelope. He took it and wrote *To the Lighthouse.* He glanced carefully at Eugène, who was sitting directly across from him. Eugène looked away. *A Sportsman's Notebook,* he wrote, and turned the envelope around so that Sabine could read it.

Shortly after that, Eugène got up and went out into the corridor and stood by an open window. After Orléans, Barbara and Sabine went out into the corridor also and stood by another window, and when Barbara came back into the compartment she said in a low voice: "I asked Sabine if she knew what was the matter with Eugène, and she said he was moody and not like other French boys." Though, during the entire journey, Eugène had nothing whatever to say to the three people he was traveling with, he had a long, pleasant, animated conversation with a man in the corridor.

In the train shed in Paris, they met up with the house party again, and this time Jean Allégret acknowledged the acquaintance with a smile and a wave of his hand, as if not he but his double had had doubts in the station at Blois about the wisdom of accepting an American as a friend.

Harold put his two suitcases down and searched through his pockets for the luggage stubs. After four hours of ignoring the fact that he was being ignored, it was difficult to turn casually as if nothing had happened and ask where he should go to see about the two big suitcases and the dufflebag. Eugène shrugged, looked impatient, looked annoyed, looked as if he found Harold's French so inaccurately pronounced and so ungrammatical that there was no point in trying to understand it, and Harold felt that his education had advanced another half-semester. (Though there is only one way of saying "Thank you" in French, there are many ways of being rude, and you don't have to stop and ask yourself if the rudeness is sincere. The rudeness is intentional, and harsh, and straight from the closed heart.)

Too angry to speak, he turned on his heel and started off to find the baggage office by himself. He had only gone a short distance when he heard light footsteps coming after him. Sabine found the right window, took the stubs from him, gave them to the agent, and in her calm, soft, silvery voice dictated the address of her aunt's apartment.

The four of them took the Métro, changed at Bastille, and stepped into a crowded train going in the direction of the Porte de Neuilly. More and more people got on. Farther along the aisle a man and a woman, neither of them young, stood with their arms around each other, swaying as the train swayed, and looking into each other's eyes. The man's moist mouth closed on the woman's mouth in a long, indecent kiss, after which he looked around with a cold stare at the people who were deliberately not watching him.

Harold and Barbara found themselves separated from Sabine and Eugène. Barbara whispered something that Harold could not hear, because of the train noise. He put his head down.

"I said 'I think we'd better go to the Vouillemont.' "

"So do I. But I'm a little worried. It's after eleven o'clock, and we have no reservations."

"If there's no room at the Vouillemont, we can go to some other hotel," she said. "I'd rather spend the night on a park bench than put up with this any longer."

"But why did he ask us?"

"Something is wrong. He's changed his mind. Or perhaps he enjoys this sort of thing."

"The son of a bitch. You saw what happened when I asked him where to go about the big suitcases? . . . The only reason I hesitate at all is Alix and Mme Cestre. I hate to have them know we were—"

"He may not tell them what happened."

"But Sabine will."

The train rushed into the next station. They peered through the window and saw the word *Concorde*. Over the intervening heads, Eugène signaled that they were to get off.

Harold set the suitcases down and extended his hand. "We'll leave you here," he said stiffly. "Good night."

"But why?" Eugène demanded, astonished.

"The hotel is near this station, and we don't want to put you to any further trouble. Thank you very much."

"For what?"

"For taking care of us on the way up to Paris," Harold said. But then he spoiled the effect by blushing.

There was a brief silence during which both of them struggled with embarrassment.

"I am extremely sorry," Eugène said, "if I have given you any reason to think—"

"It seemed to us that you are a trifle distrait," Harold said, "and we'd rather not put you to any further trouble."

"I am not distrait," Eugène said. "And you are not putting me to any trouble whatever. The apartment is not being used. There is no need for you to go to a hotel."

A train drew in, at that moment, and Harold had the feeling afterward that that was what decided the issue, though trains don't, of course, decide anything. All decisions are the result of earlier decisions; cause, as anyone who has ever studied Beginning Philosophy knows, is another way of looking at effect. They got on the train, and then got off several stations farther along the line, at the Place Pierre-Joseph Redouté. A huge block of granite in the center of the square and dark triangular buildings, with the streets between them leading off in six directions like the rays of a star, were registered on Harold's mind as landmarks he would need to know if they suddenly decided to retrace their steps.

Sabine took her suitcase from Eugène. Then she shook hands with Barbara and Harold. "I am leaving you here," she said, and walked off down a dark, deserted avenue.

The other three turned into a narrow side street, and the Americans stopped when Eugène stopped, in front of the huge door of an apartment house. The door was locked. He rang the bell and waited. There was a clicking noise and the door gave under the pressure of his hand and they passed through a dimly lighted foyer to the elevator. Eugène put the suit cases into it, indicated that Harold and Barbara were to get in also, pressed the button for the sixth floor, and stepped out. "It only holds three," he said. "And with the suitcases it would not rise."

He shut the elevator door, and as they went up slowly, they saw him ascending the stairs, flight after flight. He was there in time to open the elevator door for them. He let them into the dark apartment with his key and then proceeded down the hall, turning on lights as he went, to the bedroom they were to occupy. "It is our room when Alix is here," he explained.

"But we don't want to put you out of your room," Harold protested.

"During the summer I prefer to sleep in the study," Eugène said.

He showed them the toilet, in a separate little room off the hall, and the bathroom they were to use. The gas hot-water heater was in the other bathroom, and he led them there and showed them how to turn the heater on and off when they wanted a bath.

They went back to the room that was to be theirs, and Eugène opened the window and unlatched the metal shutters and pushed them outward, letting in the soft night air. They saw that the room opened onto an iron balcony. Eugène removed the pillows from a big studio couch, and then he drew the Kelly-green bedspread off and folded it and put it over the back of a chair. They watched him solemnly, as if he were demonstrating the French way to fold a bedspread. He showed them how to unhook the pillow covers and where the extra blankets were, and then he said good night. During all this, everybody was extremely polite, as if they had tried everything else and found that nothing works but politeness and patience.

Chapter 13

IN THE FIRST LUMINOUS QUARTER-HOUR of daylight, the Place Pierre-Joseph Redouté in the 16th arrondissement of Paris was given over to philosophical and mathematical speculation. The swallows skimming the wet rooftops said: *What are numbers?*

The sky, growing paler, said: *What is being when being becomes morning?*

What is "five," asked the birds, *apart from "five" swallows?*

The French painter and lithographer who belonged in the center of the Place and who from his tireless study of natural forms might have been able to answer those questions was unfortunately not there any more; he had been melted down and made into bullets by the Germans. The huge block of rough granite that was substituting for him said: *Matter is energy not in motion,* and the swallows said: *Very well, try this, then, why don't you . . . and this . . . and this . . .*

Though proof was easy and the argument had long ago grown tiresome, the granite refrained. But it could not resist some slight demonstration, and so it gave off concentric circles of green grass, scarlet salvia, curbing, and cobblestone.

The wide, wet, empty streets that led away from the Place Redouté like the rays of a star or the spokes of a wheel also at the very same time returned to it—returned from the Etoile, the Place d'Iéna, the Place Victor Hugo, the Trocadéro, and the Bois de Boulogne. The sky went on turning lighter. The pissoir, ill-smelling, with its names, dates, engagements, and obscene diagrams, said: *Everything that happens, in spite of the best efforts of the police, is determined by the space co-ordinates x, y, and z, and the time co-ordinate t.*

God is love, said the leaves on the chestnut trees, and the iron church bell filled the air with a frightful clangor.

Across an attic window in the rue Malène a workshirt hanging on a clothesline to dry grew a darker blue as it absorbed the almost invisible rain.

On the other side of the street, at the same sixth-floor level, a pair of metal shutters folded back gave away the location of a bedroom. The sleepers, both in one bed, were turned toward each other. She moved in her sleep, and he put his hand under her silken knees and gathered them to his loins and went on sleeping. Shortly afterward they turned away from each other, as if to demonstrate that in marriage there is no real resting place. Now love is gathered like great long-stemmed summer flowers, now the lovers withdraw from one another to nourish secretly a secret life. He pulls the blanket and sheet closer, shutting off the air at the back of his neck. She has not committed the murder, the police are not looking for her, and there is just time, between the coming and going of the man in the camel's-hair coat and the footsteps outside the door, to hide the papers. But where? If she puts them inside a book, they will be found, even though there are so many books. She will explain and they will not listen. They will not believe her. And he is asleep, dreaming. She has no one to stand by her when they come. She goes to the closet and finds there the camel's-hair coat worn by the murderer, who knew she was innocent and good, and slipped in and out of the apartment without being seen, and so who will believe her? . . . *Help! Help!* takes the form of a whimper.

Across the room a long-deferred, often-imagined reconciliation is taking place on the wall, behind glass. The Prodigal Son, wearing a robe of stone, kneels on one knee before the Prodigal Father. One arm reaches out and touches the old man's side. One arm, upraised, touches his face. The old man sits, bearded, with a domed forehead, a large stone mouth, blunt nose, and eyes nearly closed with emotion. He has placed one hand against the young man's head, supporting it, but not looking (why is that?) at the face that is looking up at his with such sorrow and love.

The iron balcony, polished by the rain, turns darker, shines, collects puddles. Water dripping from the eaves is caught in the first fold of the awnings.

The sleepers' breath is shallow. His efforts to take her in his arms meet with no response. He cannot blame her for this because she is asleep. The sky goes on turning lighter and whiter. It has stopped raining. A man (out of whose dream?) comes up the rue Malène and, noiseless as a cat, his vibrations sinister, crosses the Place Redouté and disappears down the same street that Sabine Viénot took. But that was last night and now it is morning.

Crowded to the extreme edge of the bed by his half-waking and half-sleeping lust, she turns.

"Are you awake?" he says softly.

"Yes."

"We're back in Paris."

"So I see."

Beside the door to the hall a bookshelf, too far away to read the titles. Then an armchair, with her dress and slip draped over the back and on the seat her bra, panties, and stockings in a soft heap. Her black wedge-soled shoes. Back of the chair a photograph—a detail of sculpture from a medieval church.

"Why the Prodigal Son?"

There is no answer from the other side of the bed.

He continues his investigation of the room. A low round table, elaborately inlaid, with two more period chairs. The radiator, and then the French windows. The room is high up, above the treetops, and there are windows directly across the way, an attic floor above that, and a portion of blue sky. Love in a garret. A door leading into the next room. A little glass table with knick-knacks on it. Another chair. On this chair, his clothes. Beside it his huge shoes—careless, scuffed, wide open, needing to be shined. Then the fireplace, with a mirror over it. Then an arm-chair, with the green spread and pillow covers and bolster piled on it. And over the bed an oil painting, a nude lying on a bed, plump, soft-fleshed, blonde. Alix—but not really. It is eighteenth century. He turns over.

"She was living for his return," he said. "That's all she talked about. And then when he came, they quarreled."

"Perhaps they didn't quarrel. Perhaps they just said good-by and she went back to the château."

"Then why was she avoiding us? It doesn't make sense. She must not have gone home by the road that goes past the cemetery. She probably didn't want us to see that she had been crying. All week long she kept waiting for a letter and there wasn't any letter."

"He called."

"That's true. I forgot that he called on Thursday. But all week end he wasn't himself. He wouldn't go swimming. And he didn't have a good time at the party. Did she?"

"Apparently."

"And the rest of the time, they were off somewhere by themselves. In the back part of the house . . . You don't think it has something to do with us?"

"No."

"I feel that it must have something to do with us. . . . She may not have wanted us here, sleeping in their bed and all."

"She said she was very glad."

"Then it must be all right. She wouldn't lie about it, just to be polite. If they quarreled, I can understand his not wanting to talk afterward. But in that case, why the long cheerful conversation with the man in the corridor?"

She turned over on her back and looked at the ceiling. "It's an effort for them. They have to choose their words carefully in order to make us understand."

"It's an effort for us too."

"They may not always feel like making the effort."

"Nothing was too much effort at first. . . . Did Sabine say 'Eugène is not like other French boys'? That may be what she meant—that he was friendly one minute and not the next. Or maybe when his curiosity is satisfied, he simply isn't interested any more. . . . I suppose the streets of Paris are safe, but I felt very queer watching her go off alone at that time of night. You think she got home all right?"

"Oh yes."

"I would have offered to take her home myself, but I didn't see how I could leave you, at that point. . . . How can she go on being nice to him?"

"She knows him better than we do."

He turned back again and, finding that she was curled up in a ball and he couldn't get at her, he put his hand between her knees. He felt her drifting back into sleep, away from him.

"What time is it?"

He drew his bare arm out from under the covers and looked at his wrist watch. "Five minutes of eight. Why?"

"Breakfast," she said. "In a strange kitchen."

He sat up in bed. "Do you wish we'd gone to a hotel?"

"We're here. We'll see how it works out."

"I could call the Vouillemont. . . . I didn't know what to do last night. He seemed genuinely apologetic. . . . If we never had to see him again, it would be simpler. But the suitcases are coming here."

She pushed the covers aside and started to get up, and then, suddenly aware of the open window and the building across the street, she said: "They can see us in bed."

"That can't be of much interest to anybody. Not in Paris," he said, and, naked as he was, he went to the curtained windows

239

and closed them. In the dim underwater light they dressed and straightened up the room, and then they went across the hall to the kitchen. She was intimidated by the stove. He found the pilot light and turned on one of the burners for her. The gas flamed up two inches high. They found the teakettle and put water on to boil and then searched through the icebox. Several sections of a loaf of dark bread; butter; jam; a tiny cake of ice. In their search for what turned out to be the right breakfast china but the wrong table silver, they opened every cupboard door in the kitchen and pantry. While she was settling the tea-cart, he went back across the hall to their bedroom, opened one of the suitcases, and took out powdered coffee and sugar. She appeared with the teacart and he opened the windows.

"Do you want to call Eugène?"

He didn't, but it was not really a question, and so he left the room, walked down the hall to the front of the apartment, hesi-tated, and then knocked lightly on the closed door of the study. A sleepy voice answered.

"Le petit déjeuner," Harold said, in an accent that did credit to Miss Sloan, his high-school French teacher. At the same time, his voice betrayed uncertainty about their being here, and con-veyed an appeal to whatever is reasonable, peace-loving, and dependable in everybody.

Since ordinary breakfast-table conversation was impossible, it was at least something that they were able to offer Eugène the sugar bowl with their sugar in it, and the plate of bread and butter, and that Eugène could return the pitcher of hot milk to them handle first. Eugène put a spoonful of powdered coffee into his cup and then filled it with hot water. Stirring, he said: "I am sorry that my work prevents me from doing anything with you today."

They assured him that they did not expect or need to be entertained.

Harold put a teaspoonful of powdered coffee in his cup and

filled it with hot water, and then, stirring, he sat back in his chair. The chair creaked. Every time he moved or said something, the chair creaked again.

Eugène was not entirely silent, or openly rude—unless asking Harold to move to another chair and placing himself in the fauteuil that creaked so alarmingly was an act of rudeness. It went right on creaking under his own considerable weight, and all it needed, Harold thought, was for somebody to fling himself back in a fit of laughter and that would be the end of it.

Through the open window they heard sounds below in the street: cartwheels, a tired horse's plodding step, voices. Harold indicated the photograph on the wall and asked what church the stone sculpture was in. Eugène told him and he promptly forgot. They passed the marmalade, the bread, the black-market butter, back and forth. Nothing was said about hotels or train journeys.

Eugène offered Harold his car, to use at any time he cared to, and when this offer was not accepted, the armchair creaked. They all three had another cup of coffee. Eugène was in his pajamas and dressing gown, and on his large feet he wore yellow Turkish slippers that turned up at the toes.

"Ex-cuse me," he said in Berlitz English, and got up and left them, to bathe and dress.

The first shrill ring of the telephone brought Harold out into the hall. He realized that he had no idea where the telephone was. At that moment the bathroom door flew open and Eugène came out, with his face lathered for shaving, and strode down the hall, tying the sash of his dressing gown as he went. The telephone was in the study but the ringing came from the hall. Between the telephone and the wall plug there was sixty feet of cord, and when the conversation came to an end, Eugène carried the instrument with him the whole length of the apartment, to his bathroom, where it rang three more times while he was shaving and in the tub. Before he left the apartment he knocked on their door and asked if there was anything he could do for them. Harold shook his head.

"Sabine called a few minutes ago," Eugène said. "She wants you and Barbara to have dinner with her tomorrow night."

He handed Harold a key to the front door, and cautioned him against leaving it unlocked while they were out of the apartment.

When enough time had elapsed so that there was little likelihood of his returning for something he had forgotten, Harold went out into the hall and stood looking into one room after another. In the room next to theirs was a huge cradle, of mahogany, ornately carved and decorated with gold leaf. It was the most important-looking cradle he had ever seen. Then came their bathroom, and then a bedroom that, judging by the photographs on the walls, must belong to Mme Cestre. A young woman who looked like Alix, with her two children. Alix and Eugène on their wedding day. Matching photographs in oval frames of Mme Bonenfant and an elderly man who must be Alix's grandfather. Mme Viénot, considerably younger and very different. The schoolboy. And a gray-haired man whose glance—direct, lifelike, and mildly accusing—was contradicted by the gilt and black frame. It was the kind of frame that is only put around the photograph of a dead person. Professor Cestre, could it be?

With the metal shutters closed, the dining room was so dark that it seemed still night in there. One of the drawing-room shutters was partly open and he made out the shapes of chairs and sofas, which seemed to be upholstered in brown or russet velvet. The curtains were of the same material, and there were some big oil paintings—portraits in the style of Lancret and Boucher.

Though, taken individually, the big rooms were, or seemed to be, square, the apartment as a whole formed a triangle. The apex, the study where Eugène slept, was light and bright and airy and cheerful. The window looked out on the Place Redouté

—it was the only window of the apartment that did. Looking around slowly, he saw a marble fireplace, a desk, a low bookcase of mahogany with criss-crossed brass wire instead of glass panes in the doors. The daybed Eugène had slept in, made up now with its dark-brown velours cover and pillows. The portable record player with a pile of classical records beside it. Beethoven's Fifth was the one on top. Da-da-da-dum . . . Music could not be Eugène's passion. Besides, the records were dusty. He tried the doors of the bookcase. Locked. The titles he could read easily through the criss-crossed wires: works on theology, astral physics, history, biology, political science. No poetry. No novels. He moved over to the desk and stood looking at the papers on it but not touching anything. The clock on the mantel piece was scandalized and ticked so loudly that he glanced at it over his shoulder and then quickly left the room.

THE CONCIERGE CALLED OUT to them as they were passing through the foyer. Her quarters were on the right as you walked into the building, and her small front room was clogged with heavy furniture—a big, round, oak dining table and chairs, a buffet, with a row of unclaimed letters inserted between the mirror and its frame. The suitcases had come while they were out, and had been put in their room, the concierge said.

He waited until they were inside the elevator and then said: "Now what do we do?"

"Call the Vouillemont, I guess."

"I guess."

Rather than sit around waiting for the suitcases to be delivered, they had gone sight-seeing. They went to the Flea Market, expecting to find the treasures of Europe, and found instead a duplication of that long double row of booths in Tours. Cheap clothing and junk of every sort, as far as the eye could see. They looked, even so. Looked at everything. Barbara bought some cotton aprons, and Harold bought shoestrings. They had lunch at a sidewalk café overlooking the intersection of two broad, busy, unpicturesque streets, and coming home they got lost in the Métro; it took them over an hour to get back to the station where they should have changed, in order to take the line that went to the Place Redouté. It was the end of the afternoon when he took the huge key out of his pocket and inserted it into the keyhole. When he opened the door, there stood Eugène, on his way out of the apartment. He was wearing sneakers and shorts and an open-collared shirt, and in his hand he carried a little black bag. He did not explain where he was going, and they did not ask. Instead, they went on down the hall to their room.

"Do you think he could be having an affair?" Barbara asked, as they heard the front door close.

"Oh no," Harold said, shocked.

"Well, this is France, after all."

"I know, but there must be some other explanation. He's probably spending the evening with friends."

"And for that he needs a little bag?"

They went shopping in the neighborhood, and bought two loaves of bread with the ration coupons they had been given in Blois, and some cheese, and a dozen eggs, and a bag of oranges from a peddler in the Place Redouté—the first oranges they had seen since they landed. They had Vermouth, sitting in front of a café. When they got home Harold was grateful for the stillness in the apartment, and thought how, under different circumstances, they might have stayed on here, in these old-fashioned, high-ceilinged rooms that reminded him of the Irelands' apartment in the East Eighties. They could have been perfectly happy here for ten whole days.

He went down the hall to Eugène's bathroom, to turn on the hot-water heater, and on the side of the tub he saw a pair of blue wool swimming trunks. He felt them. They were damp. He reached out and felt the bath towel hanging on the towel rack over the tub. Damp also. He looked around the room and then called out: "Come here, quick!"

"What is it?" Barbara asked, standing in the doorway.

"I've solved the mystery of the little bag. There it is . . . and there is what was in it. But where do people go swimming in Paris? That boat in the river, maybe."

"What boat?"

"There's a big boat anchored near the Place de la Concorde, with a swimming pool in it—didn't you notice it? But if he has time to go swimming, he had time to be with us."

She looked at him in surprise.

"I know," he said, reading her mind.

"I don't know what I'm going to do with you."

"It's because we are in France," he said, "and know so few people. So something like this matters more than it would at home. Also, he was so nice when he *was* nice."

"All because I didn't feel like dancing."

"I don't think it was that, really."

"Then what was it?"

"I don't know. I wish I did. The tweed coat, maybe. The thing about Eugène is that he's very proud."

And the thing about hurt feelings, the wet bathing suit pointed out, is that the person who has them is not quite the innocent party he believes himself to be. For instance—what about all those people Harold Rhodes went toward unhesitatingly, as if this were the one moment they would ever have together, their one chance of knowing each other?

Fortunately, the embarrassing questions raised by objects do not need to be answered, or we would all have to go sleep in the open fields. And in any case, answers may clarify but they do not change anything. Ten days ago, high up under the canvas roof of the Greatest Show on Earth, thinking *Now* . . . Harold threw himself on the empty air, confidently expecting that when he finished turning he would find the outstretched arms, the taped wrists, the steel hands that would catch and hold him. And it wasn't that the hands had had to catch some other flying trapeze artist, instead; they just simply weren't there.

He lit the hot-water heater, went back to their room, threw open the shutters, and stepped out on the balcony. He could see the Place Redouté, down below and to the left, and in the other direction the green edge of the Bois de Boulogne. The street was quiet. There were trees. And there was a whole upper landscape of chimney pots and skylights and trapdoors leading out onto the roof tops. He saw that within the sameness of the buildings there was infinite variety. When Barbara joined him on the balcony, he said: "This is a very different neighborhood from the Place de la Concorde."

"Do you want to stay?" she asked.

"Do you?"

"I don't know."

"I do and I don't want to stay," he said. "I love living in this apartment instead of a hotel. And being in this part of Paris."

"I don't really think we ought to stay here, feeling the way we do about Eugène."

"I know."

"If we are going to leave," she said, "right now is the time."

"But I keep remembering that we wanted to leave the château also."

"Mmm."

"And that we were rewarded for sticking it out. And probably would be here. But I really hate him."

"I don't think we'd be seeing very much of him. The thing I regret, and the only thing, is leaving that kitchen. It isn't like any kitchen I ever cooked in. Everything about it is just right."

"Yes?" he said, and turned, having heard in her voice a sound that he was accustomed to pay attention to.

"If we could only take our being here as casually as *he* does," she said.

He leaned far out over the balcony, trying to see a little more of the granite monument. "Let's not call the hotel just yet," he said. "The truth is, I don't want to leave either."

⚜ ⚜
⚜

THEY HAD DINNER in a restaurant down the street and went to a movie, which turned out to be too bad to sit through. They walked home, with the acid green street lights showing the undersides of the leaves and giving their faces a melancholy pallor. Since it was still early, they sat down at a table in front of the café in the Place Redouté and ordered mineral water.

"In Paris nobody is ever alone," Barbara said.

He surveyed the tables all around them, and then looked at the people passing by. It was quite true. Every man had a woman, whom he was obviously sleeping with. Every woman had her arm through some man's arm. "But how do you account for it?" he asked.

"I don't."

"The Earthly Paradise," he said, smiling up into the chestnut trees.

They sat looking at people and speculating about them until suddenly he yawned. "It's quarter of eleven," he said. "Shall we go?"

He paid the check and they got up and went around the corner, into the rue Malène. Just as he put out his hand to ring the bell, a man stepped out of a small car that was parked in front of their door. They saw, with surprise, that it was Eugène. He made them get into the car with him, and after a fashion—after a very peculiar fashion—they saw Paris by night. It was presumably for their pleasure, but he drove as if he were racing somebody, and they had no idea where they were and they were not given time to look at anything. "Jeanne d'Arc, Barbara!" Eugène cackled, as the car swung around a gilded monument on two wheels. Now they were in a perfectly ordinary street, now they were looking at neon-lighted night clubs. "La Place Pigalle," Eugène said, but they had no idea why he was pointing it out to them. Politely they peered at a big wind-mill without knowing what that was either.

The tour ended in Montmartre. Eugène managed to park the car in a street crowded with Chryslers and Cadillacs. Then he stood on the sidewalk, allowing them to draw their own con-clusions from the spectacle provided by their countrymen and by the bearded and sandaled types (actors, could they be, dressed up to look like Greenwich Village artists of the 1920's?) who circulated in the interests of local color. He showed them the lights of Paris from the steps of the Sacré-Coeur, and then all his gaiety, which they could only feel as an intricate form of insult, suddenly vanished. They got in the car and drove home, through dark streets, at a normal rate of speed, without talking. And perhaps because he had relieved his feelings, or because, from their point of view, he had done something for them that (even though it was tinged with ill-will) common politeness required that he do for them, or because they were all three tired and ready for bed, or because the city itself had had an effect on them, the silence in the car was almost friendly.

Chapter 14

THE RINGING OF AN ELECTRIC BELL in the hour just before daylight Harold heard in his sleep and identified: it was the ting-a-ling of the Good Humor Man. He wanted to go right on dreaming, but someone was shaking him. He opened his eyes. The hand that was shaking him so insistently was Barbara's. The dark all around the bed he did not recognize. Then that, too, came to him: they were in Paris.

"There's someone at the door!" Barbara whispered.

He raised himself on his elbows and listened. The bell rang twice more. "Maybe it's the telephone," he said. He could feel his heart racing as it did at home when the telephone woke them —not with its commonplace daytime sound but with its shrill night alarm, so suggestive of unspecified death in the family, of disaster that cannot wait until morning to make itself known. If it was the telephone they didn't have to do anything about it. The telephone was in the study.

"No, it's the door."

"I don't see how you can tell," he said, and, drunk with sleep, he got up out of bed and stumbled out into the pitch-dark hallway, where the ringing was much louder. He had no idea where the light switches were. Groping his way from door to door, encountering a big chair and then an armoire, he arrived at a jog in the hallway, and then at the foyer. After a struggle with the French lock, he succeeded in opening the front door and peered out at the sixth-floor landing and the stairs, dimly lighted by a big window. Confused at seeing no one there, he shut the door, and had just about convinced himself that it was a mistake, that he had dreamed he heard a bell ringing somewhere in the apartment, when the matter was settled once and for all by a repetition of the same silvery sound. So it *was* the telephone after all. . . .

He started across the foyer, intending to wake Eugène, who must be sleeping the sleep of the dead. Before he reached the door of the study a new sound stopped him in his tracks: someone was beating with both fists on a door. Feeling like the blindfolded person who is "it" in a guessing game, he retraced his steps down the dark hallway, as far as the door into the kitchen. The pounding seemed to come from somewhere quite near. He crossed the threshold and to his surprise and horror found that he was walking barefoot in water. The kitchen floor was awash, and there was another sound besides the voices and the pounding—a sound that was like water cascading from a great height. He found the back door and couldn't unlock it. Angry excited voices shouted at him through the door, and try as he might, turning the huge key back and forth and pulling at the spring lever that should have released the lock, he couldn't get the door open. He gave up finally and ran back into the hallway, shouting "Eugène!"

Even so, Eugène did not waken. He had to open the study door and go in and, bending over the bed, shake him into sensibility.

"Il y a un catastrophe!" Harold said loudly.

There was a silence, and then Eugène said, without moving: "Une catastrophe?"

The pounding was resumed, the bell started ringing again, and Eugène sat up and reached for his dressing gown. Harold turned and ran back to the kitchen. Awake at last, he managed to get the door open. The concierge and a boy of fifteen burst in upon him. They were both angry and excited, and he had no idea what they were saying to him. The single word "inondation" was all he understood. The concierge turned the kitchen light on. Harold listened to the cascade. A considerable quantity of water must be flowing over the red-tiled floor and out the door and down six flights of the winding metal stair that led down into the courtyard, presumably. And maybe from there the water was flowing into the concierge's quarters. In any case, it was clear that she blamed him, a stranger in the apartment, for everything.

Eugène appeared, with his brocade dressing gown over his pajamas, and his massive face as calm and contained as if he were about to sit down to breakfast. Without bothering to remove the Turkish slippers, he waded over to the sink and stood examining the faucets. He and the concierge and the boy carried on a three-way conversation that excluded foreigners by its rapidity, volubility, and passion. They turned the faucets on and off. With their eyes, with their searching hands, they followed the exposed water pipes around the walls of the kitchen, and, passing over the electric hot-water heater, arrived eventually at a small iron stove—for coal, apparently, and not a cooking stove. (There were three of those in the kitchen.) It was cylindrical, five feet high, and two feet in diameter, with an asbestos-covered stove pipe rising from the top and disappearing into a flue in the wall. The concierge bent down and opened the door of the ash chamber. From this unlikely source a further quantity of water flowed out over the floor and down the back stairs. For a moment, as if he had received the gift of tongues, Harold understood what Eugène and the concierge and the boy were saying. Eugène inquired about the apartment directly below. The people who lived there were away, the concierge said, and she had no key; so there was no way of knowing whether that apartment also was being flooded. A plumber? Not at this hour, she said, and looked at Harold balefully. Then she turned her attention to the pipes in the pantry, and Eugène stood in front of the electric hot-water heater, which was over the sink. Yesterday morning he had put the plug into the wall socket and explained that the heater took care of the hot water for the dishes. He said nothing about removing the plug when they were finished, and so, remembering how the light in the elevator and the light on the sixth-floor landing both extinguished themselves, barely leaving time to reach the door of the apartment before you were in total darkness, they had left the heater in charge of its own current. Foolishly, Harold now saw, because it must be the heater. Unless by some mischance he had forgotten to turn the gas off after Barbara's bath, last night. He distinctly remembered turning the gas off, and even so the thought was enough to make him have to sit down in a chair until the strength came back into his knees. Once more he inquired if the flood was something that he and Barbara had done. Eugène glanced around thoughtfully, but instead of answering, he joined the search party in the pantry. Cupboard doors were opened and shut. Pipes were examined. Hearing the word "chauffage" again and again from the pantry, Harold withdrew to the bathroom at the end of the hall, expecting to discover the worst—the gas heater left burning all night, a burst pipe, and water everywhere. The heater was cold and the bathroom floor was dry. He was on the point of absolving himself of all responsibility for the inundation when a thought crossed his mind—a quite hideous thought, judging by the expression that accompanied it. He went down the hall past the kitchen and opened the door of the little room that contained the toilet.

As a piece of plumbing, the toilet was done for. It only operated at all out of good will. Last night, while they were getting ready for bed, he had heard it flushing, and then flushing again, and again; and thinking to avoid just such a situation as had now happened, he got the kitchen stepladder, climbed up on it, reached into the water chamber, and closed the valve, intending to open it when they got up in the morning. By so doing, he now realized, he had upset the entire system. It could only be that; they hadn't been near the iron boiler in the kitchen from which water so freely flowed. And it was only a question of time before the search, now confined to the pantry, would lead Eugène, the concierge, and the boy to the real source of the trouble. Nevertheless, like Adam denying the apple, he climbed up on the stepladder and opened the valve. The water chamber filled slowly and then the pipes grew still.

As he reached the kitchen door, the search party brushed past him and went into Eugène's bathroom. Harold turned and went back to their bedroom. Barbara had got up out of bed and was sitting at the window, with her dressing gown wrapped around her, smoking a cigarette.

"Look up the word 'chauffage,' " he said. "The dictionary is in the pocket of my brown coat," and he went on down the hall. Ignoring the gas heater, Eugène searched for and found a valve behind the tub. As soon as the valve was closed, the bathtub began to fill with rusty red water gurgling up out of the drainpipe. He hurriedly opened the valve, and the water receded, leaving a guilty stain.

" 'Chauffage' means heating or a heating system," Barbara said, as Harold came into the bedroom. He closed the door behind him.

"Did he say it was our fault?" she asked.

"I asked him five times and just now he finally said 'Heureusement oui.' "

"That doesn't make any sense, 'heureusement oui.' "

"I know it doesn't, but that's what he said. It *must* be our fault. We ought never to have come here."

The voices and the heavy footsteps passed their door, returning to the kitchen, and wearily he went in pursuit of them. They still had not found the valve that controlled the water pipes, and the cascade down the back stairs was unabated. The landing and the stair well were included in the area under investigation. Locating a new valve, Eugène left his sodden Turkish slippers inside the kitchen door and went into the front of the apartment;

opened the door of the huge sculptured armoire and took out a cigar box; opened the cigar box and took out a pair of pliers.

"There is something I have to tell you," Harold said. "I'm awfully sorry but last night the toilet didn't work properly and so I got the kitchen stepladder and . . ."

Eugène listened abstractedly to this confession and when it was finished he asked where Harold had put the stepladder. Then he went into the little room where the toilet was, picked up the stepladder, and carried it out to the back landing. With the pliers, standing on the stepladder, he closed a valve in the pipeline out there. He and the concierge and the boy listened. Their faces conveyed uncertainty, and then hope, and then triumph, as the sound of falling water began to diminish. It took some time and further discussion, a gradual letting down of tension and a round of congratulations, before the concierge and the boy left. Eugène put away the stepladder and picked up the mop. As he started mopping up the red tiles, Harold said: "Barbara and I will clean the kitchen up."

Eugène stopped and stared at him, and then said: "The floor will be dirty unless it is mopped." They stood looking at each other helplessly. He must think we don't understand anything at all, Harold thought.

"I'm very sorry that your sleep has been disturbed," Eugène said.

Harold studied his face carefully, thinking that he must be speaking sarcastically. He was not. The apology was sincere. Once more, with very little hope of a sensible answer, Harold asked if they had caused the trouble.

"This sort of thing happens since the war," Eugène said. The building is old and needs new plumbing. Now that the water is turned off, there is nothing more that we can do until the plumber comes and fixes the leak."

"Was it caused by turning the water off in the toilet?"

Eugène turned and indicated the little iron stove, inside which a pipe had burst, for no reason.

"Then it wasn't our fault?"

For a few seconds Eugène seemed to be considering not what Harold had just said but Harold himself. He looked at him the way cats look at people, and did something that cats are too polite ever to do: he laughed. Then he turned and resumed his mopping.

Standing on the balcony outside their room, Harold lit a cigarette. Barbara was in bed and he couldn't tell whether she was asleep or not. The swallows were darting over the roof tops. Directly below him, so straight down that it made him dizzy to look, an old man was silently searching through the garbage cans. On the blue pavement he had placed four squares of blue cloth, and when he found something of value he put it on one or the other of them.

The stoplights at the intersection at the foot of the hill changed from red to green, from green to red. The moon, in its last quarter, was white in a pearly pink sky. The discovery that it was not their fault had come too late. They had had so much time to feel they were to blame that they might just as well have been. Too tired to care any longer, he left the balcony and got into bed. A moment later, he got up and took his wallet out of his coat and found a five-hundred-franc note and then returned to the balcony. When the old man looked up he would make signals at him. Though he waited patiently, the old man did not look up. Instead, he tied his four pieces of cloth at the corners and went off down the street, which by now had admitted it was morning.

AWAKENED OUT OF A DEEP SLEEP by a silvery sound, Harold sat up in bed. It was broad daylight outside. The telephone? he thought wildly. The front door? Or the back? Whatever it was, Barbara was sleeping right through it.

He got up and followed his own wet footprints down the gray carpeting until he came to the foyer. This time when he opened the front door someone was there—the concierge, smiling and cordial, with three blond young men. One of them had a brief case, and they didn't look at all like plumbers. The concierge asked for M. de Boisgaillard, and Harold knocked on the study door and fled.

Ten minutes later, he heard a faint tap on their door.

"Yes?"

As he sat up in bed, the door opened and Eugène came in. Keeping his voice low because Barbara was still asleep, he said: "The people you let in— They just arrived in Paris this morning, from Berlin." He hesitated.

Harold perceived that Eugène was telling him this because there was something they could do for him. Eugène was not in the habit of asking for favors, and it was painful for him to have to now. What he was going to say would alter somewhat the situation between them and him, but he was going to say it anyway.

"They have no money, and they haven't had any breakfast."

"You'd like Barbara to make breakfast for them?" Harold asked, and found himself face to face with his lost friend, Eugène the way he used to be before that picnic on the banks of the Loire.

Bread, oranges, marmalade, eggs, honey—all bought the afternoon before, and with their money. Nescafe in the big suitcase, sugar cubes in the small one. All the wealth of America to feed the hungry of Europe.

"There is plenty of everything," he said.

"Plenty?" Eugène repeated, unconvinced.

"Plenty," Harold said, nodding.

"Good."

The image of a true friend was dimmer; was fading like a rainbow or any other transitory natural phenomenon, but it was still visible. When Eugène left, Harold woke Barbara, and as he

was hurriedly getting into his clothes he began to whistle. It was
their turn to do something for Eugène. And if they cared to,
they could be both preoccupied and moody as they went
about it.

When Barbara wheeled the teacart into Mme Cestre's drawing
room, the four heads were raised. The four men rose, and the
Germans clicked their heels politely as Eugène presented them
to her and then to Harold, who had come in after her. All three
were pale, thin, and nervous. One had pink-tinted rimless glasses,
and one had ears that stuck straight out from his head, and one
was tall and blond (the pure Nordic abstraction, the race that
never was) with wide, bony shoulders, concave chest, hollow
stomach, and the trousers of a much heavier man hanging from
his hip bones.

"Do sit down," Barbara said.

Herr von Rothenberg, the Nordic type, spoke French and
English fluently, and the two others told him what they wanted
to say and he translated for them. They had traveled as far as
the French border by plane, and from there by train. They had
arrived in Paris at daybreak.

"We were very surprised," Herr von Rothenberg said to the
Americans. "We did not expect to find Paris intact. We had
understood that it was largely ruins, like London and Berlin."

He was not entirely happy that Paris had been spared. It offended his sense of what is fair. But he did not say this; it only
came out in his voice, his troubled expression.

The Germans politely took the cups that Eugène handed
them, but allowed their coffee to grow cold. Barbara had to urge
it on them, and point again and again to the bread and butter on
their plates, before they could bring themselves to eat. Their
extreme delicacy in the presence of food seemed to say: *It was
most kind of M. de Boisgaillard to offer us these cigarettes, and
surely something is to be gained from a discussion of the kind
we are having, between the people who have lost a war and
those who, for reasons history will eventually make clear, have*

won it. But as for eating—we do not care to impose on anyone,
we are accustomed to being faint with hunger, we have much
more often than not, the last few years, gone without breakfast.
We would prefer to continue with what M. de Boisgaillard was
saying about the establishment of a central bureau that would
have control over credit and . . .

In the end, though, the bread was eaten, the coffee was drunk,
and on two of the plates there was a pile of orange peelings. The
third orange remained untouched. Barbara looked inquiringly
from it to the young man whose ears stuck out, and whose
orange it was. He smiled at her timidly and then looked at
Eugène, who was telephoning and ignored his appeal. Pointing
to the orange, the young man whose ears stuck out said, in halt-
ing English: "The first in twelve years." He hesitated and then,
since Eugène was still talking into the telephone and Barbara
was still waiting and the orange had not been snatched from
him, said: "I have a wife. And ten days ago a baby is born. . . .
Could I take this orange with me, to give to her?"

Barbara explained that there were more oranges, and that he
could eat this one. He put it in his pocket, instead.

Eugène was trying to find a place for the Germans to stay.
They listened to the one-sided telephone conversations with a
sympathetic interest, as if it were the welfare of three other
young men he was devoting himself to with such persistence.

Finally, as the morning dragged on, the Americans excused
themselves and left the drawing room, taking the teacart with
them.

"Terrible," Harold said.

"Terrible," she agreed.

"I didn't know there were Germans like that."

"Did you hear what he said about the orange?"

"Yes, I heard. We must remember to send some back with
them."

"But what will become of them?"

"God knows."

"Do you think they were Nazis?"

"No, of course not. How could they have been? Probably they never even heard of Hitler."

At noon, Barbara wheeled the teacart out of the kitchen again, and down the hall to Mme Cestre's drawing room, which was now murky with cigarette smoke. The men sprang to their feet and waited for her to sit down, but she shook her head and left them. She and Harold ate in the kitchen, sitting on stools. They had just finished cleaning up when Eugène appeared in the doorway.

"I am much obliged to you, Barbara," he said. "It is a very great kindness that you do for me."

"It was nothing," she said. "Did you find a place for them to stay?"

He shook his head. "I have told them that they can stay here. But you will not have to do this any more. I have made other arrangements. The person who comes in by the day when we are all here will cook for them. Her name is Françoise. She is a very nice woman. If you want anything, just tell her and she will do it for you. I did not like to ask her because her son was in a concentration camp and she does not like Germans."

"But what are they doing in Paris?" Harold asked.

"They are trying to get to Rome," Eugène said. "They want to attend an international conference there. Arrangements had been made for them to go by way of Switzerland, but they decided to go by way of Paris, instead. They used up their money on train fare. And unfortunately in all of Paris no one knows of a fund that provides for an emergency of this kind or a place that will take them in. Herr von Rothenberg I met at an official reception in Berlin, last year. He is of a very good family. The other two I did not know before. . . . You have Sabine's address? She is expecting you at eight."

⚜ ⚜
⚜

259

THE ADDRESS that Eugène gave them turned out to be a modern apartment building on a little square that was named after a
poet whose works Harold had read in college but could no
longer remember; they had joined with the works of three other
romantic poets, as drops of water on a window pane join and
become one larger drop. A sign by the elevator shaft said that
the elevator was out of order. They rang Sabine's bell and
started climbing. Craning his neck, he saw that she was waiting
for them, six floors up. She called down over the banister: "I'm
sorry you have such a long climb," and he called up: "Are you
as happy to see us as we are to see you?"

She had on a little starched white apron, over her blouse and
skirt. She shook hands with them, took the flowers that Barbara
held out to her, and, looking into the paper cone, exclaimed:
"Marguerites! They are my favorite. And a book?"

"*A Passage to India,*" Harold said. "We saw it in the window
of a bookstore."

"I will be most interested to read it," she said. "This is my
uncle's apartment—did Eugène tell you? The family is away
now. I am here alone. My uncle collects paintings and objets
d'art. There is a Sargent in the next room. . . . I must put these
beautiful flowers in water. You will not mind if I am a little distracted? I am not used to cooking."

She and Barbara went off to the kitchen together, and Harold
stood at the window and peered down at the little square. Then
he started around the room, looking at Chinese carvings and
porcelains and at the paintings on the walls. When the two girls
came back with a bottle of Cinzano and glasses, he was standing
in front of a small Renoir.

"It's charming, isn't it?" Sabine said.

"Very," he said.

"In my aunt's apartment there is a bookcase with art books in
it— Have you found it yet?"

"In the front hall," he said. "By the study door. But it's
locked."

"I know where the key is kept," she said, but before she had a chance to tell him, the doorbell rang. "Are you comfortable in the rue Malène?" she asked as she started toward the hall.

Harold and Barbara looked at each other.

"Something has happened since I saw you?" Sabine asked.

"A great deal has happened," he said. "It's a very long story. We'll tell you later."

The young man she introduced to them was in his middle twenties, small, compact, and alert-looking, with hair as black as an Indian's and dark skin. For the first few minutes, he was self-conscious with the Americans, and kept apologizing for his faulty English. They liked him immediately, encouraged him when he groped for a word, assured him that his English was fine, and in every way possible took him under their wing, enjoying all his comments and telling him that they felt as if they already knew him. The four-sided conversation moved like a piece of music. It was as if they had all agreed beforehand to say only what came into their heads and to say it instantly, without fear or hesitation. In her pleasure at discovering that Sabine had such a handsome and agreeable young man on a string, Barbara was more talkative than usual. She was witty. She made them all laugh. Sabine was astonished to learn of the presence of three Berliners in her aunt's apartment, and said doubtfully: "I do not think that my aunt would like it, if she knew."

"But if you saw them!" Harold exclaimed. "So pale, so thin. And as sensitive as sea horses." Then he began to tell the story of the burst water pipe.

They sat down to dinner at a gateleg table in the drawing-room alcove. The Americans dug out of the young Frenchman that he was in the government. From his description of his job, Harold concluded that it was to read all the newspaper articles and summarize them for his superior, who based his statements to the press on them. This explanation the Frenchman rejected indignantly; it was he who prepared the statements for the press. Looking at him, Harold thought that if he had had to draw up a set of requirements for a husband for Sabine, they would have added up to the young man across the table. Though he must be extremely intelligent to hold down a position of responsibility at his age, there was nothing pompous in his manner or his conversation. He was simply young and quick-witted and unsuspicious. They felt free to tease him, and he defended himself without attacking them or being anything but more agreeable. The evening flew by, and when they left at eleven, they tried to do it in such a way that he wouldn't feel he had to leave too. But he left with them, and as they were passing under a street lamp in the avenue Victor Hugo, they learned that he was not the person they thought he was; he was Sabine's brother-in-law, Jean-Claude Lahovary.

"Mme Viénot told us about you," Barbara said.

"Yes?"

"She told us about your family," Barbara said.

Oh no, Harold begged her silently. *Don't say it*. . . .

But Barbara was a little high from the wine, and on those rare occasions when she did put her trust in strangers, she was incautious and wholehearted. As if no remark of hers could possibly be misunderstood by him, she said: "She said your mother was hors de siècle."

The Frenchman looked bewildered. Harold changed the subject. Exactly how offensive the phrase was, he didn't know, and he hadn't been able to tell from Mme Viénot's tone of voice because her voice was always edged with one kind of cheerful malice or another. Trying to cover up Barbara's mistake he made another.

"Do you know what you remind me of?" he asked, though an inner voice begged him not to say it. (He too had had too much wine.)

"What?" the Frenchman asked politely.

"An acrobat."

The Frenchman was not pleased. He did not consider it a compliment to be told that he was like an acrobat. The tiresome inner voice had been right, as usual. Though table manners are the same in France, other manners are not. We shouldn't have gone so far with him, the first time, Harold thought. Or been quite so personal.

The conversation lost its naturalness. There were silences as they walked along together. They quickly became strangers. As they crossed one of the streets that went out from the Place Redouté, they were accosted by a beggar, the first Harold had seen in Paris. Always an easy touch at home, he waited, not knowing if beggars were regarded cynically by the French, and also not wanting to appear to be throwing his American money around. The future minister of finance reached in his pocket quickly and brought out a hundred-franc note and gave it to the beggar, and so widened the misunderstanding: the French have compassion for the poor, Americans do not, was the only possible conclusion.

They shook hands at the entrance of the Métro and said good night. Still hoping that something would happen at the last minute, that he would give them a chance to repair the damage they had done to the evening, they stood and watched him start down the steps, turn right, and disappear without looking back. Though they might read his name years from now in the foreign-news dispatches, this was the last they would ever see of Mme Viénot's brilliant son-in-law.

As they were walking home, past shuttered store fronts, Barbara said: "I shouldn't have said that about his mother, should I?"

"People are very touchy about their families."

"But I meant it as a compliment."

"I know."

"Why didn't he realize I meant it as a compliment?"

"I don't know."

"I liked him."

"So did I."

"It's very sad."

"It doesn't matter," he said, meaning something quite different—meaning that there was nothing either of them could do about it now.

He called out who they were as they passed through the foyer of the apartment building. They went up in the elevator, and the hall light went out just as he thrust his key at the keyhole. He stepped into the dark apartment and felt around until he found the light switch. The study door was closed and so was the door of Mme Cestre's bedroom.

Lying in bed in the dark, looking through the open window at the one lighted room in the building across the street, he said: "What it amounts to is that you cannot be friends with some-body, no matter how much you like them, if it turns out that you don't really understand one another."

"Also—" he began, five minutes later, and was stopped by the sound of Barbara's soft, regular breathing. He turned over and as he lay staring at the lighted room he felt a sudden first wave of homesickness come over him.

Chapter 15

T HE FIRST DAYLIGHT, whitening the sky and making the windows shine, revealed that the three Berliners had spent the night in Mme Cestre's bedroom. Their threadbare, unpressed, spotty coats and trousers, neatly folded, were on three chairs. Also, their shirts and socks and underwear, which had been washed without soap. Two of them slept in the narrow bed, with their mouths open like dead people and their breathing so quiet they might have been dead. The third slept on the floor, with a rug under him, his head on the leather brief case, his pink-tinted glasses beside him, and Mme Cestre's spare comforter keeping him from catching pneumonia. So pale they were, in the gray light. So unaggressive, so intellectual, so polite even in their sleep. *Oh heartbreaking—what happens to children*, said the fruitwood armoire, vast and maternal, bound in brass, with brass handles on the drawers, brass knobs on the two carved doors. The dressing table, modern, with its triple way of viewing things, said: *It is their own doing and redoing and undoing.*

"BONJOUR, monsieur-dame," said the tall, full-bosomed woman with carrot-colored hair and a beautiful carriage. She raised the front wheels of the teacart and then the back, so that they did not touch the telephone cord. When she had gone back to the kitchen, Harold said: "There are plates and cups for three, which can only mean that he is having breakfast with us."

"You think?" Barbara said.

"By his own choice," Harold said, "since there is now some-one to bring him a tray in his room."

They sat and waited. In due time, Eugène appeared and drew the armchair up to the teacart.

It was a beautiful day. The window was wide open and the sunlight was streaming in from the balcony. Eugène inquired about their evening with Sabine, and the telephone, like a spoiled child that cannot endure the conversation of the grownups, started ringing. Eugène left the room. When he came back, he said: "It is possible that I may be going down to the country on Friday. A cousin of Alix is marrying. And if I do go—as I should, since it is a family affair—it will be early in the morning, before you are up. And I may stay down for the week end."

They tried not to look pleased.

He accepted a second cup of coffee and then asked what they had done about getting gasoline coupons. "But we don't need them," Harold said, and so, innocently, obliged Eugène to admit that he did. "I seldom enjoy the use of my car," he said plaintively, "and it would be pleasant to have the gasoline for short trips into the country now and then."

He reached into his bathrobe pocket and brought out a slip of paper on which he had written the address of the place they were to go to for gasoline coupons.

"How can we ask for gasoline coupons if we don't have a car?" Harold said.

"As Americans traveling in France you are entitled to the coupons whether you use them or not," Eugène said. "And the amount of gasoline that tourists are allowed is quite considerable."

Harold put the slip of paper on the teacart and said: "Could you tell us— But there is no reason you should know, I guess. We have to get a United States Army visa to enter Austria."

"I will call a friend who works at the American Embassy," Eugène said, rising. "He will know."

Five minutes later, he was back with the information Harold had asked for.

Walking past the open door of the dressing room, Harold saw the Germans for the first time that morning. They were crowded around Eugène, and pressing on him their latest thoughts about their predicament. He avoided looking at whoever was speaking to him, and his attention seemed to be entirely on the arrangement of his shirt tails inside his trousers.

Later he stopped to complain about them, standing in the center of the Americans' room, with the door open, so that there was a good chance that he might be overheard. It was already too late for the Germans to get to the conference in Rome in time to present their credentials, he said. Their places would be taken by alternates.

"What will they do?" Harold asked. "Turn around and go home?"

"There are other conferences scheduled for other Italian cities," Eugène said, "and they hope to be allowed to attend one of these. Unfortunately, there isn't the slightest chance of their getting the visas they need to cross the Italian border. The whole thing is a nuisance—the kind of silliness only Germans are capable of."

Though Eugène was bored with the Germans' dilemma and despised them personally for having got themselves into it, they had thrown themselves on his kindness, and it appeared that he had no choice but to go on trying to help them.

The Americans spent the morning getting to know parts of Paris that are not mentioned in guidebooks. The address on Eugène's slip of paper turned out to be incorrect; there was no such number. Harold was relieved; he had dreaded exposure. The information about where to go to get the Austrian visa was also wrong. They talked to the concierge of the building, who gave them new and explicit directions, and in a few minutes they found themselves peering through locked doors at the marble foyer of an unused public building. Eventually, by asking a gendarme, they arrived at the Military Permit Office. There they stood in line in a large room crowded with people whom no country wanted and whom France could not think what to do with. When Harold produced their American passports, the man next to him turned and looked at him reproachfully. All around them, people were arguing tirelessly with clerks who pretended (sometimes humorously) not to understand what they wanted, not to speak German or Italian, not to know that right there on the counter in front of them was the rubber stamp that would make further argument unnecessary. As Harold and Barbara went from clerk to clerk, from the large room on the first floor to a smaller office on the third floor, and finally outdoors with a new address to find, they began to feel less and less different from the homeless people around them, even though they had a perfectly good home and were only trying to get to a music festival. At the right place at last, they were told that they had to leave their passports with the application for their visas, which would be ready the next day.

After lunch, they walked through the looking glass, leaving the homeless on the other side, and spent the afternoon sightseeing. They took the Métro to the Place du Trocadéro, descended the monumental stairs of the Palais de Chaillot, went through the aquarium, and then strolled across the Pont d'Iéna in the sunshine.

At the top of the Tour Eiffel there was a strong wind and they could not bear to look straight down. All that they remembered afterward of what they saw was the colored awnings all over Paris. They took a taxi home, and as they went down the hall to their own room they could hear the Germans talking to each other, behind the closed door of theirs.

Meeting Herr Rothenberg in the hall, they learned that he and his friends had spent the day going the rounds of the embassies and consulates.

"But you ought to be seeing Paris," Harold said. "It's so beautiful."

"We will come back and see the museums another time," Herr Rothenberg said, smiling and quite pleased with the Paris they had seen.

Shortly afterward, he appeared at their door and said that Françoise had gone home and could they please have some bread and butter and coffee?

Harold followed Barbara into the kitchen and as she was putting the kettle on he said: "Do you suppose they don't realize that all those things are rationed?"

"I don't know," she said, "but let's not tell them."

"All right. I wasn't going to. It just occurred to me that maybe the national characteristics were asserting themselves."

"I'm so in love with this kitchen," Barbara said. "If it were up to me, I'd never leave."

The two Americans and the three Germans had coffee together in Mme Cestre's drawing room, with the shutters open and the light pouring in. The Germans showed Barbara snapshots of their wives, and Harold wrote their names and addresses in his financial diary, and then they all went out on the balcony so that Barbara could take the Berliners' pictures. They stood in a row before her, three pale scarecrows stiffly composed in attitudes that would be acceptable to posterity.

Still in a glow from the success of the tea party, Harold went down into the Place Redouté and found the orange peddler and bought a bag of oranges from him, which he then presented to Herr Rothenberg at the door of their room, with a carefully prepared little speech and three thousand-franc notes, in case the Germans found themselves in need of money on the next lap of their journey. The effect of this act of generosity was partly spoiled because, out of a kind of Anglo-Saxon politeness they were unfamiliar with, he didn't give them a chance to finish their speeches of gratitude. But at all events the money got from his wallet into theirs, where it very much needed to be.

At twenty-five minutes after six, he walked into the study with a calling card in his hand and stood by Eugène's desk, waiting until his wrist watch and the clock on the mantelpiece agreed that it was half-past six. On the back of the card Mme Straus-Muguet had scrawled the telephone number of the convent in Auteuil, and "coup de fil a 6h½." During the three and a half weeks that they had been in France he had managed, through the kindness of one person and another, not to have to talk over the telephone. He would just as soon not have done it now.

A woman's voice answered. He asked to speak to Mme Straus-Muguet and the voice implored him not to hang up. He started to say that he had no intention of hanging up, and then realized by the silence that if he did speak no one would hear him. It was a long, long discouraging silence that extended itself until he wondered why he continued to hold the telephone to his ear. At last a familiar voice said his name and he was enveloped in affectionate inquiries and elaborate arrangements. Mme Straus's voice came through strong and clear and he had no trouble understanding her. They were to meet her on Saturday evening at eight thirty sharp, she said, on the corner of the rue de Berry and the avenue des Champs Elysées. They would dine at the restaurant of her goddaughter and afterward go to the theater to see Mme Marguerite Mailly.

"At the Comédie Française?" he asked. They had not yet crossed that off their list.

Mme. Mailly had had a disagreement with the Comédie Française, Mme Straus said, and had left it to act in a modern comedy. The play had had an enormous success, and tickets were impossible to obtain, but knowing that they were arriving in Paris this week, she had written to her friend, and three places for the Saturday performance would be waiting at the box office.

"I don't know that we should do that," Barbara said doubtfully, when he told her about the arrangements. "It sounds so expensive, and she may not be able to afford it."

"I don't know that I'm up to dissuading her," he said. "Tactfully, I mean, over the telephone, and in French. Besides, it is no longer 6h½, and if I called her back I probably wouldn't reach her. Do *you* want to call her?"

"No, I don't."

"Maybe she'll let us pay for the dinner," he said.

At breakfast the next morning, Eugène surprised them by saying, as he passed his coffee cup across the tray to Barbara: "I am having a little dinner party this evening. You are free? . . . Good. I have asked Edouard Doria. He is Alix's favorite cousin. I think you will like him."

From the way he spoke, they realized that he was giving the dinner party for them. But why? Had Alix asked him to? And were the Berliners invited?

Meeting them in the hall, a few minutes later, Harold stepped aside to let them pass. They greeted him cheerfully, and when he inquired about their situation, they assured him that progress was being made, in the only way that it could be made; their story was being heard, their reasons considered. What they wanted was in no way unreasonable, and so in time some action, positive or negative, surely must result from their efforts. Meanwhile, there were several embassies they did not get to yesterday and that they planned to go to today. . . .

Harold stood outside the dining-room door and listened while Eugène consulted with Françoise about the linen, the china, the menu. They reached an agreement on the fish and the vegetable.

There would be oysters, then soup. He left the soup to her discretion. For dessert there would be an ice, which he would pick up himself on the way home.

The Americans left the apartment in the middle of the morning, and crossed over to the Left Bank. They walked along the river as far as Notre Dame, and had lunch under an awning, in the rain. In the window of a shop on the Quai de la Mégisserie they saw a big glass bird cage, but how to get it home was the question. Also, it was expensive, and the little financial diary kept pointing out that, even though they had no hotel bill to pay, they were spending quite a lot of money on taxis, flowers, books, movies, and food.

As they came through the Place Redouté, they picked up the kodak films they had left to be developed. They were as surprised by what came out as if they had had no hand in it. Some of the pictures were taken on shipboard, and some in Pontorson and Mont-Saint-Michel. But there was nothing after that until the one of Beaumesnil, with the old trees rising twice as high as the roofs, and a cloud castle in the sky above the real one. The best snapshot of all was a family picture, taken on the lawn, their last morning at the château. This picture was mysterious in that, though the focus was sharp enough, there was so much that you couldn't see. Alix's shadow fell across Mme Bonenfant's face. There was only her beautiful white hair, and her hand stretched out to steady herself against the fall all old people live in dread of. Alix's hair blacked out the lower part of Harold's face, and what you could see of him looked more like his brother. Barbara had taken the picture and so she wasn't in it at all. A shadow from a branch overhead fell across the upper part of Mme Cestre's face, leaving only her smile in bright sunlight and the rest in doubt. The two small children they had hardly set eyes on were nevertheless in the picture, and Mme Viénot was wearing the green silk dress with the New Look. Beside her was a broad expanse of white that could have been a castle wall but was actually Eugène's shirt, with his massive face above it looking strangely like Ludwig van Beethoven's. And Sabine, on the extreme right, standing in a diagonal shaft of light that didn't come from the sun but from an inadvertent exposure as the film was being taken from the camera.

"I don't see how we could not have taken more than one roll in all this time," Barbara said.

"We were too busy looking."

"We have no picture of Nils Jensen. Or of Mme Straus-Muguet."

"With or without a picture, I will never forget either of them."

"That's not the point. You think you remember and you don't."

When they got home, she made him go straight out on the balcony where, even though it was late in the afternoon and the light was poor, she took a picture of him in his seersucker suit and scuffed white shoes, peering down into the rue Malène, and he took one of her in her favorite dress of black and lavender-blue, with the buildings on the far side of the Place Redouté showing in the distance and in the foreground a sharply receding perspective of iron railing and rolled-up awnings.

There were no sounds from behind the closed door of Mme Cestre's room. Nothing but a kind of anxious silence. Were they gone? Had somebody at last reached for a rubber stamp?

The Germans were not at the dinner party, and Eugène did not mention them all evening. The dinner party was not a success. The food was very good and so was the wine, and Alix's cousin was young and likable, but when he spoke to the Americans in English, Eugène fidgeted. Barbara never came out from behind the shy, well-bred young woman whom nobody could ever have any reason to say anything unkind to, and Harold did not want to repeat the mistake they had made with Jean-Claude Lahovary, and so he did not proceed as if this was the one moment he and Edouard Doria would ever have for knowing each other (though as a matter of fact it was). He did not ask per-

273

sonal questions; he tried to speak grammatically when he spoke French; he waited to see what course the evening would take. In short, he was not himself. Edouard Doria sat smiling pleasantly and replied to the remarks that were addressed to him. Eugène did not explain to his three guests why he had thought they would like one another, and neither did he take the conversation into his own hands and make tears of amusement run down their cheeks with the outrageous things he said. As the evening wore on, the conversation was more and more in French, between the two Frenchmen.

✤ ✤
✤

IN THE MORNING, the study door was open and the room itself neat and empty. All through breakfast the Americans breathed the agreeable air of Eugène's absence from the apartment, and they kept assuring each other that he would not possibly return that night; it was a long hard journey even one way.

When Harold took the mail from Mme Emile there were several letters for M. Soulès de Boisgaillard, which he put on the table in the front hall, by the study door, and one for M. et Mme Harold Rhodes. It was from Alix, and when Barbara drew it out of the envelope, they saw that she had put a four-leaf clover in it.

" '. . . I was so sad not to say good-by to you at the station on Sunday. But I love writing to you now. It was delightful to know you both, and I wish you to go on in life loving more and more, being happier and happier, and making all those you meet feel happy themselves, as you did here—' "

"Oh God!" Harold exclaimed.

Barbara stopped reading and looked at him.

"Read on," he said.

" 'We miss you a lot. Do write and give some of your impressions of Paris or Italy. And I hope we shall see one another very often in September. I should like to be in Paris with you and Eugène now. I hope you have at least nice breakfasts. I suppose you are a little too warm—but I will know all that on Friday as Mummy and I will join Eugène in the train for Tours. Good-by, dear you two, and my most friendly thoughts. Alix.' "

He put the four-leaf clover in his financial diary, and then said: "It's a nice letter, isn't it? So affectionate. It makes me feel better about our staying here. At least her part wasn't something we dreamed."

"If she were here, it would be entirely different," Barbara said.

"Do you think he will tell her how he has acted?"

"No, do you? . . . On the other hand, she may not need to be told. That may be the reason she waited so long to speak about our staying here."

"But the letter doesn't read as if she had any idea."

"I don't think she has."

They went and stood in the kitchen door, talking to Françoise, who was delighted with the nylon stockings that Barbara presented to her. Holding up a wine bottle, she showed them how much less than a full liter of milk (at twenty-four times the price of milk before the war) they had allowed her for the little one, who fortunately was now in the country, where milk was plentiful. They told her about their life in America, and she told them about her childhood in a village in the Dordogne. They asked if the Germans had gone, and she said no. She had given them their dinner the night before, in their room.

"What a queer household we are!" she exclaimed, rolling her eyes in the direction of Mme Cestre's room. "Nobody speaks anybody else's language and none of us belong here." But they noticed that she was pleasant and kind to the Germans, and apparently it did not occur to them that she might have any reason to hate them. They did not hate anyone.

The door to Mme Cestre's room was open, and the sounds that came from it this morning were cheerful; those mice, too, were enjoying the fact that the cat was away. The Americans left their door open also, and were aware of jokes and giggling down the hall.

"When we need butter, speak to Mme Emile," Eugène had said, and so Harold went downstairs and found her having a cup of coffee at her big round table. She rose and shook hands with him and he took out his wallet and explained what he had come for. While she was in the next room he looked at the copy of *Paris Soir* spread out on the dining table. The police had at last tracked down the gangster Pierrot-le-Fou. He had been surprised in the bed of his mistress, Catherine. The dim photograph showed a young man with a beard. Reading on, Harold was reminded of the fire in Pontorson. No doubt the preparations had been just as extensive and thorough, and it was a mere detail that the gangster had got away. Mme Emile returned with a pound of black-market butter, which she wrapped in the very page he had been reading, and since her conscience seemed perfectly clear, his did not bother him, though he supposed they could both have been put in jail for this transaction.

Shortly afterward, he went off to pick up their passports and the military permit to enter Austria, and when he returned at two o'clock, he found Barbara half frantic over a telephone call from Mme Straus-Muguet. "I didn't want to answer," she said, "but I was afraid it might be you. I thought you might be trying to reach me, for some reason. I tried to persuade her to call back, but she said she was going out, and she *made* me take the message!"

What Barbara thought Mme Straus had said was that they were to meet her on the steps of the Madeleine at five.

They left the apartment at four, and took a taxi to the bank, where they picked up their mail from home. Then they wandered through the neighborhood, going in and out of shops, and at a quarter of five they took up their stand at the top of the flight of stone steps that led up to the great open door of the church. For the next twenty minutes they looked expectantly at everybody who went in or out and at every figure that might turn out to be Mme Straus-Muguet approaching through the bicycle traffic. The more they looked for her, the less certain they were of what she looked like. Suddenly Barbara let out a cry; her umbrella was no longer on her arm. She distinctly remembered starting out with it, from the apartment, and she was fairly certain she had felt the weight of the umbrella on her arm as she stepped out of the taxi. She could not remember for sure but she thought she had laid it down in the china shop, in order to examine a piece of porcelain.

They left the steps of the Madeleine, crossed through the traffic to the shop, and went in. The clerk Barbara spoke to was not the one Harold had wanted her to ask. No umbrella had been found; also, the clerk was not interested in lost umbrellas. As they left the shop, he said: "Don't worry about it. You can buy another umbrella."

"Not like this one," she said. The umbrella was for traveling, folded compactly into a third the usual length, and could be tucked away in a suitcase. "If only we'd gone to the Rodin Museum this afternoon, as we were intending to," she said. "I'd never have lost it there."

He went back to the Madeleine and waited another quarter of an hour while she walked the length of the rue Royale, looking mournfully in shop windows and trying to remember a place, a moment, when she had put her umbrella down, meaning to pick it up right away. . . .

"I'm sure I left it in the china shop," she said, when she rejoined him.

"It's probably in that little room at the back, hidden away, this very minute. . . ."

He led her through the bicycle traffic to a table on the sidewalk in front of Larue's and there, keeping one eye on the steps of the church, they had a Tom Collins. It was possible, they agreed, that Barbara had misunderstood and that Mme Straus might have been waiting (poor old thing!) on the steps of some other public monument. Or it could have been another day that they were supposed to meet her.

"But if it turns out that I did get it right and that she's stood us up, then let's not bother any more with her," Barbara said. "We have so little time in Paris, and there is so much that we want to do and see, and I have a feeling that she will engulf us."

"We've already said we'd have dinner with her and go to the theater, tomorrow night."

"If she knows so many people, why does she bother with two Americans? She may be making a play for us because we're foreigners and don't know any better."

"To what end?"

"Oh, I don't know!" Barbara exclaimed. "I don't like it here! Should we go?"

She was always depressed and irritated with herself when she lost something—as if the lost object had abandoned her deliberately, for a very good reason.

The waiter brought the check, and while they were waiting for change, Harold said: "She may call this evening."

They crossed the street one last time, to make sure that their eyes hadn't played tricks on them. There were several middle-aged and elderly women waiting on the steps of the Madeleine, any one of whom could have explained the true meaning of resignation, but Mme Straus-Muguet was not among them.

That night, when they walked into the apartment at about a quarter of eleven, after dinner and another movie and a very pleasant walk home, the first thing they saw was that the mail on the hall table was gone. The study door was closed.

"Oh *why* couldn't he have stayed!" Barbara whispered, behind the closed door of their room. "It was so nice here without him. We were all so happy."

Chapter 16

"ALIX SENT YOU HER LOVE," Eugène said when he joined them at breakfast.

He did not explain why he had not stayed in the country, or describe the wedding. They were all three more silent than usual. The armchair, creaking and creaking, carried the whole burden of conversation. It had come down to Eugène from his great-great-grandfather. In a formal age that admired orators, military strategists, devout politicians, and worldly ecclesiastics, Jean-Marie Philippe Raucourt, fourth Count de Boisgaillard, had been merely a sensible, taciturn, unambitious man. He lived in a dangerous time, but, having bought his way into the King's army, he quickly bought his way out again and put up with the King's displeasure. He avoided houses where people were dying of smallpox and let no doctor into his own. He made a politic marriage and was impatient with those people who prided them-selves on their understanding of the passions. He had children both in and out of wedlock, escaped the guillotine, noticed that there were ways of flattering the First Consul, and died at the age of fifty-two, in secure possession of his estates. His son, Eugène's great-grandfather, was a Peer and Marshal of France under the Restoration. Eugène's grandfather was an aesthete, and his taste was the taste of his time. He collected grandiose allegorical paintings and houses to hang them in, married late in life, and corresponded with Liszt and Clara Schumann. His oldest son, Eugène's uncle, had a taste for litigation. The once valuable family estates were now heavily mortgaged and no good to anyone, and the house at Mamers stood empty. But scattered over the whole of France were the possessions of the fourth Count de Boisgaillard—beds and tables and armchairs (including this one), brocades, paintings, diaries, letters, books, firearms—and through these objects he continued, though so long dead, to exert an influence in the direction of order, restraint, the middle ground, the golden mean. But even he had to give way and became merely a name, a genealogical link, one of thousands, when the telephone started ringing. Seeing Eugène in his study, with his hat on the back of his head and the call going on and on in spite of his impatience and the air of distraction that increased each time he glanced over his shoulder at the clock, one would have said that there was no end to it; that it was a species of blackmail. The telephone seemed to know when he left the apartment. Once he was out the front door, it never rang again all day.

At nine o'clock, Mme Emile brought up the morning's mail, and Eugène, leafing through it, took out a letter and handed it to Harold, who ripped the envelope open and read the letter standing in the hall:

Petite Barbara Chérie
Petit Harold Chéri

I am a shabby friend for failing to keep my word yesterday evening, and not coming to the rendezvous! But a violent storm prevented me, and no taxi in the rain. I was obliged to mingle my tears with those of the sky. Forgive me, then, petits amis chéris. . . . Yes, I say "chéris," for a long long chain of tenderness will unite me to you always! It is with a mother's heart that I love you both! My white hairs didn't frighten you when we met at "Beaumesnil," and at once I felt that a very sincere sympathy was about to be established between us. This has happened by the grace of God, for your dear presence has given back to me my twentieth year and the sweetness of my youth, during which I was so happy! . . . but after! . . . so unhappy! May these lines bring you the assurance of my great and warm tenderness, mes enfants chéris. Je vous embrasse tous deux. Votre vieille amie qui vous aime tant—

Straus-Muguet

This evening on the stroke of 8h½ if possible.

He put the letter in the envelope and the envelope in his pocket, and said: "Did you ever hear of a restaurant called L'Etoile du Nord?"

"Yes," Eugène said.

"What is it like?"

"It's a rather night-clubby place. Why do you ask?"

"We're having dinner there this evening, with Mme Straus-Muguet."

Eugène let out a low whistle of surprise.

"Is it expensive?"

"Very."

"Then perhaps we shouldn't go," Harold said.

"If she couldn't afford it, she wouldn't have invited you," Eugène said. "I have been making inquiries about her, and it seems that the people she says she knows definitely do not know her."

Harold hesitated, and then said: "But why? Why should she pretend that she knows people she doesn't know?"

Eugène shrugged.

"Is she a social climber?" Harold asked.

"It is more a matter of psychology."

"What do you mean?"

"Elle est un peu maniaque," Eugène said.

He went into the study to read his mail, and Harold was left with an uncomfortable choice: he could believe someone he did not like but who had probably no reason to lie, or someone he liked very much, whose behavior in the present instance . . .

He took her letter out and read it again carefully. Mme Straus's hair was not white but mouse-colored, and though the sky had been gray yesterday afternoon, it was no grayer than usual, and not a drop of rain had fallen on the steps of the Madeleine.

When he and Barbara went out to do some errands, they saw that a lot more of the rolling metal shutters that were always pulled down over the store fronts at night had not been raised this morning, and in each case there was a note tacked up on the door frame or the door of the shop explaining that it would be closed for the "vacances." Every day for the last three days it had been like this. Paris seemed to be withdrawing piecemeal from the world. At first it didn't matter, except that it made the streets look shabby. But then suddenly it did matter. There were certain shops they had come to know and to enjoy using. And they could not leave Harold's flannel trousers at the cleaners, though it was open this morning, because it would be closed by Monday. The fruit and vegetable store where they had gone every day, for a melon or lettuce or tomatoes, closed without warning. Half the shops in the neighborhood were closed, and they had to wander far afield to get what they needed.

Shortly after they got home, there was a knock on their door, and when Barbara opened it, there stood the three Berliners in a row. They had come to say good-by. Herr Rothenberg and the one whose ears stuck out were going home. The one with the pink glasses had managed to get himself sent to a conference in Switzerland. There was something chilling in their manner that had not been there before; now that they were on the point of returning to Germany, they seemed to have become much more German. When they had finished thanking the Americans for their kindness, they took advantage of this opportunity to register with these two citizens of one of the countries that were now occupying the Fatherland their annoyance at being made a political football between the United States and the U.S.S.R.

I: *Leo and Virgo*

And the war? Harold asked silently as they shook hands. *And the Jews?*

And then he was ashamed of himself, because what did he really know about them or what the last ten years had been like for them? Herr Doerffer and Herr Rothenberg and Herr Darmstadt were in all probability the merest shadow of true Prussian aggressiveness, and its reflection in them was undoubtedly something they were not aware of and couldn't help, any more than he could help disliking them for being German. And feeling as he did, it would have been better—more honest—if he had not acted as if his feelings toward them were wholly kind. They carried away a false impression of what Americans were like, and he was left with a feeling of his own falseness.

As they stepped out of the taxi at eight thirty Saturday evening, they saw a frail ardent figure in a tailored suit, waiting on a street corner with an air of intense conspiratorial expectancy. She's missed her calling, Harold thought as he was paying the driver; we should be spies meeting in Lisbon, and recognizing each other by the seersucker suit and the little heart encrusted with diamonds.

Mme Straus embraced Barbara and then Harold, and taking each of them by the arm, she guided them anxiously through traffic and up a narrow street. With little asides, endearments, irrelevancies, smiling and squeezing their hands, she caught them up in her own excitement. The restaurant was air-conditioned, the décor was nautical; the whole look of the place was familiar but not French; it belonged in New York, in the West Fifties.

They were shown to a table and the waiter offered a huge menu, which Mme Straus waved away. From her purse she extracted a scrap of paper on which she had written the dinner that—with their approval—she would order for them: a consommé, broiled chicken, dessert and coffee. They agreed that before the theater one doesn't want to stuff.

When the matter of the wine had been disposed of, she made them change seats so that Barbara was sitting beside her ("close to me") and Harold was across the table ("where I can see you"). She demanded that they tell her everything they had seen and done in Paris, all that had happened at the château after her departure.

Barbara described—but cautiously—their pleasure in staying in Mme Cestre's apartment, and added that they had grown fond of Mme de Boisgaillard.

"An angel!" Mme Straus-Muguet agreed. "And Monsieur also. But I do not care for *her*. She is not *gentille*. . . ." They understood that she meant Mme Viénot.

"Do you know anything about M. Viénot?" Harold asked. "Is he dead? Why is his name never mentioned?"

Mme Straus did not know for sure, but she thought it was— She tapped her forehead with her forefinger.

"Maniaque?" Harold asked.

She nodded, and complimented them both on the great strides they had made in speaking and understanding French.

Under her close questioning, he began to tell her, hesitantly at first and then detail by detail, the curious situation they had let themselves in for by accepting the invitation to stay in Mme Cestre's apartment. No one could have been more sane in her comments than Mme Straus, or more sympathetic and understanding, as he described Eugène's moods and how they themselves were of two minds about everything. A few words and it was all clear to her. She had found herself, at some time or another, in just such a dilemma, and there was, in her opinion, nothing more trying, or more difficult to feel one's way through. But what a pity that things should have turned out for them in this fashion, when it needn't have been like that at all!

Having found someone who understood their ambiguous situation, and did not blame them for getting into it, they found that it could now be dismissed, and it took its place, for the first time, in the general scheme of things; they could see that it was not after all very serious. Mme Straus was so patient and encouraging that they both spoke better than they ever had before, and she was so eager to hear all they had to tell her and so delighted with their remarks about Paris that she made them feel like children on a spree with an indulgent aunt who was ready to grant every wish that might occur to them, and whose only pleasure while she was with them was in making life happy and full of surprises. This after living under the same roof with kindness that was not kind, consideration that had no reason or explanation, a friend who behaved like an enemy or vice versa —it would be hard to say which. And she herself spoke so distinctly, in a vocabulary that offered no difficulty and that at moments made it seem as if they were all three speaking English.

Mme Straus was dissatisfied with the consommé and sent it back to the kitchen. The rest of the dinner was excellent and so was the wine. As Harold sat watching her, utterly charmed by her conversation and by her, he thought: She's a child and she isn't a child. She knows things a child doesn't know, and yet every day is Bastille Day, and at seventy she is still saying *Ah!* as the fountains rise higher and higher and skyrockets explode.

While they were waiting for their dessert, Mme Straus's goddaughter came over to the table, with her husband. They were introduced to Harold and Barbara, and shook hands and spoke a few words in English. The man shook hands again and left. Mme Straus's goddaughter was in her late thirties, and looked as if she must at some time have worked in a beauty parlor. Harold found himself wondering on what basis godparents are chosen in France. It also struck him that there was something patronizing—or at least distant—in the way she spoke to Mme Straus. Though Mme Straus appeared to rejoice in seeing her goddaughter again, was full of praise for the food, for the service, and delighted that the restaurant was so crowded with patrons, the blonde woman had, actually, nothing to say to her.

When they had finished their coffee, Mme Straus summoned the waiter, was horrified at the sight of Harold's billfold, and insisted on paying the sizable check. She hurried them out of the restaurant and into a taxi, and they arrived, by a series of narrow, confusing back streets, at the theater, which was in an alley. Mme Straus inquired at the box office for their tickets. There was a wait of some duration and just as Harold was beginning to grow alarmed for her the tickets were found. They went in and took their seats, far back under the balcony of a small shabby theater, with twelve or fifteen rows of empty seats between them and the stage.

Mme Straus took off her coat and her fur, and gave them to Barbara to hold for her. Then she gave Harold a small pasteboard box tied with yellow string and Barbara her umbrella, and sat back ready to enjoy the play. With this performance, she explained, the theater was closing for the month of August, so that the company could present the same play in Deauville. Pointing to the package in Harold's lap, she said that she had bought some beautiful peaches to present to her friend when they went backstage; Mme Mailly was passionately fond of fruit. He held the carton carefully. Peaches were expensive in France that summer.

Only a few of the empty seats had been claimed by the time the house lights dimmed and went out. Mme Straus leaned toward Barbara in the dark and whispered: "When you are presented to Mme Mailly, remember to ask for her autograph."

The curtain rose upon a flimsy comedy of backstage bickering and intrigue. The star, a Junoesque and very handsome woman, entered to applause, halfway through the first scene. She played herself—Mme Marguerite Mailly, who in the play as in life had been induced to leave the Comédie Française in order to act in something outside the classic repertory. The playwright had also written a part for himself into the play—the actress's husband, from whom she was estranged. Their domestic difficulties were too complicated and epigrammatic for Harold to follow, and the seats were very hard, but in the third act Mme Mailly was given a chance to deliver—on an offstage stage—one of the great passionate soliloquies of Racine. An actor held the greenroom curtain back, and the entire cast of the play listened devoutly. So did the audience. The voice offstage was evidence enough of the pleasure the Americans had been deprived of when Mme Mailly decided to forsake the classics. It was magnificent—full of color, variety, and pathos. The single long speech rose up out of its mediocre setting as a tidal wave might emerge from a duck pond, flooding the flat landscape, sweeping pigsties, chicken coops, barns, houses, trees, and people to destruction.

The play never recovered from this offstage effect, but the actress's son was allowed to marry the ingénue and there was a reconciliation between the playwright and Mme Mailly, who, Harold realized as she advanced to the apron and took a series of solo curtain calls, was simply too large for the stage she acted on. The effect was like a puppet show when you have unconsciously adjusted your sense of scale to conform with small mechanical actors and at the end a giant head emerges from the wings, the head of the human manipulator, producing a momentary surprise.

The lights went on. Mme Straus, delighted with the comedy, gathered up her fur, her umbrella, her coat, and the present of fruit. She spoke to an usher, who pointed out the little door through which they must go to find themselves backstage. They went to it, and then through a corridor and up a flight of stairs to a hallway with four or five doors opening off it and one very bright light bulb dangling by its cord from the ceiling. Mme Straus whispered to Harold: "Don't forget to tell her you admire her poetry. You can tell her in English. She speaks your language beautifully."

Four people had followed them up the stairs. Mme Straus knocked on the door of the star's dressing room, and the re-markable voice answered peremptorily: "Don't come in!"

Mme Straus turned to Harold and Barbara and smiled, as if this were exactly the effect she had intended to produce.

More people, friends of the cast, came up the stairway. The little hall grew crowded and hot. The playwright came out, wearing a silk dressing gown, his face still covered with grease paint, and was surrounded and congratulated on his double accomplishment. Mme Straus knocked once more, timidly, and this time the voice said: "Who is it?"

"It's me," Mme Straus said.

"Who?" the voice demanded, in a tone of mounting irritation.

"It's your friend, chérie."

"Who?"

"Straus-Muguet."

"Will you please wait. . . ." The voice this time was shock-ing.

Harold looked at Mme Straus, who was no longer confident and happy, and then at Barbara, who avoided his glance. All he wanted was to push past the crowd and sneak down the stairs while there was still time. But Mme Straus-Muguet waited and they had no choice but to wait with her until the door opened and the actress, large as Gulliver, bore down upon them. She nodded coldly to Mme Straus and looked around for other friends who had come backstage to congratulate her. There were none. Barbara and Harold were presented to her, and she acknowledged the introduction with enough politeness for Bar-bara to feel that she could offer her program and Mme Straus's fountain pen. The actress signed her name with a flourish, under her silhouette on the first page. When Harold told her that they had read her poems, she smiled for the first time, quite cordially.

Mme Straus tore the string off the pasteboard carton and presented it open to her friend, so that Mme Mailly could see what it contained.

"No, thank you," Mme Mailly said. And when Mme Straus like a blind suppliant continued to show her peaches, the actress said impatiently: "I do not care for any fruit." Her manner was that of a person cornered by some nuisance of an old woman with whom she had had, in the past and through no fault of her own, a slight acquaintance, under circumstances that in no way justified this intrusion and imposition on her good nature. All this Harold could have understood and perhaps accepted, since it took place in France, if it hadn't been for one thing: in his raincoat pocket at that moment were two volumes of sonnets, and on the flyleaf of one of them the actress had written: "To my dear friend, Mme Straus-Muguet, whose sublime character and patient fortitude, as we walked side by side in the kingdom of Death, I shall never cease to remember and be grateful for. . . ."

In the end, Mme Mailly was prevailed upon to hold the pasteboard box, though nothing could induce her to realize that it was a present. The stairs were spiral and treacherous, requiring all their attention as they made their way down them cautiously. The passageway at the foot of the stairs was now pitch dark. By the time they found an outer door and emerged into the summer night, Mme Straus had had time to rally her forces. She took Barbara's arm and the three of them walked to the corner and up the avenue de Wagram, in search of a taxi. No one mentioned the incident backstage. Instead, they spoke of how clever and amusing the play had been. As they parted at the taxi stand, Harold gave Mme Straus the two books that were in his coat pocket, and she said: "I'm glad you remembered to ask for her autograph. You must preserve it carefully."

⚜ ⚜
⚜

On Sunday morning, Eugène showed his membership card at the gate in the stockade around the swimming pool in the Bois de Boulogne. Turning to Harold, he asked for their passports.

"You have to have a passport to go swimming?" Harold asked in amazement.

"I cannot get you into the Club without them," Eugène said patiently.

"I don't have them. I'm so sorry, but it never occurred to me to bring them. In America . . ."

With the same persistence that he had employed when he was trying to arrange for food and lodging for the Berliners, Eugène now applied himself to persuading the woman attendant that it was all right to let his American guests past the gate. The attendant believed that rules are not made to be broken, and the rule of the Racing Club was that no foreigner was to be admitted without proof of his foreignness. There are dozens of ways of saying no in French and she went through the list with visible satisfaction. Eugène, discouraged, turned to Harold and said: "It appears that we will have to drive home and get your passports."

"But the gasoline— Couldn't we just wait here while you go in and have a swim?" Harold asked, and then he started to apologize all over again for causing so much trouble.

"I will try one last time," Eugène said, and, leaving them outside the gate, he went in and was gone for a quarter of an hour. When he came back he brought with him an official of the Club, who told the attendant that it was all right to admit M. de Boisgaillard's guests.

Harold and Barbara followed Eugène into a pavilion where the dressing rooms were. There they separated, to meet again outside by the pools, in their bathing suits. Though he had seen French bathing slips at Dinard, Harold was astonished all over again. They concealed far less than a fig leaf would have, and the only possible conclusion you could draw was that in France it is all right to have sexual organs; people are supposed to have them. Even so, the result was not what one might have expected.

I: *Leo and Virgo*

The men and women around him, standing or lying on canvas mats and big towels or swimming in the two pools, were not lightened and made happier by their nakedness, the way people are when they walk around their bedroom without any clothes on, or the way children or lovers are. Standing by herself at the shallow end of one of the pools was a woman with a body like a statue by Praxiteles, but the two young men who were standing near her looked straight past her, discontented with everything but what they themselves exposed. It was very dreamlike.

Having argued energetically for half an hour to get Harold and Barbara into the Club, Eugène stretched out in a reclining chair, closed his eyes, and ignored them. Sitting on the edge of the pool with his feet in the water, Harold thought: So this is where he comes every afternoon. . . . What does he come here for? The weather was not really hot. And what about his job? And what about Alix? Did she know that this was how he spent his free hours?

From time to time, Eugène swam, or Harold and Barbara dived into the deeper pool and swam. But though they were sometimes in the water at the same time, Eugène didn't swim with them or even exchange remarks with them. Nothing in the world, it seemed—no power of earth, air, or water—could make up to him for the fact that he had had to go to the Allégrets' dressy party in a tweed jacket.

The sun came and went, behind a thin veil of clouds. Harold was not quite warm. He offered Barbara his towel and she wouldn't take it, so he sat with it around his shoulders and looked at the people around him and thought that this was a place that, left to himself, he would never have succeeded in imagining, and that the world must be full of such surprises.

Barbara went into the pool once more, and this time Harold stayed behind. Instinct had told him that something was trying to break through Eugène's studied indifference. Instinct was wrong, apparently. Eugène's eyes stayed closed, in spite of all there was to stare at, and he said nothing. Barbara came back from the pool, and Harold saw that she was cold and suggested that she go in and dress. "In a minute," she said. He tried to make her take his bath towel and again she refused. He looked at Eugène and thought: *He's waiting for someone or something. . . .*

Suddenly the eyelids opened. Eugène looked around him mildly and asked: "How well do you know George Ireland?"

"I know his parents very well, George hardly at all," Harold said. "Why?"

"I thought you might be friends."

"There is a considerable difference in our ages."

"Oh?" Eugène said. And then: "Have you had enough swimming, or would you like to stay a little longer? I do not think the sun is coming out any more."

"It's up to you," Harold said. "If you want to stay, we'll go in and get dressed and wait for you."

"I am quite ready," Eugène said.

They drove home to the apartment, and Barbara made lunch for them. They ate sitting around the teacart in the bedroom. Eugène congratulated Barbara on her mastery of the French omelet, and she flushed with pleasure. "It's the stove," she said. "They don't have stoves like that in America."

The swimming and the food made them drowsy and relaxed. The silences were no longer uncomfortable. Without any animation in his voice, almost as if he were talking about people they didn't know, Eugène began to talk about Beaumesnil and how important it was that the château remain in the family, at whatever cost. When his daughter came of age and was ready to be introduced to society, the property at Brenodville must be there, a visible part of her background. Seeing it now, he said, they could have no idea of what it was like before the war. He himself had not seen it then, but he had seen other houses like it, and knew, from stories Alix had told him, what it used to be like in her childhood.

The Americans had the feeling, as they excused themselves to dress and keep an appointment with Mme Straus, that Eugène was reluctant to let them go, and would have spent the rest of the day in their company. The last two days he had been quite easy with them, most of the time, but they couldn't stop thinking that they shouldn't be here in the apartment at all, feeling the way they did about him. Against their better judgment, they had come here when they knew that they ought to have gone to a hotel. Tempted by the convenience and the space, and by the game of pretending that they were living in Paris, not just tourists, they had stayed on—paying a certain price, naturally. During those times when they were with Eugène, they avoided meeting his eyes, or when they did look directly at him, it was with a carefully prepared caution that demonstrated, alas, how easily he could have got through to them if he had only tried.

At five o'clock that afternoon, while Barbara waited in a taxi, Harold went into the convent in Auteuil and explained to the nun who sat in the concierge's glass cage that Mme Straus-Muguet was expecting them. He assumed that men were not permitted any farther, and that they would all three go out for tea. The nun got up from her desk and led him down a corridor and into a large room with crimson plush draperies, a black and white marble floor, too many mirrors, and very ugly furniture. There she left him. He stood in the middle of the room and looked all around without finding a single object that suggested Mme Straus's taste or personality. Surprised, he sat down on a little gilt ballroom chair and waited for her to appear. He felt relieved in one respect; the room was so large that in all probability they didn't need to worry for fear Mme Straus couldn't afford to entertain them at an expensive restaurant.

It was at least five minutes before she appeared. She greeted him warmly and, as he started to sit down again, explained that they were going to take tea upstairs in her chamber; this room was the public reception room of the convent. He picked up his hat, went outside, paid the taxi driver, and brought Barbara back in with him. The rest of the building turned out to be bare, underfurnished, and institutional. Mme Straus led them up so many flights of stairs that she had to stop once or twice, gasping, to regain her breath. Harold stopped worrying about her financial condition and began to worry about her heart. It *couldn't* be good for a woman of her age to climb so much every day.

"I am very near to heaven," she said with a wan smile, as they arrived on the top floor of the building. They went down a long corridor to her room, which was barely large enough to accommodate a bed, a desk, a small round table and, crowded in together, three small straight chairs. The window overlooked the convent garden, and opening off the room there was a cabinet de toilette, the walls of which were covered with photographs. Mme Straus opened the door of her clothes closet and brought out a box of pastries. Then she went into the cabinet de toilette and came out with goblets and a bottle of champagne. There being no ice buckets in the convent, she had tried to chill the champagne by setting it in a washbasin of cold water.

They drank to each other, and then Mme Straus, lifting her glass, said: "To your travels!" And then nobody said anything.

Barbara asked the name of a crisp sweet pastry.

"Palmiers," Mme Straus said—from their palm-leafed shape—and apologized because there were no more of them. She opened a drawer of the desk and brought out two presents wrapped in tissue paper. But before she allowed them to open their gifts, she made Barbara read aloud the note that accompanied them: "Mes amis chéris, before we part I want you to have a souvenir of France and of a new friend, but one who has loved you from the beginning. Jolie Barbara, in wearing these clips give a thought to the one who offers them. Harold, smoke a cigarette each day so that the smoke will come here to rejoin me."

The Americans were embarrassed by the note and by the fact

that they had not thought to bring Mme Straus a present, but she sat back with the innocent complacency of an author who has enjoyed the sound of his own words, and did not appear to find anything lacking to the occasion.

Barbara put the mother-of-pearl clips on her dress, which wasn't the kind of dress you wear clips with, and so they looked large and conspicuous. Harold emptied a pack of cigarettes into the leather case that was Mme Straus's gift to him. He never carried a cigarette case, and this one was bulky besides. He hoped his face looked sufficiently pleased.

He and Barbara stood in the door of the cabinet de toilette while Mme Straus showed them the framed photographs on the walls of that tiny room—her dead son, full-faced and smiling; and again with his wife and children; various nieces and god-daughters, including the one they had met the night before; and another, very pretty girl who was a member of the corps de ballet at the Opéra. The last photograph that Mme Straus pointed out was of her daughter, who did not look in the least like her. The old woman said, with her face suddenly grave: "A great egoist! Her heart is closed to all tenderness for her mother. She refuses to see me, and replies to my communications through her lawyer."

After a rather painful silence, Harold asked: "Was your son like you?"

"But exactly!" she exclaimed. "We were alike in every respect. His death was a blow from which I have never recovered."

Harold turned and looked at the picture of him. So pleasure-loving, so affectionate, so full of jokes and surprises that were all buried with him.

When they sat down again, she showed them a small oval photograph of herself at the age of three, in a party dress, kneeling, and with her elbows on the back of a round brocade chair. A sober, proud child, with her bangs frizzed, she was look-ing straight at the click of the shutter. Mme Straus explained that in her infancy she had been called "Minou." Barbara expressed such pleasure in the faded photograph that Mme Straus took it to her desk, wrote "Minou à trois ans" across the bottom, and presented it to her. Then she asked Harold to bring out from under the bed the pile of books he would find there. He got down on his hands and knees, reached under, and began fishing them out: Mme Mailly's verses, the memoirs of General Weygand in two big volumes handsomely bound, and, last of all, the plays of Edmond Rostand, volume after volume. The two books of verse were passed from hand to hand and admired, as if Harold and Barbara had never seen them before. The General's memoirs had an inscription on the flyleaf and looked highly valued but unread. Mme Straus explained that she had enjoyed Rostand's friendship during a prolonged stay in the South of France. Each volume was inscribed to the playwright's charming companion, Mme Straus-Muguet; and Mme Straus described to Harold and Barbara the moonlit garden in which the books were presented to her, on a beautiful spring night shortly before the First World War. "These are my treasures," she said, "which I have no place to keep but under the bed."

When the books were returned to their place of safekeeping, they went downstairs and walked in the garden. It was a gray day, and from the rear the convent looked dreary and like a nursing home. The only other person in the garden was a young woman who was sitting on a bench reading a newspaper. As they approached, Mme Straus explained that it was one of her dearest friends, a charming Swedish girl. They were presented to her, and the Swedish girl acknowledged the introduction blankly and went on reading her newspaper.

They sat down on a bench in the far end of the garden, but after a minute or two the chill in the evening air made them get up and walk again. Barbara suggested that Mme Straus come out and have dinner with them. There was a little restaurant nearby, Mme Straus said, very plain and simple, where she often went. The food was excellent, and she was sure they would find it agreeable.

I: *Leo and Virgo*

The restaurant was dirty, and they sat under a harsh, white overhead light. The waitress, whom Mme Straus addressed by her Christian name, was brusque with her, and the food was not good. They were all three talked out.

On the way back to the convent, Mme Straus saw a lighted pastry shop, rushed in, bought all the palmiers there were, and presented them to Barbara. Still not satisfied with what she had given the Americans, she opened her purse while they were standing on a street corner waiting for their bus and took out two religious stamps that were printed on white tissue paper. She gave one to Harold and the other to Barbara. The design was Byzantine—the Virgin and the Christ child, with two tiny angels hovering like birds, one on either side of the Virgin's rounded shoulders. The icon from which the design was taken was in a church in Rome, Mme Straus said, where they must go and pray for her. Meanwhile, the stamps, through their miraculous efficacy, would conduct her two dear children safely on their journey and bring them back to her in September.

Chapter 17

O N THE FOURTH OF SEPTEMBER, with their faces pressed to the window of the San Remo–Nice motorbus, they saw a little harbor surrounded by cliffs. They saw the masts of fishing boats. They saw a bathing beach. They turned their heads and saw, on the other side of the road, a small three-story hotel. "Since we don't have any hotel reservation in Nice," he said, "what about staying here?" She nodded, and, rising from his seat, he pulled the bell cord. The bus came to a stop on the brow of the next hill, and the driver, handing the suitcases down to Harold, said: "Monsieur, that was a very good idea you just had."

The small hotel could accommodate them, and sent a busboy back with Harold to help with the luggage. When Harold tipped him, he also asked if the tip was sufficient, and the boy looked at him the way people do at someone who is obviously running a fever. Then, serene and amused, he smiled, and said: "Mais oui." In Beaulieu nobody worried about anything.

Very soon Harold and Barbara stopped worrying also. Right after breakfast, they went across the road to the beach. They read for a while, and then they stretched out on the sand and surrendered themselves to the sun. When it grew hot they swam, with their eyes open so that they could watch their shadows on the sandy floor of the harbor. Barbara walked slowly up the beach and back again, searching for tiny pieces of broken china which the salt waves had rounded and faded and made velvet to the touch. She was collecting them, and she kept sorting over her collection, comparing and discarding, saving only the best of these treasures that no one else cared about. Harold sat watching her and eavesdropping. At first the other people on the beach thought Barbara had lost something: a ring, perhaps. And one of the life guards offered his help. When they found out that it was only an obsession, they paid no more attention to her searching. They did not even make jokes about it. If Harold grew tired of looking at sunbathers, he looked at the cliffs, or at the sails on the horizon. Or he got up and went into the water.

By noon they were ravenous. After a long heavy nap they got dressed, yawning, and went out again. They walked the streets of Beaulieu, stopping in front of shop windows or to stare at the huge, empty Hôtel Bristol. They found a café that sold American cigarettes. They bought fruit in an open-air market. They went to the English tea shop. They had a quick swim before dinner. In the evening they sat in a canvas tent on the beach, drinking vermouth and dancing, or watching the hotel chambermaids dancing with each other or with the life guards, to a three-piece band that played "Maria de Bahia" and "La Vie en Rose." Or they walked, under a canopy of stars, with the warm sea wind accompanying them like an inquisitive dog. Now and then they stopped to smell some garden that they could not see: box and oleander, bay leaves, night-blooming stock.

One afternoon they took a bus into Nice to see what they were missing. Half an hour after they had stepped off the bus they were on their way back to Beaulieu. Nice was like Miami, they decided, without ever having been to Miami.

They walked all the way around Cap Ferrat. Behind one of the high, discolored stucco walls was the villa of Somerset Maugham; behind which was the question. Instead of becoming friends with Somerset Maugham, they took up with a couple fifteen years older than they were—a cousin of Mme la Patronne and his English wife. The four of them climbed the Moyenne Corniche and saw Old Eze; lingered in the dining room of the Hôtel Frisia, drinking brandy and Benedictine; went to Monte Carlo and saw the botanical gardens. In the Casino at Beaulieu, Barbara won four hundred francs at roulette, and a life of gambling opened before her.

On all the telephone poles there were posters announcing a Grand Entertainment under the Auspices of the Jeunesse de Beaulieu. Harold and Barbara went. Nothing could have kept them away. The Grand Entertainment was in a big striped circus tent. The little boy from the carnival in Tours came and sat at their table—or if it was not that exact same little boy, it was one just like him, his twin, his double. They supplied him with confetti and serpentines and admiration, and he supplied them with family life. The orchestra played "Maria de Bahia" and "La Vie en Rose." Fathers danced with their two-year-old daughters tirelessly. At midnight the little boy's real mother claimed him. Harold and Barbara stayed till the end, dancing. When they rang the bell of their hotel at two o'clock in the morning, the busboy let them in, his eyes pink with sleep, his good night unreproachful. He was their friend. So was the single waiter in the dining room. Also the chambermaids, and—but in a more reserved fashion—Mme la Patronne.

Their hotel room was small and bare but it looked out over the harbor. Undressing for bed, Harold would step out onto their balcony in his bathrobe, see the lanterns hanging from the masts of fishing boats, hear God knows what mermaid singing, and reach for his bathing slip. At night the water was full of phosphorescence. They slept the sleep of stones. The man in the camel's-hair coat could not find them. Those faint lines in her forehead, put there prematurely by riddles at three a.m., by curtains that did not hang straight in the dark, by faults there was no correcting, disappeared. With his lungs full of sea air, he held himself straighter. "I feel the way I ought to have felt when I was seventeen and didn't," he said. Their skin grew darker and darker. Their faces bloomed. The very bed they made love on was like a South Sea Island.

They should never have left Beaulieu, but they did; after ten days, he went and got bus tickets, and she packed their suitcases, and he went downstairs and paid the bill, and early the next morning they stood in the road, waiting for the bus to Marseilles. It is impossible to say why people put so little value on complete happiness.

They arrived at Marseilles at five o'clock in the evening. The city was plastered with posters advertising the annual industrial fair, and they were turned away from one hotel after another. They decided that the situation was hopeless, and Harold told the taxi driver to take them to the railway station. The next train to anywhere left at seven thirty a.m. They drove back into the center of town and tried more places. While Harold was standing on the sidewalk, wondering where to go next, a man came up to him and handed him a card with the name of a hotel on it. Harold showed the card to the taxi driver, who tore it up. Though they had no place to stay, they had a friend; the driver had taken them under his protection; their troubles were his. He remained patient and optimistic. After another hour and a half, Harold dipped a pen into an inkwell and signed the register of the Hôtel Splendide. It had a hole right down through the center of the building, because the elevator shaft was being rebuilt. The lobby was full of bricks and mortar and scaffolding, and their room was up five flights and expensive, but they knew how lucky they were to have a roof over their heads. And besides, this time tomorrow they would be in Paris.

They went for a walk before dinner and found the Old Port, but whatever was picturesque had been obliterated by the repeated bombings. They saw some sailboats along an esplanade that could have been anywhere, and left that in favor of a broad busy boulevard with shops. After a few blocks they turned back. As a rule, the men who turned to stare at Barbara Rhodes in public places were generally of a romantic disposition or else old enough to be her father. Even more than her appearance, her voice attracted and disturbed them, reminding them of what they themselves had been like at her age, or throwing them headlong into an imaginary conversation with her, or making them wonder whether in giving the whole of their affection to one woman they had settled for less than they might have got if they had had the courage and the patience to go on looking. But this was not true here. In the eyes that were turned toward her, there was no recognition of who she was but only of the one simple use that she could be put to.

Harold had the name of a restaurant, and the shortest way to it was an alley so dark and sinister-looking that they hesitated to enter it, but it was only two blocks long and they could see a well-lighted street at the other end, and so they started on, and midway down the alley encountered a scene that made their knees weak—five gendarmes struggling to subdue a filthy, frightened, ten-year-old boy. At the corner they came upon the restaurant, brightly lighted, old-fashioned, glittering, clean. The waiters were in dinner jackets, and the food was the best they had had in Europe. They managed to relegate to the warehouse of remembered dreams what they had just seen in the alley; also the look of considered violence in faces they did not ever want to see again.

THE PORTER who carried their heavy luggage through the Gare Montparnasse informed them that there was a taxi strike in Paris. He put the luggage down at the street entrance, and pointed to the entrance to the Métro, directly across the street. "If you'll just help me get these down into the station," Harold said. The porter was not permitted to go outside the railway station, and left them stranded in the midst of their seven pieces of luggage. Though they had left the two largest suitcases here in Paris with the American Express, during their travels they had acquired two more that were almost as big. Harold considered moving the luggage in stages and found that he didn't have the courage to do this. Somewhere—in Italy or Austria or the South of France—he had lost contact with absolutes, and he was now afraid to take chances where the odds were too great. While they stood there helplessly at the top of a broad flight of stone steps, discussing what to do, a tall, princely man with a leather strap over his shoulder came up to them and offered his services.

"Yes," Harold said gratefully, "we do need you. If you'll just help me get the suitcases across the street and down into the Métro—" and the man said: "No, monsieur, I will go with you all the way to your hotel."

He draped himself with the two heaviest suitcases, using his strap, and then picked up three more. Harold shouldered the dufflebag, and Barbara took the dressing case, and they made their way through the bicycles and down the stairs. While they stood waiting for a train, the Frenchman explained that he was not a porter by profession; he worked in a warehouse. He had been laid off, the day before, and he had a family to support, and so he had come to the railway station, hoping to pick up a little money. At this moment, he said, there were a great many people in Paris in his circumstances.

At his back there was a poster that read, incongruously: *L'Invitation au Château.* Harold thought of Beaumesnil. Then, turning, he looked up into the man's eyes and saw that they were full of sadness.

Each day, the Frenchman said, things got a little worse, and they were going to continue to get worse. The only hope was that General de Gaulle would come back into power.

"Do you really think that?" Harold said, concerned that a man of this kind, so decent and self-respecting, so courteous, so willing to take on somebody else's heavy suitcases while weighted

303

down by his own burdens, should have lost all faith in democracy.

They talked politics all the way to the Concorde station, and made their way up the steps and across the rue de Rivoli and past the Crillon and down the narrow, dark, rue Boissy d'Anglas. In the lobby of the Hôtel Vouillemont, the Frenchman divested himself of the suitcases, and Harold paid him, and shook hands with him, and thanked him, and thought: *It isn't right to let him go like this when he is in trouble*, but did let him go, nevertheless, and turned to the concierge's desk, thinking that their own troubles were over, and learned that they were just beginning. They had wired ahead for a reservation but the concierge was not happy to see them. The delegates to the General Assembly of the United Nations, the secretarial staff, the delegates' families and servants—some three thousand people—had descended on Paris the day before, and the Hôtel Vouillemont was full; all the hotels were full. How long did monsieur expect to stay? . . . Ah no. Decidedly no. They could stay here until they had found other accommodation, but the sooner they did this the better.

So, instead of unpacking their suitcases and hanging up their clothes and having a long hot bath and deciding where to have dinner their first night back in Paris, they went out into the street and started looking for a hotel that would take them for five weeks. Avoiding the Crillon and places like it that they knew they couldn't afford, they went up the rue du Mont-Thabor and then along the rue de Castiglione. They would have been happy to stay in the Place Vendôme but there did not seem to be any hotels there. They continued along the rue Danielle Casanova and turned back by way of the rue St. Roch. Nobody wanted them. If only they'd thought to arrange this in July. If they'd only been able to imagine what it would be like . . . But in July they could have stayed anywhere.

Early the next morning, they started out again.

Harold removed his hat and with a pleasant smile said: "Bon-

jour, madame. Nous désirons une chambre pour deux personnes
. . . pour un mois . . . avec un—"

"Ah, monsieur, je regrette beaucoup, mais il n'y a rien." The
patronne's face reflected satisfaction in refusing something to
somebody who wanted it so badly.

"Rien du tout?"

"Rien du tout," she said firmly.

He did not really expect a different answer, though it was
possible that the answer would be different. Once he had been
refused, nothing was at stake, and he used the rest of the conversation to practice speaking French. Within the narrow limits
of this situation, he was becoming almost fluent. He even tried
to do something about his accent.

"Mais la prochaine semaine, peut-être?"

"La semaine prochaine non plus, monsieur."

"C'est bien dommage."

He glanced around the lobby and at the empty dining room
and at the glass roof over their heads. Then he considered the
patronne herself—the interesting hair-do, the flinty eyes, the
tight mouth, the gold fleur-de-lys pin that had no doubt belonged to her mother, the incorruptible self-approval. She was
as well worth studying as any historical monument, and seemed
to be made of roughly the same material.

"C'est un très joli hôtel," he said, and smiled experimentally,
to see whether just this once the conversation could be put on
a personal or even a sexual basis. All such confusions are, of
course, purely Anglo-Saxon; the patronne was not susceptible.
He might as well have tried to charm one of her half-dozen telephone directories.

"Nous aurions été très contents ici," he said, with a certain
pride in the fact that he was using the conditional past tense.

"Ah, monsieur, je regrette infiniment qu'il n'y a rien.
L'O.N.U., vous savez."

"Oui, oui, l'O.N.U." He raised his hat politely. "Merci,
madame."

"De rien, monsieur." The voice was almost kind.

"Nothing?" Barbara asked, when he got outside. She was standing in front of a shop window.

"Nothing. This one would have been perfect." Then he studied the shop window. "That chair," he said.

"I was looking at it too."

"It would probably cost too much to ship it home, but we could ask, anyway." He put his hand to the door latch. The door was locked.

They started on down the street, looking for the word "hôtel." The weather was sunny and warm. Paris was beautiful.

In the middle of the morning, they sat down at a table under an awning on a busy street, ordered café filtre, and stretched their aching legs. Barbara opened her purse and took out the mail that they had picked up at the bank but not taken the time to read. They divided the letters between them. It was not a very good place to read. The noise was nerve-racking. Every time a big truck passed, the chairs and tables and their two coffee cups shook.

"Here's a letter from the Robertsons," she said.

"Are they still here?" he asked, looking up from his letter with interest.

Among the American tourists whom the Austrian government had billeted at a country inn outside Salzburg because the hotels in town were full of military personnel there was an American couple of the same age as Harold and Barbara and so much like them that at first the two couples carefully avoided each other. But when day after day they ate lunch at the same table and swam in the same lake and took the same crowded bus into Salzburg, it became more and more difficult and finally absurd not to compare notes on what they had heard or were going to hear. The Robertsons had no hotel reservations in Venice, and so Harold told them where he and Barbara were staying. And when they got to Venice they were welcomed in the hotel lobby by the Robertsons, who had already been there two days and showed them the way to the Piazza San Marco. With the mail that was handed to Harold at the American Express in Rome there was a note from Steve Robertson: he and Nancy were so sorry to miss them, and they must be sure and go to the Etruscan Museum and the outdoor opera at the Baths of Caracalla. The note that Barbara now passed across the table contained the name and telephone number of the Robertsons' hotel in Paris.

He finished reading the mail that was scattered over the table and then said suddenly: "I don't think we are going to find anything."

"What will we do?"

"I don't know," he said. He signaled to the waiter that he was ready to pay the check. "Close our suitcases and go home, I guess."

After lunch they started out again. There was only one small hotel in the neighborhood of the Place Redouté and it was full. Rien, monsieur. Je regrette beaucoup. They tried the Hôtel Bourgogne et Montana, the Hôtel Florida, the Hôtel Continental. They tried the Hôtel Scribe, and the Hôtel Métropolitain, and the Hôtel Madison. The Hôtel Louvre, the Hôtel Oxford et Cambridge, the Hôtel France et Choiseul . . . Rien, monsieur. Je n'ai rien . . . rien du tout . . . pas une seule chambre pour deux personnes avec salle de bains, pas de grand lit . . . Absolument rien . . . And all the while in his wallet there was that calling card, which he had saved as a souvenir. Used properly, the card of M. Carrère would have got them into any hotel in Paris, no matter how crowded. He never once thought of it.

From their room in the Hôtel Vouillemont, Harold called the Robertsons' hotel. The voice that answered said: "Ne quittez pas," and then after several minutes he heard another voice that was like an American flag waving in the breeze. "Dusty? How wonderful! You must come right over! It's our last night in Paris, we're taking the boat train in the morning, and what could be more perfect?"

The Robertsons' hotel was on the other side of the river, in the rue de l'Université, and as Harold and Barbara walked up the street from the bus stop, they saw Steve coming to meet them. He was smiling, and he embraced them both and said: "Paris is marvelous!"

"If you have a place to lay your head," Harold said.

They told him about the trouble they had been having, and he said: "Let's go talk to the proprietor of our hotel. We're leaving in the morning. I'm sure you can have our room. You'll love it there, and it's dirt cheap." The proprietor said that he would be happy to let them have the Robertsons' room, but for one night only. So they went on upstairs.

"Oh, it's just marvelous!" Nancy said as she kissed them. "We've had the most marvelous two weeks. I know it's a terrible thing to say but neither of us want to go home. We're both heartsick at the thought of leaving Paris. Wasn't Rome wonderful!"

The Robertsons had friends who were living here and spoke perfect French and had initiated them into the pleasures of the Left Bank. They took Barbara and Harold off to have dinner at a place they knew about, where the proprietor gave the women he admired a little green metal souvenir frog, sometimes with a lewd compliment. He was considered a character. The restaurant was full of students, and Harold and Barbara felt they were on the other side of the moon from the Place Redouté, where they belonged.

Saturday morning, Harold came down in the elevator alone, and, avoiding the reproachful look of the concierge as he passed through the lobby on his way to the street door, went to the Cunard Line office to see if their return passage could be changed to an earlier date, and was told that they were fortunate to be leaving as soon as the middle of October; the earliest open sailing was December first.

"I think it's a sign," Barbara said.

"We might as well take what we have," he said. "While we have it."

They got into a taxi and went back to the Left Bank and fanned out through the neighborhood of St. Germain-des-Prés—the rue Jacob, the rue de l'Université, the rue des Saints Pères, the rue des Beaux-Arts . . . The story was always the same. Their feet ached, their eyes saw nothing but the swinging hotel sign far up the street. Harold had tried to get Barbara to stay in their room while he walked the streets, but she insisted on keeping him company.

At one o'clock she said: "I'm hungry," and he said: "Shall we try one more?" The concierge was eating his lunch when they walked into the hotel lobby. The smell of beef casserole pierced the Americans to the heart. It was the essence of everything French, and it wasn't for them.

When they returned to their hotel, the concierge called to Harold. Expecting the worst, he crossed the lobby to the desk. The concierge handed him a letter and Harold recognized Steve Robertson's tiny, precise handwriting. Inside there was an advertisement clipped from that morning's Paris *Herald*. The Hôtel Paris-Dinard, in the rue Cassette, had a vacancy—a room with a bath.

⚜ ⚜
⚜

THEY MOVED across the river the first thing Sunday morning, and by lunchtime their suitcases were unpacked and stored away under the bed, their clothes were hanging in the armoire, the washbasin in the bathroom was full of soaking nylon, the towel racks were full, the guidebooks were set out on the rickety little table by the window, and they had all but forgotten about that monotonous dialogue between the possessor and the dispossessed, which began: "Nous désirons une chambre pour deux personnes . . ."

The hotel was very quiet, there were no other Americans staying there, and they were delighted with the room and the view from their window. They were up high, in the treetops, and could see through the green leaves the greener dome of a church. They looked down into a walled garden directly across the street from the hotel. The room was not large, but it was not too small, and it was clean and quiet and had a double bed and a bathroom adjoining it, and it was not expensive. Fortune is never halfhearted when it decides to reverse itself.

The green dome was in their guidebooks; it was the Church of the Ancient Convent of the Carmelites. During the Reign of Terror, a hundred and sixteen priests had had their throats cut on the church steps, and every morning, in the darkness and the cold just before dawn, Harold was wakened by a bell tolling, so loud and so near that it made his heart race wildly. Barbara slept through it. Leo is sleepy at night and easily wakened in the morning; the opposite is true of Virgo.

When the bell stopped tolling, he drifted off. Three hours later the big breakfast tray was deposited on their laps, before they were wholly awake or decently clothed. Though white flour was illegal, by paying extra they could have, with their coffee, croissants made of white flour. They were still warm from the bakery oven. Through the open window came the massed voices of school children in the closed garden, so like the sound of noisy birds. After they had finished their breakfast they fell asleep again, and when they woke, the street was quiet; the children had been swallowed up by the school. At recess time they reappeared, but the racket was never again so vivid during the rest of the day.

The owner of the hotel sat at a high desk in the lobby, behind his ledger, and nodded remotely to them as they came and went. If they turned right when they emerged from the hotel, they came to a street of religious-statuary shops, which took them into the Place St. Sulpice, with its fountain and plane trees and heavy baroque church. If they turned left, they came to the rue

Vaugirard, which was busier, and if they turned left again, they eventually came to the Palais du Luxembourg and the gardens. Sitting on iron chairs a few feet away from the basin where the children sailed their boats, they read or looked at the faces— narrow, unhandsome compared to the Italian faces they had left behind, but intense, nervously alive. Or they got up and walked, past the palace, between the flower beds, down one of the formal avenues.

In an alley off the Place St. Sulpice they found the perfect restaurant, and they went there every day, for lunch or dinner or both. Harold held the door open for Barbara, and they were greeted as they came in—by madame behind her desk and then by monsieur with his hands full of plates—and went on into the back room, where they usually sat at the same table in order to be served by a waiter called Pierre, who took exquisite care of them and smiled at them as if he were their affectionate older brother. Here in this small square room, eating was as simple and as delightful as picking wildflowers in a wood. They had artichokes and pâté en croûte, green peas and green beans from somebody's garden, and French-fried potatoes that were rushed to their table from the kitchen. They had little steaks with Béarnaise sauce, and pheasant, and roast duck, and sweetbreads, and calf's liver, and brains, and venison. They had raspberries and pears and fraises des bois and strawberry tarts, and sometimes with their dessert Pierre smuggled them whipped cream. They drank Mâcon blanc or Mâcon rouge. They ate and drank with rapture, and, strangely, grew thinner and thinner.

Though there were always people in the Place St. Sulpice, they almost never saw anybody in the rue Cassette. It had not always been so quiet. Walking home one day they saw there wasn't a single house that didn't have pockmarks that could only have been made by machine-gun bullets in the summer of 1944.

They learned to use the buses, so that they could see the upper world of Paris when they went out, instead of the underworld of the Métro. They also walked—down the rue Vaugirard to the

Odéon and then down the rue de l'Odéon to the boulevard St. Germain; down the boulevard St. Germain to the Place St. Germain-des-Prés. Over and over, as if this were a form of memorizing, they walked in the rue Bonaparte and the rue Jacob, in the rue Dauphine and the rue du Cherche-Midi, in the rue Cardinale and the Carrefour de l'Odéon, in the rue des Ciseaux and the rue des Saints Pères, in the boulevard St. Germain and the boulevard Raspail.

In their hurry to move into a hotel that wanted them, they neglected to leave behind their new address. Their first piece of mail, forwarded by the bank, was a letter from Mme Straus-Muguet:

Sunday

Dear Little Friends:
    What a disappointment! I passed by your hotel a little while ago and you had taken flight this very morning. But where? And how to rejoin you? Have you returned to the country? In short, a word guiding me, I beg of you, for I am leaving for Sarthe for six days, and I had so much hoped to spend this past week with you. Well, that's life! But your affectionate Minou is so sorry not to see you, and fondly embraces you both!
Straus-Muguet

Harold called the convent in Auteuil, and was told that Mme Straus-Muguet had left. Barbara wrote and told her where they were, and that they would be here until the nineteenth of October. She also wrote to Alix, who answered immediately, inviting them down to the country for the week end.

"Do you think that means we're to pay or are we really invited?" he said.

"I don't know. Do you want to go? I'd just as soon."

"No," he said. "I don't want to leave Paris."

They heard a gala performance of *Boris Godounov* at the Opéra, with the original Bakst settings and costumes. On a rainy night they got into a taxi and drove to the Opéra Comique. The house was sold out but there were folding seats. Blocking the center aisle, and only now and then wondering what would happen if a fire broke out, they heard *Les Contes d'Hoffman*.

They went to the movies, they went to the marionette theater in the Champs-Elysées. They went to the Grand Guignol. They went to the Cirque Médrano.

"What I like about living in Paris," he said, "is planning ahead very carefully, so that every day you can do something or see something that you wouldn't do if you weren't here."

"That isn't what *I* like," Barbara said. "What I like is *not* to plan ahead, but just see what happens. Couldn't we do that for a change?"

"All right," he said. But his heart sank at the thought of leaving anything to chance. The days would pass, would be frittered away, and suddenly their five weeks in Paris would be used up and they wouldn't have seen or done half the things they meant to. He managed to forget what she had said. He waited impatiently for each new issue of *La Semaine de Paris* to appear on the kiosks, and when it did, he studied it as if he were going to have to pass an examination in the week's plays, concerts, and movies. They did not understand one word in fifty of Montherlant's *La Reine Morte*, and during the first intermission he rushed out into the lobby to buy a program; but they were in France, the rest of the audience did not need a résumé of the plot, the program was not helpful.

At Cocteau's *Les Parents Terribles* the old woman who opened the door of their box for them came back while the play was going on and tried to oust them from their seats in order to put somebody else in them. With one eye on the stage—the mother was in bed with a cold, the grown son was kneeling on the bed, he accused, she admitted to remorse, incest was in the air—Harold fought off the ouvreuse. They were in their right seats, and indignation made him as eloquent as a Frenchman would have been in these circumstances. But by the time the enemy had retired and he was free to turn his attention to the play, the remarkable love scene was over.

313

Barbara went off by herself one morning, while he stayed home and wrote letters. When she came back, she reported that she had found a store with wonderful cooking utensils—just the kind of thin skillets that were in Mme Cestre's kitchen and that she had been looking for for years.

"I would have bought them," she said, "except that I decided they would take up too much room in the luggage. . . . Now I'm sorry I didn't."

"Where was this shop?" he asked, reaching for his hat.

She didn't know. "But I can find my way back to it," she said.

It was a virtuoso performance, up one street and down the next, across squares and through alleys, beyond the sixth arrondissement and well into the fifth. At last they came on the shop she was searching for. They bought four skillets, a nutmeg grater, a salad basket, some cooking spoons, a copper match box to hang beside the stove, and a paring knife. In the next street, they came upon a bookshop with old children's books and Victorian cardboard toy theaters. They bought the book of children's songs with illustrations by Boutet de Monvel that was in the bookcase of the red room at Beaumesnil. While Barbara was trying to decide between the settings for *La belle au bois dormant* and *Cendrillon*, he said suddenly: "Where did Sabine sleep while we were occupying her room?"

"In the back part of the house, probably. Why?"

"Or one of those dreary attic rooms," he said. "It's funny we never thought about it at the time. Do you think she minded our being in her room?"

That evening while Barbara was dressing, he gave M. le Patron the number of the apartment in the rue Malène and waited beside the bed, with the telephone held to his ear. The phone rang and rang. But she's too thin, he thought, watching her straighten the seam of her stockings. She isn't getting enough rest. . . .

Reaching into the armoire, she began pushing her dresses

along the rod. She could hardly bear to put any of them on any more.

"Mme Viénot's affectionate manner with you I took at the time to be disingenuous," he said. "Looking back, I think that it wasn't."

The cotton print dress she had bought in Rome was out of season. The brown, should she wear, with a green corduroy jacket? Or the lavender-blue?

"I think she really did like us. And that we totally misjudged her character," he said.

She chose the brown, which had a square neck and no sleeves, and so required the green jacket. "We didn't misjudge her character."

"How do you know?"

"From one or two remarks that Alix made."

"They do not answer," M. le Patron said.

In her letter Alix had said that she would be coming back to Paris soon, but a week passed, and then two, and there was still no answer when they called the apartment in the rue Malène. One morning they made a pilgrimage to the Place Redouté and stood looking affectionately around at the granite monument, the church, the tables piled on top of each other in front of the café, the barber shop. Standing in the rue Malène, they saw that all the windows of Mme Cestre's apartment were closed, and the shutters as well. "Shall we go in and ask when they are coming back?" Barbara said.

Mme Emile shook hands cordially but had no news. They were all away, she said. Monsieur also. She did not know when they were returning.

"Do you think she wrote and the letter got lost in the mails?" Barbara asked as they were walking toward the bus corner.

"I don't know," he said. "I don't think so. Perhaps their feelings were hurt that we didn't accept the invitation to come down to the country."

"We should have gone," Barbara said with conviction.

"But then we would have had to leave Paris."

"What do you think really happened?"

"You mean the 'drame'? They lost their money."

"But how?" Barbara said.

"There are only about half a dozen ways that a family that has money can lose it. They can run through it—"

"I don't think they did."

"Neither do I," he said. "Or they can lose it through inflation —which could have happened, because the franc used to be twenty to the dollar before the war. But then what about the drama? Maybe they were swindled out of it."

"Not Mme Viénot, surely."

"Well, something," he said.

SUMMER DEPARTED without their noticing exactly when this happened. Fall was equally beautiful. It was still warm in the daytime. The leaves were turning yellow outside their window. He started wearing pajamas because the nights were cold. So was their room when they got up in the morning. Soon, even in the middle of the day it was cool in the shade, and they kept crossing the street to walk in the sun. They discovered the Marché St. Germain, and wandered up and down the aisles looking with surprise at the wild game and enjoying the color and fragrance and appetizingness of the fruit and vegetables. They walked all the way down the rue de Varennes, and saw the Rodin Museum and Napoleon's tomb. They took a bus to the Jardin des Plantes and walked there. They took the Métro to the Bois de Vincennes. Walking along the Left Bank of the Seine in the late afternoon, they examined the bookstalls, but with less interest than they had shown in the shabby merchandise in the avenue de Grammont in Tours. The apparatus of rejection was fatigued; they only looked now at what there was some possibility of their wanting, and the bookstalls were too picked-over.

Coming home on the top of a bus just as the lights were turned on in the shops along the Boulevard St. Germain, they saw a china shop, and got off the bus and went inside and bought two small ash trays of white porcelain, in the shape of an elm and a maple leaf.

Barbara bought gloves in the rue de Rivoli, and in a little shop in the rue St. Honoré she found a moss-green velours hat with a white ostrich feather that curled charmingly against her cheek. It was too small, and after the clerk had stretched it Barbara knew suddenly that it was not right. It was too costumy. But the clerk and Harold both begged her to take it, and so, against her better judgment, she did.

He was looking for the complete correspondence of Flaubert, in nine volumes, and this was not easy to find and gave him an excuse to stop in every bookstore they came to.

In a little alley off the rue Jacob they saw a small house with a plaque on it: *Ici est mort Racine.* Across the door of a butcher shop in the rue Vaugirard they saw a deer hanging head down, with a sign pinned to its fur: *Will be cut up on Thursday.*

They took the train to Versailles, and walked all the way around the palace and then a little way into the park, looking for the path to the Petit Trianon. They couldn't find it, but came instead upon a fountain with a reclining goddess whose beautiful vacant face was turned to the sky. Leaves came drifting down and settled on the surface of the pool and sailed around the statue like little boats. For the few minutes that they stood looking at the fountain, they were released from the tyranny of his wristwatch and the calendar; there was no time but the time of statues, which seems to be eternity, though of course they age, too, and become pitted, lose a foot or a hand, lichen grows in the folds of their drapery, their features become blurred, and what they are a statue of nobody knows any longer.

Finding themselves in the street where Jean Allégret lived, they stopped and rang his bell. There was no answer. Harold left a note for him, in the mailbox. There was no answer to that, either.

Passing through the Place St. Sulpice on their way home, they raised their eyes to the lighted windows and wondered about the people who lived there. As far as they could see, nobody wondered about them.

The woman who had helped Barbara write those two mildly misleading letters to Mme Viénot had also given Harold the name and telephone number of two old friends from the period when she and her husband were living in Paris. One was a banker. She had not heard anything from him for a long time and she was worried about him. The other was her doctor. Both men were cultivated and responsive and just the sort of people Harold and Barbara would enjoy knowing. Harold called the Hanover Bank and learned that the banker was dead. Then he telephoned the doctor, and the doctor thanked him for giving him news of his friends in America and hung up. Harold looked at the telephone oddly, as if it must in some way be to blame. As for their own French friends, he had been conscious for some time of how completely absent they were—Alix, Sabine, Eugène, Jean Allégret, Mme Straus. Not one word from any of them.

Though they were very happy in Paris, they were aware that a shadow hung over the city. The words "crise" and "grève" appeared in the newspaper headlines day after day. The taxi strike had lasted two weeks. One day the Métro was closed, because of a strike. Two days later, to save coal, the electric utilities shut off all power for twelve hours, and as a result the elevator in their hotel did not run and their favorite restaurant was lit by acetylene lamps. Tension and uncertainty were reflected in the faces they saw in the streets.

They made one more attempt to find the château with the green lawn in front of it—they went to Fontainebleau. They

enjoyed seeing the apartment of Mme de Maintenon and Napoleon's little bathtub, and from across the water the château
did look like a fairy-tale palace, but not the right one. It was too
large, and it was not white.

When they got back to their hotel, M. le Patron handed them
a letter. Mme Straus-Muguet's handwriting dashed all the way
across the face of the envelope, which was postmarked *Sarthe:*

> My dear little friends, what contretemps all along the line,
> since I miss you at every turn! Because of the beautiful weather
> I have not had the courage to remain in Paris, and here I am
> in paradise! Sun, flowers, and the dear nuns, who are so good
> to me! But let us put an end to this game of hide-and-seek. I
> must return to Paris on Thursday, the fourteenth, but if it is
> necessary I shall advance the date of my return in order to see
> you. What are the sorties, plays, operas that will be performed
> on these dates, and what would you like to see? Find this out
> in *La Semaine* or from the billboards, and write me at once if
> between the fifteenth and your departure there is to be a
> Wednesday soirée de ballet, for I will then write immediately
> to Paris to the Opéra. If I return on Sunday—the eleventh
> that would be—is that better for you? Have you still many
> things to do before the final departure? And from where do
> you sail? And on what boat? Behind all these questions, my
> dear children, is only the desire to please you and see you again
> before the complete separation that will be so hard for me to
> bear. . . . I will continue to write to your present hotel, and
> do not change without telling me. What have you done up to
> this moment that was delightful and interesting? I so much
> wanted to show you all the beautiful things—but you have al-
> ready seen many of them! . . . Au revoir, dear little friends.
> I clasp you to my heart, both of you, and embrace you with all
> my tenderness—the tenderness of a friend and of a mother.
>
> Madame Minou
Straus-Muguet
October 4

⚜ ⚜
⚜

THERE WAS NO BALLET between the twelfth and the nineteenth, and so Harold got seats for *le Roi d'Ys* instead. He wrote to Mme Straus that they had seats for the opera for the fourteenth of October and were looking forward to her return. Also that they were enjoying Paris very much, and that on Sunday they were going to Chartres for the day.

Chartres was wonderful; it was one of the high points of their whole trip. There was no streetcar line, just as Mme Viénot had said, and so no little church at the end of it, but they got off the train and found that it was only a short walk to the cathedral from the station. To their surprise, in the whole immense interior there was no one. The greatest architectural monument of the Middle Ages seemed to be there just for them. The church was as quiet as the thoughts it gave rise to. They stood and looked at the stained-glass prophets, at the two great rose windows, at the forest of stone pillars, at the dim, vaulted ceiling, at a little side altar with lighted candles on it. They felt in the presence of some vast act of understanding. When they spoke, it was in whispers. Their breathing, their heartbeat, seemed to be affected.

They climbed one of the towers, and saw what everybody in Chartres was doing. Then they went down and had a very good lunch in a little upstairs restaurant, where they were the only patrons, and walked through the old part of town until dusk. They went back to the cathedral, and walked all the way around it, and came upon the little vegetable garden in the rear; like every other house in Chartres, it had its own potager. This time, when they went inside, there was no light at all in the sky, and it was a gray evening, besides. The stained-glass windows were still glorious, still blazing with their own color and their own light.

I: *Leo and Virgo*

"NOTHING FROM ALIX?"

"Nothing," he said, and sat down on the edge of the bed, ripped open an envelope, and commenced reading a long letter from Mme Straus-Muguet.

"What does she say?" Barbara asked when he turned the first page.

"I'll start at the beginning: '*Sunday . . . Mes petits enfants chéris, I am sad at heart at the thought that you are going to leave France without my being able to find you again—*'"

"No! She's not coming?"

"'*—and embrace you with all my heart. But it is impossible*' —underlined—'*for me to return the fourteenth donc pas d'opéra le R.*'—whatever that means."

"Let me see," she said, looking over his shoulder. "'*Therefore not of the opera le Roi d'Ys*' . . . But she said for you to get tickets. What will we do with the extra one?"

"Take Sabine," he said, "if she's here by then. '*. . . but there is at Mans a charity fête for "the work of the prisons" of my dear Dominicans, of which I occupy myself so much. It takes place Sunday the seventeenth and Monday the eighteenth, and it will be only after the twentieth that I will be returning! . . . And to say that during eight days in August I was alone in Paris! Then my poor dears, understand my true chagrin at not seeing you again, and just see how all the events are against us! Of more I was*'— Is that right?"

"Let me see . . . '*de plus j'étais à une heure de Chartres . . . all the more since I was only one hour from Chartres and it was there that I would have been able to join you . . .*'"

He continued: "'*And you would have passed the*' . . . or '*we*' would. Her handwriting is really terrible. '*. . . passed the day together. You would even have been able to come to Mans, city so interesting, superb cathedral! That all that is lacking, my God, and to say that in this moment (nine o'clock in the morning) when I am writing you, you are perhaps at Chartres.*

321

But where to find you? . . . Little friends, it is necessary to combler mon chagrin'—what's 'combler'?"

"You'll have to look it up," Barbara said. "The dictionary is in my purse."

The dictionary was not in the purse but in the desk drawer.

" 'Combler' means 'to fill up,' 'to overload,' 'to heap,' " he said. " '. . . *it is necessary to try to heap my sorrows by a kindness on your part. It is of yourselves to make photographs, tous les deux ensemble, and to send me your photo with dédicace—dedication—underneath. 19 rue de la Source, that will be a great joy for me, and at Paris there are such good photographers. Make inquiries about them and'*—it could be 'épanchez.' "

"Exaucez," Barbara said, and read from the dictionary.

" 'Exaucer: to grant, give ear to, answer the prayer of someone.' "

" '. . . *grant the prayer that I make of you. You will be thus with me, in my chamber that you know, and I will look at you each day, and that will be to me a great happiness. . . . Thank you in advance! . . . I am enchanted that you are going to the Opéra to hear Le Roi d'Ys—so beautiful, so well sung, such beautiful music. But to avoid making the queue at the location'*—the box office, I guess she means—*'do this: go take your two places at the Opéra at the office of the disection—'* "

"That can't be right," Barbara interrupted.

" '. . . *direction,'* then. *'Boulevard Haussman. Enter by the large door which is in back of the Opéra. On entering, at right you will see the concierge, M. Ferari. He will point out the office of M. Decerf or his secretary Nelle'*—no, Mlle.—*'Simone cela de ma part. Both are my friends, and you will have immediately two good places à la corbeille'*—But we have the seats already, and it took exactly ten minutes in line at the box office, and they're the best seats in the opera house . . . *'where it is necessary to be to see all, salle et scène. I'm writing to M. Decerf by this same courier to reserve you two places, and it is Wednesday morning at eleven o'clock that it is necessary to go there to take them. In this fashion all will go well and I will be tranquil about you. Servez-vous de mon nom dans tout l'Opéra et à tout le monde. . . . In mounting to the premier étage, to the office of M. Decerf (they speak English, both of them) speak to M. Georges, on arriving, de ma part. He will lead you to M. Decerf. I hope I have explained sufficiently the march to follow to arrive à bien, and to all make my good compliments. . . . On your arrival in New York I pray you to write me immediately to tell me your voyage is well passed. Such is my hope, and above all do not leave alone in France your Maman Minou, who loves you so much and has so many regrets. But "noblesse oblige" says the proverb, and to the title of president I owe to be at my post. I will send you tomorrow the book of Bethanie Fontanelle's work of the prisons. Perhaps they will go one day to America. I know the* Mauretania, *splendid boat, and I am going to make the crossing with you—in my thoughts. Et voilà, mes petits amis . . . a long letter that you are going to find too long, perhaps, but I was desirous of writing to you. An idea comes to me: if you have the time Saturday or Sunday to come to Le Mans, a train toward eight o'clock in the morning brings you here at eleven. We will lunch together, and that evening a train takes you to Paris, arriving at nine o'clock.'* That makes seven hours on the train. *'Mais c'est peut-être grosse fatigue pour vous. Anyway, at need you may telegraph me at Arnage, Straus, Sarthe. Au revoir, au revoir, mes chéris, je vous embrasse de tout mon cœur et vous aime tendrement. . . . Madame Minou.'"*

He closed the window, and the cries from the school yard became remote.

"Chartres isn't a very big place," Barbara said thoughtfully. "And there is only one thing that people go there to see. She could probably have found us all right, if she had come. But anyway, I'm not going to Le Mans."

"The trains may not even be running," he said. "There is a railroad strike about to begin at any minute. We might get there and not be able to get back. Also, I never wanted to hear *Le Roi d'Ys*. I wanted to hear *Louise* and they aren't giving it this week. *Le Roi d'Ys* was entirely Mme Straus's idea."

"I can't bear it!" Barbara exclaimed. "It's so sad. *'Use my name all through the Opéra, and to everybody. . . .'*"

⚜ ⚜
⚜

THE BOOK on the prison work of the Dominican nuns did not arrive, and neither did Harold search out the office of M. Decerf and tell him they already had three tickets for *Le Roi d'Ys*. He could not believe that Mme Straus had written to the manager of the Paris Opéra, any more than he could believe that after a stay of three weeks in Arnage she was in charge of a charity bazaar in Le Mans; or that it is possible for it to rain on the sixteenth arrondissement of Paris and not on the eighth. As the gypsy fortuneteller could have told him, this was perhaps not wise. The only safe thing, if you have an ingenuous nature, is to believe everything that anybody says.

In spite of his constant concern that she dress warmly enough, Barbara caught a cold. They were both showing signs of a general tiredness, of the working out of the law of diminishing returns. There were still days when they enjoyed themselves as keenly as they had in the beginning, but the enjoyment was never quite complete; they enjoyed some things and not others; they couldn't any more throw themselves on each day as if it were a spear. Also, their appetite was beginning to fail. They found that once a day was all they could stand to eat in the little restaurant in the alley off the Place St. Sulpice. They bought bread and cheese and a bottle of wine, and ate lunch in their room, and at dinnertime were embarrassed by the welcome they received when they walked into the back room of the restaurant. Or they avoided going there at all.

Sometimes he dreamed in French. He found, at last, the complete correspondence of Flaubert. In a shop in the Place St.

Sulpice he saw a beautiful book of photographs of houses on the Ile St. Louis, but it cost twenty dollars and he did not buy it. Their American Express checkbook was very thin, and he had begun to worry about whether they were going to come out even.

Barbara saw a silk blouse in the window of a shop in the rue Royale, and they went inside, but she shook her head when the clerk told her the price. The clerk suggested that, since they were Americans, all they had to do was get their dollars changed on the black market and then the blouse would be less expensive, but Harold delivered a speech. "Madame," he said, "j'aime la France et je ne prends pas avantage du marché noir." The clerk shook hands with him and with tears in her eyes said: "Monsieur, il n'y a pas beaucoup." But she didn't reduce the price of the blouse.

Barbara's cold got worse, and she had to go to bed with it. Harold stopped at the desk and asked if her meals could be sent up to her until she was feeling better. The hotel no longer served meals, but M. le Patron and his wife ate in the empty dining room, and so he knew that what he was asking for was possible, though it meant making an exception. One of the ways of dividing the human race is between those people who are eager to make an exception and those who consider that nothing is more dangerous and wrong. M. le Patron brusquely refused.

Burning with anger, Harold started off to see what could be done in the neighborhood. Their restaurant was too far away; the food would be stone-cold by the time he got back with it; and so he tried a bistro that was just around the corner, in the rue Vaugirard, and the bartender sent him home with bread and cheese and a covered bowl of soup from the pot-au-feu. It was just the kind of food she had been longing for. After that, he ate in the bistro and then took her supper home to her. Shopping for fruit, he discovered a little hole-in-the-wall where the peaches were wrapped in cotton and where he and the proprietress and her grown daughter discussed seriously which pear madame should eat today and which she should save till tomorrow.

He kept calling the apartment in the rue Malène and there was never any answer. It was hard not to feel that there had been a concerted action, a conspiracy, and that the French, realizing that he and Barbara had got in, where foreigners are not supposed to be, had simply put their heads together and decided that the time had come to push them out. It was not true, of course, but that was what it felt like. And it wasn't wholly not true. Why, for example, didn't Alix write to them? She knew they were only going to be here eight days longer, and still no word came from her; no message of any kind. Was she going to let them go back to America without even saying good-by?

The next morning, as if someone at the bank were playing a joke on them, there was a letter, but it was from Berlin, not Brenodville. It was an old letter that had followed them all around Europe:

Dear Mr. Rhodes:

A few days before, we returned to Berlin, only our friend Hans got clear his journey to Switzerland at the consulate in Baden-Baden. And now I want to thank you and Mrs. Rhodes once more, also in the name of my wife and of my children. You can't imagine how they enjoyed the oranges and the chocolate and the fishes in oil and the bananes, etc; many of these things they never saw before. They begged me to send you their thanks and their greetings and a snapshot also "that the friendly uncle and the friendly aunt from America may see how we look." (I beg your pardon if the expression "aunt" in U.S.A. is less usual than in Germany for a friend of little children.)

In Paris I was glad that I could report you over the circumstances under which we are living and working. But I am afraid that we saw one side only of the problem. We came from a poor and exhausted country into a town that seemed to be rich and nearly untouched by the war. And personally we were in a rather painful situation. So it could happen that we grew more bitter and more pessimist than it is our kind.

We told you from the little food rations—but we did not speak from all the men and women who try to get a little harvest out of each square foot bottom round the houses or on the public places. We did not speak from the thousands who leave Berlin each week end trying to get food on the land, who are hanging on the footboards or on the buffers of the railway or wandering along the roads with potatoes or corn or fruit. We did not speak from all those who are working every day in spite of want of food or clothes or tools. And we did not speak from the most important fact, from all the women who supply their husbands and their children and know to make something out of a minimum of food and electricity and gas, and only a small part of all these women is accustomed to such manner of living by their youth.

To me it seems to be the greatest danger in Germany: on the one side the necessity to live under rather primitive conditions —on the other side the attempts of an ideology to make proletarians out of the whole people with the aim to prepare it for the rule of communisme. A people within such a great need is always in the danger to loose his character, to become unsteady. And the enticement from the other side is very dangerous.

And another point seems important to me: there are two forms of democracy in Germany, the one of the western powers, the other of communisme in the strange form of "Volksdemokratie." It is not necessary to speak about this second form, but also the first is not what we need. The western democracy may be good for the western countries. Also the German people wants to bear the whole responsibility for his government, but it is not prepared to do so. It is very dangerous to put it into a problem that it cannot solve. Our people needs some decades of political education (but it does not need instructors which try to feed it with their own ideas and ideologies) and in the meantime it ought to get a strong goverment of experts assisted by a parliament with consultative rights only. German political parties incline to grow dogmatical and intolerant and radical— even democratical parties—and it is necessary to diminish their influence in administration and legislative and, later on, specially in foreign affairs.

I am sure that my opinion is very different from the opinion of the most Germans but I don't believe in the miracle of the majority.

Dear Mr. Rhodes, I suppose you are smiling a little about my manner of torturing your language, but I am sure that you hear what I want to say and that you will not be inconvenienced by the outside appearance.

May I ask you for giving my respects to Mrs. Rhodes?

Would you allow me to write you then and now.

Always your faithfully
Stefan Doerffer.

"Let's see the picture of the children," Barbara said when he had finished reading the letter to her.

The children were about four and six. Both were blond and sturdy. The little girl looked like a doll, the boy reminded Harold of those fat Salzburgers whose proud stomachs preceded them and whose wives followed two steps behind, carrying the luggage. It was partly the little boy's costume—he had on what looked like a cheap version of Bavarian lederhosen—and partly his sullen expression, which might have been nothing more than the light the picture was taken by or a trick of the camera, but it made him look like a Storm Trooper in the small size. The children's feet were partly covered by a large square block of building stone. It could have been ruins or a neglected back yard. The little boy's hands made it clear that he was only a child and that there was no telling what kind of German he would be when he grew up.

"I don't feel like being their uncle," Harold said as he put the letter back in its envelope. "'A strong government of experts, assisted by a parliament with consultative rights only . . .' It's all beyond me. It depresses me."

"Why should it depress you?" Barbara said. "It's a truthful letter."

"But they haven't learned anything—anything at all. He feels sorry for the German women but not a word about the others, all over the world. Not a word about who started it. Not a word about the Jews."

"What can he say? They're dead. Maybe he doesn't speak about it because he can't bear to."

"He could say he was sorry."

"Maybe. But you aren't a Jew. What right have you to ask for or receive an apology in their name? And how do you know they would accept his apology if he said it? I wouldn't—not if it was my relatives that were sent to the gas chambers."

"I don't know," he said sadly. "I don't know anything. All I know is I'm tired, and I guess I'm ready to go home."

She looked at him, to see if he really meant it. He didn't. But she was ready to go home, and had been for some time. In Beaulieu her period was five days late. This disappointment she was not able to leave behind her in the South of France. She woke to it every morning, and it confronted her in the bathroom mirror when she washed her face. For his sake she concealed the weight on her heart and did not allow herself so much as a sigh. But more and more her pleasure was becoming second-hand, the reflection of his.

Chapter 18

Just when they had got used to the idea that they had been cast out, and had managed to accept it philosophically, they discovered that they were not cast out; there had been no change in the way that the French felt about them.

Sabine was the first to call. Harold asked about Alix, and Sabine said that they were back too—they had all come up from the country together.

And while he was out doing an errand, Alix called and asked them to tea on Monday.

"What did she sound like?" he asked.

"Herself," Barbara said.

"You didn't hear anything in her voice that might indicate she was hurt or anything?"

"No. She was just affectionate, as always."

"Perhaps we imagined it," he said. "It will be so nice to see them and the apartment again. Did she say Eugène would be there?"

"She said he wouldn't be there."

The next morning, Barbara heard him say: " 'My dear little friends, do not come to Le Mans,' " and called out from the bathroom, where she was brushing her teeth: "It's too far!"

"Nobody's going to Le Mans," he said, and doubled over with laughter.

"Then what are you talking about?"

"Mme Straus. She's coming after all. Just listen: '*Tuesday ...*
Mes petits amis chéris, Do not come to LeMans'—underlined—
'*It is I who will arrive in Paris Saturday evening, Gare Mont-*
parnasse, at six o'clock. I have arranged all in order to see
you . . ."

In the same mail, there was an invitation from Jean Allégret,
who had been in the country, and had just returned to Paris and
found their note, and was inviting them to have dinner with him
at his club on Friday.

"Do you want to?" Barbara asked dubiously.

"It might be interesting," Harold said.

His pajamas had split up the back and, later that morning, he
went out to buy a new pair. When he came back, he showed
them to her and said: "Look—they're made of parachute cloth."

"Not really?"

"So the clerk said. I guess they don't have anything else. Anyway, something wonderful happened. I asked him if they
weren't too large and he looked at me and said no, they were the
normal size. . . . In France *I'm* the normal size. *Not* football
players. The first time in my life anybody has ever said that.
. . . It's so beautiful out. No matter which direction you look.
The clerk was the normal size too. Everything in France is
normal. It doesn't seem possible that Tuesday morning we're
going to get on a train and— Except that maybe we won't. The
railway strike is supposed to start Monday or Tuesday."

"What will we do if there are no trains?"

"There probably will be," he said.

"Would you like to stay?"

"A few days longer, you mean?"

"No, for good."

"We can't," he said soberly. "There is no way that it is possible, or reasonable. And besides, they tried that, in the twenties,
and it didn't work. In the end they all had to come home."

He read in *La Semaine de Paris* the plays that were to be

performed at the Comédie Française and the Odéon, the movies, the concerts, for the first three days after they would be gone. Like a man sentenced to execution, he had a sudden stabbing vision of the world as it would be without him. The day after they left, there was to be a performance of *Louise* at the Comique.

And he was haunted by that book he felt he shouldn't buy—the book of photographs of the old houses on the Ile St. Louis. And by the Ile St. Louis itself. Every time he went across the river, there it was, in plain sight, just beyond the Ile de la Cité. He kept trying to get there, and instead he found himself going to the American Express, getting a haircut, cashing traveler's checks, standing at the counter at the Cunard Line. These errands all seemed to take more time than they would have at home, and time—time running out—was what he kept having to deal with.

It did not interest him to wonder if he could stay, if there was after all some way of arranging this, because he did not want to stay here as an observer, an outsider, an expatriate; he was too proud to do that. He wanted to possess the thing he loved. He wanted to be a Frenchman.

When he got home in the late afternoon, a group of school boys would be having choir practice out of doors under the trees in the school yard. There was no music teacher—only an older boy with a pitch pipe—and the singing that rose from the walled garden was so beautiful that it made him hold his head in his hands. This and other experiences like it (the one-ring circus on the outskirts of Florence; the big searchlight from the terrace of Winkler's Café picking out a baroque church, which they then ran through the streets to, and then moving on to a palace, and then to a fountain—all the churches and palaces and fountains of Salzburg, bathed in lavender-blue light; the grandiose Tiepolo drawn in white chalk on the pavement of the Via Venti-due Marzo in Venice by a sixteen-year-old boy out of another century, who began his work at eight in the morning and finished at four in the afternoon and was rewarded with a hatful of lira notes; arriving in Venice at midnight, leaving Pisa at six in the morning, taking an afternoon nap in Rome, eating ice cream under a canvas awning by the Lake of Geneva during a downpour; the view from the Campanile at Siena in full sunshine—a medieval city constructed on the plan of a rose; the little restaurant on a jetty in San Remo, where they ate dinner peering out through the rain at the masts of fishing boats; the carnival in Tours, the Grand Entertainment in Beaulieu, dinner at Iznard, dinner at Doney's, the dinner with Sabine at Le Vert Gallant, just before they left for Switzerland, with the river only a few yards from their table, and with their vision concentrated by the candle flame until they saw only their own three faces, talking about what they believed, what they thought, what they felt—so intently that they did not know exactly when it got dark or even at what point the tables all around them were taken by other diners. And so on, and so on) —these ecstatic memories were, he thought, what made the lines in his face, and why he had lost so much weight. He felt that he was slowly being diminished by the succession of experiences that he had responded to with his whole heart and that seemed to represent something that belonged to him, and that he had not had, and, not having, had been starved for all his life, without knowing it. He was being diminished as people are always diminished who are racked with love, and that it was for a place and not a person was immaterial.

⚜ ⚜
⚜

JEAN ALLÉGRET'S CLUB was in a little narrow street behind the Chamber of Deputies, and they did not allow enough time to get there from their hotel, and had trouble finding it, and when they walked into the courtyard, half an hour late, Jean Allégret was standing on the steps of the building. They felt that he felt that in not being punctual they had been guilty of rudeness, and so the evening began stiffly. Through dinner, they talked about Austria and Italy, and he talked about his farm—about how the people he was living with—the two old gardeners who had been in the family for fifty years—were sick, and would have to go, since they could not help him any longer, and he did not know who he would find to do his cooking, for he could not do it himself; and about the water system, which would be running at the end of the month; and about his efforts to bring a few improvements to his little village. There was no doctor or chemist nearer than four miles, and he had decided that there must be a dispensary. With the help of the men and boys of the place, he had fixed up an old uninhabited house, and got two nuns to come there, and provided them with supplies. The money they needed for this had been raised through benefits—plays given by boys and girls, bicycle races, that sort of thing; and a few days ago they had celebrated the hundredth case treated there. In his spare time he had been drawing, doing sketches of rabbits, pheasants, wild ducks, stags, wild boars, or of people working in the fields or going to market. Someday, perhaps, he would publish some of them in a book.

The club was an army-officer's club, and he had done murals for it, which he showed them after dinner. Looking at the people around them, they thought: This is not at all the sort of place Americans usually see. . . . Neither was it very interesting. Then they sat down again and, over a glass of brandy, went on talking. But something was missing from the conversation. There were moments when they had to work to make it go. Why does it have to go, Harold wondered. *Because it went before* was the answer. His eyes came to rest on one figure after another at the nearby tables—the neat blond mustache, the trim military carriage, the look of cold pride.

He heard Barbara saying: "They gave Gluck's *Orpheus* in the Riding Academy, and there was a wonderful moment. The canvas roof was rolled back without our knowing it, and as Or-

pheus emerged from the Underworld we saw the lights of Salzburg. . . ."

Jean Allégret nodded politely, and Harold thought: Has she
left out something? The music, of course. The most important
part of all.

"*Orpheus* is a beautiful opera," he said, but Jean Allégret's
expression did not change.

There is something he's not saying, Harold thought, and that's
why the evening has gone this way. Instead of listening, he
watched Jean Allégret's face. It told him nothing, and he decided that, as so often happened, he was imagining things that
did not really exist.

"In the mountains," Jean Allégret was saying, "the political
struggle and all the unsolved problems of modern life belong to
a tiny lost spot over there in the evening fog, miles away in the
bottom of the valley . . . the last village. We slept in any deserted hut or rolled up in our blankets in a hole between rocks.
Our only concern was the direction of the winds, the colors of
the sunset, the fog climbing from the valley, the bucks always
on the top of the following peak . . ."

"My older brother loved to hunt," Harold said.

Jean Allégret turned and looked at him with interest.

"He took me rabbit hunting with him when I was about
eight years old. It was winter, and very cold, and there was deep
snow on the ground. I still remember it vividly. We got up at
five o'clock in the morning, to go hunting, and he missed three
rabbits in a row. I think it flustered him, having me there
watching him. And he swore. And then we went home."

It seemed hardly worth putting beside a shooting expedition
in the Pyrenees, but Harold, too, was holding something back,
and it was: *I never had a gun. I never wanted one. I always
thought I couldn't bear to kill anything. But once when we were
staying in the country—this was after Barbara and I were married—there was a rabbit in the garden every day, and it was
doing a lot of damage, and I killed it with a borrowed shotgun,*

335

and I didn't feel anything. People are so often mistaken about themselves. . . .

Though they were close enough to have reached out and touched each other (and it would perhaps have been better if they had) the broad Atlantic Ocean lay between them. That first conversation, under the full moon, had been so personal and direct that it left no way open for increasing intimacy, and so they had reverted; they had become an aristocratic Frenchman and an American tourist.

Outside on the steps of the building, they thanked Jean Allégret for a very pleasant evening, and shook hands, and at the last possible moment the brandy brushed Harold's hesitations aside and spoke for him: "There were no brown-eyed people in Austria."

"Why not?" Jean Allégret said.

"You know why not," Harold said solemnly.

"Yes, I'm afraid I do," Jean Allégret said, after a moment.

"I kept looking for them everywhere. All dead. No brown-eyed people left. Terrible!" And then: "It was all right before, and now it isn't. . . . Home, I'm talking about . . . not Austria. I didn't know about any other place. Or any other kind of people. I didn't have to make comparisons. I will never be intact again."

"In the modern world," Jean Allégret said gently, "nobody is intact. It is only an illusion. When you are home, you will forget about what it is like here. And be happy, as you were before."

"No I won't!"

"Well, you will be busy, anyway," Jean Allégret said, looking into Harold's eyes, the same person, suddenly, that he had been on that moon-flooded terrace in the Touraine. Having reached each other at last, they shook hands once more, and Jean Allégret said: "If you come back to France one day, come and spend a few days with me."

I: *Leo and Virgo*

WITH SABINE they did not feel any constraint. She came to their hotel on Saturday evening, and they took her to the restaurant in the alley off the Place St. Sulpice. She had a job, she told them. She was going to work for an elderly man who published lithographic reproductions of paintings and some art books. The salary was a little less than she had been earning at *La Femme Elégante,* but it was work that she would enjoy doing, she liked the man she would be working for, and perhaps it might lead to something better, in time. The job was to start on the first of November, and she had come up to Paris a few days early.

She was wearing the same white silk blouse and straight skirt that she invariably wore. Doesn't she have any other clothes, Harold wondered. But it turned out to be one of those things men don't understand; the white silk blouse was beautifully tailored, Barbara said later, and right for any occasion.

There were no awkward silences, because they never ran out of things to say. The few things Sabine told them about herself were only a beginning of all there was to tell, and each time they were with her they felt they knew her a little better. But there was something elusive about her. The silvery voice that was just right for telling stories and the faintly mysterious smile, though charming in themselves, were also barriers. It is possible to see the color of flowers by moonlight, but you can never quite read a book.

While Pierre was changing the plates, Harold said suddenly: "Would you like to hear a ghost story? . . . In Marseilles, all the hotels were full, because of a big fair of some kind, and we went to one after another, and finally one that the taxi driver had never heard of, and he didn't even think it was a hotel, but it was listed in the Michelin, so I made him stop there and I got out and went inside. There was no hotel sign, and when I opened the door and walked in off the street, there wasn't any lobby either. Nothing but a spiral stairway. I decided the lobby must be one flight up. On the second floor there was a landing, but no doors led from it. So I went on, and while I was climbing the stairs I heard footsteps."

"This is not a true story?" Sabine said. "You are inventing it just to please me?"

"No, no, it all happened. . . . Someone was climbing the stairs ahead of me. I called out and there was no answer. I stood still and listened. The footsteps continued, and I felt the hair rise on the back of my neck. I went a little farther, and when there were still no doors, I stopped again. This time there wasn't any sound. My heart was pounding. I could feel somebody up there waiting for me to climb the last few steps. I turned and ran all the way down the stairs and burst through the doorway into the open air. . . . What was it, do you think? Was it really a hotel?"

"I think it was a nightmare," Sabine said.

"But I was wide awake."

"One is, sometimes," she said, and he thought of the drama that had happened in her family. He had a feeling that if he leaned forward at that moment and asked: "What *did* happen?" she would tell them. But the next course arrived, and put an end to the possibility.

Sabine said to Barbara: "Where did you find your little heart?"

The little heart was of crystal, bound with a thin band of gold, and Barbara had noticed it in the window of an antique shop in Toulon, during the noon bus stop. "It wasn't very expensive," she said. "Do you think it's a child's locket? Do you think I shouldn't wear it?"

"No, it's charming," Sabine said. "And perfectly all right to wear."

"Do you remember," Barbara said, "that little diamond heart that Mme Straus always wore?"

They began to talk about the gloves and scarves and purses in the window of Hermès, and he picked up his fork and started eating.

After dinner they walked through the square and back to the

hotel, and sat on the big bed, leaning against the headboard or the footboard, with their legs tucked under them, talking, until eleven thirty. He knew that Sabine liked Barbara, and had always liked her, but as he was walking her to the Métro station he realized with surprise that she liked him too. She could not say so, directly and simply, as Alix said such things; it came out, instead, in her voice, in the way she listened to his account of their last days in Paris, and how queer he felt about going home. It was something he had been refusing to think about, but apparently he had been carrying the full weight of it around, because now that he had spoken to somebody about it, he felt lighter. He had the feeling that, no matter what he told her, she would get it right; she wouldn't go off with a totally wrong idea of what he was feeling or thinking.

He was going to take her all the way to her door but she wouldn't let him. At the entrance to the Métro, they stopped and he started to say good-by, under a street lamp, and she said: "I will be at my aunt's house on Monday."

"Oh, that's good," he exclaimed. "Then I won't say good-by. . . . I keep trying to get to the Ile St. Louis. It's as if my life depended on it. As if I *must* see it. And every day something keeps me from going there. What is it like?"

"From the Ile St. Louis there is a beautiful view of the back of Notre Dame," she said. "Voltaire lived there for a while. So did Bossuet. And Théophile Gautier, and Baudelaire, and Daumier. In the Ile St. Louis you feel the past around you, more than anywhere else in Paris. The houses are very old, and the streets are so silent. Perhaps you will go there tomorrow. . . ."

He suggested to Mme Straus, over the telephone on Sunday morning, that she take a taxi directly to their hotel, and she said

Mon dieu, she would be taking the bus, and that they should meet her at one o'clock in front of the church of St. Germain-des-Prés, which was only five minutes' walk from where they were staying.

Barbara was still dressing when the time came to start out to meet her, and since Mme Straus was usually prompt and they did not want to keep her waiting outside on a damp, raw day, he went on ahead. As he crossed the boulevard St. Germain, he saw standing in front of the church a figure that could have been Mme Straus; he wasn't sure until he had reached the sidewalk that it wasn't. In the two months since they had seen her, her face had grown dim in his mind. The old woman at the foot of the church steps was poorly dressed, and when he got closer to her, he saw she had a cigar box in her hand. The purpose of the cigar box became clear when people began to pour out of the church at the conclusion of the service. Harold stood in a doorway where he could keep an eye on the buses arriving from Auteuil and from across the river. One bus after another arrived, stopped, people got off and other people got on, but still no Mme Straus.

The beggarwoman was also not having much luck. About one person in fifty, he calculated. He found himself judging the people who came out of the church solely in relation to her. Those who gave her something were nice, were good, were kind. Those who ignored her outstretched box, or were annoyed, or raised their eyebrows, or just didn't see her, he disliked. He watched a young woman who was helping an older woman down the steps—mother and daughter, they must be. So like Alix, he thought. The young woman didn't notice the box at first, and then when she did see it, she immediately smiled at the old woman, stopped, opened her purse—all in such a way that there could be no questioning her sincerity and goodness of heart. As for the others, perhaps they had been stopped by too many beggars, or knew the old woman was a fraud, or just didn't have ten francs to spare.

I: *Leo and Virgo*

He kept expecting the old woman to come over to him, and she did finally. She came over and spoke to him—a rushing speech full of bitterness and sly derision at the churchgoers—that much was clear—though most of it he could not understand. He looked at her and listened, and smiled, and didn't say anything, thinking that she must know by his clothes that he was an American, and waiting for her to present the box. She didn't, and so he didn't put his hand in his pocket and draw out his folded French money. Something more personal was happening between them. Either he was serving her well enough by listening so intently to what she said, or else she recognized in him a character somehow on the same footing with her—a beggar holding out his hand for something if not for money, a fraud, a professional cheat of some kind, at odds with society and living off it, a blackmailer, a thief—somebody the police are interested in, or if not the police then the charity organizations. . . . A poor blind tourist, that's what he was.

While he was listening, his eyes recorded the arrival of Mme Straus-Muguet. She stepped down to the cobblestones from the back platform of a bus, and as he went toward her, looking at her clothes—her fur piece, her jaunty hat with a feather, her lorgnette swinging by its black ribbon—he wondered how he could, even at a distance, have mistaken the old beggar woman with the cigar box and a grievance against society for their faithful, indomitable, confusing friend.

Her voice, her greeting, her enthusiasm, the pressure on his arm were all affectionate and unchanged. She could not bear to leave the vicinity of such a famous church, the oldest church in Paris, without going inside for a moment. They stood in the hushed empty interior, looking down the nave at the altar and the stained-glass windows, and then they came out again. As they were crossing the street, she said that she knew the quarter well. Her sister had an apartment in the boulevard Raspail, and as a child she had lived in the rue Madame, a block from their hotel.

"But you are thin!" she exclaimed.

"Too much aesthetic excitement," he said jokingly, and she said: "You must eat more!"

Barbara was waiting for them in the rue des Canettes. Mme Straus kissed her, admired Barbara's new hat, and then, turning, perceived that she knew the restaurant; she had dined here before, with satisfaction. As they walked in, monsieur and madame bowed and smiled respectfully at Mme Straus and then approvingly at Harold and Barbara for having at last got themselves a sponsor. Pierre led them to their regular table, and recommended the pâté en croûte. Mme Straus ordered potage instead. The restaurant was unusually crowded, and the waiters were very busy. Though Barbara had explained to Mme Straus that Pierre was their friend, she called "Garçon!" loudly. And when he left what he was doing and came over to their table, she complained because the pommes de terre frites weren't hot. He hurried them away and came back with more that had just been taken from the spider. She continued to be condescending to him, but as if she were acting for Harold and Barbara—as if this were one more lesson they ought to learn. He kept his temper but something passed between them, an exchange of irritable glances and cutting phrases that the Americans could not follow and that made them uneasy. They felt left out. Pierre and Mme Straus were like two members of the same family who know each other's sore spots and can't resist aggravating them. As Pierre hurried off to bring the coffee filters, Mme Straus assured them that their friend was an intelligent boy. And a few minutes later, when Harold got up and went into the front room to pay the check, Pierre stopped, on his way past, and remarked gravely (but kindly, as if what he was about to say was dictated solely by concern for them): "Your guest—that old lady—is not what she pretends to be. The girl you brought yesterday—she's the real thing."

After lunch they walked in the square, and Mme Straus pointed out that the fountain, which they had never really looked at before, was in commemoration of Bossuet, Fénelon,

Massillon, and Fléchier—the four great bishops who should have been but were not made cardinals. "How they must have hated each other!" she exclaimed merrily.

Barbara took a snapshot of Harold and Mme Straus standing in front of the fountain, and then they walked to their hotel. She approved of their room and of the view, and asked how much they paid. She considered seriously the possibility of taking a room here. She was in mortal terror lest the nuns raise the price of her small chamber among the roses, in which case she could no longer afford to stay there.

They left the hotel and wandered up the rue Vaugirard to the Luxembourg Gardens, and walked up and down looking at the flower beds, the people, the Medici fountain, the balloon man, the children sailing their boats in the shallow basin. A gas-filled balloon escaped, and they followed it with their eyes. Since we last saw her, Harold thought, there has been a change—if not in her then in her circumstances.

Mme Straus kept looking at her wrist watch, and at five o'clock she hurried them out of the Gardens and up the street to a tea shop, where she had arranged for her grandson Edouard to meet them. Edouard was seventeen and in school; he was studying to be an engineer, Mme Straus said, and he had only one desire—to come to America.

After so big a lunch, they had no appetite. Barbara crumbled but did not eat her cupcake. Harold slowly got his tea and three cakes down. Edouard did not appear. Mme Straus sat with her back to the wall and glanced frequently at the doorway. Conversation died a dull death. There was no one at the surrounding tables, and the air was lifeless. The tea made them feel too warm. Done in by so much walking and talking, or by Edouard's failure to show up for the tea party, Mme Straus reached out for her special talent, and for the first time in their experience it was not there. She sat, silent and apparently distracted by private thoughts. She roused herself and said how disappointed Edouard would be, not to make their acquaintance. Something must have happened, of a serious nature; nothing else would account for his absence. And a few minutes later she considered the possibility that he had gone to the cinema with friends. Harold found himself wondering whether it is possible to read the mind of someone who is thinking in a language you don't understand. What he was thinking, and did not want Mme Straus to guess that he was thinking, was: Does Edouard exist? And if there really is an Edouard, does he regard his grandmother with the same impatience and undisguised contempt as the celebrated actress, her friend, to whom she is so devoted?

Mme Straus called for the check, and either misread the amount or absent-mindedly failed to put down enough to pay for the tea and cakes and *service*. The waitress pointed out the mistake, and while it was being rectified, Harold looked the other way, for fear he would see more than Mme Straus intended them to see.

They parted from her at dusk. She announced that she was coming to the boat train on Tuesday, to see them off. As they stood on a corner of the boulevard St. Germain, waiting for the bus, she pointed out the Cluny Museum to them, and was shocked that they hadn't heard of it.

The bus came and she got on it and went up the curving steps. Waving to them from the top of the bus, she was swept away.

"Do you think he forgot?" Barbara asked as they started on down the street.

"I don't even think he exists," Harold said. "But does *she*, is the question. You don't think she is something we made up?"

"No, she exists."

They crossed over, so that she could look in the window of a shoe shop.

"So courageous," he said. "Always taking life at the flood. . . . But what is she going to do—Who or what can she turn to, now that the flood has become a trickle?"

I: *Leo and Virgo*

THE LAST DAY was very strange. He had hoped that there would be time to go to the Ile St. Louis in the morning, and instead he found himself on the top of a bus going down the rue Bonaparte with another suitcase to leave at the steamship office. The sun was shining, the air was cool, and there was a kind of brilliance over everything. The bus turned left and then right and went over the Pont du Carrousel, and as he looked up and down the river, the sadness that he had managed to hold at arm's length for the last four days took possession of him.

The bus went through the south gate of the Louvre and out into the sunshine again and stopped to take on passengers. The whole of the heart of Paris lay before him—the palace, the geometrical flower beds, the long perspective down the gardens, which had been green when he came and were now autumn-colored, the people walking or bicycling, the triumphal arch, the green statues, the white gravel, the grass, the clouds coming over from the Left Bank in a procession. Looking at it now, so hard that it made his eyes burn and ache, he knew in his heart that what he loved was here, and only for the people who lived here; it wasn't anywhere else. *I cannot leave!* he cried out silently to the old buildings and the brightness in the air, to the yellow leaves on the trees, and to the shine that was over everything. *I cannot bear it that all this will be here and I will not be. . . . I might as well die. . . .*

⚜ ⚜
⚜

AT NOON they turned into the rue des Canettes for the last time. When Harold had finished ordering, he made a little farewell speech to Pierre and, after the waiter had gone off to the kitchen, thought: How foolish of me. . . . What does he care whether we love France or not? . . . But then, though they had asked for Perrier water, Pierre brought three wine glasses and a bottle of Mâcon rouge. First he assured them that the wine

345

would not be on their bill, and then he opened the bottle ceremoniously, filled their two glasses, and poured a little wine into his. They raised their glasses and drank to each other, and to the voyage, and to the future of France. Pierre went on about his work, but from time to time he returned, with their next course or merely to stand a moment talking to them. They dallied over lunch; they had a second and then a third cup of coffee. They were the last clients to leave the restaurant, and the wine had made them half drunk, as usual. They shook hands with Pierre and said good-by. They stopped to shake hands with the other waiter, Louis, and again, in the front room with Monsieur and Madame, who wished them bon voyage. As they stepped out into the street, they heard someone calling to them and turned around. It was Pierre. He had shed his waiter's coat and he drew them into the restaurant across the street, to have a cognac with him. Then they had another round, on Harold, and before he and Barbara could get away, Louis joined them, as jealous as a younger brother, insisting that they have a cognac with him. Harold said no, saw the look of hurt on both men's faces, and said: "Why not?"

Pierre went off, and came back a few minutes later with his wife, who worked in a nearby department store. The two women talked to each other, in English. They had one last round, and shook hands, and said good-by, and the Americans promised to come back soon.

They got into a taxi and went to the bank. With the floor tilting dangerously under him, Harold stood in line and grinned foolishly at the teller who counted out his money.

To clear their heads, they rode to the Place Redouté on the top of a bus, and they were able to walk straight by the time they stopped to shake hands with Mme Emile, on their way into the building.

"Are you all right?" Barbara asked as they stepped into the elevator.

"Yes. How about you?"

"I'm all right," she said. "But we probably smell to high heaven of all that we've been drinking."

"It can't be helped," he said, and pressed the button.

Alix was just the same, and they were very happy to see her, but the apartment was different. With the shutters thrown back in the drawing room, it was much lighter and brighter and more cheerful.

Shortly after they arrived, Mme Viénot came in, with Sabine, and took possession of the conversation. While she sat listening, Barbara had a question uppermost in her mind, and it was why didn't Mme Viénot or Alix or Mme Cestre mention the soap? Didn't it ever arrive? Or weren't they as pleased with it as she had thought they would be?

Harold was telling how they couldn't find the Simone Martinis in Siena and finally gave up and climbed the bell tower of the very building the paintings were in, without knowing it. When he finishes I'll ask them, she thought, but she didn't because by that time she had another worry on her mind: what if Françoise should show Alix the stockings she had given her, which were the same kind that Barbara had presented to Alix and Mme Cestre and Mme Viénot in the country, and that they had been so pleased with. She wished now the stockings had been of a better quality. She had economized on them, but she could not explain this without bringing in the fact that they were to give to the chambermaids in hotels in place of a tip.

"You must excuse me," Alix said. "I am going to get the tea things."

"Can I help?" Barbara asked, but Alix did not hear her, and so she sat back in her chair. The thing she had hoped was that she would have one last look at the kitchen. It was very queer, having to act like a guest in a place where they were so much at home. Neither Alix nor Mme Cestre made any reference to the fact that she and Harold had spent ten days in this apartment. One would almost have thought that they didn't know it. Or that it hadn't really happened.

Speaking very distinctly, Harold said to Mme Cestre: "In Italy I saw with my own eyes how fast the earth is turning. We went to hear *Traviata*. It was out of doors—it was in the Baths of Caracalla—and during the second act the moon came up so fast that it was almost alarming to watch. Within five minutes from the time it appeared above the ruins it was high up in the sky."

"You saw St. Peter's? And the Vatican?" Mme Viénot asked.

Right after she had finished her tea, she rose and shook hands with her sister, and then with Barbara and Harold. In the hall she presented her cheek to Alix to be kissed, and said: "Good-by, my dear. I'll call you tomorrow afternoon, before I leave for the country. . . . I won't say good-by now, M. Rhodes. I am seeing someone off on the boat train tomorrow—a cousin who is going to America on the *Mauretania* with you."

"You think the boat train will be running?" he asked.

"For your sake, I hope it is," Mme Viénot said. "You must be quite anxious."

"I have a present for you," Sabine said as she was shaking hands with them. "I am making you a drawing, but it isn't quite finished."

"We'd love to have one of your drawings," Barbara said.

"Maman will bring it to the train tomorrow."

When she and Mme Viénot had left, the others sat down again, and the Americans waited until a polite interval had passed before they too got up to go.

Mme Cestre told them that she had been at Le Bourget when Lindbergh's plane appeared out of the sky.

"You were in that vast crowd?" Harold said.

"Yes. It was very thrilling," she said. "I will never forget it. I was quite close to him as they carried him from the field."

Harold thought he heard someone moving around in the study, and looked at Alix, to see if she too had heard it. She said: "I also have a present for you." She opened a door of the secretary and took out a small flat package wrapped in tissue paper and tied with a white ribbon. This present gave Barbara a chance to ask about the soap.

"I should have thanked you," Alix said. "Oh dear, you will think we are not very grateful. We thought it might be from you. But there are also some other people, cousins who are now traveling in America, who could have sent it, and so I was afraid to speak about it. . . . Mummy, you were right. It was Barbara —that is, it was Barbara's mother who sent us the beautiful package of soap!"

On their way out of the building, they shook hands one last time with Mme Emile, who wished them bon voyage, and when they were outside in the street, Barbara opened the little package. It was a book—a charming little edition of Flaubert's *Un Coeur Simple* with hand-colored illustrations. On the flyleaf, Alix had written their names and her name and the date and the words: "Really with all my love."

"Wasn't that nice of her," Barbara said. And then, as they were crossing the square: "What about dinner?"

"Are you hungry?" he asked.

She shook her head. "There was somebody in the study."

"I know," he said. "Eugène."

"You think?"

"Who else."

"Françoise, maybe."

"What would she be doing in there?"

"I don't know. Do you feel like walking?" she asked.

"All right. . . . He gave me four Swiss francs, to buy sugar for him in Switzerland. I didn't do it."

"Why not?"

"It would have been a lot of trouble, and it turned out that we didn't have much time. Also, I didn't feel like doing it."

"Do you still have the money?" she asked.

"Yes. It's not very much. About a dollar. I guess we can forget about it."

They turned and took one last look at the granite monument.

"Do you think there was something going on that we didn't know about?" he said.

"Like what?"

"That's just it, I have no idea what."

"If you mean the 'drama' that—"

"I don't mean the 'drama.' That was two or three years ago. I mean right now, this summer."

"There would be no reason for them to tell us if there was," she said thoughtfully.

"No," he agreed.

"You think they're all right? You don't think they're in any kind of serious trouble, all of them?"

"Maybe not all of them. Maybe just Alix and Eugène. It would explain a lot of things. The way he was with us. And why they stayed in the country so long. I don't suppose we'll ever know what it was."

"Then you think there was something?"

"Yes," he said.

"So do I."

"Even when we thought we were on the inside," he said, "we weren't really. Inside, outside, it's nothing but a state of mind, I guess. . . . Except that if you love people, you can't help wanting to—"

"Alix is having another baby."

He took her hand as they walked along but said nothing. He was not sure at this moment what her feelings were, and he did not want to say something that would make her cry in the street.

They skipped dinner entirely and instead took the Métro halfway across Paris to a movie theater that was showing *Le Diable au Corps*. Harold wanted to see it, and they had missed it when they were here in the summer, and it had not been showing anywhere since they got back. In America it would be cut.

They were half an hour early, and walked up and down, rather than go in and sit in an empty theater. Over the ticket booth there was an electric bell that rang insistently and continuously; the whole street was filled with the sound. They looked at all the shop windows on both sides of the street. He glanced at his wrist watch. It was still twenty minutes before it would be time to go inside, and at the thought of twenty minutes more of that dreadful ringing, and then the hocus-pocus and the delay that always went on in French movie theaters, and people passing through the aisles selling candy, while they waited and waited for the picture to begin, he suddenly stopped, swallowed hard, and, taking Barbara's arm, said: "Let's go home. I can't stand that sound. . . . And even if we do wait, I won't be able to enjoy the movie. I've had all I can manage. I'm through. I can't take in any more."

⚜ ⚜
⚜

THEY ARRIVED at the Gare St. Lazare, with their hand luggage, an hour early. The boat train was running. It was due to leave at eleven ten, and they would get to Cherbourg about five. They walked down the platform, looking for their carriage and compartment, and found it. Barbara waited in the train, while Harold walked up and down outside. Magazine and fruit venders had come to see them off, and a flower girl whose pushcart was covered with bouquets of violets, but there was no sign of Mme Straus. Minute after minute passed. The platform grew crowded. There was a sense of growing excitement. Harold wandered in and out among the porters and the passengers, who, standing in little groups along the track, were nearly all Americans. For the first time in four months it didn't require any effort on his part to overhear scraps of conversation. He didn't like what he heard. The voices of his compatriots were loud, and what they said seemed silly beyond endurance. It was like having home thrown at him.

At three minutes of eleven, he gave up all hope of finding Mme Straus in the crowd that was milling around on the plat-

form and started back to their coach, telling himself that it didn't
matter that she had failed to come. It wasn't so much that she
was insincere as that she loved to arouse expectations it wasn't
always convenient or even possible to satisfy, when the time
came. . . . Only it did matter, he thought, still searching for
her among the faces. Now that they were leaving, he wanted
some one person out of a whole country that they had loved on
first sight and never stopped loving—he wanted somebody to be
aware of the fact that they were leaving, and come to say
good-by.

At the steps of their carriage he took one last look around and
saw her, talking agitatedly to one of the train guards. He was
close enough that he could hear her asking the guard to point
out the carriage of M. and Mme Rhodes. The guard shrugged.
Harold went up to her and took hold of her elbow, and she
cried: "Ah, chéri!" and kissed him.

She had been delayed. She thought that she would never find
them in the crowd.

Barbara saw Mme Straus from the train window and came out
onto the platform. Mme Straus kissed her and then presented her
with a farewell gift, a pasteboard box containing palmiers.
"They're to eat on the train," she said.

Edouard's mother had been taken ill on Sunday afternoon
and he couldn't leave her. He was sorry to have missed them.

She wanted to see their compartment, so they mounted the
steps and went down the corridor and showed her their reserved
seats and their luggage, safely stowed away on the overhead
rack.

"By the window," she said approvingly. "Now that I have it
firmly in mind, I can go with you." She squeezed their hands in
both of hers.

They went outside again and stood talking together on the
platform. Mme Viénot appeared out of the crowd, with a bou-
tonniere for Barbara. "From the garden at Beaumesnil," she
said. She and Mme Straus greeted each other with the comic

cordiality of two women who understand the full extent of their mutual dislike and are not concerned about it. Then, turning to Barbara and Harold, she said: "Sabine had something that she wanted me to bring you—a drawing. But she didn't get it finished in time. She said to tell you that she would be mailing it to you. I saw it. It is quite charming. It is of the old houses on the Ile St. Louis. . . . Au revoir, my dears. Have a good trip home."

She went off to rejoin her cousin.

The train guards called out a warning, and Mme Straus embraced them both one last time and urged them back on the train. When they sat down, she was at the window, dabbing her eyes with a tiny white handkerchief. They tried to carry on a conversation in pantomime.

She said something but they couldn't hear what it was. Harold said something back and she shook her head, to show that she didn't understand. They got up and went down the corridor to the end of the car. The door was still open. Mme Straus was there waiting, with the tears running down her cheeks. They leaned down and touched her hands, as the train began to move. For reasons that there was now no chance of their knowing, she clung to them, hurrying along beside the slowly moving train, waving to them, calling good-by. When she could no longer find them among the other heads and waving arms they could see her, still waving her crumpled handkerchief, old, forsaken, left in her own sad city, where the people she knew did not know her, and her stories were not believed even when they were true.

Part II

SOME EXPLANATIONS

Chapter 19

I s THAT ALL?

Yes, that's all.

But what about the mysteries?

You mean the "drama" that Mme Viénot didn't tell Harold Rhodes about?

And where M. Viénot was.

Oh, that.

And why Hector Gagny didn't go up to Paris with the Americans. And why Alix didn't say good-by to them at the station. And why the actress was so harsh with poor Mme Straus-Muguet, when they went backstage. And why that woman who kept the fruit and vegetable shop—Mme Michot—was so curious about what was going on at the château.

I don't know that any of those things very much matters. They are details. You don't enjoy drawing your own conclusions about them?

Yes, but then I like to know if the conclusions I have come to are the right ones.

How can they not be when everything that happens happens for so many different reasons? But if you really want to know why something happened, if explanations are what you care about, it is usually possible to come up with one. If necessary, it can be fabricated. Hector Gagny didn't go up to Paris on Bastille

Day because Mme Carrère invited him to go driving with them, and he was perfectly happy to put off his departure until the next day. And the reason that Mme Michot was so curious is that her only daughter was married and had left home, and M. Michot had left home, too, years before, in a crowded box car bound for the German border, and there had been no word from him since. It is only natural that, having to live with an unanswered question of this kind, she should occupy her mind with other questions instead. . . . But if you concentrate on details, you lose sight of the whole. The Americans fell in love with France, the way Americans are always doing, and they had the experience of knowing some French people but not knowing them very well. They didn't speak French, which made it difficult, and they were paying guests, and the situation of the paying guest is peculiar. It has in it something of the nature of an occupation by force. Once they were home, they quickly forgot a good many of the people they met abroad and the places they stayed in, but this experience with a French family, and the château, and the apartment in Paris, they couldn't forget. Hearing the blast that departing liners give as they turn in the Hudson River, Harold Rhodes raised his head and listened for a repetition of the sound. For those few seconds his face was deeply melancholy. And he took a real hatred—briefly—to an old and likable friend whose work made it possible for him to live in Paris. Neither of these things needs explaining. As for those that do, when you explain away a mystery, all you do is make room for another.

Even so. If you don't mind.

No, I don't mind. It's just a question of where to begin.

Begin with the drama.

Which one?

Were there two?

There was a drama that occurred several years before the Americans came to stay at the château, and there was another, several years after. One was a tragedy, the other was a farce.

They don't belong together, except as everything that happens to somebody, or to a single family, belongs together. In that case, though, there is no question of why anything happened, but only what happened, and what happened then, and what happened after that—all of it worth looking at, as a moral and a visual spectacle.

Well, what happened to the money, then?

That's the first drama. You're sure you want to hear about it? . . . "Somebody will tell us," Harold said, and sure enough somebody did. A cousin turned up, in New York, and called Mrs. Ireland, who invited her to lunch. She was the same age as Sabine and Alix, but a rather plain girl, and talkative. And what she talked about was the sudden change in the situation of the family at Beaumesnil. She said that shortly after the war ended, M. Viénot sold all the securities that Mme Bonenfant had been left by her husband, who was a very rich man, and bought shares in a Peruvian gold mine. The stocks and bonds he disposed of were sound, and the gold mine proved to be a swindle.

Then he was a crook?

It may have been nothing more than a mistake in judgment. . . . The cousin said that he himself profited by the transaction, but then she may not have got the facts straight. People seldom do.

But how could he have profited by reducing his wife's family from affluence to genteel poverty? It doesn't make any sense.

No, it doesn't, does it? Neither did his explanations. So Mme Viénot left him and went to live with her mother. But quite recently Barbara had a letter from Sabine in which she said that her mother and father were living in Oran, and Beaumesnil was closed. So they must have gone back together again.

The day young George Ireland arrived to spend the summer, M. Viénot turned up at the château, in an Italian sports car, with a blonde on the seat beside him. She was young, George said. And pretty. They were invited to stay for lunch, and they did, and drove back to Paris that night.

How extraordinary.

After which Mme Viénot communicated with him only through her lawyer, but Sabine continued to see her father, and so did her sister. The family could only suppose that his reason had been affected, what he did was so out of character, so unlike the man he had always been. And since Mme Bonenfant had always loved him like a son, she particularly clung to this explanation of his disastrous behavior. But there were certain signs they ought to have paid attention to. He had begun to wear less conservative clothes. He drove his car recklessly, was inattentive and irritable, sighed in his sleep, and showed a preference for the company of young people. He had even ceased to look like the man he used to be. These changes were gradual, of course, and they saw him with the eyes of habit.

So much for the tragedy. The second drama, the farce, began when two men appeared at the door one day and asked to speak to Mme Viénot. They said that they had heard in the village that she took guests and they wanted to stay at the château. Mme Viénot said that surely the person who told them this also told them that she only took guests who came to her with a proper introduction. They said they'd be back in an hour with a proper introduction and Mme Viénot said that she was sorry they had had this long walk for nothing, and shut the door on them. After lunch, at the moment when Thérèse should have appeared in the drawing room with the coffee tray, she appeared without the coffee tray, and informed Mme Viénot that the cook wanted to speak to her. This was unprecedented, and Mme Viénot foresaw, as she excused herself, that on the cook's face too there would be a look of fright.

This was Mme Foëcy?

This was a different cook. Mme Foëcy was there only that summer. She was not in the habit of staying very long in any one establishment. . . . The same two men had turned up at the kitchen door, it seems, and asked for something to eat. The cook gave them a sandwich but wouldn't let them come inside. They wanted her to leave the kitchen window open that night, so they could get into the house. She threatened to call out for help, and so they left. That same afternoon, at teatime, Mme Viénot saw the gardener hovering in the vicinity of the drawing room windows.

As soon as she could, she slipped outside. The gardener was in a state of excitement. He too had had a visit, and the two men said that there was a treasure hidden somewhere in the house.

No!

Gold bullion. Left by the Germans, because they didn't have the means or the time to take it with them.

And was it true?

It is true that there was such a rumor in the village. The same story was told of other country houses after the war, and probably had its origin in a folk tale. The story varied, according to who told it. Sometimes the treasure was buried in the garden, in the dead of night. Sometimes it was hidden inside the walls. Great importance was attached to the fact that no member of Mme Bonenfant's family had ever denied this story, but actually it had never reached their ears.

The gardener told the men he would help them. He agreed to leave a cellar window open for them, but not that night. It was not a good time, he said; the house was full of people. And if they'd wait until there was no one here but the women, their chances would be better. They decided upon a signal, and as soon as the two men were off the property, the gardener came to find Mme Viénot.

Then what happened?

She went to the police, and together they worked out a plan. The only men in the house, Eugène and Mme Viénot's son-in-law, Jean-Claude Lahovary, were to leave as conspicuously as possible in Eugène's car and come back after dark, on foot. The gardener would hang the lantern in the potting shed—the signal that had been agreed upon—and the police would be nearby, waiting for a telephone call saying that the robbers were actually inside the house. It was all very melodramatic and like a British spy movie, except for one characteristically French touch. When the police cars came up the drive, they were blowing their sirens.

So the robbers got away?

No, they were caught. They must not have heard the sirens. Or else they were confused, or couldn't find their way out of the house in the dark. They were convicted of housebreaking, and sentenced to a term in jail. At the trial it came out that one of them had had some education; he had been a government clerk. Later, in the woods back of Beaumesnil, somebody found the remains of a campfire, and it was assumed that the robbers hid out there, while they were waiting for the signal.

What an amazing story.

Yes, isn't it. What would you like to know about next?

I think I'd like to know about Eugène—why he acted the way he did. Was he in the study, the day the Americans came to say good-by?

Of course.

And Alix knew that he was there?

Her hearing was excellent. It was her mother who suffered from deafness. There was no one Eugène could not make love him if he chose to, but he blew hot and cold about people. He blew hot and they mistook it for friendship; he blew cold and they had to learn, in self-defense, to despise him. This deadly, monotonous pattern did not occur with his wife. In spite of his belief that married people change and grow less fond of one another with time, this did not happen in his case. Their marriage had its ups and downs, like all marriages, but it did not become absent-minded or perfunctory. Would you like to see them sleeping together?

Well, I don't know that I—

It's quite all right. No trouble at all. The workshirt hanging across the attic window has been replaced by a potted geranium, and the Prodigal Son is gone. Someone, unable to stand the sight of so much raw emotion any longer, took it down and put it away in a closet. If you look closely, you will see that the fauteuil that belonged to Eugène's great-great-grandfather has been mended. The dresses and skirts in the armoires throughout the apartment are of a different length, and Alix and Eugène have three children now. But certain things are the same: the church bell, the rays of the star arriving and departing simultaneously, and whoever it is that at daybreak comes through the rue Malène and silently searches through the garbage cans for edible peelings, cheese rinds, moldy bread, good rags, diamond rings, broken objects that can be mended, shoes with holes in their soles, paper, string, and other treasures often found in just such refuse by old men and women with the will to live. The sky, growing lighter, says: *What is being but being different, night from day, the earth from the air, the way things were from the way things are?* The newspaper lying in the gutter announces that a turning point has been reached in the tide of human affairs, and the swallows, skimming the rooftops—

I've really had enough of those swallows.

For some reason, I never grow tired of them. The swallows, in their quick summarizing trip over the rooftops prove conclusively that there *is* no point of turning, because turning is all there is—constant, never-ending patterns of turning.

The shutters are open, the awnings are rolled. Alix and Eugène are sleeping with their backs turned to each other but touching. When she moves in her sleep, his body accommodates itself to the change without waking. Now they are facing each other. Of his forearm, shoulder, and cheek he makes a soft warm box for her head. Over her bent knees he extends protectively a relaxed weightless leg. Shortly afterward they turn away from each other. In their marriage also there is no real resting place; one partner may dominate, may circumscribe, the actions of the other, briefly, but nothing is fixed, nothing is final.

His moods—what were they all about?

Those recurring periods of melancholy, of a kind of darkness of the soul, had nothing to do with her.

What did they have to do with?

Money, chiefly. Money that is lost becomes a kind of magic mirror in which the deprived person sees himself always in the distorted landscape of what might have been. When they were living in Marseilles, Eugène did not think about money, largely because everyone else was poor also. But in Paris he was reminded continually that his father had always lived in a certain way, and so had his grandfather, and he would have liked to live in the same way himself and he couldn't, and never would be able to, because they have made no provision for him to do this.

Shouldn't they have?

Perhaps.

Then why didn't they?

Life was beautiful, and they thought it couldn't go on being this way—about this they were quite right—and in any case it would have meant sacrificing their pleasures and they needed their pleasures; they needed all of them. His father's desk was a mosaic of unpaid bills, which he never disturbed. When he wanted to write a letter, he used his wife's desk.

What about Alix? Did she mind it that they were poor?

Not for herself. But she listened carefully to what Eugène had to say about rich young men like Jean Allégret and René Simon, and what she perceived was that it was not the money itself but that he felt the loss of it had cast a shadow over their lives so dense that they could not be seen. They were no longer part of the world. They did not move among people who counted. They might as well be the children of shopkeepers.

It would have been better if she had not made him give up his work among the poor in Marseilles.

She didn't. That was only Mme Viénot's idea of what happened. Since he had renounced his spiritual vocation in order to marry her, she was prepared to give up everything for his sake, but unfortunately it turned out that he did not really have a spiritual vocation. If he had, he would not have taken it so to heart when the men he was trying to educate failed him by falling asleep over the books he lent them, or by getting drunk and beating their wives, or simply by not understanding what it was that he wanted from them. Two or three years later, he threw himself into politics in the same high-minded way. He dedicated every free moment to working for the M.R.P.—the Mouvement Républicain Populaire, the Catholic reform party. Then he decided that all political efforts were futile, and found himself once more committed to nothing, nothing to cling to, no foothold, and totally outside the life around him. And though he was patient—no one was ever more patient—he was not always easy to live with. Or pleasant to people. Anyone in trouble could count on his help, and the telephone rang incessantly, but he had no friends. If he met someone he liked, someone who interested him, he was intensely curious, direct, personal, and charming. And then, his curiosity satisfied, he was simply not interested any more. The friends of his school days called up, made arrangements to see him, were startled by what they found, and didn't return.

That painful train journey, do you remember? the time he went up to Paris with Sabine and the Americans? What really happened?

He had quarreled with Alix on the way to the station, just as the Americans thought, and the quarrel was about them. After a few days of staying in the apartment by himself, he had found that he liked being alone, and he was sorry he had invited them. On the way to the station he proposed to Alix that she tell the Americans that it was not convenient to have them stay in the apartment at this time, and she refused. He said he would tell them himself, then, and she said that she could at least not be present when he did. After she left him, he decided that instead of telling the Americans outright that he didn't want them, he could make them understand, from his behavior, that he had changed his mind about having them.

And they didn't understand.

No, they did understand, and started to go to the Hôtel Vouillemont. But in the Métro, when they tried to leave him, he changed his mind again. For a moment, he felt something like affection for them. He continued to teeter in this fashion, between liking and not liking them, the whole period of their stay in the apartment.

But why did he act the way he did? Was it because Barbara did not dance with him? She really should have. It was inexcusable, her refusing to dance with him at the Allégrets' party.

She would have danced with him, except that he was so sullen when he asked her. But that wasn't why he changed.

Was it something Harold did?

It was something he was, I think.

What was he?

A young man with a beautiful wife and the money to spend four months traveling in Europe. An American. A man with a future, and no shadow across his present life.

But that isn't what his life was like.

No, but that's what it looked like, from the outside.

It was also wrong of them, very wrong, not to accept Alix's invitation to come down to the country for the week end. And not to call on M. and Mme Carrère, after M. Carrère had given Harold his card, was—

True. Perfectly true. Their behavior doesn't stand careful inspection. But on the other hand, you must remember that they were tourists. This is not the way they behaved when they were at home. And it is one thing to hand out gold stars to children for remembering to brush their teeth and another to pass moral judgment on adult behavior. So much depends on the circumstances.

In short, it is something you don't feel like going into. Very well, what happened to Hector Gagny?

He divorced his wife, and married a woman with a half-grown boy, and she made him very happy. I always felt that his first wife was more—but she was impossible, as a wife. Or at least as a wife for him. The little boy in the carnival is grown up now and has a half interest in the merry-go-round. The gypsy fortuneteller dealt herself the ace of spades. Anybody or anything else you'd like to know about?

That drawing Sabine was going to send to the Americans. Did it ever arrive?

Yes, it arrived, about a month after Harold and Barbara got home, and with it was a rather touching letter, written the day they took the boat train:

> Here is the little drawing promised, I hope it will not oblige you to lengthen your list for the douane!— Thanks still for all your kindness— You don't know what it meant for me, nor what both of you meant to me—. It's difficult to explain specially in English—. I think you represent like Aunt Mathilde and Alix an atmosphere *kind*, gay and harmonious, where everything is in its real place. And seeing you was a sort of rest through the roughness of existence, a bit like putting on fairy shoes.
>
> Perhaps did you guess there was, a few years ago, a sad drama in our family. Since then many things changed, and I lived in one place and then in another—missing baddly that sort of atmosphere I just described. That's why perhaps I bored you a bit like Mme Straus, in trying to see you often— I am very sorry if I did. But you know: qu'il est encore plus difficile de diriger ses bons mouvements que ses mauvais, car, contrairement à ces derniers on ne peut jamais prévoir exactement leur résultat. En tout cas sachez que vous m'avez fait grand plaisir. . . .

It is so curious how, in the history of a family, you have one drastic change after another, all in a period of two or three years, and then for a long long time afterward no change at all. Sabine continued to live now in this place and now in that. The one place where she was always welcome at any time, and for as long as she cared to stay there, the apartment in the rue Malène, she would not make use of. But she turned up fairly often, and stayed just long enough to take her bearings by what she found there. "You will stay and eat with us?" Mme Cestre would say, but she did not urge her. And a few minutes later, Alix would say: "Françoise has set a place for you. . . . Well, come and sit down with us anyway," and Françoise waited and when the others were halfway through dinner she brought in a plate of soup, which Sabine allowed to grow cold in front of her, and then absent-mindedly ate. And then she went home—only it wasn't home she went to but the apartment of a cousin or an uncle or an old school friend of her grandmother's; and the bed she slept in was only a few feet away from an armoire that was crammed with somebody else's clothes.

But the family stood by her. And people were kind; very kind. ("Such a pleasure to have you, dear child"—until the end of the month, when this large room overlooking the avenue Friedland would be required for a granddaughter whose parents were traveling in Italy, and who was therefore coming here for the school holidays.) And Sabine was still invited to the larger parties, but when she went, wearing the one dress she had that was suitable, what she read on the faces of older women— friends of her mother or her grandmother, women she had known all her life—was: "It is a pity that things turned out the way they did, but you do understand, don't you, that you are no longer a suitable match for any of the young men in our family?"

And did she mind?

The way children mind a bruise or a fall. She cried sometimes, afterward, but she did not mind deeply. She did not want the kind of life that a "brilliant" marriage would have opened up to her. And the waters did not close over her head, though there was every reason to think that they would. Or perhaps there wasn't every reason to think that. It all depends on how you look at things. She did have talent; it was merely slow in revealing itself. And failure—real failure—has a way of passing over slight, pale, idealistic girls with observant eyes and a high domed forehead, in favor of some victim who is too fortunate and whose undoing therefore offers a chance for contrast and irony. You know those marvelous windows in Paris?

In the Sainte Chapelle, you mean? And the rose windows of Notre Dame?

No. They're marvelous too, God knows. But I meant the windows of the shops in the rue St. Honoré and the place Vendôme. She had a talent for designing window displays that were original and had humor and appealed to the Parisian mind. For example, she did a small hospital scene, in which the doctor and the patient in bed and the nurses were all perfume bottles dressed up like people. It created a small stir. She worked very hard, but her work was valued. The hours were long, and sometimes she overtaxed her strength. The family worried about her lungs. But she was well paid. And happy in her work. And she did not have to go to a fortuneteller because Eugène had a way of sardonically announcing the future. It was a gift the family stood in some fear of. "Would you like to know what is going to happen to Sabine?" he demanded one day. "She is going to be introduced to a man without any papers. Of good family, but dispossessed; a refugee. And he will not become a French citizen because he is a patriot and cannot bring himself to renounce his Polish, or Hungarian, or Spanish citizenship, and therefore, even though he speaks without an accent, and is educated, and has a first-class mind, he cannot even get a job teaching school. And Sabine, unequipped as she is, is going to take care of him, and they are going to marry, and her mother will never accept him or forgive her. . . ."

His name was Frédéric. His father was a well-to-do banker in——. In the fall of 1939, when the sky was full of German planes day after day, the house Frédéric grew up in, along with whole blocks of other houses, was destroyed by a bomb. The family was in the country when this happened. The caretaker was killed, but no one else. Then the Russians came, and they were allowed to keep one room in that enormous country place, and Frédéric's father arranged for him to escape in a Norwegian fishing vessel. Or perhaps it was on foot, across the border, with a handful of other frightened people. His father remained, to avoid the confiscations of his property, and his mother would not leave his father. For a year and a half, Frédéric lived in the Belleville quarter of Paris. Would you like to see him the way he was at that time? He is stretched out on a bed, in an ugly furnished room that he shares with a waiter in a café in the rue de Menilmentant. He is fully dressed, except for his bare feet, which are thin and aristocratic. The bulb in the unshaded ceiling fixture is not strong enough to bother his eyes. The one window is open to the night. The soft rain fills the alleyway outside with small sounds, sounds that are all but musical, and he is quite happy, though the walls are mildewed and the bedclothes need airing and the sheets are not clean and shortly he will have to get up and spend the rest of the night on the stone floor. He turns on his back, and with his hands clasped under his head, he thinks: *She is hearing this rain.* . . .

The girl who hid out from the Gestapo in Mme Cestre's apartment had brought him to a party where Sabine was, and he saw her home from the party, but she could not, of course, ask him in. One of the ways by which Ferdinand and Miranda are to be distinguished from all commonplace lovers is that, along with Prospero, Ariel, and Calaban, they have no island. It has sunk beneath the sea. Sometimes Frédéric and Sabine meet in an English tea room that is one flight up and rather exposed to the street, but there is one table that is private, behind a huge chart of the human hand showing the lines of the head and the heart, and the mountains of Venus, Jupiter, Saturn, the Sun, Mercury, and Mars. Also the swellings of the palmar faces of the five fingers, indicative of (beginning with the thumb) the logical faculty and the will; materialism, law and order, idealism; humanity, system, intelligence; truth, economy, energy; goodness, prudence, reflectiveness. When the weather permits, the lovers meet on the terrace in front of the Jeu de Paume.

This time, she arrives first. She goes up that little flight of marble steps and crosses the packed dirt to where there are two empty iron chairs. It is a beautiful evening. There are pink clouds against a nearly white sky. Shortly afterward he comes. There is a greenish pallor to his skin. His hands are beautiful and expressive. And he is just her height and just her age, and he speaks French without an accent. His suit is threadbare, but so are most people's suits in France at this time. The part of the terrace they are sitting in now is like the prow of a ship. They look down at the bicycles and motorcars and taxis that come over the bridge and disappear into the delta of wide and narrow streets that flows into the Place de la Concorde. He says: "You are looking at the hole in my shoe?"

"I was looking at your ankle," she says.

"You don't like it?" he says anxiously. "It is the wrong kind of ankle?"

"I was thinking I would like to draw it."

"I was afraid you thought it looked Polish," he says. (Or Hungarian. Or Spanish. I forget which he was.)

They see that the old woman who collects rent for the chairs is coming toward them. He digs down in his coat pocket and produces a five-franc note. Wrinkled and dirty and sad, the old woman gives him his change and moves on.

"You have never thought of committing suicide?" he asks after a time.

She shakes her head.

"I think I used to be in love with death," he says. "I sat in a cold room on an unmade bed with the barrel of a loaded revolver in my mouth, counting to . . . the number varied. Sometimes it was three, sometimes it was seven, and sometimes it was ten."

Farther along the balustrade, the old woman has got into an altercation with a middle-aged couple, and the altercation is being carried on in two languages.

"I was not in any particular trouble, and one is supposed to want to live. . . . What are they saying? They speak too fast for me."

"The man is saying that in America it does not cost anything to sit down in a public park."

"And is he indignant?"

"Very."

"Good," Frédéric says, nodding. "I have hated that old woman for a year and a half. And is she giving him as good as she is taking?"

"Yes, but he does not speak French, and she does not understand English."

"Too bad, too bad. Shall we go and translate for him? With a little help from us, it may become an international incident—the start of the war between the United States and the U.S.S.R." He starts to rise, and she puts a hand on his wrist, restraining him.

A few minutes later, he turns to her and says: "You are going to your aunt's?"

She nods. "You could come too. She has told me to bring you. And you would like them."

"I'm sure I would."

And then, after an interval, in a toneless voice, he says: "I must not keep you."

She gets up from her chair and walks with him to the head of the stairs. In the sky the two colors are now reversed. The clouds are white, and the sky they float in is pink. As they shake hands he does not say: "Will you marry me?" but this question hangs in the air between them, and is why she looks troubled and why he steps out into the traffic like a sleepwalker. Oblivious of the horns and shouts of angry drivers, he arrives safely at the other side. She stands watching him until he passes the Crillon and is hidden by a crowd of people who are waiting in a circle around the red carpet, hoping to see the King of Persia.

Would you like to know about the King of Persia?

Not particularly. What I would like to know is the name of that white château with the green lawn in front of it that Barbara Rhodes was always looking for.

One time when Eugène and Sabine were going down to the country together, there was a picture, behind glass, in their compartment. Eugène was furious at her because she had given her seat to an old woman who was sitting on her suitcase in the corridor, and so had made him sit next to a stranger. Or perhaps it was because the old woman was large and crowded him in his corner. Or it might not have been that at all, but something that had nothing to do with her that was making him cold and abstracted. Ultimately the cause of his black moods declared itself, but first you had the mood in its pure state, without any explanation. She stood in the corridor for a while, looking at the landscape that unreeled itself alongside the train, and when the old woman got off at Orléans, she went back into the compartment. She was eager for the trip to be over. The compartment was airless and cramped. With her head against the seat back she sat watching the sunset and noting the signs that meant she was nearing the country of her childhood. She found herself staring at the photograph opposite her. It was of a white château that looked like a castle in a fairy tale. Was it Sully, she wondered. Or Luynes? Or Chantilly? There was a metal tag on the frame, but it was tarnished and could not be read.

You don't know what château it was?

There is every reason to be grateful that these losses do occur, that every once in a while something that is listed in the inventory turns up missing. Otherwise people couldn't move for the clutter that they make around themselves.

I do not take such a charitable view of Eugène's behavior as you seem to. Many people have had to live with disappointment and still not—

He was also capable of acts of renunciation and of generosity that were saintlike. We all have these contradictions in our natures. . . . In the family they were accustomed to his moods and did not take them seriously. There was a time when Alix thought that their life might go differently (though not necessarily better)—that he had reached a turning point of some kind. His dark mood had lasted longer than usual, and one morning she sat up in bed and looked at him, and was frightened. What he looked like was a drowned man.

It was a Saturday, so he did not go to his office. And suddenly, in the middle of the morning, she missed him. She went through the apartment, glancing in the baby's room, then in their bedroom, then in the dressing room. The bathroom door was open. She turned and went back down the hall. He must have gone out. But why did he go out without telling her where he was going? And how could he have done it so quietly, so that she didn't hear either the study door open or the front door close. Unless he didn't want her to know that he was going out. She had a sudden vision of him ill, having fainted in the toilet. She opened the door of that little room. It was empty.

"Eugène?" she said anxiously, and at that moment the front door closed. She turned around in surprise.

There was still time to stop him, to ask where he was going. When she opened the front door, she heard the sound of feet descending the stairs and, leaning far over the banister, caught a glimpse of his head and shoulders, which were hidden immediately afterward by a turn in the staircase.

"Eugène!" she called, and, loud and frightened though her voice sounded in her own ears, he still did not stop. The footsteps reiterated his firm intention never to stop until he had arrived at a place where she could not reach him. When they changed from the muffled sound made by the stair carpet to the harsh clatter of heels on a marble floor, she turned and hurried back into the apartment, through the hall, through the drawing room, and out onto the balcony, where she was just in time to see him emerge from the building and start up the sidewalk. She tried to pitch her voice so that only he would hear her calling him, and a man on the other side of the street looked up and Eugène did not. He went right on walking.

Step by step, with him, she hurried along the balcony to the corner of the building, where she could look down on the granite monument and the cobblestone square. Hidden by trees briefly, Eugène was now visible again, crossing a street. There was a taxi waiting, but he did not step into it. He kept on walking, past the café, past the entrance to the Métro, past the barbershop, past the trousered legs standing publicly in the midst of the odor that used to make her feel sick as a child. Again he was hidden by trees. Again she saw him, as he skirted a sidewalk meeting of two old friends. He crossed another ray of the star, and then changed his direction slightly, and she perceived that the church steps was his destination. There, in the gray morning light, one of the priests (Father Quinot, or Father Ferron?) stood with his hands behind his back, benevolently nodding and answering the parting remarks of a woman in black.

The image that Alix now saw before her eyes—of Eugène on his knees in the confessional—was only the beginning, she knew. More was required. Much more. The heart that was now ready to surrender itself was not simple. There would be intellectual doubts, arguments with Father Quinot, with Father Ferron, appointments with the bishop, a period of retreat from her and from the world, in some religious house, where no one could reach him, while he examined his faith for flaws. Proof would be submitted to him from the writings of St. Thomas, St. Gregory, St. Bonaventure. And when he returned to her, with the saints shielding him so that each time she put out her hand she touched the garment of a saint, his mind would be full of new knowledge of how men *know*, how the angels *know*, how God in his infinite being becomes all *knowledge* and all *knowledge* is a *knowledge* of Him.

This being true, clear, and obvious even to a slow mind like hers, a person given to looking apprehensively at mirrors and clocks, and there being also no way of joining him on his knees (though there were two stalls in the mahagony confessional, the most that was given to Father Quinot or Father Ferron to accomplish would be to listen to their alternating confession, not their joint one)—this being true, she would not go down and wait for him in the street, as she longed to do, even though it be hours from now, past midnight, or morning, before he reappeared. She would stay where she was, and when he came home she would try not to distract him, or to seem to lay the slightest claim upon his attention or his feelings, in order that . . .

Each of the woman's parting remarks seemed to give rise to another, and as Eugène drew closer, Alix thought: *What if she doesn't stop talking in time?* For Eugène would not wait. He was much too proud to stand publicly waiting, even to speak to the priest. "Oh, please," she said, under her breath. The woman turned her head, as if this supplication had been heard. But then she remembered something else that she wanted to say, and Eugène kept on going, and disappeared down the steps of the Métro.

Shortly after this, he went to see M. Carrère, who was exceedingly kind. Eugène outlined his situation to him, and M. Carrère asked if Eugène had any objection to working for an American firm that he was connected with through his son. "The job would be over there?" Eugène asked, and M. Carrère said: "No, here. I assume that Mme de Boisgaillard would not want to live so far from her mother. Suppose I arrange for an interview?"

The interview went well, and after an hour's talk, Eugène was asked to come back the next day, which he did. They made him an offer, and he accepted it.

A few nights later, when Mme Viénot went in to say good night to her mother, Mme Bonenfant said: "I wonder if Eugène will be happy working for an American firm. He doesn't speak any English."

"If it is like other foreign firms that have a branch in Paris, the personnel will be largely French," Mme Viénot said. "I have heard of this one, as it happens. In America they make frigidaires. Sewing machines. Typewriters. That sort of thing."

"It doesn't sound very intellectual," Mme Bonenfant said. "Are you sure that you understood correctly."

"Quite sure, Maman. . . . In France, the firm manufactures only machine guns."

M. and Mme Carrère never came back to the château. They found another quiet country house that was more comfortable and closer to Paris. But from time to time, when Mme Viénot went into the post office, she was handed a letter that was addressed to him. The letters no doubt contained a request of some sort; for money, for advice, for the use of his name. And how it was answered might change the lives of she did not like to think how many people. In any case, the letter had to be forwarded, and it gave her acute pleasure to think that he would recognize her handwriting on the envelope.

Hector Gagny never came back either, with his new wife. But Mme Straus came at least once a year. Her summer was a round of visits. For a woman past seventy, without a place of her own in which to entertain, with neither wealth nor much social distinction, she received a great many invitations—many more than she could accept. And if the friends who were so eager to have her come and stay with them did not always invite her back, there were always new acquaintances who responded to her gaiety, opened their hearts to her, and—for a while at least—adjusted the salutation of their letters to conform with the rapidly increasing tenderness of hers.

A blank space in her calendar between the end of June and the middle of September meant a brief stay at Beaumesnil. She was at the château just after the affair of the robbers, and she brought two friends with her, a M. and Mme Mégille. Monsieur was a member of the permanent staff of the Institut Océanographique, and very distinguished. And since he had been brought up in the country he did not mind the fact that there was no electricity.

They never found that short circuit?

Oh yes. This was a piece of foolishness on Mme Viénot's part. You won't believe it, but she could not get that gold bullion out of her mind. She induced the priest at Coulanges to come and go all through the house with her, holding a forked stick. There was one place where it responded violently, and in opening up the wall the gardener sawed through the main electric-light cable.

But surely Mme Viénot was too intelligent to believe that—

Yes, she did. Mme Viénot is the Life Force, with dyed hair and too much rouge, and the Life Force always believes. Defeated, flat on her back, she waved her arms and legs like a beetle, and in a little while she was walking around again.

Every novel ought to have a heroine, and she is the heroine of this one. She is a wonderful woman—how wonderful probably no one knows, except an American woman she met only once, on a train journey—a woman who, curiously enough, knew Barbara and Harold Rhodes, though only slightly. The two women opened their hearts to each other, as women sometimes do on a train or sharing a table in the tea room of a department store, and they have continued to write to each other afterward, long letters full of things they do not tell anyone else.

What Mme Viénot did the summer Barbara and Harold were with her was miraculous. She had nothing whatever to work with, and bad servants, and somehow she kept up the tone of the establishment and provided meals that were admirable. Singlehanded, she saved the château. It would have gone for back taxes if she had not done what she did. No one else in the family could have saved it. As a person, Mme Cestre was more sympathetic, perhaps, but she was an invalid, and introspective. And the men . . .

What about the men?

II: *Some Explanations*

Well, what about them?

I guess you're right. Go on with what you were saying.

Once more they dined by candlelight. When they went up to bed, they were handed kerosene lamps at the foot of the stairs. There was no writing desk in Mme Straus's room, and so, sitting up in bed, she used a book to write on. Her hair was in two braids and her reading glasses were resting far down on the bridge of her nose. She wrote rapidly, with no trace of a quaver:

> . . . Maman Minou finds that she has been a long time without news of her dear American children. The last letter from Harold, written in English, was translated for me by a friend, but tonight I am not in Paris. I beg him not to be vexed with me. Can he not find, at his office, a good-natured comrade who knows how to read French and will translate this letter into English? But my dear friend, why this sudden change? Your old letters, and those of dear Barbara, were perfectly written. It makes me wonder whether you perhaps no longer wish to correspond with poor Minou in France.

The fountain pen stopped. The old eyes went on a voyage round the room, searching for something to say (one does not create an atmosphere of concert pitch out of accusations of neglect) and came to rest on a large stain in the wallpaper:

> Your presence surrounds me here. I go looking for you, and find my friends occupying your room. I put flowers there for them but Oh miracle! the moment the flowers are in their vase, they fly off toward you. Take them, then, my dears, and may their perfume spread around you. Here it is gray, cheerless, cold. The surroundings are agreeable, even so. M. and Mme Mégille are charming. Sabine pleases me very much. The lady of the manor dolls herself up for each new arrival. So droll! Alix is adorable. She is going off to visit cousins in Toulon next week. I shall miss her. Have you pretty concerts and plays to see? In this moment when we are in summer, are you not in winter? And at the hour when I am writing to you—eleven o'clock at night—your hour of the omelette, the good odor of which I smell even here?

She thought the United States was in South America?

Apparently. Some people have no sense of geography.— The letter ended:

> Life is rather difficult here, but I am so eager to obey our dear President Pinay, whom we admire so much, that all becomes easy. Your dear images still have a place in my little chamber, which you know. Pray for your old Maman Minou, who embraces you with all her loving heart.
>
> Antoinette Straus-Muguet
> Please put the date and the year of your letters. Thank you.

Why didn't they answer her letters? It isn't like them.

I'll get around to that in a minute. One thing at a time. She blew the lamp out—

We have to hear about the lamp?

Yes. And settled herself between the damp sheets. And it was at that moment that the odor of kerosene brought back to her something priceless, a house she had not seen for half a century.

The youngest of a large family, she had all through her childhood been the charming excitable plaything of older brothers and sisters. When evening came, so did Charles and Emma and Andrée and Edouard and Lucienne and Maurice and Marguerite and Anna. They gathered in the nursery to assist in putting Minou to bed, invented new games when her head hung like a heavy flower on its stalk, and, as they peeled her clothes off over her head, cried: "Skin the rabbit! Don't let the little white bunny get away." "Stop her!" "Catch her, somebody!" And when she escaped from them, they tracked her down with all the cruelty of love, and carried her on their shoulders around the nursery, a laughing overexcited child with too bright eyes and a flushed face and a nature that was too highstrung and delicate to be playing such games at the end of the day.

All dead, the pursuers; long dead; leaving her no choice but to pursue.

As for the Americans, it was much harder to think in French when they were not in France. They had to sit down with a

French-English dictionary and a French grammar, and it took half a day to answer one of Mme Straus's letters, and they were leading a busy life. Also, he hated to write letters. He used to wait for days before he opened a letter from Mme Straus, because of his shame at not having answered the last one. But they did answer some of the letters. They did not altogether lose touch with her.

Quite apart from the effort it took, and the fact that year after year the friendship had nothing to feed on, her letters to them were really very strange. ("The monsieur who is at Fifth Avenue is not my relative, but my niece is flying over soon, on business for the house, of which she is administrator, director, in place of her dead husband. She will be, *alone,* in our confidence, but see you, become acquainted with you, speak to you of Maman Minou. You will see how nice she is. Answer her telephone calls above everything. She will give you news of me, and fresh news . . .) None of the people she said were coming to America and that Harold and Barbara could expect to hear from ever turned up. And there was one frantic, only half-legible letter, which they had to take to the friend who had lived in the Monceau quarter, to translate for them. She found it distrait, full of idioms that she had never seen and that she didn't believe existed. The letter was about money. Mme Straus' income, with inflation, was no longer adequate to meet her needs. Her daughter had refused to do anything for her, and Mme Straus was afraid that she would be put out of the convent. In the next letter it appeared that this crisis had passed: Mme Straus-Muguet's children, to whom her notary had made a demand, had finally understood that it was their duty to help her. "Forgive me," she wrote, "for boring you with all my miseries, but you are all my consolation." Her letters were full of intimations of increasing frailty and age, and continually asked when they were coming back to France. At last they were able to write her that they were coming, in the spring of 1953, and she wrote back: "If Heaven wills it that I have not already departed for my great journey, it will be with arms wide open that I will receive you. . . ."

And was she there to receive them?

They went first to England, and had two weeks of flawless weather. The English countryside was like the Book of Hours, and they loved London. They arrived in Paris on May Day Eve, and by nightfall they were in the Forest of Fontainebleau, in a rented car, on their way south. They spent the night in Sens, and in the morning everyone they saw carried a little nosegay of muguets. After their other trip, they enrolled in the Berlitz, and spent one winter conscientiously studying French. Though that was years ago now, it did seem that their French had improved.

The boy learns to swim in winter, William James said, and to skate in summer.

From Provence, Barbara wrote to Mme Straus that they would be in Paris by the end of the second week in May. When they were settled in—someone had told them about a small hotel whose windows overlooked the gardens of the Palais-Royal—Harold telephoned, and the person who answered seemed uncertain of whether Mme Straus could come to the telephone. *The stairs have become too much for her*, he thought. There was another of those interminable waits, during which he had a chance to reflect. *Five years is a long time, and to try and pick up the threads again, with people they hardly knew, and with the additional barrier of language . . . But they couldn't not call, either. . . .*

Mme Straus's voice was just the same, and she seemed to be quite free of the doubts that troubled him. They settled it that she would come to their hotel at seven that evening.

At quarter after six, as they were crossing the Place du Palais-Royal, Barbara said: "Aren't we going to have an apéritif?"

They had only five weeks altogether, for England and France, and there was never a time, it seemed, when they could sit in front of a sidewalk café, as they used to do before, and watch the people. They were both tired from walking, and he very much wanted a bath before dinner, but he decided that with luck they could do it, in spite of the crowd of people occupying the tables of that particular café, and the overworked waiter. They did it, but without pleasure, because he kept looking at his watch. They hurried through the gardens, congratulating themselves on the fact that it was still only twenty minutes of seven—just time enough to get upstairs and bathe and dress and be ready for Mme Straus.

"You have company," Mme la Patronne said as they walked into the hotel. "A lady." There was a note of disapproval in her voice. "She has been waiting since six o'clock."

The Americans looked at each other with dismay. "You go on upstairs," he said, and hurried down the hall to the little parlor where Mme Straus was waiting, with two small parcels on the sofa beside her. His first impression was that she looked younger. Could he have misjudged her age? She kissed him on both cheeks, and told him how well he looked. They sat down and he began to tell her about Provence. Then there was an awkward pause in the conversation, and to dispell it they asked the questions people ask, meeting after years. When Barbara came in, he started to leave the room, intending to go upstairs and at least wash his face and hands, but Mme Straus stopped him. It was the moment for the presentation of the gifts, and again they were dismayed that they had not thought to bring anything for her. They were also dismayed at her gifts—a paper flower for Barbara, a white scarf for Harold that had either lain in a drawer too long or else was of so shoddy a quality that it bore no relation to any man's evening scarf he had ever seen. Mme Straus had learned to make paper flowers—as a game, she said, and to amuse herself. "Oeillet," she said, resuming her role of language professor, and Barbara pinned the pink carnation on her dark violet-colored coat, where it looked very pretty, if a trifle strange.

They left the hotel intending to have dinner at a restaurant in the rue de Montpensier, but it was closed that night, and so Mme Straus led them across the Place du Théâtre-Français, to a restaurant where, she assured them, she was well known and the food and wine were excellent. It was noisy and crowded; the maître d'hôtel received Mme Straus coldly, but at least the waiter knew her and was friendly. "He is like a son to me," she said, as they sat down.

There were a dozen restaurants in the neighborhood where the food was better, and Harold blamed himself for not insisting that they go to some place more suited to a long-delayed reunion, but Mme Straus seemed quite happy. Nobody had very much to say.

The Vienna Opera was paying a visit to Paris, and during dinner he explained that he had three tickets for *The Magic Flute*. She said: "Quelle joie!" and then: "Where are they?" He told her and she exclaimed: "But we won't be able to see the stage!"

The tickets had cost five times what tickets for the Opéra usually cost, and were the most he felt he could afford. He said: "They're in the center," and she seemed satisfied. And would they arrange for her to stay at their hotel that night, since the doors of her convent were closed at nine o'clock?

Arm in arm, they walked to the bus stop, and waving from the back of the bus, she was swept away.

"It isn't the same, is it?" he said, as they were walking back to their hotel.

"We're not the same," Barbara said. "She took one look at us and saw that the jig was up."

"Too bad."

"If you hadn't got tickets for the opera—"

"I know. Well, one more evening won't kill us."

Harold found that Mme Straus could stay at their hotel the night of the opera, and when she arrived—again an hour early—she was delighted with her room. "It's just right for a jeune fille," she said, laughing. And did Barbara have a coat she could wear? And wouldn't it be better if they had dinner in the same place, because the service was so prompt, and above all they didn't want to be late.

When they arrived at the Opéra, she introduced them to the tall man in evening clothes who was taking tickets, and they were introduced again on the stairs, to an ouvreuse or someone like that. They climbed and climbed and eventually arrived at their tier, which was above the "basket." Their seats were in the first row and they had a clear view of the stage and the stage was not too far away. Mme Straus arranged her coat and offered Harold and Barbara some candy. Stuffed with food and wine, they said no, and she took some herself and then seized their hands affectionately. She made them lean far forward so that she could point out to them, in the tier just below, the two center front-row seats that her father and mother had always occupied. She regretted that *Les Indes Galantes* was not being performed during their stay in Paris. A marvelous spectacle.

The Magic Flute was also something of a spectacle, and the soprano who sang the role of Pamina had a very beautiful voice.

Harold had failed to get a program and so they didn't know who it was. In the middle of the first act, he became aware of Mme Straus's restlessness. At last she leaned toward him and whispered that this opera was always sung at the Comique; that it did not belong on so large a stage. The Opéra was more suited to *Aida*. She found the singing acceptable but the opera itself did not greatly interest her. Did he know *Aida?* It was her favorite. Again she pressed the little bag of candy on him in the dark, and he suddenly remembered the strange behavior of Mme Marguerite Mailly, when they went backstage after her play. A few minutes later, hearing the rustle of the little bag again coming toward him, he was close to hating Mme Straus-Muguet himself. They left their seats between the acts, and as they walked through the marble corridors, he noticed a curious thing: because their French had improved, Mme Straus understood what they were saying, but not always what they meant, and when they explained, it only added to the misunderstanding. Wherever her quick intuitive mind was, it wasn't on them.

After the performance, she insisted that they go across the street, as her guests, and have something to eat. Harold and Barbara drank a bottle of Perrier water, and Mme Straus had a large ham sandwich.

"I am always hungry," she confessed.

Worn out with the effort of keeping up the form of an affectionate relationship that had lost its substance, they sat and looked at the people around them. Mme Straus borrowed the souvenir program of a young woman at the next table, and they learned the name of the soprano with the beautiful voice: Irmgard Seefried. Then Mme Straus brought up the matter of when they would see her next. Barbara said gently that they were only going to be in Paris a few more days, and that this was their last evening with her.

"Ah, but chérie, just one time! After five years!"

"Two times," Barbara said, and Mme Straus smiled. She was not hurt, it seemed, but only pretending.

They said good night on the stairs of the little hotel, and the Americans went off early the next morning, to Chartres; they wanted to see the cathedral again. When they got back to the hotel, Mme Straus had gone, leaving instructions about when they were to telephone her. There were several telephone calls during the next two days and in the end they found themselves having lunch with her, in that same impossible restaurant. She took from her purse a postcard she had just received from her daughter, who was traveling in Switzerland. It was simple and affectionate—just such a card as any daughter might have sent her mother from a trip, and Mme Straus seemed to have forgotten that they knew anything about her daughter that wasn't complimentary.

At the end of the meal, Mme Straus asked for the *addition*, and Harold, partly out of concern for her but much more out of a deep desire to get to the bottom of things, reached for his wallet. In the short time that remained, perhaps it was possible to discover the simple unsentimentalized truth. At the risk of being crass and of hurting her feelings, he insisted on paying for the luncheon she had invited them to, and, smiling indulgently, she let him. So I could have paid for all the other times, he thought. And should have.

"Now what would you like to do?" she asked. "What would you like to see? Do you like looking at paintings and old furniture?"

They got into a taxi and drove to the shop of a cousin of Mme Straus's husband. It was a decorator's shop, and the taste it reflected was not their taste, in furniture or in objets d'art. Finding nothing else that she could admire, Barbara pretended to an interest in a Chinese luster tea set. "You like it?" Mme Straus said. "It is charming, I agree." She could not be prevented from calling a salesman and asking the price—three hundred thousand francs. Mme Straus whispered; "I will speak to them, and tell them you are my rich American friends." She giggled. "Because of me, they will give you a prix d'ami."

Barbara said that the tea set was much too expensive. As she turned away, her short violet-colored coat swept one of the cups out of its saucer. With a lunge Harold caught it in mid-air.

They went upstairs and looked at what they were told were Raphaels. "Copies," Harold said, committed now to his disagreeable experiment. "And not necessarily copies of a painting by Raphael."

The salesman did not disagree, or seem offended. Seeing that they were not interested in what he showed them, he asked what painters they did like.

"Vuillard and Bonnard," Harold said.

They were shown a small, uninteresting Bonnard and told that there were more in the shop if they would like to see them. Harold shook his head. It was tug of war, with Mme Straus endeavoring to give her husband's cousin the impression that

Harold and Barbara were rich American collectors and might buy anything, and Harold and Barbara trying just as hard to convey the truth.

Mme Straus started to leave the shop with them, and then hesitated. "I have some business to discuss with monsieur upstairs," she said, and kissed them, and said good-by, and perhaps she would come to the airport.

In the taxi Harold said: "Is that the explanation? All this elaborate scheming so she can get her commission?"

"No," Barbara said. "I don't really think it is that. . . . I think it is more likely something she thought of on the spur of the moment. A role she performed just for the pleasure of performing it. But I kept thinking all the time we were with her, there is something about her manner and her voice. I couldn't place it until we were in that shop. She is like the women in stores who try to sell you something. Whatever she is, or whoever she was, she knows that world. I think that's why Pierre disapproved of our being with her. . . . But it is the young she likes. Now that we are no longer young, it isn't worth her while to enchant us."

The other reunions were not disappointing. They liked Sabine's husband, and she was exactly as they remembered her. It was as if they had bicycled home in the moonlight from the Allégrets' party the night before. She did not even look any older. The questions she asked were the right questions. They could convey to her in a phrase, a word, the thing that needed to be said. She is all eyes and forehead, Harold thought, looking at her. But what he was most aware of was how completely she took in what they said to her, so that talking to her was not like talking to anybody else. Walking to her door from the restaurant where they had had dinner, he heard their four voices, all proceeding happily like a quartet for strings. Allegro, andante, etc. While he was telling Frédéric about an experience with some gypsies outside the walls of Aigues-Mortes, she began to tell Barbara about the robbers. Harold stopped talking to listen.

Then, turning to Frédéric, he asked: "She's not making this up?" and Frédéric said: "No, no, it all happened," and Harold said: "I guess when anything is that strange you can be sure it happened." Looking up at the lamplit underside of the leaves of the chestnut trees, he thought: We're in Paris, I am not dreaming that we are in Paris. . . .

The next day, they met Eugène and Alix for lunch, and that too was easy and pleasant. Eugène spoke English, which made a difference. And he was in a genial mood. Their eyes had no trouble meeting his. They did not have to make conversation out of passing the sugar back and forth. *We're not the same, are we?* they all three agreed silently, and after that he treated them and they treated him with simple courtesy. And unwittingly, Harold saw, they had pleased Eugène by inviting him to this restaurant. He informed them that Napoleon used to play chess here, and that the décor was unchanged since that time. With its red curtains, its red plush, it was exactly right, and what a classical restaurant should look like. . . . He enjoyed his lunch as well. And the wine was of his choosing. He was sardonic only once, with the waiter, who urged them a shade too insistently to have strawberries.

After lunch they strolled through the gardens of the Palais-Royal, and Barbara took a picture of the three others, standing in front of the spray of a fountain. When Eugène left to go back to his office, Alix said, somewhat to their surprise, that, yes, she would like to go and see the rose garden at Bagatelle with them. In appearance she was totally changed. She was not an unconfident young woman with a baby; she was a stylish Parisian matron. Her hair was cut short, in a way that was becoming to her. Her black suit had the tailoring of Paris, and what made them instantly at ease and happy with her was that she didn't pretend she wasn't pleased with it. "All my life I've wanted a black suit," she said, when Barbara spoke of it. If she understood the meaning of pretense, she did not understand the need for it. It had no part in her nature. We thought all these years that we remembered her, Harold said to himself—her voice, her face, how nice she is, how much we liked being with her. But all we had, actually, was a dim recollection of those things. And it didn't even include the most important fact about her—that she would never under any circumstances turn away from the presence of love, happy or unhappy.

Because she was wearing a tight skirt, they stopped off first at the apartment in the rue Malène, and Barbara and Harold saw Alix's children, who were charming, and had a visit with Mme Cestre while Alix was changing her clothes. At Bagatelle, something awaited them—a red brick wall almost a hundred feet long, and trained against it were climbing roses and white and blue clematis, demonstrating their cousinship. Both flowers were at the very perfection of their blooming period. It was one more ecstatic experience, to put with the lavender-blue searchlight, the rainy night in San Remo, the one-ring circus, and the medieval city that was enclosed in itself like a rose. Sitting on a bench, with the wall in front of them, Alix talked about her present life. All that Harold remembered afterward was the one sentence: "I don't mind doing the washing and ironing, or anything else, so long as I don't have to sit with them in the park." It reduced the Atlantic Ocean to a puddle, and he began to tell her about their efforts to adopt a child. Then they looked at the roses some more. And then they made their way to a bus stop, and back into the city. She got off first, and they waved until they couldn't see her any longer. They saw her once more after that. Sabine had a party for them, an evening party, and invited Alix and Eugène and also her sister and brother-in-law.

The man who looked like an acrobat but wasn't?

He was a performer. Their instinct about him was right. But his performance was intellectual; he balanced budgets in the air. He had changed so in five years that they didn't recognize him. He didn't refer to the evening they had spent together, and they didn't remember until afterward who he was.

And Sabine was different, Harold suddenly realized. In one

respect she had changed. That strange suggestion of an unprovoked or unrelated amusement was not there any longer. Was this because it was now safe to be serious? In any case, she was happy.

Feeling that the party was for them, they tried too hard, and didn't really enjoy themselves, but it didn't matter; they had already reached the people they wanted to reach. Including that waiter, Joseph.

Pierre, you said his name was.

His name was Joseph, but they didn't know it. The patron's name being Joseph also, he called himself Pierre, to avoid confusion. But his name was really Joseph. The simplest things are often not what they seem. . . . The restaurant in the alley off the Place St. Sulpice had gone downhill. The patron had taken to drink, and their friend was now working in a brasserie on the boulevard St. Germain. The first time they stopped in, he was off duty. They left a message—that they would be back two days later. They almost didn't go back. Though they had exchanged Christmas cards with him faithfully, would they have anything to say to him? It didn't seem at all likely. When they walked in, there he was, and he saw them and smiled, and they knew that they didn't have to have anything to say to him. They loved him. They had always loved him.

He led them to a table and they asked him what to order and he told them, just as he used to do; but when Harold asked him to bring three glasses with the bottle of wine, he shook his head and said warningly, as to a younger brother: "This is a serious restaurant." He stood by their table, talking to them while they ate, or left them to go look after another table and then returned to pick up where they had left off. They found they had too much to say to him. When they left, they promised to meet him at noon on Sunday—for an apéritif, they assumed. On Sunday, the four of them—Joseph's wife was there beside him—sat for a while in front of the brasserie, watching the people who passed, and talking quietly, and when the Americans got up to go, they discovered that they had been invited to lunch, in Joseph's apartment, seven flights up, in the rue des Ciseaux. It was a tiny apartment, with two rooms, and only two windows. But out of each they could see a church tower, Joseph's wife showed them. And they could hear the bells. She confessed to Barbara that they greatly regretted not having children, and that all their affection should be heaped on a canary. It was wrong, but they could not help it. And Barbara explained that at home they had a gray cat to whom they gave too much affection also. The canary's name was Fifi, and all that love it had no right to poured back out of its throat, and remarks were frequently addressed to it from the lunch table. Lunch went on for hours. Joseph had cooked it himself, that morning and the day before, and they saw that there is, in France, a kind of hospitality that cannot be paid for and that is so lavish one can only bow one's head in the presence of it. They drank pernod, timidly, before they began to eat. They drank a great deal of wine during lunch. They drank brandy after they stopped eating. From time to time there were toasts. Raising his glass drunkenly, Harold exclaimed: "A Fifi!" and a few minutes later Joseph pushed his chair back and said: "A nos amis, à nos amours!" The Americans were just barely able to get down the stairs.

Side by side with what happens, the friendship that unexpectedly comes into full flower, there is always, of course, the one that could and does not. Among the clients of the little restaurant in the rue de Montpensier there was a tall interesting-looking man, in his late forties, and his two barely grown sons. The father usually arrived first, and the sons joined him, one at a time. In their greeting there was so much undisguised affection that the Americans found them a pleasure to watch. But who were they, and where was the boys' mother? Was she ill? Was she dead? And why, in France, did they eat in a restaurant instead of at home? Like a fruit hanging ripe on the bough, the acquaintance was ready to begin. All it needed was a word, a smile, a small accident, and they would all five have been eating together.

II: *Some Explanations*

If they had been on shipboard, for instance—but they were not on shipboard.

And who were they? Were they aware of the Americans?

Of course. How could they not be? The Americans went to a movie that was on the other side of Paris, and when the lights came on, there sitting in the row ahead of them were the father and his two sons. It was all Harold could do not to speak to them. . . . Though their story is interesting, and offers some curious parallels, I don't think I'd better go into it here.

The Americans continued to see things, and to be moved by what they saw, and to love France. During the few days they were in Paris, there was an illumination of Gothic and Renaissance sculpture at the Louvre, and a beautiful exhibition of medieval stained-glass windows, at the Musée des Arts Décoratifs.

And Mme Viénot?

They didn't see her. And neither did they try to see Jean Allégret. They were afraid it would be pushing their luck too far, and also they were in Paris such a short time, and there were so many things they wanted to see and do. They saw a school children's matinee of *Phèdre* at the Comédie Française and a revival of *Ciboulette* at the Comique. Harold got up one morning at daybreak and wandered through the streets and markets of Les Halles. Coming home with his arms full of flowers, he stopped and stared at an old woman who was asleep with her cheek pressed against the pavement. His eyes, traveling upward, saw a street sign: rue des Bons Enfants. The scene remained intact in his mind afterward, like a vision; like something he had learned.

Did they adopt a child?

No. It is not easy, and before they had managed to do it, Barbara became pregnant. It was as if someone in authority had said Since you are now ready and willing to bring up anybody's child, you may as well bring up your own. . . . So strange, life is. Why people do not go around in a continual state of surprise is beyond me. In the foyer of the Musée Guimet, Barbara saw a Khmer head—very large it was, and one side of the face seemed to be considering closely, from the broadest possible point of view, all human experience; the expression of the other half was inward-looking, concerned with only one fact, one final mystery.

Those people whose windows look out on the gardens of the Palais-Royal know that though the palace is built of stone it is not gray but takes its color from the color of the sky, which varies according to the time of day. In the early morning, at daybreak, it is lavender-blue. In the evening it is sometimes flamingo-colored. If you walk along the rue La Feuillade shortly after five o'clock in the morning, you will come to a bakery that is below the street level, and the smell of freshly baked bread is enough to break your heart. And if you stand late at night on the Pont des Arts, you will find yourself in the eighteenth century. The lights in the houses along the Quai Malaquais and the Quai de Conti are reflected in the river, and the reflections elongate as if they were trying to turn into Japanese lanterns. The Louvre by moonlight is a palace, not an art gallery. And if you go there in the daytime you must search out the little stairway that leads up to a series of rooms where you can buy, for very little money, engravings of American flowers—the jack-in-the-pulpit, the May apple, the windflower—that were made from specimens collected by missionaries and voyageurs in the time of Louis XIV. At the flower market there is a moss rose that is pale pink with a deeper pink center, and you will walk between trenches of roses and peonies that are piled like cordwood. And though not every day is beautiful (sometimes it is cold, sometimes it is raining) there will be days when the light in the sky is such that you wonder if—

I know, I know. Everybody feels that way about Paris. London is beautiful too. So is Rome. So, for that matter, is New York. The world is full of beautiful cities. What interests me is

Mme Viénot. It is a pity that they did not bother to see her.

She was in the country. But just because the Americans didn't see her is no sign we can't. . . . It is a Tuesday. The sky in Touraine is a beautiful, clear, morning-glory blue. She wheels her bicycle from the kitchen entryway, mounts it, and rides out of the courtyard. The gardener and his wife and boy are stacking the hay in the park in front of the house, and a M. Lundqvist is leaning out of the window of Sabine's room. He waves to her cheerfully, and she waves back.

She stops to talk to the gardener, who is optimistic about the hay but thinks it is time they had rain; otherwise there will be no fodder for the cows, and the price of butter will go sky-high, where everything else is already.

Halfway down the drive she turns and looks back over her shoulder. The front of the house, with its steep gables, box hedge, raked gravel terrace, and stone balustrade, says: "If one can only sustain the conventions, one is in turn sustained by them . . ." Reassured, she rides on. She is going to haggle with the farmer, five miles away, who supplies her with cream and butter and the plain but admirable cheese of the locality. When she looks back a second time, the trees have closed in and the château is lost from sight. But it can be seen again from the public road, across the fields—a large, conspicuous white-stone house, the only house of this size for several miles around.

M. and Mme Bonenfant celebrated their son's coming of age here, and the marriages of their two daughters, and of one of their granddaughters. Like all well-loved, well-cared for, hospitable, happy houses, the Château Beaumesnil gives off a high polish, a mellowed sense of order, of the comfort that is felt by the eye and not the behind of the beholder. A stranger walking into the house for the first time is aware of the rich texture of sounds and silences. The rugs seem to have an affinity for the floor they lie on. The sofas and chairs announce: "We will never allow ourselves to be separated under any circumstances." "This is rightness," the house says. "This is what a house should be; and to have to live anywhere else is the worst of all possible misfortunes."

The village is just the same—or practically. M. Canourgue's stock is now on open shelves instead of under the counter or in the back room. There is a clock in the railway station, and the station itself is finished. Though the travel posters have been changed and the timetables are for the year 1953, the same four men are seated on the terrace of the Café de la Gare.

The village is proud of its first family, and also of the fact that the old lady chose to throw in her lot with theirs. Mme Bonenfant is eighty-eight now, and suffers from forgetfulness. Far too often she cannot find her handkerchief or the letter she had in her hand only a moment ago. On her good days she enjoys the quickness and clarity of mind that she has always had. She is witty, she charms everyone, she is like an ivory chess queen. On her bad days chère Maman sits with her twisted old hands in her lap, quiet and sad, and sometimes not really there; not anywhere. It bothers her that she cannot remember how many great-grandchildren she has, and she says to Sabine: "Was that before your dear father died?" and realizes from the look of horror that this question gives rise to that she has confused a son-in-law who is dead with one who is very much alive. She leaves the house only to go to Mass on Sunday, or to the potager with her wicker garden basket and shears. She is still beautiful, as a flower stalk with its seed pod open and empty or a tattered oak leaf is beautiful. The potager never ceases to trouble her, because ever since the war the fruit trees, flowers, and vegetables have been mingled in a way that is not traditional. And terrible things have happened to the scarecrow. "Look at me!" he cries. "Look what has happened to me!" Mme Bonenfant, snipping away at the sweet-pea stems, answers calmly: "To me also. All experience is impoverishing. A great deal is taken away, a little is given in return. Patience is obligatory—the patient acceptance of much that is unacceptable."

II: *Some Explanations*

Now it is evening, but not evening of the same day. The house is damp, and it has been raining since early morning. There are no guests at the moment. With her poor circulation Mme Bonenfant feels the cold, and so sometimes even in summer a small fire is lit for her in the Franklin stove in the petit salon. Mme Viénot is sitting at the desk, going over her accounts. Alix is on the divan. And Mme Bonenfant is going through a box of old letters.

"This is what the world used to be like," she says suddenly. "It is a letter from my father to his sister in Paris. 'The two young people'—Suzanne and Philippe, he is referring to— 'evinced a delicate fondness for each other that we ought to be informed of. . . .' "

"And were they informed of it?" Alix asks.

"Yes. Shortly afterward," Mme Bonenfant says, and goes on reading to herself. When she finishes the letter, she puts it back in its envelope and drops it into the fire. The paper bursts into flame, the pale-brown ink turns darker for a few seconds and then this particular link with the remote past is gray ashes, and even the ashes are consumed.

"But surely you aren't destroying old letters!" Mme Viénot exclaims.

"When I am gone, who will be interested in reading them?" Mme Bonenfant says.

"*I* am interested," Mme Viénot says indignantly. "We all are. I have implored you—I implore you now—not to burn family letters."

"You didn't know any of the people," Mme Bonenfant says with finality, as though Mme Viénot were still a child.

Though she is very old, and tired, and forgetful, she is still the head of the family.

Now suppose I pass my hand over the crystal ball twice. What do we see? The furniture is under dust covers, the shutters are closed, the grass is not cut in the park, the potager is a tangle of weeds and briers. Sometimes in the night there are footsteps on the gravel terrace in front of the house, but no one lies in bed with a wildly beating heart, hearing them. All the rooms of the house are quiet except the third-floor room at the head of the stairs. The shutters here have come loose; they must not have been fastened securely. At some time, the ornamental shield has been removed from the fireplace, and occasionally there is a downdraft that redistributes the dust. Wasps beat against the windowpanes. In the night the shutters creak, the black-out paper flaps softly, the room grows cold. The mirrors recall long-forgotten images: the Germans; the young American couple; M. Lundqvist; Mme Viénot as a girl, expectant and vulnerable. Moonlight comes and goes. The mirrors remember the poor frightened squirrel that got in and could not get out. And in the hall at the foot of the stairs—this is really very strange—the grandfather's clock chimes again and again, though there is nobody to wind it.

You are not asking me to believe that?

No. The wheels turn, revealing (but in the dark, and to nobody) the exact hour of the day or night when footsteps are heard on the gravel. The children on their teeter-totter on the clock face are not afraid. They go right on recording the procession of seconds. Time is their only concern: the relentless thieving that nobody pays any attention to; or if they have become aware of it, they try not to think about it.

If you are of a certain temperament, you do think about it, anyway. You think about it much too much, until the sense of deprivation becomes intolerable and you resort to the Lost-and-Found Office, where, by an espèce de miracle, everything has been turned in, everything is the way it used to be. It requires only a second to throw open the shutters and remove the dust covers and air out musty rooms. "Do, do, l'enfant, do . . ." Alix sings, pushing the second-hand baby carriage back and forth under the shade of the Lebanon cedar, until Annette lets go of her thumb and falls fast asleep. The departure is as abrupt as if she had stepped into a little boat. The baby carriage has become a familiar sight on the roads around the château. Propped up on a fat pillow, the fat baby stares at the barking dog, at M. Fleury when he drives past in his noisy camion, at the little boy, Alix's friend, who has now fully mastered the art of riding a bicycle and rides round and round the baby carriage, sometimes not using his hands. Watching Alix go off down the driveway, Mme Viénot is sometimes tempted to say to her sister: "She does not look happy," but it is not the kind of remark one shouts into a hearing aid, if one can avoid it, and also, Mme Viénot reflects, it is quite possible that Mathilde's daughters do not confide in her, either.

During the daytime, Sabine reads or draws. She makes drawings of grasses and leaves and fruit from the garden. She makes a drawing of the two rain-stained statues, with the house in the background. Mme Viénot observes that no letters come for her, and that she does not seem to expect any. There is a note from a cousin, and Sabine leaves it unopened on the table in her room for three days. The sound of her voice coming from her grandmother's room is cheerful, but that is perhaps nothing more than the effect chère Maman has on her, on everybody. Mme Bonenfant arranges bouquets in the manner of Fantin-Latour, who is her favorite painter, in the hope that Sabine will be tempted to paint them. Sabine draws the children instead.

For the second week in a row, Eugène does not come down from Paris. Neither does he write, though Alix writes to him. In the evenings, Mme Viénot works at her desk in the petit salon. The two girls sit side by side on the ottoman, sharing the same pool of lamplight. Alix is knitting a sweater for the baby, Sabine is reading *Gone With the Wind* in French, Mme Bonenfant and Mme Cestre face each other across the little round table, with the *diamonoes* spread out on the green baize cloth. If she plays with anyone else, Mme Bonenfant finds that the game tires her. But Mme Cestre, far from being impatient with her mother when it takes her so long to decide where to place her counter, does not even notice, and has to be reminded that it is now her turn. The evenings pass very much as they did during the war, except that everybody is a little older, trucks do not come and go in the courtyard all night, and the only male in the house is a little boy of four, who shows no signs of ever becoming a professional soldier.

When they have all gone up to bed, the grandfather's clock in the downstairs hall chimes eleven fifteen and eleven thirty and a quarter of twelve and midnight.

Hearing the clock strike, Mme Viénot gets up from her desk, where she is writing a letter, and goes into the room across the hall. Mme Bonenfant is sitting up in bed, and when Mme Viénot takes the book from her hands, she sees that her mother has been reading Bossuet's funeral oration on the Grand Condé. The white bedspread is lying on a chair, neatly folded. The room's slight odor of camphor and old age Mme Viénot has long since become accustomed to. Mme Bonenfant removes her spectacles, folds them, and puts them on the night table, beside the photograph of her dead son.

Mme Viénot takes away the pillows at her mother's back, and the old woman lies flat in the huge double bed, as she will lie before very long in her grave. Is she afraid, Mme Viénot wonders. Does she ever think about dying?

There is little or no point in asking. Her mother would not consider this a proper subject for conversation. Actually, there are a good many subjects that chère Maman, close as she is to the end of her life, does not care to speak of. To question her about the past, to try to get at her secrets, is merely to provoke a smile or an irrelevant remark.

As she opens the window a few inches, Mme Viénot suddenly remembers how when she was a child her mother, smelling of wood violets, used to come and say good night to her. If one only lives long enough, every situation is repeated. . . .

Back in her own room, she undresses and puts on her nightgown and the dark-red wrapper, which is worn at the cuffs, she notices. Seated at the dressing table, she digs her fingers into a jar of cleansing cream and, having wiped away powder and rouge, confronts the gray underface. She and it have arrived at a working agreement: the underface, tragic, sincere, irrevocably middle-aged, is not to show itself until late at night when everyone is in bed. And in return for this discreet forbearance, Mme Viénot on her part is ready to acknowledge that the face she now sees in the mirror is hers.

She goes over to the desk and takes up the letter where she left off. When it is finished, she puts it in its envelope, licks the flap, seals it, and puts it with several other letters, all written since she came upstairs. The pile of letters represents the future, which can no more be trusted to take care of itself than the present can (though experience has demonstrated that there is a limit, a point beyond which effort cannot go, and many things happen, good and bad, that are simply the work of chance).

She begins a new letter. After a moment her pen stops moving, and she listens to the still house. Again there is a creaking sound, but it is in the walls, not in the passage outside her door. The pen moves on again, like a machine. Mme Viénot is waiting for Sabine to come and say good night. The poor child must be disheartened at losing her job with *La Femme Elégante,* and it is indeed a pity, but such things happen, and she is prepared to offer comfort, reassurance, the indisputable truth that what seems like misfortune is often a blessing in disguise. She glances impatiently at her wrist watch, and sees that it is quarter of one. She writes two more letters, even so. Her acquaintance, now that she no longer lives in Paris, shows a tendency to forget her unless prodded regularly with letters and small attentions. Paying guests, when they leave, cannot be counted on to remember indefinitely what an agreeable time they have had, and so may fail to return or fail to send other clients. A note, covering one page and part of the next, serves to remind them, if it is a question of someone's searching out a pleasant, well-situated, wholly proper establishment, that they know just the place—a handsome country house about two hundred kilometers from Paris and not far from Blois.

Mme Viénot takes off the red dressing gown and puts it over the back of a chair, gets into bed, and opens the book on her bedside table. She reads a few lines and then turns out the light. It is time that Sabine learned to be more thoughtful of others.

Stretched out flat, she discovers how tired she is, and for a moment or two she passes directly into that stage of conscious dreaming that precedes sleep. Between dreams, she reflects that the younger generation has very little affection for Beaumesnil. It is important only to Eugène.

The telephone rings, and when Mme Viénot answers it, she hears the voice of Mme Carrère. Monsieur has had a slight relapse—nothing serious, but the doctors think it would be advisable for him to be in the country, where there is absolute quiet, in a place that did him so much good before. They arrive that afternoon by car, and find their old rooms waiting for them. "You will want to rest after your long drive," Mme Viénot says. "Thérèse will bring you a can of hot water immediately. Then you need not be disturbed until dinnertime." And closing the door behind her, she passes happily over the border into sleep, but the ratching, scratching sound draws her back into consciousness. The sound continues at irregular intervals. A squirrel or a fieldmouse, she tells herself. Or a rat.

After half an hour she sits up in bed, turns on the light, props the pillows behind her back. With a sigh at not being able to go to sleep when she so much needs a good night's rest, she reaches for the book. It is the memoirs of Father Robert, an early nineteenth-century Jesuit missionary, who lived among the Chinese, and was close to God. Mme Viénot puts what happened to him, his harsh but beautifully dedicated life, between her and all silences, all creaking noises, all failures, all searching for answers that cannot be found.

Also by

WILLIAM MAXWELL

"Maxwell's voice is one of the wisest in American fiction;
it is, as well, one of the kindest." —John Updike

ALL THE DAYS AND NIGHTS
The Collected Stories

The twenty-one stories in *All the Days and Nights* (eight of which
appear in book form for the first time) take us from a small town
in turn-of-the-century Illinois to a precariously balanced enclave
of the good life in Manhattan; together they make up what
William Maxwell calls "a Natural History of home," a tour of a
world that engages us entirely, and whose characters command
our deepest loyalty and tenderness.

Fiction/Literature/0-679-76102-0

ANCESTORS
A Family History

Ancestors is the history of William Maxwell's family, which he re-
traces branch by branch across the wilderness, farms, and small
towns of the nineteenth-century Midwest. Out of letters and
journals, memory and speculation, Maxwell takes his readers
into the lives of settlers, itinerant preachers, and small businessmen and makes us understand the way they saw their world and
imagined the world to come.

Literature/Memoir/0-679-75929-8

The Presidency of George W. Bush

THE PRESIDENCY OF

George W. Bush

A First Historical Assessment

JULIAN E. ZELIZER, *Editor*

Princeton University Press   Princeton and Oxford

Library of Congress Cataloging-in-Publication Data
The presidency of George W. Bush : a first historical assessment /
Julian E. Zelizer, editor.
p. cm.
Includes bibliographical references and index.
ISBN 978-0-691-13485-7 (hardcover : alk. paper) — ISBN 978-0-691-14901-1
(pbk. : alk. paper)   1. United States—Politics and government—2001–
2009.   2. Bush, George W. (George Walker), 1946–—Political and social
views.   I. Zelizer, Julian E.
E902.P695 2010
973.931092—dc22   2010000524

British Library Cataloging-in-Publication Data is available

In memory of Julio and Rosita Rotman

CONTENTS

CONTRIBUTORS

MARY L. DUDZIAK is Judge Edward J. and Ruey L. Guirado Professor of Law, History, and Political Science at the University of Southern California Gould School of Law.

GARY GERSTLE is James G. Stahlman Professor of American History and professor of political science at Vanderbilt University.

DAVID GREENBERG is associate professor of history and of journalism and media studies at Rutgers University.

MEG JACOBS is associate professor of history at the Massachusetts Institute of Technology.

MICHAEL KAZIN is professor of history at Georgetown University and co-editor of *Dissent*.

KEVIN M. KRUSE is associate professor of history at Princeton University.

NELSON LICHTENSTEIN is professor of history and director, Center for the Study of Work, Labor, and Democracy, at the University of California, Santa Barbara.

FREDRIK LOGEVALL is John S. Knight Professor of International Studies and professor of history as well as director of the Mario Einaudi Center for International Studies at Cornell University.

TIMOTHY NAFTALI is the author of books on the cold war and American presidency.

JAMES T. PATTERSON is emeritus professor of history, Brown University.

JULIAN E. ZELIZER is professor of history and public affairs, Princeton University.

ACKNOWLEDGMENTS

I WOULD LIKE TO THANK ANNE-MARIE SLAUGHTER, NOLAN McCarty, and Jeremy Adelman for providing the financial support that was needed to organize the conference that resulted in this volume. Michele Epstein and Helene Wood handled the organizational component of the event in impeccable fashion.

I would also like to thank Anthony Badger, Larry Bartels, Charles Cameron, George Edwards, Fred Greenstein, Dan Rodgers, Bruce Schulman, John Thompson, Keith Whittington, and Brandice Canes-Wrone, who offered insightful commentary on the various chapters. All the participants in the Boston University–Clare College, Cambridge University–Princeton University Political History Conference provided a wonderful forum for discussing the initial drafts of these chapters. The anonymous reviewers of the manuscript offered very useful suggestions. And finally, thanks to Brigitta van Rheinberg and Clara Platter for their editorial enthusiasm and guidance. Natalie Baan and the production team smoothly brought this to a conclusion.

The contributors to this volume made the book a pleasure to edit. They produced outstanding and original pieces on time and offered excellent suggestions to fellow authors, including myself.

I dedicate this book to my late grandparents, Rosita and Julio Rotman, who always provided me with endless love and support from their home in Argentina.

The Presidency of George W. Bush

1

ESTABLISHMENT CONSERVATIVE

The Presidency of George W. Bush

JULIAN E. ZELIZER

FOLLOWING THE TRAGIC EVENTS OF 9/11, WHEN AL QAEDA TER-
rorists crashed three airplanes into the World Trade Center and the
Pentagon, Americans turned their frightened eyes toward George W.
Bush to see just what kind of president he would be.

Most people weren't sure what they would find. The new president
was still hard to define. His campaign in 2000 had sent mixed signals
on a variety of issues. Bush, the son of former president George H. W.
Bush (1989–93), had run as a "compassionate conservative" who understood that in certain areas the federal government was necessary.
He assured supporters he would use the power of the federal government to ameliorate problems such as inadequate primary education
programs. "Big government is not the answer," Bush told Republicans
at his acceptance speech at the Philadelphia convention. "But the alternative to bureaucracy is not indifference. It is to put conservative
values and conservative ideas into the thick of the fight for justice
and opportunity."

At the same time, Bush remained loyal to the Reagan Revolution
by assuring voters he would pursue tax cuts, deregulation, and reduced spending. He was determined to avoid the fate of his father,
who had accepted a tax increase in 1990, contradicting his famous
campaign pledge, "Read my lips: no new taxes," and had thus alien-
ated conservatives from his administration. On foreign policy, Bush

criticized President Bill Clinton and his opponent, Vice President Al Gore Jr., for having deployed troops on international peace-keeping missions that were not vital to the national interest. Yet at the same time, Bush called for a tougher posture against rogue states such as Iraq and North Korea and supported increased funding for the Pentagon.

Further complicating Bush's presidency was the fact that he had been elected in an extraordinarily close and contested election. Problems with the ballots in Florida had resulted in a recount, court battles, and a controversial Supreme Court decision in December in *Bush v. Gore* that was needed to cement his victory. As a result, some Americans did not accept his presidency as legitimate, feeling that the election had literally been stolen from Gore. Many others who accepted the outcome of the judicial process, including some Republicans, remained skeptical that Bush had the skills and gravitas to succeed.

In his first few months in the White House, Bush did not fully reveal what his agenda would be. In some cases he appeared to be exactly the conservative that the right wing had hoped for. The president started his term with an executive order that weakened clean water standards. He then pushed a regressive tax cut through Congress by employing a highly partisan strategy. Pleasing the right wing of the GOP, Bush announced in August that he was sharply curtailing embryonic stem-cell research. But the administration was not entirely predictable. In his first year, Bush worked with Senate Democrats to enact the No Child Left Behind law, legislation that extended the role of the federal government in education. Bush also made a number of high-level cabinet appointments of African Americans and Latino Americans, moves that Gary Gerstle in chapter eleven demonstrates reflected a genuine commitment to pursue ethnic and racial diversity.

Nor was there a clear trajectory on foreign policy before 9/11. The administration had rejected multilateralism when it aggressively pushed to reinvigorate the missile shield program and withdrew from several international agreements. Bush talked tough against the Chinese government but walked away from a military confrontation after the Chinese captured a downed U.S. spy plane and the pilots on board.

While questions about Bush's core agenda lingered throughout his eight years in the White House, what did become clear, to the surprise of many of his opponents, was that the administration developed four relatively coherent objectives, some of which they arrived in Washington ready to pursue and others that evolved only after they had control of the White House and lived through the crisis of 9/11, in an effort to bring to fruition the battles conservatives had been waging since the 1940s.

The administration's first objective was to craft federal policies that facilitated the economic and demographic shift that had been taking place since the 1970s, with the transfer of economic and political power to the service-, high-tech-, and oil-based economic sectors of the Sun Belt. The shift in power had been occurring over several decades as the South and Southwest experienced sizable increases in population and surging economic growth. Southern states, boasting of their nonunionized workforces and low tax rates, had worked hard to entice businesses through tax incentives and direct economic subsidies. Workers moving to this region left behind stagnant economies in the Northeast and Midwest. Retirees moved to these low-tax states because air conditioning made living conditions more tolerable.[1]

As Nelson Lichtenstein and Meg Jacobs show in their respective chapters, Bush's election had depended on the growing influence of these states, as they were populated by voters who formed the electoral base of the modern Republican Party and were key to his electoral success. A number of Bush's domestic policies would benefit the economic interests of these states. According to Lichtenstein, for instance, the Department of Labor agreed to a request from Wal-Mart to provide fifteen days' advance notice before it would investigate allegations of child labor standards violations. With Republican control of the White House and Congress after the 2002 midterm elections, the president had the political muscle he needed to pursue policies that were beneficial to the nonunionized, low-wage, low-priced Wal-Mart economy.

The second, related objective of the Bush presidency was to accelerate progress on the twin policy goals of deregulating industry and instating tax reductions that had been central to the conservative agenda to weaken the capacity of the federal government and unleash market activity. The administration relied on executive authority to relax workplace as well as environmental regulations. The impact of the supply-side economics revolution of the 1980s on the administration's agenda was quite powerful, James T. Patterson argues in chapter six. By constraining the role of the government in the workplace and lowering the tax burden for upper-middle-class and higher Americans, Bush sought to weaken the fiscal standing of the Treasury and to roll back those areas of government that were most vulnerable politically. He also wanted to distribute government benefits, through tax cuts, to wealthy Americans, who constituted a core component of the Republican coalition. Bush also continued the practice, used by Republican presidents Richard Nixon and then Ronald Reagan, of filling important bureaucratic positions with politically motivated administrators who were unsympathetic to the programs they managed.

The third objective was to aggressively pursue the use of executive-centered national security programs that conservatives had championed since Vietnam. Republicans had pushed for expansive intelligence investigations at home and unilateral, targeted military operations abroad that flexed America's military muscle without overcommitting U.S. forces. Though this was all on their agenda upon winning office, the attacks of September 11, 2001, dramatically intensified their drive to see these policies enacted into law and caused the president to expand his reach into areas such as nation building with the war in Iraq. They undertook a radical expansion of interrogation techniques, including the use of torture, that broke with national precedent and circumvented international accords on the treatment of detainees. Timothy Naftali in chapter four and Fredrik Logevall in chapter five recount the broader strategic shift that took place during this presidency through the response to the events of 9/11.

Like Reagan and his father before him, however, Bush learned he was still operating in the shadow of Vietnam. Americans were unwilling to tolerate high numbers of casualties, would not accept the restoration of the draft, and were leery of the government's violating civil liberties in pursuit of enemies. But within that framework, as a result of 9/11, George W. Bush pushed for more expansive national security operations than his Republican predecessors had in the 1980s and 1990s.

The final objective was the boldest of all: to construct a governing Republican coalition that was comparable in strength to what Democrats had achieved after 1932. Bush's strategy for achieving this coalition, however, moved in contradictory directions. The contributors to this book reveal a tension at the heart of this coalition-building operation. One the one hand, following the Republican Party's failure to build a broad coalition in the 2000 election, there were numerous moments when the administration focused on building a coalition of the willing by ignoring moderates and focusing on policies that, as political scientists Jacob Hacker and Paul Pierson said, were "off-center."[2] The goal was to remake politics by governing with slim majorities and energizing activists on the right of the political spectrum, who voted at higher rates than the rest of the population, through symbolic issues such as attacks on liberal institutions and cultural values. In the short term, winning over moderates or Democrats was not the most efficient way to go, according to this strategy. By winning with slim margins in congressional and presidential elections, Republicans could maintain control and have the strength in numbers to remake government.[3]

On the other hand, there is substantial evidence that at other moments the administration did seek a more traditional "big tent" approach, as Bush's team had originally sought in the 2000 campaign. Most important, following the traumatic events of 9/11, what came to be called the war on terrorism had the potential to bring sizable segments of the population, including some Democrats, into the Republican fold. Bush also pushed for domestic programs that benefited broad portions of the population, not just the base, including the No Child Left Behind provisions and Medicare prescription drug benefits, the largest expansion of Medicare since its creation in 1965 (to this list should be added his failed attempt to liberalize immigration laws). A potential Republican coalition, according to Bush's political guru Karl Rove, would be rooted in noncoastal states while securing the Republican base to include voting blocs traditionally thought Democratic, from working-class white voters in the industrial sectors of the Midwest (who had already been tempted by Reagan's GOP in the 1980s) to new immigrants in the Southwest, such as Hispanics. After the narrow 2000 election victory, Rove said, "I look at this time as 1896, the time where we saw the rise of William McKinley and his vice president, Teddy Roosevelt. . . . That was the last time we had a shift in political paradigm." Gary Gerstle, Kevin M. Kruse, and Michael Kazin in their chapters all explore the ambitions and frustrations involved in these efforts to capitalize on a divided, red/blue America.

In pursuing all four objectives, the exercise of presidential power became one of the defining characteristics of Bush's administration, as Mary L. Dudziak and I show in our respective chapters. The expanding authority of the executive branch was a primary objective of President Bush and Vice President Cheney since the day they took office in January 2001. While continuing the trend that had been evident since the Progressive Era, they moved more aggressively in scale and scope than any of their immediate predecessors. The Bush administration formed in direct conversation with the 1970s. This was a decade when many members of the administration came of professional age, several working in Richard Nixon's and Gerald Ford's White House, as they watched an assertive Congress respond to Watergate by revitalizing legislative power through the War Powers Act of 1973, the Budget Reform Act of 1974, and the creation of national surveillance regulations and the Office of the Independent Counsel in 1978. Conservatives came to see presidential power, grounded in a distinct interpretation of the law, as the best available tool for combating the liberals who dominated Congress and federal agencies. Bush would spend an enormous amount of political energy, before and after 9/11, trying to vest more power in his office. The administration constantly privileged voices from the executive branch over other realms of society, tapping into traditions such as anti-intellectualism, as David Greenberg argues in chapter nine, to discredit individuals and organizations that opposed their policies.

The contributors to this book seek to evaluate Bush's presidency as he set out to accomplish these four objectives. To do so, they place Bush's presidency in a broader historical context, trying to discern what he was responsible for changing and when his administration was shaped by broader historical forces that had been developing for many years.

THE BUSH PRESIDENCY AND THE HISTORY OF CONSERVATISM

Throughout the essays, the authors find that one theme shaped George W. Bush's time in the White House. Within every policy area, Bush struggled with the central quandary of conservatism in the twenty-first century: what were the challenges conservatives faced, now that they had become the governing establishment?

The history of the Bush presidency marked the culmination of the second stage in the history of modern conservatism, a period that began in the early 1980s when conservatives switched from being an oppositional force in national politics to struggling with the challenges of governance that came from holding power.[4] Between the 1940s and the 1970s, conservatives had concentrated on trying to build a political movement. Conservatism consisted of a number of different factions, none of which sat very comfortably alongside any other. The factions depended on the theme of anti-communism and other common enemies, such as the Great Society, to create some semblance of a movement. The Religious Right harnessed the energy of evangelical leaders and churchgoers around issues such as the tax treatment of private religious schools and representations of sexuality in popular culture. Business leaders fought for tax reductions and economic deregulation. Libertarians championed the virtues of individual freedom and markets over the state. Neoconservative intellectuals and policymakers warned about the unintended consequences of Great Society programs, as well as the need to take a more aggressive military stand toward international communism. A small faction of extremist organizations explicitly played off racial animosity and fears about feminism to try to persuade former working-class Democrats into the Republican camp by fomenting a backlash against the civil rights laws from the 1960s.

In the first stage of this history, conservatives focused on building organizations, nurturing activist networks, and developing a financial infrastructure capable of challenging Democrats and liberalism. Conservatives formed political action committees, volunteer operations, radio talk shows, think tanks, and direct mail networks that facilitated the transmission of ideas and electing candidates.[5] They tried to create a movement, and they were successful.

The second stage in the history of conservatism started around 1980, with the election of Ronald Reagan to the presidency, and continued through 2008, when Republicans lost control of both branches of government and found themselves facing an internal crisis of leadership. During this period in the evolution of conservatism, Republicans struggled with the challenges that emanated from the process of governance.[6] To be sure, conservative Republicans enjoyed a number of important victories. There was, for example, the dismantling of economic regulatory programs that had been put into place during the Progressive Era and the New Deal. President Reagan also obtained congressional support for a historic tax cut in 1981 that weakened the fiscal strength of the American government, as President George W. Bush in his turn would do in 2001. By failing to update programs such as the minimum wage law, conservatives were able to diminish the value of the benefits.[7] Finally, unions, the heart of the New Deal coalition, continued to see their power decline, partially as a result of public policies unfavorable to labor.

From the moment Reagan started his presidency, conservatives also learned about the difficult compromises they would have to make because of the continued power of liberal policies, politicians, and activists in the post-1960s period. Conservatism did not remake politics but rather built its influence on top of existing structures. Conservative politicians quickly became aware of the popularity of many domestic programs that on paper were easy to attack but in practice were almost impossible to retrench. Reagan and the Republican Senate were unable to eliminate most portions of the federal government. After flirting with reductions in Social Security in 1981, the administration backed off when it encountered stiff opposition. Federal spending increased significantly in the 1980s. As James T. Patterson found, federal spending reached 23.5 percent of GDP in 1983, falling only to 21.2 percent in 1989, which was still higher than in the 1970s. At the same time, the number of federal employees *expanded* to 3.1 million from 2.9 million when Reagan was in office.[8]

When dealing with national security, conservatives found that the legacy of Vietnam and the challenges from liberals to the national security state were deeply rooted. Reagan started his time in the White House by using vitriolic rhetoric about how he intended to weaken communism in areas such as Central America. However, by 1982 and 1983, Reagan found himself hamstrung by congressional Democrats as well as by public opinion, which was notably tepid about military intervention. An international nuclear freeze movement placed immense pressure on Republicans to tone down their aggressive stance toward the Soviets.[9]

Policy resilience was only one problem in the period of conservative governance. Once conservatives had power, it became clear that holding together the different factions of the movement would be difficult. Social conservatives were frustrated with Republican politicians for ignoring their issues. Many neoconservatives were angry when Reagan softened his position toward the Soviets during his second term. When the cold war came to an end in 1991 and conservatives lost their unifying issue of anticommunism, the internal tensions became more severe.

Following the 1994 Republican takeover of Congress, when

Democrat Bill Clinton was president, conservatives encountered similar problems on Capitol Hill. The Republican majority was razor thin in both the House and the Senate. This limited much of what conservatives could accomplish, given the veto power of the Senate minority. When Republicans forced a government shutdown in 1995–96 as they demanded steeper cuts in domestic spending than President Clinton was willing to accept, public opinion turned against the GOP, and the Republican leadership backed off many of its key demands. With the exception of Aid to Families with Dependent Children (which Clinton and Congress ended in 1996), most of the welfare state remained intact.

The biggest test of governance began in 2001. By then, conservatives were not only dealing with issues of governance, they had become the political establishment—a far cry from the 1964 presidential campaign, when Senator Barry Goldwater and his supporters were seen as renegade mavericks trying to shake up Washington. In Congress, Republicans after 1994 developed close working alliances with interest groups on K Street. Conservatives controlled Congress and the White House after 2002 (in 2001 the parties split control of the Senate until Senator Jim Jeffords bolted from the GOP in the summer, leaving Democrats in control), as well as the well-established universe of conservative think tanks, advocacy organizations, publications, and media outlets. Congressional reforms in the 1970s and 1990s had left the party leadership in both chambers with a formidable arsenal of procedural weapons to impose discipline on members of their own caucus and to stifle the participation of the opposition party. The Republican leadership consisted of seasoned veterans in the legislative process, such as Tom DeLay, who as both a minority and a majority party member had built the strength of the GOP in Congress by mastering the nuances of procedural conflict to undermine the Democrats.[10]

The presence of a conservative establishment was essential to Bush's pursuit of his broader political and policy objectives and his attempt to overcome the immense obstacles conservatives had struggled with over the preceding three decades. Without a clear electoral mandate before his reelection in 2004 and facing thin governing majorities in Congress and high unpopularity ratings in his second term, the organizational and financial infrastructure of conservatism played a crucial role in providing him with the political muscle he had.

But the assistance from the conservative establishment that helped Bush achieve some of his objectives came at great political cost. Congressional Republicans struggled with the problems of corruption. Scandals involving the relationship of Republicans to corrupt lobbyists and their reliance on federal spending to pay off political loyalists brought down several key players, including House Majority Leader Tom DeLay, and were pivotal to bringing Democrats into power in the 2006 midterm elections.

Since the time of the Reagan administration, Republicans had also weakened the federal bureaucracy by underfunding key agencies and stacking administrative bodies with political loyalists. Whereas the strategy to weaken government without trying to directly retrench it had been shrewd, and to some extent successful, it became hugely problematic when Bush needed a stronger federal infrastructure to deal with issues ranging from hurricanes in the bayous to reconstructing a democratic Iraq.

Because conservatives had enjoyed power for a substantial amount of time, they had come to rely on federal spending and government largesse to satisfy their own electoral base. It was hard to wean the party from this spending habit. Republicans thus had trouble substantially reducing spending, not just because liberalism remained stronger than they had believed but also because Republicans feared offending key constituents and organized interest groups within the Republican coalition. The result was that spending continued to grow at a brisk pace after 2000.

One of the unexpected effects of Bush's presidency was to stimulate new forces and tactics within the Democratic Party. In 2004, many younger voters who had not participated in politics threw their support behind Vermont Governor Howard Dean's unsuccessful campaign for the Democratic nomination. Dean drew on new internet-based fund-raising and organizational tactics, and appealed to many voters who had become disillusioned with the political system by taking a strong and forceful stand against Bush. While Dean lost the nomination, he redirected the party in fundamental ways. Many of the same sources of support returned to the campaign trail four years later.

During the 2008 campaign, Democrat Barack Obama tapped into this discontent by combining an antiestablishment and anti-conservative campaign to propel himself into the Democratic nomination and defeat his rival, Hillary Clinton. Obama connected Clinton to the conservative establishment, particularly on issues such as Iraq, and undercut her ability to capitalize on her experience.

With conservatives looking like the establishment in the eyes of many Americans, activists in the conservative movement started to rebel against their own leadership. The result was fractious and contentious debate among the Right.

The Republican presidential candidate, John McCain, and vice presidential candidate Sarah Palin predictably ran as agents of change and positioned themselves as opponents of the conservative establishment from which they came. At the convention, they reiterated the theme of change—though it was their party that was in power—and competed with Democrats not by defending the status quo but by calling for fundamental reform. Governor Palin told one audience that "John McCain has used his career to promote change. He doesn't run with the Washington herd. Let's send the maverick of the Senate to the White House."

The transition of conservatism from an opposition movement to the governing establishment seemed complete, with Republicans rebelling even against their own predecessors. It was the particular challenges from the stage of governance that defined George W. Bush's presidency.

Politically, the Bush presidency was not what Republicans had hoped for. If conservatives hoped for a coalition, which most did, the outcome could not have been more disappointing. The 2008 election resulted in a Democratic White House and Congress. The events surrounding the campaign raised questions about the basic policies, ideas, and leaders of the Republican Party. The aftermath of the election revealed a striking dearth of respectable conservative leaders. With America battling an economic crisis as Bush exited the White House and with continued instability overseas, Bush's presidency concluded with conservatism in a state of political instability, raising serious questions about the future of the movement.

President Obama is unsure what will happen next, displaying skepticism that the conservative era is actually over. "What Reagan ushered in was a skepticism toward government solutions to every problem," Obama said, "a suspicion of command-and-control, top-down social engineering. I don't think that has changed. I think that's a lasting legacy of the Reagan era and the conservative movement, starting with Goldwater. But I do think [what we're seeing] is an end to the knee-jerk reaction toward the New Deal and big government."[11] In his first year in the White House, President Obama encountered significant difficulty moving forward most of his agenda and saw conservatives reenergized in their opposition to his signature measure, national health care reform. But if conservatism is to survive as a political movement, it will have to be by overcoming the condition it found itself in in the aftermath of the Bush presidency rather than as a result of what he accomplished.

It is impossible to tell how history will judge President Bush, given that interpretations of his tenure in office will change many times and be open to ongoing debate. Some historians who have weighed in point to decisions such as the surge of U.S. troops in Iraq, which stabilized conditions, as evidence of successful presidential leadership. Donald Critchlow has argued that "Bush's remaking of the Republican party was a major achievement. By strengthening party organization at the national and state levels, Bush . . . enabled the GOP to harness grassroots activism to win control of Congress and the White House."[12] Yet a majority of professional historians (who do tend to come from the liberal side of the political spectrum) have been less sanguine. For a cover story in *Rolling Stone*, "The Worst President in History?," Sean Wilentz began by saying, "Bush's presidency appears headed for colossal historical disgrace."[13]

The historians whose essays appear in this book do not attempt to resolve this debate. The chapters catalogue some of the successes of the administration, ranging from counterterrorism efforts against al Qaeda between 2001 and 2003 through AIDS policy in Africa to the appointment of minorities to prominent government positions. They also examine some of the failures, including the damage caused by the war in Iraq, the bungled response to Hurricane Katrina, and the devastating collapse of financial markets following years of deregulation in the fall of 2008. Rather than speculate whether he was the worst or the best president in U.S. history, the contributors have attempted to place the Bush White House in a broader historical perspective by understanding his presidency in relationship to the conservative movement.

The authors of the essays in this book are trying to write a first take on the history of this period, but one that builds on the rich literature on the history of conservatism in modern America. We hope the essays provoke further investigation. Since this is an early effort to write the history of the George W. Bush presidency, the work is necessarily incomplete. We do not yet have access to some archival materials that will become available in the future. Yet, in addition to the substantial documentation instantaneously available in the age of the Internet, the contributors also have the advantage of producing this interpretation at a time when the emotions and sentiment and context of President Bush's actions are still vivid. We hope these essays offer the opening to a conversation that will continue for centuries.

2

HOW CONSERVATIVES LEARNED TO STOP WORRYING AND LOVE PRESIDENTIAL POWER

Julian E. Zelizer

THE VAST EXPANSION OF PRESIDENTIAL POWER UNDER PRESIDENT George W. Bush was as troubling for many on the right as it was for those on the left. The conservative columnist George Will lamented that "conservatives' wholesome wariness of presidential power has been a casualty of conservative presidents winning seven of the past 10 elections."[1]

There is certainly a grain of truth to the claims of conservatives who didn't want to link themselves to a strong presidency, and in this respect they legitimately disassociated themselves from Bush. Twentieth-century liberals, until the 1970s, were the people who most actively promoted the importance of a powerful president. Following the presidency of Theodore Roosevelt, contemporary liberals came to believe that executive power was integral to achieving domestic reform, designing internationalist foreign policies, and overcoming the obstacles from the legislative and judicial branches. Franklin Roosevelt's presidency during the Great Depression and World War II became a model for liberal governance. Even liberal internationalists in Congress, such as Senator William Fulbright, who promoted diplomacy and warned of the need to avoid overextending the military, accepted the superiority of the presidency as an institution relative to the legislature.[2] One need only look at Arthur Schlesinger Jr.'s magisterial three-volume history of the New Deal, published in 1957, 1958, and 1960, to gain a sense of just how much capacity liberals saw in the office of the president. In Schlesinger's narrative, Roosevelt heroically saved the nation from the depths of its economic crisis while preventing equally dangerous threats from the left and the right. Liberals continued to champion this vision until frustration among the New Left with President Lyndon Johnson's policies toward race and war, as well as the scandals of President Richard Nixon, created overwhelming fears of an "imperial presidency." These anxieties shattered liberal confidence in the executive branch.

Before the 1970s, moreover, there were some conservative activists skeptical of, if not downright hostile toward, presidential power. Contemporary conservatives had cut their teeth railing against the presidency in the 1930s. Senator Frederick Steiwer of Oregon said in 1933, "Italy is under a dictatorship; Russia is under a dictatorship; Germany is under a dictatorship, and those who are here pressing this legislation [the Economy Act and banking legislation] are seeking to put the United States of America under a dictatorship!"[3] Formed in 1934, the American Liberty League made such attacks central to their agenda. Roosevelt's court-packing plan and executive reorganization subsequently become symbols of how the president aimed to create the same kind of dictatorial government that existed in Japan and Germany. These kinds of arguments informed the writing of conservatives who feared the future of constitutional government. The warnings gained more power after the midterm elections of 1938, when conservative Democrats and Republicans were elected to Congress in large numbers. The bipartisan coalition of southern Democrats and Republicans used the committee system to block civil rights and union legislation that threatened their mutual interests. The conservative intellectual James Burnham published a book in 1959 in which he claimed that the founding fathers privileged the legislature: "Legislative supremacy was thus not a novelty for the Fathers, but a starting assumption. . . . [T]he primacy of the legislature in the intent of the Constitution is plain on the face of that document [the Constitution]."[4]

Nonetheless, recent conservative criticism of the Bush presidency ignores how deeply ingrained presidential power has become to the conservative movement. Starting early in the cold war, and vastly accelerating during the succeeding three and a half decades, a growing number of conservatives have learned to love the presidency. While conservatives have justified their position through arguments that the presidency is often the best way to achieve smaller and more accountable government, they have also counted on an aggressive and centralized presidency to pursue the aims of the conservative movement. Bush's presidency thus falls on a larger historical trajectory, even as he has clearly pushed this tradition far beyond its previous limits.

A key turning point was the 1970s, a decade that has come to be seen as more important in recent years.[5] For many conservatives, the congressional reforms that were passed in the aftermath of Watergate dangerously weakened the power of the executive branch and were a symbol of what went wrong as a result of the 1960s. The gradual delegation of authority to independent agencies, in this line of thought, had resulted in decisions being made by bureaucrats who were beyond the control of elected officials.[6]

THE NIXON YEARS

Some conservatives, such as William Buckley, had come to accept during the early cold war years that broader executive power would be essential in the fight against communism. Under President Dwight Eisenhower, some conservatives joined the president in warding off efforts by Republicans such as Senator John Bricker to curtail executive power. Buckley wrote that conservatives had to "accept Big Government for the duration—for neither an offensive nor a defensive war can be waged . . . except through the instrument of a totalitarian bureaucracy within our shores." He explained that Republicans "will have to support large armies and air forces, atomic energy, central intelligence, war production boards, and the attendant centralization of power in Washington—even with Truman at the reins of it all."[7]

But the conservative embrace of presidential power really began to take shape with the presidency of Richard Nixon between 1969 and 1974. Merging conservatism and presidential power was one of Nixon's most lasting achievements. Nixon identified as a conservative Republican who came of age during the anticommunist crusades of the early cold war era. From the beginning of his presidency, Nixon demonstrated how presidential power could be an effective tool against liberalism. He entered office convinced that liberalism was powerful because the ideology had proponents that were entrenched in Congress, the media, the bureaucracy, and academia.

The fact that he took office in a time of divided government reified this perception. Despite his victory in 1968, Democrats had retained control of the House, 243 to 192, and the Senate, 57 to 43. Not only did Democrats control Congress, liberals had been gaining more power in the House and Senate as elections and reforms weakened the power of older southern Democrats and their conservative coalition. The president believed he faced a more difficult political atmosphere than had the last Republican president, Dwight Eisenhower. Nixon and his advisers felt that congressional Democrats were being driven by the party's most partisan figures and that the administration should use this in its public relations campaigns.[8] Nixon was infuriated when Senate liberals blocked two nominations for the Supreme Court in 1969. Top advisers lamented that "not since Zachary Taylor has a new President had to try to form a new Administration with a hostile Congress second-guessing every move."[9] In October 1969, Nixon told congressional Republicans that he wanted a "systematic program of putting the blame on Congress for frustrating the legislative program." Nixon targeted the "super-partisans" in the Democratic leadership, and he presented Congress as inefficient and incapable of governing.[10] Nixon perceived that liberals would work through the bureaucracy and regulatory bodies to defend their programs.[11] Therefore, presidential power was essential, Nixon believed, to undercut liberal power.

Nixon used several tools to curtail the influence of the Democratic Congress. For instance, the president relied on the impound-ment of funds to prevent the use of money Congress had appropri-ated for specific domestic programs. He also attempted to expand domestic programs in ways that would be politically detrimental to Congress. When a debate emerged between 1969 and 1972 over the need to liberalize Social Security benefits to meet the rate of inflation, Nixon supported indexing rather than relying on the tra-ditional route of discretionary increases by Congress. Legislators immediately realized this would deny them the credit—and the power—they had enjoyed since 1950, when Congress made benefit increases a normal part of the congressional calendar. In the end, Congress passed indexation and discretionary increases to satisfy both sides. In foreign policy, Nixon conducted national security operations in Southeast Asia without congressional knowledge. The liberal historian Arthur Schlesinger Jr. noted in his diaries that "Nixon has gone further, I guess, than any President in ignoring even the forms of congressional consultation. I fear that those un-critical theories of the strong presidency that historians and politi-cal scientists, myself among them, were propagating with such en-thusiasm in the fifties have come home to roost."[12]

Most famously, Nixon depended on presidential power in his struggles against congressional investigation. He attempted to block the *New York Times* from publishing the *Pentagon Papers* (documents that held the real history of the Vietnam War) in 1971 by claiming executive privilege. He was stopped only when the Su-preme Court deemed his actions unconstitutional. During the Watergate process, Nixon tried to withhold the famous White House tapes until the courts once again ruled he had to relinquish them. He also came under intense fire for authorizing covert pro-grams through the White House to intimidate domestic protest-ers. Nixon claimed executive privilege on six different occasions.[13]

In response to Nixon, Congress passed reforms such as the War Powers Act (1973) and the Budget Reform Act (1974), which at-tempted to strengthen the role of Congress in key areas of the policymaking process. Although those reforms turned out to be less effective than their creators had hoped, at the time they were perceived as significant efforts to restore the balance between the branches of government.[14]

While Nixon demonstrated to conservatives how effective presidential power could be when turned against liberalism, his own relationship with the conservative movement became tenuous toward the end of his term. As president, Nixon attempted to build a broad coalition that could ensure his reelection. He took positions on domestic and foreign policy that angered many on the right. The passage of landmark environmental policies and the indexing of Social Security defied any claims that this Republican was truly committed to reducing the size of the welfare state. Nixon's foreign policy of détente, moreover, opened diplomatic ties with Communist China and led to arms agreements with the Soviet Union. These dramatic steps by the administration angered right-wing Republicans like Ronald Reagan, who defined themselves in large part through their staunch anticommunism.

Notwithstanding Nixon's tensions with conservatives, as well as the embarrassment that Watergate caused the GOP, his use of presidential power against liberal objectives offered a model for the Right as the conservative movement took form in the 1970s. Many up-and-coming conservative policymakers would come out of the Nixon and Ford White House, including Richard Cheney and Donald Rumsfeld. They were deeply influenced by his strategy even as they distanced themselves from his tarnished legacy. In the November 1974 issue of the *National Review*, Jeffrey Hart called on conservatives to reexamine their long-standing opposition to a strong presidency, given that the executive was needed to tame the bureaucracy and liberal media.[15]

CONGRESS REFORMS THE NATIONAL SECURITY STATE

Whereas Nixon demonstrated the strategy for conservatives to use presidential power, heightened congressional activism between 1974 and 1978 helped liberals see that a strong Congress was in their interest. The feeling of betrayal by Lyndon Johnson over

Vietnam caused many Democrats to rethink their glorification of the White House as an instrument of progress. Those frustrations greatly intensified when a Republican was in the White House. One of Senator Fulbright's first major legislative moves in the Nixon era occurred on June 25, 1969, when the Senate, by a resounding vote of 70–16, passed the National Commitments Resolution stating that the Senate needed to repair the balance among the three branches of government when dealing with foreign policy.

The sense of optimism among liberals in the legislature further increased as a result of turnover in the membership, and institutional reforms that weakened the power of senior southern conservatives who had benefited from the committee system. This movement culminated in the election of the "Watergate Babies" in 1974, mostly Democratic legislators who promised to reform government and give Congress a greater role in policymaking and oversight. Senator Barry Goldwater called them the "most dangerous Congress" the country had seen, while CIA director William Colby noted that the new members were "exultant in the muscle that they had used to bring a President down, willing and able to challenge the Executive as well as its own Congressional hierarchy, intense over morality in government, [and] extremely sensitive to press and public pressures."[16]

During the presidencies of Gerald Ford and Jimmy Carter, congressional reforms to constrain the extraconstitutional powers and common abuses of presidents angered many conservatives. Given the dynamics of the era, reform of the executive branch came to be seen as a liberal objective. Ford vetoed sixty-six bills in the span of his short tenure. He also created various policy commissions to enhance his influence. For instance, Ford created the Economic Policy Board (EPB) by executive order on September 30, 1974. The EPB was a joint cabinet-staff agency, headed by the secretary of the treasury and including a number of cabinet secretaries, the director of the Office of Management and Budget (OMB), the chairman of the CEA, and sometimes the chairman of the Federal Reserve. The president also created an Energy Resources Council and an Intelligence Oversight Board.[17] When Cambodia captured an American ship and its crew of thirty-nine in May 1975, the president sent in the Marines. The operation was a success, although forty-one Americans were killed. The president took these military steps in Cambodia without congressional authorization, despite the recently passed War Powers Resolution.

Notwithstanding this exercise of presidential power, many top members of the administration felt they were constantly on the defense. Congress was aggressive and, just as important, Ford's exercise of executive power was limited. Ford had to be cautious, given the turmoil that had unfolded surrounding Nixon's use of the presidency against his adversaries. As the historian Douglas Brinkley wrote in 2007, "throughout his 896 days in the White House, it seemed that Ford, the veteran Congressman from Michigan's Fiftieth District, didn't fully comprehend the massive executive power at his disposal."[18] Conservatives who were working in these administrations in the 1970s watched as Congress, sometimes with the hesitant endorsement of the president, rapidly expanded social regulations, including federal intervention in environmental issues, consumer protection, workplace safety, transportation, and more.[19]

The tensions over executive power were central to the CIA crisis that unfolded after an internal report in 1975 revealed the agency had sponsored assassination plots against foreign leaders. In the legislative branch, Idaho senator Frank Church chaired hearings that received substantial coverage in the press. The committee staff numbered ninety-two people at a cost of $2 million a year. Church's committee issued a report making a number of recommendations for reform, including restrictions on wiretapping, the harassment of domestic protest groups, assassination plots, and other forms of surveillance. "In the absence of war," Church argued, "no Government agency can be given license to murder. The President is not a glorified Godfather."[20] As the Senate deliberated, Church released portions of the findings on his own. Church also published articles in *Playboy* and *Penthouse*, to the chagrin of some of his advisers, who were thinking about his 1976 presidential run and conservative voters in Idaho. The Senate soon published a six-volume report and expanded oversight of the CIA. Representative Otis Pike organized similar hearings in the House, and information was leaked to papers such as the *Village Voice.* National Security Advisor Henry Kissinger called these leaks a "new version of McCarthyism."[21]

Ford, feeling pressure to disprove charges that he had attempted to whitewash the revelations about the CIA, issued an executive order on February 18, 1976, that granted the National Security Council greater power over intelligence gathering, established a Committee on Foreign Intelligence and Operations Advisor Group to monitor the CIA, as well as an Intelligence Oversight Board, imposed restrictions on surveillance, and banned assassinations of foreign leaders. Ford told Congress his reforms would "help to restore public confidence in these agencies and encourage our citizens to appreciate the valuable contribution they make to our national security."[22] In response to the Senate revelations, the FBI crafted a set of strict guidelines that curtailed the authority of officials in investigations.

Congress drafted legislation that mandated warrants for domestic surveillance. Despite the opposition of Ford, Cheney, and Rumsfeld, this would eventually pass as the Foreign Intelligence Surveillance Act (FISA) of 1978. President Carter, who had accepted the creation of the Senate and House Intelligence Committees in 1976 and 1977, agreed to this reform. He had made this promise in the campaign, in response to the Church committees. The bills were handled through the Intelligence and Judicial Committees, so Church did not play a central role in this final stage as much as Senator Birch Bayh (D-IN) and Edward Kennedy (D-MA) did. In the House, Eddie Boland (D-MA), who was the first House Intelligence Committee chairman, handled the bill. The House and Senate passed it over the objections of conservatives, who claimed that many of the prohibitions on intelligence gathering would hamper executive power, while at the same time many felt the creation of an independent court to monitor intelligence would remove this authority from a democratically elected president and give it to an unaccountable body of judges. Senator Bayh, who took over this issue in this final phase of the process as Church turned his attention to other issues, such as managing the SALT II agreements on the Senate floor, promised the bill would remove intelligence activities from the total control of the executive branch.

The boldest move was to give the courts authority over this matter, not just Congress. The conference committee made compromises, including the addition of a provision that exempted the National Security Agency from many of these regulations as long as the attorney general certified that a surveillance program met certain guidelines, a decision Kennedy said would place a high burden on the attorney general to ensure the guidelines were not violated. Boland insisted the exemption was needed to pass the measure in the House. Conservatives complained that the legislation would prevent the executive branch from conducting the kind of operations needed for national security. The four Republicans on the House Intelligence Committee—Ashbrook (OH), Robert McClory (IL), Bob Wilson (CA), and Kenneth Robinson (VA)— offered this as their dissenting view.

Building on a 1972 Supreme Court decision that deemed electronic domestic surveillance to be unconstitutional, the legislation created strict, judicially enforced procedures that had to be followed when any agency conducted foreign intelligence surveillance. The legislation thus established a legal infrastructure that criminalized particular national security activities by the executive branch. The new standard, according to Chairman Bayh, aimed to create "safeguards, against unjustified wiretaps of Americans on the basis of political activities."[23]

Although the final reforms were much milder than many critics had hoped for, and Congress did not dismantle executive power in the area of national security (Seymour Hersh lamented that the investigations "generated a lot of new information, but ultimately they didn't come up with much"),[24] conservatives did perceive the hearings and ensuing legislation as far-reaching, and the congressional decisions profoundly shaped right-wing perceptions about why the legislature was the most dangerous branch of government.

In addition, the 1978 Ethics in Government Act created the Office of the Independent Counsel (Title VI). The legislation was a response to Watergate and an effort to prevent future presidents from taking the kind of steps Nixon had taken with the Saturday Night Massacre (when he fired the special prosecutor investigating the scandal). Under the law, the attorney general would request the appointment of a prosecutor if there was evidence of wrongdoing in the executive branch. The attorney general was instructed to seek a prosecutor upon receiving "specific information" about violations of the law. Following the request, a three-person panel drawn from the U.S. Court of Appeals for the District of Columbia would appoint a special prosecutor to conduct an investigation. The prosecutor would have few budgetary or political restraints. The legislation constituted a substantial blow to presidential power by creating an unelected mechanism outside the full control of the executive branch to pursue charges of corruption.

Conservatives criticized the law as an unconstitutional and dangerous delegation of power. One congressional Republican warned that "if an attorney general cannot be trusted to enforce the law against the executive, the remedy is impeachment and not the cloning of an additional attorney general to do the job of the first."[25] Former president Ford lamented to the American Enterprise Institute that Congress was making an "imperial presidency . . . an imperiled presidency."[26]

THE CONSERVATIVES' PRESIDENT

Ronald Reagan strengthened the marriage between conservatism and presidential power that had begun under Richard Nixon. Like Nixon, Reagan believed in the centrality of the presidency. His political role model was Franklin Roosevelt. However, Reagan quickly learned that Congress presented a major obstacle to conservatives, even when Republicans controlled the Senate between

1980 and 1986. When the president attempted to cut Social Security spending in 1981, he suffered a major defeat. A bipartisan coalition of legislators, under intense pressure from voters and interest groups, forced the administration to abandon its plans. Following the 1982 midterm elections, the number of liberal northern Democrats in the House increased. Congress took a number of steps that angered the White House, including a decision to increase taxes in order to cut deficits. House Democrats also passed amendments restricting assistance in Central America. Reagan believed in peace through strength. He thought the United States needed to demonstrate its willingness to use force in areas such as Central America if it wanted to create viable conditions for negotiating with the Soviet Union and its communist allies.[27] In the president's mind, congressional Democrats did not understand that by failing to support a strong defense, they undermined the possibility for peace.

In response, Reagan and his cabinet aggressively relied on executive power to achieve conservative objectives that otherwise would have been defeated. Through executive orders, for instance, Reagan attacked environmental policies that Congress defended. Under Reagan, the Executive Office of the President supported regulations that allowed the federal government to intervene in state authority over environmental programs. The White House enhanced the power of the OMB to exert more control over agencies and how they spent funds. [28]

Conservatives attempted to reconcile their acceptance of muscular presidential power with their antigovernment arguments. They claimed that stronger presidents were needed since twentieth-century liberals had abandoned the nondelegation doctrine (Article I, Section 1, of the Constitution, which granted all legislative power to the legislative branch) in favor of agencies that could make regulatory decisions. Centralizing control in the White House, they said, was thus needed to curtail other forms of government. At the same time, enhancing presidential authority could diminish the influence of institutions such as Congress or bureaucracies that were more prone to creating intrusive federal initiatives.

According to their writing, there were three reasons to support expansive presidential power on organizational grounds. The first was that centralized power produced a more efficient administration of policy. The second was that the president had greater capacity than Congress to coordinate decision making and achieve the best results. The final argument was that a centralized presidency was more democratically accountable than other power-sharing arrangements.

Besides an acceptance of more expansive executive power to achieve conservative ends, there was a cohort of young attorneys in the Department of Justice that promoted the theory of the unitary executive. The ideas flowed out of a growing body of conservative legal scholarship in the mid-1980s that opposed the Office of the Independent Counsel on the grounds that it violated the president's total control over the executive branch (given that the courts appointed the prosecutor).[29] Proponents of these arguments insisted that all executive power should be vested in the president rather than disbursed among independent agencies.

Attorney General Edwin Meese's Justice Department became a nursery for conservative legal arguments that promoted an expansive vision of presidential authority. Lawyers associated with the Federalist Society helped to craft a new understanding of the separation of powers that enhanced the freedom of executive branch officials. Justice officials in the Reagan administration expanded the theory of the unitary executive so far as to claim that the Constitution created a total separation of powers so that no branch could infringe on the power of any other.[30]

Throughout the 1980s, the Department of Justice led the opposition to the Office of the Independent Counsel. Their constitutional concerns were probably compounded by the fact that Meese himself came under investigation from an independent prosecutor for being complicit in a scandal involving the Wedtech Corporation. The company had received generous no-bid defense contracts from the Department of Defense when Meese was their lobbyist (Meese resigned from the Justice Department in 1988).

Republicans in Congress defended executive power. Between 1968 and 1986, according to one study, conservatives in Congress voted for the pro-presidential-authority positions more often than other legislators. Presidents Nixon, Ford, and Reagan received far more votes from Republicans than from Democrats when seeking legislation concerning the power of the presidency.[31]

One of the most important moments for congressional Republicans took place during the Iran–Contra arms scandal in 1986. The scandal involved revelations that National Security Council officials had sold arms to Iran and used the money to provide assistance to the Nicaraguan Contras, assistance that Congress had prohibited. Congressional Republicans were not apologetic about what had happened, dismissing Democratic criticism as partisan and supporting the principles behind the administration's policies. The minority report, signed by eight Republicans on the Iran-Contra Committee, rested on the claim that the nation needed to vest tremendous power and accountability directly in the president.[32]

When all the major players implicated had escaped significant political or legal damage by the end of Reagan's presidency, conservatives became more willing to defend strong presidential power. The courts reversed the convictions of Oliver North and Admiral Poindexter. When President George H. W. Bush pardoned former secretary of defense Casper Weinberger, former national security advisor Robert McFarlane, and former assistant secretary of state Elliot Abrams shortly before the 1992 election, he did not apologize for their actions.

Conservatives were also furious with Independent Counsel Lawrence Walsh, who conducted a multi-million-dollar investigation of the administration on this matter (he was appointed in 1987). Congress extended the Independent Counsel Reorganization Act in 1987. Reagan signed the bill, though he thought it was unconstitutional. Upon signing the legislation, the president reiterated his concern that the policy allowed the judiciary to appoint prosecutors for the executive branch, thus violating the separation of powers. He expressed his disappointment with the fact that the legislature "has not heeded these concerns, apparently convinced that it is empowered to divest the president of his fundamental constitutional authority to enforce our nation's laws." The following year, the U.S. Court of Appeals for the District of Columbia struck down the law as a violation of the appointments clause of Article II of the Constitution and an infringement of the separation of powers.

But the Supreme Court in *Morrison v. Olson* ruled that the law was constitutional. Chief Justice William Rehnquist joined six other justices to argue that the independent counsel was an "inferior officer" and could be appointed by a panel of judges. The office was not independent because it remained subordinate to the attorney general. Justice Anton Scalia dissented, arguing that the law clearly aimed to undermine executive power: "That is what this suit is about. Power. The allocation of power among Congress, the President, and the courts in such fashion as to preserve the equilibrium the Constitution sought to establish . . . frequently an issue of this sort will come before the Court clad, so to speak, in sheep's clothing: the potential of the asserted principle to effect important change in the equilibrium of power is not immediately evident, and must be discerned by a careful and perspective analysis. But this wolf comes as a wolf."[33]

George H. W. Bush continued to champion executive power. In July 1989, William Barr, head of the Office of Legal Council, sent a memo to the counsels of each executive agency defending the concept of the unitary executive.[34] Throughout December 1990, Bush and his top advisers, including Secretary of Defense Cheney, insisted that congressional authorization to send troops to defend Kuwait against Iraq was unnecessary. The administration obtained a congressional resolution of support from Congress, but it never sought a declaration of war. In case there was any confusion on Capitol Hill, Bush stated that "my signing this resolution does not constitute any change in the long-standing positions of the executive branch on either the president's constitutional authority to use the armed forces to defend vital U.S. interests or the constitutionality of the War Powers Resolution."[35] Republicans in Congress were still in agreement about the presidency. In 1992 they blocked the renewal of the independent counsel law as they were furious about Walsh's multi-million-dollar investigation, which concluded shortly before the presidential election, producing a report that suggested Bush played a larger role in the scandal than he had previously indicated. Senate Republican leader Robert Dole called Walsh and his assistants "assassins," while the *Wall Street Journal* wrote that he had attempted to "criminalize policy differences."[36] Senator Carl Levin of Michigan complained that Republicans were "killing the most important single Watergate reform on the books."[37] Republican William Cohen, one of the architects of the original law, agreed, saying that if Clinton won the election, Republicans "might rue the day they presided over the final rites of this legislation."[38]

But most congressional Republicans agreed with Dole. In response to Levin, they pointed out that many Democrats were happy to let the law expire as they dealt with a series of scandals that rocked the House. Clinton and Attorney General Janet Reno persuaded Congress to restore the law in 1994. More Republicans supported the law, as Clinton was facing charges about his and his wife's role in an Arkansas land deal connected to the Whitewater Development Company (although many, like Iowa's James Leach, said that the attorney general was fully capable of making sure that a prosecutor remained independent).[39] Dole now said that "if there was ever a need, it is when one party controls everything."[40]

FACING ANOTHER DEMOCRATIC WHITE HOUSE

During most of the Clinton years, Republicans held control of Congress (with the 1994 elections) as Democrats secured their hold on the White House. Clinton continued the aggressive use of executive power. As partisan polarization and the frequent use of the Senate filibuster had made legislative deal-making more difficult on Capitol Hill, presidents from both parties saw incentives to working around Congress rather than through the institution. For example, Clinton withheld materials from Hillary Clinton's health care task force. He also created programs by using executive orders, such as prohibiting the construction of roads throughout national forests, providing Medicare coverage to patients who were participating in clinical trials, improving water quality standards, and more.[41] One of Clinton's most controversial actions was to rely on the 1906 Antiquities Act, which enabled the president to place sites under federal protection, to create numerous national monuments. The act did not allow subsequent presidents to reverse the decision through proclamations but only through legislation. Clinton protected more than two million acres of land in his final months as president.[42]

Republicans responded, but not consistently. Although conservatives had become much more comfortable with presidential power, they still harbored older fears about the executive branch and exhibited a sort of institutional schizophrenia. One factor behind their push against the presidency had to do with ideology. There were many Republicans who, like Newt Gingrich, believed in a strong role for the legislature in the nation's polity. Equally important, they had pragmatic reasons to resist presidential power now that their party no longer controlled the White House. Congressional Republicans tried to pass legislation and amendments that would limit presidential discretion in sending troops under UN command and for specific "nation-building" efforts. Most of these proposals failed. The most dramatic example of congressional attacks on the executive branch occurred later in the decade when Republicans slowly whittled away at executive privilege during various fights over investigations and Clinton's impeachment.

Despite these efforts, the 1990s did not witness a complete philosophical reversal among conservatives against the presidency. Indeed, the Republicans' 1994 Contract with America, widely promoted by Newt Gingrich, included proposals for a line-item veto for the president. Speaker Gingrich and the 1994 Republicans attempted to repeal the War Powers Act. Unlike in the 1970s, when Democrats railed against the presidency once a Republican was in office and tried to pass reforms to constrain executive power, numerous prominent conservatives in the 1990s remained comfortable with a strong presidency despite having a Democrat in the White House. When the independent counsel law, one of the greatest symbols of congressional resurgence from the 1970s, expired on June 30, 1999, after the failed effort to remove Clinton from office, there were few members of either party excited about extending the measure. The Republican Congress happily allowed this measure to expire.

There were also a number of prominent conservatives who defended President Clinton when he bombed Kosovo without the authorization of Congress in 1999, and continued the operation even after the House of Representatives failed to authorize it. Berkeley law professor John Yoo, a young star in the world of conservative legal thought, argued that the Constitution supported Clinton's actions.[43]

Many of the conservative legal scholars who worked in Reagan's Department of Justice spent most of the 1990s working in the court system or teaching at law schools, where they refined arguments about the unitary executive theory and presidential power. These conservative legal minds would influence younger scholars and lawyers who found themselves on the front line of political debate in the next decade.[44]

THE WAR ON TERRORISM

When George W. Bush was elected president in 2001, he continued to build on the conservative pro-presidential-authority tradition. Working with a cooperative and disciplined Republican majority, he pushed that tradition far beyond anything that had preceded it. Starting with Richard Cheney as vice president, he staffed the White House with conservative veterans of the 1970s and 1980s who believed that the executive branch remained the most effective base from which to assert themselves without having to compromise, as in Congress. Expanding presidential power was a central objective.[45]

The arguments that Republicans made in defense of the White

House during the Iran–Contra arms scandal served as an intellectual foundation for how they felt domestic and national security issues should be handled in the twenty-first century.[46] Bush targeted the executive orders Clinton had used to circumvent Congress—by using executive orders. For instance, he issued orders that stopped the provision of assistance to international family planning groups and reversed Clinton's regulations on arsenic levels in drinking water.[47] Vice President Cheney crafted the administration's energy program in secrecy by coordinating with private industry officials. When Congress attempted to force the White House to release the records from these meetings, Cheney relied on an expanded claim of executive privilege—one that covered the vice president—to withhold the documents.

Indeed, Vice President Cheney was the driving force within the administration pushing for this understanding of executive power. Cheney, who had cut his political teeth in the interbranch battles of the 1970s while serving as chief of staff for President Ford, believed that congressional reforms had dangerously undercut executive power and that no president, including Reagan, had been able to reestablish a sound balance. Cheney, as he had explained in the Iran–Contra hearings, did not believe that Congress was an efficient institution and he felt that sometimes extraordinary measures were needed to make sure the nation was safe.[48]

Influenced by Cheney, the president focused his efforts on expanding what might be called the hard power of the presidency. It is useful to think about the distinction that diplomatic scholars have made between "soft" and "hard" power to describe how the United States influences nations overseas. In foreign policy, hard power involves the use of military force and economic sanctions to coerce opponents into accepting American demands. In contrast, soft power refers to a reliance on exporting cultural and ideological values—using the power of argument and the power of persuasion—to expand America's influence in a much more subtle fashion.

Bush's White House focused on expanding hard presidential power in terms of strengthening the institutional muscle of the office and using brute force to achieve its objectives. President Clinton had made these kinds of arguments as well, but he had followed the post–World War II route of justifying such actions on technical interpretations of the law while accepting certain congressional limitations on his authority. In contrast, the Bush administration made dramatic constitutional arguments about unbounded presidential power and was defiant, if not downright hostile, about any kind of congressional restrictions whatsoever.[49]

When responding to the 9/11 attacks, Alberto Gonzales (White House counsel), John Yoo (Department of Justice), and David Addington and Lewis Libby (both Office of the Vice President) claimed that executive power was essential to fighting the war. Convinced that congressional restraints on executive power had been responsible for the failure of the government to stop al Qaeda, the president's advisers sought authority to overcome the barriers imposed by FISA, which they said had hampered domestic intelligence operations. Gonzales argued there was a strong precedent to grant the commander in chief virtually unlimited power in war and that the president could not be bound by congressional law or international treaties. A high level of executive authority was needed, they added, in the current crisis, given that speed was essential to stopping irrational enemies of the United States who were stateless and capable of lethal attacks.

Gonzales designed a plan to liberate the executive branch and military officials from most international and domestic constraints when dealing with the detainment and prosecution of prisoners. The Office of the Vice President was the driving force, pushing Justice Department officials beyond their comfort zone, in obtaining an expansive view of how much torture was tolerable.[50] Based on the memos of Yoo and Addington, Gonzales insisted that the United States needed to abandon the "cops and robbers" model that had previously been used to deal with captured terrorists, a model that relied on normal judicial channels and due process protections, and instead shift toward a war powers model. By strengthening the hand of the president, Gonzales claimed, the government could achieve faster, speedier, and more efficient results. On November 13, President Bush signed a directive that called for the use of military tribunals to prosecute alleged terrorists. The Department of Justice would also produce a series of memos justifying the use of torture, including waterboarding.

Notably, the administration had the consent and cooperation of Congress. With Congress under Republican control from 2000 to 2006 (except for a brief period when the Senate was split in 2001), Republicans used the procedural rules to push through Bush's proposals. Congressional Republican leaders and the White House converged on an executive-centered approach to governance, from domestic to national security policies.

By 2004 and 2005, the media, third parties, and some members of both parties were criticizing Bush's understanding of presidential power. In April, for instance, the media reported that Bush had relied on presidential signing statements as a means of circumventing the legislature.[51] In *Hamdan v. Rumsfeld*, the Supreme Court ruled on June 29 that the military tribunals at Guantánamo violated the Geneva Conventions as well as the Uniform Code of Military Justice.

But the backlash against Bush's executive power had limited effect. After taking over Congress in the 2006 midterm elections, Democrats were unable to roll back the institutional changes implemented since 2001. Legislative efforts to curtail programs such as the national surveillance program have failed. Many conservatives, particularly with the issue of national security, remain firmly committed to a strong presidency and have no intention of reverting back to the nineteenth or even the early twentieth century. In January 2007, the Democratic Congress seemed flummoxed when Bush signed a directive that empowered the president to shape rules and policy statements related to public health, safety, the environment, and civil rights. The directive stipulated that all agencies would establish regulatory offices, run by political appointees, to oversee material that had an impact on industry.[52] Even with his presidential ratings reaching historical lows and conservatives in the presidential primaries openly nervous about the possible demise of the Reagan coalition, President Bush did not flinch from his defense of executive power. In March 2008, the president vetoed legislation that would have prohibited the CIA from using various types of interrogation techniques such as waterboarding.

As Bush's time in office came to an end, no apologies were made. Vice President Cheney told one reporter that "If you think about what Abraham Lincoln did during the Civil War, what F.D.R. did during World War II. They went far beyond anything we've done in a global war on terror. But we have exercised, I think, the legitimate authority of the president under Article II of the Constitution as commander in chief in order to put in place policies and programs that have successfully defended the nation."[53]

One of the great ironies of this presidency is that George W. Bush's administration, which worked harder than almost any other in recent memory to expand presidential power, ended with Americans thinking so poorly of the institution. According to a Gallup poll released in September 2008, public satisfaction with the executive branch reached its lowest level seen since Watergate. Only 42 percent of Americans said they had a "great deal" or a "fair amount" of trust in the executive branch, compared with 40 percent in April 1974.

The chances for restoring a better balance of power remain unclear. There was a notable silence in the 2008 campaign about this issue from either candidate. Since the election, the prospects for change remain murky. While congressional Democrats and President Obama have been extremely critical of Bush's muscular approach to the executive branch, with Obama having promised to reverse a number of executive decisions made by his predecessor, it is hard to tell how far he is willing to go. In the first few months of his administration, Obama made a few important moves to distinguish himself from Bush. He signed an executive order announcing that the Guantánamo interrogation facility would be closed, and he released top-secret documents from the Bush administration that revealed how certain forms of torture had been authorized. Yet there is still minimal evidence that Obama will substantially roll back the gains in presidential power. Of note, it has been extremely rare for presidents in the postwar period to voluntarily relinquish power. Democrats in Congress might not be willing to do to Obama what they did to Richard Nixon or even to Jimmy Carter in the 1970s. After decades of Republican rule, Democrats now believe they have an opportunity to build a new majority, and in a time of true crisis there will be less incentive to challenge the institutional prerogatives of their president. When Obama threatened to use executive power if Congress attempted to gain the release of interrogation photographs, some Democrats complained, but ultimately agreed to let the issue go. The Department of Justice has protected secret spying programs established as part of the war on terror, and the administration has continued to take similar positions in court as Bush did with regard to the treatment of detainees. Since Obama's first year as president was a time of economic crisis and continued international danger, Democrats govern under the exact conditions that have traditionally been used since World War II to justify granting presidents expanded, not contracting, power.

CONCLUSION

Recent events have confirmed how conservatism and presidential power have become intertwined since the 1970s. The Right cannot legitimately divorce itself from strong presidential power. The war on terrorism has highlighted the reality that presidential power is integral, rather than aberrational, to modern conservatism. The relationship is more than simply a product of political pragmatism under conditions of divided government. Since the 1960s, the Right, rather than the Left, has been a much more vociferous champion of an all-powerful White House.

This historical account of conservatism and presidential power contributes to an expanding historical literature that is attempting to revise our knowledge about conservatism by demonstrating how conservatives have had a more complex and less adversarial relationship with the modern state than we previously assumed.[54] But even with their arguments about how centralized presidential power is necessary as a tool to restrain other forms of government intervention, conservatives must acknowledge that their movement, too, has helped build big government in America. Regardless of the reasons behind its expansion, centralized presidential authority is a significant form of government power, and the impact has been clear during the war on terrorism. Conservatives must reassess their own antigovernment rhetoric and reexamine the impact of the enormous expansion in executive power they have promoted over the decades.

3

A SWORD AND A SHIELD

The Uses of Law in the Bush Administration

MARY L. DUDZIAK

The Bush administration has been criticized by the Right as well as the Left for departures from the rule of law. Yet within the administration, law was not ignored. Instead, although the president and his advisers feared law as a potential threat to the operation of the executive branch, they turned to law as a means of achieving important goals. What is ultimately most interesting about law in the Bush administration is not the formal legal question of how "lawful" its actions were, on which there will be varying judgments, but instead what the basic conception was of law and the presidency in the Bush era. How is it that a president christened in court rather than through the ballot box would proceed to avoid the jurisdiction of courts and the lawmaking power of Congress? The facile answer often offered is that the nation was at war, and war changes the rules. But the presence of a "war on terror" provided a context for the administration's legal strategies, not their justification.[1]

Two narratives of law in the Bush administration compete for attention. In an era when the legality of torture was debated not only within the White House but on television talk shows, the deployment of law in wartime seemed the most immediate issue. At the same time, however, a decades-long conservative movement to change American law was both significantly furthered and complicated, as Supreme Court appointments moved the Court to the right but the lack of a common jurisprudence hampered the consolidation of a new conservative constitutional vision.

As courts became increasingly conservative, they would seem to have been a safe haven for the president, less likely to challenge the actions of a conservative administration, but the Bush administration had a complicated relationship with courts. The Bush Justice Department sought out the courts to further aspects of a social policy agenda, such as restricting abortion rights and gun control. But when it came to the executive branch, the administration used creative means to avoid court jurisdiction, including constitutional theories about executive power. Law was both a sword and a shield: it was a tool used to further some conservative objectives, and it was a shield intended to protect executive autonomy.

THE SUPREME COURT ENDS AN ELECTION

Our story opens in Palm Beach, Florida, December 9, 2000. That day, a recount of ballots in the disputed presidential election came to a halt when the Supreme Court issued a stay. Justice Antonin Scalia released an opinion explaining the order: "The counting of votes that are of questionable legality does in my view threaten irreparable harm to petitioner [President Bush], and to the country, by casting a cloud upon what he claims to be the legitimacy of his election." With the recount halted in Florida, the die was cast, though the rest of the legal drama continued to play out. Following a highly compressed schedule, the Court took briefs, heard arguments, wrote opinions, and issued a ruling in *Bush v. Gore* in just a few days. If an impasse in Florida had continued, George W. Bush would most likely have been selected by the House of Representatives as the nation's president if the dispute had followed the process laid out in the Constitution. But instead the Court put an end to the controversy, overturning a Florida Supreme Court ruling ordering the recount and effectively ending the election controversy with a very narrow margin for Bush in Florida. Among the most surprising elements was that conservative justices who usually argued for a narrow reading of the equal protection clause embraced a novel and expansive reading to reach their result. In doing so, they announced that their equal protection analysis was applicable to this case only.[2]

Many were outraged by what they saw as judicial activism on the part of conservatives who had themselves decried it. For others, concerned that uncertainty about the election would lead to a constitutional crisis, the Court had fallen on its sword, having taken a step of questionable legitimacy for the good of the nation.[3]

Democratic presidential candidate Al Gore quickly announced he would not pursue other avenues to challenge the outcome.[4] This cleared the path for George W. Bush's inauguration, but it would take another event, on a bright and tragic morning in September, to make him the country's leader. September 11 did more than rally a frightened nation behind a weak president. It provided an argument for the powers of his presidency.

THE "TERROR PRESIDENCY"

War and emergency powers are often invoked as the basis for the Bush administration's conception of executive power, but the effort to expand executive power was a priority from the very beginning. While the scope of presidential power had recovered from the post-Watergate era, Charlie Savage suggests that the Bush administration came into office motivated by a concern that the Clinton years had damaged the presidency, and the president instructed his staff that they needed to rehabilitate the office, leaving it "in better shape" than they found it. One way to protect executive prerogative, Bush officials believed, was to protect secrecy, and so an initial battle was over an effort to shield from disclosure records of Vice President Cheney's energy task force, which was challenged by both Congress and private litigants. After September 11, the administration expanded its efforts to make executive actions secret, using national security as the rationale, even though secrecy extended to non-security-related matters.[5]

President Bush sought to exercise power in a way that was insulated from the usual checks and balances provided by Congress and the courts. That did not leave him without legal cover, however. The Office of Legal Council (OLC) in the Justice Department often serves as a minor brake on executive action, offering its opinion on the legality of proposed presidential initiatives. The office took on particular importance during the Bush presidency, even though, when its services were most sorely needed, the OLC was without a director.[6]

Following the terrorist attacks on September 11, 2001, as the rest of the staff at the OLC evacuated, John Yoo, the only lawyer with experience with foreign affairs issues, was asked to stay behind. Soon, wrote Tim Golden, Yoo "found himself in the [Justice] department's command center, on the phone to lawyers at the White House." The young lawyer was on his way to becoming a crucial insider in the war on terrorism. Yoo's views on expansive presidential power were outside the mainstream but in keeping with the direction the administration had favored from the beginning.[7]

Yoo was not on his own, of course. David Addington, Vice President Cheney's chief of staff and legal adviser, liked to carry around a copy of the Constitution in his pocket. He found in its sparse words the same robust vision of executive power as did Yoo, and he devoted the energies of his office to realizing it. Addington has at times been characterized like the man behind the curtain in *The Wizard of Oz*, directing the development of a conservative legal agenda, perhaps at the behest of the vice president. It is important, however, to see Addington not as a legal innovator but as a staff person positioned to further a legal agenda much longer in the making. Addington would carry out this role in part through vetting presidential appointees, using appointments to proliferate a broad view of executive power throughout the Bush administration.[8]

Congress, stunned by the September 11 attacks, responded by quickly passing the Patriot Act and an Authorization for the Use of Military Force. While these actions were intended to give the president the authority he sought to act effectively at home and abroad, there was just one difficulty. The Bush administration did not want to concede that Congress's support was needed. If that was the case, then Congress would be able to withdraw its grants of power. Yoo began crafting OLC opinions based on the idea that the president could act alone. On September 20, 2001, he wrote that congressional resolutions had recognized the presidential response to terrorism, but they could not "place any limits on the president's determinations as to any terrorist threat, the amount of military force to be used in response, or the method, timing and nature of the response." International law was also not a limit; he would later write that the Geneva Conventions did not apply to the conflict in Afghanistan, and he authored a particularly controversial memo legitimizing torture. Yoo's basic justification was that the U.S. Constitution granted broad executive power to the president, and Congress and the courts did not have power to undermine it. This was based on a reading of Article II of the Constitution, which provides that "the executive Power shall be vested in a President of the United States of America" and that "the President shall take care that the laws be faithfully executed." In essence, these clauses were read as vesting *all* power that is executive in nature in the president, with incursions on presidential power therefore unconstitutional. A more modest version of the "unitary executive" thesis had been argued for in earlier years by conservative legal scholars. During the Bush years, it entered the broader political debate.[9]

The unitary executive thesis was especially important to OLC decision making on torture. An August 1, 2002, OLC memorandum on interrogation stated that "Any effort by Congress to regulate the interrogation of battlefield detainees would violate the Constitution's sole vesting of the Commander-in-Chief authority in the President." Congress could not play a role, leaving the president to determine appropriate policy. At the same time, governing statutes were interpreted in a way that gave the administration as broad authority as possible. A federal statute banning torture was interpreted to prohibit only "the most extreme acts." For physical pain to be torture, "it must be equivalent in intensity to the pain accompanying serious physical injury, such as organ failure, impairment of bodily function, or even death." An effort to keep judgments like this secret reinforced the administration's efforts to retain broad, unilateral power over detainees.[10] Documents released by the Justice Department in 2009 showed that actual interrogation practices went beyond the brutal tactics authorized by the memos. For example, CIA operatives used waterboarding 183 times in one month against September 11 planner Khalid Sheik Mohammed.[11]

The unitary executive thesis embraced such a robust view of presidential power that it would seem to have given the administration plenty of room to maneuver. But the embrace of this analysis would be only one of the steps taken to expand the scope of presidential power. One way to shield executive acts from judicial oversight was to take them outside the jurisdiction of courts.

The effort to avoid judicial review illustrates an important aspect of the Bush administration's perspective on the role of law. The majority of federal judges had been appointed by Republican presidents, and by 2005 conservatives would be in the majority in ten of the thirteen U.S. courts of appeals. This might have made the courts a welcome forum, but the Bush administration viewed judicial review of its own actions as an affront to its conception of the presidency.[12] Taken together, the successful efforts to place conservatives on the courts and to avoid submission of executive action to the courts illustrate a two-pronged approach to law. Conservative courts could aid the administration's legal agenda by striking down gun control laws or upholding restrictions on abortion, but the courts were not to be the president's overseer.

Two strategies were used to insulate administration actions in the war on terror from judicial review. The first was to place detainees outside U.S. territory, on the theory that U.S. constitutional protections would not apply to those held by the U.S. government in another country. The second strategy was to create a new category of legal persons, "illegal enemy combatants." As enemy soldiers during wartime, it was argued, they were not entitled to the protections of domestic courts that attended criminal prosecutions. But as *illegal* enemy combatants they were also not protected by the laws of war. The president claimed the right to designate the status of individuals as illegal enemy combatants and applied it not only to suspected al Qaeda operatives captured on the battlefield in Afghanistan but also to U.S. citizens apprehended on American soil.[13]

On November 13, 2001, President Bush issued an order authorizing the detention of terrorists and their trial by military commission. In early 2002, construction began of a new prison facility at Guantánamo Bay, Cuba. Soon, prisoners from the conflicts in Iraq and Afghanistan were incarcerated there, potentially keeping them outside the jurisdiction of American courts. With no apparent end to a war on terrorism, there seemed to be no limits to the prisoners' detention.[14]

President Bush did not seek legislation authorizing military tribunals, and argued that congressional authorization was unnecessary. Why not put such important initiatives on stronger legal footing? Bush's lawyers advised against it. Addington and other White House insiders "believed cooperation and compromise signaled weakness and emboldened the enemies of America and the executive branch," writes Jack Goldsmith, who served as director of the OLC from 2003 to 2004.[15]

Although the Bush administration sought to avoid judicial review, lawyers were front and center in White House decision making. According to Goldsmith, faced with concerns about the possibility of another terrorist attack and fearful of being blamed for not avoiding it, the president could only justify the failure to take protective action if he had a good reason. "A lawyer's advice that a policy or action would violate the law, especially a criminal law, was a pretty good excuse." The White House was "haunted" by 9/11, Goldsmith argues, and "obsessed with preventing a recurrence of the expected harsh blame after the next attack." Because of this, "the question, 'What should we do?' . . . often collapsed into the question 'What can we lawfully do?'. . . It is why there was so much pressure to act to the edges of the law." The central role played by lawyers had limitations, however. Lawyers "look to *legal sources* to find the answers," said 9/11 Commission executive director Philip Zelikow. This left out other important factors, such as the impact of a policy on U.S. foreign relations and on domestic public opinion.[16]

Addington and Vice President Cheney in particular "viewed every encounter outside the innermost core of most trusted advisors as a zero-sum game that if they didn't win they would necessarily lose," according to Goldsmith. In this context, arguments about law were volleys in an international struggle for power; they were "strategic lawfare." The fusion of war and law—lawfare, or warlaw—is usually thought of as law on the battlefield, the way the laws of war might characterize as lawful a soldier shooting one person (an enemy soldier) but not another (a civilian). But after September 11, the fusion of war and law seeped into the basic domestic administration of justice. Legal actors saw their lawmaking role as affecting the course of the war on terror. And judgments about legality were infused by questions of security.[17]

In this rendering, law appears as a tool of power, not a practice of democratic constraint. Such a conception may seem lawless, as if the avoidance of law was essential to maintain sovereign power. But Ruti Teitel provides a different logic for the Bush administration's law avoidance. Faced with post-9/11 fears about international terrorism, she argues, the U.S. government acted as the "sovereign police," as if it were a global enforcer of law. It is inconsistent with that position to submit to the enforcement power of others. From this perspective, the operating paradigm would not be the maxim that necessity knows no law, but instead that necessity has required that the sovereign *be* the law.[18]

In the post-9/11 environment, laws that had once been seen as tools of domestic governance became securitized. For example, immigration law, once fueled by concerns about economic policy and humanitarianism, was now the door through which the next terrorists might slip through the borders. The Immigration and Naturalization Service was folded into the Department of Homeland Security, and a barrier at the Mexican border was recast as a means of thwarting terrorism. Overall, the security threat was real, but many initiatives pushed through quickly as 9/11-related matters had been part of a preexisting political agenda. Whether because of real links with security or because of the political opportunities opened by the new national security environment, across categories, law became implicated in the war on terror.[19]

NO BLANK CHECK?

Terror-related cases would ultimately find their way into court. President Bush did not suspend the writ of *habeas corpus*, and lawyers for detainees invoked the great writ on behalf of prisoners at Guantánamo and elsewhere. A series of Supreme Court cases concerning detainees reveals a conflict over the basic conception of wartime during the Bush years. The parties and the Court initially framed their arguments within the traditional paradigm, assuming that wartime was temporary and its impact on law would eventually wane. Toward the end of the Bush administration, however, the seemingly endless character of the war on terror challenged the idea that war is necessarily bounded in time.[20] Eventually, this affected the Court's willingness to place limits on executive power.

The Supreme Court had addressed the problem of wartime detention before. During World War II, the Court justified the exclusion and relocation of persons of Japanese heritage from the West Coast based on the wartime context. It posed a hardship, but, wrote Justice Black for the Court in *Korematsu v. United States*, a case soon vilified as one of the great tragedies in American legal history, "hardships are part of war."[21] The temporary character of the program was thought to be inherent in its wartime circumstances. But wartime's inherent limits were fraying by the time the Guantánamo cases came before the Court.

In the detainee cases, the Bush administration argued that the Supreme Court lacked authority to rule. To a large degree, the Court's rulings in these cases simply reasserted the Court's own role in American governance. *Rasul v. Bush* (2004) was the opening volley. Fourteen detainees, citizens of Kuwait and Australia, argued they had been unlawfully detained without charges. The Supreme Court rejected the Bush administration's argument that the Court lacked power to hear the case because the men were held outside U.S. territory. The *Rasul* ruling was limited to the power of federal courts to hear such a case, and the case was sent back to the district court to consider the merits. Meanwhile, the Department of Defense set up military tribunals on Guantánamo. According to Benjamin Wittes and Zaahira Wyne, the tribunals were "clearly intended to place the military in a stronger litigation position" in subsequent *habeas* cases.[22]

Also in 2004, the Court decided the case of a U.S. citizen, Yasser Esam Hamdi, who had been captured by American forces in Afghanistan and held first at Guantánamo, then at a U.S. naval facility in South Carolina. Hamdi argued that he was not an "unlawful combatant." Could the federal courts hear his case? Hamdi's U.S. citizenship complicated the legal context, for a federal statute required that "no citizen shall be imprisoned or otherwise detained by the United States except pursuant to an Act of Congress." The Fourth Circuit Court of Appeals held that Congress's authorization of the use of force in Afghanistan was sufficient to satisfy this requirement, and that searching *habeas* review was not constitutionally required. In a split opinion, the Supreme Court stepped back. Justice Sandra Day O'Connor, writing for a plurality of four, was troubled by the potentially indefinite character of Hamdi's detention. Her concern, O'Connor wrote, was not "the lack of certainty regarding the date on which the conflict will end, but . . . the substantial prospect of perpetual detention." She believed that

> If the Government does not consider this unconventional war won for two generations, and if it maintains during that time that Hamdi might, if released, rejoin forces fighting against the United States, then the position it has taken throughout the litigation of this case suggests that Hamdi's detention could last for the rest of his life.

The Court did not have to face the prospect of endless detention, however, at least not yet. Justice O'Connor found that the war on terror, at that moment in time, fit within conventional understandings of military conflict, bounded by time, for there were "active combat operations" against the Taliban in Afghanistan. It was appropriate to detain enemy combatants "for the duration of these hostilities."[23]

The plurality found, however, that detention must be subject to judicial review. "We have long since made clear that a state of war is not a blank check for the president when it comes to the rights of the nation's citizens," O'Connor wrote. Hamdi's right to a hearing would be limited by the security context, however. He was entitled to a lawyer, but evidence based on hearsay need not be barred. Justice Antonin Scalia went further in his concurrence, arguing that the only lawful options for the government were for Congress to suspend the right to *habeas corpus*, which Congress may do only in times of invasion or rebellion, or Hamdi must be tried using the usual procedures in criminal cases. Only Justice Clarence Thomas agreed with the federal government that the Court lacked the power to act. For him, Hamdi's detention fell "squarely within the Federal Government's war powers, and we lack the expertise and capacity to second-guess that decision." The Constitution placed all necessary war-related powers in a "unitary Executive."[24]

While *Hamdi* was touted as an example of constraints on the executive, in practice the decision was "little more than slaps on the wrist," Goldsmith writes, for "it did not at that time require the President to alter many of his actions." Instead, it merely showed that Guantánamo was not a complete legal black hole. It was, however, a counterforce against the administration's go-it-alone efforts. President Bush finally sought statutory authorization for military commissions to try detainees.[25]

In 2005, a Republican-dominated Congress sought to limit the Court's role, passing the Detainee Treatment Act, which stripped jurisdiction of U.S. courts over *habeas corpus* petitions from Guantánamo detainees. The statute seemed to be aimed at cases in the pipeline to the Supreme Court, but the Court did not back down. In *Hamdan v. Rumsfeld*, a detainee argued that the military commissions created to try detainees violated military and international law. The Bush administration argued that the Court lacked power to hear the case. Coming in June 2006, well after the exposure of abuses of prisoners at Abu Ghraib and allegations of improper treatment at Guantánamo, and amid growing dissatisfaction with the administration's war efforts, this case would put a more serious brake on executive autonomy. Justice John Paul Stevens, writing for the Court, found that abstention by the Court would be improper, that the commissions were not authorized by Congress, and that their procedures violated both the Uniform Code of Military Justice and the Geneva Conventions. Congress, still dominated by Republicans, again responded, giving the president more power over detainees than he had had prior to the *Hamdan* ruling.[26]

Jurisdiction-stripping legislation was not the only strategy to keep a case out of the Supreme Court, as the strange case of José Padilla would reveal. A U.S. citizen, Padilla was arrested in Chicago, suspected of plotting to detonate a "dirty bomb" in the United States, but he was not immediately charged with a crime. Instead, he was held in military detention for three years as an illegal enemy combatant. Padilla challenged his indefinite detention and was successful in the Second Circuit Court of Appeals, but the Supreme Court dismissed the case on jurisdictional grounds, shifting it to a more conservative jurisdiction. The Fourth Circuit Court of Appeals denied relief in 2005. Padilla again sought Supreme Court review, but then something unusual happened. While his case was pending, the federal government took the extraordinary move of asking the Fourth Circuit to withdraw its opinion and seeking to transfer Padilla to civilian custody in Florida. The Bush administration now sought to charge Padilla with a crime and accord him the protections of the U.S. justice system that, they had previously argued, would undermine American national security. Padilla would no longer be an unlawful enemy combatant but an ordinary criminal. This move was too much for Judge Joseph Luttig, a staunch conservative on the Fourth Circuit who had been on short lists of possible Supreme Court nominees and who wrote the Fourth Circuit opinion in the *Padilla* case. In a step widely seen as taking him out of contention for the Court, Luttig blasted the administration in a surprisingly sharp opinion denying the government's motions and suggesting that the government's new strategy was an effort to avoid review of the case in the Supreme Court.[27]

The Court then declined to consider Padilla's appeal. Although the case raised "fundamental issues respecting the separation of powers, including consideration of the role and function of the courts," the Court was wary of addressing claims that had now become "hypothetical," particularly since Padilla was now getting what he had originally sought, a transfer to the civilian criminal court system. The strategy of shifting Padilla's confinement to avoid a potentially negative Supreme Court assessment had worked. Padilla was then tried in Miami and convicted on August 16, 2007, of terrorist conspiracy and of material support for terrorists. Padilla's sentence of more than seventeen years in prison was less than the prosecution had sought, reflecting the judge's concern about the harsh treatment Padilla had received while in confinement. In the meantime, Judge Luttig, considered "one of the brightest conservative stars in the federal judiciary," resigned from the bench.[28]

The detainee cases captured the headlines and showed that wartime would not completely displace the Court's role, but while these rulings limited the president's autonomy, it was only at the margins. They established the power of courts to review detainee cases, but so far had not altered an executive decision to detain anyone. And plaintiffs challenging widespread warrantless datamining of telephone and Internet communications found that the government escaped judicial scrutiny because the data they needed to bring a lawsuit was itself a government secret. Secrecy itself undermined the ability of those targeted to challenge their surveillance.[29]

The Supreme Court and Congress continued to assume that

wartime's temporal limits mattered to legal decision making. War legitimated restrictions on liberties in part because it was thought to be temporary. The framing of wartime seemed to slip, however, in the last important Guantánamo case during the Bush years. *Boumediene v. Bush* was a *habeas corpus* case brought by six men captured overseas and held at Guantánamo who claimed they were not al Qaeda terrorists and were not supporters of the Taliban. A 5-4 Supreme Court majority found unconstitutional the latest and broadest statute attempting to strip federal courts of jurisdiction over *habeas corpus* challenges brought by detainees. The Court noted that it was lawful to detain those who had fought against the United States "for the duration of the conflict." But Justice Anthony Kennedy, writing for the majority, was troubled by this war's lack of boundaries. The present conflict, "if measured from September 11, 2001, to the present, is already among the longest wars in American history." One of the reasons *habeas corpus* was needed was that "the consequence of error may be detention of persons for the duration of hostilities that may last a generation or more." The lack of time boundaries made this conflict different from past wars, Kennedy reasoned, requiring more judicial oversight.[30]

And so the troublesome nature of twenty-first-century war, with no end in sight, would lead the Court to limit the Bush administration's power, but, as before, this ruling had its limits. Months after the ruling, detainees were still waiting for their *habeas* challenges to be resolved, even though the Court had stressed that "the costs of delay can no longer be borne by those who are held in custody." On November 20, 2008, Federal District Judge Richard J. Leon granted *habeas* relief to five detainees, finding their detention unlawful. They had been held at Guantánamo for seven years. Judge Leon urged the administration not to appeal the case because the evidence was so weak, and to release these detainees "forthwith." Finally, on December 16, 2008, three of the men were repatriated to Bosnia. Lakhdar Boumediene himself would remain five more months.[31]

THE COURT AND THE CONSERVATIVE AGENDA

That the exigencies of a war on terror did not place unlimited power in the hands of the president was clear when George W. Bush stood in the Cross Hall of the White House on October 31, 2006, and announced his second choice to replace Justice Sandra Day O'Connor on the U.S. Supreme Court. In 1968, Lyndon Johnson had underestimated the degree to which his power had waned and nominated a friend, Homer Thornberry, for the Court, only to find little support for his lackluster nominee. Harriet Meirs was George Bush's Homer Thornberry. Unlike LBJ, whose presidency was in its last months, after the Meirs nomination collapsed, President Bush had time to recover. He did so with Samuel Alito, placing a more qualified and more predictably conservative justice on the Court. Alito would solidify an effort many years in the making. To many, it appeared that the Right finally had its Court. While some legal analysts stressed the continuing uncertainty created by deep divisions on the Court, by the end of the 2006–7 term, others, such as Thomas Goldstein, suggested it was "quite clear by the numbers that the Court took a genuine step to the right."[32]

The Meirs nomination was a temporary setback for a conservative legal movement that had built a legal infrastructure in lower courts and American law schools and was hoping for the day when a staunchly conservative Supreme Court majority would finally be achieved. For these lawyers, Republican Party affiliation was certainly not enough. Membership in the Federalist Society and a career record of conservatism were more reliable predictors of a justice who would move the court to the right.[33]

A conservative effort to remake American law was long in coming. Richard Nixon ran for president in 1968 on a platform of reversing liberal Warren Court rulings. Once he was in office, the argument for judicial restraint was also relied on to insulate executive power from judicial review. Alexander Bickel's thesis in *The Least Dangerous Branch*, that judicial review is inherently problematic in a democracy because it is countermajoritarian, was the touchstone in the Nixon administration. In later years, after *Roe v. Wade*, the Supreme Court became an even more pressing target of conservatives. By the Bush years, Bickel had been relegated to the sidelines, and the work of a new generation of scholars emerged as influential. Their starting point was not Bickel's, that the design of our constitutional system required a restrained role for courts. Instead, they argued that the original meaning of the Constitution set the appropriate terms of government power and determined the nature of rights. Bickel's theory of judicial restraint left policy choices largely to the political branches, but originalism was consistent with a more prominent role for the courts, which could restrain Congress and the states when they violated an original understanding of the Constitution. Under a reading of constitutional provisions on executive power championed by some conservatives, however, judicial power diminished when it came to the president.[34]

One aspect of a broader conservative legal movement was the Federalist Society. Organized by Yale and Chicago law students in the early 1980s, it was initially intended simply as a way for conservatives to find each other in a predominantly liberal law school environment. It grew into an effective organization that facilitated mentorship and networking among legal conservatives. In the Bush years the organization became a pipeline for legal positions at all levels in the administration. Meanwhile, religious groups focused on cultural issues such as prayer in school and abortion, new conservative public interest law firms handled cases challenging affirmative action programs and gun regulations, and an academic law and economics movement sought to reshape academic thinking about private law. One of the goals was a more conservative judiciary.[35]

Abortion rights were a principal target of the effort to move the Court to the right. Despite the Court's conservative majority, *Roe v. Wade* had not been formally overturned. In *Planned Parenthood of Southeastern Pennsylvania v. Casey* in 1992, the Court abandoned *Roe*'s analytical structure and its insistence that abortion restrictions impinged on fundamental rights, therefore requiring strict judicial scrutiny. *Casey* allowed to stand regulations burdening abortion rights that would have been invalid under *Roe*. The Court appeared to draw a line in a case about a late-term abortion procedure called by its opponents "partial-birth abortion." In *Stenberg v. Carhart* (*Carhart I*) in 2000, a 5–4 majority struck down a Nebraska law that outlawed the procedure, with no exception for situations in which a doctor thought it necessary to protect a woman's health. Without an exception for health reasons, the Court held that the law constituted an "undue burden" on women's right to reproductive privacy. Justice O'Connor voted with the majority.[36]

Congress responded to the case, passing a new ban on the procedure in 2003. The Court then granted review in a case that seemed a mirror image of *Carhart I*. Justice O'Connor resigned in July 2006, before the case was argued, raising the question of whether a change in Court personnel would result in a reversal. *Gonzales v. Carhart* (*Carhart II*) was decided the next April. With Justice Alito joining a new five-vote majority, the Supreme Court upheld the ban on the procedure. More striking than the different outcome, however, was the rhetoric of Justice Kennedy's surprisingly graphic majority opinion, which described the intimate details of the way the body of a fetus would be torn apart and expressed concern about the impact of such a procedure on women's mental health. Called "wrenching" and "melodramatic" by Tony Mauro, the opinion laid out the new terms of the Court's reproductive rights jurisprudence. The narrative structure of *Carhart II* placed the perspective of the fetus itself front and center. The fetus had not attained formal legal personhood, but it nevertheless gained a powerful spokesperson: a majority on the U.S. Supreme Court.[37]

Another focus of the conservative legal strategy was an attack on government programs related to race, such as affirmative action. The Court upheld the limited use of affirmative action in higher education in *Grutter v. Bollinger* in 2003, with Justice O'Connor providing a crucial vote. In 2007, after O'Connor's departure, the Court struck down voluntarily adopted student assignment plans that took race into account to maintain some degree of racial balance in public schools in *Parents Involved in Community Schools v. Seattle School District.* Chief Justice John Roberts argued in the Court's plurality opinion that constitutional equality required colorblindness, relying for support on *Brown v. Board of Education*, sparking a debate over whether the historic ruling that schools may not be segregated by race required as well that any use of race, even to maintain desegregation, was unlawful. Geoffrey Stone characterized the reliance on *Brown* in this case as "willful ignorance of American history." The Court's colorblindness analysis, many argued, would ironically lead to the result that more children would go to predominantly one-race schools, reinforcing a racial identifiability that was in tension with the premise underlying colorblindness, that race should no longer matter.[38]

The Court furthered a conservative constitutional agenda in other areas, but the Court did not predictably embrace conservative outcomes. In *District of Columbia v. Heller* (2008), the Court struck down a District of Columbia ban on handguns, ruling that the Second Amendment protects an individual's right to bear arms. In the area of gay rights, however, a ruling in *Lawrence v. Texas* (2003), finding a sodomy conviction to be unconstitutional, seemed downright liberal. Relying on an analysis of constitutional liberty, the Court reversed a 1986 ruling and held that consensual sex between adults of the same gender was protected by the due process clause.[39]

Federalism was long a favorite of constitutional conservatives hoping to limit the scope of federal government power by protecting state autonomy. During the Bush years the Court first advanced but then appeared to retreat from a conservative "federalism revolution." Chief Justice William Rehnquist was "the Court's leading advocate" of the New Right critique of the welfare state, as Thomas Keck puts it. Rehnquist's view was that the Tenth Amendment and the role of states in the U.S. constitutional system required limitation of federal power in order to maintain the proper role for the states. This approach promised to roll back the expansion of federal power since the New Deal, reversing a trend in Supreme Court decisions since the late 1930s. In this area, Keck argues, "conservative justices proved willing to abandon their commitment to restraint in an effort to enforce what they saw as fundamental principles of limited government." This "revolution" had its limits, however. Kathleen Sullivan argues that "the Court did more to change the constitutional jurisprudence of federalism than it did to realign actual constitutional power."[40]

The most important Rehnquist Court federalism cases were decided before George W. Bush took office. In the early years of the Bush administration, the Court furthered its federalism-related rulings in the area of state sovereign immunity under the Eleventh Amendment, which protects state autonomy by limiting the ability of individuals to sue states. Outcomes were not predictable, however, and Rehnquist himself authored a 2003 opinion allowing individuals to sue states that violated the Family and Medical Leave Act. It remains unclear whether the Roberts Court will build on Rehnquist-era federalism jurisprudence. Christopher Banks and Jon Blakeman have suggested that "although there is a reconfigured 'States' Rights Five' voting coalition," neither Roberts nor Alito endorses rigid viewpoints about federalism, and it "remains uncertain if the Court will return to the type of aggressive new federalism which arguably defined the legacy of the Rehnquist Court." Differences over federalism were just one example of the way the lack of a unified approach limited the ability of the conservative majority to consolidate its power.[41]

When it came to actions of the executive branch, however, national security put new strains on federalism. "The war on terror has created new frontiers of federalism," Susan N. Herman argues, as the federal government "has attempted to enlist state and local law enforcement officials as its 'hands and feet.'" This turn was consistent with broader Bush administration policy. The president embraced "big government conservatism" and called on Congress to expand federal power in areas beyond national security. In education, for example, the No Child Left Behind Act established federal standards for school achievement and enforced costly penalties on schools that failed to meet them, expanding the federal government's role in an area where states and local governments hoped to maintain some autonomy.[42]

LAW AND THE CRISIS PRESIDENCY

The dangers facing the nation took on a new character in the last months of the Bush administration as the United States and the world plunged into an economic crisis. President Bush, by now weakened and unpopular, was nevertheless able to get through Congress broad authority to intervene in the economy. Americans worried about the impact of an economic downturn on their communities and on U.S. national security and the nation's standing as a world power, as global skepticism about American security policy was now supplanted by criticism of American economic policy. This new crisis was the bookend to an administration launched in a political crisis and then legitimated by a security crisis.

The Bush administration invoked security to pursue its goals, but the strategy threatened to collapse on itself. Fear was needed to justify expansive power, but if fear persisted, that suggested the powers granted had not achieved their purpose. And there were too many things to be afraid of in the waning days of the Bush presidency. Amid the deepening economic downturn, former advocates of the free market found federal economic regulation suddenly comforting. As his hold on power frayed, President Bush worked to embed remnants of the conservative legal agenda in federal regulations, from a rule that allowed greater dumping of mine waste in rivers to one that enabled medical personnel to refuse services that conflicted with their religious faith, even if that included refusing to prescribe birth control.[43] In these and other actions, the president deployed law to isolate and insulate his power, as long as he could.

4

GEORGE W. BUSH AND THE "WAR ON TERROR"

Timothy Naftali

> People are going to analyze my presidency for
> a long time. All you can do is do the best you can,
> make decisions based upon principles, and lead.
> And that's what I have done and will continue to do.
>
> —*George W. Bush*[1]

George W. Bush came to office assuming he would be a peacetime president whose leadership would be judged by how he managed long-term domestic challenges to American society. "Our national courage has been clear in times of depression and war," he said in his first inaugural address, "when defending common dangers defined our common good. Now we must choose if the example of our fathers and mothers will inspire us or condemn us. We must show courage in a time of blessing by confronting problems instead of passing them on to future generations." The few foreign shadows that he mentioned in "this time of blessing" were cast by weapons of mass destruction (WMDs). "We will confront weapons of mass destruction," he pledged, "so that a new century is spared new horrors." Nowhere in his first speech to the nation as president did Bush mention terrorism, the issue that would ultimately determine his legacy.

Bush inherited an intelligence community that had already embraced terrorism as a threat to U.S. security. The 1995 sarin gas attack on the Tokyo subway by the millenarian terrorist organization Aum Shinrikyo had drawn the attention of the highest levels of the Clinton administration to a coming revolution in the capabilities of terrorists. In the 1980s the Iranian-backed Shi'a group Hezbollah, using conventional weapons, had committed acts that killed hundreds. The new terrorists of the 1990s were scheming to kill many more, using biological, chemical, and perhaps someday nuclear weapons. Three years later the simultaneous attacks on U.S. embassies in Nairobi and Dar es Salaam demonstrated that the Sunni extremist Osama bin Laden led an organization with the sophistication to stage a mass-casualty event. U.S. intelligence had earlier noted bin Laden's enmity toward Americans. In 1996 the Central Intelligence Agency formed a special unit to operate against the Saudi and his terrorist organization, al Qaeda. But until the East African bombings in August 1998 there had been some question whether bin Laden and al Qaeda had the skills to make good on their rhetoric of hate. Following those attacks, the U.S. intelligence community received covert-action authority. "These documents spelled out in detail why it was necessary to continually ratchet up the pressure against Bin Laden," Bush's first director of Central Intelligence (DCI) George Tenet later wrote. "These written authorities made clear that Bin Laden posed a serious, continuing, and imminent threat of violence to U.S. interests around the world."[2]

The issues that shaped the 2000 election showed, however, that a vast chasm separated public views of national priorities from the U.S. national security establishment's concerns about terrorism. Whereas fears of a turn-of-the-century technology meltdown, known by the shorthand Y2K, had dominated the news as New Year's Day 2000 approached, intelligence experts had spent that period equally concerned about the possibility of an Islamist wave of terrorism to usher in the new millennium. In December 1999, an alert customs agent at the U.S.-Canadian border had foiled the plans of Ahmed Ressam, an Algerian terrorist, to blow up sections of the Los Angeles international airport. Similarly, the issue of terrorism played no role in the presidential campaign. Neither Vice President Gore nor Texas governor Bush raised the issue in the campaign. Indeed, Bush never linked Clinton's handling of bin Laden to his general charge of administration incompetence in foreign policy. As the Supreme Court decided that George Bush would become president, Clinton's national security advisor, Sandy Berger, asked the CIA what it would do about al Qaeda if resources were unlimited. In response, the CIA sent what it called its Blue Sky memorandum.

The Bush administration wasted no time in signaling a shift away from the foreign policy priorities of the Clinton White House. Instead of focusing on the challenges of globalization—with terrorism being its dark side—and problems in the former Yugoslavia, the new administration appeared to want to return to traditional U.S. concerns over the power of Russia and China and Saddam Hussein's weakening of international sanctions. As its first foreign policy initiative, the administration pressed forward with missile defense by suspending U.S. participation in the thirty-year-old Antiballistic Missile Defense Treaty. Foreign policy crises, unlike initiatives, are rarely a matter of choice, and the Bush administration faced its first one in April 2001, when the Chinese captured the crew of a U.S. Navy reconnaissance plane that had made an emergency landing in China after it collided with a Chinese air force jet shadowing it. China, however, had already been high among the incoming administration's foreign policy concerns. Bush's new team had already captured the change in U.S. policy toward China by declaring its status would be downgraded from "strategic partner" to "strategic competitor."

Despite this change in priorities and concerns, the Bush administration retained enough elements of the Clinton national security bureaucracy that concern about terrorism did not dissipate entirely at the working level in the administration's nine months of peace. Bush retained both DCI George Tenet and, until September, the incumbent director of the Federal Bureau of Investigation, Louis Freeh. Incoming National Security Advisor Condoleezza

Rice also kept Richard Clarke as the National Security Council's special advisor on counterterrorism. Nevertheless, the portfolio seemed to have been downgraded. Richard Clarke, who lacked the relationship with Rice that he had had with Sandy Berger, lost his seat at the table in the cabinet-level Principals Committee. He argued, unsuccessfully, that "Al Qida is not some narrow, little terrorist issue that needs to be included in broader regional policy."[3]

The president and his chief aides viewed al Qaeda more as a symptom than as an illness. Instead of deploying U.S. resources against bin Laden with a sense of urgency, they sought a concerted strategy for the Afghanistan-Pakistan region that would eventually deny al Qaeda its safe haven. The wheels of that policy review turned very slowly. It took until the first week of September 2001 for the Principals Committee to get around to discussing al Qaeda as a group and approve a draft presidential directive on covert action for Afghanistan.[4]

The lack of any high-level focus on bin Laden had the additional effect of magnifying the existing flaws in the structure of U.S. intelligence. Although FBI director Freeh and DCI Tenet got along very well, and their two bureaucracies had taken steps to overcome decidedly different organizational cultures and two generations of mistrust and competition, there were real impediments to sharing information. The Bush White House's tepid interest in al Qaeda before 9/11 also meant that the U.S. government was no closer to resolving larger, related policy questions that had stymied the Clinton administration.

President Bill Clinton told the new president that bin Laden was a huge piece of unfinished business.[5] After the East African bombings, Clinton had authorized the CIA to let the agency's allies in southern Afghanistan kill al Qaeda's leader, if a successful capture proved impossible.[6] Meanwhile the CIA and the U.S. Air Force had jointly developed a reconnaissance drone, the Predator, to locate him in Afghanistan.[7] But the delay between a sighting and a cruise missile attack was still too long for the new system to ensure a successful assassination. In the waning months of the administration, the CIA and the air force began discussing arming the Predator. The fact that al Qaeda enjoyed the support of the Taliban government in Afghanistan posed the second great policy challenge. Although the CIA was permitted to develop fissures within the Taliban's leadership, regime change was not yet the policy of the United States, nor was the Clinton administration prepared to arm the Northern Alliance, the Taliban's rival for power in the country. Pakistan was the reason for the U.S. government's caution. The U.S.-Pakistan relationship, which had weakened after the end of the cold war, hit a new low in 1998 when the government of Nawaz Sharif tested an atomic weapon, forcing congressionally mandated economic and military sanctions to kick in. It was assumed that if mishandled, U.S. policy toward Afghanistan could undermine that already fragile relationship. Gaining Pakistan's assistance in dealing with bin Laden and his Taliban supporters was further complicated by the role that Pakistan's intelligence service, the ISI, and the Pakistan military had played in supporting the mujahideen resistance against the Soviets, of which bin Laden had been a part, and, more recently, of the Taliban as a regional counter to India.

Also key to understanding the surprise to come was the fact that even those elements in the administration that continued to beat the drum about bin Laden did not anticipate an attack on the United States in the short term. Clarke and his team were pushing for a three- to five-year program for neutralizing al Qaeda. Their greatest fear was that bin Laden would acquire WMDs, and it was assumed that al Qaeda was still five years away from realizing that nightmare scenario. As a result, for even the most attentive in the intelligence and policy bureaucracies, al Qaeda was primarily a foreign threat, and the vulnerability of the U.S. homeland remained a blind spot to the entire intelligence community.[8]

"GO, GO, GO"

Presidents are allowed only one "Pearl Harbor" attack by the American people. Franklin D. Roosevelt established the modern model for recovering from strategic military surprise. Despite efforts by his political adversaries to use December 7, 1941, to tarnish his stature as a leader, Roosevelt was ultimately forgiven for the federal government's lapse that Sunday morning because America won the war. Harry S. Truman's political difficulties in Korea did not arise from the North's surprise invasion in June 1950 but from the stalemate that ensued. Besides the human desire to punish aggression and murder, Bush instinctively understood that his effectiveness as president depended on how quickly and comprehensively his administration responded to the attacks on New York and Washington, D.C., on September 11, 2001. Bush and his leadership team had misjudged the urgency of dealing with bin Laden before, but history would perhaps give him a second chance. It was clear, however, that there could be no more surprises in the United States before bin Laden and al Qaeda were stopped.

The CIA was the only agency with a plan to retaliate against al Qaeda.[9] Director Tenet took a variation of the Blue Sky memorandum off the shelf and on September 13 presented it to the NSC. Boasting that the agency had more than one hundred sources and subsources in Afghanistan, Tenet suggested that al Qaeda could be stripped of its safe haven in Afghanistan and its leadership captured through primarily a paramilitary operation. In the latter years of the Clinton administration, the CIA had established contacts (or in some cases had reestablished former cold war contacts) with leaders of the Northern Alliance, the largely Uzbek and Tajik resistance to the Taliban. Meanwhile, the CIA had also launched a covert plan to sow dissention among the Taliban themselves.[10] The plan now was to find a way to get the non-Arab Pashtun Afghans in the south to ally pragmatically with a U.S. drive to force bin Laden and his Arab forces out of their country. Although it would turn out that the CIA had overestimated the value of its efforts among the southern tribes, especially its covert action to divide the Taliban by working with six of Taliban leader Mullah Omar's military commanders, Tenet's optimism was not misplaced.

Unlike the CIA, the Pentagon did not have any serious contingency plans for operating in Afghanistan or dealing with al Qaeda.

Indeed, the post of assistant secretary of defense for special operations and low-intensity conflict, the central office for counterterrorism policy in the Pentagon, was still vacant on 9/11.[11] Incoming secretary of defense Donald Rumsfeld's main focus had been on creating a nimble military for twenty-first-century conflicts against other national armies.[12] What could have been a debilitating Washington turf fight at the outset between the CIA and the Pentagon over which approach to take did not happen because the U.S. military had nothing to offer a president hungry for a plan of action.

So much went very wrong on 9/11, but it was helpful to future U.S. policy that the head of the Pakistani ISI happened to be in Washington that day. General Mahmood Ahmed witnessed a nation experience shock and arouse itself in anger. Bush administration officers, most notably Colin Powell's deputy at State, Richard Armitage, underlined for the visiting spy chief that Pakistan faced a historic choice. The United States could no longer tolerate ambivalence toward al Qaeda and the Taliban. The head of the ISI was impressed, but the man who was actually moved by the warning was his boss, President Pervez Musharraf. Musharraf authorized contacts with the Taliban to make clear that if they did not turn bin Laden over to the United States, Afghanistan would come under U.S. attack. At the same time as these Pakistani warnings, the CIA sent through back channels a similar message to the Taliban's Mullah Omar. Although not dismissing these requests outright, Omar ultimately refused to cooperate. Despite the failure of its own entreaties to the Taliban, Pakistan's about-face was one of the most important positive consequences of the 9/11 surprise and would be of enormous value in the struggle to come.

"WAR ON TERROR"

In the thirty years since international terrorism had made its debut with a series of dramatic airline hijackings by the Popular Front for the Liberation of Palestine, the United States had tended to accept the existence of terrorism as one of the unfortunate costs of doing business as a superpower.[13] Against the backdrop of the smoking ruins of the World Trade Center, calculations of what was and was not an acceptable risk had changed dramatically in Washington, D.C. In the wake of the attack, Bush asked Tenet for a country-by-country briefing on how well the United States had done against Islamic extremism since 2000. He had never requested anything like this before. "The president . . . became engaged in the matter in a way he had never been before the attacks," wrote Tenet in his memoirs.[14]

President Bush quickly concluded that a paramilitary operation against al Qaeda and its Taliban ally in Afghanistan would be only the initial phase of America's response to 9/11. In National Security Presidential Decision 9, which formalized American war aims in October 2001, Bush established a high, and some would later come to believe unrealistic, standard for victory. It was "the elimination of terrorism as a threat to our way of life." Al Qaeda was merely the first on a list of terrorist groups targeted for destruction or neutralization.[15] Behind this war strategy lay the conviction that the world had become too dangerous and too small a place to tolerate anti-American violent extremists anywhere, anymore.

President Bush announced the start of this broad offensive in a solemn address to a joint session of Congress on September 20, 2001. "Our war on terror begins with al Qaeda, but it does not end there. It will not end until every terrorist group of global reach has been found, stopped and defeated." Not since John F. Kennedy promised in 1961 "to bear any burden" to fight the cold war had an American president made as expansive a pledge: "We will direct every resource at our command—every means of diplomacy, every tool of intelligence, every instrument of law enforcement, every financial influence, and every necessary weapon of war—to the disruption and to the defeat of the global terror network."[16] Bush was also straightforward about how long this war might be: "Americans should not expect one battle, but a lengthy campaign, unlike any other we have ever seen. It may include dramatic strikes, visible on TV, and covert operations, secret even in success. We will starve terrorists of funding, turn them one against another, drive them from place to place, until there is no refuge or no rest." Finally, he made clear that the United States would not simply target shadowy groups: "And we will pursue nations that provide aid or safe haven to terrorism. Every nation, in every region, now has a decision to make. Either you are with us, or you are with the terrorists. From this day forward, any nation that continues to harbor or support terrorism will be regarded by the United States as a hostile regime." In its plan of September 13, the CIA stated its goal of going after al Qaeda in ninety-two countries and seeking broader cooperation with Uzbekistan, Pakistan, Libya, Syria, Iran, Turkey, and Tajikistan.[17]

As the president had pledged, the offensive against terrorists quickly took many forms. The NSC gave the Treasury Department responsibility for tracking and deterring terrorist financing. Under pre-9/11 law the Treasury Department had the authority to identify and freeze terrorist accounts and had even established an Office of Foreign Assets Control, but it had done little with this authority. The National Commission on Terrorist Attacks Upon the United States (9/11 Commission) later found that the office had also lacked access to the kind of intelligence that would have allowed it to freeze bin Laden's assets had it wanted to.[18] At a meeting of Treasury Department officials on September 17, the "first priority was to end the indifference of higher-level Treasury policymakers."[19] On Monday, September 24, Bush ordered U.S. financial institutions to freeze the assets of twenty-seven individuals and organizations. Another thirty-nine people or groups had their financial assets frozen by October 12, and by the end of the year the list numbered 162 people or organizations.[20]

Freezing assets would have little effect if limited to U.S. financial institutions alone. In this as in the other elements of the Bush administration's initial response to the challenge of 9/11, international cooperation was considered necessary. Starting almost immediately, Treasury conferred with its counterparts in the other major economies. At a meeting of the Group of Seven on October 6, the participants created a comprehensive G7 action plan to track and freeze terrorist funding. At the UN Security Council, the Bush administration successfully pushed through resolutions that called on member countries to freeze all terrorist funding. By 2007, 172 states had participated in the initiative, freezing 1,400 terrorist accounts.[21] International cooperation also involved the sharing of financial intelligence. The United States and its allies gained access to the database of the Society for Worldwide Interbank Financial Telecommunications, "a messaging system to transmit information related to financial transactions between banks around the world."[22]

The CIA's and Treasury's response fit a pattern of the entire government in the fall of 2001. In haste to do something against al Qaeda, Washington did not have the time to create new organizations or to reform old ones. The Bush administration set out to empower and unleash what it had. Bush issued a notification— what in an earlier period would have been called an Intelligence Finding—that had the effect of granting to the CIA additional authorities to capture and kill suspected terrorists. Working with Congress, the administration set about broadening authorities for domestic intelligence gathering. The USA PATRIOT Act, which Bush signed into law in October 2001, contained provisions that the Clinton administration had unsuccessfully sought to pass in 1996 when it had first awakened to the threat of Islamist terrorism. The act attempted to reshape the domestic surveillance laws of the 1970s in light of new technologies. It was also designed to ease the granting of warrants for domestic wiretapping by the Foreign Intelligence Surveillance Court, a secret court in Washington that operated round the clock. Existing law required that the FBI prove that an individual was an "agent of a foreign power" and that the wiretap was primarily for intelligence gathering purposes before it could be given. Now a warrant could be granted if the target could be linked to an independent terrorist group, such as al Qaeda, and even if the tap might produce information for eventual prosecution.

There was some limited institutional change in the wake of 9/11. Bush brought a political ally to Washington as a domestic security czar. Governor Tom Ridge of Pennsylvania was put in charge of the new Office of Homeland Security within the White House. Bush wanted Ridge and his staff to nudge the many domestic agencies with responsibility for domestic law enforcement and security. And Congress, with the support of the White House, created a new agency, the Transportation Security Administration, thus federalizing baggage screeners at U.S. airports. The closed-circuit video of Mohammed Atta, the lead 9/11 hijacker, easily going through security on that fateful day and the evidence that the terrorists had carried box cutters onto the four doomed planes made the continued outsourcing of airport security to private contractors intolerable.

The public largely accepted these changes, including the increased restriction of one's zone of privacy, especially at airports. What the public would not know for another four years was that parallel with the open legislative effort to expand intelligence capabilities at home, the White House had launched a highly secret domestic intelligence program on October 4, 2001, with little significant congressional involvement.[23] As the Bush administration ended, the precise parameters of what became known as "the Terrorist Surveillance Program" remained secret.[24] In congressional hearings over broadening the Foreign Intelligence Surveillance Act (FISA), the Bush administration explained in 2007 that this program was deemed necessary to monitor telephone calls where at least one of the participants was overseas. The presidential authorization swept away the requirement that law enforcement and intelligence agencies needed to seek a warrant from the FISA Court, which had handled these kinds of requests for domestic surveillance since 1978. There are other reports that the program also included cooperation with private telecommunications companies to acquire access to their digital switches and databases. Set up secretly, the "program" was apparently briefed to some members of Congress in 2002.

To some extent, the U.S. government moved as it did because Washington knew so little about al Qaeda's capabilities and immediate plans in the fall of 2001. There were realistic fears of a second wave of attacks, led possibly by al Qaeda sleeper cells in the United States. There was a pervasive sense of urgency and ignorance. Especially frightening was a series of anthrax attacks that may not have killed many Americans—five died and seventeen were sickened—but revealed weaknesses in the U.S. government's ability to protect its citizens from biological weapons. Although quickly forgotten by the public, the case heightened Bush administration fears about the likely effectiveness of unconventional weapons in the hands of terrorists.[25]

Even allowing for the exigencies of the moment, however, George Bush's opting for limited institutional innovation and increased secrecy at home reflected something else. Although the president had identified the country's enemy broadly and had warned of a long war, it was assumed that the structures developed in the cold war for the struggle with the Soviets could be adapted to this new struggle. It was also assumed that the public consensus that had allowed the U.S. government to sustain a largely secret domestic surveillance program through the first half of the cold war could be reestablished in this new time of peril. In part, this reaction may be ascribed to conservative ideology. The Bush team shared the mistrust of government bureaucracies associated with modern American conservatism. But it was equally the product of a reaction to the 1970s by some of the influential graybeards around the inexperienced president. In the wake of Vietnam and Watergate, Congress and the judiciary had placed new restraints on executive power. Lyndon B. Johnson's and Richard Nixon's assumption of a blanket authority for fighting the war in Vietnam, the FBI's and the White House's unregulated use of wiretaps, and Nixon's use of executive power against his political enemies had all created a toxic political brew that produced the War Powers Act, FISA, and congressional oversight of intelligence. Vice President Dick Cheney had watched the congressional counterrevolution from a perch in both the Nixon and Ford White Houses and believed that Congress had gone too far. Indeed, in the wake of the Iran–Contra arms scandal Cheney, who was by then a leading minority member of the U.S. House of Representatives, had co-authored a defense of Ronald Reagan's use of executive power.[26] For Cheney, who believed the White House had all the power it needed to defend the country if only the president opted to use it, the most important way to deal with the new threats of the millennium was to unleash the American executive. Cheney's role in shaping the administration's initial response was extraordinary. Before 9/11, Bush had designated his vice president to lead a study of how the U.S. government should deal with the threat of the proliferation of WMDs, but following 9/11 it became clear that Cheney's office was shaping the entire national security strategy of the United States. The cold war nostalgia of the new approach seemed more reflective of a longtime veteran of Washington, Cheney, than of a baby boom president.

Although innovative, even the approach to Afghanistan reflected the lessons of the cold war, where U.S.-led covert action had defeated the Soviet occupation. The first CIA officers entered Afghanistan on September 27 and were joined on October 17 by a twelve-man Special Forces A-team.[27] Ultimately 110 CIA officers and 316 Special Forces personnel would serve in the combat phase of the Afghan war.[28] CIA optimism that the Taliban would sacrifice Osama bin Laden to save their regime proved unfounded. U.S. go-betweens sent messages to Taliban leader Mullah Omar that Afghanistan would be spared the wrath of the United States if the Taliban turned over bin Laden, allowed him to be captured, or simply executed him. A U.S. bombing campaign began on October 7 after the Taliban provided their final refusal.

Once fully joined, the Afghan conflict produced a strong tug-of-war in Washington. The White House found itself having to deflect Defense Secretary Rumsfeld's disappointment at not being in charge of this campaign. Both President Bush and Vice President Cheney gave the CIA plan room to work. Cheney turned down Rumsfeld's effort to place the CIA teams in Afghanistan under CENTCOM, the military command led by General Tommy Franks. Within the CIA, the local teams working with the Northern Alliance believed that the U.S. Air Force's bombing campaign was too tentative. But senior CIA leaders refused to give up hope that their clever covert operation to split the Taliban would lead some of Omar's rivals to deliver up bin Laden and his associates. It was believed that a stronger bombing campaign would alienate the country's Pashtun majority, which was suffering most of the casualties. Meanwhile the Pentagon chafed at not being allowed to unload on the Taliban and al Qaeda. As October ended, doubts were growing that the CIA plan would work before the onset of winter made military operations difficult.

U.S. support for the Northern Alliance and the terror created by the U.S. bombing campaign ultimately proved the most decisive factors. Taliban control of the country disintegrated. On November 10, Mazar-i-Sharif fell. An important town in the north, it was needed as a land bridge to allow waves of supplies to come south from Uzbekistan (much as the capture of Cherbourg was key to setting up the logistical network required to liberate France after the D-Day invasion in 1944). Four days later, having been abandoned by the Taliban, Kabul was captured by the Northern Alliance. On November 16, the bombing campaign scored its first big victory. Mohammed Atef, bin Laden's military commander, died in a Predator missile attack in Gardez, just south of Kabul.

The Afghan campaign, however, did not achieve it most important objective, the capture of Osama bin Laden. As the hunt for the al Qaeda chief dragged on, the cost of relying so heavily on the CIA's paramilitary strategy—which, owing to a lack of manpower, had the effect of minimizing the U.S. military presence in the Afghan-Pakistani borderlands—became painfully obvious.

Following the fall of Kandahar in the south, the leadership of al Qaeda and elements of the Taliban regime fled to the Tora Bora Mountains near the border with Pakistan. U.S. intelligence pinpointed bin Laden in the caves of that region.[29] As efforts to dislodge him by means of an air campaign proved ineffective, the CIA found that it could not motivate its Afghan allies to engage in a cave-by-cave search for him. The CIA's subsequent requests for immediate U.S. military assistance were equally unsuccessful. CENTCOM responded that it could not send any major military reinforcements for weeks. There had never been any planning for a major deployment of U.S. troops to the region. According to a *New York Times* report, there were only about thirty-six Special Forces troops sent to Tora Bora. The Marines had a force of four thousand under Brigadier General James N. Mattis in Afghanistan, but when the general requested permission from CENTCOM to join the battle at Tora Bora, he was turned down.[30] On December 17, 2001, it is believed that bin Laden and his remaining lieutenants crossed the border into the lawless tribal region of Pakistan.

"MISSION ACCOMPLISHED"

Over the course of 2002 and 2003, the Bush administration would make its greatest mistakes in the name of counterterrorism. The nearly costless collapse of the Taliban regime had the simultaneous effect of emboldening hawks in the Bush administration who believed in the necessity of a broad offensive against all terrorism and worrying those who wondered what a wounded but not dead al Qaeda could achieve now that it was on the run. This potent admixture of hubris and fear caused the Bush administration to expand even further the meaning of a "war on terror." The result was a series of decisions that would hamper the administration's concerted effort against Islamist terror and undermine domestic and international support for the U.S. struggle with Islamic extremists in the remaining years of the Bush presidency.

The first evidence of this expansion came in four sentences in the president's 2002 State of the Union address. After making direct reference to Iran, North Korea, and Iraq, Bush enunciated a new war aim: "States like these, and their terrorist allies, constitute an axis of evil, arming to threaten the peace of the world. By seeking weapons of mass destruction, these regimes pose a grave and growing danger. They could provide these arms to terrorists, giving them the means to match their hatred. They could attack our allies or attempt to blackmail the United States. In any of these cases, the price of indifference would be catastrophic." Three months earlier, Bush had threatened states that sponsored terrorists; now he expanded that threat to include unfriendly regimes that were pursuing WMDs. The shift was subtle, but it reflected a return to the state-based concerns that had dominated the early months of his administration and to the sole external threat he had mentioned in his first inaugural address.

Events conspired both to increase the administration's confidence in its management of the terrorist threat and to complicate it. On March 27, 2002, the Bush administration caught its first big fish in Faisalabad, Pakistan. The capture of Abu Zubaydah, a high-level al Qaeda manager, was made possible by cooperation between Afghan militiamen, the CIA, and Pakistani intelligence, a troika that would have been impossible a year earlier.[31] Zubaydah, who was badly wounded in the operation, recovered and was moved to a secret CIA interrogation facility. Zubaydah's interrogation, which started in May 2002, forced the Bush administration to decide two issues that would later shape domestic and international public opinion of U.S. counterterrorism: what to do with so-called high-value detainees (HVDs) and whether U.S. officers would be permitted to employ torture to extract information from them.[32] The most important al Qaeda operative ever in U.S. custody, Zubaydah potentially knew of future operations and certainly knew the names of trained al Qaeda operatives unknown to the United States or its allies. "Despite what Hollywood might have you believe," George Tenet would write later, "in situations like this you don't call in the tough guys; you call in the lawyers."[33] To protect Zubaydah's CIA interrogators from future prosecution on U.S. torture laws, the Justice Department issued an "interrogation" opinion on August 1, 2002. The opinion defined torture as narrowly as possible—as acts that caused pain "associated with a sufficiently serious physical condition or injury such as death, organ failure, or serious impairment of bodily function"—and then made it clear that even if U.S. interrogators committed that much pain, they would be immune from prosecution by claiming self-defense on behalf of the United States.[34] As the CIA established its own network of secret prisons, the Pentagon was in the first phase of managing its own special terrorist interrogation and detention facility at the U.S. military base at Guantánamo, Cuba. Having found itself with about one thousand low-level al Qaeda detainees in Afghanistan, some of whom had been bought from the Northern Alliance, the Pentagon, it appears, reluctantly agreed to take responsibility for them. The first detainees reached Guantánamo in January 2002. The same gaggle of Justice Department lawyers who would draw on a pinched constitutional theory to empower the CIA to use torture against Zubaydah determined that the al Qaeda detainees would not have to be treated as prisoners of war, and were therefore exempt from the Geneva protections. The detainees at Guantánamo would become a public relations and constitutional problem for the administration.

Sources vary on what torturing Zubaydah produced for the United States. George Tenet credits Zubaydah with crucial leads that resulted in the capture of Ramzi Bin al-Shibh, who had been selected to be one of 9/11 hijackers but had served instead as a conduit between them and al Qaeda's headquarters when he could not get a visa to enter the United States.[35] Newspaper reports also credit him with pointing U.S. intelligence in the direction of Jose Padilla, a U.S. citizen later found guilty of belonging to al Qaeda.[36] Yet the CIA's own inspector general, in a 2004 special review of the use of "enhanced interrogation techniques," refused to reach any conclusion as to whether these techniques were the reason Zubaydah produced useful information. The CIA did learn more from Zubaydah after he was waterboarded eighty-three times in August 2002, but, the agency concluded, "it is not possible to say definitely that the waterboard is the reason for Abu Zubaydah's increased production." And the CIA's inspector general did not attempt to compare the value of this "increased production" to what had been learned before the use of these techniques.[37] Indeed, FBI sources told journalist Jane Mayer that the U.S. government obtained its best information from Zubaydah, including the tip-off about Padilla, before the CIA began torturing him, when the FBI was engaged in "rapport building" with the prisoner.[38] In April 2009, one of the FBI interrogators, Ali Soufan, explained publicly that traditional legal methods had extracted all that Zubaydah had to offer before the CIA took over.[39]

Over the course of the spring of 2002 the president began to fill out the doctrine that lay behind his "axis of evil" declaration. Issued as the National Security Strategy in September 2002, this formal statement endorsed military preemption as a legitimate strategy. With al Qaeda's leadership scattered but undefeated, and lacking confidence in international controls of biological, chemical, and nuclear weapons, the Bush administration decided on a throw of the strategic dice. "It has taken almost a decade for us to comprehend the true nature of this new threat," the document stated. "Given the goals of rogue states and terrorists, the United States can no longer solely rely on a reactive posture as we have in the past. The inability to deter a potential attacker, the immediacy of today's threats, and the magnitude of potential harm that could be caused by our adversaries' choice of weapons, do not permit that option. We cannot let our enemies strike first."[40] Comparing the new era to the cold war, the strategy expounded the chilling proposition that unlike the Soviets, who were deterred by nuclear weapons, the new enemies, both states and terrorist organizations, could not be deterred. One year after 9/11, "rogue states" had been elevated to the same level in this new war as al Qaeda and Islamist terrorism. In essence, the Bush administration was basing U.S. policy on a conspiracy theory that assumed operational links between terrorists and regional rogue states, irrespective of ideology, with the implication that both kinds of threats had to be treated alike. Iraq was at the top of the new list of targets in this ever-expanding world war.

For the rest of 2002, the Bush administration was consumed with making a case for invading Iraq, a secular state detested by bin Laden. Vice President Cheney and key deputies in the Department of Defense repeatedly queried the CIA about possible connections between al Qaeda and the Hussein regime. In their minds, Hussein's secrecy about his WMD programs—which had existed before the Gulf War, and which he had lied about afterward— fused with knowledge that various al Qaeda operatives had been able to move around parts of the autonomous Kurdish region in

Iraq's northeast to produce a conviction that these two American enemies were conspiring to produce a mass-casualty attack. Had al Qaeda seemed more threatening in late 2002 or had Iran been an easier target, Iraq might not have been an acceptable option, but the war against al Qaeda in Afghanistan had gone both too well and not well enough. Mindful of the pitfalls of historical analogies, to some extent the Bush administration was making the same strategic calculation as the Reagan administration when faced with the frustrations of fighting a shadowy terrorist threat in the mid-1980s. Frustrated by its inability to inflict a mortal blow on Iranian-backed Hezbollah following successive attacks on U.S. diplomatic and military personnel in Lebanon, the administration chose to go after a convenient enemy. Iran was too difficult a target; but Libya offered many advantages. It too supported terrorists and was resistant to U.S. pressures.[41] The main difference between 1986 and 2002 was that twenty years earlier the Reagan administration had waited (and schemed) for a Libyan provocation before attacking. The Bush administration believed that in the new threat environment it was foolhardy to wait. And this time it would be Iraq that would be made an example of. In the words of Cheney's staff, defeating Saddam Hussein would have a salutary "demonstration effect" on U.S. enemies everywhere. [42]

As U.S. armies amassed in Kuwait and Saudi Arabia for an invasion of Iraq, a Pakistani tipped off U.S. intelligence to the whereabouts of Khalid Sheik Mohammed, the mastermind of the 9/11 attacks. Historically, the best intelligence agents have been "walkins," literally sources that walk into a foreign facility with information to share.[43] In this case, the informant knew the location of the safe house where Mohammed was hiding for the night. U.S. and Pakistani authorities moved swiftly, and a bedraggled Mohammed was taken into custody on March 1, 2003. With the fall of Baghdad a month later after a deceptively easy military campaign and Mohammed's capture, there seemed to be some truth underlying the presidential boast on the USS *Abraham Lincoln* of "Mission Accomplished." Unbeknownst to any of the principal actors in this drama, May 2003 was the height of the Bush counterterrorism offensive. Iraq was under U.S. occupation, and three-quarters of the pre-9/11 leadership of al Qaeda had been captured or killed.

THE TIDE TURNS

A crisis occurred in the U.S. counterterrorism effort in 2004. In part, it was a reaction to the Islamist attack on the Madrid railway system in March 2004, which resulted in the electoral defeat of a conservative U.S. ally in Spain. Although not ordered by bin Laden, the attack involved individuals who had been inspired by Islamicist propaganda. Until 2004, public expert discussion of al Qaeda had tracked with threat assessment within the government. But after Madrid, these discussions began to diverge sharply. Outside experts believed that al Qaeda's leadership of world jihadism had been diluted because of the loss of the Afghan sanctuary and effective counterterrorism efforts in Pakistan and elsewhere. The main terrorist threat, it was argued, now stemmed from smaller, homegrown groups, such as had organized the attack in Madrid. Although as murderous in their intent as al Qaeda, these groups were less likely to be able to launch a WMD attack.[44] Inside government, however, there were rising fears of a second 9/11 attack by al Qaeda itself. "By July 2004," recalled George Tenet, "we believed that the major elements of the plot were in place and moving toward execution and that the plot had been sanctioned by the al-Qa'ida leadership. We believed that al-Qa'ida facilitators were already inside the United States, in an organized group—which to the best of my knowledge has never been found—and that they had selected non-Arab operatives to carry out the attacks."[45]

The divergence in the expert community only served to magnify the wider loss of confidence in the U.S. government's strategy to meet the terrorist challenge and of trust in what the government was telling the American people about the struggle. The inability of U.S. inspectors to find WMDs in Iraq, combined with revelations in April 2004 of prisoner abuse at the Abu Ghraib prison in Baghdad, deepened public concerns about the turn that the response to 9/11 had taken in 2002. The use of the generic "war on terror" as an issue by the president and the vice president in the election campaign and the raising of alerts by the Department of Homeland Security (reflecting the intelligence community's actual fears that summer) only increased public cynicism about Bush's counterterrorist strategy. At the same time, overseas support for U.S. counterterrorism operations continued the steady decline that had begun with the invasion of Iraq. Although the National Security Strategy of 2002 had mentioned public diplomacy, the administration seemed untroubled by the apparent trade-off between a successful hearts-and-minds campaign among Muslims outside Iraq and its drive to control the situation inside that war-torn country.

Meanwhile, an elite bipartisan commission put a nail in the coffin of the Bush administration's institutional approach to Islamic extremism. Created by both the U.S. Congress and President Bush on November 27, 2002, the 9/11 Commission was tasked to explain why this generation's Pearl Harbor surprise had occurred and to provide recommendations so that nothing similar happened again. The commission's public hearings in 2003, which called National Security Advisor Condoleezza Rice and former counterterrorism czar Richard Clarke to the stand, accelerated the steady erosion of legitimacy for existing counterterrorism institutions, especially in the intelligence community. Witness after witness underscored both the inadequacies of the nation's existing national security structure to handle the terrorist menace and the likelihood of future attacks at home. But it was the publication of the 9/11 Commission report on July 22, 2004, with its list of concrete recommendations, that provided the catalyst for the deep changes in U.S. national security institutions that the public knew instinctively was needed. The official document became an immediate bestseller and an instant factor in the 2004 presidential election. The Bush administration had no choice but to embrace much broader and deeper structural changes than it had ever thought necessary. Until the summer of 2004, the administration had preferred to broaden the authority and power of existing intelligence and foreign policy agencies rather than create new ones. Its one major institutional innovation, the creation of the Department of Homeland Security in the fall of 2002, had involved only domestic defense. And even though no one could doubt the significance of this change, there was room to doubt whether the amalgamation of twenty-two distinct domestic agencies, with different organizational cultures, into one bureaucracy would actually lead to more security at home. As the 9/11 Commission pointed out, the Bush administration still had not adequately addressed the problem of ensuring effective coordination of foreign and domestic intelligence activities.

The 9/11 Commission did what the administration had refused to do since September 2001. It questioned the utility of cold war institutions in fighting an international extremist conspiracy and found those institutions wanting. Efforts by the intelligence community to improve coordination were still far less effective than what the U.S. military had instituted through the Joint Chiefs of Staff as far back as World War II. Although the CIA had established an interagency intelligence fusion center (the Terrorist Threat Integration Center) in early 2003, the center's mandate was limited to intelligence coordination. There was no operational coordination among the government's civilian and military services. The U.S. Air Force and the CIA did manage the Predator project to allow for instant action on the receipt of sensitive information, but this example of synergy was an outlier in the struggle against al Qaeda. As a result, the commission proposed the formation of a national counterterrorism center. Aware of the history of weaknesses in the management of the U.S. intelligence community since the formation of the CIA in 1947, the commission also proposed the creation of the post of director of national intelligence, to force better intelligence sharing and smarter intelligence collection and analysis by giving one person the authority to coordinate the use of resources by the country's fifteen intelligence agencies.[46]

Hidden from public view, the Bush administration managed an even tougher internal institutional challenge. In March 2004, the top level of the Justice Department signaled to the White House that it had concerns about the civil liberties implications of the Terrorist Surveillance Program. In establishing a legal framework for this secret initiative, the Bush administration required that the attorney general of the United States certify the program every forty-five days. Since October 2003, Attorney General John Ashcroft's Office of Legal Counsel had advocated taking a new look at all of the legal aspects of the administration's approach to fighting the war on terror, including the terrorism listening program. By early 2004 Ashcroft himself had doubts. In March, the program was due to be reauthorized, and though Ashcroft was hospitalized with a serious illness, the White House hoped to pressure him to sign once more. But in a dramatic hospital confrontation with Bush's two emissaries, White House Chief of Staff Andrew Card and White House Counsel Alberto Gonzales, at his bedside, a weakened Ashcroft denounced the program and pointed to his deputy, James Comey, an opponent of the program as originally conceived, and said, "*There* is the attorney general." Comey, who had become acting attorney general because of Ashcroft's illness, then refused to certify the program. When President Bush decided to ignore Ashcroft's concerns and alter the legal niceties so that Gonzales could certify the program instead, both Acting Attorney General Comey and FBI Director Mueller threatened to resign. A few days later the president changed his mind. Comey and Mueller stayed, and the program was altered in ways still secret but sufficient to satisfy his own Justice Department.[47]

The Justice Department's quiet rebellion was also directed at the U.S. policy toward detainees. The arrival of Jack Goldsmith at the White House's Office of Legal Counsel in October 2003 had caused the review of the legal basis for the war. In June 2004, he withdrew the legal document prepared by his predecessors, the August 2002 "torture memo" by John Yoo and Jay S. Bybee, that had given the CIA legal cover for its use of torture.[48] Only days later the third branch of government, the judiciary, added its weight to pressuring the White House to change its ways. In two decisions issued on June 28 (*Hamdi* and *Rasul*), the U.S. Supreme

Court ruled that the war's detainees, whether they were at Guantánamo or not, had a right to legal representation and could contest their arrest under U.S. law.[49] With these challenges to the surveillance program and to the treatment of detainees, the legal foundation for the administration's maximalist approach to counterterrorism was crumbling.

Following George W. Bush's reelection in November, the bottom also fell out of the situation in Iraq, which, because of the failure of the occupation, even critics of the war began to see as a front in the struggle against al Qaeda. The number of terrorist attacks worldwide, compiled by the CIA on behalf of the State Department, jumped above 11,000 in 2005, causing 14,200 deaths. More than half of these deaths occurred in Iraq. Far from making the world safe, the so-called war on terrorism seemed to have unleashed the greatest wave of terrorism in world history. Al Qaeda's leader in Iraq, Abu Musab al-Zarqawi, led a group of foreign jihadists who were responsible for many of these killings, and bin Laden's lieutenant was using Iraq to train even more terrorists. Iraq seemed to be replacing Afghanistan as an al Qaeda sanctuary.

THE RETURN OF LEGALITY AND PRAGMATISM

Comparing and contrasting George W. Bush's first and second terms will be a major challenge for historians for years to come. As in other areas of administration policy, the public face of counterterrorism did not change in the second term. The administration refused to change its justifications, its tropes—most notably the use of the much-discredited label "war on terror"—or to acknowledge a strategic misstep in Iraq. Yet the second term brought significant changes in how the administration managed the struggle with Islamic extremists.

Condoleezza Rice's arrival at the State Department coincided with the emergence of more flexibility in the U.S. approach to rogue states, which since 2002 had been linked to the larger war with militant Islam.[50] U.S. rhetoric regarding North Korea was brought down a notch, and the Bush administration supported regional negotiations to encourage Pyongyang to dismantle its nuclear program. Meanwhile, Washington subtly opened a new diplomatic and intelligence front against terrorism by establishing a strategic relationship with India, despite the suspicions of Pakistan. In September 2006, the White House issued a document titled "National Strategy for Combating Terrorism," which in recalling the importance of international as well as domestic institutions in fighting the cold war argued that similar "transformational structures" were needed in the current war. The strategy stressed the importance of strengthening coalitions and partnerships around the world, and, in a subtle dig at the arrogance inherent in the approach of the first term, the position paper added, "we will ensure that such international cooperation is an enduring feature of the long war we will fight."[51]

There were limits to this pragmatic diplomacy. In the summer of 2006, the White House supported the costly Israeli invasion of Lebanon to destroy the military capacity of Iran's ally, Hezbollah, and in the last weeks of the administration Washington appeared to do little to discourage Israel from invading Gaza in search of the leadership of Hamas. In both cases, it appeared that Israeli actions did little to enhance Israel's regional security while once again providing Islamic militants with a rallying cry against the United States.

A new pragmatism was also apparent in the administration's conduct of military operations, especially after the replacement of Secretary of Defense Donald Rumsfeld by Robert Gates in December 2006. In Iraq, under the imaginative leadership of then Lieutenant General David Petraeus, the U.S. armed forces established coalitions with local Sunni warlords, accepting a distinction between accidental and global guerrillas. Young Sunnis who only a few weeks before had been constructing roadside bombs to kill U.S. soldiers were enlisted in a common struggle against al Qaeda's surrogates in Iraq.[52] In January 2007, George W. Bush announced an increase in the numbers of troops deployed to Iraq, a "surge," to facilitate this new strategy. By the end of 2008, U.S. military deaths had plummeted by two-thirds in Iraq over 2007 and Iraqi civilian deaths were down 60 percent.[53]

Pragmatic realism could also be seen in the policy toward a relative backwater. The Bush administration showed flexibility in its approach to the rise of the radical Islamic Court Union (ICU) in Somalia. Washington and regional ally Ethiopia had supported an alliance of secular warlords, the Alliance for the Restoration of Peace and Counterterrorism. After the Islamists gained control over all of the Somali capital, Mogadishu, in June 2006, Ethiopia began sending troops into the country. By Christmas 2006, the ICU regime had collapsed and the Ethiopian military was patrolling Mogadishu in support of the newly installed Transitional Federal Government (TFG), a ragtag group of secular warlords. The United States made little attempt to hide its support for the Ethiopian operation. In January 2007, U.S. warships launched missile attacks on suspected Islamist hideouts in Somalia.

But the Ethiopian operation did not bring stability. The foreign intervention was unpopular in Somalia, not least because of the bloodshed and dislocation—1.3 million people—associated with Ethiopia's local ally.[54] In response, the Bush administration gradually varied its tactics. When U.S. efforts to replace the Ethiopians with peacekeepers from the African Union stalled, Ethiopia negotiated a pullout agreement directly with the Somalis. This agreement, reached in November 2008, laid the groundwork for the complete withdrawal of Ethiopian forces and the deployment of 3,400 African Union peacekeepers. More surprisingly, the agreement also allowed for the return to power in January 2009 of some elements of the deposed ICU government.

In the wake of the failure of the Ethiopian intervention, Washington chose to take advantage of factionalism among the Islamists in Somalia. Between 2006 and 2008, a more radical Islamic element had broken off the ICU, making the ICU seem moderate in comparison. In the final year of the Bush administration, the Ethiopians and the United States opted for dealing with the ICU, even helping the ICU leadership regain control over their movement, rather than betting on the unpopular secular warlords of the TFG. In August 2008, for example, U.S. Tomahawk missiles killed the leader of the radical Islamic splinter group.[55]

At home, the second term also brought changes in how the United States conducted counterterrorism. The legalists' revolt that had started in 2004—both inside and outside the administration—began achieving some success in reestablishing limits on presidential authority in wartime. Those successes were largely due to pressure from the courts and Congress. An internal effort to put U.S. counterterrorism on a sounder legal footing, endorsed by Secretary of State Rice and led by Philip Zelikow, counselor of the Department of State, and Deputy Secretary of Defense Gordon England, stalled in the face of Rumsfeld's opposition and tepid support from the National Security Council staff. In a June 2005 draft paper entitled "Elements of Possible Initiative," Zelikow and England made both a pragmatic and moral argument for ending the current detention and interrogation system. The reformers at State and in the Pentagon argued that not only had the recent experience in fighting al Qaeda in Iraq proved that humane treatment of captives could produce actionable intelligence, but continuing to violate the Geneva Conventions held long-term moral and diplomatic costs.[56] Meanwhile, by mid-2005 Comey and Goldsmith had left the Justice Department, allowing the temporary restoration of legal cover for use of "enhanced interrogation techniques" by the CIA.[57] Pressure from outside the administration, however, would soon force President Bush to accept some of the arguments made by the internal reformers. On June 29, 2006, the Supreme Court ruled in *Hamdan v. Rumsfeld* that the administration was bound by the Geneva Conventions on torture and the treatment of prisoners of war. Two months later, President Bush revealed that in the wake of 9/11, the U.S. government had been holding prisoners at secret sites overseas. The president then announced that these sites would be closed and all of the remaining detainees would be transferred to Guantánamo to face military trials. In early September, after two years of skirmishing between a coalition of State Department officials and military lawyers and a White House skeptical of international law, the Pentagon also issued a new army field manual that restored the authority of the Geneva Conventions in determining the treatment of detainees.[58] Congress also played a role in reining in the Bush administration. In October 2006 it passed the Military Commissions Act, which reestablished the authority of the Geneva Convention over all U.S. personnel.[59] Finally, in early 2008, Congress provided a legal foundation for domestic surveillance of terrorist suspects that brought the administration's activities back under the supervision of the FISA courts.

As the Bush administration came to a close, the twilight war against Islamic extremism seemed no closer to resolution than it had on September 12, 2001. Under the leadership of Osama bin Laden, al Qaeda continued to organize or inspire the organization of terrorist activities directed at the United States and its allies. In late November 2008, Islamists from Pakistan launched an audacious terrorist assault on the center of Mumbai, India, followed by a three-day siege that altogether killed nearly two hundred people.[60] If, as President Bush had suggested, his administration would be judged according to how well it handled the challenge of terrorism, then the scorecard appeared decidedly mixed. On the one hand, the U.S. homeland had been spared a second attack since 9/11, the operational effectiveness of al Qaeda appeared to have been severely reduced, and Osama bin Laden, though likely still alive, had been forced into perpetual hiding. Although much of the struggle remained shadowy, there was publicly available evidence that good intelligence and investigative work in the United States, Great Britain, and Pakistan (among others) led to the disruption of plots and the detainment of Islamic extremists, not necessarily linked to bin Laden, who wished to kill Americans. The Lackawanna or Buffalo Six and the so-called 2006 UK airlines terror plotters, for example, were serious in their intent, if not necessarily sophisticated enough to pull off spectacular events.[61] There was also overt evidence of gains made against al Qaeda allies in Southeast Asia. Since 2002 local authorities have scored large victories against the leadership of Jemaah Islamiyah in Singapore and Malaysia and Abu Shayyaf in the Philippines. The United States' role in these successes is unclear, though in the wake of 9/11 the U.S. military publicly stepped up its role in training and assisting the Filipino army, especially in counterterrorism.[62]

On the other hand, in its zeal to reorder the international system, the Bush administration created a Petri dish for massive amounts of terrorism in Iraq between 2003 and 2007, with immeasurable damage to U.S. soft power in the Muslim world. And although the United States had maintained widespread support for its goals in Afghanistan, by the end of 2008, U.S. and Allied casualties in that war were increasing, along with evidence of a resurgent Taliban.[63] In the 2008 presidential election, the administration faced bipartisan criticism for having neglected Afghanistan as a consequence of mishandling Iraq. Meanwhile, the U.S. detainee facility at Guantánamo, which had been a lightning rod for international criticism, remained open, with nearly two hundred fifty inmates as of January 2009.[64] The Bush way of counterterrorism also had its costs at home. Unwilling to question residual cold war institutions, the administration instead raised serious constitutional issues and divided the American public by overriding the late cold war consensus on privacy rights and the proper restraints on executive power.

Changes in the administration's handling of counterterrorism in President George W. Bush's second term, however, underscored the self-corrective elements of the American system of government. A broad coalition of legalists and pragmatic realists, both within all three branches of the U.S. government and outside government, played a significant role in rolling back perceived excesses and in reordering the administration's priorities. This quiet rebellion, which is not yet fully understood and deserves more study as more documents become available, had very positive consequences for U.S. national security and for the U.S. government's standing at home and around the world.

5

ANATOMY OF AN UNNECESSARY WAR

The Iraq Invasion

FREDRIK LOGEVALL

F— Saddam. We're taking him out.

—*George W. Bush, March 2002*[1]

Today, if we went into Iraq, like the president
would like us to do, you know where you begin. You never
know where you are going to end.

—*George F. Kennan, September 2002*[2]

HOW THE UNITED STATES GOT INTO IRAQ IS ONE OF THE GREAT foreign policy questions of our time. For decades to come, historians will be debating the developments that culminated in the launching of the "shock and awe" aerial bombardment on March 19, 2003, and the ground invasion the following day. George W. Bush and his top advisers from the start explained their decision for war in varying and often contradictory ways, and their explanations changed over time. Some motives they left unstated. Seven years later, the bloodshed continues, albeit at a reduced level, having killed more than four thousand American soldiers and seriously injured many times that figure, having devastated Iraq and left at least a hundred thousand of its citizens dead, and having weakened America's traditional alliances and caused precious resources to be diverted from the struggle in Afghanistan and the broader campaign against terror.

Much remains to be learned about what went on in the halls of power in the weeks and months leading up to the invasion. Parts of the story may forever remain elusive, out of reach to even the most diligent and discerning historian in 2030 or 2050. But there's also much that we already know. We know that the keys to the outbreak of war lay in Washington, not in Baghdad or another world capital, and not at the United Nations. We know that the Bush administration launched the invasion with British backing but without UN authorization and despite opposition from leading allied governments. And we know that Iraq was a war of choice, not of necessity, and that it was understood as such by top officials in Washington. As Richard N. Haass, a close adviser to Secretary of State Colin L. Powell, put it not long after the invasion, "[T]he administration did not have to go to war against Iraq, certainly not when it did. There were other options."[3]

How then to explain what occurred that late winter day in 2003? Thanks to an outpouring of memoirs and journalistic accounts and the leaking of key documents, enough information now exists to begin to piece together the answer to that question. It is contemporary history, incomplete history, based on a partial record, but hardly less important for that. For if getting the United States out of Iraq will be a challenging task—and who would suggest otherwise, notwithstanding the relative improvements in the security situation after early 2007?—a necessary first step is to give careful attention to how it got in. What emerges is the story of an administration that decided early for military action and then manipulated the truth to make its case. It is also a story about a permissive decision-making environment in which Congress, the press, and the American public were mostly content to go along, unwilling to raise the tough questions that might have halted or slowed the rush to war.

• • •

From the administration's first days, Iraq was high on the agenda. It was discussed at the first meeting of the National Security Council (NSC) on January 30, 2001, with CIA director George Tenet showing a large, grainy aerial photograph of a building in Iraq that he said could be "a plant that produces either chemical or biological materials for weapons manufacture." At a second NSC meeting two days later Colin Powell was laying out a plan for targeted sanctions against Saddam Hussein's government when Secretary of Defense Donald Rumsfeld interrupted him: "Sanctions are fine, but what we really want to think about is going after Saddam. Imagine what the region would look like without Saddam and with a regime that's aligned with U.S. interests." According to Treasury Secretary Paul O'Neill, who was in attendance, Rumsfeld talked at the meeting "in general terms about post-Saddam Iraq, dealing with the Kurds in the north, the oil fields, the reconstruction of the country's economy, and the 'freeing of the Iraqi people.'"[4]

O'Neill recalled, "There was never any rigorous talk about this sweeping idea. From the start, we were building the case against [Saddam] and looking at how we could take him out and change Iraq into a new country. And if we did that, it would solve everything. It was all about finding *a way to do it*. That was the tone of it. The president was saying, 'Fine. Go find me a way to do this.'" In an interview some months earlier, during the presidential campaign, Bush had expressed frustration that the Iraqi leader still lived, and had issued a warning: "I will tell you this: If we catch him developing weapons of mass destruction in any way, shape, or form, I'll deal with him in a way that he won't like."[5]

Many senior policymakers had wanted to oust Saddam Hussein for years, indeed since the end of the 1991 Gulf War, in which a U.S.-led coalition drove Iraq's army out of Kuwait but did not continue on to Baghdad, thereby allowing Saddam to remain in power. For these officials, and especially those such as Vice President Dick Cheney and Deputy Defense Secretary Paul Wolfowitz, who had served under then president George H. W. Bush in 1991, it was a piece of unfinished business.[6] They were not mollified by the UN arms and economic embargo maintained after 1991, or by the specific UN Security Council resolutions designed to severely limit Iraq's weapons program, or by the creation of northern and southern no-fly zones prohibiting Iraqi aircraft flights. The Clinton administration's bombing attacks on Iraqi targets in 1993 and 1998 they dismissed as feckless and insufficient.

Neoconservatives, foremost among them Paul Wolfowitz, were especially insistent. Fed up with the Clinton administration's policy of keeping Saddam Hussein contained through a mix of sanctions and military coercion and the refusal of France and Russia to back a tougher sanctions regime, Wolfowitz in 1997 co-authored a *Weekly Standard* article in which he wondered whether Clinton's most notable foreign policy legacy would be "letting this tyrant get stronger." The following year Wolfowitz joined other neoconservatives in signing a letter to Clinton arguing that "containment" of the Iraqi dictator had failed and that "removing Saddam Hussein and his regime from power . . . needs to become the aim of American foreign policy." In a prophetic comment, the letter said, "American policy cannot continue to be crippled by a misguided insistence on unanimity in the UN Security Council." Of the eighteen signatories to the letter, eight would hold senior positions during George W. Bush's first term.[7]

Measuring the impact of the "neocons" on the foreign policy debate in the late 1990s remains difficult, but they were certainly now a major presence within the GOP fold. Consisting primarily of academics and intellectuals, many of them former Democrats, the group had embraced Ronald Reagan's aggressively anti-Soviet posture in the early 1980s but parted ways with him as he shifted toward détente with reformist Kremlin leader Mikhail Gorbachev. Many neocons also faulted Reagan for being insufficiently supportive of Israel, while the more idealistic among them criticized his acceptance of authoritarian regimes simply because they were anti-Soviet. The neoconservatives were emboldened by the collapse of the Soviet Union in 1991 and the unipolarity that resulted. As the 1990s progressed, they pushed hard on a number of themes, none of them new to American discourse about foreign policy but all uttered with unprecedented fervor: that U.S. global dominion

was good both for America and for the world; that collective security, in the words of neoconservative writer Charles Krauthammer,
was a "mirage," the "international community . . . a fiction"; that
the United States should enhance its military superiority and not
hesitate to put that military to use; and that realism, whether man-
ifested in the cynical pragmatism of Henry Kissinger or the inor-
dinate caution of Colin Powell, was a dangerous and outmoded
concept. Rather, the United States should henceforth aggressively
promote democracy and freedom around the world, using force if
necessary, thereby creating a world order friendly to American security and values.[8]

Not all of the principal architects of the Iraq invasion endorsed
each of these principles. Donald Rumsfeld, for example, though he
signed the 1997 letter to Clinton, cared little about democracy
promotion or remaking the Middle East; for him, ousting Saddam
would complete a job left undone and would serve America's geo-
political interests. The same was true of Vice President Dick Cheney
(who was not a signatory to the letter). But the neoconservative
influence was nevertheless highly significant; by the end of the
1990s the neocons were no longer insurgents but had, in Andrew
Bacevich's words, "transformed themselves into establishment figures." Their views had become mainstream views, promulgated
not only in the pages of the *Weekly Standard* but in top newspapers and on weekend television talk shows. "Ideas that even a decade earlier might have seemed reckless or preposterous," Bacevich
notes, "now came to seem perfectly reasonable." This included
forcibly removing Saddam Hussein from power in Iraq. Clinton
might have showed scant interest in working hard to actually bring
about regime change, but the discourse in Washington had clearly
shifted—and as a result of the neoconservative agitation. Just as
no politician after 1945 wanted to be called soft on communism,
so no Democrat or Republican half a century later was going to
take chances on being labeled irresolute on Saddam.[9]

Still, notwithstanding this new political climate and the attention given to Iraq in the early NSC meetings after Bush's inauguration, it took 9/11 to move the issue to the forefront. The hijackers

who carried out the attacks that day—fifteen Saudi Arabians, two Emiratis, one Lebanese, and, leading them, an Egyptian—had ties to al Qaeda, the radical Islamic organization led by Osama bin Laden. Al Qaeda operated out of Afghanistan with the blessing of the ruling Taliban, a repressive Islamic fundamentalist group that had gained power in 1996 in the turmoil following the defeat of the Soviet-backed government in 1989. Bush and his aides accordingly decided immediately to attack Afghanistan with large-scale military force. Bush also announced a sweeping "war on terrorism," ignoring skeptics who wondered whether such a war could ever be won in a meaningful sense, given that the foe was a nonstate actor weak in the traditional measures of power—territory and governmental authority—and with little to lose. The president spoke in Manichean terms about a global struggle against "evil forces," in which America would "rout out terror wherever it might exist."

Even now, in the early hours and days after the 9/11 attacks, Iraq entered into the high-level deliberations. On the morning of September 12—"Day Two of the march to war," in Thomas Powers's words[10]—CIA director George Tenet happened upon neoconservative agitator Richard Perle (another signatory to the 1997 Clinton letter) as Perle was leaving the West Wing of the White House. "Iraq has to pay a price for what happened yesterday," Perle said as Tenet reached the door. "They bear responsibility." That evening, Tenet hosted three British officials for dinner at the agency's headquarters in Langley, Virginia. David Manning, foreign policy adviser to Prime Minister Tony Blair, already suspected that officials close to Bush wanted to go after Saddam Hussein. "I hope we can all agree," he told Tenet, "that we should concentrate on Afghanistan and not be tempted to launch any attacks on Iraq."[11]

The Langley dinner took place on Wednesday. On Saturday, Bush and senior aides met at Camp David to discuss possible responses to 9/11. Wolfowitz and Rumsfeld argued that hitting Afghanistan alone would be too weak a response to the terror attacks and that the United States should concentrate its efforts on ousting Saddam Hussein. Others disagreed. Bush heard the arguments, and then determined that Afghanistan would get first priority. Iraq would not be included in the immediate attack plans. But it likely would be added later. "We won't do Iraq now," Bush told National Security Advisor Condoleezza Rice that same day, September 15, "but eventually we'll have to return to that question." To Tony Blair's urging, during a dinner at the White House on September 20, that the focus ought to remain on overthrowing the Taliban, Bush responded, "I agree with you, Tony. We must deal with this first. But when we have dealt with Afghanistan, we must come back to Iraq."[12]

• • •

In early October, the United States launched a sustained bombing campaign against Taliban and al Qaeda positions and sent special operations forces to help a resistance organization based in northern Afghanistan. Within two months the Taliban had been driven from power, although bin Laden eluded capture. So did top Taliban leaders, who would live to fight another day. All the while, Iraq planning continued behind the scenes. A prime mover in this work was Dick Cheney. Already in May 2001, in an interview with the *New Yorker*, Cheney had linked North Korea, Iran, and Iraq as threats to American security. Now, in the wake of September 11, he came to accept the power of Wolfowitz's message: that hitting Afghanistan was not enough, that the moment had come to take care of Saddam as well. Under the tutelage of Middle East academic specialists Bernard Lewis and Fouad Ajami the vice president even began to shed some of his skepticism regarding the prospects for democracy in the region; he became, if not a neocon of sorts, at least an ally. Lewis and Ajami argued that democracy could take hold in the Middle East, and that a necessary first step was ousting autocratic regimes such as Saddam Hussein's, using American arms if necessary.

By late November, with the Taliban in retreat, Bush began shifting his attention to Iraq. According to Bob Woodward in *Plan of Attack*, the president told Rumsfeld on the twenty-first, "Let's get started on this." In late December General Tommy Franks, commander of the U.S. Central Command (CENTCOM), briefed him on current Pentagon Iraq war planning. And in his State of the Union address a month after that Bush named Iraq, North Korea, and Iran as states that posed a threat to American interests either because they supported terrorists or because they had developed weapons of mass destruction (WMDs), or both. The three constituted an "axis of evil" that posed "a grave and growing danger" to the United States and its allies, Bush declared, and he called the Iraqi regime one of the most dangerous in the world, not least for its efforts to develop nuclear, chemical, and biological weapons. "We'll be deliberate," he added ominously, "yet time is not on our side. I will not wait on events, while dangers gather. I will not stand by, as peril draws closer and closer."[13]

The "axis of evil" speech, it came to be called, and it generated intense discussion both in the United States and abroad. At home many Americans were ready to believe, but in Europe and elsewhere Bush's language solidified growing concern about the direction of U.S. policy. Bush's bellicosity and good-versus-evil terminology had put off many foreign observers right from 9/11, but they initially swallowed their objections in order to show solidarity with Washington's plight. The "axis of evil" phraseology, however, and the alarmist tone of the speech generally, caused leading allies to speak out—and foreshadowed divisions to come. The Russian government expressed unease about the speech and declared itself opposed to military action against Iraq; Germany and France did likewise. "The French Foreign Ministry said it was a simplistic description of the situation," remarked *Le Monde* senior editor Alain Frachon of the "axis of evil" formulation. "People were afraid of introducing this religious language in the political landscape. . . . This kind of language sounds very odd to us, very bizarre, and it does not cross the ocean well."[14]

In Britain there were similar murmurings of discontent and apprehension, but not where it mattered most: at 10 Downing Street. Tony Blair was far more comfortable with the president's language than were his continental counterparts; he not infrequently spoke in such terms himself, and often seemed more in tune with the neoconservative message than were some senior players in the Bush inner circle. "No European leader of his generation speaks so unblushingly of good and evil," one unsympathetic historian later observed.[15] Determined to maintain close relations with Washington and to back the Americans to the hilt in the struggle against terror, Blair in the months to come would be a principal, perhaps even an indispensable, ally on Iraq.

Blair made clear his unequivocal support for ousting Saddam Hussein from an early point, and then stuck firmly to that position. Historians of the future may attach considerable importance to a meeting at Bush's ranch in Crawford, Texas, in early April 2002, during which the Iraq issue was a main item of discussion. Already the previous month David Manning had assured Condoleezza Rice of Blair's unstinting support for removing Saddam (and had reported back to London that "Condi's enthusiasm for regime change is undimmed"); that same month Christopher Meyer, Britain's ambassador in Washington, made the same vow to Paul Wolfowitz.[16]

But it was in Crawford that the two leaders could meet for extended conversations. Neither man, and certainly not Bush, needed to be persuaded about the basic objective. "I made up my mind that Saddam needs to go," the president told Trevor McDonald of Britain's ITV on April 4, two days before Blair's arrival—a message intended, no doubt, to set the framework for the talks. Some days before that Bush had made the same point more graphically in Rice's office, poking his head in as she and three senators discussed Iraq options. "F— Saddam. We're taking him out," Bush said, eliciting nervous laughter from the senators.[17] Yet the Crawford talks were important, both for cementing the bond between Bush and Blair and for yielding an agreement that would remain inviolate for the next eleven months. Saddam Hussein, the two men concurred, would be removed from power.[18]

The question was how to do it. The British were not opposed to using military force, but they warned against going to that option too quickly, lest international support—and therefore domestic support in Britain—be undermined. Important preparatory work had to be done. Saddam must be cast as the villain, and the way to do it was to highlight his serial rejection of UN resolutions. Said British foreign secretary Jack Straw in a memo prepared for Blair's Crawford visit, "That Iraq is in flagrant breach of international legal obligations imposed on it by UNSC provides us with the core of a strategy. . . . I believe that a demand for the unfettered readmission of weapons inspectors is essential, in terms of public explanation, and in terms of legal sanction for any subsequent military action."[19]

Straw appended a paper from the Foreign Office political director, Sir Peter Ricketts, who saw the immediate challenge as explaining why Iraq constituted a pressing concern. "The truth is that . . . even the best survey of Iraq's WMD programs will not show much advance in recent years on the nuclear, missile or CW/BW fronts: the programs are extremely worrying but have not, as far as we know, been stepped up," Ricketts wrote. "We are still left with a problem of bringing public opinion to accept the imminence of a threat from Iraq. This is something the Prime Minister and President need to have a frank discussion about."[20]

Discuss it they did, but Bush was cool to Blair's plea that military action should come only after the UN weapons inspections had been given a real chance to succeed. For Bush and many of his subordinates the military option was always preferred. Saddam, they maintained, would play cat-and-mouse with the inspectors, dragging things out, until enthusiasm in American public opinion for invading and occupying Iraq gradually withered, leaving an unrepentant Iraqi dictator in power. Far better, they said, to take him out by force. To ITV's McDonald and others that spring Bush offered the assurance that "I have no plans to attack on my desk." This may have been technically true—we don't know what was on his desk—but it was really just truthiness: several times that winter and spring (in February, April, May, and June) Bush was briefed on revised versions of CENTCOM's war plan.[21]

In July, the British received further confirmation of the administration's commitment to military action against Iraq. Sir Richard Dearlove, the head of Britain's MI6 (the equivalent of the CIA), flew to Washington that month to check the temperature of American thinking. He met with CIA director George Tenet, among others, and upon his return to London briefed the prime minister and the cabinet. The now-famous record of that meeting, the so-called Downing Street Memo (leaked to a British journalist in September 2004), could hardly have put the core issues more succinctly:

> C [the traditional designation for the chief of MI6] reported on his recent talks in Washington. There was a perceptible shift in attitude. Military action was now seen as inevitable. Bush wanted to remove Saddam, through military action, justified by the conjunction of terrorism and WMD. But the intelligence and facts were being fixed around the policy. The NSC had no patience with the UN route, and no enthusiasm for publishing material on the Iraqi regime's record. There was little discussion in Washington of the aftermath after military action.[22]

The historian would like to have high-level American documents from this same period, and will suspend firm judgments until such a time (if it ever comes) as they are available. Yet there is little reason to doubt the basic accuracy of Dearlove's recapitulation of the Bush team's thinking, consistent as it is with other evidence from the period.[23] The quoted passage reveals several things: that by no later than mid-2002 Bush had decided "to remove Saddam, through military action"; that war was now "inevitable"; that it would be justified "by the conjunction of terrorism and WMD" and that the "intelligence and facts were being fixed around the policy"; that top U.S. officials did not want to seek approval from the UN; and that few in Washington thought much about Iraq after the war.

The point bears emphasizing: more than half a year before the invasion, and many months before high-stakes deliberations on Iraq at the UN and a major congressional vote, war had been decided upon. The task now was merely to justify it, to "fix" what Tony Blair would call the "political context." Specifically, in British eyes, broad international backing would have to be secured before the actual hostilities commenced. Yet that would be no easy task, London officials conceded among themselves, for the legal case for war was thin: Saddam Hussein was not threatening his neighbors, and his WMD capacity was lower than that of Libya, North Korea, and Iran. The desire for "regime change" alone did not justify invasion in legal terms. What to do? The cabinet came back to what Jack Straw and others had said in March: that a plan to "wrong-foot" Saddam through the UN was essential. If he could be coaxed to reject one final demand to disarm, phrased delicately to make UN stipulations seem fair, then the world could come around to seeing war as just and necessary.

Blair accordingly worked through the late summer to convince Bush to go the UN route, and he received strong assistance in this endeavor from Secretary of State Powell. It was a tough sell. On August 5, Tommy Franks briefed the White House on CENTCOM's latest war plan. He described an early attack on Baghdad and principal Iraqi command centers, and pleased Donald Rumsfeld by saying the total force package would not need to be huge. Rumsfeld on August 9 said publicly that containment of Saddam had not worked, implying that the use of force would be necessary, and Dick Cheney, in a speech before the Veterans of Foreign Wars (VFW) in late August, said that "a return of inspectors would provide no assurance whatsoever of [Saddam's] compliance with UN resolutions. On the contrary, there is great danger that it would provide false comfort that Saddam was somehow 'back in his box.'" A top-secret National Security Presidential Directive entitled "Iraq: Goals, Objectives and Strategy" and signed by Bush on August 29 spoke unambiguously about the need to "free Iraq in order to eliminate Iraqi weapons of mass destruction, their means of delivery and associated programs, to prevent Iraq from breaking out of containment and becoming a more dangerous threat to the region and beyond."[24]

During a meeting at Camp David on September 7, at which Blair was also in attendance, the issue came to a head. "Colin Powell was firmly on the side of going the extra mile with the UN," recalled George Tenet of the session, "while the vice president argued just as forcefully that doing so would only get us mired in a bureaucratic tangle with nothing to show for it other than time lost off a ticking clock. The president let Powell and Cheney pretty much duke it out."[25]

Bush in effect split the difference. Entirely in sympathy with his vice president's position, he agreed to bring the issue of Saddam's WMD to the United Nations one last time, but he cautioned Blair and Powell that war would probably still occur in the end.

• • •

Thus began a phase we might call the "selling of the war." The American public was starting to pay attention, to realize that George W. Bush might attack Iraq, and the administration's task now would be to convince Americans that such action would be justified. The basic pitch had already been decided on: it would be "the conjunction of terrorism and WMD." But there was a problem: the principal argument offered, that Saddam possessed weapons of mass destruction and intended to use them, was not substantiated by American intelligence agencies. In his speech to the VFW Cheney minced no words: "Simply stated, there is no doubt that Saddam Hussein now has weapons of mass destruction. There is no doubt that he is amassing them to use them against our friends, against our allies, and against us." These assertions went well beyond the CIA's assessments at the time, and didn't jibe with Tommy Franks's assertions during a meeting of the NSC a few days after the VFW speech: "Mr. President, we've been looking for Scud missiles and other weapons of mass destruction for ten years and haven't found any yet."[26]

Bush was undaunted. In early September he told members of Congress that he considered Saddam a greater menace than al Qaeda. "The war on terror is going okay," he said. "We are hunting down Al Qaeda one by one. The biggest threat, however, is Saddam Hussein and his weapons of mass destruction." Later that month Bush told the nation in his weekly radio address, "The Iraqi regime possesses biological and chemical weapons, is rebuilding the facilities to make more and, according to the British government, could launch a biological or chemical attack in as little as 45 minutes after the order is given. . . . The regime is seeking a nuclear bomb, and with fissile material could build one within a year."[27]

Whether and to what degree Bush believed what he was saying is hard to determine. Most U.S. and allied officials, it seems clear, felt certain that Saddam Hussein possessed at least some WMDs. Even many critics of the administration's aggressive posture on Iraq thought so. But the utter certainty with which the president and his advisers expounded on the issue in these months is nevertheless striking, not merely in hindsight but in the context of the time as well. Administration spokespersons didn't argue that Saddam had *some* WMDs; they implied he had vast amounts hidden away in secret storage facilities. They warned darkly that he was readying to use these weapons, or to hand them over to terrorist organizations, and that he was working hard to get nukes. Never mind that their own intelligence agencies didn't support these claims. Never mind that British officials, UN inspectors, and other informed observers had concluded that the Iraqi dictator's WMD capacity had been drastically weakened by a decade of sanctions, and that, by implication, the containment policy followed since 1991 had in this respect succeeded much more than it had failed.

Nor did U.S. intelligence estimates back up the second prong in the propaganda offensive, that Saddam had ties to al Qaeda and could be linked to the 9/11 attacks. Quite the contrary, here the evidence was almost entirely lacking, as senior officials surely knew. When asked by reporters in July if the Iraqi leaders had relationships with al Qaeda figures, Rumsfeld offered a one-word answer: "Sure." A few weeks later he said at a news conference that the link between Saddam and al Qaeda was "not debatable." In a weekly radio address in late September, Bush warned that al Qaeda terrorists were "inside Iraq." In early October he elaborated the point in a speech in Cincinnati. Yet an assessment by the Defense Intelligence Agency at midyear found no "compelling evidence demonstrating direct cooperation between the government of Iraq and Al Qaeda." This followed other intelligence estimates that likewise could find no close ties between the two entities. Not a single one of the thousands of documents found after the Taliban's ouster in Afghanistan substantiated a meaningful Iraq–al Qaeda connection.[28]

Other observers, too, found this administration argument lacking in substance. Brent Scowcroft, national security advisor under Gerald Ford and under George H. W. Bush during the Persian Gulf War and a principal mentor to Condoleezza Rice, put the matter plainly in a widely read op-ed piece titled "Don't Attack Saddam" in the *Wall Street Journal* on August 15. "[T]here is scant evidence to tie Saddam to terrorist organizations, and even less to the Sept. 11 attacks," Scowcroft wrote. "Indeed Saddam's goals have little in common with the terrorists who threaten us, and there is little incentive for him to make common cause with them." Scowcroft denied that the Baghdad regime represented a direct and immediate threat to American security or American interests and said that Saddam, although "thoroughly evil," was above all a power-hungry survivor.[29]

Scowcroft's misgivings were echoed by other veterans of the first Bush administration, including Lawrence Eagleburger and James Baker, and by seasoned analysts such as diplomat-historian George Kennan. And they were echoed, if quietly, by many senior officers in the American military, including much of the top brass. "I can't tell you how many senior officers said to me, 'What the hell are we doing?'" recalled Marine Lt. Gregory Newbold, director of operations on the joint staff, of that summer and fall. Many of them feared that Saddam would use WMDs against U.S. troops, or that an invasion would enmesh their forces in urban warfare, or that the postwar occupation would be costly and messy. Almost none saw war as necessary at this point in time, with containment seemingly working and with work still to do in Afghanistan. "Why Iraq? Why now?" Newbold remembered them asking. Wouldn't hitting Iraq undercut the mission against al Qaeda? "All of us understood the fight was against the terrorists, and we were willing to anything in that regard—so, 'Why are we diverting attention and assets?'"[30]

What these skeptics failed to realize, or at least acknowledge, was that the administration's relentless public focus on the WMD-terrorism "conjunction" masked other motivations for war, ones less "salable" to the American people and hence kept largely under wraps. Neoconservatives saw in Iraq a chance to use U.S. power to reshape the region in America's image, to oppose tyranny and spread democracy. Ousting Saddam, they said, would enhance the security of Israel, the key U.S. ally in the Middle East, and would likely touch off a reverse "domino effect" that would extend democracy throughout the region. Americans would welcome this prospect, the neocons were confident, but not to the point of sacrificing U.S. soldiers' lives to make it happen. Oil, too, entered the picture, though not quite in the way many antiwar activists, with their cries of "No blood for oil!," assumed. For Bush and his aides, it was not so much about gaining direct access to Iraqi oil as about preventing an unpredictable and hostile Baghdad regime from destabilizing an oil-rich region.

White House political strategists, meanwhile, thinking in crass but for them vital terms, believed a swift and decisive removal of a hated dictator would cement Republican domination in Washington and virtually ensure Bush's reelection two years hence. Top Bush aide Karl Rove, in a speech to the Republican National Committee in January 2002, declared openly that the war on terror represented the path to victory for the GOP in the upcoming midterm elections. Candidates "can go to the country on that issue," Rove said, for voters trusted Republicans to keep them safe. He left unstated that it might be necessary to up the ante. The political glow from September 11 was fading. Afghanistan had become a sideshow, to the public as well as to the administration, and Osama bin Laden continued—embarrassingly—to elude capture. In the late winter of 2002 polls for the first time showed erosion in popular support for the administration's response to 9/11. By Memorial Day, a *USA Today*–CNN–Gallup survey found that only 35 percent of Americans believed the United States was winning the war on terror, a dramatic drop from three months earlier, when almost two-thirds thought so. "Rove could see," columnist Frank

Rich acidly concluded, "that an untelevised and largely underground war . . . might not nail election victories without a jolt of shock and awe. It was a propitious moment to wag the dog."[31]

Most of all, it seems, George W. Bush wanted to attack Iraq because he could. The bold neoconservative vision of remaking the Middle East via Iraq appealed to him; in Jacob Weisberg's apt words, it was "just the kind of game-changing idea he went for." Bush believed, moreover, that only wartime presidents achieve greatness.[32] He sought regime change in Baghdad, not a changed regime, and he wanted American arms to bring it about. Publicly he suggested otherwise, to be sure, telling the public in October that no decision for war had been made, and that he "hope[d] the use of force will not become necessary." It was not really true. Intoxicated by their power in the wake of 9/11, by their swift (if, as it turned out, incomplete) success against the Taliban in Afghanistan, and by their stratospheric poll numbers, the president and his lieutenants, virtually none of whom had ever seen combat themselves, relished the prospect of a preventive war against the tyrant who had thumbed his nose at them for so long, who had allegedly plotted to kill the president's father.[33] He presented an easy target, moreover, much easier than the other two axis of evil members, Iran and North Korea.

None of this was said, of course. Publicly, it was all about presenting Saddam Hussein as a direct and immediate threat to America's security, who would do immense harm to the United States if given the chance. Not everyone bought the argument. More so than is generally remembered, millions of Americans rejected the administration's case, and showed it by taking part in antiwar demonstrations organized in communities across the country starting in the fall of 2002. Most, however, across the political spectrum, were prepared to sign on. Some did so unhesitatingly; others, including self-described liberal internationalists, claimed to be reluctant converts to the notion that ousting Saddam by force was this era's grim historical necessity.[34] But accept it they did. They endorsed the worst-case scenarios vividly depicted by the White House and chose to trust the government's claim that it possessed classified information about exactly how close Saddam Hussein was—read: extremely close—to having usable nuclear warheads or other WMDs. They embraced, some of them, the notion of a transformed, democratized Middle East following Saddam's overthrow. And they took comfort in the fact that Britain's Blair provided such unstinting and articulate support for an aggressive policy.

Like his father in 1991, Bush claimed he did not need congressional authorization to launch military action against Iraq; like his father, he nevertheless sought such backing. If he anticipated a tough fight, it didn't happen. The vote was anticlimactic. The debate in both chambers yielded little in the way of fireworks, as less than 10 percent of members generally showed up. The outcome seemed preordained, as Republicans lined up to support the president and most Democrats appeared eager to get the matter over with as fast as possible and to move on to the economic issues they thought would help them more in the election. In 1991, the resolution authorizing Bush Sr. to use "all necessary means" to drive the Iraqis out of Kuwait had encountered stiff opposition also in the House of Representatives and had barely squeaked by in the Senate; this time, with the Iraqi army invading no one but with an election looming, the vote passed comfortably: 296–133 in the lower chamber and 77–23 in the upper. A majority of Senate Democrats voted yea, often after giving varying versions of the same basic message: there ought to be no rush to war, but the thug of Baghdad was an evil tyrant who threatened American interests. Many of them pointed to a new National Intelligence Estimate (rushed through to be available for the debate) claiming, contrary to the underlying intelligence reporting, that Iraq possessed chemical and biological weapons and sought to reconstitute its nuclear program.

Preordained or not, the vote was a huge victory for the White House. Bush had covered his congressional flank and had given Republican candidates an achievement to trumpet on election day (which they did to good effect, expanding their majority in the House and regaining control of the Senate). Even so, cautionary words continued to be heard, both inside and outside Congress. Critics complained that the president had not presented evidence that Saddam Hussein constituted an imminent threat or was connected to the 9/11 attacks. Republican senator Chuck Hagel of Nebraska, a Vietnam veteran who had voted yes on the resolution, protested that "many of those who want to rush this country into war and think it would be quick and easy don't know anything about war." Internationally, too, alarms were raised against early military action, complicating Bush's pledge to seek UN support. He switched to a less hawkish and unilateral stance and in so doing gained UN backing: in early November, the UN Security Council unanimously approved Resolution 1441, imposing rigorous new arms inspections on Iraq.

Behind the scenes, though, the Security Council was deeply divided over what should happen next. When Washington's UN ambassador John Negroponte asserted that Baghdad's failure to comply fully with the inspections would justify the use of military force, his French counterpart Jean-David Levitte issued a flat denial: 1441, he declared, was not an automatic "trigger." In December, as Saddam Hussein agreed to let the inspectors in and said Iraq would fully comply with the resolution, Bush dispatched troops to the region, sending 25,000 that month and 62,000 more in early January. The buildup deepened fears in European capitals that Bush actively wanted a war, despite his claims to the contrary. The suspicion was amply justified: on December 18, Bush told a meeting of the NSC that "war is inevitable."[35]

In late January 2003 a report by chief UN weapons inspector Hans Blix castigated Iraq for failing to carry out "the disarmament that was demanded of it," but also said it was too soon to tell whether the inspections would succeed. While U.S. and British officials emphasized the first point and said the time for diplomacy was up, France, Russia, and China emphasized the second point and called for more inspections. "Since we can disarm Iraq through peaceful means," French foreign minister Dominique de Villepin asserted at a press conference on January 20, "we should not take the risk to endanger the life of innocent civilians or soldiers, to jeopardize the stability of the region. . . . We should not take the risk to fuel terrorism."[36] Some at the UN also warned that toppling the regime could cause an explosion of sectarian bloodshed between Iraq's Sunni Muslims and the majority Shi'ites who had suffered so grievously under the Sunni Saddam's rule. As the UN debate continued, and as massive antiwar demonstrations took place around the world, Bush boosted the U.S. troop count in the region to 250,000. Britain, meanwhile, sent about 45,000 soldiers.

White House strategists assumed that France would come around in the end. "This is what the French do," scoffed one senior American official at the time. "They resist, and then when the time comes, they move to the head of the parade."[37] It didn't happen. On February 5, Secretary of State Colin Powell, whose private views during this period remain hard to decipher, made a dramatic appearance before the UN Security Council, laying out what he termed irrefutable evidence of Iraq's ongoing WMD programs. "How much longer," Powell asked, "are we willing to put up with Iraq's noncompliance before we, as a council, we, as the United Nations, say: 'Enough. Enough.'" The presentation won rave reviews in the American media, but continental European officials were unimpressed, both by the claims regarding WMDs and by Powell's suggestions of an Iraq–al Qaeda link. "Nonsense. It just wasn't true," the *Washington Post* quoted the French intelligence chief as saying after the session.[38]

In late February the United States and Britain floated a draft resolution to the UN that proposed issuing an ultimatum to Iraq, but only three of the fifteen Security Council members affirmed support. Faced with an embarrassing political defeat, Bush abandoned the resolution and all further diplomatic efforts on March 17 when he ordered Saddam to leave Iraq within forty-eight hours or face an attack. "Should Saddam Hussein choose confrontation," he had the audacity to add, "the American people can know that every measure has been taken to avoid war, and every measure will be taken to win it."[39] Saddam failed to comply, and on March 19 the United States and Britain launched an aerial bombardment of Baghdad and other areas. A ground invasion followed soon thereafter. The Iraqis initially offered stiff resistance, but soon the advancing forces gained momentum. On April 9, Baghdad fell to American troops.

· · ·

If everything after that April 9 date had gone as planned in Iraq—if the celebrations in Baghdad's streets had been real and durable, if stability had quickly returned to the country and with a minimum of bloodshed, and if the reverse domino effect had kicked in throughout the region—there would still very troubling questions about the war, about why it was launched and whether it could have been avoided. The outcome on the ground in Iraq in this respect is immaterial.

The same goes for the WMD issue, which is so often seen as the heart of the matter, down to the present day. If Saddam Hussein had been shown to possess WMDs, so the argument goes, the war would have been justified. Even some opponents of the invasion seem ready to concede this point. It misses the mark on two grounds. First, the WMD issue was in all likelihood a rationale for the invasion more than a reason for it. Second, if he had the weapons, so what? Did that necessarily make military action justified? Surely not. Making the case for preventive war, if it can be done at all, requires providing proof that the threat is massive and acute and that any further delay in taking military action is likely to have disastrous consequences. In the critical weeks of early 2003, no amount of pressure by Washington and London could convince more than a small minority of Security Council members that the case was there, or even to pretend for the sake of allied unity that it was.[40] In hindsight, it looks thinner still.

Why, then, did war happen? This essay has emphasized the determination for military action at the highest levels in Washington and the important support provided by the British government. It has noted the galvanizing effect of 9/11 and of the swift success of the initial action in Afghanistan. A comprehensive answer would of course have to go further and examine the wider context in which U.S. decisions were made. In a previous study of a previous war of choice, Vietnam in 1964–65, I looked closely at this broader arena and concluded that American policymakers operated in a "permissive context."[41] The same appears to have been true in 2002–3. In the press, for example, senior reporters for several leading newspapers, including the *New York Times,* in the key months of decision accepted with little question administration claims regarding Saddam Hussein's intentions and capabilities. By and large, they failed to probe beneath the surface, to ask tough questions, to give serious attention to the views of skeptics. Editorial writers at the *Washington Post* and elsewhere largely seconded White House talking points. Recognizing these realities, in 2004 the *Times* and the *Post* took the unusual step of publicly apologizing for their coverage in the lead-up to the invasion. "Administration assertions were on the front page. Things that challenged the administration were on A18 on Sunday or A24 on Monday," said the *Post*'s Pentagon correspondent Thomas Ricks, which about sums it up.[42]

Columnists and television pundits were often even more unquestioning. Following Powell's speech to the UN in February 2003—a culmination of sorts to the administration's six-month sales pitch—the *Washington Post*'s liberal columnist Mary McGrory wrote that the secretary of state "persuaded me, and I was as tough as France to convince." Another liberal at the paper, Richard Cohen, declared that Powell's testimony "had to prove to anyone that Iraq not only hasn't accounted for its weapons of mass destruction but without a doubt still retains them. Only a fool—or possibly a Frenchman—could conclude otherwise." On television, CNN's Bill Schneider said that "no one" disputed Powell's findings, while the *Post*'s Bob Woodward, asked by Larry King what would happen if the United States went to war and didn't find any WMDs, answered, "I think the chance of that happening is about zero. There's just too much there."[43]

On Capitol Hill, meanwhile, most lawmakers of both parties were content to avoid asking tough questions—or, if they did ask them, to quickly add that they too wanted to be "tough on Saddam." Many more legislators voted against the authorization to use force than had voted against the Gulf of Tonkin resolution on Vietnam in 1964, but the White House got the affirmative vote it sought, and by a comfortable margin. Some who voted yes (especially Democrats) would later claim they were not authorizing war but merely giving Bush the ability to use coercive diplomacy to bring Saddam into line (i.e., only if he really believed force might be used would he comply with the UN demands). They were duped by the administration, they would insist, a claim that, while not untrue, didn't exactly reflect well on them. None acknowledged that naked political calculation had anything to do with their vote. It's hard to escape the conclusion that there was among lawmakers a certain willingness to be deceived, a willingness to be strong-armed by the White House. Many were quite content to escape responsibility from a policy issue for which few had a clear prescription. Only a handful of them read more than the five-page executive summary of the October 2002 National Intelligence Estimate report.

Lincoln Chafee of Rhode Island, the only Republican senator to vote no, in his memoirs chastises senior Democrats for their lack of courage in the debate. "The top Democrats were at their weakest when trying to show how tough they were," he writes. "They were afraid that Republicans would label them soft in the post-September 11 world, and when they acted in political self-interest, they helped the president send thousands of Americans and uncounted innocent Iraqis to their doom." Time and again, Chafee continues, these Democrats "went down to the meetings at the White House and the Pentagon and came back to the chamber ready to salute. With wrinkled brows they gravely intoned that Saddam Hussein must be stopped. Stopped from what? They had no conviction or evidence of their own. They were just parroting the administration's nonsense. They knew it could go terribly wrong; they also knew it could go terribly right. Which did they fear more?"[44]

The permissive context extended also to the general public. Notwithstanding the many antiwar demonstrations in small and large cities across the country in late 2002 and early 2003 and the caustic commentary on numerous blogs, most Americans in these months were content to go along with administration claims. Few had a deep knowledge of the issues at stake, and as such many were inclined to follow the government's lead. Polls showed little popular enthusiasm for hitting Iraq but broad trust in Bush's leadership, and widespread anger at France in particular for its allegedly obstructionist stance. Whereas right after 9/11 a mere 6 percent believed that bin Laden had collaborated with Saddam Hussein, by the eve of war that figure had risen to 66 percent. A majority now even believed that Iraqis had been among the hijackers.[45] Few lawmakers reported serious pressure from their constituents to hold more hearings or pressure the administration for more proof that preventive war was needed. Most college campuses were sleepy places in the weeks prior to the invasion.

Saddam Hussein's own actions in those weeks obviously were part of the wider context, and thus must be included in any assessment of why war happened. Future historians will look closely at Baghdad's decision making in 2002–3, but even now certain elements are clear. The official U.S. position, elaborated in speech after speech, both before the invasion and since, is that Saddam bore full responsibility for what occurred, because he defied the UN over the WMD issue and because he misled the world into believing he still possessed the weapons. The reality was much cloudier, in that Saddam can be said to have complied with Resolution 1441 by declaring (accurately, we now know) that he had disposed of his WMD stockpiles and by permitting UN inspectors to examine any site of their choosing. Yet it's also true that he was cagey, and less than fully forthcoming; up to early January 2003, in particular, he left hints that he still possessed WMDs. Why? It's plausible to believe that he saw the bluffing as an effective and inexpensive deterrent, especially vis-à-vis neighboring Iran. In the words of Hans Blix, "[The Iraqis] didn't mind the suspicion from the neighbors—it was like hanging a sign on your door saying 'Beware the dog' when you don't have a dog." Blix came away convinced that war was avoidable, that a few more months—"not weeks, not years"—of inspections would have conclusively demonstrated that the weapons in fact did not exist. He allows, however, that Saddam's behavior did not do much to help those who wanted more time for the inspections.[46]

All of which says we should be careful about branding this "Bush's war." The president was first among equals, by virtue both of his position of authority and his preference for using military force. It was his war if it was anyone's. But Bush had assistance every step of the way—from his top aides (including, not least, Colin Powell), from the media and Congress and the American people, from Tony Blair, from Saddam Hussein. Moreover, the phrase "Bush's war" may miss the degree to which the president's freedom of action had diminished by the final weeks. He and his aides had painted themselves into a tight corner with their tough talk and constant demands that Baghdad must disarm or be disarmed. "The failure to take on Saddam after what the president said," Richard Perle revealingly noted before the invasion, would lead to a "collapse of confidence."[47] In other words, America's credibility was on the line, and so was Bush's own. If he failed to stand firm now, after all the saber rattling, he would be revealed as a weak man, an ineffectual man.

The calendar and the heavy troop commitment likewise narrowed Bush's options. In November 2002 Condoleezza Rice startled Chuck Hagel by saying, "we have to get in there before it gets too hot," meaning by March 2003 at the latest. "We've got to get this done within a window."[48] U.S. commanders made the same point, and there's every indication the administration got the message. Hans Blix has made the intriguing argument that Bush should have halted the buildup at about 50,000 troops, the point at which Saddam became almost fully cooperative yet Bush retained some flexibility regarding courses of action. Instead, the numbers kept rising, portending war. "Once there got to be 250,000 troops sitting in the hot desert sun," Blix concludes, "there was a momentum built up that couldn't be halted."

An interesting counterfactual, but in the end only that. What matters is that George W. Bush did not step back. He took the plunge, with huge consequences. How will his Iraq adventure end? It's too soon to know. The so-called surge of troops in 2007, implemented by the administration in the face of deep skepticism among outside experts that it could work, succeeded in drastically reducing the level of violence and shifting the focus to a counter-insurgency strategy emphasizing protection of the population (though it is unclear how much of the progress was due to the modest increase in force levels and how much of it resulted from other factors, such as the prior "ethnic cleansing" that separated the opposing groups). The surge did not, however, achieve tangible results in its second goal, that of promoting political reconciliation among the contending political factions in Iraq. That objective remained elusive when Bush left office in early 2009.

And regardless of the ultimate outcome in Iraq, the damage done by this unnecessary and reckless war has been enormous in terms of lives lost and resources squandered, in terms of America's standing in the region and the world, in terms of the impact on the broader struggle against terrorism. Brent Scowcroft's haunting comment in an interview in late 2005, as the insurgency raged, remains as apt as ever. Perhaps the United States will win in Iraq in the end, Scowcroft said. "But look at the cost."[49]

6

TRANSFORMATIVE ECONOMIC POLICIES

Tax Cutting, Stimuli, and Bailouts

JAMES T. PATTERSON

WELL BEFORE GEORGE W. BUSH LEFT OFFICE IN 2009, HE HAD SUC-ceeded in securing major cuts in federal taxes that contributed over time to mounting deficits and rising income inequality. This dramatic turn in fiscal policy was the most significant domestic legacy of his presidency.[1]

Equally dramatic, though neither foreseen nor welcomed by the Bush administration, was a desperate series of measures, notably multi-billion-dollar stimulus packages and bailouts, that he felt obliged to approve in 2008 in order to deal with a crisis in the American economy. These unprecedented measures, too, promised to have very large and long-run consequences.

• • •

There was little doubt in 2000 where Bush stood on fiscal issues: strongly in step with Republican activists, who since the late 1970s had begun demanding large-scale tax cuts. Many of these activists supported one or another version of supply-side economics. Federal taxes, they argued, had to be cut, especially for people in high brackets, in order to offer much-needed incentives to employers and investors, who would therefore spend more heavily on productive enterprises. This spending, in turn, would promote a new, postindustrial age of advanced technology.[2] As George Gilder, whose *Wealth and*

Poverty (1981) became a Bible for supply-siders, emphasized, "the crucial question in a capitalist country is the quality and quantity of investment by the rich."[3]

Some of the most fervent supply-siders were fiscal conservatives who predicted that lower taxes of this sort, by boosting investment and taxable profits, would enable federal revenues to rise even with lower rates in place, thereby reducing deficits that had been mounting since 1970. Others who were attracted to supply-side ideas, however, did not care very much if deficits persisted. Cutting taxes, they said, would "starve the beast" of big government.[4] Millions of tax-cut advocates in the late 1970s, moreover, knew little if anything about supply-side theories. Afflicted by inflation and "bracket creep," they were mobilizing behind popular campaigns at the state and local levels, such as the widely noted Proposition 13 that cut taxes in California in 1978.

A great many economists—and most liberals—vigorously opposed supply-side ideas, which they viewed as simplistic. Such policies, they complained, would pamper the rich and subvert social programs. Wealthy people would fritter away tax windfalls on idle speculative ventures or on luxuries—yachts, McMansions, and other high-end consumer goods—that did not greatly benefit society at large.

Many moderates, including a sizable number of Republicans, also rejected supply-side approaches. Indeed, fiscal conservatives (such as Gerald Ford, while president) generally valued deficit reduction above tax cutting, and they remained influential in the GOP and on Capitol Hill until the late 1980s. They included George H. W. Bush, who in his race against Ronald Reagan for the GOP presidential nomination in 1980 famously dismissed supply-side ideas as "voodoo economics."

Keynesian approaches aimed at stimulating demand, however, had obviously failed in the late 1970s to prevent extraordinarily high rates of inflation and unemployment—"stagflation"—thereby bolstering the case of tax cutters and of free-marketers. Leading a supply-side surge on Capitol Hill in 1978, Congressman Jack Kemp of New York and Senator William Roth of Delaware championed a

30 percent reduction in federal income taxes, to be achieved over a three-year period.

Reagan, a convert to the Kemp-Roth cause, featured income tax cuts as a central issue of his presidential campaign in 1980. Congress responded in 1981 by enacting across-the-board reductions of 25 percent over the next three years. The marginal tax rate at the highest income level was cut from 70 percent to 50 percent.[5] The largest tax reductions in American history, these were the most important domestic accomplishments of the "Reagan Revolution."

Reagan's fiscal innovations, however, did not work the wonders that many supply-siders had predicted. Domestic business investment remained sluggish; per capita income tax revenue dipped in real dollars and as a percentage of gross domestic product (GDP); and once a recession ended in 1982, the economy grew only modestly. Nor did supply-side economics do much to starve the beast of big government: real increases in domestic spending, along with huge new outlays for the military, helped create enormous deficits, which rose from 2.7 percent of GDP in 1980 to a postwar record of 5.1 percent by 1985.

Even before 1985, alarmed fiscal conservatives had demanded tax increases, which Reagan felt obliged to support in 1982 and 1984. In 1986 he signed another tax law, which lowered the top marginal income tax rate (for all but a few) to 28 percent. Though the tax hikes of 1982 and 1984 helped lower the deficit to 2.8 per cent of GDP in fiscal 1989, annual deficits were still high, and the gross federal debt nearly tripled during the Reagan years, jumping from 33.3 percent of GDP in 1980 to 53.1 percent in 1989.[6]

Undeterred, well-funded antitax lobbies, notably Grover Norquist's Americans for Tax Reform (ATR), gathered momentum in the late 1980s and thereafter. Republicans in Congress gradually abandoned fiscal conservatism and climbed aboard a deregulatory and tax-reduction bandwagon that barged ahead in the years to come. Their commitment to cuts was as often rooted in populist political considerations as in deep understanding of supply-side theories. Still, this "base" of deregulators and tax reducers, boosted by moderates and Democrats here and there, had developed formidable political clout by 1990.

Tax cutters, however, still did not win them all. The enormous federal debt, which a recession in 1990–91 was increasing, led President Bush and congressional allies (mostly Democrats) to reach a budget compromise in 1990 that included yet another tax hike. Polls at the time, moreover, suggested that grassroots agitation for tax cutting, which had been especially powerful between 1978 and 1981, had weakened: no longer terrified of inflation, a majority of Americans in the 1990s favored deficit reduction and better support of schools and health care over tax reduction.[7]

The budget compromise of 1990, however, enraged GOP tax cutters on Capitol Hill. Bush, after all, had promised "Read my lips: No new taxes!" in accepting the GOP presidential nomination in 1988. Furious at the president's change of heart, the conservative *New York Post* headlined, "Read My Lips: I Lied." Thereafter, House Republicans, directed by Representative Newt Gingrich of Georgia, became especially zealous about tax cutting, notably in a Contract with America in 1994.[8] GOP presidential candidate Robert Dole, who had scorned supply-siders in the past, made an across-the-board tax cut of 15 percent the centerpiece of his campaign in 1996. Well before George W. Bush ran for the presidency in 2000, tax-cutting zealotry within the GOP had paved the way for passage of legislation that Ronald Reagan would have envied.

•　•　•

During his campaign in 2000, Bush positioned himself as a "compassionate conservative." But he also made it clear that he was cool to federal outlays for social purposes.[9] He often remarked, "I've learned that if you leave cookies out on a plate, they always get eaten."[10] Moreover, he remembered vividly the political price his father had paid when he raised taxes in 1990.[11] Fully aware of the power of the GOP base, he intended to avoid his father's fate. As the *New York Times* observed, there was "something almost Oedipal in Bush's revitalization of Republican stereotypes, as if by invoking them he can void the conservative revolt on taxes that upended his father's presidency."[12]

The budgetary situation in early and mid-2000, vastly more promising than it had been in the deficit-ridden 1980s and early 1990s, further encouraged tax cutters. Thanks in part to the package that Bush had signed in 1990, and to another tax hike/spending-cut agreement that Clinton and congressional Democrats managed to accomplish in 1993, federal deficits started to decline. In the mid-1990s, moreover, the economy began to boom. Careful management of interest rates by Chairman Alan Greenspan of the Federal Reserve helped maintain price stability while encouraging consumer spending. Such expenditures ratcheted up personal debt, but also became the most powerful force driving the economy.

Buoyed by these developments, the federal government, which had incurred deficits every year since 1969, ran surpluses for four straight fiscal years between 1998 and 2001. Prominent Democrats in 2000, including presidential nominee Al Gore Jr., favored modest income tax cuts but urged that surpluses be otherwise used to retire federal debt so as to shore up Medicare and Social Security in the future. Bush's more grandiose tax-cutting ideas, Gore proclaimed, would offer irresponsible handouts to the rich.

Bush flatly rejected Gore's approach. Like many of his top advisers, he did not worry much about balancing the budget. (Vice President Dick Cheney, a determined tax cutter, later said, "The Reagan years proved deficits don't matter.")[13] Instead, the president made tax "relief" (as he called it) his top priority. "Today," he said in accepting the GOP nomination, "our high taxes fund a surplus. Some say that growing federal surplus means that Washington has more money to spend. But they've got it backwards. The surplus is not the government's money; the surplus is the people's money." He added, "On principle, no one in America should have to pay more than a third of their income to the federal government."[14]

In January 2001, the Congressional Budget Office (CBO) over-optimistically estimated that accumulated federal government surpluses would reach $5.6 trillion by 2010. Already, however, the vibrant economy of the late 1990s had begun to tremble. A recession started in March 2001. Bush then shifted gears, talking less about supply-side principles and more about income tax reductions to counter the downturn. "A tax cut now," he declared in February 2001, "will stimulate the economy and create jobs. . . . This is not a time for government to be taking more money away from the people who buy goods and create jobs." This argument—that tax cuts would aid consumers and revitalize the economy—artfully combined Keynesian theories and supply-side tax-cutting ideas.[15]

Some Republicans, notably Treasury Secretary Paul O'Neill, believed correctly that the CBO estimates were far too rosy. Greenspan, a free-market conservative, also had doubts, advising Congress to exercise fiscal restraint and to bring down the federal debt. But he also testified that the high surpluses justified reductions. As a widely revered guru, he gave substantial cover to Bush's case.[16] When O'Neill, still worried, urged the president to move slowly, he received what he later described as a "flat, inexpressive stare." O'Neill reflected, "there were no let's-look-at-the-facts brokers in any of the key White House positions." Instead, he grumbled, there was a "team of ideologues."

O'Neill, a maverick, was replaced as secretary in December 2002. But he was hardly alone in recognizing that Bush brushed aside serious internal debate over economic matters. In 2001, as throughout his time in the White House, the president relied on his own strongly held convictions and on the advice of politically engaged counselors, notably Karl Rove, not on his various teams of economic advisers.[17] John DiIulio, a centrist Democrat who briefly served in 2001 as director of the newly created White House Office of Faith-Based and Community Initiatives, later lamented, "On social policy and related issues, the lack of even basic policy knowledge, and the only casual interest in knowing more, was somewhat breathtaking. . . . Even quite junior staff would sometimes hear quite senior staff pooh-pooh any need to dig deeper for pertinent information on a given issue."[18]

Wasting no time, in early 2001 Bush presented Congress with a request for $1.6 trillion in tax cuts, to be fully implemented by

2010. To appeal to social conservatives, he emphasized that his proposals would strengthen American families. These initiatives included a doubling of the existing child tax credit, from $500 per child to $1,000, and the elimination of federal estate taxes, or "death taxes," as he cleverly called them. These levies, he asserted, damaged the ability of farmers and small businesspeople to pass on the benefits of their hard work to their children.

To stimulate the economy in the short run, Bush asked Congress to approve rebates in 2001 for taxpayers, with maximums of $300 to single payers, $500 to single parents, and $600 to married payers. Filers in all brackets would also receive cuts in rates, which Bush proposed to cut by a third, from 15 percent to 10 percent, on the first $6,000 for single payers (and the first $12,000 for families). These provisions would mainly help taxpayers in the bottom brackets. Payers in middle brackets, while receiving smaller percentage cuts, would also benefit from reductions. Supply-side thinking lay behind the most significant element of the legislation: a reduction for the highest-bracket payers at the top marginal rate, which would drop over the next few years from 39.6 percent to 33 percent.

Republicans in both houses, having become extraordinarily well disciplined by the late 1990s, moved quickly and virtually unanimously to approve most of Bush's requests; the only changes of note more gradually phased in the cuts, thereby reducing the total reduction over ten years from $1.6 trillion to $1.35 trillion, and lowered the top marginal rate to 35 percent instead of 33 percent.

By shrewdly seeing to it that rebates reached taxpayers quickly, Bush's supporters managed to front-load the good news. This was smart politics. Congress also stipulated that the cuts, including the complete elimination of federal estate taxes as of the tax year 2010, would expire not later than January 2011. This "sunset" approach was also shrewd, making it appear that the reductions would be temporary. Bush, however, anticipated that Congress would never permit the cuts to expire in 2011. To allow that, after all, would be to "raise" taxes. He happily signed the measure in early June.

Then and later, controversy swirled concerning the wisdom of the law. Defending it, Bush and the supply-siders emphasized a number of points. First, they said, total federal revenues as a percentage of GDP, at 20.9 in 2000, had become two to three percentage points higher than they had been between the mid-1980s and mid-1990s: it was time to give taxpayers a break.[19] They added that the reductions, if fully implemented, would be smaller as a percentage per year of GDP than Reagan's cuts had been in 1981.[20] They also maintained that the law, because of the increase in child tax credits and the new 10 percent rates, did not significantly change the distribution of taxes.[21]

Supporters of the cuts also argued that the new top marginal rate of 35 percent for the highest-income earners, though reduced, would not be particularly generous compared to the lows that had been established between 1986 and 1993. These, having been at a high of 91 percent in 1964, had been cut at that time to 70 percent, in 1981 to 50 percent, and in 1986 to 28 percent, before being raised a little to 31 percent in 1990, and to 39.6 percent in 1993.[22]

Critics, led by liberals in Congress, retorted that the tax burden (federal, state, and local) was already considerably lower in the United States than in virtually all other industrialized nations.[23] More progressive taxation, they said, would help finance needed social programs, which were relatively ungenerous in America.[24] Turning to recent history, they stressed a key point: that Reagan's reductions in 1981 had not sparked especially rapid growth, whereas the tax increases that Clinton and congressional Democrats had crafted in 1993 had helped to ignite a boom. Red ink, they added, would soon swamp the national till.

Pointing to the downturn in the economy, critics employed Keynesian arguments to complain that the one-shot rebates of 2001 were too modest and therefore of relatively little use as a stimulus. Millions of low-income people, already paying no federal income taxes, would not receive rebates; those who did would likely bank them rather than spend them on consumer goods. Opponents also argued that the income tax rate cuts, increasing in steps over time, would not stimulate the economy in the short term; one critic later quipped that a ten-year-plan for stimulus was "like going to the doctor with a headache and ending up with an appendectomy."[25]

Above all, opponents emphasized that the amounts to be saved under the law by middle- and low-income taxpayers were puny compared to the bonanzas to be enjoyed by the wealthy. Indeed, some four-fifths of American taxpayers paid more in payroll levies, which were unaffected by the act, than in income taxes. Critics also assailed the law's provisions regarding estates. Prior to passage of the act, only 2 percent of estates—those worth $675,000 or more—had been subject to federal taxation; contrary to the picture painted by the administration, very few small businesspeople or farmers left estates large enough to benefit from Bush's changes. Yet the law helped the rich by raising this exemption limit over time: up to $3.5 million per person in 2009, with the tax eliminated altogether for the 2010 tax year.

Rich people, moreover, would enjoy windfalls from income tax reductions in the higher brackets.[26] Taxes for an individual earning $10,000, for instance, would drop by $300, whereas taxes for an individual earning $100,000 would fall by $2,489. Taxes for an individual earning $500,000 would drop by $17,731. This was a tax break worth fifty-nine times as much as for the person earning $10,000.[27] The cuts, therefore, would sharpen income inequality, which had been growing since the early 1970s. Bill Gates, America's richest man, declared that the reductions would "widen the growing gap in economic and political influence between the wealthy and the rest of America."[28] It was later estimated that 45 percent of total tax reductions under the act went to people in the top 1 percent of the income pyramid, compared to only 13 percent to those in the poorest 60 percent.[29]

A number of unforeseen developments—9/11, funding for a new Department of Homeland Security, the war in Afghanistan, the war in Iraq, Hurricane Katrina—accelerated federal spending in the next few years, and therefore complicated subsequent efforts to resolve debates over the 2001 tax act. Defenders of the law, however, confidently reiterated three points: first, that the real after-tax incomes of people in the low and middle brackets did increase a little over the next few years; second, that the new rates for wealthy people, far from being supergenerous, would nonetheless be higher than they had been between 1986 and 1993; and third—this was a fundamental assumption of supply-siders—that money left in the hands of private investors would be managed far more productively than if handed over to public officials who were operating a wasteful "nanny state."

Later, in the mid-2000s, when the economy had recovered, defenders of the cuts further emphasized that the share of federal income taxes paid by the very rich grew substantially after 2004. Though the wealthy obviously benefited from the cuts, they earned so very much more in the next few years—in many cases from enormously higher corporate salaries, bonuses, and stock options—that, as a group, they ended up paying higher percentages of total income tax receipts than they had in the past.[30]

Opponents of the tax law of 2001, however, kept up their attack. Though subsequent analyses of the impact of the rebates differed, it seemed that many people were in fact cautious about spending their rebates on consumer goods. In any event, the rebates did not give much of a boost to the economy, which grew only slowly until expanding more rapidly as of mid-2003. One critic later joked that the rebates "were as direct a route to economic stimulus as a flight to Chicago or Miami that happened to stop in Moscow."[31]

The tax law (like Reagan's cuts in 1981) also failed to support a central assumption of supply-siders: that reductions, by expanding the after-tax income and profits of employers and entrepreneurs, would rapidly stimulate private investment in productive enterprise and promote strong economic growth. Instead, wealthy investors tended to save their tax windfalls or to engage in high-end spending and speculative pursuits. Private investment in domestic ventures did not exceed its level in 2001 until 2004.[32]

The tax act, finally, did not bear out the predictions of those supply-siders who had imagined that reduced rates, by encouraging investment, would greatly increase taxable incomes, and therefore enlarge government receipts even at the lower rates. Income tax revenue declined sharply in 2002 and 2003, both in constant dollars and as a percentage of GDP. Overall federal revenues fell from 20.9 percent of GDP in 2000 to 16.3 in 2004, the lowest percentage since 1950. Though federal income tax revenue grew substantially in current dollars after 2004, it was not until 2006 that it surpassed the level of 2000.[33]

For this reason, and because federal expenditures rose steadily in constant dollars after 2001, large deficits returned. In fiscal 2001 (ending on September 30, 2001), the government ran the last of its four successive surpluses—of $125 billion in 2000 dollars. Deficits mounted thereafter, cresting in those dollars at $375 billion in fiscal 2004 before subsiding a little in the next three years. Gross federal debt as a percentage of GDP increased from 57.4 percent in 2001 to an estimated high in the Bush years of 65.3 percent in 2007. This was almost as high as the peak percentage in the 1990s, which had reached 67.3 in 1996.[34]

Not all of these figures, of course, were entirely the result of the tax act of 2001 (or of a subsequent tax measure in 2003, which accelerated the phasing in of the cuts and added new tax breaks). Revenue shortfalls in constant dollars, worsened by the downturn in the economy that had begun in 2000, were appearing prior to passage of the law. Federal spending for wars in Afghanistan and Iraq added to deficits in fiscal 2003 and afterward.

But it remained clear that the law worsened the capacity of the federal government to expand domestic social and economic programs, let alone to deal with the substantial obligations it was certain to face in the future in order to fund entitlements such as Social Security and Medicare. Above all, critics reiterated, the cuts contributed substantially to a worrisome aspect of American economic life: rising inequality of income.

• • •

Though focusing on foreign affairs after 9/11, Bush and GOP conservatives in the House nonetheless pressed for more supply-side tax cuts in 2002. The Democratic Senate, however, demanded instead measures to combat unemployment, which had risen from a rate of 3.8 percent in April 2000 to 5.8 percent in December 2001. In March 2002, the Senate version prevailed. Though it offered modest new depreciation benefits to businesses, its major thrust extended the duration of payment of unemployment benefits to millions of Americans.[35]

But the president did not give up. Indeed, it was becoming ever more evident that he had an ambitious long-range goal in mind: the abolition of federal taxes on investment income and accumulated wealth.[36] And in November 2002, when the GOP made gains in congressional elections, he resolved to press again for tax cuts. A delighted Cheney told O'Neill that major tax reform remained a priority. "We won the midterms," he exclaimed. "This is our due."[37]

Bush agreed. In January 2003 he appealed for a package of tax reforms: acceleration of the cuts of 2001, permanent repeal of estate taxes, and reduction of tax rates on long-range capital gains (from a top rate of 20 percent to 15 percent) and on dividends. He also asked Congress to allow individuals to move up to $60,000 a year into tax-free savings accounts. As he had done in 2002, he said that these proposals would stimulate the economy.

Opponents in Congress, almost all of them Democrats, countered angrily that Bush was once again disguising significant long-range changes as stimulus programs. As they had in 2001, they exclaimed that Bush underestimated future declines in revenue (which the head of the CBO in February placed at $2.7 trillion) and that rising deficits would sabotage efforts to fund needed social programs. High deficits would also be likely to raise interest rates, thereby increasing the already daunting costs of debt service. Bill Gates and Warren Buffett, both billionaires, publicly denounced the effort to repeal estate taxes.

Bush and fellow supply-siders predictably dismissed these complaints. Greenspan, though he urged Congress to practice fiscal discipline, once again avoided opposing the administration's proposals. And Milton Friedman forcefully backed the proposed reductions in a widely cited contribution to the *Wall Street Journal*. "There is one and only one way," he wrote, of cutting "government down to size." This is "the way parents control spendthrift children, cutting their allowance." He added, "a major tax cut will be a step toward the smaller government that I believe most citizens of the U. S. want."[38]

Republicans in the House, most of whom had signed pledges not to back tax increases, quickly backed Bush's proposals.[39] Senators, however, worried that war and reconstruction in Iraq, which began in March, would further enlarge the deficit. Administration officials retorted that no one would suffer financial sacrifice because of the war. John Snow, O'Neill's replacement as treasury secretary, testified, "we can afford the war and we'll put it behind us."[40]

In the end, Bush accepted legislation that the CBO estimated would result in smaller cuts, of around $320 billion. But the law did offer substantial increases in depreciation allowances for small businesses, and it accelerated implementation of the rate cuts enacted in 2001, thereby increasing the total reduction anticipated from that law.[41] It also lowered top rates for capital gains taxes from 20 percent to 15 percent and for dividends to 15 percent. For Americans in the lowest two tax brackets these two rates would be 5 percent.

Even in its downsized version, the act represented a victory for the president. It was in fact a substantial tax reduction that the CBO reckoned would increase deficits in 2003 and 2004 by a total of $270 billion. Other analysts, anticipating that Congress would at some point extend the cuts, later estimated the revenue loss from the 2003 law at $1 trillion over ten years, and the combined loss over ten years from the 2001 and 2003 laws at $4 trillion.[42]

What of the law's shorter-term effects on the economy? Within the next few years, Bush and other administration officials repeatedly insisted that the cuts, along with those approved in 2001, greatly boosted growth, which revived by late 2003. They also predicted—accurately, as it turned out—that economic expansion (leading to larger tax collections) would enable deficits to decline both absolutely and as a percentage of GDP.[43]

Liberal critics, however, countered that these and other reductions did not greatly spur investment or economic growth, either in the short or the long term. They added that the real wages of nonsupervisory production workers, which had stagnated for many years, barely improved after 2003.[44] As earlier, they emphasized that economic expansion had been slowly appearing, even before the tax cuts of 2003. Recovery thereafter owed more, they said, to larger economic trends and low interest rates than to supply-side policies.[45]

Critics of the package of 2003 were especially persuasive in pointing out that it bestowed special blessings on wealthy investors.[46] According to Citizens for Tax Justice, a respected liberal organization, 62 percent of tax savings from the reduced rates on capital gains and dividends between 2003 and 2007 went to individuals with incomes of $1 million or more. The very rich fared best of all: 28 percent of tax savings went to 11,433 of 134 million taxpayers, who saved an average of almost $1.9 million, for a total of $21.7 billion. The nearly 90 percent of taxpayers who made less than $100,000 a year gained an average of $318, for a total of 5.3 percent of total tax savings under the law.[47]

• • •

Bush still hoped after mid-2003 to steer two of his cherished economic policies through Congress: partial privatization of Social Security, and permanent cuts in income and estate taxes. Private retirement accounts of that sort, however, had little popular appeal, and Bush had to drop the idea in 2005. Congress, though approving a modest tax cut in 2006, also failed to advance his larger agenda. Instead, powerful interest groups, such as agribusiness and AARP, often dominated debates over economic issues on Capitol Hill after mid-2003. Their demands, which led to rising government spending, notably for a prescription drug plan added to Medicare in late 2003, sparked mounting criticisms of the administration's fiscal policies and widened splits dividing American conservatives.

Many fiscal conservatives complained loudly after 2003 that Bush was a wastrel.[48] Reeling off statistics, they emphasized that he had never presented a balanced budget and that he had presided over the greatest real per capita growth of federal spending since the LBJ years. His first budget called for $2 trillion, his last for $3.1 trillion. Expenditures for the wars in Iraq and Afghanistan, these conservatives insisted, accounted for but part of the spending increases, amounting to roughly a third (approximately $324 billion) of record-high budget deficits totaling $979 billion that Bush and Republican Congresses produced in the three fiscal years between 2004 and 2006.[49]

Most of these critics (along with many liberals) complained also that politicians of both parties were not dealing seriously with the long-range funding problems facing highly expensive entitlements such as Social Security, Medicaid, and (especially) Medicare. One well-informed conservative estimated that the money required for these three programs, which had amounted to 4 percent of GDP in 1970, had leapt to 9 percent in 2007 and would jump to as much as 15 percent by 2030.[50] Comptroller General David Walker warned repeatedly of a "fiscal cancer" and an "explosion of debt" that if ignored would have "catastrophic consequences."[51]

Some observers, pointing out that the Social Security trust fund would not require use of general revenues until 2017 (and that the Medicare hospital insurance fund would not become insolvent until 2019), accused officials such as Walker of scaremongering. They had a point. But warnings proliferated. Robert Samuelson, economic columnist for *Newsweek*, wrote in 2007 that federal entitlements seemed destined to swallow 70 percent of the federal budget by 2030. To balance accounts the government would have to eliminate funding for Homeland Security, national defense, and most domestic programs. It would also have to raise taxes by between 30 and 50 percent.[52]

• • •

Confronted by criticisms such as these, and by Democratic majorities on Capitol Hill after 2006, Bush was forced on the defensive. As campaigning for the election of 2008 intensified, candidates in both parties jumped in to debate his economic record.

There was much about the economy as of mid-2007 that Republicans, Bush included, could and did brag about. From 2002 on, it had grown irregularly but without interruption. Unemployment fell from a high of 6.3 percent in mid-2003 to 4.7 percent in September 2007. Inflation, notwithstanding rising oil and food prices, remained moderate. Consumer spending continued to be robust.[53] The Dow Jones Industrial Average, which had dropped below 8,000 in 2002, reached 14,164 in October 2007. David Brooks, a moderately conservative columnist for the *New York Times*, celebrated America's economic progress by declaring in July 2007, "we're in the middle of one of the greatest economic eras ever."[54]

Opponents of Bush's policies painted a gloomier portrait, especially after the economy began to decline in late 2007. The costs of health care, they emphasized, had risen rapidly over the previous forty years and were considerably higher per capita and as a percentage of GDP than in most other wealthy nations.[55] Boosted in part by surging immigration, the number of people who lacked health insurance jumped between 2000 and 2008 from 40 million to 47 million—more than 15 percent of the population.[56] Millions more were underinsured. Yet the administration had opposed all efforts for comprehensive reform.

Liberal critics deplored other aspects of the administration's domestic record. By refusing to raise taxes to pay for war, they said, Bush scrimped on federal support of science, student aid programs, funding for development of renewable energy, social programs, and all manner of infrastructure maintenance. The percentage of people in poverty, though decreasing slightly between 2004 and 2007, remained considerably higher than in almost all other advanced economies. America's poverty rate for children under the age of eighteen, rising from 15.8 percent in 2001 to 17.4 in 2006 (36 percent for black children), was scandalous.[57]

Other observers grumbled that the Bush administration had presided over very high imbalances in the nation's global transactions. Thanks primarily to rising oil prices and to explosive growth of imports—much of it from low-wage nations such as China—the trade deficit rose from $365 billion in 2001 to nearly $800 billion, a record high, in 2006. To encourage exports, Bush had allowed the dollar to fall dramatically against other major currencies, thereby lifting American exports to record levels in 2007. But at some point the debt from international transactions would have to be repaid with interest. If Asian central banks, which had accumulated trillions in dollar-denominated assets, were to stop purchasing U.S. Treasury bills, stocks, and properties, the American economy could take a major hit.[58]

Most critics of Bush fiscal policies zeroed in, as earlier, on the income tax cuts, which had magnified economic inequality. This reached a level in 2005 equal to that of the late 1920s, in large part because of extraordinary income gains amassed by the super-wealthy in the previous three years.[59] In 2005, the richest three million people had as much income as the bottom 166,000,000, more than one-half the American population.[60] The share of all federal taxes paid by the richest 1 percent of people grew between 2002 and 2005 at a rate that was slightly more than half the rate of their growth in incomes.[61]

• • •

Some of these statistics, however, also reflected long-range structural trends. The stagnation of manufacturing wages in the United States, for instance, dated to the early 1970s. Labor unions, whose influence had peaked in the 1950s and 1960s, had lost power; in 2007 they represented only 12.1 percent of American workers (and only 7.5 percent of those in the private sector).[62] These were developments that no prior presidential administration or Congress had managed to overcome.

Income inequality in the United States also had a considerable history. After lessening between the 1930s and the 1960s, it had begun to grow again in the 1970s and had continued to increase during the presidential administrations of Jimmy Carter, Reagan, Bush senior, and Clinton. Similar, though considerably less pronounced increases in inequality affected other industrial nations at the same time.

Cuts in top marginal tax rates during the Reagan years and in the George W. Bush era strengthened this trend in the United States.[63] But significant nongovernmental developments had also abetted inequality.[64] As married women entered the labor force in ever larger numbers, the average incomes of most two-earner households far exceeded those with one earner. People with specialized training and skill in new technologies raced up the income ladder, leaving others scrambling at the lower rungs.[65] The acceleration of globalization devastated some blue-collar workers while benefiting many white-collar employees in companies able to compete in world markets. Bull markets in stocks between 1995 and 1999 and again between 2003 and 2007 enriched corporate executives, money managers, and wealthy investors and contributed to spectacular spikes in the uppermost levels of the income pyramid.[66]

Structural forces also widened the income pyramid at lower levels. These included historically large racial gaps in earnings and wealth, dramatic increases in the number of low-income immigrants, and growth in the number of female-headed families. The relentless expansion of low-wage jobs in the service sector, in which more than 60 percent of American employees worked in 2008, depressed the relative earnings of millions of people.

Developments in education further enlarged inequality. Chronically failing public schools in low-income areas saddled millions of already disadvantaged young people with lifelong educational and occupational handicaps.[67] Costs at colleges and universities after the early 1970s shot upward more than three times as rapidly as inflation. Students who finish college may or may not learn a great deal more, but many surely earn more: in 2005, Americans aged thirty-five to forty-four with high school diplomas had average annual incomes of $32,220; those with bachelor's degrees averaged $55,083, or 70 percent more. The difference in total earnings over a forty-year span of employment came to $903,320.[68]

If masses of people had protested against income inequality, politicians might have listened. But throughout their history Americans have more strongly supported the goal of equality of opportunity than the goal of equality of outcome. They have believed—at least some of the time—in the American dream of social mobility, which remained real for the majority of poor immigrants during the early 2000s. Cultural attitudes such as these persisted even during the recession-ridden days of 2001: a considerable majority of Americans, dreaming that they might leave riches to their children, supported Bush's efforts to repeal estate taxes. Though millions of people continued to feel insecure after the economy recovered, they did not coalesce in a populist crusade against inequality.

Friends as well as critics of Bush-era economic policies would have been wise to keep these larger structural and cultural realities in mind and therefore to recognize that there are limits to the capacity of governmental fiscal policies to transform the economy. Bush's tax policies had a large effect on a range of economic indicators, notably deficits, debt, and inequality at the top. America's gross federal debt (in 2000 dollars) increased from $5.6 trillion at the end of fiscal 2000 to an estimated $9.2 trillion in February 2008. But the independent impact of federal fiscal policies should not be exaggerated. Structurally enhanced income inequality, having risen for more than a generation, preceded the tax reductions. And it remains hard to weigh the role of the tax cuts, as opposed to a host of powerful domestic and global market forces, in accounting for the resumption in 2003 of encouraging growth in the economy.

America's economic resilience between late 2003 and mid-2007 depended, after all, on a host of nongovernmental blessings that helped, as throughout U.S. history, to promote affluence and growth—notably the nation's huge domestic and continental market, superabundant resources, stable political institutions, durable legal protections, technological innovativeness, entrepreneurial spirit, industrious workers, and eager consumers. In the early 2000s, as at many times in the past, these helped to promote productivity, facilitate growth, and maintain the United States as the economic colossus of the world.

Once the recession of 2001 ended, and before Bush's first tax reductions went into effect, these dynamic forces enabled America's economy to move ahead slowly. Thereafter they were keys to a welcome recovery that lasted until late 2007. Still, growth in these years was less robust than during the boom of the mid- to late 1990s.[69] Real median household income remained below its peak in 1999.[70] Personal indebtedness mounted alarmingly. Unimpressed by the Bush administration's record, critics of supply-side ideas kept up their attacks.

As Walter Mondale had learned in 1984, however, it is politically perilous to call for higher taxes, especially in an economic downturn such as the one that began to descend in late 2007. John McCain, who had been one of only two Senate Republicans to oppose the tax laws of 2001 and 2003, changed his mind as an aspirant for the presidency in 2007–8, exclaiming, "tax cuts, starting with Kennedy, as we all know, raise revenues."[71] Like most Republicans, he not only favored making the Bush tax cuts permanent, he also called for further reductions in corporate and capital gains levies and championed larger tax credits for business investment.

Democrats in 2008 countered by advocating various economic reforms. Most, including Barack Obama, demanded that the Bush administration's income tax cuts benefiting the wealthy, as well as cuts in capital gains and dividend taxes, be allowed to lapse at the end of 2010. It was far from clear, however, that Democrats could accomplish much of this agenda. Indeed, even in 2009, high hurdles loomed before Democratic reformers: the institutionalization since 2001 of supply-side thinking, which had seemed radical in 1980, had done much to enrich the wealthy and to deplete the federal till.

Moreover, concerns over the economy, which was faltering badly in late 2007 and 2008, increasingly dominated the election campaign. Hoping to encourage investment, the Federal Reserve Board lowered the federal funds rate seven times, from 5.25 percent in September 2007 to 2.25 percent as of March 2008. These reductions were the most aggressive in modern American history. The Fed, acting with resolve, also guaranteed $29 billion of the assets of Bear Stearns, a failing investment bank. Meanwhile, the Bush administration and a Democratic Congress worked out a substantial stimulus package of $168 billion. It featured tax rebates of some $117 billion for some 130 million taxpayers in low- and middle-income families and measures to promote business investment.[72]

Though most economists welcomed this show of bipartisanship, fiscal conservatives complained that the package would enlarge the already burdensome federal debt, and in so doing further complicate future efforts to deal with unfunded obligations, notably Medicare. Some liberals complained that it was too small. Other critics predicted—accurately, as it turned out—that many people, worried about the future, would save their rebates, thus doing little to revive the economy.

• • •

Few experts, however, predicted the stunning decline of the American economy that occurred during the late summer and fall of 2008. By the end of the year, the Dow Jones Industrial Average had plunged from its high (of 14,164 in October 2007) to 8,776—a drop of some 37 percent. The unemployment rate, 4.7 percent in October 2007, had increased to 6.7 percent. Consumer spending, which had been the driving force behind prosperity, fell by more than 3 percent during each of the last two quarters of 2008. The federal deficit for fiscal 2008 (ending on September 30, 2008) soared to a record post-World War II high of $455 billion.

Staggered by numbers such as these, economists and others struggled to pinpoint the causes. Though their explanations differed considerably, it was clear as of early 2009 that several developments had played a role. One was the Reagan-era passion for deregulation, followed by the bipartisan dismantling in the 1990s of Depression-era legislation (the Glass-Steagall Act) that had separated commercial and investment banks. (The final move in this direction, the Gramm-Leach-Bailey Act of 1999, had passed in the Senate by a vote of 90–8). So encouraged, major commercial banks had gone public and merged with investment banks, creating such behemoths as J. P. Morgan Chase, Citigroup, and Bank of America. Raising billions of dollars via sales of stock, these institutions borrowed billions more and engaged in levered lending on an enormous and escalating scale. By 2007, Bear Stearns, Lehman Brothers, and Merrill Lynch had more than $30 of investments on their books for every $1 of capital they possessed.

Few investments seemed more lucrative than home mortgages. Between 2002 and 2006, housing values increased astoundingly, by 16 percent per year. Lenders, including quasi-governmental institutions such as Fannie Mae and Freddie Mac, offered a range of attractive subprime and adjustable-rate mortgages. Many buyers were people who had only a dim idea at best of the terms of their mortgages and were serious credit risks. The lenders, moreover, bundled many of their mortgages into gigantic and exotic "derivatives" and "collateralized debt obligations" and sold them to other investors. The hugely complicated market in these impenetrably complex derivatives expanded exponentially.

Had government regulators stepped in to curb such high-risk practices, they might have averted serious trouble. But until late 2008 they did not. Bush administration officials, foes of regulatory activism, were partly to blame for what was happening. The Securities and Exchange Commission, for example, had failed to exercise oversight. But few people had warned of the trouble ahead, and there was plenty of blame to go around. Greenspan, heading the Federal Reserve until replaced by Ben Bernanke in February 2006, had opined that the market would be able to regulate itself. Congressmen, eager to expand home-ownership, had pressed Fannie Mae and Freddie Mac to loosen their requirements for loans. As in the heady days of the late 1920s, regulators as well as investors had been caught up in an overoptimistic herd mentality, and they ignored the signs of danger.

When the bubble burst, as it did with frightening force in mid- and late 2008, it shattered the housing market. Home values plunged by 20 percent between January and October. It was later reported that 860,000 properties had been repossessed in 2008— more than two times the number in 2007. Major banks, trapped with more than a trillion dollars in toxic assets, reeled under the strain. When Lehman Brothers, a major investment house, collapsed in September, it sent waves of panic through the financial community. Terrified banks and financial institutions refused to lend money, even to one another. Many businesses, squeezed in a disastrous credit crunch, laid off workers, filed for bankruptcy, or went under. Consumers with savings hoarded rather than buy goods. As of September 2008, a crisis of confidence threatened to paralyze the overall economy and to drive the United States into the worst depression since the 1930s.

As a foe of governmental regulation of the economy, Bush could hardly have been expected to intervene in a major way to deal with these developments. But the magnitude of the crisis as of September—which the series of interest rate cuts and $168 billion stimulus package had failed to alleviate—left him little choice. The result: the Treasury, working with the Democratic Congress and the Federal Reserve, acted in a transformative way. The Fed cut its federal funds rate three more times, thereby lowering it to zero in December, and injected some $800 billion to buy mortgage-based debt incurred by Fannie Mae, Freddie Mac, and other institutions. These and other commitments and guarantees by the Treasury and the Fed—via insurance, investments, and loans—totaled many trillions of dollars as of December. Taken together, they established considerably greater government control (one observer, though exaggerating, called it "a weird, shadow nationalization") of the banking industry.

Congress, meanwhile, authorized a $700 billion stimulus package, most of which was used to bail out large banks and financial institutions. Half the money went out between October and the end of December. Smaller amounts (some $13.4 billion in 2008) propped up General Motors and Chrysler, which seemed on the verge of collapse. The CBO estimated in January 2009 that the federal deficit for the first three months (October–December 2008) of the new (2009) fiscal year had been $485 billion—or $40 billion more than the deficit had been for the entire 2008 fiscal year—and that the total deficit for the 2009 fiscal year would be at least $1.2 trillion—or more than one-fourteenth of the overall economy of $14 trillion. In such a new world, the hotly contested deficits that Bush's tax cuts had created seemed puny indeed.

By the time Obama became president on January 20, 2009, hope existed that these extraordinary efforts would help to prevent catastrophe. No major banks had gone under after the fall of Lehman Brothers. But relatively little of the stimulus money had gone to help struggling mortgagees. The stock market had continued to fall and unemployment to rise. Consumption still lagged. And the major banks, despite having used bailout money to pay down debts—rather than lending—were still hemorrhaging money. The credit crunch, therefore, persisted. Congress, digging deeper, approved yet another stimulus package, this one for $787 billion, as well as a bailout of $700 billion to help auto companies, banks, and other sectors of the economy. Estimates of the federal deficit for the 2009 fiscal year then escalated to $1.8 billion and counting.

No one could be sure, however, in early 2009 if such unprecedented measures would turn the economy around. Indeed, the wrenching developments since late 2007 unsettled policymakers as well as economists of varying persuasions. These developments revealed, though not for the first time, that key assumptions of classical economics—that people mostly make rational economic decisions, and that markets are by and large efficient—rest on shaky foundations, and that government regulators cannot always be relied on to curb excesses. The crisis also raised questions about the capacity of public officials to pick up the pieces. Many experts, watching in dismay as unprecedented monetary and fiscal interventions failed to turn the tide, wondered if *any* combination of government policies could cope with the extraordinarily complicated consequences of the millions of decisions that people and institutions, at home and abroad, make every day in the marketplaces of the world.

Though the economic crisis continued to dominate headlines in early 2009, further controversies over Bush's economic policies, notably the significant supply-side tax cuts, still loomed ahead. Indeed, most of the formidable fiscal edifice that Republicans had erected since 2000 was scheduled to come down at the end of 2010. Would Congress let the edifice (or parts of it) fall so as to allow it to be replaced with a more progressive tax code such as had existed in 2000? Extend it, thereby forgoing as much as $400 billion a year (one of many estimates) in federal revenue? Or, as some advocates hoped, approve still deeper cuts (and deficits) in an effort to stimulate recovery? If Congress were to extend or increase the Bush-era tax reductions, it would enshrine a supply-side revolution that had erected the boldest monuments of Bush's domestic agenda.

7

WREAKING HAVOC FROM WITHIN

George W. Bush's Energy Policy in Historical Perspective

MEG JACOBS

WHEN GEORGE W. BUSH ENTERED OFFICE IN 2001, ONE OF HIS TOP priorities was crafting a comprehensive new energy policy. Within nine days, the president had set up the National Energy Policy Development Group, an executive task force chaired by Vice President Richard Cheney. The goal was to reverse thirty years of environmental and energy policy, specifically through deregulation, tax reform, and the opening up of new lands to exploration and drilling. Since the Arab oil embargo of 1973, Republican presidents had sought to stimulate domestic production to reduce dependence on foreign oil. In his 2007 State of the Union address, Bush explained, "For too long, our nation has been dependent on foreign oil. And this dependence leaves us more vulnerable to hostile regimes and to terrorists who could cause huge disruptions of oil shipments and raise the price of oil and do great harm to our economy."[1]

The Bush energy agenda was not new. For three decades, conservatives had pushed to overturn the regulatory world put in place during the early 1970s, from energy price controls to environmental regulations. In addition to boosting production, they also sought to militarize the Persian Gulf as a way to protect access to the free flow of Middle Eastern oil. Increasing production and military commitments stood in contrast to Democratic alternatives of heavily regulated oil markets and environmentally inspired conservation. As the United States moved into a post-Vietnam, post–cold war world, conservatives met with success in shifting American foreign policy, as became clear in the First Persian Gulf War. But the results have been mixed on the domestic side. American politics have shifted rightward since the 1970s, but conservatives have not dismantled big government, especially environmental regulations and restrictions on energy production. Over the last generation, popular support for environmentalism on Capitol Hill has grown.

As a result, Bush and his allies did not realize all their goals. The 2005 Energy Policy Act, which grew out of Cheney's energy task force, was largely regarded as a boon to the energy industry. But the administration did not achieve its central legislative demand, the opening of the Arctic National Wildlife Reserve (ANWR) in Alaska. Nor was it able to resist congressional mandates to increase fuel economy standards and invest in renewable energies.

These efforts were not total failures, far from it. While Bush and his top-level officials faced some congressional roadblocks, they did succeed in undercutting and blunting some of the environmental and energy regulatory apparatus in place since the early 1970s. With Vice President Dick Cheney at the helm, they enhanced the independence and power of the executive office as a way around congressional opposition. Building on strategies of conservative governance learned over thirty years, the Bush administration figured out how to give industry greater protections through bureaucratic warfare. Its tools included executive secrecy, nonenforcement of existing regulations, and administrative rewriting and reinterpretation of bureaucratic rules. As one environmentalist presciently explained about Bush's choice for energy secretary, Spencer Abraham, a former senator from Michigan who had twice sponsored legislation to abolish the Department of Energy, "we fear[ed] he would try to wreak havoc from within."[2]

PROJECT INDEPENDENCE

Crafted during the Arab oil embargo of 1973–74, Project Independence, as President Nixon first called it, became a central part of the Republican agenda and has remained at the core. It was designed as a reaction against the liberal response to the Arab oil embargo, when a Democratic-controlled Congress passed legislation that put the oil industry under New Deal-type price and allocation controls. Weakened by Watergate and often willing, under pressure, to adopt the economic programs of his opponents, Nixon was unable to stop this dramatic governmental intrusion into the energy markets. Earlier in his administration, Nixon had signed the Environmental Protection Act and the Clean Air Act, both of which also regulated industry and prompted serious concerns. Kenneth Lay, then deputy secretary of the interior, told the White House, "our problem . . . has resulted from outmoded government policies—from excessive tinkering with the time-tested mechanisms of the free market."[3]

The goal of Project Independence, from Nixon to Ronald Reagan, was to remove the controls and environmental regulations of the early 1970s. In the Ford administration, a group of young conservative insiders sought to construct a market-oriented energy policy from within the White House. Donald Rumsfeld, Ford's chief of staff, his thirty-four-year-old assistant Dick Cheney, and others, such as Alan Greenspan, whom Ford appointed chairman of the Council of Economic Advisors, feared America's growing dependence on foreign oil. Between 1970 and 1973, American imports of oil doubled, with imports accounting for one-third of oil consumption by 1975. Energy prices were also rising. On the eve of America's bicentennial, these policymakers worried deeply about the decline of American oil independence, and with it the potential end of American strength as a political and economic superpower. As Irving Kristol, one of the founders of neoconservatism, explained in a *Wall Street Journal* editorial, energy dependence threatened the "preservation of America's status as a world power, with the capability of conducting a foreign policy free from black-mail."[4]

Given the post-Vietnam constraints on the United States's ability to use military force to protect its national security interests, the alternative was to boost American domestic production. Frank Zarb, in charge of energy under Ford, told the president, "What is essentially at stake is the economic balance of power achieved by the Western World over the last century and a half. . . . The restoration of American dominance in setting the goals and establishing the price of energy must be the ultimate objective of our national energy policy." To make America once again the price-setter of oil required increasing domestic production. On January 13, 1975, Ford warned the nation, "Americans are no longer in full control of their own national destiny, when that destiny depends on uncertain foreign fuel at high prices fixed by others." Energy dependence, he explained, is "intolerable to our national security."[5]

Ford and conservative advisers knew it would be no easy task to get rid of regulations on American production. They had seen firsthand, during the winter of 1973– 74, how the petroleum shortage had led to the regulation of the energy industry. The Federal Energy Administration, which later became the Department of Energy, set prices for petroleum products, decided which products refiners would make, and allocated their distribution. The Ford White House sought to dismantle these controls. But with Democrats still strong in Congress and the public fearful of high prices, Michael Duval, a Ford adviser, contended that Ford would have a tough time defeating the "powerful momentum, pulling our energy choices towards the sanctuary of government controls." "We face a nation scared by their economic crisis and conditioned to expect a government-oriented solution," Duval explained. "The center of gravity of the political forces which exist in this country is clearly against a solution to a national problem, such as our energy crisis, which relies on the individual and the marketplace."[6]

After nearly a year of negotiations between the White House and the Hill, the energy bill that ended up on Ford's desk in December 1975, the Energy Policy and Conservation Act, was a conservative's nightmare. In essence, it extended price controls for another four years. In addition, it imposed a host of new environmental restrictions, with the main one creating corporate average fuel economy (CAFE) standards for the automobile industry, which required a 40 percent improvement in efficiency in ten years.[7] In the end, without the numbers he needed to win in Congress, Ford signed the bill, fearful of public resentment over rising fuel prices.

For conservatives, the Carter years were an unmitigated failure, especially on energy policy, with the creation of the Department of Energy and a massive government commitment to alternative fuels. In the 1970s the American Right was becoming increasingly visible, vocal, and politically organized. The oil lobby mobilized against Carter's plan, and so too did conservative think tanks, public intellectuals, and popular publications. The debate over energy policy served as a dress rehearsal for Reaganite arguments against regulation, taxes, and bureaucracy and in favor of market efficiency, innovation, and free enterprise. Conservative activists and intellectuals developed a right-leaning ideological perspective on Carter's proposal to oppose the liberal viewpoint. They told the public and legislators on Capitol Hill that environmentalists advocated a return to an agrarian past, moralists wanted to subject everyone to self-denial, and bureaucrats interfered in affairs they were ill-equipped to monitor.[8] "The Carter proposal is a monstrosity. Its end result would be less energy," wrote economist Milton Friedman. Putting it bluntly, he said, "Big brother is the problem not the cure."[9]

The second oil shock in 1979, in the wake of the Iranian Revolution, undermined Americans' faith that government had the solutions to the energy crisis. The lengthening gas lines in the summer of 1979 discredited the Department of Energy and lent credibility to the conservative thesis that government was the problem. Still, Carter proposed a massive government program to create synthetic fuels. He pushed this program through Congress, along with a windfall profits tax on oil corporations to pay for it. But the program had little popular support and would get eliminated soon after he left office.

ENERGY POLICY IN THE AGE OF REAGAN

The best hope for a production-oriented energy policy came when Ronald Reagan entered the executive office in 1981. The new Republican president signed an executive order on January 27 ending all price controls on oil. Reagan came into power as the leader of a conservative movement dedicated to trimming government and reasserting American power abroad. By ending price controls, the hope was to stimulate domestic production of oil and decrease dependence on insecure Middle Eastern oil. Reagan also wanted to signal his commitment to a new production- and market-oriented deregulatory agenda. But even as Reagan got rid of the New Deal–style controls, the environmental regulations that limited the energy industry were still in place, leaving much work to be done.

Under Reagan, conservatives developed new strategies that would be honed, refined, and ultimately yield success under George W. Bush. Republicans won the Senate in 1980, but Democrats retained a large majority in the House. To overcome congressional roadblocks, the Reagan administration looked to nonlegislative tools to roll back environmental regulations. Reagan appointed James Watt secretary of the interior and Ann Gorsuch head of the Environmental Protection Agency (EPA). Both were hostile to the regulations they were meant to enforce and sought to gut many provisions from within. Outspoken and aggressive in pursuing their agenda, each was forced to resign. Still, from within the White House, conservatives began to discover techniques of conservative governance, including nonenforcement of liberal policies. Specifically, they sought to subject environmental regulations to cost-benefit analysis, they appointed judges who required agencies to assess the economic trade-offs of regulation, they pushed for budget cuts as a way to dampen the influence of regulators, and they revised rules to favor industry. Given the continuing strength of environmental groups, they met with mixed results.

Reagan also pursued a shift in foreign policy to militarize the Persian Gulf as another means of guaranteeing American energy independence. President Carter had begun this policy. When the Soviet Union invaded Afghanistan, Carter formulated the Carter Doctrine in 1980 to commit the United States to protecting oil interests in the Gulf with a military buildup. Reagan continued this policy, which would come to fruition in the First Gulf War under his successor, George H. W. Bush.

The George H. W. Bush years were mixed. Bush's background as an independent oilman from Texas with connections around the world made him sympathetic to the interests of the oil industry. But from the mid-1980s into the early 1990s, world oil prices were low, and as a result, many independent oilmen went out of business. At the same time, environmentalists succeeded in pushing through the Clean Air Act of 1990, which Bush came under pressure to sign new regulations to require that cities meet beefed-up standards of air quality. Those regulations only further dampened expansion of the domestic energy industry. As domestic supply continued to fall, U.S. oil imports rose. The initial vision of Project Independence was to free the United States from reliance on foreign oil. By 1991, at the time of the Persian Gulf War, the United States imported more than half its oil.

When Saddam Hussein sent troops into Kuwait in August 1991, the Bush administration made it clear that this action would not stand. President Bush, along with Secretary of Defense Dick Cheney and most American lawmakers, justified the war as the necessary defense of open access to oil. At first, Bush and the oil industry were hopeful that the war would enable broad reform of energy regulations. Certainly, independent oilmen hoped to use the war as an excuse to roll back environmental restrictions, arguing that Saddam Hussein's actions underscored the danger of relying on oil from insecure sources. The industry also wanted to open ANWR in Alaska to drilling. But the war was over quickly, and as oil prices dropped and supplies remained plentiful, there was little momentum for reform, especially as Democrats retained control of Congress. Bush devoted only a single sentence of his 1992 State of the Union address to energy policy.[10] The Energy Policy Act of 1992, which Bush ultimately signed, was so watered down that it passed in the Senate 94–4 and in the House 381–37. The *Washington Post* described it as "the dog that didn't bark."[11]

Under the Clinton administration, it became clear there would be a showdown over energy policy. On the one hand, with gas prices at a low, Americans started to switch to bigger cars, such as sport utility vehicles, which used more gasoline and got less mileage per gallon. These light trucks, which were not subject to emissions controls, accounted for half of all new American vehicle sales. Business-oriented Republicans and their Democratic allies from auto-producing states prevented any moves to improve CAFE standards. Between 1995 and 1999, House majority whip Tom DeLay (R-TX) successfully blocked the Transportation Department from investigating new standards.[12]

On the other hand, environmentalists gathered additional strength as concern about global warming grew. Liberal Democrats and moderate Republicans, reflecting the wishes of their middle-class constituents who cared about the environment, began to a push for greater reductions in pollution and improved emissions standards. In the last year of the Clinton administration, environmental lobbyists got ninety members of the House to sign a letter urging the president to raise CAFE standards by administrative action. In March 2000, actor and environmental activist Leonardo DiCaprio interviewed President Clinton on ABC, signaling a surge in popularity in environmental issues.[13]

ENTER BUSH

By the time of the 2000 election, the stage was set for a confrontation between advocates of greater conservation and supporters of greater consumption. As presidential candidate in the 2000 election, Vice President Al Gore pressed environmental issues, going so far as to suggest that Detroit would have to figure out how to eliminate internal combustion engines.[14] The Big Three were worried about the challenge on emissions standards. "This is the most important public policy issue to the auto industry," said Andrew Card. At the time of this statement, Card was vice president of government relations at General Motors and would soon become George W. Bush's chief of staff.[15]

On the campaign trail, George W. Bush and his running mate, Dick Cheney, made a virtue out of their backgrounds as oilmen. To them, all energy problems could be solved by greater production. Cheney had formerly served as chief executive of Halliburton, the oil services corporation. Bush and Cheney made it clear that they would push for an energy policy focused on increasing domestic production, starting with opening up the Alaskan ANWR to drilling. The proposal was to open 1.5 million acres of the 19 million-acre refuge. In 1980, President Carter had signed the Alaska National Interest Lands Conservation Act, which required congressional approval for opening the area to drilling. The Reagan and Bush administrations had tried and failed. Environmentalists argued that this area was an essential breeding ground for caribou, whereas the oil industry insisted that new technologies would enable drilling with minimal ecological costs. Proponents said that the oil from this area would result in over one million barrels a day, or roughly 5 percent of Americans' daily usage. Before a group of automobile workers in Saginaw, Michigan, Bush said, "My plan opens the door to more energy to fuel a growing economy and a new economy. We take the path of exploration and innovation and national self-reliance. . . . My opponent takes a different path. In a long Washington career, he has supported higher energy taxes and higher energy prices, more regulation and more central controls." There was little question what energy policies Bush would pursue as president.[16]

After the 2000 election was settled, Bush and Cheney wasted no time. Signaling their pro-industry attitude, Bush nominated Spencer Abraham as secretary of energy. Abraham, a Michigan Republican, lost his seat in 2000 after serving only one term. In his brief tenure in Congress, Abraham had co-sponsored one bill in 1995 and another in 1999 to dismantle the Department of Energy. The son of an autoworker, he went to Harvard Law School, became the chairman of the Michigan Republican Party Committee, and then was deputy chief of staff to Vice President Dan Quayle.

Abraham won election to the Senate in 1993 and established a conservative record. The League of Conservation Voters placed Abraham, a leading recipient of contributions from the oil, gas pipeline, and electrical utilities, at the top of its "Dirty Dozen" list and worked successfully for his defeat in the 2000 election. When Bush announced Abraham's nomination, environmentalists were concerned. Abraham was on record calling for drilling in ANWR and opposing the Kyoto Protocol, increased fuel efficiency standards, and funds for renewable energy research.

Just as Bush took office, a massive electricity shortage in California was making front-page news. Even though the problem stemmed from mismanaged deregulation of electricity markets, the administration and their allies on the Hill jumped on the rolling blackouts in California to provide the rationale for opening up domestic oil production. Within days of Republicans returning to power in the Senate, Alaska senator Murkowski introduced a bill to open up ANWR to oil and gas drilling. He explained, "We have an energy crisis in this country." He also proposed major tax breaks for oil exploration and also for coal and nuclear industries, even greater than what Bush had promised on the campaign trail. Republicans continued to argue that promoting domestic production was essential to preserving international power. "We have allowed this drift to go on too long," said Senator Chuck Hagel (R-NE). "We can't leave this country subject to international blackmail because of our reliance on foreign oil. It's far too dangerous."[17]

A showdown on the Hill between environmentalists and pro-industry advocates became increasingly likely. One side, concentrated largely in the Democratic Party, pushed for conservation as a way to save fuel, reduce dependency, and lower prices; the other side, mostly in the Republican Party, pushed for increased production as the way to attain those same goals. With concerns about global warming and conservation gaining steam, the Bush administration had to not only advance its agenda but also fend off new regulations. Cheney took a hard line. "Conservation might be a sign of personal virtue, but it is not a sufficient basis for a sound, comprehensive energy policy."[18] In response to the California en-

ergy shortage, Bush said from the White House, "you cannot con-
serve your way to energy independence. We can do a better job in
conservation, but we darn sure have to do a better job of finding
more supply."[19] The contrast with Carter in 1979 was striking.
Whereas Carter had asked Americans to cut back on driving, obey
the speed limit, and carpool once a week, Bush pushed for greater
supply. As far as global warming was concerned, which was the
main reason that conservation was becoming politically attractive,
the administration refused to acknowledge the problem existed.[20]

In August 2001 the House, under Republican control, passed a
comprehensive energy bill, which, with its massive tax breaks, was
roundly denounced as a giveaway to the energy industry. The bill
included $33.5 billion in energy tax breaks through 2011. The mea-
sure most certain to trigger fury was the opening of ANWR to
drilling. Support came not only from Republicans but also from
three dozen Democrats, who hoped that drilling would create
jobs.[21] The Teamsters ran radio ads saying that drilling in ANWR
would produce 750,000 jobs. With Bush's popularity high and
after spending time, along with Cheney, hosting town meetings to
drum up support, many moderate Republicans held ranks. "You
can't always cave in to the environmental wackos," explained Peter
King, a moderate Republican representative from New York. "I'm
not against conservation, but there's no reason why we can't walk
and chew gum at the same time." The bill passed, 240–189.[22]

The Bush energy plan met a different fate in the Senate, where
Democrats held a razor-slim majority that enabled them to take
the lead in drafting legislation. In December, Majority Leader Tom
Daschle (D-SD) introduced the Democratic response to the House
bill. Instead of drilling and exploration, the Senate bill stressed
conservation, efficiency, and the development of alternative energies.[23] Instantly, oil lobbyists put ads in South Dakota newspapers
with side-by-side pictures of Saddam Hussein and Daschle, suggesting that Daschle's blocking of drilling in ANWR helped keep
Hussein in power.[24] Daschle would ultimately lose his bid for reelection. But polls showed that a majority of Americans opposed
the president on energy and the environment. Few believed that

measures like $3.3 billion in tax credits for "clean-coal" technology was, as advertised by the White House, a conservation measure as opposed to a break for industry.[25] Here moderate Republicans played a key role, feeling vulnerable to public opinion. The one issue they backed away from was supporting drilling in the Arctic.[26]

After almost a year in office, Bush had made little progress on the Hill. In response to the terrorist attacks on September 11, 2001, Bush justified his energy bill on national security grounds. On October 11, Bush said Congress should pass the House version as an essential part of fighting the war on terrorism. "It's important for our national security to have a good energy policy."[27] Promoting his bill as a security measure, Bush told the public, "The less dependent we are on foreign sources of crude oil, the more secure we are at home."[28]

BUSH'S ENERGY TASK FORCE AND EXECUTIVE POWER

In 2001, while the administration was pushing its legislative agenda in Congress, the White House energy task force was working more quietly behind the scenes. By executive order, Bush created the National Energy Policy Development Group, which became known as the energy task force, on January 29, in his second week in office. The director was Andrew Lundquist, a Fairbanks, Alaska, native who had served as an aide to both senators from Alaska and staff director of the Senate Energy and Natural Resources Committee chaired by his former boss and long-time advocate of drilling in the Arctic, Senator Frank Murkowski. The other top staff member on the task force, Karen Knutson, also was an aide to Murkowski. Lundquist and Knutson nicknamed themselves the Alaska Jihad.[29]

No one did more to design the administration's energy policy than Vice President Cheney, who chaired the task force. He sought to avoid the failures of Hillary Clinton's health care task force. Not only had the Right criticized Clinton's plan as socialized medicine, conservatives had attacked the high-handed tactics Clinton used to design a major social reform out of public view. Cheney's task force operated with even more discipline and relied on a much smaller staff. Whereas Clinton's staff numbered around five hundred, Cheney's was under fifty.[30] Made up of several cabinet members, the policy development group felt less like an arena for each department to push its own agenda, and instead the task force maintained tight control over its operations.

Almost instantly there were challenges to the task force's secrecy. In April 2001, the National Resources Defense Council requested a list of interest groups the task force consulted. The Department of Energy denied the request, saying these documents were "pre-decisional" and thus not subject to public disclosure.[31] Pressure for openness also came from Democrats on the Hill. Henry A. Waxman (D-CA), a leading liberal voice on the environment, asked the Government Accountability Office (GAO), the audit and investigative arm of Congress, to get documents from the task force.

The White House made it clear it would fight. David Addington, Cheney's counsel, rejected the requests for disclosure. According to Addington, the vice president did not have to comply with the Federal Advisory Committee Act, which required public disclosure of information when advisory bodies included people from outside the government. Addington claimed that all staff members were government employees and thus the meetings were not subject to the law. In December the environmental group, joined by Judicial Watch, a conservative group committed to openness, sued in the U.S. District Court for the District of Columbia to force release. The GAO would take the matter to the courts as well.

"What's Cheney hiding?" journalist E. J. Dionne asked in the *Washington Post*. "It's hard to know why Cheney is so insistent on keeping his task force's deliberations out of public view. If we learned that the oil companies and other energy corporations played a large role in the formation of President Bush's energy policy, would a single American be shocked?"[32] It was common knowledge, for example, that Kenneth Lay, chairman of Enron, a massive *Fortune* 500 energy-trading company, was good friends with Bush and Cheney. He and two other Enron executives contributed $300,000 to the inauguration, and the company was one of the largest contributors to the campaign. The day after the inauguration, Lay attended a private luncheon at the new Bush White House.[33] It was widely reported that many cabinet members held stock in Enron and other oil companies.[34]

Did Big Oil have unique influence? Yes. That was the short answer. A year later, when reporters pieced together the records of the task force meetings, it became clear that oilmen had disproportionate access. Of the roughly four hundred groups that had asked for meetings with the task force, about half got appointments, and of those, 158 represented energy companies and trade associations. There were also representatives from twenty-two labor unions, thirteen environmental groups, and one consumer organization. Eighteen of the energy industry's top twenty-five financial contributors to the Republican Party met with the task force.

Did this influence buy support? Again, the short answer is yes. An oil lobbyist explained, "We give money to these people to have a business environment we want to work in. And the thing we're proposing is to have an increase in the domestic energy supply." But they did not have to work hard to make their case; the influence was more organic, with the industry and the task force having a similar approach and outlook. The chief lobbyist of the world's largest coal-mining company explained, "We're all on the supply side—the electric utilities, the coal companies—and the energy plan is basically a supply side plan, but that's not the result of back room deals or lobbying the vice president of the United States." He went on, "People running the United States government now are from the energy industry, and they understand it and believe in increasing the energy supply, and contribution money has nothing to do with it." If anything, industry representatives claimed that they had lobbied even harder during the Clinton years precisely because that administration was less friendly. "This is a natural alliance," said Eric Schaeffer, an EPA enforcer who would resign over nonenforcement of clean air laws. "The administration didn't need a lot of persuading."[35]

Covering up connections was not the point of Cheney's secrecy; instead, the vice president was protecting executive privilege. Given the strength of environmentalism on Capitol Hill, it was not easy to write energy policy anew. Cheney was aware that to make progress he would have to use other means, namely, enhancing executive powers. And that begins to explain why, in part, Cheney refused to release task force documents.

At stake in Cheney's insistence on task force secrecy was the power of the executive office. "These are vital matters dealing with constitutional prerogatives vested in the presidency," said White House press secretary Ari Fleisher. According to Fleisher, that was why Cheney would not release the list of people who attended task force meetings.[36] Cheney came to the Bush White House with a real vision of reclaiming executive privilege for the White House. The obvious reference point was the investigations of the Clinton years, but for Cheney this view of the White House losing power dated back to the Nixon era.[37] "There's a feeling of some in the current administration that they want to draw a line in a different spot than previously has been drawn in the separation of powers. As a result of Watergate and the challenges that Clinton had, Congress has been much more involved in a range of areas they don't believe are appropriate," said David M. Walker, the comptroller general from the GAO.[38] Walker understood the stakes. The vice president's "attorneys are engaged in a broad-based frontal attack on our statutory authority," Walker told the *Washington Post*. "We cannot let that stand."[39]

On May 17, 2001, the task force delivered its final report. The emphasis was on market-based approaches, such as cap-and-trade emissions programs, tax credits for fuel-efficient cars, and scaling back or eliminating regulations on exploration, coal burning, and the construction of pipelines and refineries. This was, as President Bush had charged them to craft, a national energy policy "designed to help the private sector."[40] Many of the recommendations called for regulatory changes and executive orders such as instructing federal agencies to expedite permits for new energy plants that did not require congressional action. Representative Edward Markey (D-MA), a longtime environmental advocate, denounced the Bush plan as a "Trojan horse to take health and environmental laws passed in the last generation off the books."[41]

The attack on 9/11 made Cheney even more committed to protecting executive privilege. The plan to enhance executive powers, including the right to secrecy and protection from public scrutiny, existed before 9/11. Before 9/11 Attorney General John Ashcroft had crafted a memo instructing agencies to resist Freedom of Information Act requests. "When you carefully consider FOIA requests and decide to withhold records . . . you can be assured that the Department of Justice will defend your decisions."[42] After 9/11 Cheney dug in his heels further and continued to block GAO requests to release task force records. He and his advisers were aware of a likely showdown over executive privilege on issues of defense and homeland security, particularly the right of the administration to detain and, if necessary, torture enemy combatants.

Only a commitment to principle over politics explains Cheney's steadfast defense of secrecy in the face of the Enron scandal that unfolded that same winter. In December 2001, Enron filed the largest corporate bankruptcy case in American history. The connections between Enron and the administration were clear. Enron got its start in 1985 as a gas pipeline company, but then became a multi-billion-dollar trader of gas, electricity, and other commodities. It had long lobbied for regulatory reform that would benefit its ability to trade energy futures. It was common knowledge that Kenneth Lay and other Enron executives had contributed more than half a million dollars to the Bush campaign. But now there was intense political pressure to flesh out exactly what, if anything, the administration had done to help Enron in its final months as it imploded under the pressure of a major accounting scandal. Accusations that Enron illegally manipulated California's energy markets during the electricity crisis put additional pressure on the administration. Still, Cheney insisted that releasing the task force records would infringe on the constitutional balance of power.[43]

Even as the GAO made it clear it was going to sue Cheney, the vice president stood strong. "There's a principle involved," explained Ari Fleisher. On ABC's *This Week*, Cheney said, "We are weaker today as an institution because of the unwise compromises that have been made over the last 30 to 35 years."[44] All the GAO was asking for, at this point, was a list of whom the task force had met with, not even the minutes of the meetings. It was already widely reported that Enron had met with the task force six times. Reporters had easily compiled an informal list of other industry executives to whom the task force had also granted access. But Cheney made it clear the administration would fight, even challenging the constitutionality of the GAO if necessary, to rebuff what one senior Bush aide described as "an unconstitutional infringement on the powers of the presidency."[45] As Cheney made this choice, the political hazards it created were clear. Both the oil industry and many Republicans on the Hill were eager to have Cheney comply with the release request in order to clear the air of any overt mishandling of the Enron case. "I understand philosophically why the vice president may be doing this, but this sure puts us in a pickle," said one oil industry executive.[46] But Cheney would not budge.

Many legal battles later, Cheney would prevail. In October 2002, U.S. district judge Emmet Sullivan ordered Cheney to turn over the list of people who had met with the task force.[47] But Cheney appealed that decision and won on jurisdictional grounds. At the same time, Judicial Watch, the conservative watchdog group, and the Sierra Club jointly filed suit in the U.S. Court of Appeals for the D.C. Circuit. When they got a favorable hearing, Cheney appealed, and the Supreme Court took up the case in 2004. The close connections between Supreme Court justice Antonin Scalia and the vice president, who had served together in the Ford administration when Scalia was an assistant attorney general, became a source of controversy after the two went on a duck-hunting trip together as the case was being considered.[48]

In the end, the vice president won, with the Supreme Court ruling that the White House's internal discussions could be protected from outside investigation. The Justice Department argued that there is a "zone of autonomy" in which the executive office can receive confidential advice. "Congress does not have the power to inhibit, confine or control the process through which the president formulates the legislative measures he proposes or the administrative actions he orders," argued Solicitor General Theodore Olsen. To which Thomas Fitton, president of Judicial Watch, responded, "It is an extraordinary assertion of the executive power and privilege."[49]

REWRITING THE RULES

So what would the administration do with its executive power? The Reagan era as well as the Gingrich years showed the difficulty of scaling back existing policies and programs, especially when they were popular. While Bush's energy package was stalled in Congress, the energy task force pursued real change, especially in environmental rules, through bureaucratic measures and regulatory reform. In the most basic way, the White House sought to hamper the EPA by cutting its staff by two hundred. In addition, out of sight of much of the public, the task force began rewriting regulations governing coal plants. It was clear to interested parties that the task force sought to undo environmental regulations that were adverse to coal-burning utilities in the South and Midwest, where a number of large utility companies were facing lawsuits by the EPA. Eric Schaeffer, who directed EPA's office of regulatory enforcement, and who would quit in dismay, complained he was "fighting a White House that seems determined to weaken the rules we are trying to enforce."[50]

The central battle played out over a technical program called New Source Review (NSR), which required factories to install modern pollution controls when they upgraded their plants. When the Clean Air Act had originally passed in 1970, the bill allowed existing coal-fired plants and refineries to delay adoption of pollution controls because of the substantial cost involved. At the time, lawmakers assumed that companies would build new plants that were, under the new rules, more environmentally friendly and that older, dirtier plants would simply shut down. As it turned out, many companies opted to repair and expand existing plants rather than invest in new plants, and thus were not subject to the provisions of the Clean Air Act. In 1977, as a way of making sure that older plants complied with the law, Congress added a new-source review regulation to require adoption of pollution controls anytime a plant expanded its operations.

When Bush came into office, the EPA had a number of billion-dollar lawsuits pending. Throughout the Reagan years, the EPA did not investigate compliance with the NSR program. After lying dormant, the rule gained attention from state attorneys general, especially New York's Elliot Spitzer, who began to sue companies for upgrading their facilities without putting in pollution controls. In 1999 the Clinton administration initiated several major cases once EPA officials discovered rampant noncompliance. The result was a serious public health problem. According to the EPA, there were at least twenty thousand premature deaths because of air pollution, generated largely by factories that did not comply with EPA standards. Under Clinton, the EPA cited fifty-one power plants for NSR violations, with more than half owned by three large utility companies. At stake were tens of billions of dollars to bring plants into compliance, not to mention to substantial settlements.

The Bush administration had intimate ties with many of the companies under investigation. Southern Company, the second biggest utility operator and one of the three large companies cited for violations, was a major contributor to Bush's campaign, aware that his victory would increase the chances of EPA dropping its lawsuit. Their chief lobbyist was Haley Barbour, former chairman of the Republican National Committee. Thomas Kuhn, president of Edison Electric Institute, the major trade association for utilities, had gone to college with Bush and was a major fundraiser for his campaign.[51] Kuhn encouraged associates in the energy industry to bundle their contributions to "ensure that our industry is credited" for what it gave.[52] Beyond these connections, Bush had campaigned on promises to boost coal production and won three swing states, Kentucky, Tennessee, and West Virginia, which were also major coal-producing states.

As soon as Bush had established the energy task force in January 2001, the utility companies took their case to the vice president. On March 21, 2001, a Southern lobbyist e-mailed Joseph Kelliher, a political appointee in the Department of Energy, that NSR was a top priority. (Days earlier Kelliher had e-mailed many energy lobbyists asking them, "If you were King or Il Duce, what would you include in a national energy policy?")[53] The NSR rules, the lobbyist for Southern explained, threatened the nation's energy supply, and a more lax interpretation should be an essential part of the Bush energy plan. According to a story in the *New York Times*, the task force added NSR to its agenda a week later. "There was a real flurry of activity after the Southern Company e-mail to put N.S.R. on the energy policy agenda," reported one of the task force participants. "And it didn't go away." At the same time, Southern's Haley Barbour lobbied Cheney directly.[54]

In May 2001, the task force ordered a ninety-day interagency review of NSR. That move was understood by all sides as the beginnings of an effort to relax the rules, a major priority for the energy industry. The pending legal cases ground to a halt, and the Bush administration did not initiate a single new case. Christie Todd Whitman, the EPA administrator, engaged in a losing battle against Cheney. In private, she wrote to Cheney, "We will pay a terrible political price if we decide to walk away from the enforcement cases; it will be hard to refute the charge that we are deciding not to enforce the Clean Air Act."[55] After a protracted bureaucratic struggle with EPA, the administration began to announce its new policy in March 2002. Environmental groups denounced the move. "Enforcement is not a lobbying process," complained John Walke of the National Resources Defense Council. "Once that law is firm, we expect it be enforced according to the letter."[56] The administration had different plans.

The EPA's Whitman strained to fall in line. She was not nearly as committed as Cheney; as governor of New Jersey she had sued one of the biggest utility companies to clean up its coal-fired plants, and, in an odd way, that had helped her to win her appointment. The lesson from the Reagan years was to not appoint someone as outspoken and as identified with the New Right as James Watt. Instead, the Bush White House focused on second-tier appointments, people who had served in industry and therefore knew what rules to undo. The key person on NSR was Jeffrey Holmstead, an electric utility lobbyist, whom Bush appointed assistant EPA administrator for air and radiation.[57] The report that EPA issued on NSR in June 2002 reflected the tensions and competing pressures on the agency. The report acknowledged that NSR might impede current plants from expanding or updating, which is what the task force and the industry contended, and therefore could be blamed for slowing the growth of the domestic supply of fuel. But, the report concluded, "there is little evidence that these delays and costs are preventing new source construction."[58]

Whitman's days were numbered. Feeling increasingly beleaguered, she issued a hollow statement that "enforcement is still a critical part of what we do." The energy industry executives "need to understand that we are not backing away from that." But these clearly defensive statements belied what insiders knew was already in the works.[59] Senator James Jeffords, who had broken with Republicans the previous summer, said, "Why anyone would pick smog and soot over clean air is beyond comprehension." As chairman of the Environment and Public Works Committee, he promised to subpoena the records of the EPA to see how the decision to back away from NSR was being made.[60]

On this issue, industry scored a major victory. The official change to the rules came in November 2003. As energy legislation continued to stall, EPA was rewriting the NSR rules out of the public's eye. Unwilling to go along, Whitman had resigned. Under the new rules, only renovations that exceeded 20 percent of the value of the existing plant would require a company to install pollution controls. That was a radical departure, one that effectively killed NSR. In preparation for this shift in policy, Jeffrey Holmstead had asked the career EPA staff what percentage the renovations should be of the total value of each generator, and the response was 0.75 percent. That meant that if a generating unit was worth a billion dollars, a power company could spend $7.5 million on modifications without having to put in pollution controls. Any investment beyond $7.5 million would be considered an addition of a new source, and therefore the rules would require the plant to install pollution controls. Twenty percent, the amount that Holmstead came up with for the new NSR rules, obviously vastly exceeded this allowance. According to experts, that figure was so high that requirements for new pollution controls would virtually never come into effect. A career EPA enforcement lawyer said, "I don't know of anything like this in 30 years."[61]

BACK TO THE HILL

The administration knew that this was a shaky victory, at best, subject to challenge in the courts. The only way to secure a permanent victory would be to get new legislation on the Hill. But there the task force's recommendations met with less success. In February 2002, Bush introduced his Clear Skies initiative to Congress, calling for a two-thirds reduction in most power plant emissions by 2018. The president intended this measure to replace the Clean Air Act, including the NSR provisions. Instead of the current plant-by-plant standards under the Clean Air Act, Clear Skies would set a national pollution cap, and companies could trade their excess pollution with other companies that polluted less. Although it appeared tough and allowed Bush to say he had an environmentally friendly initiative in advance of the 2002 midterm elections, in fact, Clear Skies was a retreat, because the overall cap was less than what the Clean Air Act was already mandating. The measure went nowhere.

In 2003, with both chambers again in Republican control, Republican leaders pressed for enactment of the Bush plan, including Clear Skies as well as other producer-friendly initiatives. Bush sold his pro-industry proposals, which consisted largely of tax benefits and subsidies to the oil, gas, and coal industries, as part of a larger antigovernment agenda. "Today we have a chance to move beyond the environmental debates of the past, debates that centered around regulation and lawsuit—what I like to call the command-and-control era of environmental policy, where all that wisdom that seemed to emanate of Washington, D.C., where things got hamstrung and stuck because lawyers got more involved in the process than people on the frontlines of actually improving our environment."[62] Instead of regulations, Bush suggested, the government had to give tax breaks to industry as a way to spur innovation and production. Though Americans continued to be more pro-environment than Bush, the president's popularity remained high. Since the Reagan era, this kind of antigovernment rhetoric had played well among conservative and even moderate voters.

The main controversy over the Bush agenda continued to be drilling in Alaska. Bill Richardson, governor of New Mexico and energy secretary under Clinton, explained, "ANWR is the Holy Grail for Democrats because of the environmental ties to the party, and ANWR then became the Holy Grail for the oil and gas Republican stalwarts."[63] In August 2003, a massive blackout that put fifty million Americans and Canadians in the dark gave some momentum to energy reform. There was broad agreement on the need for tax incentives for energy production and conservation, research for cleaner-burning coal, pipeline safety, and funds for fuel assistance for low-income people. But the Republican-designed energy bill failed to pass in Congress, Bush's Clear Skies initiative died, and there was no agreement on ANWR. [64]

After the 2004 elections, which increased the Republican majorities on the Hill slightly, the administration made another push for legislation. This time the context was rising fuel prices. The price of crude oil had doubled in two years, and continued upward, as a result of growing world demand. The other major factor, of course, was the war in Iraq. Unlike the First Gulf War, the Bush administration justified this war as an effort to fight terrorism and spread democracy in the Middle East. While U.S. forces quickly brought down Saddam Hussein's regime, establishing peace and stability proved elusive. In light of this instability, the administration expressed concern over dependence on Middle Eastern oil. "Our dependence on foreign oil is like a foreign tax on the American Dream," said Bush in a handful of energy addresses in 2005.[65]

On August 8, 2005, President Bush finally signed a comprehensive energy bill into law. The heart of the Energy Policy Act consisted of tax incentives to boost production of traditional fossil fuels. Critics denounced the measure as a massive giveaway to oil, gas, and coal producers at a time when prices were already high. As much as this measure constituted a clear victory for Bush's energy policy, there were limits to what the Republicans could gain. The leadership failed again on ANWR. And they also had to remove a controversial provision to protect manufacturers of a gasoline fuel additive called MTBE from product liability suits. MTBE was supposed to make fuel cleaner, but, as it turned out, this chemical contaminated groundwater. Lawmakers from the Gulf Coast, where MBTE is made, insisted on a liability waiver to protect producers. But lawmakers from the Northeast, fearful their states would get stuck paying the expensive clean-up costs, threatened to filibuster any bill with this waiver, so the administration had to let it go. The Republican leadership also had to compromise on renewable energies. To secure enough votes to pass the bill, Senate and House leaders had to cut a deal on ethanol production, which is made from corn. By mandating ethanol production as a way to lower carbon emissions of gasoline, the energy bill won support from Senate Minority Leader Tom Daschle (D-SD) and other lawmakers from Midwestern corn-growing regions. Overall, in spite of modest conservation measures, the measure was seen as a boon to the energy industry.

The energy industry continued to fare well, even as it came under public scrutiny for its record high profits. Soon after Bush signed the energy bill, Hurricane Katrina ripped through the Gulf Coast, shutting down refineries and leading to a spike in gas prices. In the months that followed, congressmen from both parties took oil executives to task for earning huge profits, even calling them to Washington for a hearing. The scene was reminiscent of one that played out during the Arab oil embargo, when, in January 1974, with oil company profits up 45 percent, leading Democrats subpoenaed the executives from the seven largest American oil companies to appear before them in Washington. In both hearings, Washington politicians accused the executives of reaping "obscene profits." But those superficial similarities only underscored the very real political differences. In 2005, there was no serious discussion of windfall profits taxes, price controls, rollbacks at the pump, and divestiture. Instead, as Representative Edward Markey (D-MA) explained, he and his liberal allies were too busy fighting to reduce oil subsidies. Indeed, the Bush administration used the Katrina crisis to push its agenda once again. Explaining the need to boost production, the White House tried to write into law changes to new source review, given that attorneys general who wanted to still sue power companies for noncompliance were contesting EPA's 2003 NSR change in courts. The White House also sought to get an oil refineries bill passed, which would have given additional tax breaks at a time when the industry was posting record profits. They failed on both counts, but their efforts confirmed Markey's point about liberals rebuffing conservative efforts rather than going on attack.[66]

HOW LASTING?

While the first six years of the Bush presidency yielded much success on energy policy, the last two years proved that a change in political fortune could reverse those gains. Bureaucratic warfare resulted in nonenforcement of rules already on the books. But a permanent victory required new laws. Beginning in 2006, especially with the midterm elections, the Bush energy agenda started to look less durable. The Republican Party under Bush had consolidated its power in the South and Southwest, where much of the energy interests were concentrated. But coastal liberals, who continued to support environmentalism, rivaled the power of the GOP. In addition, the courts also upheld much of the environmental legislation of the 1970s. Therefore, without a decisive victory on the Hill, the effort to implement a regulatory rollback would remain incomplete.

In March 2006, a federal appeals court overturned the NSR regulation by the Bush EPA. The court ruled that the new interpretation of the NSR amounted to an evasion of the Clean Air Act's intentions. In an editorial, the *New York Times* remarked, "it is nice to hear someone say that you cannot rewrite an act of Congress just because you do not like it."[67] A year later the Supreme Court dealt the administration an even greater blow by ruling that the EPA had the authority to regulate emissions of greenhouse gases. In effect, that ruling gave momentum to the environmentalists' claim that the EPA had to consider auto emissions under its purview, an extension of its authority that the Bush White House did not want. By the time the Court issued its decision, the White House was already losing the battle over auto emissions on Capitol Hill.

After the 2006 elections, the Bush agenda stalled in the fight over fuel economy standards. To oppose higher standards, the White House had counted on an alliance of business-oriented Republicans and blue-collar Midwestern Democrats in auto-producing states. Senate Minority Leader Trent Lott (R-MS) denounced efforts to boost standards as an attack on consumer choice, criticizing tighter regulations as part of a "nanny state." "This is still America," said Lott. "We should be able to make our own choices. We shouldn't have the federal government saying you're going to drive the purple people eater here," pointing to a purple European mini-car. Right-wing organizers sought to link business interests with social conservatives around issues like CAFE standards. Grover Norquist, head of Americans for Tax Reform and a leading conservative organizer, reached out to Phyllis Schlafly's Eagle Forum, saying that higher fuel efficiency would endanger the minivan, the iconic family vehicle.[68] "I don't want to tell a mom in my home state that she should not get an SUV because Congress decided it would be a bad choice," said Representative Chris Bond (R-MO).

This alliance could not counter the growing appeal of environmentalism. Al Gore's *An Inconvenient Truth* raised awareness about global warming. Representative John Dingell (D-MI), who had protected Detroit's interests for decades, recognized that the industry would have to make some concessions on fuel economy. As it became clear that reform was gaining momentum, Bond proposed a desperate measure to transfer authority over CAFE standards out of Congress and back to the Department of Transportation, where he and his allies hoped for a more favorable policy.[69]

In the end, the White House lost. On June 22, 2007, with a gallon of gas over the $3 mark, a bill to raise the fuel economy standards on cars, light trucks, and SUVs by ten miles per gallon by 2020 won bipartisan support, passing the Senate 65–27.[70] The final measure, the Energy Independence and Security Act, passed the House in December, 314–100. Along with an increase in fuel efficiency, the measure included mandates for renewable fuels and a fivefold increase in ethanol production.[71]

As historic as it was, the passage of the bill was not the complete story. The Bush team had honed its bureaucratic battle plan, where the main fight was taking place. It turned out that the real threat to the auto industry came not from the Energy Act but from the state of California. On the same day that President Bush signed the bill, the EPA made an unprecedented announcement. For the first time, it would deny California's request for a federal waiver to set its own emissions standards. Under the Clean Air Act, states were allowed to set their own clean air standards if they received a federal waiver. California had routinely applied for Clean Air Act waivers to set its tougher standards, and the EPA had always granted them. This time was different. In light of the Supreme Court's ruling that EPA could regulate tailpipe emissions, California, joined by sixteen other states, was appealing to the Bush administration to allow it to set rigorous carbon dioxide emission standards. California's standards would have required automakers to cut greenhouse gas emissions by 30 percent in new cars and light trucks. That reduction would in turn require automakers to improve fuel economy at a rate that was in fact double what was required in the energy bill Bush had signed earlier in the day, and in a shorter time frame. Together, these seventeen states accounted for at least half of all vehicles sold in the United States. By signing the Energy Act and rejecting the California waiver on the same day, the Bush administration was choosing the lesser of two evils. The effect of that decision was devastating for environmentalists and an enormous victory for the auto industry.

Instantly, environmentally friendly Democrats said they had been had. The administration justified its actions by saying it wanted one national solution rather than a "patchwork." But few were fooled. Senator Dianne Feinstein (D-CA) denounced the EPA decision. "I find this disgraceful. The passage of the energy bill does not give the EPA a green light to shirk its responsibility to protect the health and safety of the American people from air pollution." The charge was that the auto industry had, in the end, supported the energy bill because the administration had given assurances that it would decide against the waiver request. Senator Carl Levin, a Michigan Democrat who had made a career protecting the auto industry, said on the floor that he would vote for the bill only if he was certain that EPA would not "undercut" it with tougher standards. An auto company official revealed that the California waiver was "one of our worry beads." The *New York Times* editorial page did not mince words: "The Bush administration's decision to deny California permission to regulate and reduce global warming emissions from cars and trucks is an indefensible act of executive arrogance that can only be explained as the product of ideological blindness and as a political payoff to the automobile industry."[72]

The final fate of the Bush bureaucratic battles would be determined by the 2008 election. As oil prices soared to new highs in 2008, it looked as though energy would be a winning issue for the Republicans. When it came to energy policy, the majority of Americans were placing pocketbook issues ahead of, or at least on par with, environmental concerns. In 1990, a Gallup poll found that Americans preferred to protect the environment over economic growth by a margin of 71 percent to 19 percent. In 2007, with energy prices at a historic peak, that spread shrank to 49 percent over 42 percent.[73] As prices at the pump went up to $4 a gallon, the White House saw its last chance to advance its agenda. Laying blame on the Democratic Congress's unwillingness to open up areas for drilling, the GOP leadership denounced what they called "Pelosi premium." Speaker of the House Nancy Pelosi, a committed environmentalist, refused to bend to pressure for more drilling and instead called for new taxes on oil companies reaping record profits to pay for alternative energy development. The sides of the debate, with Democrats pushing for conservation and Republicans pushing for more production, remained the same.

On July 14, in the middle of the 2008 election season, President Bush lifted the executive ban on offshore drilling, putting pressure on the Democratic Congress to do the same. House Republicans pushed again for opening up ANWR. Republican candidate Senator John McCain, who had long been a supporter of environmental causes, supported the move for more drilling. Though he opposed opening up ANWR, his choice of Alaska governor Sarah Palin, who instantly became associated with the slogan "Drill, Baby, Drill," cemented the idea that the Republicans wanted to do something about high gas prices while the Democrats stood in their way. Aware that the public overwhelmingly favored lifting the Congressional ban on offshore drilling, Pelosi agreed to a compromise.[74]

The election of Barack Obama and the Democrats in 2008 put the Bush energy accomplishments in jeopardy. When Pelosi agreed to compromise on drilling, she was hopeful, as were her Democratic allies, that a win in the White House would lead to a reinstatement of the drilling ban. Representative Henry Waxman, a longtime environmental advocate, challenged Representative John Dingell for his position as chairman of the House Energy and Commerce Committee, signaling a renewed Democratic Party commitment on emissions regulation and fuel efficiency. In one of his first presidential directives, President Obama ordered the EPA to reconsider California's appeal for a waiver. Approval meant the state, along with sixteen others, could begin regulating tailpipe emissions. In addition, Obama's inclusion of clean energy investments in his economic stimulus package signaled a switch from

Bush's focus on production and drilling to a Democratic emphasis on regulation and conservation.

The Bush energy agenda had deep roots. Since the Arab oil embargo there have been two conservative strategies for achieving energy independence. The first consisted of putting troops in the Persian Gulf to protect American oil interests. On that front, conservatives largely succeeded. The second consisted of scaling back environmental and energy regulations, and here the story was mixed. The most heavy-handed New Deal-style government measures of the 1970s, from price controls to divestiture to windfall profits taxes, were off the table. And there were some real successes, such as the 2005 Energy Policy Act. In addition, the energy task force, under Dick Cheney, successfully enhanced executive power, going around the legislative process and using bureaucratic strategies to score additional victories, as was clear with the 2003 NSR rule and the 2007 EPA decision. But the Bush energy plan did not realize all its goals. Given the strength of environmentalism, the administration was not able to open up the Arctic to drilling, nor was it able to thwart the momentum for congressionally mandated conservation.

Understanding the Bush energy policy is not as simple as saying that this was an administration run by two oilmen, though that certainly matters. Nor can the administration's policies be explained as a crude payback to political backers, though again, energy industry contributions were not insignificant. Conservatives came into power with long-held convictions since the Ford administration days about America's energy policy. Although their ideology pointed in the direction of smaller government, they were unable to dismantle the state and instead had to craft strategies of conservative governance. Since the 1970s, conservatives have been learning how to wreak havoc from within. This was a story about how conservatives tried to reshape America from the centers of power, at times succeeding, but also failing.

8

IDEOLOGY AND INTEREST ON THE SOCIAL POLICY HOME FRONT

Nelson Lichtenstein

IDEOLOGY AND INTEREST STRUCTURED THE DOMESTIC SOCIAL policy over which George W. Bush presided during his two-term administration. The former represented a remarkably consistent, neoliberal impulse hostile to most of the institutions of economic regulation first installed by the Progressives and the New Dealers decades before. The latter is more complex, reflecting both the rise of a new set of business enterprises that have become influential in the policy debates of early twenty-first-century America and the continuing weight of those institutions and demographic strata that have retained a social democratic outlook in U.S. politics. Indeed, the social policies advanced by the Bush administration often accommodated those corporations emblematic of the increasingly powerful retail sector of the economy, but they never commanded true majority support, which accounts for the dramatic collapse of its political potency after the Hurricane Katrina debacle so graphically encapsulated all that seemed inadequate in the Bush policy agenda.

George Bush became president at a moment of capitalist transformation that privileged the market power, political influence, and labor standards generated by the giant retailers of our time and their cousins in the restaurant, food-processing, and hospitality sectors of the economy. Indeed, our era is one of retail supremacy, in contrast to the century-plus era, extending from 1860 to 1980, when manufacturing stood atop the commanding heights of the U.S. political economy. Today the firms that import, distribute, and sell goods and services are politically and economically most potent. In this world, the old relationship between increasing productivity and wage growth has been severed. Instead, and until very recently, wage stagnation within the working class was ameliorated by cheap imports, easy credit, an overpriced dollar, and an array of new financial products that widened the range of assets (mainly houses) that both homeowners and bankers could borrow against.

The Bureau of Labor Statistics reports there are now almost five times as many service sector jobs as those in mining, agriculture, manufacturing, and construction, the "goods-producing" industries that once constituted the core of the U.S. economy. Today the retail trade alone employs some 15.5 million workers, about the same as in all manufacturing, which lost an astounding three million workers during the first term of George W. Bush. Likewise, "accommodation and food services," another low-wage, high-turnover employment sector, gained a million and a half workers during the administration of George Bush, so that some 11.5 million are now employed in U.S. hotels and restaurants.[1]

Much has been made of the Bush administration's close ties to the oil and gas sector and its solicitude toward the fortunes of the Texas entrepreneurs who made and lost fortunes searching for energy at home and abroad. The influence of Enron, Halliburton, and the various oilmen that have partnered with every member of the extended Bush family has not been hard to discern inside and outside the Washington corridors of power. When considering the Bush administration's effort to weaken environmental regulations, loosen antitrust laws, push through Congress the huge tax reduction bills of 2001 and 2003, and wage war in the Middle East, it would be foolish to discount the influence of the rich and influential domestic energy industry.[2]

But when it comes to trade, labor, health care, and retirement policies the Bush administration has been even more aligned with the interests of a U.S. industry whose most prominent firm topped the *Fortune* 500 list of large corporations during six of the eight years when George Bush was president. Wal-Mart, a southern, thoroughly Republican firm, employed more than a million workers, operated in almost every county in the nation, and enjoyed sales of more than $400 billion in 2007. Like other retailers and branded merchants—Home Depot, Disney, Nike—Wal-Mart stands at the top of a global supply chain that has thoroughly subordinated tens of thousands of manufacturing "vendors" to the interests of these market-shaping, labor-intensive enterprises. Reflecting the shifting contours of power at the very apex of U.S. capitalism, Wal-Mart supplanted General Motors as the largest U.S. firm in 2002, only to be replaced by Exxon Mobile in 2006, when surging oil prices handed the energy companies an unexpected and unearned bonanza. For a time, the nation's largest oil companies made a lot of money and earned gigantic profits, but when it came to social policy, their impact was more akin to that of a burdensome but distant taxing agency than an institution whose payroll was the largest in the nation save that of the federal government itself. Indeed, Wal-Mart employed more than fifteen times the number of people who worked for Exxon Mobile. There are a lot of oil wells in Texas, but also more than four hundred huge Wal-Mart stores, with sales of $50 billion in that state alone.[3]

Bush-era Republicans saw the world in much the same way as did top executives in the retail sector. Both were free trade militants who had little stake in the continuing viability of an American manufacturing base. As employers of many low-wage workers, most retailers favored the lightest possible regulatory hand, especially when it came to welfare-state mandates such as those covering employee health insurance, retirement pay, and health and safety issues. Of course, an intense hostility to trade unionism characterized both the big discounters and their like-minded friends in the Bush administration. There was a cultural affinity as well. Unlike the urban, Jewish milieu out of which many old-line department stores arose, the discount retailers came out of the South or Midwest, sited their big box stores in suburban or exurban areas, and often aligned themselves with an evangelical Protestant ethos. Vice President Dick Cheney recognized these affinities when he told headquarters staff on a visit to Bentonville, "The story of Wal-Mart exemplifies some of the very best qualities in our country—hard work, the spirit of enterprise, fair dealing, and integrity."[4]

BUSH GETS DOWN TO BUSINESS

President George Bush's domestic policy statecraft reflected this political alignment. As an anti-union conservative, Bush was just as willing as Ronald Reagan to challenge the beleaguered trade union movement when the occasion presented itself. Thus, in 2001 he deployed long-standing but rarely used presidential authority to forbid strikes by airline mechanics at Northwest and United Airlines, thereby undercutting union negotiating leverage.[5] The next year he ordered thousands of "locked out" West Coast longshoremen and women back to work for eighty days in an effort, coordinated with key big box shippers and maritime firms, to forestall an economically damaging strike that might have allowed the still powerful International Longshore and Warehouse Union to expand its jurisdiction.[6] But such interventions in traditional labor-management conflicts were rare during the Bush years, if only because large strikes, or their threat, had virtually disappeared in the twenty-first-century United States.

The Bush administration's control of the regulatory apparatus proved of far greater import. In setting policy and staffing these agencies and departments, Bush and his Texas coterie relied not only on business personnel and industry association operatives but also on the many right-wing think tanks, advocacy groups, and foundations that had flourished since the late 1970s. Edwin Feulner of the Heritage Foundation, which passed on more than a thousand names and résumés to the Bush transition team, thought the new crowd "more Reaganite than the Reagan Administration." Likewise Grover Norquist, president of the highly influential Americans for Tax Reform, asserted, "There isn't an us and them with this administration. They is us. We is them." In a March 2001 *New York Times* interview, Norquist outlined his strategy. "Part of what we're doing is bring K Street and the business community in," he said, "They should be an integral part of the center-right coalition. What does the business community want? Deregulation. Free trade. Tax cuts."[7]

Staffing at the Department of Labor proved one arena in which Bush demonstrated his ideological and business commitments. Republican presidents had often installed moderate politicians from their own party or businessmen familiar with a unionized workforce at this post. But George Bush broke with this genteel pattern. He first attempted to make the neoconservative cultural warrior Linda Chavez secretary of labor. She was a leading opponent of both affirmative action and bilingual education, a vocal critic of the trade union alliance with the Democrats, and a Zionist hawk on Middle Eastern affairs. She would soon publish *Betrayal: How Union Bosses Shake Down Their Members and Corrupt American Politics*. But the Chavez nomination collapsed when it appeared she had failed to pay the legally required Social Security taxes on her undocumented Guatemalan housekeeper.[8]

She was replaced by Elaine Chao, who, from a Bush administrative perspective, was actually a far better choice for labor secretary than Chavez, a polarizing figure still fighting the cultural battles that began in 1968. Chao, who remained secretary of labor longer than anyone else in U.S. history except FDR's Frances Perkins, was deeply engaged in the deregulatory, free trade politics that constituted the core of the new administration's economic and social agenda.[9] Chao was the eldest daughter in a Twainese shipping family with increasingly close ties to China. At the Heritage Foundation, where she worked in the 1990s, she helped make that conservative, anticommunist institution amenable to an open trading relationship with a country that anchored the trans-Pacific supply chains feeding America's big box merchants. Chao's influence, at both Heritage and in the Frances Perkins building, was enhanced by her 1993 marriage to Kentucky Republican senator Mitch McConnell, who rose to GOP leadership posts after Bush became president. McConnell's support for China's membership in the World Trade Organization did much to persuade conservatives to put no qualifications on an open trading relationship with an authoritarian country many now considered the new "workshop of the world."[10]

With Elaine Chao installed at Labor, it did not take long for the Bush administration to transform political ideology into policy. As trade unionism waned throughout the North Atlantic, the development and enforcement of what the Progressives first called "labor standards" became the key battleground in the low-intensity class warfare found everywhere throughout the American workplace. Therefore, the first thing Bush and Chao did was nothing. In the Labor Department's Wage and Hour Division, enforcement hours declined by 13 percent in the six years after 2002, and the number of cases concluded declined by nearly 23 percent. The division even boasted that registered complaints had dropped by almost 20 percent, reflecting an agency effort to "screen incoming calls and correspondence to ensure that the issue raised is properly within WHD's enforcement jurisdiction."[11]

Nor did Chao and Bush put forward a viable proposal for an increase in the minimum wage, which was then sinking to an all-time low in terms of its real purchasing power. The president said he would support a minimum wage boost, but only if it were marbled with plenty of tax breaks for business and if it included a provision allowing any state to opt out should it choose. This was tantamount to an abolition of the minimum wage itself, especially since many northern and western states had their own higher minimum wages, permitted under a law the Clinton Democrats had pushed through Congress in 1993. The federal minimum wage would not rise until the Democrats once again took control of Congress in 2007.[12]

DEREGULATING THE WORKPLACE

Another place where a social policy vacuum had an enormous impact came in those jobs where the lifting, shifting, keyboarding, and scanning of millions of products and billions of pages had reconfigured the dangers and difficulties faced by tens of millions of workers in their white-, pink-, or gray-collar jobs. While the traumatic, dramatic injuries characteristic of the industrial age still take place, soft-tissue musculoskeletal injuries, most notably carpel tunnel syndrome, have become the characteristic maladies of the information age. The Department of Labor reports that each year 1.8 million American workers are disabled by injuries caused by physical stress on the job.

To protect workers subject to these chronic, progressive injuries, ergonomics, the shop floor science that aims to make heavy or repetitive work less destructive to workers' bodies, had become a subject of much investigation, debate, rule-making, and adjudication over the previous two decades. By 2000 it had taken twelve years for a moderately useful set of ergonomics regulations to make its way through the federal bureaucracy. These standards, put into effect through a Clinton executive order in December of that year, represented a hard-fought compromise between the AFL-CIO and business groups. Northern Republican senators Arlen Specter of Pennsylvania and Lincoln Chaffee of Rhode Island offered their support.[13]

But for economic conservatives, the repeal of these Clinton-era regulations became a cause célèbre. "No issue was as important to Bush in establishing his bona fides among K Street lobbyists who had backed his campaign," observed journalist John Judis in the early months of the new administration.[14] The National Retail Federation, Wal-Mart at the fore, offered monetary and moral support, as did the National Association of Manufacturers. And no lobbyist was more active in seeking the overturn of the Clinton ergonomics order than Eugene Scalia, the thirty-seven-year-old son of the Supreme Court justice. He was a smart, energetic, corporate labor lawyer who had devoted almost his entire career to an assault on any and all policies and politicians that might advance an ergonomics standard of the sort advocated by the unions, the occupational health and safety experts, and the Democratic Party. Scalia thought ergonomics a "junk science." He called the standards based on such medical-occupational studies just a new form of featherbedding. The whole effort, he wrote in the *Wall*

Street Journal, was "a major concession to union leaders, who know that ergonomic regulation will force companies to give more rest periods, slow the pace of work, and then hire more workers (read: dues-paying members)."[15]

Republicans did not quite have the votes to actually overthrow the Clinton rule, so President Bush's April 2001 nomination of Eugene Scalia to the number three spot in the Department of Labor proved an early, sensational instance demonstrating the efficacy of the conservative claim that personnel is policy. As solicitor general, Scalia would be in charge of five hundred attorneys across the nation responsible for enforcing 180 federal laws covering everything from workplace safety to child labor, not to mention the "voluntary guidelines" on ergonomics that the Labor Department promised to announce. Since the Democrats, who then controlled the Senate, felt betrayed by the Scalia nomination, they held off a vote on his nomination and promised a real battle when and if it finally took place.

But no matter. President Bush installed Scalia as solicitor general through a recess appointment in August 2001. Scalia remained in the position for eighteen months, never got an actual confirmation vote, and then returned to his K Street law firm, where he happily represented a series of big corporations seeking to eviscerate even more of the tattered regulatory regime that still cloaked millions of U.S. workers. Among his key clients was Wal-Mart, which Scalia successfully represented when the Retail Industry Leaders Association, a Wal-Mart-dominated trade group, blocked Maryland's effort to force the big discounter to contribute at least 8 percent of its payroll to cover the health care costs of its employees in that state. Meanwhile, Scalia's replacement at Labor, the lower-profile Howard M. Radzely, continued the deregulatory work he had begun. In one controversial instance, Radzely agreed to a Wal-Mart request that the Labor Department give the company an unusually generous fifteen days' notice before investigating any stores facing complaints that managers had violated child labor laws.[16]

The Scalia nomination was characteristic of Bush's approach to the nation's labor standards regime: put an ideological fox in the regulatory henhouse, and then watch the fireworks explode. Even if the appointment is unsuccessful, the tenor of the debate will have been changed. In any event, the seemingly more amenable successors will continue the work, if at a somewhat lower level of public visibility and debate.

Thus, for example, the absence of Scalia did nothing to stop the Labor Department from seeking a radical change in the overtime laws that would "update" them to accord with the requirements of an economy where service sector workers were the predominant employees. Overtime pay was a hypersensitive issue both in the retail and hotel sector of the economy and for many firms in the financial and insurance world, where the ranks of "supervisors" and "professionals" had ballooned far beyond the imagination of any New Deal rule maker. By the end of the twentieth century, between 19 and 26 million full-time workers were classified as executive, administrative, and professional personnel, almost half of them women, which may give the reader a hint that most of these jobs were neither high-paying nor genuinely managerial or professional in their actual duties. However, such workers were "exempt" from the overtime pay standards of the Fair Labor Standards Act.[17] Wal-Mart, for example, employed upward of 30,000 assistant managers in its 4,000 stores. They were salaried employees earning about $40,000 a year. None got overtime, so the company worked them mercilessly, with weeks of sixty and eighty hours not uncommon.[18]

Naturally, there was a proliferation of lawsuits. The Heritage Foundation found that in 2001, there were more suits filed about overtime pay than suits alleging discrimination in the workplace.[19] In California, auto insurance adjusters and employees of Radio Shack and Starbucks won multi-million-dollar claims for improper classification and denial of overtime pay. "Non-exempt" workers won large settlements from Wal-Mart because the firm either refused to pay overtime compensation or forced thousands of employees to work "off the clock" before they could leave the store. "This is an extremely significant issue for employers," asserted a lawyer for Jackson Lewis, one of the most militant of the management-side labor law firms." There is so much activity in this area because the litigation lends itself to class-action lawsuits with large damage awards."[20]

Tammy McCutchen agreed. She was the Chicago management-side labor lawyer and former Federalist Society activist who now headed up the Labor Department's Wage and Hour Division. Conservatives had long complained that the department's overtime regulations had not been revised since Elvis was an exciting new act. Labor and the liberals were pleased when McCutchen raised the wage ceiling, below which all workers were automatically entitled to overtime. But they were outraged by McCutchen's effort to expand the definition of a wide array of exempt occupations and positions. [21] For example, under the new regulations, the definition of an executive was expanded to allow employers to deny overtime pay to workers who did very little supervision and a great deal of manual or routine work. This included employees, such as the team leaders or department heads in many retail stores and white-collar bureaucracies, who could recommend—but not carry out—a "change of status" to those workers, as few as just two, whom they "supervised" during the course of their otherwise routine work. In this category were hundreds of thousands of chefs, editors, office department heads, mortgage loan officers, nurses, computer programmers, and supervising cashiers—in short, many of the jobs that were proliferating as the U.S. economy moved from manufacturing to services. An AFL-CIO-sponsored report estimated that as many as six million workers would lose overtime protection by the time corporations had implemented the new rules.[22] Said an officer of the National Retail Federation in early 2004, "We're pleased that after having to live with 50-year-old regulations that no longer fit today's workplaces, we finally face an update."[23]

In the fight over ergonomics and overtime rules, the Bush administration had used the routine levers of administrative power to put into effect an agenda long advanced by business and conservative ideologues. But that agenda was hardly exhausted, nor were the opportunities to push it forward. This became clear in two moments of national crisis, the first of which came in the wake of the attacks of September 11, the second in the immediate aftermath of Hurricane Katrina. That the administration was far more successful in the first instance than in the second tells us much about the staying power of Bush-era conservatism; that it tried to use both emergencies to eviscerate long-standing labor standards and marginalize the unions tells us even more about the steadfast and consistent ideology of the men and women loyal to George Bush.

SEPTEMBER 11 ON THE HOME FRONT

The events of September 11, 2001, gave the Bush administration a chance to move on a multitude of fronts, domestic as well as foreign. "For the next few months Mr. Bush will have enormous political capital to do whatever he says must be done to help the war effort and buttress national strength," editorialized the *Wall Street Journal* on September 19, 2001. "But the lesson of history is that Presidents must spend political capital or they will lose it."[24]

An obvious place to start was airport security. As of 9/11 the airlines contracted with private companies to screen baggage and passengers boarding America's airlines. As a result, workers were often paid $6 or $7 an hour, annual turnover ranged from 100 percent to 400 percent, and the screeners were poorly trained. Getting the airlines out of the security equation and making the baggage screeners federal employees would solve a lot of problems, argued the Aviation Security Association, a new trade group that represented large security companies. "It's the single biggest impediment to increasing wages and benefits and lowering turnover."[25]

But Republicans opposed the federalization of airport screeners. As Congressman Bob Barr of Georgia put it, "To me as a conservative, I look at a problem and ask, is this a federal function?"[26] The GOP was willing to set standards, but it choked at an actual increase in the federal payroll, which contravened the Bush administration's propensity to outsource as many governmental functions as possible. Although the Senate, by unanimous vote, passed a bill federalizing 28,000 screeners on October 11, the House resisted for six more weeks, with some in the Republican majority asserting that the new Transportation Security Administration (TSA) was akin to socialism. Commented Paul Krugman in a *New York Times* column published just one month after 9/11, "Whatever the explanation, the dispute over airport security leaves no doubt about one thing: The right's fanatical distrust of government is the central fact of American politics, even in a time of terror."[27]

President Bush signed on to this hard-line approach, but the Democrats held the advantageous ground in this dispute.[28] With stories pouring out of New York every day celebrating the heroism and sacrifice of firemen, policemen, and government rescue workers, it was difficult even for the most committed conservatives to resist the federalization of the men and women who were also be responsible for ensuring the safety of the traveling population. The legislation was being "held hostage by Republicans who are ideologically opposed to a larger federal role," charged Senator Ron Wyden, Democrat of Oregon. Privately, some House Republicans admitted they were being "pummeled" on this issue.[29] They finally caved in late November, sending the White House a bill that effectively doubled the wages, increased the benefits, and put in uniform tens of thousands of new federal employees.

Bush signed the bill, prompting the *Wall Street Journal* to editorialize, "big government won the day after Bush folded to the political-media pressure."[30] But the president soon took his pound of flesh out of the new Homeland Security Administration, of which these federalized screening personnel would soon be a part. Despite much Democratic prodding, the Bush administration did not agree to create a Department of Homeland Security until June 2002. The new department combined twenty-two separate agencies, from the Coast Guard to the Immigration and Naturalization Service, encompassing more than 170,000 employees, including the newly federalized TSA screeners. But the proposal quickly stalled because the president insisted that the director of the new agency must have the power to abrogate existing collective bargaining contracts and civil service rules in order to secure the "flexibility" necessary to more easily hire and fire federal workers and move them at will among various jobs and posts. Few experts on public administration agreed with this approach; after all, state and local police and fire personnel were among the most heavily unionized of all public servants. But these new powers would threaten the union status of some 44,000 existing workers and forestall the unionization of the new TSA screeners. "For President Bush, it's his way or the highway," said Bobby L. Harnage, president of the American Federation of Government Employees. "I'm not used to crumbling to those kinds of demands. He's got a fight on his hands."[31]

For a moment it seemed as if the labor and the Democrats might also win this one. In September 2002 they won a significant victory when they persuaded Lincoln Chafee, a moderate Republican senator from Rhode Island, to join Democrats and form a majority to limit the president's ability to revoke or revise existing job protections. Chafee and the Democrats proposed that a presidentially appointed panel would arbitrate the dispute once the new Homeland Security Department was set up. But Bush rejected the compromise, insisting that the commander in chief had to have the unfettered authority to determine the employment regime in Homeland Security. "I hope we're going to start to be as hard on terrorists as we are on these union members," said the reliable laborite, Barbara A. Mikulski, Democrat of Maryland. "It's been over one year, and we haven't found bin Laden, but we're going to nitpick over whether you have a union or not?"[32]

But when it came to playing the war-on-terror card in the 2002 election cycle, the Republicans far outclassed their detractors. With the skillful Bush operative Karl Rove calling the shots, Republican candidates painted the Democrats and their labor allies as unpatriotic or worse. In September, President Bush asserted that "the Senate is more interested in special interests in Washington and not interested in the security of the American people"; the next month GOP Senator Phil Graham explained the stalemate by blaming the Democrats: "Their problem is they love public employee labor unions more than they love homeland security."[33] In Georgia and Missouri, Democratic senators Max Cleland and Jean Carnahan were pummeled with the accusation that they had voted against the war on terror at the behest of selfish union leaders. Cleland, a highly decorated Vietnam veteran, now a triple amputee confined to a wheelchair, was slandered by Republican Saxby Chambliss in a notorious ad that distorted Cleland's effort to maintain civil service protections for Homeland Security workers. "He says he supports President Bush at every opportunity, but that's not the truth," ran the Saxby advertisement. "Since July, Max Cleland voted against President Bush's vital homeland security efforts 11 times." One television ad morphed Cleland's face into Saddam Hussein's while suggesting that the Democratic senator was indifferent to the safety of the American people. The ad proved so controversial that Republican senators Chuck Hagel of Nebraska and John McCain of Arizona both protested it.[34]

It worked, however. Both Carnahan and Cleland were defeated in a midterm election that saw conservative Republicans regain control of the Senate and make substantial gains in the House. Facing this new reality, the Democrats acquiesced to the president's demands in a brief postelection session designed to finally establish the new Department of Homeland Security. The administration now had an essentially free hand to bypass civil service rules in promoting and firing workers in the DHS, and it permitted the president to exempt other unionized federal workers from collective bargaining agreements in the name of national security.[35] Bush administration appointees prohibited more than 40,000 employees at the new TSA from participating in the federal government's system of collective bargaining, a dictate to which President Bush held fast even after the Democrats regained control of Congress in 2007 and sought to restore unionization rights to TSA workers. After Bush threatened to veto any such legislation, even when contained in a comprehensive antiterrorism bill, the Democrats backed down.[36]

AN OWNERSHIP SOCIETY

When in his second inaugural address President George W. Bush described his vision of an "ownership society," he specified not only the ownership of homes, businesses, and retirement savings but also of health insurance. This philosophical shift from collective to individual responsibility would become a lightning rod in Bush's 2005 effort to begin the privatization of Social Security, but the concept had a dress rehearsal earlier in his administration when Bush and his conservative allies made health savings accounts (HSAs) a fiscally small but ideological potent part of the much larger 2003 Medicare law that subsidized pharmacy drugs for seniors. Conservatives labeled these HSAs the centerpiece for a new era of "consumer-driven health care." Former Speaker Newt Gingrich thought these accounts "the single most important change in health care policy in 60 years."[37]

The HSA is a portable financial vehicle, akin to an individual retirement account, to which contributions may be made with pretax dollars and from which balances may be withdrawn to pay medical claims, again without payment of a tax. If not spent in the year they are made, contributions accumulate, are invested, and can be spent on health services in later years. HSAs receive favorable tax treatment only when they are accompanied by an insurance policy with a high deductible, at least $2,000 for a family enrolled in an employer-subsidized insurance plan, but often well above $5,000 when the insurance policy is purchased on the open market. When paying health expenses, the enrollee first uses funds from the HSA until the balance is exhausted, then dips into personal savings for payments until expenses reach the deductible threshold. But personal expenses don't stop there because the enrollee then continues paying part of the costs, typically 20 to 30 percent, until an annual maximum for out-of-pocket payments is reached, often as much as $10,000 per year.[38]

The Right saw these tax-advantaged HSAs as the cornerstone of an ideological and policy assault on liberal efforts to preserve or expand the welfare state, including a more inclusive and equitable system of health insurance. Among the early activists in this effort was J. Patrick Rooney, a wealthy and influential Republican whose Indianapolis-based Golden Rule Insurance Company sold low-premium insurance to a "cherry-picked" cohort of young and healthy individuals. John Goodman, an economist originally at the Dallas Federal Reserve, offered the Rooney program intellectual heft and political sophistication. His think tank, the National Center for Policy Analysis, was bankrolled by all the key right-wing foundations, including Bradley, Olin, and Scaife.[39] With Rooney, Goodman recognized that two-thirds of all Americans supported a government-run, universal system of health care provision. However, by offering an attractive set of HSAs, a large segment of the population would now have the opportunity to withdraw from the comprehensive, risk-sharing, employer- and taxpayer-subsidized health insurance system. This would generate a large "poison pill," forestalling liberal efforts to pass a government-run or -mandated health program. "It's going to be real hard to socialize the system if everybody has their own account," explained Goodman right after passage of the 2003 Medicare bill.[40]

That conservative Republicans could declare the creation of a new and expensive health care entitlement a bulwark against the socialization of the system tells us quite a lot about Bush-era social policy. The Medicare Modernization Act signed by President Bush in December 2003 was designed to make affordable to millions of seniors the pharmaceuticals that had been left uncovered in the original 1965 Medicare law. Because such medicinals were an increasingly important, and expensive, part of their health care costs, coverage under a new Medicare program—it would be called "Part D"—had long been a pressing political issue for both parties. Liberals wanted a straight expansion of Medicare so that the government would buy prescription drugs in bulk, drive down the price, and then subsidize and sell them to seniors on the cheap. Most Republicans wanted to make prescription drugs more affordable as well, but they insisted that market principles had to govern any expansion of Medicare. Drugs would therefore be purchased through one of several competing private plans and costs to the beneficiary would vary according to income and the kind of plan chosen, even as the government would be prohibited from negotiating directly with the pharmaceutical companies to lower drug costs. And the new law banned importation of cheaper, publicly regulated drugs from abroad.[41] By 2008, Medicare Part D covered 25 million seniors, but it remained a complex and expensive entitlement. There were some 1,824 different prescription drug plans, all covering a different set of drugs at varying cost to the consumer.[42] Because of the widespread adoption of generic drugs, the costs of the new program were about a third less than expected in 2003, but on a ten-year basis, Medicare Part D still represented a $400 billion expenditure.[43]

Although insurance companies and pharmaceutical makers had lobbied hard for the new law, and the Bush administration saw it as a big political plus, many conservative Republicans balked. It was a huge new entitlement that threatened to balloon the federal deficit. But that right-wing darling, the HSA, greatly expanded in the new Medicare law, helped save the day. Perhaps as many as forty conservative Republicans who might otherwise have opposed a law then expected to cost more than half a trillion dollars voted yes in order to advance the HSA concept. "This will spark a consumer revolution in health care," said Republican Paul Ryan, a staunch proponent of the HSA idea who was otherwise cool to Bush's pharmaceuticals-for-seniors bill.[44] Indeed, the revolution might be even more far-reaching. "I'm in favor of dramatically broadening tax-free savings accounts," declared Stephen Moore, president of the free-market Club for Growth. Moore observed that if the government continued to facilitate the creation of accounts for health care, education, child care, and other needs, a section of the middle class might well gravitate toward the Bushite vision of an "ownership society," thereby "short-circuiting the left's ability to create new government programs, because if people have enough money in these accounts, they don't need new government programs."[45]

The revolution was a bit tardy in getting off the ground. By the end of the Bush presidency only about five million Americans had established any sort of HSA, with just 10 percent of all large corporations participating. Not unexpectedly, the main takers were the low-wage, high-turnover firms in the retail industry. "They're moving the risk from their balance sheet to the employees," concluded Richard T. Evans, a health care analyst with Sanford C. Bernstein and Co. "The risk is being transferred without the consumer really realizing it."[46] Wal-Mart, for example, offered a bewildering array of low-premium, high-deductible, HSA-linked insurance plans designed, in part, to finally entice a simple majority of all of its own employees to sign up for one of the company's health insurance plans, an effort that might deflect some of the public disdain faced by the company. Wal-Mart and other proponents of the HSA concept argued that if employees had to pay a substantial amount of their health care expenses out of pocket, they would be more careful in their health care spending (fewer visits to the emergency room), and in return the company could provide health plans with smaller premiums. "The greatest incentive for health and wellness is high deductibles," Wal-Mart vice president Tom Emerick told a friendly Dallas business audience. "We'll tell anybody in America how we did it and how it works."[47]

President Bush was a booster, of course. In February 2006 he flew to the Dublin, Ohio, headquarters of Wendy's International, the hamburger chain. Like Wal-Mart, Wendy's was the kind of low-benefit, high-turnover firm for which the HSA had been designed. The insurance would be cheap and, in addition, pack an ideological punch. As the president told Wendy's managers, "We've got to choose between two competing philosophies when it comes to health care. . . . On the one hand, there's some folks . . . who believe that government ought to be making the decisions for the health care industry. And there are some of us who believe that the health care industry ought to be centered on the consumer." The latter worked best, said the president, because "The fundamental problem with traditional coverage is that there's no incentive to control how their health care dollars are spent. . . . If patients controlled how their health care dollars are spent, the result is better treatment at lower cost."[48]

Most liberals understood the stakes as well. *Consumer Reports* summed up much of the empirical research, which had shown that while healthy and affluent people might save some money, for the rest, high-deductible HSA accounts were a considerable gamble: "A promotional pamphlet for an HSA boasts, 'If you plan correctly, you may find that you spend far less for health care than ever before.' True, if you could plan to avoid cancer, being hit by a car, or growing older. But you can't."[49] Equally important, noted most critics on the left, "consumer-driven health insurance" essentially abandons older and sicker workers to the "adverse selection" that occurs in any system of insurance when people with the lowest medical risks opt out of the existing coverage pool, either that of a government program or employer-subsidized comprehensive health coverage. The HSA scheme, noted the politically liberal *New England Journal of Medicine*, "is analogous to efforts to translate part of the Social Security insurance structure into personally owned and management retirement accounts. . . . The language of individual ownership weakens society's sense of collective responsibility for its most vulnerable members, but emphasizes the importance of individual effort in generating the economic resources that underlie any system of care."[50] Editorialized *Consumer Reports*, "The health-care system needs fixing, but HSAs are a sham substitute for comprehensive reform."[51]

THE SOCIAL SECURITY GAMBIT

For conservatives, Social Security was the big, collectivized entitlement that stood athwart a final erasure of the New Deal state and the progressive, redistributive ethos that it embodied. As the *American Prospect*'s Robert Kuttner put it in 2002, when the Bush administration was just gearing up to "reform" it, "Social Security serves, and reinforces, a kind of collective solidarity rarely articulated explicitly in the ordinary idiom of American politics. But it has precisely expressed the modern liberal view of social entitlement—the collectivity taking responsibility for unearned misfortune, not by singling out (and thus stigmatizing) the certifiably needy, but with a universal system. . . . It cultivates a politics of social empathy and, in turn, an astonishing level of political support."[52]

No wonder the Bush conservatives found it anathema, no matter the rhetoric about strengthening and sustaining it over the long run. But "reform" would be difficult because the post-New Deal Republican Party had been rehabilitated only by making a fundamental concession to the Democrats on maintenance of this program. As Dwight D. Eisenhower wrote to his more conservative brother Edgar in 1954, "Should any political party attempt to abolish Social Security, unemployment insurance, and eliminate labor laws and farm programs, you would not hear of that party again in our political history."[53] Ike's warning seemed entirely justified when the Democrats crushed Barry Goldwater in the 1964 elections. The Republican candidate's political "extremism" had been signaled by two policy stands: a willingness to let military commanders in the field have more control over the use of nuclear weapons; and a proposal that Social Security become a "voluntary" retirement system. Few liberals could say which was more odious.

Though Ronald Reagan had been a leading Goldwater supporter in 1964, he was fully consignant of Social Security's residual popularity when he became president. The severe slowdown in employment and economic growth during the 1970s, combined with high inflation, had raised questions about the system's long-range solvency, which some ideologically attuned Reaganites sought to parlay into an initiative cutting benefits and privatizing the program. Reagan spent about a week entertaining these right-wing proposals, but he quickly retreated when the Republican-controlled Senate passed a resolution, on a 96 to 0 vote, asserting that "Congress shall not precipitously and unfairly penalize early retirees." The aphorism that Social Security is the "third rail" of American politics originated in the aftermath of this vote. Reagan therefore took his small lumps and appointed a genuinely bipartisan commission headed by Alan Greenspan to suggest fiscally reasonable reforms. With staunch Social Security pioneers such as

Robert Ball and Claude Pepper on board, the commission did precisely what it was intended to do: ensure the viability of the program through a slight increase in payroll taxes and a year or two delay in the age when young people would become eligible to receive their retirement checks. The system seemed set for another seventy-five years.[54]

But it wasn't. During the next twenty years Social Security became increasingly vulnerable to attack. Despite its enormous size, Social Security became structurally isolated as virtually every other institution of collective, redistributive economic provision came under political and fiscal attack. "Above" Social Security, the stability and payout of many corporate retirement plans came into question; "below," both unemployment insurance and means-tested forms of aid for the very poor were increasingly underfunded and subject to social and political disdain.[55] The long stock market boom, which began in 1992, fattened IRA accounts and made private investment decisions look easy and lucrative. Thus, Social Security seemed increasingly anomalous as the only part of the American system of social provision that was both universal, guaranteed, and economically progressive.

This opened it up to ideological assault, often couched in terms questioning Social Security's long-term financing. The payroll tax generated a huge income stream, enough to support the increasingly high proportion of retirees to contributors, but only if the real wages of American workers continued to rise at the historic rate generated during the era of postwar manufacturing prowess, union strength, and technological innovation. But for more than two decades, wages had stagnated and labor force participation had declined, producing a shortfall in Social Security's anticipated income stream. Liberals saw the solution arising out of a very modest improvement in these underlying economic structures. For example, a reduction in the unemployment rate by just 1 percent or a shift in the distribution of income back to that existing in 1980 would virtually eliminate the prospect of a long-range Social Security deficit, even without an overall boost to economic growth.[56]

But none of this had much impact on the growth of the think tanks, foundations, and front groups that challenged the Social Security system's solvency or its social rationale. Opponents argued that since younger recipients would never get their anticipated benefits, it would be fairer and wiser to allow them to divert some of their payroll tax money into the stock market, not a bad prospect during the era 1982–2000, when the Dow Jones Industrial Average rose more than tenfold. In addition to holding out a vision of retirement wealth for Generation X, Social Security privatization advocates such as Boston University economist Lawrence Kotlikoff, the inventor of "generational accounting," saw Social Security as an ongoing Ponzi scheme in which the undeserving elderly robbed the industrious young. Neoliberal critics such as Charles Peter denigrated the logic of universal entitlement as nothing more than "bribing the middle class."[57]

The most persistent and influential organization pushing for Social Security privatization was the Cato Institute, a libertarian think tank founded in the 1970s by the Koch industrial clan of Kansas, whose patriarch, Fred Koch, had been a charter member and financial backer of the John Birch Society a decade before. Among the most influential Cato "scholars" was Jose Pinera, who as a cabinet minister in the Chilean government of dictator Augusto Pinochet had played the leading role in the creation of a retirement system based on private personal accounts. As one of the "Chicago boys" drawing inspiration from the work of Milton Friedman, Pinera's transition to the Washington world of right-wing think tanks had been smooth. With Cato president Ed Crane, Pinera paid a 1997 visit to the governor's mansion in Austin. According to Crane, Bush told them that privatization is "the most important policy issue facing the United States today."[58] He may have been telling the truth. Collegiate friends of George Bush recalled that the transformation of Social Security had been one of the few public policy issues that had captured his attention after he read Barry Goldwater's *Conscience of a Conservative* in prep school.[59]

During his presidential campaign Bush hit all the notes that had by then become standard in the privatization chorus. The system was facing a crisis; we should "trust younger workers to manage some of their own money"; the Republican plan would "save" the system. Bush was always fuzzy on the math, as Al Gore was ridiculed for pointing out, but when it came to political imagery he was crystal-clear. "Ownership in our society should not be an exclusive club," argued the Republican candidate. "Everyone should be part owner in the American dream." Cato economist Michael Tanner understood what Bush—and his longtime political adviser Karl Rove—were proposing. "What does it mean when every truck driver and waitress becomes a stockholder?" asked Tanner, one of the architects of the private-account movement. "You can create inheritable wealth for low-income people and minorities. If you turn those truck drivers and waitresses into stockholders, they vote and behave very differently."[60]

By the spring of 2001 President Bush had established the Commission to Strengthen Social Security, through which he recruited a cohort of true believers, many from Cato or the larger privatization movement.[61] Even Bush's secretary of the treasury, Paul O'Neill, though fearful of large budget deficits, was nevertheless a hawk on Social Security, favoring "wealth accumulation rather than generational transfer," as he often preached.[62] Unlike the Greenspan Commission of twenty years before, the Bush commission made little pretense of bipartisanship. There were some Democratic commissioners, former senator Daniel Patrick Moynihan first among them, but none were staunch proponents of maintaining the integrity of the existing system, and some, such as former congressman Tim Penny of Minnesota, had actually served on the board of Cato's Project on Social Security Privatization. Many of the key staff jobs also went to Cato veterans, including that of the chief economist, Andrew Biggs, whom Bush would later appoint assistant commissioner for policy at the Social Security Administration, where he championed privatization, a true fox in the henhouse.[63]

As expected, the commission produced the report that Bush and Cato wanted: Social Security faced a crisis of insolvency in which the only viable solutions involved substantial benefit cuts combined with some form of privatization. But in December 2001 no one was listening. Not only did the country face an expensive "war on terror," but the bursting of the Internet stock market bubble, the Enron collapse, and the scandals that besmirched a whole series of once high-flying companies all soured the public on the prospect of stock market riches, via a private Social Security account or otherwise.[64] And beyond all this, advocates of Social Security privatization could never figure out a way to actually pay the enormous extra cost entailed in diverting a large portion of the payroll tax to individual accounts while still adequately funding existing pensions. Had the conservatives been satisfied with putting a sizable proportion of the trust fund into the stock market it would have been risky, but all the dividends and capital gains would have been available to actually fund the system, albeit in a collective fashion. But even this capitalist road failed the political test, which demanded that the under-forty set own and control their individual accounts and thereby transform the psychology and politics of a whole new generation of citizen capitalists.

Whether one labels it stubbornness or tenacity, George Bush would not give up. After his reelection in 2004, the president declared he would spend some of the political capital he had accumulated to press forward with a radical restructuring of Social Security. It was the centerpiece of the domestic agenda in his February 2, 2005, State of the Union Address, but the Bush administration and its conservative allies did make one linguistic "concession" to their critics. From now on "privatization" was out and in its place a new set of phrases appeared: "personal accounts," "trust between generations," "security in retirement," and "strengthen and save Social Security."[65] But the words always had an Orwellian flavor, as did the cohort of front groups and advocacy organizations that conservatives had built in expectation of a new battle to dismantle the system. These included "For Our Grandchildren," "RetireSafe.org," "Third Millennium," "Alliance for Worker Retirement Security," and "Women for a Social Security Choice." All were funded by the now familiar list of right-wing foundations, conservative businesses, and Bush "Pioneers" who had contributed so generously to his recent reelection campaign.[66]

President Bush barnstormed the country in the winter of 2005, but he faced staunch opposition from the Democrats and won only tepid support from big business and Wall Street. Although many investment firms were sure to earn billions managing personal accounts in any privatization scheme, at mid-decade there were lots of other ways to make a bundle that did not subject them either to public scrutiny or to charges of "profiteering."[67] Nor were all Republican legislators on board. Most supported some version of privatization, but another budget-busting federal expenditure made many conservatives nervous. Indeed, George Bush's decision to "spend" on a $1.3 trillion tax cut the Clinton-era budget surpluses he had inherited in 2001 deprived the administration of the money that would have been essential to fund the transition costs, variously estimated at well above a trillion dollars, necessary to move from a public to a partially privatized old-age retirement system.[68] In short, the Bush effort to make privatization a postelection priority represented an ideological victory for the Republican right, but it did not reflect a similar shift in public sentiment, business self-interest, or fiscal policy.[69] All this was reflected in the anemic support the president won for his Social Security reform. Never above 50 percent in the polls, it seemed to drop the more people learned of the details of the plan. Said House Minority Whip Steny Hoyer, "The president says he wants to educate the public. God bless him—keep at it. The education is working."[70]

KATRINA

The demise of the Bush-Cato Social Security scheme was a defeat, but that setback did little to temper White House interest in pushing forward a free-market social policy agenda, even in the face of the president's declining popularity. When Hurricane Katrina blasted its way through New Orleans and the Gulf Coast on the last day of August 2005, Bush administration officials had their second great opportunity to use a national catastrophe to enact a set of reforms that would deregulate the labor market and open the door to the "opportunity society." Katrina is now synonymous with Bush administration cronyism and bungling, but from an ideological standpoint, the Katrina aftermath may well have represented the apogee of the Bush administration's ambition to delegitimize the regulatory state and the social democratic ethos. Thus, as late as early 2008, when Mitt Romney was still a viable Republican candidate for president, he expected that conservatives would not be the only ones to nod when he offered yet another slap at governmental efforts to solve a complex social problem: "I don't want the people who ran the Katrina cleanup to manage our health care system."[71]

Indeed, the institution that came out of this natural catastrophe with the greatest credibility was neither a federal agency nor a local government but Wal-Mart, whose entire ethos sustained the values and vision of the GOP right wing. At its height, more than 126 Wal-Mart stores were closed or damaged by the storm, but the company quickly put into overdrive its remarkable logistics system. Within days, Wal-Mart had dispatched 2,500 truckloads of merchandise, both for donation and sale, food for 100,000 meals, and teams of workers to get its stores up and running again.[72] Dozens water damaged or without electricity turned their parking lots into de facto relief centers from which emergency workers distributed tons of perishable food and cases of soft drinks and water. Wal-Mart was therefore in full-bore rescue mode days before either the National Guard or the Federal Emergency Management Agency made their tardy way to the disaster area.[73]

During a tearful September 4 interview on NBC's *Meet the Press*, Aaron Broussard, the president of Jefferson Parish, told host Tim Russert that if "the American government would have responded like Wal-Mart has responded, we wouldn't be in this crisis."[74] This was a theme the national press and many conservatives quickly endorsed. The *Wall Street Journal* declared, "The Federal Emergency Management Agency could learn some things from Wal-Mart Stores, Inc," and the *Washington Post* editorialized that "Wal-Mart is being held up as a model for logistical efficiency and nimble disaster planning."[75] David Vitter, the Republican senator from Louisiana, promised to introduce a bill abolishing FEMA and contracting its job out to the private sector. John Tierney, a conservative columnist for the *New York Times*, nominated Wal-Mart CEO Lee Scott as the man the government should put in charge of rebuilding the Gulf Coast. His new organization: WEMA, the Wal-Mart Emergency Management Agency.[76]

Liberal Democrats initially thought that the devastation wrought by the hurricane offered their cause a historic opportunity. After all, the nation had committed itself to the largest emergency reconstruction effort since the New Deal. And the issues they most cared about—health care, housing, jobs, race—were suddenly staples on the nightly news. But as the *New York Times* reported, "what looked like a chance to talk up new programs is fast becoming a scramble to save the old ones." Even as Bush cashiered FEMA chief Michael Brown, he was taking his policy cues from the same group of conservative ideologues who had played such a large role in the days after 9/11 and in the recent Social Security debate. [77]

The Bush administration quickly developed a reconstruction program that paralleled Wal-Mart's own evisceration of many U.S. labor and environmental standards. Key federal departments and agencies put forward a broad set of waivers and directives that rolled back numerous regulations in the devastated region. Indeed, the Katrina disaster served as a kind of domestic stand-in for September 11, enabling Bush to refashion social policy for a wide swath of the Gulf Coast. In a speech announcing the White House's multi-billion-dollar reconstruction plan, the president included a reference to a "Gulf Coast Opportunity Zone," mirroring the Heritage Foundation language that called for an across-the-board repeal of health, safety, and labor protections. Thus the Federal Motor Carrier Safety Administration waived most safety regulations for trucks and their drivers entering the disaster area, and the Environmental Protection Agency dropped fuel refinement and emissions standards that would otherwise have been highly controversial. President Bush also suspended rules requiring federal contractors to file affirmative action plans, which conservative allies of the administration called "cumbersome" in this emergency.[78]

A presidential executive order suspending the Bacon-Davis Act came on September 8. The 1931 law, which prohibited federally financed construction jobs from paying wages less than the local, "prevailing" rate, had long sustained construction trades unionism, although in the case of New Orleans the wage thus mandated was only about $10 an hour. Nevertheless, abolition of Bacon-Davis was an absolute fetish among conservatives. The *Wall Street Journal* editorial page had campaigned in 2002 to eliminate prevailing wage requirements among the contractors hired by the new Department of Homeland Security, asserting at one point, "Let's hope Osama bin Laden pays his operatives union scale and requires them to file their forms in triplicate too."[79] That battle was lost, but the *Wall Street Journal* returned to the fray even before the New Orleans waters had stopped rising on September 1, 2005, when it called on the Bush administration to suspend Bacon-Davis, since the paper claimed the law "excluded" non-union workers and contractors from the reconstruction process "while adding billions in costs."[80]

Rehousing hundreds of thousands of displaced people proved another site of ideological contestation. Vouchers had worked well in the aftermath of the 1994 Northridge earthquake, but the Bush administration feared that an even more extensive distribution of housing vouchers along the Gulf Coast would legitimize an entitlement for even more low-income people. The "danger" was acute because many conservatives supported the housing voucher idea: they were, after all, a market-oriented solution, in contrast to the much derided public housing projects of decades past. But that was precisely the approach adopted by the Bush administration, focusing its efforts on the creation of public housing in the form of temporary trailer parks, which were slow to take shape, ghettoized survivors, and almost always cost more than a mere expansion of the existing voucher program. "What's going on here?" asked the liberal columnist Paul Krugman. "The crucial point is that President Bush has been forced by events into short-term actions that conflict with his long-term goals. His mission in office is to dismantle or at least shrink the federal social safety net, yet he must, as a matter of political necessity, provide aid to Katrina's victims. His problem is how to do that without legitimizing the very role of government he opposes."[81]

STALEMATE AND COLLAPSE

So the policy and political aftermath of Katrina ended in a stalemate. Some of the most egregious of the Bush initiatives, such as the suspension of Bacon-Davis, were quickly reversed by Congress, where Republican representatives who had long relied on building trades support revolted against the Bushite war on the unions.[82] But reconstruction along the Gulf Coast hardly assumed a New Deal flavor. Although President Bush and the advocates of limited government sank in the public opinion polls, the Democrats, the liberals, and the laborites were unable to put forward any effective alternative, even after they recaptured control of Congress in 2006. There were many good individual proposals, but for the most part the Democrats played defense, pushing for more reconstruction money and keeping a close eye on the racial dynamics of the rebuilding project but unable to offer any overarching schema that linked a physical reconstruction of the Gulf Coast to a larger neo-New Deal project.

The heirs of Franklin Roosevelt got their chance in the fall of 2008 when the financial crisis, the onset of a severe recession, and the election of Barack Obama transformed the policy landscape. Their victory, electoral as well as ideological, made it clear that the Bush administration, unlike that of Ronald Reagan, was at best a holding action. President Bush did not construct an "ownership society"; he did not privatize Social Security or take the demand for higher labor standards, national health insurance, or a more equitable distribution of wealth off the nation's policy agenda.

Indeed, in the very last weeks of 2008, division and retreat eviscerated key elements of the Bush coalition. In December, when southern Republican senators blocked a congressional effort to bail out America's unionized automobile companies, the Bush administration itself broke ranks with many of its most steadfast, anti-union, free-market supporters. From monies originally appropriated to rescue banks and insurance companies the Bush Treasury Department loaned Chrysler and General Motors more than $17 billion, in the process extracting little more than symbolic concessions from a beleaguered United Automobile Workers. Equally dramatic was the Wal-Mart turnabout that same month. Recognizing that an era of political indulgence and regulatory neglect was fast coming to an end, the nation's largest private employer announced it would resolve sixty-three wage-and-hour lawsuits in forty-two states by paying upward of half a billion dollars to settle accusations that it forced employees to skip lunch breaks, work off the clock, and sidestep overtime laws.[83] On the social policy home front, the era of George W. Bush was over.

9

CREATING THEIR OWN REALITY

The Bush Administration and Expertise in a Polarized Age

DAVID GREENBERG

CONSERVATISM HOLDS FEW TENETS MORE SACRED THAN THE EXISTENCE of immutable truths. All strains of conservative thought, including that which united the Republican Party in late twentieth-century America, have rested on moral absolutism and an abhorrence of relativism. So it was a bit strange during the years of George W. Bush's presidency to hear how people used the term "reality-based." It was coined as a term of scorn by an administration official—widely guessed to be Bush's chief political aide, Karl Rove—speaking anonymously in 2004 to the reporter Ron Suskind. "The aide said," Suskind reported in the *New York Times Magazine*, "that guys like me were 'in what we call the reality-based community,' which he defined as people who 'believe that solutions emerge from your judicious study of discernible reality.' I nodded and murmured something about enlightenment principles and empiricism. He cut me off. 'That's not the way the world really works anymore,' he continued. 'We're an empire now, and when we act, we create our own reality.'"[1]

Many of the critics whom the aide derided—liberals, for the most part—were soon brandishing the label as a badge of honor. Amid the new century's shrill verbal warfare, they deployed the phrase "reality-based" partly to mock the government-funded religious programs that Bush euphemistically called "faith-based," but more often to refer in shorthand to a popular critique of the Right's newly pervasive contempt for scientific and professional expertise. Whether bemoaning the politicization of intelligence before the Iraq War or of programming at the Public Broadcasting System, whether denouncing the doctoring of environmental data or the muzzling of the surgeon general, liberals during the Bush years came to see themselves as old-fashioned empiricists, loyal to nonpoliticized evidence, while casting their antagonists as making policy decisions without regard for the facts.

Although the taunts of Bush's critics frequently descended into glibness, the president's denigration of independent expertise was real, and it marked one of the more significant and all-encompassing features of his administration. A century earlier, in the Progressive Era, reformers had enshrined a respect for authorities with specialized training in professional or academic disciplines. Government officials turned to these experts for technically informed, nonpartisan policy advice in fields from science and medicine to law and economics. To be sure, the reign of experts had always been contested. Critics over the decades had noted how these experts became handmaidens of power, or operated with blinkered perspectives. Some argued that experts disagreed too much among themselves to produce clear guidance for officials; others said that they constituted a fundamentally undemocratic aspect of public life, to be tolerated rather than welcomed. All the same, in a vast range of policymaking realms, technical knowledge trumped political preferences. Reports from the Centers for Disease Control or the Bureau of Labor Statistics, conclusions from the American Bar Association or the surgeon general's office—these sorts of findings usually enjoyed the trust of most policymakers and citizens, and rightly so.

Under Bush, all that changed. As never before, administration officials and their allies in politics and the news media openly disregarded the empirically grounded evidence, open-minded inquiry, and expert authority that had long underpinned governmental policymaking. Such politicization was hardly unknown in the past, but what had been aberrations now became standard practice. And to justify its disregard for expertise, the Right under

Bush found itself promoting a view of knowledge in which any political claim, no matter how objectively verifiable or falsifiable, was treated as simply one of two competing descriptions of reality, with power and ideology, not science or disciplined inquiry, as the arbiters.

Several factors account for this undermining of expertise under Bush. Most obvious was the dominance of conservatism. With Bush's ascent, those who billed themselves as a "conservative movement" held a near monopoly on power for the first time, arguably, in seventy years. Largely through their chief instrument, the Republican Party, they controlled the White House, the Federal courts, and, for much of Bush's tenure, Congress. The terrorist attacks of September 11, 2001, forged a climate that chilled dissent and blunted opposition, augmenting the conservatives' power. More than under Richard Nixon and Ronald Reagan, the Right felt emboldened to disregard expert opinions that led to unwelcome outcomes.

A changed journalistic environment also played a role. In the twentieth century, objectivity had taken hold as a professional ideal at the institutions we now call the mainstream media—the newspapers, magazines, and broadcast outlets charged with providing trusted news to audiences of all political stripes. But almost from the start, reporters, like other intellectuals, found objectivity to be elusive and problematic. To prove their impartiality, they developed the practice of giving equal attention to the two main positions on any given issue, with the two-party system frequently serving as a handy if flawed proxy for political reality. Objectivity thus gave way to "balance," the idea that the two parties' stands on an issue enjoyed equal legitimacy. Although journalists had recognized for decades how this notion could serve the ends of unscrupulous politicians—many had called for a reassessment of "balance," for example, as long ago as the 1950s, in the wake of Senator Joe McCarthy's manipulations of the press—the strategies for changing journalistic practices, such as by strengthening the professional distinction between "news" and "opinion," never solved the essential problem. Indeed, when conservative activists began exploiting journalists' desire to be seen as fair by attacking the media as biased, journalists usually responded simply by redoubling their efforts to achieve balance—thus playing into conservatives' hands. "It's a great way to have your cake and eat it too," explained Matt Labash, a young writer for the conservative *Weekly Standard*, in 2003, as if revealing trade secrets. "Criticize other people for not being objective. Be as subjective as you want. It's a great little racket. I'm glad we found it actually."[2]

Journalists' inclination to hug the sidelines of political debates underscored how the specialization of knowledge complicated efforts to settle technical issues in the public realm. Most citizens, including journalists, lacked the time, motivation, and training to form sound, independent verdicts about the arcane matters that undergirded policy, whether budget projections or the effects of pharmaceuticals or the causes of the earth's temperature changes. For such information, citizens relied on journalists, who in turn relied on experts. This reliance on experts, even within the self-proclaimed "reality-based community," ultimately hinged on no small measure of trust, as citizens vouchsafed the wisdom of experts through such superficial tokens of authority as their degrees, institutional homes, or professional standing.[3]

Starting in the 1960s and 1970s, the Right systematically exploited this trust in the badges of expertise. Republicans erected a "counter-establishment," in the journalist Sidney Blumenthal's phrase[4]—an alternate universe of pseudo-experts devoted to promoting conservative policy, outfitted in the trappings of professionalism that the technocracy had ratified. If the professors ensconced in the top universities, think tanks, and research centers were producing findings and proffering advice that led to liberal policies, the Right would cultivate its own stable of wonks and graybeards who could offer clashing judgments. Thus, to combat think tanks like the Brookings Institution, the Right created the Heritage Foundation. To counteract the ABA, they founded the Federalist Society. The George C. Marshall Institute put a pseudo-scientific gloss on pro-industry positions; the Discovery Institute repackaged creationism as "intelligent design."

The cunning of these institutions was that they rested on a hidden asymmetry. Though formally similar to those of the establishment, the Right's organs were fundamentally different in that they served a plainly political purpose. Scholars at Brookings were committed, foremost, to scholarly values; the operatives at Heritage promoted the conservative cause above all. (If you opened a Brookings Institution book about tax policy, you might not be able to predict its findings; if you opened a Heritage Foundation book on the topic, you almost certainly could.) Similarly, the ABA existed to meet the needs of attorneys as professionals; the Federalist Society existed to bolster conservative lawyers' clout. Even the news organizations created by the right in later years weren't analogous to those they meant to displace. The Fox News cable channel, founded in the mid-1990s by Nixon's old adviser Roger Ailes, scarcely concealed its fealty to a conservative agenda; CNN, though sometimes referred to as Fox News's liberal cousin, operated within the mainstream twentieth-century tradition of seeking to offer news and analysis without ideological coloration, its primary commitments being professional, not political. Nonetheless, by century's end these counterestablishment organs had set themselves up as one of two dueling sets of voices given equal legitimacy in the public discourse, as if each represented a political camp.

By the Bush era, these institutions had matured. When policy debates arose, they bombarded journalists with minority opinions, and journalists, ill-equipped to make technical determinations and keen to avoid charges of bias, reported both "sides" of the issue. In extreme cases, this posture was absurd; the economist Paul Krugman, a columnist for the *New York Times*, quipped that "if President Bush said that the Earth was flat, the headlines on the news articles would read, 'Opinions Differ on Shape of the Earth.'"[5] Most readers, of course, know what science teaches about the earth's shape. In other cases, though, they were left to their own devices to separate truth from spin.

The Right thus found itself in the Bush years promoting a radical epistemological relativism: the idea that established experts' claims lacked empirical foundation and represented simply a political choice. In this position, conservatives were espousing a notion resembling that of postmodernism—or at least that strand of postmodernism that denies the possibility of objective truth claims. Of course, given conservatism's antagonism toward the idea that self-interest and power relations insidiously inform all arguments, it's a little impish to make the comparison. Most conservatives would disavow the postmodern label, and it's impossible anyway to confidently pinpoint the worldview that produced the Right's assault on expertise. Did Bush and his allies willingly embrace and accept a postmodern-like view of knowledge in which "enlightenment principles and empiricism" were passé, as the anonymous Bush aide said? Or did they consider *themselves* to be empiricists, convinced that the armies of scientists, doctors, lawyers, and policy professionals with whom they did battle were ideologically biased? Were their attacks on these experts purely cynical, with sound findings deliberately rejected in a raw political calculation because other goals mattered more? Or at least in some cases (such as the promotion of intelligent design), did the Right consciously opt for religious dogma over scientific teachings, reflecting a premodern rather than a postmodern sensibility?

These questions of motive should probably be tabled. Outsiders are always hard-pressed to discern inner motives, which at any rate are often multiple and contradictory. Yet it's noteworthy that puckish critics on the left applied the postmodern label to Bush during his presidency as a provocation—pointing up how often conservatives were, despite their traditional stance, disdaining claims to professional and scientific authority as masks for ideological agendas.[6] Conservatives fell into a position of sympathy with postmodernist claims about expertise, even if their arrival there constituted what they might refer to as an unintended consequence.

• • •

In trying to discredit expertise, Bush-era conservatives were taking on a regime that had held sway for more than a century. Before the rise of expertise, partisanship and loyalty governed politics. In the glory days of the spoils system and the machines, partisanship wasn't a problem. Voters identified proudly with their parties. Parties themselves printed the ballots that voters deposited, sometimes uninspected, in the voting box, automatically backing a party's slate. Officials doled out jobs and contracts to friends. Newspapers made no pretense of objectivity. If they weren't literally paid party mouthpieces, they trumpeted a cheerful one-sidedness, slanting the news for the home team.

Late in the nineteenth century, good-government reformers altered these arrangements. Reviling the system's corruption and inefficiency while ignoring its benefits, they replaced the hacks who had gained office through dutiful obedience with a civil service of disinterested, able public servants. Voting reforms, particularly the secret ballot, empowered the independent citizen. By the next century, this good-government worldview underpinned the Progressive movement.

A key tenet of the Progressive worldview was the cachet of expertise. In the post-Civil War years, most fields of inquiry and professional practice—law and medicine, economics and political science, journalism and education—evolved from unregulated pursuits that required scant formal training into disciplines with more rigorous norms. New societies wrote codes of behavior, set standards, and judged their members' fitness. Universities created graduate schools whose programs taught specialized knowledge and methods and whose degrees became tokens of prestige and licenses for plying the trade. Experts emerged as a new priesthood, replacing the clergymen who once dominated higher education as sources of intellectual and even moral authority.

In the newly complex society of industrial America, governments drew on experts to address an array of problems. From Woodrow Wilson's cadre of intellectuals called "the Inquiry" to Franklin Roosevelt's "Brains Trust" of economists, political scientists, and law professors, the alliance of activism, policy innovation, and academic expertise gave rise to the modern technocracy. By the 1950s, technocratic premises had gained unprecedented acceptance.

It's important to acknowledge that in one sense of the term, these technocrats were "liberal" in character. The belief that disinterested, reasoned inquiry and empirical research could improve society had been central to liberalism since the Enlightenment. The social sciences were also in some sense "activist," since the very project of studying social problems to devise solutions entailed a meliorist vision and a positive role for government. It made sense that technocrats tended to align with politicians who used the state to address social ills. Nonetheless, to describe a belief in the value of experts in policy formation as "liberal" in this generic sense is a far cry from imputing to these experts—as the Right later did—a partisan liberal "bias," a distorted picture of the world that led them unfairly to favor policies congenial to the Left. On the contrary, the experts' advice had value only if they followed their data wherever it led. The whole point of expertise was to remove the distortions of dogma, prejudice, and partisanship from the quest for sound policy.

For a time, the technocracy enjoyed virtual immunity from serious attack. Midcentury thinkers hailed, in the phrase the sociologist Daniel Bell made famous, the "end of ideology"—a cessation of the stark conflicts between all-encompassing doctrines. Depoliticized policymaking was ascendant. In a 1962 commencement address at Yale, President Kennedy endorsed the idea. "The central domestic problems of our time do not relate to basic clashes of philosophy and ideology," he maintained, "but to ways and means of recasting common goals—to research for sophisticated solutions to complex and obstinate issues." His administration established a culture of esteem for research. Lyndon Johnson followed suit. Delivering the keynote address at the fiftieth anniversary celebration of the Brookings Institution in 1966, Johnson praised the explosion of research taking place at the policy shops. "Without the tide of new proposals that periodically sweeps into this city," he declared, "the climate of our government would be very arid indeed."[7]

The regard for expertise appeared in other ways. New government bodies aimed to offer dispassionate analysis of data, free from political noise and clutter: the Council of Economic Advisors, the National Security Council, the Central Intelligence Agency. Harry Truman appointed the first dedicated science adviser. Dwight Eisenhower asked the ABA to certify his judicial nominees. These and countless other efforts represented a triumph of expertise and professionalism over politics.

In journalism, too, technocratic assumptions reigned. Sharing the Progressive Era's esteem for the disinterested pursuit of information, journalists shunned overt partisanship in favor of "straight" news coverage that could find audiences of diverse political stripes. An elite group of "opinion leaders," such as the columnist Walter Lippmann, whose classic work *Public Opinion* had championed the role of expertise in a democracy, dispensed sober, moderate analysis from a position that Lippmann's fellow columnist Stewart Alsop called "the Center," a term that implied both a midpoint on the political spectrum and a seat of authority. The most influential pundits consorted freely with leading politicians, deriving their influence from their proximity to power and from a worldview that seemed unclouded by ideology.[8]

Just when this technocracy reached its peak influence, however, two currents—one from the left, one from the right—roiled the consensus. In the 1960s, the Left honed attacks on the seats of authority in every realm. "Critics charged that urban planning created slums, that schools made people stupid, that medicine caused disease, that psychiatry invented mental illness, and that the courts promoted injustice," the sociologist and journalism historian Michael Schudson has written. "Intellectuals, no longer seen as the source of dispassionate counsel, were the 'new mandarins,' while government policy makers were called 'the best and the brightest' in a tone of most untender irony."[9] Some critics elaborated a critique of expertise that drew on John Dewey's quarrels with Walter Lippmann in the 1920s, emphasizing the undemocratic aspects of policymaking by experts. Others challenged more sweepingly the Enlightenment ideas underpinning scholarship: the reality of individual free will and agency, the desirability of value-free research, even the possibility of transparent meaning. Concerned with exposing the subtle sources of cultural power, these critiques construed traditional claims about the pursuit of knowledge as constructs that served to buttress the intellectuals' place of privilege; in some of its more radical forms, the Enlightenment bases for knowledge itself were questioned. "The [post-1960s] Academic Left," the historian John Patrick Diggins argued, "was the first Left in American or European history to distrust the eighteenth-century Enlightenment."[10]

The Left's critique found an echo on the right. In 1965 Stanton Evans, a foot soldier in the "New Right," published a Buckleyesque polemic called *The Liberal Establishment* that cast a cold eye on the supposed objectivity of political and other elites.[11] As a term, "the establishment" had originated in English church politics. But in the American context it was applied first to foreign policy elites, such as those at the Council on Foreign Relations, and then developed into a rough synonym for the Great Society technocrats. In the tumultuous 1960s, Right and Left alike invoked the word as an epithet, offering complementary arguments that policy intellectuals and the politicians who relied on them were too ensconced in their own comfort to bring about the change society needed.

Ironically, many of the theorists assailing the intellectual class were themselves intellectuals. More than a few campus liberals and highbrow journalists, recoiling from the Great Society and campus radicalism, articulated a critique that came to be known as neoconservatism. As expounded in Irving Kristol's *Public Interest* and Norman Podhoretz's *Commentary*, neoconservatism originated as a *cri de coeur* against the purported collapse of standards, a rearguard defense of timeless verities. But neoconservatism held the seeds of a paradox. For while the neocons warred against theories that denied objective truth, or that reduced ideas to power relations, they themselves viewed the Left in precisely this fashion: as dogmatists who cloaked their will to power in the garb of cutting-edge thought. "*The Public Interest* began as a journal that was anti-ideological, with the hope that a public philosophy would emerge out of reasoned discourse," wrote Daniel Bell in 1985; "it is now enlisted in an ideological campaign against liberalism."[12] They seemed to forget that the motives they attributed to the intellectuals they disparaged as "tenured radicals" might be applied equally to the traditional intellectual authorities they professed to venerate.

When Richard Nixon became president, the Right's critique of the establishment—and of what the neocons called the "New Class"—found its perfect spokesman. No occupant of the nation's highest office ever harbored a deeper grudge against the intellectual and professional classes. The ABA, the Brookings Institution, public television, the CIA, the national news media—Nixon saw these and kindred bodies, governmental and paragovernmental, as hotbeds of liberalism. He even abolished the position of science advisor (Gerald Ford would reinstate it). He railed against Ivy Leaguers, academics, and even his own administration's civil servants, whom he called, with his characteristic precision, "bastards who are here to screw us."[13] Nixon's barbs expressed more than personal animus. They reflected and stoked a hostility toward intellectual authorities that spanned the expanding conservative movement, from the anti-intellectual Old Right to the resentful avatars of the post-1960s cultural backlash. In this climate was born the counterestablishment, with its institutions that pretended to mirror the "liberal" counterparts that preceded them. And it reached its maturity precisely at an opportune moment— the arrival in the White House of George W. Bush.

• • •

Bush's denigration of empirical findings and his forays into epistemological relativism were foreseeable from early on, in the epochal fight over Florida's presidential vote tally in the month after election day, 2000. During that battle for the presidency, Bush's team did everything possible (including at one point fomenting mob violence) to forestall a manual recount of the state's ballots that might have shown Al Gore to be the rightful president-elect. In so doing, they began their assault on reality-based decision making. For the Bush team didn't just contend that a recount would fail to identify the true winner more accurately; more radically, they argued that *any* accurate tally was unattainable—that the truth was unknowable. A recount was dangerous, they said, since it would mislead people into thinking that the nation had come closer to arriving at the truth of the election outcome when it hadn't.

At the time, two intellectuals had the acuity to note echoes between these arguments adopted by pro-Bush partisans and the postmodern ideas that had long drawn the Right's scorn. "When promulgated by left-wing academics skeptical of truth claims held to be timeless and universal—such claims, they argued, denied the proclivity of dominant groups to impose their values on the oppressed or the marginalized—postmodern skepticism has faced derisive rebuttal from political conservatives," wrote the political scientist Alan Wolfe. "But when it was expressed by George W. Bush and his supporters in their efforts to explain why it was unnecessary to count votes, conservatives applauded."[14] Likewise, the journalist Ron Rosenbaum argued that Bush had embraced nothing less than "the signature attitude of postmodernism: distrust of knowledge, of evidence, of the possibility of ever knowing the truth, the futility of the search for 'facts.'"[15]

Even if the postmodern label was just being applied playfully, it hit on something important: the Bush team prevailed in the recount battle in part because it managed to delegitimize the idea that any discernible truth existed beyond the two sides' dueling claims. By and large, the media portrayed the Florida battle as the mirror-image power grabs of dueling opportunists, not as a philosophical or constitutional exercise in which Gore's side sought a recount whatever the outcome, while Bush's aimed to halt a procedure that could only derail his ascent. News reports tended to treat all arguments as mere rationalizations, depriving Gore of the moral pressure that might (conceivably) have forced the politicians and even the Supreme Court justices deciding the election's outcome to allow the recounts to proceed.

Bush and his aides, after using this rhetorical strategy during the Florida recount fight, would follow the same operating assumption once they took office. Consistently, the administration would seek to defang expert opinions that threatened its agenda, casting accepted authorities as mere political actors. The Right's solid hold on power, however, introduced an important wrinkle to its old strategy. So long as conservatives held the opposition, they had expressed their hostility to established expertise mostly as critique; it hadn't borne the burden of supporting sound policymaking. Governing now meant either tempering or implementing the rhetoric—with the risk of either alienating the base or toying with unsound policies. Placing ideology above pragmatism, Bush dared to deliver on his "anti-establishment" rhetoric to a degree that Nixon and Reagan hadn't, forging beyond those predecessors in casting aside expertise.

Examples came early and often. Two months after the inauguration, Bush terminated the ABA's fifty-year-old role in evaluating judicial nominees. The move represented the culmination of a long-standing drive. In a March press conference announcing the shift, White House counsel Alberto Gonzales revealed the Right's view of the ABA, calling it but one of "literally dozens of groups and many individuals who have a strong interest in the composition of the federal courts." ABA president Martha W. Barnett identified the move as a rebuke not just to her organization but to the idea that judicial qualifications might exist apart from ideology. "This means," she warned, "that the role of politics may be taking the place of professionalism in choosing judges."[16] Yet the move caused little stir. Journalists and the public had grown accustomed to the politicization of judicial appointments. They had learned to treat court rulings, too—most obviously the recent *Bush v. Gore*, roundly seen as a political decision masquerading as jurisprudence—as expressions of political power, far from disinterested. The dismay voiced by a few senators and editorial pages over the ABA's demotion soon petered out.

Bush's denigration of expertise moved to center stage later that spring as he pushed his tax plan, the centerpiece of his presidential bid. Although economists differed about the wisdom of passing the plan, it remained an inescapable fact that with its sizable tax cuts the plan would eat into the federal budget surplus that

Bush had inherited and would directly benefit the wealthy most of all. To counteract these inconvenient truths, the administration pitched the tax cuts as a boon to the working class and a spur to higher tax revenues. It conscripted friendly economists and budget experts willing to tout the plan, and when its Treasury Department's figures proved uncongenial, the White House modified them to make its case. Critics such as Paul Krugman, who demonstrated how the administration was cooking the numbers, were depicted as arguing from their own ideology, not a position of disinterested knowledge.[17] Without the training to crunch the numbers, however, most journalists again presented the administration's claims as one legitimate side of a two-sided debate. Having seen countless politicians of both parties fudging budget forecasts and economic projections before, many saw the administration's spin on its numbers as unremarkable. Ultimately, a significant portion of Democrats concluded they could not win the spin wars and safely oppose what were often misleadingly called "tax cuts"; pledging support for the plan, they eased its passage later that spring.

If the politicization of law and economic expertise was too familiar and common to prompt any major outcry, the administration's disregard of expertise in the realm of science, which also came into view during Bush's first year, proved more shocking. More than the social sciences, the hard sciences enjoyed a public reputation as cocooned from politics. In a democracy, some skepticism toward expertise in the political realm is common, reasonable, and ultimately healthy; experts shouldn't be treated as unaccountable. But while the public understands that scientists disagree, their disputes don't usually correlate with political viewpoints, as disputes among legal scholars, economists, criminologists, or other social scientists sometimes do; if a scientific claim enjoys a consensus, most citizens have traditionally accepted that it was reached without regard to ideological considerations. Therefore, when the administration moved into challenging the disinterested posture of not just lawyers and economists but also scientists, it crossed a frontier widely seen as inviolable. It had, in the words of physicist Kurt Gottfried, a professor at Cornell and chairman of the Union of Concerned Scientists, a group advocating the use of disinterested research in policies relating to the environment, food, energy, and similar issues, "broken an unwritten code of scientific conduct."[18]

Instances of the administration's disregard for science accumulated in the administration's first term, amounting to what critics called a "war on science," in the title phrase of a best-selling book cataloguing these violations.[19] Often, the political agenda was easy to detect. With stem-cell research having become a new bugaboo of the Religious Right, the administration limited the availability of stem-cell lines for medical research, flying in the face of scientists' recommendations. Committed to an anti-abortion agenda, the administration touted dubious claims that abortions increased the risk of breast cancer. To promote a program of sexual abstinence, the administration twisted the scientific data about the effectiveness of condoms in preventing disease and pregnancy.

But not all of these cases of denigrating science entailed promoting the agenda of the Religious Right. The most high-profile case concerned the political debate over global warming—the sharply rising temperatures that threatened to devastate the earth's environmental balance. Since the mid-1990s, scientific opinion had grown increasingly unified and confident that human industrial activity—the use of cars, airplanes, factories—was making the phenomenon significantly worse. These findings pointed to new and potentially costly regulations, a prospect that business-friendly conservatives feared. Starting in the 1990s, these conservatives set out to discredit the dominant opinion of experts and to gain a hearing for a fringe position among scientists that human activity wasn't to blame. Once Bush entered the White House, the efforts bore fruit.

The first hints that it would reject the science about global warming came in March 2001, when the White House reversed the Clinton administration policy and withdrew its support for the Kyoto Protocol, an international compact for limiting greenhouse gases in the atmosphere. In justifying its stands, the administration increasingly found that it had to ignore or rebut scientific opinion. Indeed, so thoroughgoing was the White House's denial of global warming that it even repudiated a document from its own State Department that endorsed the finding that human activity contributed to climate change, with the president shrugging that the statement was "put out by the bureaucracy." Similarly, the administration refused to heed a report that it had requested from the National Academy of Sciences. The academy, a classic Progressive-style learned society devoted to the promotion of science in the public good, concurred with the scientific consensus that human beings contributed to rising global temperatures. In keeping with normal scientific practice, however, the report allowed that, as in most efforts to establish ironclad scientific correlations, some margin of uncertainty remained. The White House seized on this pro forma disavowal of absolute certainty ("a causal linkage . . . cannot be unequivocally established") to overplay the claim that "uncertainties remain" and to justify inaction.[20]

Without endorsing the administration's line, journalists again treated it as one of two legitimate positions in a debate among experts. A study by two political scientists demonstrated the phenomenon. The scholars analyzed the content of stories about the global warming in four leading national newspapers: the *New York Times*, the *Washington Post*, the *Los Angeles Times*, and the *Wall Street Journal*. More than half gave roughly equal attention to the scientifically supported claim that human activity contributes to global warming and to the fringe position that warming results only from natural changes, while only 35 percent gave more weight to the dominant view.[21]

Nonetheless, the administration's denial of global warming, along with other antiscience positions, triggered a backlash. On Capitol Hill, Democrats held hearings, issued reports, and introduced bills to rein in the administration's behavior, mostly to little avail other than gaining publicity. As the litany of the Bush administration's abuses of scientific data grew, critics took to punning grimly about "political science."[22] But if critics were powerless to change administration policy, a picture was forming of a president beholden to ideology and contemptuous of policy expertise.

Adding credibility to this picture was the testimony of a handful of disaffected administration officials about their colleagues' views of policy expertise. Perhaps the most important came from John DiIulio, a conservative political scientist who pioneered Bush's faith-based programs. In October 2002, Ron Suskind, the journalist who later wrote of the White House's scorn for the "reality-based community," reported in *Esquire* magazine on DiIulio's consternation about the extent to which policy staff were ignored in the Bush White House. As DiIulio wrote in an e-mail to Suskind,

> In eight months, I heard many, many staff discussions, but not three meaningful, substantive policy discussions. There were no actual policy white papers on domestic issues. There were, truth be told, only a couple of people in the West Wing who worried at all about policy substance and analysis, and they were even more overworked than the stereotypical, nonstop, 20-hour-a-day White House staff. Every modern presidency moves on the fly, but, on social policy and related issues, the lack of even basic policy knowledge, and the only casual interest in knowing more, was somewhat breathtaking—discussions by fairly senior people who meant Medicaid but were talking Medicare; near-instant shifts from discussing any actual policy pros and cons to discussing political communications, media strategy, et cetera. Even quite junior staff would sometimes hear quite senior staff pooh-pooh any need to dig deeper for pertinent information on a given issue. . . . This gave rise to what you might call Mayberry Machiavellis—staff, senior and junior, who consistently talked and acted as if the height of political sophistication consisted in reducing every issue to its simplest, black-and-white terms for public consumption, then steering legislative initiatives or policy proposals as far right as possible. These folks have their predecessors in previous administrations (left and right, Democrat and Republican), but, in the Bush administration, they were particularly unfettered.[23]

DiIulio's whistle-blowing got attention and contributed to the emerging picture of an ideologically driven administration. His exposé probably would have gotten more attention, too, had it not been published just as the public and the media were fully engaged in an even more consequential debate—the debate about whether to invade Iraq.

• • •

The two issues—the decision to go to war and the valuation of ideology over expertise—were actually linked. Central to Bush's case for war, after all, was the politicization of the intelligence-gathering process that was supposed to be the basis for judging whether the weapons programs that Saddam Hussein was developing in Iraq threatened American security. In late 2002, as Bush began building his case for invading Iraq, news reports revealed that his aides were manipulating intelligence and ignoring dissenting analyses from career CIA officers and other experts. Eventually, this corruption of intelligence would lead to the angriest criticisms Bush had yet suffered.

U.S. officials had debated the wisdom of allowing Saddam to remain in power in Iraq since 1998, when he kicked out the UN weapons inspectors charged by international law with ensuring that he didn't rearm. But where the Clinton administration had only encouraged indigenous efforts to topple Saddam, Bush early on showed an eagerness to invade Iraq to depose him. In November 2001, he ordered Defense Secretary Donald Rumsfeld to draft invasion plans, and by the next fall advocating for war had become his top priority. By the end of the year, Bush had gotten the U.S. Congress to authorize military force to pressure Saddam to readmit the inspectors and the UN to issue resolutions demanding his compliance. Those preliminary steps succeeded in getting the inspectors to resume their long-delayed work. Barely had they resumed, however, when Bush prematurely charged that Saddam wasn't cooperating and signaled that an invasion would likely come soon. The UN refused to bless an invasion until the inspectors had more time to examine the state of Saddam's weaponry, yet Bush, boasting support from a small band of allies, went ahead and launched a full-scale invasion anyway.[24]

Contrary to recollections that the news media had abetted the administration with utter compliance, a hearty minority of journalists at the time looked askance at the administration's arguments for war. Debate about the invasion flourished in editorial pages, magazines, and to some degree on news shows. Reports in major media outlets noted how pro-invasion officials were misreading or misrepresenting intelligence about Saddam's weapons programs and his ties to the terrorist group al Qaeda. The *New York Times*, although rightfully faulted after the fact for publishing reporter Judith Miller's credulous, administration-fed accounts about the advanced state of Saddam's weapons program, also ran articles questioning those reports. The *Times* discovered that Rumsfeld, Vice President Dick Cheney, and other aides were second-guessing professionally prepared intelligence reports that undermined the case for war, going so far as to create a unit to review the information on Saddam's Iraq—a disclosure that brought widespread charges that they were "cherry picking" intelligence to buttress the case for war. Other national publications also aired these troubling facts.[25]

Nor did the strained claims that officials used in their public statements go unchallenged. After Bush stated in September 2002 that Iraq had sought to buy aluminum tubes for centrifuges, weapons experts publicly disputed his assertion, with the *Times*, the *Washington Post*, and other outlets airing their skepticism.[26] When Cheney and other hawks claimed that one of the 9/11 hijackers had met with Iraqi officials in Prague, the press reported that intelligence analysts considered the theory to have been debunked. Career government officials also got a forum, often with a cloak of anonymity, to question other alleged connections between Saddam and al Qaeda.[27]

The problem with the discourse in the media, in short, wasn't an absence of skepticism or even journalistic plumping for war, although there was plenty of that. The more serious obstacle to airing objections to the case for an invasion was again the convention of balance, which restrained the media's ability to forthrightly criticize the administration's claims except in those venues cordoned off for "opinion." Since the administration professed such certainty about Saddam's malign intentions, and since claims from high-placed official sources during wartime almost always enjoy a privileged status from journalists, critics of the faulty intelligence were hard-pressed to frame their arguments as the introduction of facts into the debate, as opposed to a simple matter of differing opinion. In the fearful post-9/11 climate, the doubts of experts invariably appeared next to administration rebuttals, leaving reporters and citizens once more unsure of what to believe.

The prewar spinning of intelligence had little consequence at first, when the invasion looked like a success. Within months, however, the occupation of Iraq turned sour. Saddam's weapons stockpiles never materialized; violence escalated; and the occupation proved disastrous on many fronts. By late 2003, the public was reexamining the case for war, rounding out a picture of the ways that leading administration officials, especially Cheney, had disparaged the analyses of intelligence experts to buttress their case for war. Unlike the demotion of the ABA, which directly affected few Americans, or the cooking of economic numbers to pass Bush's tax cuts, which were seen as standard Washington procedure, here the politicization of expertise had far-reaching, life-or-death consequences.

• • •

Despite some efforts to make Bush's war on expertise a campaign issue, the president won reelection in 2004 in another close race. And as he made his second-term appointments, he continued to value ideological purity and partisan loyalty over expertise. He rewarded several of his longtime aides with cabinet positions, a signal as to the course of his second term. It was as if, having dethroned the Progressive Era regime of expertise and merit, he were reviving a nineteenth-century-style spoils system.

This tendency would be Bush's undoing. Despite his confidence at the start of his second term, Bush soon found himself in the worst political peril of his presidency. For the rest of his term he would struggle with the failure of his policies, low approval ratings, the thwarting of high-priority legislation, and fissures within once-unified Republican ranks. This swift collapse had several causes, including the chaos in Iraq and Bush's misguided attempt to privatize Social Security. But critical blows came in the first year of Bush's new term, when the administration's devaluation of expertise in favor of ideological or partisan imperatives led to failures, scandals, and public relations disasters. (Both the failed Social Security initiative and the continued disaster in Iraq were themselves partly the result of hyperpoliticized staffing that devalued professional expertise.) Even former supporters now questioned Bush's competence.

One prominent if symbolic case came early in 2005: that of Terri Schiavo, a Florida woman locked irreversibly in a permanent vegetative state. Religious conservatives, opposed to euthanasia or a "right to die," organized to protest her husband's plan to let her expire. Brandishing the crackpot views of a few unorthodox doctors, national Republican leaders joined the cause, dismissing the medical consensus that Schiavo wouldn't recover. The case instantly became a cause célèbre, with liberals mostly supporting Schiavo's husband and conservatives mostly backing her parents, who wished her to remain alive. Again, the knowledge required to assess Schiavo's state was so specialized that journalists fell back on the formula of balance, and citizens had to place trust in one set of experts or another. The essayist Joan Didion, who thought of herself as a skeptic of journalistic clichés, was one of many who gave credence to the doctors showcased by the Right, throwing up her hands to sigh, "Much is unknown here. A change in diagnosis might or might not lead to a change in treatment, and a change in treatment might or might not lead to improved response."[28] Bush hurried back from a vacation to sign a bill to keep Schiavo alive, and the Right seemed poised for another political victory. Within days, however, courts upheld Schiavo's husband's right to follow the medical consensus, remove her feeding tube, and let her die. Despite predictions that the public would back the Republicans, moreover, polls showed majorities actually disapproving of their actions. In the end, the incident mostly fed the perception that Bush was putting politics above scientific—here, medical—considerations.

More detrimental to Bush's standing in the long run were several blunders in late 2005 that stemmed from his penchant for replacing the regime of technocracy with one of cronyism. The gravest breakdown in competence was the administration's disastrous response to Hurricane Katrina in August and September, in which the Federal Emergency Management Agency—the federal body tasked with disaster preparation and response—proved wholly unprepared for the relief and rescue of thousands of dispossessed and hungry citizens unable to evacuate a flooded New Orleans. Popular outrage soared when it emerged that Bush had named to run FEMA the woefully underqualified Michael D. Brown, who had previously served as an official for the International Arabian Horse Association and had gained his position through his friend Joe Allbaugh, an old political aide to the president and his first FEMA chief. Brown's unfitness for the job of FEMA's director was more than an oversight; it stemmed from the Right's very worldview. The Clinton administration had treated FEMA as a problem-solving agency, relying on disaster-management experts. It had dealt effectively with several hurricanes and the 1995 Oklahoma City bombing. But Bush shoehorned the agency into the new Department of Homeland Security and denied it attention and funding. An antigovernment ideology took hold within; it farmed out functions to private companies; valued employees quit. The decision to appoint Brown, a crony lacking the basic qualifications for the position, was part of this larger trend.

The elevation of loyalty over expertise also came back to hurt Bush in 2005 when he nominated his friend Harriet Miers, the White House counsel, to the vacated Supreme Court seat of Justice Sandra Day O'Connor. Here Bush was working within the confines of an elaborate rhetorical game surrounding judicial nominees that dated to the 1960s, in which presidents sought to blunt partisan attacks by choosing candidates with clear professional merit.[29] Earlier that fall Bush had used the strong qualifications of Circuit Court Judge John G. Roberts to speed his confirmation as Supreme Court chief justice; Roberts won the votes of half of the Senate's forty-four Democrats, many of whom cited his sterling résumé as a reason for looking past his conservative jurisprudence. But Bush broke from that strategy in selecting Miers, apparently hoping that her sex would deter Democrats from objecting to her selection as O'Connor's heir. Miers, though, lacked a paper trail that could prove her right-wing bona fides, and conservatives worried that she might, like some previous Republican appointees to the bench, drift toward a more liberal jurisprudence. Conservative senators thus seized on her relatively weak résumé as a rationale for opposing her; ironically, the rise of the technocracy had rendered untenable the once common practice of appointing political allies to the high court. Unable to claim that Miers had the Roberts-like résumé that he himself had made the standard, Bush had his friend withdraw from consideration.[30]

The cases of Brown and Miers reinforced the perception of an administration given to cronyism. Together with other embarrassing examples of the administration's misguided rewarding of loyalty, these cases chipped away at Bush's now crumbling reputation for competence and credibility. In the following months, the incidents tumbled forth onto the news pages. An oil industry lobbyist who ran Bush's Environmental Policy Council stepped down after it emerged that he had doctored Environmental Protection Agency documents to downplay links between greenhouse gas emissions and global warming. A twenty-four-year-old political appointee at NASA, who falsely claimed a college degree he had never earned, resigned after disclosures that he had ordered officials to keep a top climate scientist from talking to reporters and ordered a NASA Web designer to describe the Big Bang as just a theory. Kenneth Y. Tomlinson, a crony of Karl Rove's, resigned as the head of the Corporation for Public Broadcasting after the organization's inspector general found he had illegally politicized programming on PBS. In the summer of 2007, former surgeon general Richard Carmona told Congress that the White House had forbidden him from speaking publicly about major health issues on which its policies diverged from the medical consensus.[31]

But even after the president's sagging reputation contributed to a resounding Democratic victory in the 2006 midterm elections, the administration continued to politicize realms supposed to remain relatively free of partisanship. The Democrats' capture of both houses of Congress did not stop the administration from proceeding with a plan to dismiss several U.S. attorneys, the chief federal prosecutors situated in regional jurisdictions across the country. Some of these attorneys had launched prosecutions that were damaging to the administration; others had resisted pursuing cases that Bush officials favored; in still other cases, the administration wanted to give the jobs to loyalists who could then burnish their résumés for future political careers. Congressional Democrats convened hearings, which soon unearthed communications among White House and Justice Department officials, including thousands of e-mail messages that showed politics to be very much at work in their discussions. Both Rove and Attorney General Alberto Gonzales had been involved in selecting who should be let go, and their aides were caught speaking baldly of their political motives. As the scandal spread, it forced the resignation of several top Justice Department officials—including, in August 2007, of Gonzales himself. Again, the disregard for professionalism in favor of loyalty had backfired.

• • •

Toward the end of the Bush administration, the president and his aides showed signs that they appreciated the costs, if only the political ones, of jettisoning expertise. The replacement of Gonzales with Michael Mukasey suggested that professionalism, not loyalty, had been restored, in at least one case, to the Justice Department's appointments process, since Mukasey ended the politicized hiring. And while the administration bore much responsibility for the deregulatory excesses that enabled the disastrous financial crisis of late 2008, it had notably shied away from cronyism in appointing Henry Paulson to the Treasury Department and Ben Bernanke to the Federal Reserve Board, both of whom strove to address the crises professionally, if not necessarily with the utmost effectiveness.

Ultimately, though, the limits to the administration's contempt for expertise and professionalism proved less significant than the far-reaching nature of that contempt. Indeed, the administration's valuation of loyalty over expertise contained the seeds of its own undoing. Needless to say, the problems of the Bush presidency stemmed from more obvious and proximate causes, including the Iraq misadventure, the reversal of America's economic fortunes, and the neglect of New Orleans. But these failures in turn were able to happen because the administration shunned the counsels of those who knew better or might have done better—the analysts whose doubts about the danger posed by Saddam's weapons programs were suppressed, the economists whose warnings of the perils of huge tax cuts were dismissed, the engineers whose alarums about the Gulf Coast's unpreparedness fell on deaf ears. Catastrophe wasn't inevitable, but given how consistently expert advice was shunted aside or derided, it would have been amazing if some disasters like these had not occurred.

In January 2009, Bush left office with record-low approval ratings. The Democrats' victory in the 2008 presidential election left his party without control of the House, the Senate, or the White House—a stunning turnaround from four years earlier. Analysts declared the end of a conservative era that had begun with Reagan or Nixon.

The change of parties and of governing ideology suggested that, as the incoming president Barack Obama had promised on the campaign trail, sound research and science would again enjoy a secure place in policymaking. And yet even as Bush's contempt for expertise fostered an admiration among liberals for science and standards, there were also some on the further reaches of the Left who were now urging their political allies to in fact *mimic* the Right's politicization of expertise and its attack on establishment institutions. During the Bush years, some liberals, convinced that think tanks like the Brookings Institution were no match for the

Heritage Foundation's ideologically driven policy papers, poured money into the new Center for American Progress, which focused on shaping inside-Washington debates, not on disinterested policy research. Feeling cornered by the Federalist Society, liberal law students in 2001 created the American Constitution Society, hoping to erect a Federalist-like breeding ground for left activism. Struggling with low ratings in the later years of Bush's presidency, the cable news channel MSNBC reinvented itself as a true left-wing counterpart to Fox News, with commentators such as Keith Olbermann and Rachel Maddow, who made no pretense that they were engaging in objective or neutral journalism.[32]

Moreover, beyond the partisan debates, ancient currents of American anti-authoritarianism proved difficult to suppress. A deep strain in the nation's political culture—with roots in evangelical religion, Jacksonian democracy, and the entrepreneur's esteem for practical business horse sense—had always deemed the common individual as fit to render critical judgments as any expert; and while countervailing technocratic ideals had muted this disdain for authority in the mid-twentieth century, it came roaring back in the 1960s, with the rise of the New Left, the New Right, and a leveling impulse more generally.

Indeed, in the new century, with the rise of the Internet and other new media, a broad assault on cultural standards seemed to have champions of standards and discrimination on the run. Armchair movie fans displaced learned cinephiles as influential critics. In politics, industrious bloggers vied for clout with careerlong students of policy. Wikipedia, an unreliable on-line encyclopedia open to contributions from anyone with a keyboard, was bookmarked by college freshmen and New York Times reporters alike. Right and Left fashioned an anti-elitist rhetoric that glorified common sense. In 2006, Time magazine named as its "Person of the Year" neither a statesman nor a scientist nor an artist but, as the shiny mylar cover revealed, "You."[33]

Despite the changes in the White House and Congress, then, the deep-seated suspicion of expertise was not about to disappear.

The Right, it turned out, had been only its most hospitable incubator, not its exclusive home. Deference to technocratic managers of the midcentury sort showed little likelihood of return.

But for those in the reality-based community, this cultural shift didn't have to dictate a posture of despair. To be sure, the Left would have to guard against the self-destructive anti-elitism that had led the Right into error. But there would have been peril, too, had the Left allowed the conservative contempt for expertise to trigger a blind defense of intellectual authority. Government reliance on experts had always worked best when kept in check by grassroots forces, not reflexively rejecting expert opinion but subjecting it to scrutiny in a kind of fruitful dialectic between populism and liberal technocracy.

In this regard, many of the same technological tools that enabled and encouraged the assault on standards also made possible a transparency that held the promise of bolstering democracy. Data of all sorts, for instance, were now much more easily accessible to the layperson, who could engage in thoughtful reinterpretation as readily as mindless fulmination. To pick but one example, polling data, once left to inexpert journalists to decipher, were, by the 2008 campaign, effortlessly downloaded and pored over by droves of industrious amateurs, who could spot flaws in the journalistic accounts. Information-rich reports no longer lay squirreled away on library shelves, largely unexamined, but could be scrutinized by anyone with a high-speed Internet connection and a political agenda.

Those agendas, moreover, were often what motivated people to participate in democracy. In an age of polarization, the lapse into dogma was always a danger, and a world without institutions devoted to disinterested inquiry—a world with *only* Fox and MSNBC, but no *New York Times*; with *only* the Heritage Foundation and the Center for American Progress, but no Brookings Institution— would be immeasurably poorer. But the counterestablishments of the Left and the Right, along with the sea changes in the world of information, weren't solely sources of disinformation and spin.

They contained promise as well as peril, and no one could predict which would predominate in the years ahead. As the Bush presidency receded into history, it was at least possible to envision an outcome in which civilization's vast knowledge was deployed constructively for social betterment while the experts' own tendencies toward hubris or complacency were largely held in check by activist cadres within an emboldened public.

10

COMPASSIONATE CONSERVATISM

Religion in the Age of George W. Bush

KEVIN M. KRUSE

AT THE END OF THE TWENTIETH CENTURY, THE RELATIONSHIP BE-tween the Republican Party and religious voters stood at a cross-roads. For two decades, conservative Christians had been a crucially important constituency in the Republican coalition. Organizations of the Religious Right, such as Reverend Jerry Falwell's Moral Major-ity and Reverend Pat Robertson's Christian Coalition, became pillars of the conservative movement and quickly dedicated themselves to delivering religious voters to Republican candidates. The results were clear. Over the course of three successive elections, Republicans steadily increased their share of votes from white evangelical Chris-tians, winning by margins of 56 percent to 40 percent in 1980, 69 percent to 30 percent in 1984, and then 74 percent to 24 percent in 1988. During that same span, the GOP won majorities of the white Catholic vote as well, securing margins of 51 percent to 40 percent in 1980, 57 percent to 42 percent in 1984, and 56 percent to 43 percent in 1988. Noting the trends, political pundits came to speak of the ever-widening "religion gap" in contemporary American politics as a key factor in the success for modern conservatism.[1]

Two decades later, however, the Religious Right was wandering the political wilderness. For all their intensity, the "culture wars" of the 1990s had brought few concrete successes for religious conserva-tives, and their inability to remove President Bill Clinton from office only deepened a serious crisis of confidence. Paul Weyrich, the conservative organizer who had helped build the Religious Right, now pronounced it a failure. In a broadly circulated letter of February 1999, he even rejected the name he had used to christen the movement: "I no longer believe that there is a moral majority." Weyrich urged religious conservatives to see that their struggle had failed and "to drop out of this culture, and find places . . . where we can live godly, righteous and sober lives" away from national politics. In many ways, leading figures and organizations of the Religious Right were already marginalized. After the dissolution of the Moral Majority in 1989, Reverend Falwell searched for ways to remain relevant, but with little success. As the 1990s came to a close, he was waging war against fictional characters in children's programming whom he believed to be gay, resulting in little more than what one newspaper characterized as "coast-to-coast snickers" of derision. The Christian Coalition, meanwhile, was likewise in decline, under investigation by both the Federal Election Commission and the Internal Revenue Service. With several state chapters in disarray and many major figures leaving its leadership ranks, a former field director dismissed the organization as "defunct." The reign of the Religious Right had seemingly ended.[2]

Against this landscape, the confluence of religion and politics in the presidency of George W. Bush represented a paradox of sorts. As a candidate, the Texas Republican promised a new approach to the troubled topic of church and state. He presented himself as a proponent of "compassionate conservatism," an ideology that avoided the moral absolutism of past religious conservatives and instead promised a more inclusive and effective approach to social problems. But his efforts as president to transform the relationship between religion and politics failed. Liberals remained distrustful of his motives. But conservatives proved to be an even greater obstacle, as they co-opted the centerpiece of his efforts, the so-called faith-based initiative, and used it for their own ends. Increasingly, as old lines of division formed around him, the president dutifully took his place on the right, doing battle on perennial issues of the culture wars such as abortion and gay rights. In the immediate sense, Bush's embrace of traditional religious conservatism led to success in the 2004 election and a second term in office. But from a longer perspective, the president's capitulation to the culture wars may well represent a missed opportunity to transcend old conflicts of religion and politics.

As he entered the race for the presidency, Texas governor George W. Bush sought to present a kinder, gentler face for religious conservatism. It was a task to which Bush seemed ably suited, as his faith formed an essential part of both his private character and his public persona. At heart, his religious convictions appeared sincere and deeply felt. After a wayward youth, Bush had undergone a conversion in middle age and now thought of himself as a born-again Christian. The sincerity of Bush's faith, however, did not diminish its usefulness in political terms. To the contrary, his religious beliefs made him a more alluring option for the Religious Right and served as one of the driving rationales for his candidacy and, in time, his presidency. Bush credited his decision to run, for instance, to a sermon delivered in January 1999 by Pastor Mark Craig at Austin's First United Methodist Church. The minister's words, he said, "prodded me out of my comfortable life as Governor of Texas and toward a national campaign." In a strategic series of meetings with evangelical leaders, Bush asserted that he saw the path before him clearly. "I feel like God wants me to run for president," he told Reverend James Robison. "I can't explain it, but I sense my country is going to need me." Two decades earlier, Robison had done much to secure the support of religious conservatives for the presidential campaign of Ronald Reagan. Convinced of Bush's convictions, Robison would now do the same for him. Faith, it seemed, did have earthly rewards.[3]

On the campaign trail, Bush wore his faith openly and comfortably. During a December 1999 Republican primary debate in Iowa, for instance, when the candidates were asked about their favorite philosopher, Bush immediately named Jesus Christ, "because he changed my heart." For like-minded believers, the comment made perfect sense. As Richard Land of the Southern Baptist Convention noted, "Most evangelicals who heard that question probably thought, 'That's exactly the way I would have answered.'" Political pundits agreed that the answer resonated, but assumed it represented not heartfelt faith but a calculated appeal to evangelicals. "This is the era of niche marketing, and Jesus is a niche," observed *New York Times* columnist Maureen Dowd. "W. is checking Jesus' numbers, and Jesus is polling well." The media parsed Bush's words for their impact on the election, deciding that they would likely alienate many Americans. "This comes across as, you know, intolerant," argued *Time's* Margaret Carlson. On NBC's *Meet the Press*, host Tim Russert grilled the governor: "Fifteen million atheists in this country, five million Jews, five million Muslims, millions more Buddhists and Hindus. Should they feel excluded [by] George W. Bush because of his allegiance to Jesus?" Bush calmly replied, "It's my foundation and if it costs me votes to have answered the question that way, so be it."[4]

While Bush remained unapologetic about his personal religious belief, he also sought to assure voters that he would not seek to implement the rigid political agenda of the Religious Right. Borrowing a phrase from author Marvin Olasky, the Republican candidate characterized himself as a "compassionate conservative" who would take a softer line on social issues than the culture warriors in his party previously had. Many on the right took issue with the phrase. For some, the "compassionate" qualifier implicitly condemned mainstream conservatism as heartless; for others, the phrase seemed an empty marketing gimmick. (As Republican speechwriter David Frum joked, "Love conservatism but hate arguing about abortion? Try our new *compassionate conservatism*— great ideological taste, now with less controversy.") But the candidate backed his words with deeds, distancing himself from the ideologues of his party and illustrating just what he intended. In a single week in October 1999, for instance, Bush criticized congressional Republicans for heartlessly "balancing the budget on the backs of the poor" and lamented that, all too often, "my party has painted an image of America slouching toward Gomorrah."[5]

In concrete terms, Bush's plans for compassionate conservatism rested with his promise to empower private religious and community organizations and thereby expand their role in the provision of social services. The "faith-based initiative," as it would be known, had its clearest expression in a July 1999 address. Bush traveled to Indianapolis, where Mayor Stephen Goldsmith's Front Porch Alliance had crafted close working relationships between local government and neighborhood, community, and religious organizations. In his speech there, Bush distanced himself from party orthodoxy on economic and fiscal conservatism. "I know that economic growth is not the solution to every problem," he announced. "The invisible hand works many miracles. But it cannot touch the human heart." He proposed a massive program of government spending to support the "churches and synagogues and mosques and charities" engaged in social welfare. "Without more support and resources, both public and private," he insisted, "we are asking them to make bricks without straw." Specifically, Bush called for annual spending of $8 billion through a combination of tax credits for charitable donations and, on a smaller scale, direct government financing. Furthermore, he called for an additional $200 million annually to create a "Compassion Capital Fund" which would help smaller charities, often overlooked in national programs, strengthen their own poverty programs.[6]

In political terms, the faith-based initiative seemed unlikely to spark controversy. During the Clinton administration, Congress had instituted a rule known as "charitable choice," which encouraged proselytizing religious organizations to seek and secure federal funds for their private social service programs. The measure had first been passed as part of the 1996 welfare reform legislation, and then three more times after that, with little to no controversy. More immediately, Vice President Al Gore had outlined a similar proposal on the campaign trail. Indeed, two months *before* Bush's Indianapolis speech, the Democratic frontrunner called for a "new partnership" between the federal government and faith-based charities during a visit to a Salvation Army center in Atlanta. "I believe government should play a greater role in sustaining this quiet transformation—not only by dictating solutions from above, but by supporting the effective new policies that are rising up from below," Gore announced. "If you elect me President, the voices of faith-based organizations will be integral to the policies set forth in my administration." This common ground led liberal columnist E. J. Dionne of the *Washington Post* to proclaim the faith-based initiative "the opposite of a wedge issue." Despite differences else-where, "on this question, Gore doesn't mind if he and Bush sing from the same hymnal."[7]

As the campaign continued, however, the faith-based initiative came to be seen as a uniquely Republican policy. George W. Bush made the concept of compassionate conservatism a centerpiece of his general election campaign and focused extensively on the pro-posals in his acceptance speech in Philadelphia. There he spoke glowingly about the work of a Christian charity and enlisted the nation to support similar efforts. "Government cannot do this work. It can feed the body, but it cannot feed the soul. Yet govern-ment can take the side of these groups, helping the helper, encour-aging the inspired," the nominee argued. "My administration will give taxpayers new incentives to donate to charity, encourage after-school programs that build character, and support mentor-ing groups that shape and save young lives." As the Republican focused more on the initiative, his Democratic rival let the matter drop. "[Gore] didn't develop it; he didn't show commitment; he seemed to have abandoned it," Democratic strategist Will Mar-shall reflected. "Undoubtedly, campaign strategists saw this as an irrelevant, or worse, Bush issue. 'If Bush is talking about it, why are you?' So they get on solid Democratic turf and off the Bush turf."[8]

The election returns provided fresh evidence that religious is-sues were still widely seen as Republican ones. According to exit polls, Bush secured significant majorities from voters who claimed they frequently attended religious services—87 percent of white voters identifying with the Religious Right, 61 percent of white Protestants, and 57 percent of white Catholics. Exceptions were to be found, of course, in that the Republican won votes from only 30 percent of Latino Catholics, 20 percent of Jews, and 9 percent of black Protestants. Even though Bush secured the votes of white religious conservatives, their overall presence at the polls had dropped slightly when compared to past elections. In the previous election, the Religious Right had a larger presence—representing 17 percent of the electorate in 1996, but 14 percent in 2000—even though the Republican standard-bearer that year, Kansas senator Bob Dole, was a halfhearted ally at best. The core constituencies of the Religious Right had also weakened across the board. Turnout among white evangelicals had fallen by 6 percent, among white mainline Protestants by 2 percent, and among white Catholics by 1 percent. In previous elections, religious voters had been seen as central; after the marked ebbing of the Religious Right in the late 1990s, their importance had slipped.[9]

Once in office, President George W. Bush moved swiftly to enact the faith-based initiative. The longest section of his inaugural address offered an expansive reflection on the idea. "America, at its best, is compassionate," he observed. "Church and charity, synagogue and mosque lend our communities their humanity, and they will have an honored place in our plans and in our laws." Despite the president's rhetoric, that "honored place" had not actually been secured. The faith-based initiative still remained formless as he took the oath. During the transition period, a young Bush aide named Don Willett had stepped forward to craft plans for the program when he realized no one else had bothered. To his dismay, he found little support for the issue, with requests for funding and staff rebuffed at every turn. Then, suddenly, three days after the inaugural, political adviser Karl Rove told him that the entire faith-based initiative would be introduced to the press in six days. An astonished Willett asked how that could be accomplished when the initiative still lacked a director, a staff, an office, or even a general plan of action. "I don't know," Rove responded wearily. "Just get me a fucking faith-based thing. Got it?"[10]

The following Monday, January 29, 2001, George W. Bush issued his first two executive orders as president. The first created a new agency for the executive branch, the White House Office of

Faith-Based and Community Initiatives (WHOFBCI), which was charged with leading the administration's drive to "enlist, expand, equip, empower and enable the work of faith-based and community groups." Directed to set priorities and coordinate public education campaigns, the new office would also monitor the results of all new faith-based initiatives across the federal government. The second order, meanwhile, created faith-based programs for five cabinet-level departments—Education, Health and Human Services, Housing and Urban Development, Justice, and Labor. The offices would conduct internal audits to identify obstacles that prevented community or religious charities from providing social services. "We will encourage faith-based and community programs without changing their mission," the president promised. "We will help all in their work to change hearts while keeping a commitment to pluralism." In keeping with that inclusive spirit, he announced that John J. DiIulio Jr. would serve as WHOFBCI director. Neither a Republican nor a religious leader, DiIulio was a political scientist with expertise in the fields of social welfare, crime policy, and religious charities. A fiercely independent figure from working-class South Philadelphia, he had been christened by the *Washington Post* "Joe Pesci with a Ph.D."[11]

DiIulio accepted the position on the strict condition that the office would remain free from politics, but he soon found himself under attack from both sides of the spectrum. Liberals worried that the initiative was little more than a crusade to fund religion and turn the government into a theocracy. An editorial in the *Atlanta Journal-Constitution* captured the fears of many: "We do not need religious leaders addicted to federal money, always lobbying Congress for more. We do not need politicians using taxpayers' money to buy the support of religious leaders. And most importantly, we do not need a government that requires taxpayers to fund religious groups whose doctrines they find objectionable." Conservatives, meanwhile, argued that the program represented a wasteful "big government" approach to social problems. Even leaders of the Religious Right expressed serious reservations, concerned they would lose their independence and autonomy. "With the king's shillings come the king's shackles," warned Richard Land. Others worried that the president's words about respecting pluralism might be sincere. Pat Robertson warned that "the same government grants given to Catholics, Protestants and Jews must also be given to the Hare Krishnas, the Church of Scientology, or Sun Myung Moon's Unification Church—no matter that some may use brainwashing techniques, or that the founder of one claims to be the messiah and another that he was Buddha reincarnated."[12]

On behalf of the administration, DiIulio sought to calm critics on both sides. First, he responded to those on the left with a February 2001 column in the *Wall Street Journal*. DiIulio assured them that the effort would be neither partisan nor sectarian. "Facts, not faith; performance, not politics; results, not religion; and, we pray, humility, not hubris, will guide my office in advising President Bush and in helping the administration put flesh on the bone of compassionate conservatism," he promised. Liberals remained wary, with later events seeming to confirm their initial skepticism. In July, reports surfaced that the Salvation Army had struck a bargain with the White House. According to an internal memo, the nation's largest Protestant charity would support legislation for the faith-based initiative, and in return the Bush administration would institute a new federal regulation denying aid to state or local governments if they required religious charities to employ nondiscriminatory employment policies that clashed with their beliefs. When the *Washington Post* reported the details of the agreement, Democratic congressmen John Conyers and Jerry Nadler sent DiIulio an angry letter, citing it as proof that faith-based programs were "merely tools to permit increased discrimination" and would "inappropriately entangle religion in our public affairs." DiIulio dismissed the story as "preposterous," but soon learned to his embarrassment that the Salvation Army had, in fact, been negotiating with Karl Rove.[13]

As difficult as it was to convince liberal skeptics, DiIulio found his relationship with conservatives to be even more problematic. In a major address to the National Association of Evangelicals (NAE) in March 2001, DiIulio confronted the concerns religious conservatives had about the program. Those worried about increased secularization of their ministries should remember that participation was voluntary and that they would not be forced to take part. But, he added pointedly, other ministries were eager for government aid. In a comment that was perhaps demographically accurate but politically awkward, DiIulio told the NAE audience that "predominantly white, ex-urban evangelical and national parachurch leaders should be careful not to presume to speak for any persons other than themselves and their own churches." If anything, they could learn from urban ministries. "In all truth and grace," he continued, "I would call upon the National Association of Evangelicals to (as we say on inner-city streets) get real—and get affiliated church leaders and their congregations to get real—about helping the poor, the sick, the imprisoned, and others among 'the least of these.' We all have ears to hear and a heart to listen—and act. It's fine to fret about 'hijacked faith,' but . . . such frets would persuade more and rankle less if they were backed by real human and financial help." Not surprisingly, conservatives reacted indignantly. "Support for the president's faith-based initiative . . . is waning on the Right," warned the *National Review*. "DiIulio's speech yesterday will not do anything to stop it from waning."[14]

As the issue entered the legislative stage, things only got worse. In his public pronouncements, President Bush had outlined a moderate approach to the issue, which he hoped would lead to broad bipartisan support in Congress. In private, however, his administration never reflected his commitment to the issue. His aides seemed more concerned with politics than policy. "Just get me a damn faith bill," domestic policy aide Margaret Spellings pled with a WHOFBCI official. "Any bill. I don't care what kind of bill. Just get me a damn faith bill." Accordingly, as one congressional staffer later lamented, there was little to no direction from the White House on substance. "Legislative affairs, Domestic Policy Council, OMB—they didn't care about this," the aide confided. "Point blank, it wasn't a priority for them." "The White House lobbying people [were] worthless on this whole thing," echoed another. With little direction from the executive branch, House Republicans rallied around more conservative proposals championed by the Religious Right: little or no government oversight for grantees, complete license to discriminate in hiring, and freedom to use public funds as part of private religious endeavors. As DiIulio later observed, the House bill "bore few marks of compassionate conservatism and was, as anybody could tell, an absolute political nonstarter." Its already slim chances of passing the Senate became even slimmer when that chamber switched to Democratic control with the defection of Senator Jim Jeffords from Republican ranks in May 2001. Ultimately, no legislation was secured. Without it, the core of the president's original plan—the provision to secure a massive boost in private charitable giving through tax incentives—was lost as well.[15]

By late summer 2001, the once promising faith-based initiative had been badly crippled. The legislative struggle, according to its most comprehensive study, had transformed a "bipartisan rallying cry for the armies of compassion" into little more than "a throwback to partisan blitzkriegs of the Newt Gingrich era." This sentiment was further cemented in August when John DiIulio announced his resignation. He had agreed to serve for only a six-month period, but the news was nevertheless seen by many as a sign that the Bush administration was seeking to strengthen its relationship with evangelical and fundamentalist leaders. Barry Lynn of Americans United claimed that DiIulio had been "left out of the loop in recent weeks as Bush operatives manipulated the faith-based initiative to make the plan more palatable to the religious right." Reverend Eugene Rivers seconded that assessment, arguing that the resignation "sends a signal that the faith-based office will just be a financial watering hole for the right-wing evangelicals." Conservative leaders, meanwhile, rejoiced at DiIulio's departure. Michael Horowitz of the Hudson Institute dismissed him as "the most strategically disastrous appointee to a senior government position in the twenty-plus years I've been in Washington." Jerry Falwell agreed: "Anyone will be an improvement."[16]

After DiIulio's departure, the WHOFBCI underwent a significant transformation, becoming much more of a partisan political operation. Shortly after taking over in February 2002, the new director, Jim Towey, and deputy director, David Kuo, met with Ken Mehlman, head of political affairs at the White House, to see how they could help Republicans in the upcoming election. They planned twenty "roundtable events," local gatherings of religious and community leaders, hosted by threatened incumbents and held in their districts. The events proved incredibly successful. "In November," Kuo recalled, "we celebrated 19 out of 20 wins." Expanding on that effort, the WHOFBCI held larger conferences across the nation in preparation for the 2004 elections. Ostensibly, the conferences were meant to help local audiences learn how to secure federal grant money, but the political impact was unmistakable. Kuo invited Ralph Reed, former executive director of the Christian Coalition, to the first conference in Atlanta. He was stunned. "You've got three thousand people, mostly minorities, applauding a stinkin' *video* of the president," Reed enthused in a call to Rove. "This is unbelievable!" Buoyed by their success, the WHOFBCI held more than a dozen conferences with more than 20,000 religious and community leaders, purposefully targeting battleground states in the presidential election. "Their political power was incalculable," Kuo remembered. "They were completely off the media's radar screen."[17]

Meanwhile, funding patterns in the cabinet-level faith-based offices showed that worries of their being a "watering hole" for religious conservatives held some merit. The Associated Press conducted a thorough analysis of grants distributed in 2003 by the five federal departments with faith-based offices and determined that an overwhelming amount of the $1.17 billion had gone to Christian groups. More than 1,600 organizations had received grants, but only fifty or so were Jewish, five Muslim, and one Buddhist. As Kuo discovered, the imbalance stemmed from the fact that applications were reviewed by "an overwhelmingly Christian group" of analysts whose "biases were transparent." Proposals with obvious connections to the Religious Right were given top ratings on the hundred-point scale. Pat Robertson's Operation Blessing, for instance, received a nearly perfect rating of 95.67 for its $1.5

million request, even though the organization was then under investigation for diverting relief funds to Robertson's private diamond-mining business. Groups with a non-Christian mission, meanwhile, had a decidedly different fate. Kuo later recalled meeting a woman who had served as a reviewer. The government had given her strict orders to rate the proposals on their practical merits, according to a set list of requirements. Still, she confided, "when I saw one of those non-Christian groups in the set I was reviewing, I just stopped looking at them and gave them a zero." In the end, journalist Amy Sullivan noted, the faith-based initiative had essentially "devolved into a small pork-barrel program that offers token grants to the religious constituencies in Karl Rove's electoral plan for 2004."[18]

Of course, the effort to shore up support from religious conservatives for Bush's reelection rested on much more than the faith-based initiative. Rove, the president's chief political strategist, believed that evangelical and fundamentalist turnout had been depressed in the 2000 elections after reports surfaced that Bush had once been arrested for driving under the influence. Seeking to rally those voters around the president, Rove aggressively advocated a "play-to-the-base" strategy in which hot-button issues for the Religious Right would reemerge as central themes of future campaigns. The struggle over abortion, for instance, quickly moved to the forefront of the new president's agenda. Allies of the pro-life movement were given prominent positions in the administration, including John Ashcroft as attorney general and Tommy Thompson as secretary of health and human services. On his first full day in office, moreover, the president enacted a ban on federal funding for any organizations that provided abortion services abroad, thus restoring a Reagan executive order known by pro-choice critics as "the global gag rule." "It is my conviction that taxpayer funds should not be used to pay for abortions or advocate or actively promote abortion, either here or abroad," the president announced. Significantly, word of the decision came on the anniversary of *Roe v. Wade*. A pro-life rally at the Washington Monument welcomed the news of the president's action with cries of "We love you,

George!" "Now we have a spring in our step," said one marcher. "There is somebody who is listening to us up there."[19]

In addition to these executive decisions, the president also worked closely with congressional conservatives and leaders of the Religious Right to secure two landmark pieces of pro-life legislation at home. In November 2003, Bush signed into law the measure known by anti-abortion activists as the partial-birth abortion ban. Although the procedure in question was rarely used, the ban was heralded as a major step in the struggle to roll back abortion rights. After the signing ceremony, Bush met in the Oval Office with officials from a number of prominent evangelical organizations, including the Southern Baptist Convention, the National Association of Evangelicals, the National Religious Broadcasters, and the Ethics & Religious Liberty Commission. The president asked them to join hands and pray for God's blessings for both the nation and their efforts to protect the unborn. Participant Jerry Falwell pronounced Bush a "man of God" and later reported he had felt "humbled to be in the presence of a man . . . who takes his faith very seriously." Five months later, in April 2004, the president signed into law a second major pro-life bill. The Unborn Victims of Violence Act (UVVA) held that if a pregnant woman were murdered, the fetus would be legally considered a second victim. Again, the practical applications were limited but the legal ramifications were considerable. "What the UVVA does is give legal recognition to life in the womb," noted a spokesperson for Focus on the Family. Tony Perkins of the Family Research Council agreed, pronouncing it a "tremendous victory" for the pro-life movement.[20]

While Bush's support of the pro-life movement was in keeping with traditional demands of religious conservatives, his actions in the realm of AIDS policy represented a bold new direction. In the early years of his presidency, it seemed the new president would lead a retreat from the Clinton administration's fight against AIDS at home and abroad. Chief of Staff Andrew Card created a minor scandal in the early weeks of the new administration by announcing that the Office of National AIDS Policy would be closed. The White House quickly reversed course, but experts remained skeptical. "It's wonderful that they're going to keep the office open," said Clinton AIDS czar Sandy Thurman. "But the proof is in the pudding." Indeed, the president initially took only cautious steps in supporting the international fight against the disease. In May 2001, he announced the United States would contribute $200 million to the UN-backed Global Fund to Fight AIDS, Malaria and Tuberculosis; in June 2002, he promised to increase the contribution to $500 million. Experts in the field welcomed the money as "desperately needed," but said it wasn't nearly enough. "That is a drop in the ocean," argued Dr. Peter Lampley, director of the AIDS Institute at Family Health International. "The U.S. could do a lot more, and the amount they are spending is disappointing, very disappointing."[21]

In his January 2003 State of the Union Address, President Bush stunned the world with his announcement that the United States would commit $15 billion over the next five years to the global fight against AIDS, thereby tripling its investment in the cause. While many initially reacted with skepticism, the president and his allies in Congress quickly moved to make good on the promise. Representative Henry Hyde, a long-time ally of the Religious Right, proved invaluable in shepherding the legislation through Congress, where it came under fire from both sides of the aisle. The bill was patterned on a Ugandan program known as the "ABC approach" for its strategy of urging individuals to "abstain, be faithful, and use condoms." Liberals resented the stress on abstinence; conservatives strongly opposed the advocacy of condoms. Moreover, many on the right demanded that the bill contain an anti-abortion amendment similar to the global gag rule of 2001. Hyde personally favored that approach, but he let the matter drop in order to secure passage, and convinced his allies to do likewise. President Bush, meanwhile, lobbied aggressively for the legislation, marshalling biblical language to win over religious conservatives. "When we see a plague leaving graves and orphans across a continent, we must act," he urged. "When we see the wounded traveler on the road to Jericho, we will not—America will not—pass to the other side of the road." In May 2003, only four months after the initial proposal, the full $15 billion in funding had been secured.[22]

The president's initiative on AIDS was widely praised, even from previously skeptical members of the prior administration. Steve Morrison, an Africa specialist in the Clinton State Department, claimed it "showed leadership that was striking," while Clinton AIDS czar Sandy Thurman heralded the "unprecedented opportunity" it offered for battling the disease. Many observers were puzzled by the apparent contradiction of a conservative president, so clearly wedded to the Religious Right, getting involved in AIDS policy on the international stage. "The cynical read on this was that if he handled domestic AIDS wrong he would appear to be too aligned with Falwell and that crowd, and the global epidemic was the right opportunity to focus on compassion and treatment," argued Terje Anderson of the National Association of People with AIDS. "My noncynical version is that George W. Bush is a deeply religious man and, confronted with this apocalypse around HIV in the developing world, he wanted to do the right thing." Whatever his motivation, the results were well worth noting. Bush did more than simply challenge the conventional wisdom of the Religious Right on the AIDS issue; he enlisted its leaders as active participants in the struggle. While some liberal critics complained about the involvement of religious conservatives in the process and the demands they brought to the table, the simple fact that they had been recruited in the struggle against global AIDS at all and were now supportive of massive government action was in itself remarkable.[23]

While President Bush moved his allies in the Religious Right into new directions on AIDS policy, he more often followed their lead, as seen in the realm of gay rights. Personally, David Frum recalled, "Bush's instinct on gay-rights issues was clear and emphatic: *Do not touch them.*" Accordingly, the president successfully avoided the controversy for years. When the Supreme Court handed down the *Lawrence v. Texas* decision legalizing sodomy in June 2003, however, it sparked a backlash on the right that was impossible to ignore. In his impassioned dissent to the decision,

Justice Antonin Scalia warned that "state laws against bigamy, same-sex marriage, adult incest, prostitution, masturbation, adultery, fornication, bestiality, and obscenity" would be "called into question" by the broadly written majority ruling. Religious conservatives agreed. "We think this is the start of the court putting San Francisco values on the rest of the country," noted an analyst with the Culture and Family Institute. In particular, they worried courts would extend *Lawrence* to legalize gay marriage as well. "That's where we are headed," insisted Richard Lessner of the Family Research Council. "We're convinced this case was brought to provide the foundation for same-sex marriages."[24]

To prevent such an outcome, religious conservatives focused their energies on securing a constitutional amendment defining marriage as between one man and one woman. No effort was spared. According to James Dobson of Focus on the Family, the struggle would be "our D-Day, or Gettysburg, or Stalingrad." The Traditional Values Coalition mailed out literature at a monthly rate of 1.5 million pieces, while leading organizations such as the Family Research Council and Focus on the Family devoted themselves fully to the cause. That fall the Arlington Group, a massive umbrella organization of religious conservatives formed specifically to fight against gay marriage, announced plans to blanket 70,000 congregations with pamphlets and reach millions more through radio and television. The mass mobilization of this core constituency forced the president to inch away from his hands-off approach to gay rights. Initially, Bush offered little more than sympathy for the cause and resisted calls to endorse the amendment. Lobbying wore him down, however, and in February 2004 he threw his full support behind the campaign for the proposed federal marriage amendment. "Activist judges and local officials have made an aggressive attempt to redefine marriage," he announced. "If we are to prevent the meaning of marriage from being changed forever, our nation must enact a constitutional amendment to protect marriage in America." The campaign stalled in the Senate a few weeks later, but religious conservatives managed to keep attention on the issue, securing ballot spots for referenda on same-sex marriage in eleven states. "Make no mistake, my friends," said Gary Bauer, "the sanctity of marriage will be the defining issue of 2004."[25]

With the country at war, however, reviving the culture wars would not be easy. "People are disturbed by the idea of same-sex marriage, but right now it's just an attitude and not something they are acting on," political scientist John Green observed in July 2004. "It's the job of activists to turn those attitudes into votes." Republicans were well prepared to do just that, with a special focus on evangelicals and Catholics. Ralph Reed was recruited to lead the Bush campaign's evangelical outreach, which he did with businesslike efficiency. In Florida, for instance, he installed a state chair, who in turn installed outreach leaders in all sixty-seven counties, who in turn recruited dozens of volunteers to recruit and register fellow believers in their local communities. To attract Catholic voters, meanwhile, the Republican National Committee enlisted 50,000 volunteers to serve as "team leaders" across the country and augmented them with nearly a hundred field coordinators working the grass roots in swing states. In its outreach efforts, the campaign was incredibly aggressive. It contacted churches to distribute literature and register voters, encouraging ministers to become all-but-official surrogates for the campaign. Jay Sekulow, chief counsel of Pat Robertson's American Center for Law and Justice, mailed letters to 45,000 ministers advising them that "short of endorsing a candidate by name from the pulpit, they were free to do almost anything." As Republicans engaged in this massive crusade, Democrats barely gave it a thought. The Kerry campaign relegated much of its religious outreach to a twenty-eight-year-old newcomer with virtually no institutional support, not even an old database of contacts. "The matchup between the two parties in pursuit of religious voters wasn't just David versus Goliath," reflected journalist Amy Sullivan. "It was David versus Goliath and the Philistines and the Assyrians and the Egyptians, with a few plagues thrown in for good measure."[26]

The effectiveness of Republican religious outreach was evident in the election returns. In the targeted demographics, George W.

Bush improved on his 2000 performance by significant margins. His shares of the white evangelical vote rose from 72 to 78 percent, while his portion of the Catholic vote increased from 47 to 52 percent. These national shifts were drawn into sharp focus in swing states such as Ohio, which emerged as the central battleground in the election. Its referendum on gay marriage proved incredibly powerful in rallying conservative Christians. "I see people marching like a holy army to the voting booth," Pastor Rod Parsley told his 12,000-member evangelical church in Columbus before election day. "I see the Holy Spirit anointing you as you vote for life, as you vote for marriage, as you vote for the pulpit!" Ohio Catholics likewise trended Republican, motivated in no small part by the thousands of Bush campaign field workers dispatched to parishes across the state. In the end, the president broadened his share of the Catholic vote from 50 to 55 percent there, with a net gain of 172,000 votes. Notably, that increase was more than his 130,000-vote margin of victory in the state.[27]

While conservative Christians had proven to be an important factor in the president's reelection coalition, many observers mistakenly argued that the election represented a mandate for their agenda. In particular, reporters seized on National Election Pool (NEP) exit polling in which 22 percent of voters claimed "moral values" had mattered more to them than any other issue. Republican strategists seized on the NEP poll as a sign of success, noting that 80 percent of these "values voters" chose Bush. "I think people would be well advised to pay attention to what the American people are saying," urged Karl Rove. Closer inspection, however, showed that claims of a new "moral values" mandate were overblown. As Andrew Kohut of the Pew Research Center noted, that option ranked high in the exit polling because it was an attractive and ambiguous catchall. If options such as "terrorism" and "the Iraq war" had been combined into a single "national security" category, that would have encompassed 34 percent of voters; a similarly broad "economic" category, meanwhile, would have taken 33 percent. While the "values vote" was not as large as it first seemed, neither was it new. The NEP had never asked about "moral values" before, but another exit poll had. According to *Los Angeles Times* exit polling, 40 percent of voters cited "moral/ethical values" as one of their two most important issues in 2004, a percentage that compared closely to past elections: 35 percent in 2000 and 40 percent in 1996. Little, if anything, had changed. Nevertheless, social conservatives interpreted the results in their own way. "President Bush now has a mandate to affect policy that will promote a more decent society, through both politics and the law," argued William Bennett. "Now is the time to begin our long, national cultural renewal."[28]

To the consternation of religious conservatives, the president seemed disinclined to pursue an aggressive agenda on social issues after the election. Bush sent signals that his first priorities would be the privatization of Social Security and other economic issues and suggested that the drive for a constitutional amendment against gay marriage would be neglected. Leaders of the Religious Right refused to be ignored. "Business as usual isn't going to cut it, where the GOP rides to victory by espousing traditional family values and then turns around and rewards the liberals in its ranks," complained Robert Knight of Concerned Women for America. "If the GOP wants to expand and govern effectively, it can't play both sides of the fence anymore. It needs a coherent message, which came through loud and clear in the election." Religious conservatives soon rallied around a cause that many believed would express that message clearly. The controversy centered on Terri Schiavo, a Florida woman who collapsed in 1990 and entered what her physicians described as a persistent vegetative state. After several years, her husband petitioned to have her removed from life support. Her parents, devout Catholics, believed that such actions were violations of their faith and their daughter's, and resisted the effort. They enlisted the support of pro-life activists, including Father Frank Pavone of Priests for Life and Randall Terry of Operation Rescue, as well as sympathetic politicians such as Florida governor Jeb Bush. The protests waged on Terri Schiavo's behalf transformed what had been a local legal struggle into a national political controversy. In March 2005, after Florida courts issued rulings for her husband in his effort to remove her feeding tubes, congressional Republicans passed legislation ordering her case to be reviewed once more by federal courts. President Bush rushed back to Washington from his vacation to sign the bill in a dramatic, late-night ceremony.[29]

While many religious conservatives expressed sincere moral outrage over the Schiavo case, some calculated its political impact as well. "It has galvanized people the way nothing could have done in an off-election year," admitted Reverend Lou Sheldon of the Traditional Values Coalition, which had seen an increase in donations as a result. "That is what I see as the blessing that dear Terri's life is offering to the conservative Christian movement in America." Likewise, Gary Bauer asserted that the controversy focused attention on "the sanctity of life, and it will encourage voters to believe that it is something Republicans feel strongly about." An internal memorandum to Republican senators echoed those views, calling Schiavo a "great political issue" that would rally conservative Christians for the 2006 elections and be "a tough issue for Democrats." "This is an important moral issue," the memo argued, "and the pro-life base will be excited." While the case certainly energized the Religious Right, the government's intervention served to alienate even larger numbers of voters. An *ABC News* poll showed that Americans overwhelmingly supported the removal of Terri Schiavo's artificial life support as her husband wished, by a margin of 63 percent to 28 percent, and opposed congressional involvement, 70 percent to 27 percent. Even 54 percent of conservatives and 61 percent of Republicans supported the decision to end life support. Many of them recoiled at what they saw as overreaching by religious conservatives. "The Republican Party of Lincoln has become a party of theocracy," argued Republican representative Chris Shays. "There are a number of people who feel that the government is getting involved in their personal lives in a way that scares them."[30]

While many in the GOP were becoming restless over the influence of the Religious Right, so too were growing numbers of evangelicals themselves. As their involvement on AIDS had revealed, evangelical Christians began to demonstrate a much greater political diversity during the Bush administration. A 2003 survey by the Pew Forum on Religion and Public Life showed that rank-and-file evangelicals embraced "liberal" stances such as universal health care and increased spending on welfare programs by wide margins, even if their nominal leaders did not. After the 2004 election, and moreso after the 2005 Schiavo controversy, the diversity in evangelical politics began to make itself manifest. As the leading evangelical publication *Christianity Today* argued, "Single-issue politics is neither necessary nor wise." In that spirit, Richard Cizik of the NAE worked to enlist his fellow believers in a biblically inspired environmentalism that he characterized as "creation care." Polls showed that evangelicals were receptive to the new direction he proposed, with a February 2006 survey showing that 63 percent believed global warming was a dire threat and roughly half supported immediate government action to fight it. Leaders of the Religious Right tried to get Cizik fired for his heretical politics but found their demands airily dismissed. "The last time I checked," President Ted Haggard told critic James Dobson, "you weren't in charge of the NAE."[31]

As the Bush era came to a close, the Religious Right's old guard found itself increasingly irrelevant, supplanted by a younger generation with a new agenda and attitude. In 2006, after decades of combative conservative leadership, the Southern Baptist Convention elected as its president Frank Page, a moderate who championed the idea that Baptists needed to focus more on the religious values they supported and less on the political issues they opposed. "I believe in the word of God," Page said repeatedly. "I am just not mad about it." A similar attitude was evident in the evangelical ministries of popular megachurch leaders such as Bill Hybels and Rick Warren. Head of the Willow Creek Association, an independent network that encompassed 12,000 churches, Hybels argued that old leaders of the Religious Right had lost touch with the real concerns of evangelical Christians. "The Indians are saying to the chiefs, 'We are interested in more than your two or three issues,'" he asserted in 2007. "We are interested in the poor, in racial reconciliation, in global poverty and AIDS, in the plight of women in the developing world." Warren, the founder of Saddleback Church and a figure whom *Time* anointed "the most influential evangelical in America," was likewise a visible presence on these matters. Traveling to Davos and Damascus, he spoke out frequently on global issues of poverty, disease, and war, looking for allies wherever he could find them. When he invited Illinois senator Barack Obama to an HIV/AIDS summit in December 2006, leaders of the old guard furiously demanded that Warren retract the invitation. Obama's support for abortion rights, they argued, made him an unworthy ally. "You cannot fight one evil while justifying another," they insisted. Warren simply ignored them.[32]

The significance of these changes in the relationship between religion and politics was made manifest in the 2008 presidential election. On the Republican side, Arizona senator John McCain lacked President Bush's personal and political connections with conservative Christians. During the 2000 Republican primaries, McCain had denounced Reverends Falwell and Robertson as "agents of intolerance" and decried the influence of the Religious Right in his party. As the 2008 campaign neared, McCain recanted such claims and actively pursued endorsements from the religious leaders he once decried. Still, the relationship remained strained. At the 2007 Values Voters Summit, a national gathering of socially conservative activists, a straw poll of presidential preferences showed McCain finishing last in a field of nine candidates. Even after McCain clinched the Republican nomination, religious conservatives remained unenthusiastic. "For John McCain to be competitive, he has to connect with the base to the point that they're intense enough that they're contagious," noted Tony Perkins. "Right now they're not even coughing." Late moves in the campaign, such as McCain's selection of socially conservative Alaska governor Sarah Palin as his running mate and his willingness to keep a strong anti-abortion plank in the party platform, helped shore up his support with that base. Despite these concessions, religious conservatives never embraced Senator McCain as they had embraced President Bush. The final results seemed similar—McCain took 74 percent of white evangelical votes in 2008, only slightly less than Bush's 78 percent in 2004—but many observers argued that the vote represented little more than fear of his opponent. Richard Land captured the overall mood: "I'd rather have a third-class fireman than a first-class arsonist."[33]

Despite the lingering mistrust of conservative Christians, Democratic nominee Barack Obama worked diligently to win over religious voters of his own. Within the campaign, Pentecostal minister Joshua DuBois led an aggressive religious outreach. Several events were held at Christian colleges, with campaign workers arranging for dozens of Christian rock concerts and more than nine hundred "American values house parties" in which religiously observant Obama backers reached out to members of their own congregations. Meanwhile, liberal evangelicals helped the campaign through external organizations like the Matthew 25 Network, which spent more than $500,000 on pro-Obama advertisements in Christian media. Their combined efforts focused deliberately on moderate evangelicals, Catholics, and mainline Protestants. "There never was an aggressive outreach effort to white Southern Baptist evangelicals in the South," noted Matthew 25's Mara Vanderslice; "that wasn't the focus." Instead, the campaign concentrated its religious outreach on moderates in swing states, and with notable results. In Colorado, for instance, a battleground state that was home to a number of powerful evangelical ministries such as Dobson's Focus on the Family, Obama improved on Kerry's performance with white evangelicals by ten full points, winning the state in the process. While Obama's success with evangelicals was noticeable largely at the state level, his inroads with Catholics were apparent nationwide. He took 54 percent of the Catholic vote, reclaiming the previous advantage that the GOP had with the demographic and surpassing even the 52 percent that Bush had won in the previous election.[34]

In the end, the presidency of George W. Bush represented a crossroads in the history of religion and politics in modern America. Coming into office, the president had hoped to transcend the nation's long-standing stalemate on matters of religion and politics, sidestepping the old struggles of the culture wars with his promise of a more compassionate conservatism. Aside from the global AIDS policy, however, Bush would experience little real success in this regard. Much of the potential for compassionate conservatism rested on the president's faith-based initiative, but it ultimately proved to be a missed opportunity. Neglected by his aides in the White House and made unworkable by partisan politics in Congress, it became little more than an afterthought as national attention focused ever more on foreign policy in the wake of 9/11. The faith-based offices devolved into little more than partisan apparatuses, taking their place alongside policies on abortion rights and gay marriage that seemed focused first and foremost on electoral strategies. While the union of the Religious Right and the Bush administration would prove successful in the 2004 election, its victory there was short-lived. Both the president and his partners overreached in the Schiavo case, beginning a steady decline in their influence and straining their relationship. Jerry Falwell died in 2007, and other leaders of the old guard likewise faded from view. In their place, there arose a new generation of evangelical leaders who downplayed the traditional agenda of religious conservatives and instead embraced a new set of priorities. "Compassion" once again loomed large in their agenda, but it now stood freed from the partisan limits of "conservatism."

11

MINORITIES, MULTICULTURALISM, AND THE PRESIDENCY OF GEORGE W. BUSH

GARY GERSTLE

IN THE ORIGINAL VISION OF GEORGE W. BUSH AND KARL ROVE, the new and permanent Republican electoral majority was to emerge only in part from the relentless mobilization of conservatives and their moderate allies. It was also to emerge from the Republican Party's success in peeling significant percentages of voters away from traditional Democratic constituencies, most notably Hispanics, but even to some degree African Americans. Bush had done well among minorities in Texas during his successful races for the governorship in the 1990s, capturing 49 percent of the Texas Hispanic vote and 27 percent of the Texas black vote when he ran for reelection in 1998.[1] By 2004 Bush had almost doubled the Republican portion of the Hispanic presidential vote to 40 percent from the 21 percent that Robert Dole had achieved in 1996.[2] Success did not require winning majorities of either of the two principal minority groups. If the Republicans could consistently win 40 to 45 percent of the Hispanic vote and 25 to 30 percent of the African American vote, then the party could declare its minority strategy a success and use it to establish what it most wanted, a permanent Republican majority.

Bush and Rove believed that their Republicanism offered groups of minority voters reason to rethink their traditional hostility to the GOP. On questions of immigration and diversity, Bush was worlds apart from Patrick Buchanan and the social-conservative wing of the

Republican Party that wanted to restore America to its imagined Anglo Saxon and Anglo Celtic glory. Bush wanted relatively open borders with Mexico and a road to citizenship for illegal aliens. Bush was comfortable with diversity, bilingualism, and cultural pluralism, as long as members of America's ethnic and racial subcultures shared his patriotism, religious faith, and political conservatism. He became the first president in U.S. history to appoint a black man and a black woman to the position of secretary of state, and to make a Hispanic attorney general. During a time in which the United States was at war and Europe was exploding with tension and violence over Islam, Bush played a positive role in keeping interethnic and interracial relations in the United States relatively calm. During his presidency, too, the U.S. military continued to burnish its reputation as the most successfully integrated institution in America, at the level both of enlisted men and women and of the top brass. Generals with such names as Shinseki, Abizaid, Sanchez, and Odierno rose to prominence during the years when Bush was commander in chief.

In regard to the two controversial issues for which Bush stood to suffer at the hands of minority voters, his antagonism to the welfare state and to affirmative action, he and his advisers launched new policies to convince African Americans and Hispanics that Republicans were concerned about underlying issues of poverty, education, and jobs. The Republicans would deliver welfare through private rather than public institutions (churches in particular) and would improve minority education (and then success in the workforce) through the provisions of the No Child Left Behind (NCLB) Act. Because of its scale and boldness, NCLB is likely the most significant social policy initiative of the Bush years. Rather than promote racial equality through affirmative action, which conservatives had long decried as the promotion of the unqualified, the act held schools responsible for ensuring that all students and faculty reached satisfactory levels of competence. It is arguably the most ambitious public school initiative ever sponsored by the federal government, and it is currently convulsing education at all levels, from the first grade through the public universities.

Whatever one thinks about the particulars of this Bush program, it possessed a coherence that liberal critics of the administration too often overlooked. It promised immigrants tolerance and opportunity and African Americans achievement. It sought to appeal to the religiosity and social conservatism of many Hispanics and African Americans. Its preference for delivering welfare through churches rather than government agencies was calculated in part to resonate among minority communities in which religious institutions played an important a role.

This essay probes the roots of the Bush multicultural program, and analyzes how it fared during his presidency. It identifies several important roots: first, Bush's comfort with Hispanics and Hispanic culture, an unanticipated yet significant consequence of his family's relocation to Texas in the 1940s; second, Bush's religiosity and the commitment to *religious* pluralism it impelled him to embrace; and third, Bush's principled and strategic opposition to the "Fortress America" style of cultural politics that was dominating Republican Party conventions and political races when he entered politics in the 1990s. Bush believed that such politics were consigning the Republican Party to a minority status, a trend he was determined to reverse. The essay then examines what difference Bush's multiculturalism made to the United States during the years of his presidency. Overall, I judge it to have been a failure, if measured by its success in winning the favor of the Republican Party base and becoming a serious rival to the multiculturalism of the Democratic Party. Within that record of overall failure, however, Bush's multicultural initiatives resulted in some lasting gains, evident in the numbers of minorities holding high political office and in the demonstrated ability of a Republican to appeal to the country's largest and most rapidly growing minority, Latinos.

◆   ◆   ◆

The Bush family's move to Midland, Texas, in 1948 was part of a group effort by elite New York and New England corporate and financial families to stake their Ivy-educated sons to promising careers in the booming Permian oil fields of West Texas. The heirs of these families imagined that their sons would colonize a large portion of the Texas oil industry for corporate family interests in the Northeast. What they understood less clearly is how the migration of their sons to the Lone Star State would, over two generations, do less to expand the power of old New England elites than to create new southern elites with distinct economic and political interests. The Texas Republicanism of George W. Bush would end up a great distance away from the New England Republicanism of his grandfather, Connecticut senator Prescott Bush.[3] Partly this had to do with the web of economic associations in Texas and south of the Rio Grande in which these new Texans became enmeshed and the embrace of a political economy with deep roots in Anglo Texas politics; another part resulted from these elite Anglo migrants' exposure to and engagement with Mexicans and Mexican Americans in Texas.

Exposure to Mexicans in the oil business, in school, and at home is a consistent theme of George W.'s young life. George H. W. Bush's choice of the name Zapata Petroleum Corporation for his oil exploration enterprise signaled his transnational business ambitions, as did his decision to take as one of his partners Jorge Díaz Serrano, a Mexican oligarch and onetime candidate for the Mexican presidency. George W. saw Mexican laborers working in his father's oil fields and Mexican children at public school in Midland in the 1950s.[4]

A Mexican woman entered the Bush household in 1959 when Bush père moved the family to Houston. Hired to be the Bushes' live-in housekeeper, Paula Rendon became a fixture in the family, staying with the Bushes through all the moves they made between 1960 and 1992 (including the one that brought the family to the White House). She served as an emotional anchor for the Bush boys during their adolescence, especially as Barbara Bush became more remote, battling the depression that accompanied her growing isolation as Republican politics and public service increasingly preoccupied her husband. George W. has referred to Rendon as his second mother. Jeb Bush recalled that he "adore[d] her. . . . I got pretty good at Spanish thanks to her."[5] Jeb's comfort with the

Spanish language and Mexican culture may have played a role in his decision at age seventeen, while a student at Andover, to spend part of the year in León, Mexico, helping build a school for the poor. There he was smitten with a local convent girl who knew no English. Columba Garnica Gallo would become the love of Jeb's life and his wife, bringing Mexicanness and grandchildren of mixed Anglo Mexican descent directly into the Bush family. These grandchildren were the "little brown ones," as George H. W. affectionately (or condescendingly, depending on one's perspective) liked to refer to them.[6]

George W. returned to Midland in 1975 after a ten-year sojourn through New England's elite educational institutions (Andover, Yale, and Harvard Business School) to make his father's path to business and then political success his own. Like his father, George W. went as part of a group of Ivy Leaguers from wealthy backgrounds whose families sensed their sons could make fortunes from another Permian Basin oil rush, this one made possible by the quadrupling of oil prices in the wake of the Yom Kippur War and the formation of OPEC in 1973 and 1974.

Most of these young men quickly made fabulous amounts of money and indulged in a nouveau riche and exclusively Anglo lifestyle of mansions, private schools, private clubs, and private planes for their business and pleasure. George W., however, didn't follow this script, in part because he showed little aptitude for making money and in part because he seems to have preferred to live in a less insulated, less anglicized, and less rarified world. His closest friends were buddies from the Northeast, men such as Donald Evans, future secretary of commerce, but the social circuit of the Bush crowd revolved more around family backyard barbeques and visiting local Mexican American restaurants than around posh Anglo country clubs.[7]

Doña Anita's Mexican restaurant was one of their favorite hangouts, where they went almost every Friday night. Bush befriended the Reyes family that owned the restaurant, as he did other Mexican American men such as José Cuevas and George Veloz, also involved in thriving family restaurant businesses.[8] Bush identified with them as aspiring businessmen and grew comfortable with the biculturalism of these encounters, a biculturalism strengthened by the middlebrow Texas culture of sports, Mexican food, and beer that all these men shared. Bush's young wife, Laura, influenced his openness to Mexican American culture too, as immediately prior to her marriage to George W. she had been teaching poor Latino kids in Austin's public schools.[9] Thus the arrival of many more Mexican laborers in the Permian oil fields in the 1970s and 1980s did not disturb Bush; to the contrary, he welcomed the cultural diversity their presence generated. His friends remember how Bush developed a "'particular empathy for the new Mexican immigrants who worked hard on the farms, in oil fields and in people's homes and went on to raise children who built businesses and raised families of their own, without the advantages he had as the scion of a wealthy New England family.'"[10] Bush's long-standing interest in Mexicans prompted Israel Hernandez, an assistant secretary for commerce in the Bush administration, to remark that "in every dimension of his career, whether it was politics or the private sector or the sports world, he's been engaged with the Hispanic population."[11]

The way in which Bush took religion into his life in the 1980s further contributed to the formation of his multicultural consciousness. Bush's embrace of Christ as his savior was born of personal crisis: failure in business, his parents' disappointment in him, alcoholism, and Laura's threat to leave him. Faith in Christ gave Bush a purpose, a discipline, and an ability to inject strong moral values into his life—characteristics he felt he had lacked. Being born again made possible his recovery from addiction, the salvaging of his marriage, and the launch of a successful political career. In an unusual twist, it also imbued him with a deep respect for other religions and other ways of finding faith.

Nominally, Bush's embrace of evangelicalism prompted him to abandon Episcopalianism for Methodism. But Bush was never much interested in denominational or doctrinal battles, nor does he ever seem to have believed that there was one, or even an exclusively Protestant or Christian, path to God. His introduction to

Christ occurred not in church but in personal meetings with evangelical ministers, such as Billy Graham, and in Bible study groups, such as the Community Bible Study group he joined in Midland in 1984. What he took from such meetings and study was not a message about the superiority of the Christian God and the evangelizing zeal that this God demanded of all his faithful but rather the command to have faith and to lead a moral life. As Jacob Weisberg has observed, "Bush believes that everyone who prays prays to the same God, and that there is 'truth' in all religions." As president, Bush would come to feel a keen partnership with the Muslim prime minister of Turkey, Recep Tayyip Erdogan, because the two men shared, in Bush's words, a strong belief "in the almighty." And the Russian Orthodox cross that Bush saw Vladimir Putin wearing around his neck inclined Bush to think that he and Putin would work well together.[12] Bush's attraction to the "new" Europe of the East rested in part on his conviction that the Poles, Russians, and others who lived there were far more inclined than the "old Europeans" who lived in Western Europe to embrace a godly life.

In foreign policy, these attitudes sometimes led Bush in remarkably naive directions, as in blithe declarations that he and Putin were soul mates and that all religious groups of the world were eager, if given the chance, to interweave their faith with Western notions of freedom. But they also yielded some successes, as in Bush's ability to feel closely connected to the peoples of Africa, whom he included in his community of "God's children." This connectedness led him to authorize a massive anti-AIDS and anti-malarial campaign in Africa, a campaign that even Bush's critics concede has probably saved millions of lives.[13]

In domestic affairs, Bush's ecumenism also had positive ramifications, most of them stemming from his comfort in reaching out to religious groups in the United States that were not white or Protestant. Through such outreach to religious Catholics, Jews, and even Muslims, he laid the foundation for what we might call a multiculturalism of the godly. Bush's ability to develop an alliance with Hispanic Catholics would be the earliest and most important consequence of his godly multiculturalism.

The opportunity to pursue this sort of multiculturalism presented itself to Bush from the moment he entered Texas politics in the 1990s to run for governor. The "culture wars" were then an obsession of American domestic politics. These were battles fought between Left and Right over the place in American life of the "hard" multiculturalism that had emerged in the 1970s and 1980s. Hard multiculturalists argued that America had been so compromised by racism and sexism that the nation could never redeem its promise to minorities. Members of subordinate groups had no alternative but to craft identities for themselves that were grounded not in American patriotism but in racial, gender, or sexual communities or in a cosmopolitanism that partook of no national identity whatsoever. Conservatives reacted angrily to this rejection of America's promise and sought to extirpate hard multiculturalism wherever it had advanced in public institutions. Conservatives especially targeted the teaching of American history in public schools and the portrayals of the American past in public museums (such as the Smithsonian); in both cases they argued that the perspective on America advanced in such institutions had become unacceptably negative. Conservatives repeatedly attacked the National Endowment for the Arts and the National Endowment for the Humanities for supporting art and scholarship they regarded as immoral, anti-American, or both.[14]

Conservatives also believed that multiculturalist principles had led government social policy astray, especially in regard to the welfare state. Welfare, in their eyes, had become a way of coddling "welfare queens," tolerating a debilitating drug culture and its associated violence, and encouraging widespread promiscuity and moral laxity. A harsh vision of the inner-city poor emerged from these conservative fusillades; America's ghettoes were depicted by many conservatives as homes to a vast underclass that lay beyond the reach of civilization. These attitudes encouraged conservatives to rehabilitate old racist stereotypes, such as the use of the Willie Horton image in the 1988 presidential campaign, to associate black men with criminality and rape. The spread of these stereotypes intensified a climate of racial hatred and fear and helps to explain the savage beating that Los Angeles cops administered to a black motorist, Rodney King, arrested for speeding, actions that in turn triggered the L.A. riots of 1992. Those riots revealed not only that black-white relations were on the edge but that immigrant–native-born relations in cities like Los Angeles had become tense as well, especially as the numbers of Mexican immigrants in Los Angeles and elsewhere, many of them illegal, were increasing rapidly. Negotiations with Mexico and Canada to make North America a common market further stoked fears among some conservatives that Hispanic America was about to reconquer America's Southwest and take back what Mexico had ceded to the United States in the U.S.-Mexican War of 1846–48.[15]

These developments brought to the fore Republican politicians determined to vanquish the hard multiculturalism they blamed these problems on with a law-and-order, morally absolutist, and nativist conservatism. Leading the way was Republican firebrand Patrick Buchanan. Party leaders handed him one of most important speaking slots at the 1992 Republican convention, and he used his time to call for retaking America's cities from the "mobs" who had rendered them areas of criminality, immorality, and barbarism.[16] Vying with Buchanan for the leadership of the "Fortress America" faction was Pete Wilson, former San Diego mayor and U.S. senator who, in 1991, became governor of California. In running for reelection in 1994, Wilson became one of the most enthusiastic supporters of anti-immigrant Proposition 187, a harsh initiative meant to strip California's illegal immigrants of their access to public services, including social services, health care, and public schooling. Wilson and Proposition 187 won by large margins, making it seem as though Fortress America politics were carrying the day. Indeed, Wilson began laying plans to ride this anti-immigrant, law-and-order wave into the White House. By 1995 he was an odds-on favorite to capture the 1996 Republican nomination.[17]

From the moment George W. Bush decided to run for the Texas governorship in 1994, he cast himself as the anti-Wilson. If Wilson was going to build a national reputation by positioning himself as the enemy of Latino immigrants, Bush would construct his by posing as their friend. If Wilson was going to become the unforgiving, law-and-order Republican determined either to purge America of every last one of its criminals or else seal off every remaining crime-ridden ghetto and barrio with police force, Bush would become the "compassionate conservative," finding a way to bring the poor, even those who were sinners, into American life under the aegis of conservative values.[18]

Bush had instrumentalist reasons for positioning himself as Wilson's opposite. He may have sensed that the support for Buchanan's and Wilson's nativism was, in actuality, softer than it appeared to be at the time. With Karl Rove already at his side, Bush understood in precise, district-by-district terms how indispensable the Texas Hispanic vote had become to his and Rove's largest ambition, building a permanent Republican majority in Texas and then in the nation, and he wanted to bring those voters into the Republican tent.[19] In political-economic terms, Bush intended to seize on California's deepening anti-Latino hostility to enlarge Texas's importance as the crossroads for hemispheric trade and as the gatekeeper for the huge volume of goods already passing between the United States and Latin America (a subject to which we will return).[20] Nevertheless, Bush's willingness to give these instrumentalist concerns prominence in his thinking and in his politics revealed how comfortable he already was living in a bicultural state and how deeply he believed that a properly constructed and religiously inflected multiculturalism was compatible with the conservative values he cherished.

In this respect, it may be appropriate to see Bush as the Republican Bill Clinton. Bush was the GOP candidate who intended to lance the boil of the culture wars by putting forward a soft multiculturalism that merged diversity and patriotism. In the process of doing so, he, Clinton, and others would relieve the American body politic of the distress and distraction that the culture wars had caused. Of course, the road to soft multiculturalism was different for each man. Clinton had to attack and discredit his hard multicultural left, as he did when he condemned the black hip-hop art-ist Sister Souljah in 1992 for her separatist, antiwhite diatribes. At the same time, he embraced African Americans as few Demo-cratic presidents before him had done.[21] Bush had to attack the Fortress America faction on his hard right—the likes of Buchanan, Wilson, and then Ross Perot and his allies—and he did. And he matched Clinton's embrace of blacks with his own embrace of Hispanics.

Bush's multicultural politics as governor first became apparent in the close economic and cultural relations he sought with Mex-ico. He invited the governors of the Mexican states that bordered Texas to attend his inauguration, and seated them prominently at his swearing-in ceremony. He repeatedly expressed his support for improved relations with Mexico and endorsed the North Amer-ican Free Trade Agreement (NAFTA) from the start. In 1995 he supported a $20 billion stabilization package that the Clinton administration had proposed for Mexico.[22] That same year, Bush led the opposition to fellow Texan Ross Perot's United We Stand America Conference and its anti-NAFTA and anti-immigrant agenda. Bush expressed indignation at remarks by Buchanan, speaking at Perot's conference, that if "he [Buchanan] were elected president he would dump NAFTA, build a wall along the border and never again offer Mexico a bailout plan."[23] While Pete Wilson refused to meet with the new Mexican president, Ernesto Zedillo, Bush attended Zedillo's inauguration and visited him three times during Zedillo's first year in office.[24]

Bush matched his insistence on close relations with Mexico with a desire to make Mexican immigrants feel at home in Texas. Immigrants, Bush told reporters at one point, "come to Texas to provide for their families." And, he added, in a curious aside, "they come for love."[25] A law such as California's Proposition 187, meant to keep the children of illegal immigrants out of public schools, would have no place in Bush's Texas. "Once children are in Texas," Bush declared in 1995, "Texans know it is in our best interest and their interest to educate them, regardless of the nationality of their parents. An educated child is a child less likely to commit a crime;

an educated child is much more likely to become a responsible member of society."[26]

Bush even supported bilingualism. Bush unveiled a program in Texas that he called "English Plus" and that made clear his belief that Spanish ought to be taught in schools and spoken in Texas. "'English plus,'" he wrote in a letter to Texas Republicans, "recognizes the important richness that other languages and cultures bring to our nation of immigrants. Here in Texas, the Spanish language enhances and helps define our state's history and tradition. I think that if a bilingual education program is teaching to read and comprehend English as quickly as possible we should keep it."[27] Several years later, Secretary of State Tony Garza elaborated on Bush's remarks by saying that Bush believed that "bilingualism adds to a student's literacy in English" and that "the ability to speak several languages is an important asset for all Texans."[28]

Bush also positioned himself as a progressive Republican on the vexed issue of affirmative action. When the Fifth Circuit Court of Appeals ruled in 1996 that state universities could not consider the race of applicants in their admission decisions, Bush did not use the opportunity to take a stand against affirmative action. Instead he proposed a new plan that he called "affirmative access," by which he meant that affirmative steps needed to be taken to ensure that "every person will get a fair shot based on his or her potential or merit."[29] The phrase "affirmative access" was meant to free the discussion of affirmative action from the stigma of quotas. As Bush declared in 1999, "I support the spirit of no quotas, no preferences ... but what's important to say is not what you're against—[but] what you're for. I'm for increasing the pool of applicants and opening the door so that more people are eligible to go to the university systems."[30] In practice, Bush actually supported a quota plan, but not one explicitly grounded in race. This was the 1997 plan to admit to the University of Texas all Texas high school graduates who ranked in the top 10 percent of their class. To fulfill this 10 percent obligation, Texas expanded the University of Texas system to accommodate those eligible for admission. As a result, Texas developed one of the more rapidly growing and accessible systems of higher education in the country. As the liberal *New York Times* columnist Anthony Lewis conceded in 1999, this plan "had considerable success in maintaining student diversity."[31]

Bush himself was a supporter of diversity and believed that cultural variety strengthened America. In a 1997 speech to the U.S. Hispanic Chamber of Commerce he declared, "We are the United States of America, not the divided states of America. One of our strengths is in our differences."[32] On another occasion he said, "Texas is a diverse state enriched by its many cultures and heritages. We can achieve racial harmony by demonstrating understanding and mutual respect for our fellow Texans."[33] In an address to a group of Hispanics in Miami in August 2000, Bush became effusive in his praise for a new, multicultural America:

> America has one national creed, but many accents. We're now one of the largest Spanish-speaking nations in the world. We're a major source of Latin music, journalism, and culture. Just go to Miami, or San Antonio, Los Angeles, Chicago, or West New York, New Jersey . . . and close your eyes and listen. You could just as easily be in Santo Domingo or Santiago or San Miguel de Allende. For years, our nation has debated this change—some have praised it and others have resented it. By nominating me, my party has made a choice to welcome the New America.[34]

By 2008 it had become difficult to envision a presidential nominee of either major party talking in such open and glowing terms about the multicultural possibilities of the "New America."

Bush believed that this embrace of diversity, especially in connection to Hispanics, would strengthen his conservative political agenda. In addition to Rove, Lionel Sosa, a Republican media strategist from San Antonio, helped show him the way. Sosa had been inspired by Ronald Reagan in the late 1970s. As Sosa would later recall, Reagan had told him in 1978 that "'Hispanics are Republicans; they just don't know it.'" By that Reagan meant that Hispanic families cherished Republican values: "family, faith in God, hard work, and personal responsibility" and the belief that

"America is the greatest country in the world." Given their identification with bedrock Republican values, Sosa and Bush both believed, Hispanics' desire to preserve elements of their native culture in their home need not threaten Republican dreams or ambitions.[35] To the contrary, Republicans such as Bush believed they could harness Hispanic values to advance their conservative agenda, both on symbolic but potent matters—faith in God, love of country, family values—as well as on social policies that Bush hoped to advance, most notably the substitution of a private, faith-based set of welfare institutions for the public one that had become so expensive and had allegedly caused so much moral deterioration among the nation's poor.

The willingness of poor Hispanics in the United States to acquiesce in the dismantling of public welfare institutions was arguably the weakest link in the Bush-Rove blueprint for corralling the Hispanic vote in Texas and the United States. But it may have been the case that Bush and Rove believed that if their multicultural program was alluring enough, Hispanics would make fewer demands on the Republican Party to service the material needs of the immigrant poor. This, then, would free Bush and his economic allies in Texas, including an increasingly numerous and wealthy Mexican-Texan business elite, to pursue a hemisphere-wide capitalist free market in which the imperatives of investment and capital accumulation would take precedence over the needs of the poor and maintaining a low-tax, union-free, and weakly regulated economy would be the primary ambition of government in economic affairs. If these goals were in fact as central to the Bush business model as they appear to have been, it would not have been the first instance of multiculturalism being turned to the service of corporate expansion and enrichment.

If we shift our gaze from cultural politics to political economy, it becomes clear that part of Bush's interest in the Hispanic world emerged from his desire to make the hemisphere a single free market in which capitalists throughout the Americas would flourish. Bush and other Texans dreamed about making their state the pivot of what we might label a "Union of the Americas" (UA), a trading bloc that would rival the European Union and East Asia in size, significance, and ease of trade. Unlike the EU, which gave Brussels the power to impose binding economic rules on all EU members, the UA would eschew a centralized model of economic regulation in favor of a decentralized one: each member state would determine its own regulatory, wage, and tax regime. However, all the countries would be part of a single free trade and migration zone, thus putting the different economic regimes in competition with each other. Bush and his allies believed that corporations and investors in the hemisphere would gravitate away from Latin American countries with their burdensome welfare states and histories of interfering with free markets and toward those countries, such as the United States, that were sporting "low-tax, lightly regulated economies with modest levels of social benefits." Bush believed that his economic plan would resonate among the capitalist classes of Mexico and other Latin countries, especially those portions that had embraced what North Americans called "free market capitalism" and what Latin Americans labeled "neoliberalism."[36]

Many Texans, like Bush, believed that the Lone Star State would be at the center of this UA, attracting investment and capitalists from every part of the hemisphere and generating new businesses that would draw to the United States vast pools of underemployed labor in Mexico and other Latin countries. The United States would, in turn, became a major exporter of goods to Latin America. All these inflows and outflows would pass through Texan banks, ports, rail termini, and truck depots. Texas was a state advantaged by history, geography, and capitalist leadership to play this key hemispheric role.[37]

This king-size Texas dream was on the one hand a long-term proposition. On the other hand, its supporters were already in the 1990s discussing the infrastructural improvements that would be required to bring it into being. A city on the west coast of Mexico, Lázaro Cárdenas, had been identified as having the physical attributes necessary to make it a major port for the entry of Asian goods into the Americas, thereby siphoning the Pacific trade away from the union-strong, high-wage southern California ports of

Los Angeles and Long Beach. Making such a port a success would require other infrastructural improvements too, most notably new north-south superhighways leading from Lázaro Cárdenas through Texas to Kansas City, and then branching into several northern routes ranging from Winnipeg and Chicago to Detroit and Toronto.[38] Here were plans for capitalist growth and transformation on the grandest scale, and ones that, if successful, would substitute a north-south grid of transportation for the existing east-west one. These kinds of improvements would vault Texas over California as the most important state in the nation for international trade. These dreams came easily to Texans, both because dreaming big was part of their cultural inheritance and because of the specific ways in which this modern desire to be a hemispheric powerhouse linked up with the old antebellum Texas ambition of spreading the state's economic and cultural power (and its slavery) throughout the Caribbean and Central America.[39]

The seriousness with which Bush had internalized this dream can be gleaned from three of his earliest foreign policy initiatives as president. He became the first U.S. president to make a Latin American country, Mexico, the destination of his inaugural foreign trip. Another early initiative was a hemispheric conference in Quebec to explore elongating the hemispheric free trading zone beyond NAFTA to encompass all of the Americas, from the Arctic Circle in the North to Tierra del Fuego in the South. Bush called this zone a Free Trade Area of the Americas.[40] Third, he scheduled a summit with President Vicente Fox of Mexico in September 2001 to develop a bilateral treaty on trade, immigration, and economic development. The summit was about to convene when al Qaeda's attacks on the World Trade Center and the Pentagon not only scuttled the meeting but put dreams of a hemispheric union indefinitely on hold.[41]

Hispanics and Latin America were at the core of Bush's multiculturalist and transnational economic vision. Blacks were not as important to the Republicans' grand strategy either electorally or economically, and Bush did not expend the same kind of energy on them as he did on attempting to bring Hispanics into his coalition. Bush had had important and positive encounters with African Americans, including his work with poor black youths in Houston in 1973, a volunteer duty he undertook to mollify his father's anger toward him for his lack of focus and ambition. By one account, George W.'s casual, even hip, style and his talent for banter proved to be a big hit among his charges, and he formed strong bonds with several of them.[42] When Bush ran for reelection as Texas governor a quarter century later, he asked a group of well-heeled African American Republicans in Houston to promote his candidacy in Texas's black communities, and they succeeded in turning out for him an impressive fraction—27 percent—of the total African American vote. But neither in his gubernatorial nor in his presidential campaigns did Bush ever make the kind of effort to appear in black churches or before black secular organizations that rivaled his Hispanic initiatives in comprehensiveness or intensity. Moreover, blacks occupied no strategic place in the grand Republican hemispheric economic vision that paralleled the important role accorded Latin Americans. This may help to explain why Bush and his political gurus were willing to jettison their efforts to bring blacks into the new Republican Party. Soon after winning his first race for the governorship in 1994, Bush told a Texas reporter that "Blacks didn't come out for me like the Hispanics did. So they're not gonna see much help from me."[43]

●　●　●

Bush brought his multiculturalism to the White House. He appointed more minorities to positions requiring Senate confirmation than any Republican president in history.[44] At the highest level, these appointees included the first two African American secretaries of state, the first female African American national security advisor, and the first Hispanic attorney general in American history. Thirty years earlier these minority appointments would have been unimaginable in either a Democratic or a Republican administration. Whatever one thinks of the particular accomplishments and failures of the individuals holding these positions, their presence in or alongside the cabinet, with two of them, Attorney

General Alberto Gonzales and National Security Advisor (and then Secretary of State) Condoleezza Rice, having exceptional access to the president, broke the glass ceiling that previously limited how high minority presidential appointees could rise. In light of those advances, it is worth thinking seriously about Hendrik Hertzberg's claim that "by appointing first Colin Powell and then Rice to the most senior job in the Cabinet, a job of global scope, Bush changed the way millions of white Americans think about black public officials."[45]

Few sitting presidents (and probably no other Republican president) have had the kind of close relationship with an African American woman that Bush enjoyed with Rice. The two evidently delighted being in each other's company, a circle of friendship that included Laura, and easily shifted back and forth between their professional and personal relationships. The many white Americans who watched a black woman sit so close to the presidency and be involved with the president at so many different levels likely helped many of them envision living in an America in which an African American occupied the presidential seat itself. In such ways, perhaps, did Bush contribute to Barack Obama's pathbreaking bid for the presidency.[46]

The Bush administration also made a significant contribution toward maintaining a climate of cultural toleration in the wake of September 11, when it would have been easy and popular to make America a Buchanan-like fortress. While the administration did subject Muslim and Arab communities and immigrants to intensive and intrusive surveillance, it also insisted on distinguishing between the radical Islamic fringe and the Islamic mainstream. In one of his first public speeches after September 11, Bush called on Americans to respect the legitimacy of Islam and the law-abiding Muslims who practiced it. In so doing he distinguished himself from two of his presidential forebears, Woodrow Wilson and Franklin Roosevelt, who in the era of their own wars made no parallel effort to demand toleration for law-abiding German Americans in World War I or law-abiding Japanese Americans in World War II. World War I marked the end of public displays of German culture in the United States, as anti-German hostility drove these displays either underground or out of existence altogether. And in World War II the federal government imprisoned virtually the entire West Coast Japanese and Japanese American population in the belief that this community was, for reasons of race, uniquely prone to subversion and treason.[47]

The Bush administration undertook no such extreme action against the Muslim or Arab populations. Bush was keenly aware of the Japanese American incarceration precedent, in part because Norman Mineta, a Japanese American who had been "relocated" in 1942, sat in Bush's cabinet as secretary of transportation. At a cabinet meeting the day after September 11, Bush declared (looking at Mineta) that his administration didn't "want what happened to Norm in 1942 to happen again" to Arab and Muslim Americans.[48] Instead, the Bush administration worked to create attitudes toward the latter groups that were more tolerant than those deployed against Germans in World War I and Japanese in World War II. It often was not successful in these efforts, as anti-Arab and anti-Muslim sentiment continued to bubble up among many groups of Americans at the grass roots. But the Bush administration's efforts to encourage toleration did make a difference. The dramatic growth in interest in Muslim culture and history and in the commitment of universities to teaching Arabic during the war on terror era stands in contrast to the World War I era, when many local and state governments banned the teaching of the German language and the study of German culture in schools and eliminated the names of foods, streets, and towns that gave evidence of German influence on American culture.[49]

The greatest benefits of this predisposition to cultural toleration no doubt accrued to immigrant populations that did not originate in Muslim or Arab lands. It would hardly have been surprising if the United States had shut off immigration in the first year or two after September 11, much as the nation had done in 1921, two years after the anarchist bombings and the Red Scare of 1919. The United States did make it far more difficult for some immigrant groups to gain entry after September 11, especially those originating in Arab and Muslim countries. And pathways for some other migrants, most notably foreign students wanting to study in the United States, became so obstructed by national-security–inflected visa rules that they altered course. Europe in particular became a more popular destination for many of these Third World students than the United States, a development that now poses a long-term threat to the soft power of American imperialism. Nevertheless, for almost six full years after September 11, the United States retained its reputation as a society open to immigrants. During that time, millions of immigrants, especially from Latin America, the Caribbean, and parts of Africa and East Asia, continued to come to the United States. The Bush administration played a significant role in keeping the immigrant gates open, and it took on powerful nativist groups in the Republican Party in order to do so.[50] Hispanics in particular believed they had a friend in the White House. They expressed their gratitude to Bush in 2004 by casting 40 percent of their votes for him—a doubling of the Republican percentage of Hispanic votes over what Robert Dole had achieved for the Republican Party in 1996.

The importance of multiculturalism to the Bush domestic agenda can be gleaned, finally, from a signature piece of legislation passed just as Bush began his second year in office, the No Child Left Behind Act. This legislation required every public school in the country to ensure that a large majority of students in every one of the school's racial groups meet or surpass government-mandated achievement levels in math, English, and other basic subjects. Schools that failed to achieve these levels would be given a number of years to remedy the situation. If they failed, they would face sanctions: the loss of federal funds, the loss of students (who would be given permission to enroll in better schools), the firing of school administrators and teachers, and ultimately the closing or state-ordered takeover of the failing schools themselves. NCLB in effect shifted responsibility for achievement from the individual child and his or her family to the state: local school districts in the front lines, state governments overseeing them, and the central government as the ultimate enforcer of standards and penalties.[51]

Although the NCLB attracted bipartisan support in Congress—Senator Ted Kennedy was one of its congressional sponsors—it originated with the Bush administration and Bush himself. Other than tax cuts and immigration, education was the policy issue that Bush knew and cared about the most. Still, what could have prompted a conservative president to design legislation that so disregarded a sacred principle of American governance, local control of American public schools? And what could have prevailed on him to overlook a basic conservative belief that individuals and families, not the state, are responsible for their own well-being?

Bush's willingness to overlook such bedrock conservative principles suggests that a great deal was at stake in this legislation. Indeed it was. Through NCLB, Bush and his advisers thought they could hammer the final nails into the coffin of affirmative action by offering minorities a new route to socioeconomic achievement. The seriousness of the Republicans' effort to address racial inequities through NCLB is apparent in their insistence (written into the law) that school achievement data be disaggregated by racial group, and that each racial group in every school reach a mandated level of achievement for the school as a whole to receive a passing grade. If the Republican Party were to succeed in raising achievement standards across the board through NCLB and in closing the historic achievement gap between whites, on the one hand, and blacks and Hispanics on the other, they could then take credit for spurring minority success and advancement in ways that liberals, with their "soft bigotry of low expectations," never had.[52] Minority voters, blacks and Hispanics, would then reward Bush's "tough love" Republican Party with their votes, thus ensuring that Bush would become the architect of that which he and Karl Rove most ardently desired: a permanent and multicultural Republican majority.

By embracing the kind of "social engineering" project that conservatives repeatedly castigated liberals for undertaking, Bush revealed his willingness to challenge key conservative orthodoxies. And he did so in the interests of furthering his multicultural vision of America in which differences grounded in race would no longer impede minority advancement.

Whether or not NCLB will succeed in reducing historic racial divergences in academic achievement is not yet clear. What is clear is that the implementation of NCLB, and of Bush's multicultural program more generally, suffered from his unwillingness to modify other aspects of conservative orthodoxy. Bush was deeply committed to slashing taxes paid by the wealthy, even at the cost of depriving the government of needed revenue for the NCLB and other social programs, and Bush tolerated in his administration and in the executive branch more broadly a hostility toward public governance that undermined some of his most cherished domestic and foreign ambitions.

The package of tax cuts passed during 2001 was a signature legislative accomplishment of Bush's first term. Equally important was his administration's refusal to rescind any of those cuts between 2001 and 2008, even in light of an expensive war, exploding budget deficits, and the underfunding of social programs that were important to Bush but that languished because he did not commit sufficient funds to them. The consequences of this lack of funding for Bush's multicultural program and for the pursuit of a permanent Republican majority were severe. A month after Bush engineered the passage of NCLB, he cut its funding by $90 million. The funds appropriated for NCLB after that time were never adequate, prompting Ted Kennedy and his allies to scream betrayal and impelling local school districts and state governments throughout the country to look for ways to evade the unfunded mandates imposed on them by the federal government. Meanwhile, the Bush Administration set aside only meager funds for its faith-based welfare state, consigning what might have been a major legislative initiative and a root-and-branch reconstruction of welfare services to the status of a mere slogan.[53]

A disdain for public governance among some of those close to Bush and within important GOP circles was equally damaging to the Republican Party and to Bush's multicultural ambitions. Many Republicans had become so enamored of an extreme version of free market ideology—one that declared that the market could solve all problems and the government none—that they proved surprisingly cavalier about the discharge of even basic government duties. Some Bush lieutenants filled government posts with individuals whose only qualification seems to have been their party loyalty or their ability to channel public money into the pockets of private contractors.[54]

The Bush administration even allowed this cynical appointments policy to penetrate critical government agencies charged with rebuilding Iraq and leading relief and reconstruction efforts along the Gulf Coast in the aftermath of Katrina. In both cases the results hurt Bush. In Iraq, the U.S. occupation force failed for years to protect the lives and security of the Iraqi people. At home, the Federal Emergency Management Agency, under the direction of the political appointee Mike Brown, proved to be spectacularly inept in its response to Katrina, allowing a great American city, and its African American majority, to descend into disaster.[55]

The failure in Iraq and New Orleans became apparent at roughly the same time, in the fall of 2005, and changed the tenor of politics in the United States. Among blacks, already angered by the Republican Party's machinations to keep them from voting in 2000 and 2004, the federal government's neglect of New Orleans in the hurricane's aftermath evoked memories of a long-standing racist tradition in American life: that black life was cheap and not worth saving. Whatever gains the Republican Party had made among African Americans vanished, and it would be beyond Bush's power to repair the damage. Many whites who had supported Bush, meanwhile, began to wonder why the basic task of maintaining public order in New Orleans and Baghdad seemed beyond the capacity of the U.S. government. Some began actively to examine what they had long sensed about the Bush administration but had declined to confront: perhaps this administration did not possess the competence to lead the country either abroad or at home.

Falling prestige occasioned by administrative failures undid the greatest achievement of Bush's multicultural strategy, the Republican Party's capture in 2004 of 40 percent of the Hispanic vote.

Bush's multiculturalism had never been popular among white, socially conservative Republicans. As long as the Bush administration retained its aura of invincibility, the social conservatives held their fire. But once that prestige was damaged, and Bush's poll numbers plummeted, social conservatives revolted. Worried that Bush's slide meant that political power in Washington would slip from their grasp in the 2006 elections, they seized on immigration as a law-and-order issue that could rally the party's demoralized base and restore the party's credibility. Conservative Republicans increasingly depicted both the country's toleration of porous borders and the presence of Spanish-speaking immigrants on U.S. soil as threats to core American values. They made known their belief that there could be no compromise with the twelve million illegals in the United States, and certainly no road to citizenship for them. In December 2005 Republicans pushed through the House of Representatives a draconian anti-immigrant bill that made illegal entry into the United States a felony punishable by imprisonment. Hispanics reacted with fury and launched an immigrant-rights protest movement that brought millions into the streets in spring 2006. In its breadth, intensity, and public militancy, this immigrant-rights movement had no precedent in American history. It acted as a brake on anti-immigrant legislation, evident in the Senate's declining to take up the House bill. Senators from both parties, with the Bush administration's support, began framing a new immigration initiative that they hoped would achieve both improved border security and a road to citizenship for the undocumented.[56]

Neither the Senate nor Bush, however, could persuade the House Republican hard-liners to support this balanced effort at immigration reform. Indeed, the latter dug in their heels, becoming the mouthpieces on Capitol Hill for rising anti-immigrant sentiment among the Republican rank and file throughout the country. By the fall of 2007, the Senate immigration initiative had collapsed. Conservative Republicans, meanwhile, were compelling Republican presidential hopefuls, even those with liberal records on immigration, to take hard anti-immigrant stances. Conservatives also conscripted a reluctant but weakened Bush administration into a nationwide campaign of raids to deport thousands of immigrants directly and to scare hundreds of thousands more into leaving of their own accord.[57]

Hispanics, as a result, began exiting the Republican Party in large numbers. Bush was not the only Republican absent from the party's convention in St. Paul, Minnesota, in August 2008. So too were the Hispanic Republicans and other minorities. By every measure the convention was the least diverse one that the Republicans had sponsored in more than forty years. The proportion of Hispanics casting their votes for Republicans in November 2008 plummeted by 25 percent from the 40 percent high that Bush had achieved in 2004.[58] The administrative ineptitude that so damaged the Bush presidency in the fall of 2005 and that triggered the revolt of Republican social conservatives cost Bush a prize, Republican popularity among Hispanic voters, that he had spent his entire political career attempting to win.

• • •

What lay at the root of the collapse of Bush's multiculturalist program? We cannot yet answer this question with certainty because too many presidential documents pertinent to the subject are not yet available to historians. But we can identify four factors that an explanation ought to consider: first, Bush's personal limitations as president; second, the effect of war on Bush and his presidency; third, the way in which Bush and his closest advisers interpreted the results of the 2000 election and altered their electoral strategies as a result; and finally, the corrosive effects of the Republican Party's contempt for public governance.

Bush's personal limitations. Jacob Weisberg has argued that Bush should be understood as a tragic figure, his virtues—evident, in this case, in a serious commitment to creating a new America in which minorities and immigrants would feel at home—compromised by character flaws that undermined Bush's ability to lead either in foreign or domestic affairs.[59] We don't have to subscribe to Weisberg's preference for a psychologically inflected view of

Bush's weaknesses (most notably a love-hate relationship with his father) to acknowledge that Bush could be incurious about important policy matters, that he sometimes reached decisions without a full airing of the options before him, and that he did not always keep his subordinates to whom he delegated important tasks on a firm enough leash. David Kuo's chronicle of Bush's failure to make headway with his faith-based welfare state portrays Bush as a man of good intentions who was betrayed by his ineffectuality as commander of his own administration.[60]

The pressures of war. Bush was a wartime president for all but nine months of his eight years in office. We must consider the possibility that September 11 and the ensuing war on terror and the Iraq War profoundly changed Bush and the ambitions of his presidency. Just as World War I ended Woodrow Wilson's efforts to establish a Progressive America and the Vietnam War undermined Lyndon Johnson's efforts to create a Great Society, so too the war on terror may have compromised Bush's ability to pursue his dream of compassionate conservatism. After September 11, much of what Bush wanted to do, from a well-funded NCLB policy to inventing a faith-based welfare state, from immigration reform to pursuing a hemispheric union, became far more difficult to accomplish. Robert Draper has further argued that the burden of waging war also changed Bush, inclining him to rigidity and robbing him of the flexibility, imagination, and improvisational ability that had characterized his earlier career.[61]

Republican reactions to the 2000 election. The Republicans put forward a resolute public face in the wake of the uncertainty of the 2000 election results; indeed, their self-assurance, in combination with the skillfulness and ruthlessness of their electoral maneuverings (far more impressive than what the Democrats could muster), arguably turned Florida election laws and judicial rulings in their favor and secured the presidency for their candidate. But this impressive GOP blitzkrieg should not cause us to overlook the private shock that Bush's loss of the popular vote triggered among his inner circle of political strategists.[62] For the 2000 campaign, Karl Rove had devised for Bush a centrist, big-tent, compassionate conservative campaign, believing that independent voters would decide the election. After the election, another Bush strategist, Matthew Dowd, undertook a study to understand why the Rove strategy had failed to yield a popular vote victory. The results of his investigation stunned Republican insiders: Rove's vaunted independent electorate, Dowd claimed, had shrunk to a paltry 6 percent of the total number of voters, down from the 25 percent range it had occupied during the Reagan years. Independent voters were now too small in numbers, Dowd argued, to be a decisive force in most elections. Meanwhile, Bush's pursuit of the "phantom middle" of the electorate had cost him votes among hard-core Republicans, especially those who identified themselves as evangelicals.[63]

Influenced by Dowd's memo, Rove did not therefore give up on his big-tent vision of a permanent Republican majority. But he did decide that he had to match efforts by Republicans to reach out to independent or new voters (such as Hispanics) with efforts to mobilize much greater proportions of the socially conservative, white evangelical base. This is the strategy that Rove, with Dowd's assistance, pursued in 2004 in states such as Ohio, choosing the emotional issue of gay marriage to pry large numbers of evangelical voters out of their homes and churches and send them scurrying to the polls.[64]

Rove's adjusted strategy was brilliantly successful in the short term, bringing Bush what many observers regarded as a surprising reelection victory. But it was also a strategy that was inherently difficult to execute, for it required balancing contradictory ambitions, broadening the party's appeal while persuading the conservative base that the party was a vehicle for their views alone. The strategy unraveled only a year after the 2004 victory. The Katrina catastrophe gave Republican social conservatives, reenergized by the 2004 election, the opportunity to release themselves from the control of Bush and Rove and to scuttle, through anti-immigration agitation, the big-tent portion of the Bush-Rove strategy. The Republicans' 2006 and 2008 electoral defeats reveal how short-sighted the plan embodied in the Dowd memo had been.

A Republican contempt for public governance. From the days of Ronald Reagan until the financial crash of 2008, market fundamentalism was ideologically dominant in the Republican Party. This faith rested on two principles: first, that free markets were the source of everything that was good in society—economic growth, affluence, personal freedom, and democracy; and second, that government could do little that was right in the economy and so should be barred from interfering with the markets and the freedoms that those markets made available.[65] Many Republicans, moreover, disliked the "big government society" that liberals had built up across nearly a half century of their influence (1932–80) and wanted to dismantle the government institutions that made this society possible. The Republicans' failure, however, to eliminate sizable bureaucracies or even to shrink their size substantially during the period of Republican ascendancy (1980–2008) bred deep frustration. Too many permitted this frustration to shade into contempt for government and become an excuse for undermining the work of essential government institutions. Thus, Republicans during the Bush years filled many important government posts with political appointees whose qualifications were ideological rather than skill-based; frequently these appointees did not possess either the knowledge or the desire necessary to carry out their agency's work. Many among them became cynical, using their government positions and access to make themselves and their families rich. A general contempt for government justified such cynicism: if government were truly bad, it really didn't matter whether or not its employees abused its authority or neglected its responsibilities. So unfolded one of the extraordinary spectacles of the Bush years: critical government agencies, including the Provisional Government in Iraq, the Federal Emergency Management Agency, and the Securities and Exchange Commission, became populated by individuals who did not have either the skill or the desire to carry out the important work these agencies were charged with doing.

If Bush's own ambitions for social policy had been modest (and if Katrina had occurred on someone else's watch), the contempt for government that his administration tolerated might not have been calamitous. But Bush's ambitions for the government were in fact grand, bordering on the utopian: his determination to bring democracy to the Middle East was a project of social engineering that required a U.S.-superintended program of government reconstruction in Iraq that would exceed in cost, expertise, and duration the reconstructions that previous administrations had undertaken in Germany and Japan. The NCLB agenda was one of the most ambitious programs for minority educational achievement ever undertaken by the federal government, and Bush's desire to make America an ownership society and, in the process, to avail poor Americans, and especially racial minorities among the poor, unprecedented access to homeownership required careful government regulation of the subprime mortgage market. In none of these areas did the work of the federal government come close to matching the policy challenge Bush had set for it.[66] And the blame must lie both with Bush, for his chronic inattention to the details of his policies, and with a general contempt for public governance in which so many Republicans had for a generation indulged.

The multiple failures of the Bush administration may incline some to believe that its multiculturalist project never could have succeeded. But this would be to sell short the significance of Bush's multicultural initiatives: the commitment to appointing minorities to the highest positions in government, the search for a way to eliminate racial inequities that did not rely on affirmative action, assembling a multicultural coalition of the godly that welcomed god-fearing minorities into it ranks and that weakened the control of the Democratic Party over minority voters, and the construction of an economic and multicultural Union of the Americas. These initiatives have left their mark on America. Future Republican politicians will likely return to them as a way of building winning electoral coalitions.

Likewise, future Republican strategists will recognize, as Rove did, the centrality of a multiculturalist project to the success of the Republican Party over the long term. During his years as Bush's principal adviser, Rove was fond of invoking the presidency of

William B. McKinley (1896–1901) for its success in developing a big-tent strategy for the Republican Party that made it the majority party in American politics for thirty years.[67] Rove remarked far less on when this Republican Party lost its big-tent appeal, and on what the consequences were. But surely he knew that the McKinley era of Republican dominance weakened in the 1920s and ended in the early 1930s. This was a moment when nativist conservatives took over the Republican Party, turned the party against immigration and the New America, and, with a little help from a collapsing financial structure that brought on the Great Depression, cost their party its hold on national power for nearly forty years.

The Republican Party of today once again stands in danger of returning itself to a minority party status, its ability to win elections limited to one region, the South, and a few outlier states such as Alaska.[68] Should the tendencies that have been creating this insurmountable electoral map harden in coming years, the Republican Party may come to regret its repudiation of Bush's and Rove's embrace of the New America more than it can currently imagine.

12

FROM HUBRIS TO DESPAIR

George W. Bush and the Conservative Movement

Michael Kazin

Presidential speechwriters may be the only true idealists at work in the White House. Their job, after all, is to distill the moral, hopeful, altruistic essence from policies and deeds that an administration often adopts primarily to enhance its power or to reward a key constituency. The demands of their craft lead them to make grandiose claims about the man whom they serve that, in retrospect, often appear foolish and naive. But some of their phrases endure in popular memory as signature moments of nearly every modern presidency, from Franklin Roosevelt's 1936 "rendezvous with destiny" speech (drafted by four different writers) to John Kennedy's inaugural address (the work of Theodore Sorensen) to Ronald Reagan's denunciation of the USSR as an "evil empire" (a phrase coined by Anthony Dolan). At such times, a talented speechwriter can be critical to the making of political history at the highest symbolic level.

Thus, a clash of views between Peggy Noonan and Michael Gerson—the two best speechwriters for the only conservative Republican presidents ever to serve two terms—over the legacy of President George W. Bush as his term in office neared its end may reveal something significant about the fortunes of their movement. Conservative activists tend to care more than do liberals about big ideas: of individual liberty, a morality rooted in religion, the need for strong leadership, the claims of tradition, the exceptional merits of the American nation. Inevitably, Noonan and Gerson saw themselves as guarding the temple of conservative virtue from those who would defile it.

The movement to which both writers belong has been in continuous existence since the 1950s, far longer than any comparable effort on the liberal or radical left. At the beginning, it was a conscious project mainly among small groups of intellectuals. But as the movement grew in size, so, inevitably, did disputes among its adherents. During most of his first term, President George W. Bush seemed to have unified all factions on the right, except those "paleoconservatives" like Patrick Buchanan who opposed the invasion of Iraq. For the first time since the movement began, conservatives controlled all three branches of the federal government and enjoyed unrivaled domination of the Republican Party. But their differences broke out forcefully after Bush won reelection, revealing fault lines that may imperil the movement's fortunes in the years to come.[1]

Peggy Noonan wrote several of President Ronald Reagan's most memorable speeches and then did the same for the first President Bush. "The boys of Point de Hoc" and "a kinder, gentler nation" came from her pen, or keyboard. An Irish Catholic from a working-class family who once adored the Kennedys, Noonan represented the "ethnic" former Democrats who helped infuse the conservative movement of the 1970s and early 1980s with an energetic, populist spirit. Noonan wrote a memoir about her days in the White House that helped establish the now conventional image of Reagan as the conservative's FDR—an eloquent leader with a first-class temperament who altered the course of history. "He was probably the sweetest, most innocent man ever to serve in the Oval Office," she wrote. "'I'm not odd,' he would say, 'I'm only odd for a president.'"[2]

As a columnist for the *Wall Street Journal*, Noonan was almost as smitten by the second President Bush—at least until he was safely reelected. On the eve of the invasion of Iraq, she praised Bush for having "a steady hand on the helm in high seas, a knowledge of where we must go and why, a resolve to achieve safe harbor. More and more," she concluded with a quasi-divine metaphor, "this presidency is feeling like a gift." During the 2004 campaign, Noonan again used populist language to describe her latest conservative hero. "Mr. Bush is the triumph of the seemingly average American man. . . . He thinks in a sort of common-sense way. . . . He's not exotic. But if there's a fire on the block, he'll run out and help."[3]

But then, like other veteran commentators on the right, such as William F. Buckley and George Will, she turned sharply against the president. Policy fiascos from Iraq to New Orleans, followed by the Republican loss of Congress in the 2006 elections, had alerted Noonan to the rot within. Bush, she wrote angrily in the spring of 2007, had betrayed nearly every conservative cause. He had created expensive new federal programs, promoted a form of amnesty for illegal immigrants, and, in his second inaugural address, committed the United States "to eradicate tyranny in the world," a vow "at once so utopian and aggressive that it shocked me." When conservatives protested these heresies, the president and his closest advisers attacked them. "Leading Democrats often think their base is slightly mad but at least their heart is in the right place," Noonan retorted. "This White House thinks its base is stupid and that its heart is in the wrong place. . . . Bush . . . sundered the party that rallied to him, and broke his coalition into pieces. He threw away his inheritance. I do not understand such squandering."[4]

Michael Gerson's understanding of what George W. Bush did, or at least tried to do, could hardly be more different. But then Gerson was the president's lead speechwriter from the early months of his 2000 campaign up to the summer of 2006, a length of tenure few other members of his trade have enjoyed. Like Noonan, Gerson is a former Democrat with a strong religious faith, although he belongs to an evangelical Protestant church rather than a Catholic one. Gerson started out in politics campaigning for Jimmy Carter, and he is as likely to cite as his models such Christian leftists as William Lloyd Garrison and Martin Luther King Jr. as any Republican. Ambivalent about the death penalty, he could not bring himself to vote for Jerry Kilgore, the Republican candidate in Virginia's 2005 gubernatorial election, because of Kilgore's "just kill 'em" rhetoric.[5]

After leaving the White House, Gerson wrote a book that heralds the attempts Bush made to forge what he called, during his 2000 race, "compassionate conservatism." Gerson viewed this as a "heroic" ideology that in many ways broke from the orthodox gospel Noonan had espoused. Heroic conservatives, in his view, favor a government strong enough to aid the poor and uneducated while advancing individual "dignity" at home, through faith-based institutions and a ban on abortion. The liberatory purpose behind the Iraq War was laudable, Gerson maintained. Only the execution was flawed. And, in the future, the United States should not shrink from promoting democracy and human rights around the world.[6] This is the man who wrote the inaugural address whose messianic goals Noonan deplored.

Gerson did fault the administration for not being fully committed to the kind of conservatism he favors. Many who served the president, he wrote in sorrow, "did not embody" Bush's daring vision. In fact, "some who served" in it "did not share the vision at all." But he maintained that the president kept the flame of idealism burning throughout his term in office and that Republicans who abandon it will "face a severe judgment of history."[7]

While Noonan and Gerson both call themselves conservatives, their conceptions of what that means draw from different and sometimes hostile tendencies in their movement and in American political culture more generally. Noonan is mostly faithful to traditional conservative thought, in the spirit that led Buckley, in the first issue of the *National Review*, to express his famous intention to publish a magazine that "stands athwart history, yelling Stop. . . ." Noonan wants to limit the powers of the federal government, except for law enforcement and the military. She favors the Catholic principle of "subsidiarity": depending on local communities, parishes, small enterprises, and individuals instead of the national government to solve social problems.

In contrast, Gerson is an evangelical crusader whose influences derive as much from the traditions of Protestant reform, even radicalism, as they do from conservative values of cautious initiatives and a respect for the "cake of custom." Like the abolitionists and prohibitionists of the nineteenth century, he believes only a government actively committed to great, salvific causes is worthy of American ideals. Some conservative reviewers of his book even questioned whether he was one of them at all.[8]

This clash of judgments about George W. Bush's presidency represents more than the inevitable conflict that occurs when any presidential administration declines swiftly in public opinion and achieves few if any of its major objectives. Veterans of the Carter administration and that of George H. W. Bush did not quarrel over first principles or disagree fundamentally about whether the chief executive in question damaged or advanced their political fortunes. But in neither of these cases did key officials view themselves as part of an ideological movement. Nor did they believe they had wasted a splendid opportunity to transform the political universe for decades to come.

For most Americans on the right, George W. Bush's first term in office was the best of times. After his controversial triumph over Al Gore in 2000, Bush made clear that he meant to emulate the strategy Ronald Reagan had followed in his attempt to build a new conservative majority. Like Reagan, he appointed movement loyalists to key positions in his new administration while avoiding asking for cuts in popular government programs or indulging in harsh rhetoric that might alienate independent voters. Following the counsel of the inimitable Karl Rove, Bush also called for cuts in income taxes and denounced gay marriage, thereby satisfying the two largest cohorts on the right, the economic and religious conservatives.

Only on the issue of immigration did Bush part company with leading members of his coalition, with the significant exception of the business lobby. The president's attempt to give undocumented immigrants, particularly from Mexico, some hope to gain legal status was propelled by demographic and economic realities he had successfully negotiated in the 1990s when he was governor of Texas. It made no electoral sense to estrange the growing numbers of Latino voters by barring from school children whose parents had entered the United States illegally or to deport low-wage workers essential to many companies in the Sun Belt and elsewhere.[9]

During the 2000 campaign, Rove told reporters that he aimed to be the Mark Hanna of the twenty-first century. Like Hanna, manager of William McKinley's two victorious campaigns for the presidency, he advised his candidate to secure the Republican base among white Protestants of all classes while also appealing to groups that leaned Democratic, particularly Latinos and white Catholics. It helped that, like Reagan, Bush had a folksy personal style—and an apparent fondness for clearing brush—that encouraged sympathetic writers like Noonan to trumpet his identification with "ordinary people."[10]

The aftermath of the terrorist attacks of September 11, 2001, seemed to give Rove an excellent chance to achieve his objective of an enduring Republican majority. The president's aggressive response in securing the nation and overthrowing the Taliban regime in Afghanistan helped the GOP gain victory in the 2002 midterm election, and convinced Congress and most Americans to back the invasion of Iraq a few months later. Although his popularity had dwindled by 2004, Bush was still a more credible commander in chief than John Kerry, and his opposition to abortion and gay marriage helped him win the Catholic vote over his Catholic adversary, and to take about 40 percent of Latino votes as well.

With five sympathetic justices on the Supreme Court, conservatives, in effect, now controlled every branch of the federal government. It was a feat the Right hadn't matched since the 1920s, when "conservative" had a rather different meaning. Although Presidents Calvin Coolidge and Herbert Hoover disliked progressive taxation and mandatory regulation of business, they favored rights for women and black people more than did most Democrats at the time. Hoover, who swore by the Quaker values of individualism and unselfish service, even called himself a liberal.[11]

Early in 2003, on the eve of war with Iraq, Bill Keller, soon to be named executive editor of the *New York Times*, wrote a long and mostly admiring profile of President Bush for his newspaper. He assessed the president's chances for achieving a new conservative majority. "If he fails," predicted Keller, "my guess is that it will be a failure not of caution but of overreaching, which means it will be failure on a grand scale. If he succeeds, he will move us toward an America Ronald Reagan would have been happy to call his own."[12]

When Bush left office six years later, his failure was the most obvious fact of American political life. To understand why activists on the right fell so hard for Bush and rejected him so rudely requires a detour back to the origins of their movement.

• • •

As a self-conscious movement, modern American conservatism began in the mid-1950s, when William F. Buckley Jr., then just twenty-nine, founded the *National Review*. His magazine quickly became a forum for a variety of erudite conservatives who rejected the isolationist and often anti-Semitic views that had hampered the Right from mounting an attractive alternative to the New Deal. Early in the 1960s, Buckley and his co-editors helped spark a grassroots effort to persuade Arizona senator Barry Goldwater to run for president. The Goldwater campaign mobilized a variety of groups that had never before worked together, from the conspiracy-mongering John Birch Society to the campus-based Young Americans for Freedom to local groups that favored mandated prayer in public schools but opposed busing to integrate them.

Although Goldwater lost the 1964 election in a landslide, the movement continued to grow. Activists quickly took advantage of the failure of liberal Democrats to win the war in Vietnam or to soothe the rising fears of many white Americans about black criminals, rebellious youths, and uppity gays, college students, and feminists. From Goldwater to George W. Bush, writes one young conservative, the movement "transformed itself from a narrow claque into a broad church, embracing anyone and everyone who called themselves an enemy of liberalism, whether they were New York intellectuals or Orange County housewives." Since Lyndon Johnson left office, no avowed liberal has come close to winning the presidency. Even Barack Obama, in 2008, rejected the label, although his policies conformed to the image most Americans have of that ideological breed.[13]

While their counterparts in the New Left were distancing themselves from mainstream Democrats in the 1960s, most conservatives were taking a more practical approach to electoral politics. They made a commitment to the GOP and gradually gained power in many state parties by the end of the 1970s. At the same time, the Right built an impressive set of institutions—think tanks, legal societies, lobbying firms, evangelical colleges, and popular periodicals—that trained and financed a generation of writers and organizers. During the quarter century from Ronald Reagan's election in 1980 to George W. Bush's reelection in 2004, conservatives nurtured an alliance between large employers and optimistic white Christians that lifted many of their own into office.[14]

The Right's dominance over political debate forced even President Bill Clinton, who won office in 1992 when many Republicans split their votes between Bush's father and independent Ross Perot, to declare that "The era of big government is over." Clinton achieved two feats the Right had long demanded: a balanced budget and punitive welfare reform. Writing not long after the 2004 contest, the liberal journalist Thomas Edsall sadly observed, "The GOP is the party of the socially and economic dominant and of those who identify with the dominant." Perhaps Barry Goldwater had won after all.[15]

Yet, like any entity that manages to gain national influence and power in a democratic society, the Right had always been an assemblage of disparate parts united for a common purpose. Unlike the historic Left, which dreams of an egalitarian transformation, of rapid progress toward a better and newer world, conservatives traditionally have defined themselves by what and whom they oppose. Like Peggy Noonan, most sought, at least in principle, to preserve institutions, values, and ways of life that the Left rashly endangers, not to attempt to change the world. Yet activists in two smaller sections of the movement did favor sweeping, even radical changes. Followers of Ayn Rand believed that, if unencumbered by the state, fearless entrepreneurs would usher in a society of free, self-reliant individuals, while neoconservatives favored an aggressive foreign policy that would help topple tyrannical left-wing regimes and replace them with capitalist democracies.

In the late 1950s, Buckley and the *National Review* famously brokered a "fusion" between two groups of thinkers: traditionalist conservatives, most of them Catholic, such as Russell Kirk, who feared the moral collapse of Western civilization, and economic libertarians, such as Milton Friedman, who cared little about religion but a great deal about preserving and extending the free market in goods and labor. Ayn Rand and her dogmatic acolytes were not welcome at the party. The essential bonding agent was a shared hatred of communism and revulsion at those naive liberals who were willing to coexist with and perhaps emulate the diabolic enemy. Such eloquent apostates from communism as Whittaker Chambers and James Burnham filled a prophetic role, helping to convince the two groups of conservatives to work together, despite their conflicting ideas about what constituted a good society.

Over the next two decades, the movement swelled far beyond that small band of founding minds. Resentments, partly based on race, of rising crime rates and against welfare recipients led many white voters to vote for conservative Republicans, and some to become activists as well. Yet inside the burgeoning coalition of right-wing Christians, antitax crusaders, and champions of the white backlash there always simmered a conflict over the role of the state in the economy and about whether to ground one's ethics and politics in the self-reliant individual or in a community of the faithful. Traditionalists recoiled not so much against a welfare state but against a godless one. The rising prominence of neoconservatives, first in intellectual circles and then in the Reagan administration, provided both a new source of influence for the movement and a new source of conflict within it. Cosmopolitan in their tastes and mostly Jewish and secular, the neocons had entrée into the *New York Times*, the *Washington Post*, the major networks, and elite universities. In debates about foreign affairs, they were skillful at putting their liberal foes on the defensive. But their aggressive support of Israel infuriated such traditionalists as the journalist and speechwriter Patrick Buchanan, and they never really warmed to the libertarians' vision of a minimal state. After all, the "tax-and-spend" era of the 1930s through the 1960s had done much to lift Jews and other white ethnic groups into the middle class.

While Ronald Reagan was president, the three camps had every reason to compromise or submerge their differences. As long as the relaxed former actor sat in the White House, the virtual merger between the conservative movement and the GOP seemed a match that benefited both groups. Libertarians would have liked to cut spending as well as taxes, traditionalists longed to outlaw all abortions and not just to limit the numbers performed, and neoconservatives were wary of the president's fondness for Mikhail Gorbachev and his close ties to Saudi Arabia, the main financial supporter of the Palestinian resistance. But they knew Reagan was a movement conservative; he had launched his own political career with a stirring televised speech for Goldwater in 1964. And his rhetoric and personality were excellent recruiting forces. His strong ratings in opinion polls—at least after the economy recovered in 1983 from recession—and success at establishing "big government" as the "problem" in the minds of most Americans made him the only shared hero conservatives had possessed since their movement began.[16]

George H. W. Bush enjoyed no such status or confidence. Although he portrayed himself as the consolidator of the "Reagan Revolution," his temperament and policies seemed closer to those of the then marginal but still despised "Rockefeller Republicans" from the Northeast. Libertarians mistrusted him for raising taxes, and traditionalists like Buchanan and Pat Robertson mistrusted him for giving only tepid backing to the right-to-life cause and cooperating with the leaders of the nearly defunct Soviet Union to build "a new world order . . . in which the nations of the world, East and West, North and South, can prosper and live in harmony." Buchanan ran a strong campaign against Bush for the 1992 Republican nomination. Then, in his keynote address to that year's GOP convention, the feisty journalist sought to bind the party to his wing of the movement, declaring there was "a religious war going on in our country for the soul of America."[17]

That speech only added to the incumbent's woes. Bush's drubbing in the November election was almost a relief to true believers on the right. Over the next eight years, they were again able to unite against a common enemy: the Clinton administration, which conservatives viewed as a stealthy attempt to jerk the nation leftward. As the Right saw him, the slick-talking former southern governor talked like a moderate while he sought to federalize the provision of health care and refused to curb his libido even within the Oval Office, symbolic hub of America's civil religion.

• • •

The failure of Congress, under GOP leadership, to drive Bill Clinton from office during the Lewinsky scandal in 1998–99 demoralized some long-time activists and confirmed the image of the Right, in much of the mass media, as a movement obsessed with sexual behavior and blind hatred of its adversaries. What is more, Clinton's studied centrism on domestic policy seemed to have established a new common sense about the role of the state: Americans favored small, efficient programs designed to solve specific problems but opposed any return to the days of "big government."

Mindful of these problems, most conservatives rallied early to the presidential candidacy of George W. Bush. They calculated that the affable, born-again governor of a major state—who, thanks to his father, was also blessed with instant name recognition—had the best chance to revive their fortunes. Indeed, during the 2000 campaign, Bush's pledges to improve public schools, support the earned income tax credit, and advance other elements of "compassionate conservatism" mixed well with his evangelical creed. After securing his party's nomination, Bush even held a press conference with gay Republicans at which he declared, "These are people from our neighborhoods, people with whom all of us went to school. . . . And I'm mindful that we're all God's children."[18]

In the wake of the attacks of 9/11, all factions on the right were willing, as during the glory days of the Reagan administration, to

work out their differences in the hope of building a durable majority that would advance ends they held in common. Neoconservatives now opposed *Roe v. Wade*, evangelicals had become fervent
tax cutters, and everyone on the right, save the small group of paleoconservatives behind Patrick Buchanan, applauded the "war on
terrorism" and, at least publicly, the decision to invade Iraq. Like
Reagan, Bush may not have been carrying out every point on the
conservative agenda, but he seemed in command of a wartime nation and was making the Right and its ideas look good again. "So
long as [a conservative president] talks the talk they really don't
have to walk the walk so much," commented Sam Tanenhaus, the
journalist and historian, ". . . they can constantly make the sorts
of real-world adjustments that any real-world political figure
does."[19]

A historical analogy comes to mind: the George W. Bush who
had just defeated John Kerry was in a position similar to that which
faced his fellow Texan, Lyndon B. Johnson, exactly forty years earlier. LBJ, having retained his office with far more ease than Bush
and with a much bigger majority in Congress, set out to transform
the nation's social policy while also prosecuting a war for democracy halfway across the world. At the end of 1964, Johnson appeared to have as solid backing from the liberal stalwarts in his
party as Bush enjoyed, in late 2004, from their latter-day counterparts on the right. Of course, George W. Bush and LBJ utterly
failed in both pursuits and, in the process, fragmented their once
mighty coalitions. Each did, however, achieve some of his major
legislative goals: for Johnson, such landmark Great Society laws as
the Civil Rights and Voting Rights Act and Medicare; for Bush, a
huge tax cut, enactment of national educational standards, and a
drug benefit for senior citizens.

Bush's record did present his fellow partisans with a severe dilemma, one neither Johnson nor his liberal critics had to face: how
conservatives govern contradicts their basic ideals. Ever since
forming a disgruntled opposition to the New Deal, conservatives
have vowed to reverse the role the state, particularly the federal
state, plays in American society. Barry Goldwater once said that

the first duty of elected officials should be "to divest themselves of the power they have been given."[20]

Reagan, in his first inaugural address, declared that "government is not the solution to our problem; government is the problem." But he was unwilling and probably unable to practice what he preached. As a share of GDP, federal spending shrank by only 1 percent during his term in office, and the federal civilian workforce grew from 2.8 million to three million employees. Instead of cutting taxes on the middle class, Reagan actually increased income, payroll, and gasoline levies, in part to pay for popular and costly social programs enacted under his Democratic predecessors. During his time in office, the national debt ballooned to $2.7 billion, easily the highest total in American history. Reagan also expanded the size and cost of the national security state, both in the United States and abroad. As a political project, the Reagan Revolution certainly put liberals on the run, in part because the huge deficit made it hard for future administrations to propose and Congress to enact large and expensive new domestic programs. But the conservative hero did little to trim either the enhanced powers or responsibilities to protect citizens' rights he had inherited from his Democrat predecessors.[21]

George W. Bush had a similar record of spending but lacked Reagan's ability to quiet protests from his own side and disarm the Democrats. With overwhelming support from his fellow Republicans in Congress, Bush boosted both the domestic and military budgets and signed the prescription drug benefit under Medicare, which may cost as much as $1.2 trillion in its first decade of operation. His administration increased spending by a higher percentage than any chief executive since Lyndon Johnson. The president began to hear a few protests from the Right when he ran for reelection, but they became quite deafening during his final term. "Bush seems intent on following the LBJ model by making entitlement spending even more overgrown," complained the editors of the libertarian magazine *Reason* in 2005. "If I'd thought he was a big-spending Rockefeller Republican—that is, if I'd thought he was a man who could not imagine and had never absorbed the damage big spending does—I wouldn't have voted for him," Peggy Noonan snapped the following year.[22]

Such complaints may keep activists in fighting trim, but they fail to grasp the exigencies of governing a complex, modern society. As Alan Wolfe has put it, "A conservative in America . . . is someone who advocates ends that cannot be realized through means that can never be justified, at least not on the terrain of conservatism itself."[23]

Even those Americans who tell pollsters they are conservatives—a plurality for decades now—take for granted the welfare state constructed during the 1930s and enhanced by every administration since then. They curse "big government," but most expect, or at least hope, that public officials will keep the economy prosperous and deliver good education to their children, a decent income, and cheap medical care when they retire, and will provide swift and efficient aid whenever disaster strikes. Rhetorical fashions come and go in American politics, but FDR's vow to deliver "security" and "freedom from fear" still captures what voters most want from their politicians.

In the White House, Reagan and both Bushes emulated Dwight Eisenhower's famous 1954 comment to his brother Edgar, "Should any political party attempt to abolish social security, unemployment insurance, and eliminate labor laws and farm programs, you would not hear of that party again in our political history." Just after winning reelection, George W. Bush did announce his intention to privatize Social Security, promising that no American's benefits would be reduced. But leaders of both parties deflated that trial balloon quickly and completely. For all his belief in American exceptionalism, Bush should have learned from his fellow conservative leaders in Europe, few of whom even consider dismantling the more lavish welfare programs in their nations.

In the goals of his foreign policy, the Bush administration did break sharply with traditions on the right that date back to Edmund Burke's elegant condemnation of the French Revolution. His second inaugural address, as Noonan implied, could have been delivered by Wilson, FDR, JFK, or Bill Clinton: "no one is fit to be a master, and no one deserves to be a slave. . . . All who live in tyranny and hopelessness can know the United States will not ignore your oppression, or excuse your oppressors. When you stand for liberty, we will stand with you." Bush's messianic talk helped convince such prominent leftists as Paul Berman and Christopher Hitchens to support the invasion of Iraq.

After the war proved far more difficult than promised, a growing number of intellectuals on the right began to voice their doubts about the grand mission. Neoconservative columnists David Brooks and Charles Krauthammer questioned whether a democratic Iraq was possible and temporarily endorsed a three-way partition of the country. Francis Fukuyama compared his former allies on the right to Leninists who believed they could force their ideology on other nations. "Leninism was a tragedy in its Bolshevik version," he wrote in the *New York Times*, "and it has returned as farce when practiced by the United States."[24]

The result of such disappointments—or betrayals—was a swift and stunning desertion from the president's side. By late 2007, few activists on the right bothered to defend Bush, and the leading Republican candidates to succeed him, all of whom brandished the conservative label, condemned most of his domestic policies as well as his handling of the war in Iraq, at least until the surge of troops seemed to reduce the violence in Baghdad. No GOP hopeful asked for Bush's endorsement, and none was forthcoming. In fact, the president was fortunate that his erstwhile loyalists even invited him to address the Republican convention in the Twin Cities, although on a video hookup from the White House. In 1968, Lyndon Johnson had avoided such an ignominious farewell. Although he declined to run again, LBJ was still able to convince his party to nominate Vice President Hubert Humphrey to succeed him, and their supporters dominated the unruly convention in Chicago that summer.

• • •

How can conservatives revitalize their movement in the wake of the Bush presidency and Obama's victory? They face thorny challenges, both internal and demographic. And it will be difficult to rebound if the Democrats in control of the White House and Congress, a more liberal group than were their counterparts during the Clinton years, are able to pull the nation out of the worldwide recession and enact a national health care system and measures to curb global warming.

During the 2008 presidential campaign, internal rifts on the right were relatively muted. Conservatives did not suffer the sort of bitter split between pro- and antiwar forces that helped doom the candidacies of Democrats Hubert Humphrey in 1968 and George McGovern in 1972. In 2008, every serious contender for the Republican nomination agreed, in general, with the Bush administration's approach to combating terrorism abroad and wanted to retain a large force of combat troops in Iraq. Despite the unpopularity of the war, no vocal peace movement dogged the candidates, pressing moral claims that a potential president would have found difficult to ignore. The surge of forces in Iraq did not make the United States a more popular occupier, but it did divert the mass media from describing the war as a debacle and usually removed it from the spotlight altogether.

During the campaign, every Republican candidate dutifully paid homage to Reagan as the avatar of their cause, proof that he remained the only political figure that everyone on the right admired without significant second thoughts. But three of the four major GOP contenders represented, with uncanny precision, just one section of the conservative coalition that had come together in 1980: Mitt Romney, the free-marketers; Rudolph Giuliani, the neoconservatives; and Mike Huckabee, the white evangelicals. Only John McCain attracted a measure of support from each ideological faction, without allowing that support to limit his appeal to independents and some Democrats. It should therefore not have been surprising that he won the nomination and was running even with Barack Obama in the polls in the week after the successful Republican convention. If the U.S. financial system had not collapsed in mid-September, making a mockery of the GOP's faith in unregulated markets, the Democrats probably would not have won such a far-reaching victory just six weeks later.

The fissures on the right that cracked open during George W. Bush's second term are quite different from and may be easier to close than the ones that wrecked the Great Society. The uneasy coalition across racial lines that FDR bequeathed to LBJ did not survive the urban riots of 1965-68. In contrast, movement conservatism has always been an overwhelmingly white persuasion; the debate that erupted in 2006 between Bush and his critics on the right over how to treat undocumented immigrants involved few of the Latinos who, for familial and historical reasons, cared most about the issue. At the same time, the predominance of nativist forces in the party was one reason Latino voters punished the GOP in 2008, much as white Southerners did the Democrats in 1968 and 1972.

After McCain's defeat, however, a debate began among conservatives similar to that which engrossed liberals who had to face up to their minority status two decades before. At issue was whether to revive the movement's fortunes by sticking to first principles or to adapt those principles to more centrist concerns. The ideological stalwarts, who included such prominent figures as Rush Limbaugh, Newt Gingrich, and Sarah Palin, echoed themes similar to those Peggy Noonan articulated after the 2006 election: conservatives should call for restraining or rolling back the growth of the federal government and refuse to compromise on their resistance to abortion and homosexual marriage. It was their free market gospel that led a majority of House Republicans to vote against the $700 billion rescue of banks and investment firms in the fall of 2008 and to oppose appropriating funds to help floundering U.S. auto firms a few months later. That the lame duck administration was cooperating with Democrats to enact both "bailouts" only proved to many conservatives that George W. Bush had sold his political soul as well as squandered the esteem of the public.

In contrast, a number of intellectuals on the right called for rethinking the approach both the movement and its party took to Americans whose confidence it had lost during Bush's disastrous second term. Young journalists Ross Douthat and Reihan Salam argued that to win back the white working class, conservatives should advocate "pro-family" policies that would appeal to people scared about their economic future. They favor measures conservatives have traditionally opposed, such as wage subsidies and state-funded catastrophic health insurance. David Frum, a former speechwriter for President George W. Bush, urged the right-to-life movement to abandon its quixotic desire for a constitutional amendment and be satisfied with limiting the number of abortions. He also called for an end to the campaign against gay rights, including marriage. Most college-educated voters believe "their values are under threat from Republicans," Frum wrote, and it is this fast-growing group they needed to win back.[25] Remarkably, neither the traditionalists nor the new moderates said much about the war against terrorism, perhaps the central preoccupation of the administration that had failed to live up to their hopes.

After their landslide loss in the 1964 election, Republicans had quarreled along similar lines. But the political context was quite different. The conservative movement was just beginning to grow in the mid-1960s; not for almost two decades did the ideological Right control the GOP in most states and localities. But by 2008, outside the Northeast and a few other places there was little separation between the Republican Party and the conservative movement, particularly during election campaigns. So a crisis for one half of the partnership inevitably caused big trouble for the other.

Conservatives faced the future ensnared in a dilemma. If they faithfully adhered to the doctrine of limited government and steadfast opposition to abortion and homosexual marriage, they might confine themselves to a base of libertarian ideologues and evangelical white Christians. Yet to embrace the prescriptions espoused by the softer, gentler thinkers—and the pragmatic office-holders whom they advised—risked abandoning convictions that had made it possible to recruit thousands of smart, determined activists who had reshaped the nation's politics, if not its governance. In the 1950s, Barry Goldwater accused the "modern" Republicans who came to power with Eisenhower of carrying out a "dime store

New Deal." Half a century later, any conservative branded a "Wal-Mart Obama" would surely alienate some of the very people the movement needs to revive.

Meanwhile, the demography of the American electorate is changing in ways that may imperil the future of the kind of conservative movement that surged to power with Reagan and George W. Bush. In 2008, Barack Obama lost the votes of white voters without college educations—a common definition of "working class"—by eighteen percentage points, about the same margin as Al Gore in 2000. But he won such overwhelming margins among Latinos, African Americans, Asian Americans, professionals, and young people of all races that his deficit among white working-class people did not matter. While it may be difficult to repeat the huge black turnout in subsequent elections, every other group that overwhelmingly voted Democratic in 2008 is likely to grow as a proportion of the electorate in the years to come. On other hand, for the first time in history, white Christians, the base of the conservative movement and of the GOP since the 1980s, now make up less than half the U.S. population. And the number of small-town voters, so cherished by Sarah Palin, is dwarfed by the residents of cities and nearby suburbs, who cast a sizable majority of their ballots for Barack Obama. The growth of this "non-Christian coalition," as Democratic analyst Ruy Teixeira has dubbed it, challenges conservatives to alter their rhetoric, if not to change how they propose to govern a nation that has soured on its leaders.[26]

The failures of George W. Bush's presidency did more damage to the Right than merely giving new confidence to a Democratic Party in which liberals (or "progressives") had taken command for the first time since the 1980s. By 2008, conservatives lacked the great advantage Ronald Reagan (and his political advisers) had given them: a moral calling attractive to Americans who shun partisanship. Reagan's anti-communism and his upbeat populist challenge to liberal elites allowed the Right to appear to be talking common sense instead of mere ideology, and to promote its legislative agenda on that basis. As the liberal journalist Sidney Blumenthal wrote at the time, "without Reagan, conservatism would never have become a mass cultural experience; he gave life to abstractions."[27] In the absence of major attacks on the homeland by "Islamo-fascists," it is difficult to see how the activist Right and its favored politicians can regain that status. Like liberals after 1980, they may be in for a long period of division, rethinking, and adaptation.

Still, the conservative movement has advantages liberals did not possess at the dawn of the Reagan era. In 1980, labor unions were declining and dispirited, and neither the black movement nor the feminist movement had the élan or numbers that might have expanded the Democratic electorate. But decades of intelligent, well-financed labor produced a powerful structure of conservative institutions that can survive the loss of several national elections. These institutions include the Southern Baptist Convention and other evangelical churches, the Federalist Society and other networks of conservative lawyers and law schools, Christian colleges, both Protestant and Catholic, that give students a more coherent worldview than do the more prestigious schools led by liberals, such media outlets as Fox News and talk radio and the editorial pages of the *Wall Street Journal*, and the Republican parties of most states outside the Northeast, whose leading activists still dream of restoring the Reagan coalition. While business lobbyists tend to back whichever party is in power or seems about to achieve it, far more corporations are led by men and women with conservative backgrounds than liberal ones.

Unless Obama and the Democrats are able to use the opportunity of the deep recession to produce a new New Deal, this structure could help tilt U.S. politics rightward again, as George W. Bush becomes a fading memory instead of an irritating presence. Americans continue to want the government to help solve their problems, but they also continue to mistrust politicians who struggle to craft policies with that aim in mind. Such cynicism is nearly always a boon to the Right, which, at least in principle, favors that government which governs least. Meanwhile, as the Tea Party up-surge showed in 2009 and 2010, the individualist creed has weakened only slightly, despite such perils as economic collapse, global warming, and transnational terrorism that have promoted interdependence in other postindustrial states.

One conclusion does seem inescapable: the presidency of George W. Bush robbed conservatives of a precious mass emotion, the confidence shared by members of every dynamic political force that they are acting in harmony with the movement of history. Despite their sharp differences, both Peggy Noonan and Michael Gerson felt the same sense of despair as the administration came to an end. Sam Tanenhaus, whose own political sympathies lean to the right, told an interviewer in 2007 that George W. Bush "will have no ideological legacy."[28] If he proves correct, then the administration of the forty-third president will be remembered as a political watershed indeed.

NOTES

CHAPTER 1
Establishment Conservative

[1] Shane Hamilton, *Trucking Country: The Road to America's Wal-Mart Economy* (Princeton: Princeton University Press, 2008); Bruce J. Schulman, *The Seventies: The Great Shift in American Culture, Society, and Politics* (New York: Free Press, 2001), 102–17.

[2] Jacob S. Hacker and Paul Pierson, *Off Center: The Republican Revolution and the Erosion of American Democracy* (New Haven: Yale University Press, 2005).

[3] Thomas B. Edsall, *Building Red America: The New Conservative Coalition and the Drive for Permanent Power* (New York: Basic Books, 2006). Other interesting analyses of the president's strategies can be found in Gary C. Jacobson, *A Divider, Not a Uniter: George W. Bush and the American People* (New York: Pearson, 2007), and Fred I. Greenstein, *The George W. Bush Presidency: An Early Assessment* (Baltimore: Johns Hopkins University Press, 2003).

[4] For a historiographic review of conservatism, see Julian E. Zelizer, "Rethinking the History of American Conservatism," *Reviews in American History*, 38 (June 2010).

[5] Some of the most interesting work on the rise of the Right includes Bruce Schulman and Julian E. Zelizer, eds., *Rightward Bound: Making America Conservative in the 1970s* (Cambridge, MA: Harvard University Press, 2008); Steve Teles, *The Rise of the Conservative Legal Movement* (Princeton: Princeton University Press, 2008); Joseph Crespino, *In Search of Another Country: Mississippi and the Conservative Counterrevolution* (Princeton: Princeton University

Press, 2007); Kevin Kruse, *White Flight: Atlanta and the Making of Modern Conservatism* (Princeton: Princeton University Press, 2005); Matthew D. Lassiter, *The Silent Majority: Suburban Politics in the Sunbelt South* (Princeton: Princeton University Press, 2005); Jonathan M. Schoenwald, *A Time for Choosing: The Rise of Modern American Conservatism* (New York: Oxford University Press, 2001); and Lisa McGirr, *Suburban Warriors: The Origins of the New American Right* (Princeton: Princeton University Press, 2001).

[6] Meg Jacobs and Julian E. Zelizer, *Conservatives in Power, 1981–1989* (Boston: Bedford, forthcoming); Donald T. Critchlow, *The Conservative Ascendancy: How the Right Made Political History* (Cambridge, MA: Harvard University Press, 2007); Paul Pierson and Theda Skocpol, eds., *The Transformation of American Politics: Activist Government and the Rise of Conservatism* (Princeton: Princeton University Press, 2007).

[7] Jacob S. Hacker, "Privatizing Risk Without Privatizing the Welfare State: The Hidden Politics of Social Policy Retrenchment in the United States," *American Political Science Review* 98 (May 2004): 243; Nolan McCarty, "The Policy Effects of Political Polarization," in Pierson and Skocpol, *The Transformation of American Politics*, 223–55.

[8] James T. Patterson, *Restless Giant: The United States from Watergate to Bush v. Gore* (New York: Oxford University Press, 2005), 165.

[9] Julian E. Zelizer, *Arsenal of Democracy: The Politics of National Security from World War II to the War on Terrorism* (New York: Basic Books, 2010); Lawrence Wittner, *Resisting the Bomb: A History of the World Nuclear Disarmament Movement, 1954–1970* (Stanford: Stanford University Press, 1997).

[10] Julian E. Zelizer, *On Capitol Hill: The Struggle to Reform Congress and Its Consequences, 1945–2000* (New York: Cambridge University Press, 2004); idem, "Seizing Power: Conservatives and Congress Since the 1970s," in Pierson and Skocpol, *The Transformation of American Politics*, 105–34.

[11] Dan Balz and Haynes Johnson, "A Political Odyssey," *Washington Post*, August 2, 2009.

[12] Critchlow, *The Conservative Ascendancy*, 277.

[13] Sean Wilentz, "The Worst President in History?" *Rolling Stone*, April 2006.

CHAPTER 2
How Conservatives Learned to Stop Worrying and Love Presidential Power

[1] George F. Will, "Why Didn't He Ask Congress?" *Washington Post*, December 20, 2005.

[2] Randall B. Woods, *LBJ: Architect of American Ambition* (New York: Free Press, 2006).

[3] Paul J. Kern, "The President as 'Dictator' in the Light of Our History," *New York Times*, March 26, 1933.

[4] James Burnham, *Congress and the American Tradition* (Chicago: Regnery, 1959), 93–97.

[5] Bruce Schulman and Julian E. Zelizer, eds., *Rightward Bound: Making America Conservative in the 1970s* (Cambridge, MA: Harvard University Press, 2008).

[6] An abbreviated version of this paper can be found in Julian E. Zelizer, "The Conservative Embrace of Presidential Power," *Boston University Law Review*, April 2006, 100–105.

[7] Ronald Lora, "Conservative Intellectuals: The Cold War and McCarthy," in *The Specter: Original Essays on the Cold War and the Origins of McCarthyism*, ed. Robert Griffith and Athan Theoharis (New York: New Viewpoints, 1974), 60.

[8] "Diary of White House Leadership Meetings—91st Congress," October 7, 1969, RNP (Richard Nixon Papers, College Park, MD), box 106, file: White House–Congressional Leadership Meeting 10/7/69.

[9] Bryce Harlow to President Nixon, October 6, 1969, RNP, White House Central Files, Subject Files FG 31-1, box 5, file 4.

[10] "Diary of White House Leadership Meetings—91st Congress."

[11] Gareth Davies, *See Government Grow: Education Politics from Johnson to Reagan* (Lawrence: University of Kansas Press, 2007).

[12] Arthur M. Schlesinger Jr., *Journals: 1952–2000* (New York: Penguin, 2007), 352.

[13] Congressional Research Service, *Presidential Claims of Executive Privilege: History, Law, Practice and Recent Development*, September 17, 2007, 37.

[14] James L. Sundquist, *The Decline and Resurgence of Congress* (Washington, DC: Brookings Institution Press, 1981).

[15] Jeffrey Hart, "The Presidency: Shifting Conservative Perspectives?" *National Review*, November 1974.

[16] Kathryn S. Olmsted, *Challenging the Secret Government: The Post-Watergate Investigations of the CIA and FBI* (Chapel Hill: University of North Carolina Press, 1996), 48.

[17] John Robert Greene, *The Presidency of Gerald R. Ford* (Lawrence: University Press of Kansas, 1995), 69, 70, 106.

[18] Douglas Brinkley, *Gerald R. Ford* (New York: Times Books, 2007), 147.

[19] Hugh Graham, *Collision Course: The Strange Convergence of Affirmative Action and Immigration Policy in America* (New York: Oxford University Press, 2002), 75; Paul Pierson, "The Rise and Reconfiguration of Activist Government," in *The Transformation of American Politics: Activist Government and the Rise of Conservatism*, ed. Paul Pierson and Theda Skocpol (Princeton: Princeton University Press, 2007), 24–26; Marc K. Landy and Martin Levin, eds., *The New Politics of Public Policy* (Baltimore: Johns Hopkins University Press, 1995); David Vogel, *Kindred Strangers: The Uneasy Relationship Between Politics and Business in America* (Princeton: Princeton University Press, 1996), 141–94, 298–388; idem, "The 'New' Social Regulation," in *Regulation in Perspective: Historical Essays*, ed. Thomas McGraw (Cambridge, MA: Harvard University Press, 1981), 155–85.

[20] "Church: 'Entering the 1984 Decade,'" *Time*, March 24, 1975, 26.

[21] "Backlash over All Those Leaks," *Time*, February 23, 1976.

[22] "Text of Ford Plan on Intelligence Units and Excerpts from His Executive Order," *New York Times*, February 19, 1976.

23 David Burnham, "Compromise Bill Is Drafted on Electronic Surveillance," *New York Times,* February 8, 1978.

24 Olmsted, *Challenging the Secret Government,* 3.

25 *Congressional Quarterly Almanac* (Washington, DC: CQ Press, 1978), 843.

26 David S. Broder, "Presidential Power Is Defended by Ford," *Washington Power,* December 14, 1978.

27 Melvyn P. Leffler, *For the Soul of Mankind: The United States, the Soviet Union, and the Cold War* (New York: Hill and Wang, 2007), 346.

28 Samuel P. Hays, *Beauty, Health, and Permanence: Environmental Politics in the United States, 1955–1988* (New York: Cambridge University Press, 1987), 535–36.

29 Terry Eastland, *Ethics, Politics and the Independent Counsel: Executive Power, Executive Vice, 1789–1989* (Washington, DC: National Legal Center for the Public Interest, 1989).

30 Frederick A. O. Schwarz Jr. and Aziz Z. Huq, *Unchecked and Unbalanced: Presidential Power in a Time of Terror* (New York: New Press, 2007), 156.

31 Richard Pious, "Why Do Presidents Fail," *Presidential Studies Quarterly* 32 (December 2002): 739–40; Richard Piper, "Situational Constitutionalism and Presidential Power," *Presidential Studies Quarterly* 24 (1994): 577–96.

32 Michael A. Fitts, "The Paradox of Power in the Modern State: Why a Unitary, Centralized Presidency May Not Exhibit Effective or Legitimate Leadership," *University of Pennsylvania Law Review* 144 (1996): 847–50.

33 *Morrison v. Olson,* 487 U.S. 654, 699 (1988).

34 Charlie Savage, *Takeover: The Return of the Imperial Presidency and the Subversion of American Democracy* (New York: Little, Brown, 2007), 57–58.

35 Fisher, "War Power," 695–96.

36 Stuart Taylor Jr., "Keep the Special Counsel," *New York Times,* June 22, 1992.

37 *Congressional Quarterly Almanac,* 1992, 317.

[38] Adam Clymer, "Republicans in About-Face on Special Prosecutor Law," *New York Times*, November 18, 1993.

[39] *Congressional Quarterly Almanac*, 1994, 295.

[40] Clymer, "Republicans in About-Face on Special Prosecutor Law."

[41] Kenneth R. Mayer and Kevin Price, "Unilateral Presidential Powers: Significant Executive Orders, 1949–1999," *Presidential Studies Quarterly* 32 (June 2002): 369.

[42] William G. Howell and Kenneth R. Mayer, "The Last One Hundred Days," *Presidential Studies Quarterly* 35 (September 2005): 546–47.

[43] John Yoo, "Kosovo, War Powers, and the Multilateral Future," *Pennsylvania Law Review* 148 (2000): 1673–1731.

[44] Steven M. Teles, *The Rise of the Conservative Legal Movement: The Battle for Control of the Law* (Princeton: Princeton University Press, 2008).

[45] Savage, *Takeover*.

[46] Jane Mayer, "The Hidden Power," *New Yorker*, July 3, 2006, 44.

[47] Mayer and Price, "Unilateral Presidential Powers," 369.

[48] Barton Gellman, *Angler: The Cheney Vice Presidency* (New York: Penguin, 2008), 81–107.

[49] David J. Barron and Martin S. Lederman, "The Commander in Chief at the Lowest Ebb: A Constitutional History," *Harvard Law Review* 121 (February 2008): 1087–97.

[50] Barton Gellman and Jo Becker, "Pushing the Envelope on Presidential Power," *Washington Post*, June 25, 2007.

[51] Charlie Savage, "Bush Challenges Hundreds of Laws," *Boston Globe*, April 30, 2006.

[52] Robert Pear, "Bush Directive Increases Sway on Regulation," *New York Times*, January 30, 2007.

[53] Rachel L. Swarns, "Cheney, Needling Biden, Defends Bush's Record on Executive Power," *New York Times*, December 22, 2008.

[54] See, e.g., the contributions in Schulman and Zelizer, eds., *Rightward Bound*; Donald T. Critchlow, *The Conservative Asend-*

ency: How the GOP Right Made Political History (Cambridge, MA: Harvard University Press, 2007).

CHAPTER 3
A Sword and a Shield

For comments on earlier versions, thanks to Dan Rodgers, Julian Zelizer, David Cruz, Ingrid Wuerth, Chris Slobogin, Neil Siegel, Jason Solomon, and participants in the Conference on the Presidency of George W. Bush in Historical Perspective, Princeton University; the Rule of Law Under Pressure Seminar, Institute for Advanced Study, Princeton; and those who attended my workshops at the University of Maryland School of Law, Vanderbilt University Law School, and Duke Law School. Thanks to Abigail Perkins, Carolyn Furlong, and William Sung for research assistance, and to Paul Moorman of the USC Law Library.

[1] E.g., Louis Fisher, *The Constitution and 9/11: Recurring Threats to America's Freedoms* (Lawrence: University Press of Kansas, 2008), 361–62; David Cole, *Enemy Aliens: Double Standards and Constitutional Freedoms in the War on Terrorism*, 2nd ed. (New York: New Press, 2005), 206–7, 228–29; David Cole and James X. Dempsey, *Terrorism and the Constitution: Sacrificing Civil Liberties for National Security*, 3rd ed. (New York: New Press, 2005), 148–49, 174–75; the Constitution Project, "Statement of the Coalition to Defend Checks and Balances," October 2006, http://www.constitutionproject.org/pdf/Checks_and_Balances_Initial_Statement.pdf, 1–2. More sympathetic works include Eric A. Posner and Adrian Vermeule, *Terror in the Balance: Security, Liberty, and the Courts* (New York: Oxford University Press, 2006).

[2] *Bush v. Gore*, 531 U.S. 1046, 1047 (2000); *Bush v. Gore*, 531 U.S. 98, 109, 111 (2000); Howard Gillman, *The Votes That Counted: How the Court Decided the 2000 Election* (Chicago: University of Chicago Press, 2001), 152–59.

[3] Gillman, *The Votes That Counted*, 151–71; Keith Whittington, "Yet Another Constitutional Crisis?" *William and Mary Law Re-*

view 43 (2001–2): 2093–2149; Mark V. Tushnet, "Renormalizing *Bush v. Gore*: An Anticipatory Intellectual History," *Georgetown Law Journal* 90 (November 2001): 113–25.

⁴ Gillman, *The Votes That Counted*, 151–52.

⁵ David Savage, *Takeover: The Return of the Imperial Presidency and the Subversion of American Democracy* (New York: Little, Brown, 2007), 73–75, 85–118; John Yoo, "How the Presidency Regained Its Balance," *New York Times*, September 17, 2006, http://www.nytimes.com/2006/09/17/opinion/17yoo.html?_r=3&oref=slogin&oref=slogin&oref=slogin.

⁶ Jack Goldsmith, *The Terror Presidency* (New York: W. W. Norton, 2007), 9, 22–24, 31–32. On the history of the Office of Legal Council, see Frederick A. O. Schwarz Jr. and Aziz Z. Huq, *Unchecked and Unbalanced: Presidential Power in a Time of Terror* (New York: New Press, 2007), 187–99. On Vice President Cheney's role, see Barton Gellman, *Angler: The Cheney Vice Presidency* (New York: Penguin Press, 2008), 131–94.

⁷ Tim Golden, "A Junior Aide Had a Big Role in Terror Policy," *New York Times*, December 23, 2005, http://www.nytimes.com/2005/12/23/politics/23yoo.html?_r=1&scp=1&sq=tim%20golden%20a%20junior%20aid%20yoo&st=cse&oref=slogin; Goldsmith, *The Terror Presidency*, 22–23.

⁸ Jane Mayer, "The Hidden Power: The Legal Mind behind the White House's War on Terror," July 3, 2006, *New Yorker*, http://www.newyorker.com/archive/2006/07/03/060703fa_fact1; idem, *The Dark Side: The Inside Story of How the War on Terror Turned into a War on American Ideals* (New York: Doubleday, 2008), 48–50, 62–63; Goldsmith, *Terror Presidency*, 25–30, 77–79, 171.

⁹ *Uniting and Strengthening America by Providing Appropriate Tools Required to Intercept and Obstruct Terrorism (USA PATRIOT Act) Act of 2001*, Public Law 107-56 (2001), *U.S. Statutes at Large* 115 (2001): 272; *Authorization for Use of Military Force*, Public Law 107-40, *U.S. Statutes at Large* 115 (2001): 224; Golden, "A Junior Aide"; John C. Yoo, *The Powers of War and Peace: The Constitution and Foreign Affairs after 9/11* (Chicago: University of Chicago Press, 2005), 17–24; John C. Yoo, "Memorandum Opinion

for the Deputy Counsel to the President," September 25, 2001, http://www.usdoj.gov/olc/warpowers925.htm; Jay S. Bybee, memorandum for Alberto Gonzales, "Re: Standards of Conduct for Interrogation under 18 U.S.C. Secs. 2340–2340A," August 1, 2002, http://www.humanrightsfirst.org/us_law/etn/gonzales/memos_dir/memo_20020801_JD_%20Gonz_pdf, 1–2, 36–39; Goldsmith, *Terror Presidency*, 148; Jay S. Bybee, memorandum for Alberto R. Gonzales and William J. Haynes II, January 22, 2002, http://www.gwu.edu/~nsarchiv/NSAEBB/NSAEBB127/02.01.22.pdf, 1–2, 9–11. On the unitary executive thesis, see Steven G. Calabresi and Kevin H. Rhodes, "The Structural Constitution: Unitary Executive, Plural Judiciary," *Harvard Law Review* 105 (April 1992): 1153–1216; Steven G. Calabresi and Christopher S. Yoo, *The Unitary Executive: Presidential Power from Washington to Bush* (New Haven: Yale University Press, 2008).

The unitary executive thesis threatened to displace the analysis of presidential power articulated by Justice Robert Jackson in the Korean War–era Steel seizure case. Jackson's analysis in a concurrence, widely relied on thereafter, suggested that the president's power varied depending on whether the president was acting pursuant to a grant of power by Congress, when it was at its height; in opposition to Congress, when it was at its lowest point; or in an in-between "zone of twilight." *Youngstown Sheet & Tube Co. v. Sawyer*, 343 U.S. 579, 634 (1952) (Jackson, J., concurring) (the Steel Seizure Case). See Louis Fisher, *Presidential War Power*, 2nd rev. ed. (Lawrence: University Press of Kansas, 2004), 101–31, 190–91.

[10] Bybee, memorandum for Alberto Gonzales, "Re: Standards of Conduct for Interrogation"; Goldsmith, *Terror Presidency*, 148. The memo is signed by Bybee but according to Goldsmith was written by John Yoo.

[11] Scott Shane, "Waterboarding Used 266 Times on 2 Suspects," *New York Times*, April 19, 2009, http://www.nytimes.com/2009/04/20/world/20detain.html; Steven G. Bradbury, memorandum for John A. Rizzo, May 30, 2005, http://luxmedia.vo.llnwd.net/010/clients/aclu/olc_05302005_bradbury.pdf.

[12] Warren Richey, "Conservatives Near Lock on US Courts,"

Christian Science Monitor, April 14, 2005, http://www.csmonitor
.com/2005/0414/p01s02-uspo.html; Savage, *Takeover*, 73.

[13] Mayer, *The Dark Side*, 52, 108–10, 120–25; Fisher, *The Constitution and 9-11*, 197; Goldsmith, *Terror Presidency*, 100–101; Schwarz and Huq, *Unchecked and Unbalanced*, 74, 103.

[14] "Military Order—Detention, Treatment, and Trial of Certain Non-Citizens in the War Against Terrorism," November 13, 2001, http://www.presidency.ucsb.edu/ws/index.php?pid=63124; Amnesty International, "United States of America: No Substitute for Habeas Corpus: Six Years without Judicial Review in Guantánamo," November 1, 2007, http://www.amnesty.org/en/library/asset/AMR51/163/2007/en/7577c886-a6c3-11dc-a534-f71c530609 5d/amr511632007en.html; Cole, *Terrorism and the Constitution*, 183–84.

[15] Goldsmith, *Terror Presidency*, 126, 128.

[16] Ibid., 131–33; Philip Zelikow, "Legal Policy for a Twilight War," *Houston Journal of International Law* 30 (Fall 2007): 89–109 (lecture delivered April 26, 2007).

[17] Goldsmith, *Terror Presidency*, 126, 128. On warlaw, see David Kennedy, *Of War and Law* (Princeton: Princeton University Press, 2006).

[18] Ruti Teitel, "Empire's Law: Foreign Relations by Presidential Fiat," in *September 11 in History: A Watershed Moment?*, ed. Mary L. Dudziak (Durham, NC: Duke University Press, 2003), 198–200.

The effort to avoid the legal judgment of others informed the vociferous arguments against the reliance on "foreign law" in American courts. Compare, e.g., Steven G. Calabresi, "'A Shining City on a Hill': American Exceptionalism and the Supreme Court's Practice of Relying on Foreign Law," *Boston University Law Review* 86 (2006): 1335–1416, with Mark Tushnet, "Referring to Foreign Law in Constitutional Interpretation: An Episode in the Culture Wars," *University of Baltimore Law Review* 35 (2006): 299–312. See also "Symposium: 'Outsourcing Authority?': Citation to Foreign Court Precedent in Domestic Jurisprudence," *Albany Law Review* 69 (2006): 645–888.

¹⁹ John Yoo, *War by Other Means: An Insider's Account of the War on Terror* (2006), 71; Jennifer C. Evans, "Comment, Hijacking Civil Liberties: The USA Patriot Act of 2001," *Loyola University of Chicago Law Journal* 33 (2002): 933, 967; Beryl A. Howell, "Seven Weeks: The Making of the US Patriot Act," *George Washington Law Review* 72 (2004): 1145, 1178–79; Julie Farnam, *U.S. Immigration Laws under the Threat of Terrorism* (Algora: Algora Publishing), 50; Mary Beth Seridan, "Immigration Law as Anti-Terrorism Tool," *Washington Post*, June 13, 2005, http://www.washingtonpost .com/wp-dyn/content/article/2005/06/12/AR2005061201441.html. See also Margaret Chon and Donna E. Arzt, "Walking While Muslim," *Journal of Law and Contemporary Problems* 68 (2005): 215–54.

²⁰ The issue of war's perceived temporal boundaries and the way they affect ideas about law is taken up in Mary L. Dudziak, "Law, War, and the History of Time," *California Law Review*, 2010.

²¹ *Korematsu v. United States*, 323 U.S. 214, 219 (1944). On criticism of *Korematsu*, see, e.g., Peter Irons, *Justice at War: The Story of the Japanese-American Internment Cases* (New York: Oxford University Press, 1983); Jacobus TenBroek, Edward Norton Barnhart, and Floyd W. Matson, *Prejudice, War, and the Constitution* (Berkeley and Los Angeles: University of California Press, 1968).

²² *Rasul v. Bush*, 542 U.S. 466, 485 (2004); Benjamin Wittes and Zaahira Wyne, "The Current Detainee Population of Guantánamo: An Empirical Study," Brookings Institute, December 16, 2008, http://www.brookings.edu/reports/2008/1216_detainees_wittes .aspx.

²³ *U.S. Code* 18 (1948), § 4001(a); *Hamdi v. Rumsfeld*, 542 U.S. 507, 520–21 (2004).

²⁴ *Hamdi*, 542 U.S. at 579; *Hamdi*, 542 U.S. at 573 (Scalia, J., dissenting); *Hamdi*, 542 U.S. at 589 (Thomas, J., dissenting).

²⁵ Goldsmith, *Terror Presidency*, 135–39.

²⁶ *Detainee Treatment Act of 2005*, Public Law 109-148 §§ 1003, 1004 (2005); *Hamdan v. Rumsfeld*, 548 U.S. 557, 655 (2006); *Military Commissions Act of 2006*, Public Law 109-366 (2006). The Court held that the Military Commissions Act of 2006 was an un-

constitutional suspension of the *writ of habeas corpus* in *Boume-diene v. Bush*, 128 S. Ct. 2229 (2008).

[27] *Padilla v. Hanft*, 423 F.3d 386, 396 (4th Cir. 2005); *Padilla v. Hanft*, 423 F.3d 582, 584-86 (4th Cir. 2005). The authority cited by administration lawyers for the detention of Padilla as an unlawful enemy combatant was the *Authorization of the Use of Military Force*, which authorized the president to "use all necessary force against . . . such nations, organizations, or *persons*" (emphasis added). The jurisdictional problem in the case was that the Court ruled that Padilla had brought his *habeas* petition in the wrong federal court, for the federal district court in New York did not have personal jurisdiction over the defendant, the commanding officer of the South Carolina brig where Padilla was being held. The case was dismissed without prejudice so that Padilla could refile in a proper court in South Carolina. *Authorization for Use of Military Force*, Public Law 107-40, *U.S. Statutes at Large* 115 (2001): 224; *Rumsfeld v. Padilla*, 542 U.S. 426, 451 (2004).

[28] *Padilla v. Hanft*, 547 U.S. 1062, 1063 (2006); Peter Whoriskey, "Jury Convicts Jose Padilla of Terror Charges," *Washington Post*, August 17, 2007, http://www.washingtonpost.com/wp-dyn/con tent/article/2007/08/16/AR2007081601009.html; Debra Cassens Weiss, "Judge Lowers Padilla Sentence Because of Harsh Confine-ment," *ABA Journal*, January 22, 2008, http://www.abajournal .com/news/judge_lowers_padilla_sentence_because_of_harsh_ confinement; Liz Aloi, "Luttig leaves bench for corporate post," SCOTUS Blog, May 10, 2006, http://www.scotusblog.com/wp/ luttig-leaves-bench-for-corporate-post.

[29] *American Civil Liberties Union v. National Security Agency*, 467 F.3d 590, 653, 687–88 (6th Cir. 2007). Some detainees were released, but not pursuant to court orders. Some releases resulted from pressure from human rights organizations or from the de-tainee's home country. According to Pierre-Richard Prosper, American Ambassador-at-Large for War Crimes Issues, 207 de-tainees were transferred or released following military tribunal hearings and other reviews by February 25, 2007. "U.S. Releases Juveniles from Guantanamo Prison," MSNBC.com, January 29,

2004, http://www.msnbc.msn.com/id/4096774/; "Guantanamo Inmates back in France," BBC News.com, July 27, 2004, http://news.bbc.co.uk/2/hi/americas/3928767.stm; Declaration of Pierre-Richard Prosper, *el-Mashad v. Bush*, no. 2005-0270 (U.S. District Court for the District of Columbia, February 25, 2005), 2–3, http://www.state.gov/documents/organization/45849.pdf.

[30] *Boumediene v. Bush*, 128 S. Ct. 2229, 2277, 2270 (2008). For Justice Scalia in dissent, however, a traditional wartime frame should continue to guide the Court.

[31] *Boumediene*, 128 S. Ct. at 2275; William Glaberson, "Despite Ruling, Detainee Cases Facing Delays," *New York Times*, October 4, 2008, http://www.nytimes.com/2008/10/05/us/05gitmo.html; Lyle Denniston, "Judge orders five detainees freed," SCOTUS Blog, November 20, 2008, http://www.scotusblog.com/wp/judge-orders-five-detainees-freed/; William Glaberson, "U.S. Is Set to Release 3 Detainees From Base," *New York Times*, December 15, 2008, http://www.nytimes.com/2008/12/16/washington/16gitmo.html?scp=4&sq=guantanamo%20detainees%20released%20obosnia&st=cse; Steven Erlanger, "Ex-Detainee Describes His 7 Years at Guantána-mo," *New York Times*, May 26, 2009, http://www.nytimes.com/2009/05/27/world/europe/27paris.html?scp=8&sq=guantanamo%20detainees%20released%20obosnia&st=cse. See also Wittes and Wyne, "The Current Detainee Population of Guantánamo."

[32] David Alistair Yalof, *Pursuit of Justices: Presidential Politics and the Selection of Supreme Court Nominees* (Chicago: University of Chicago Press, 1999), 91–94; Greenberg, *Supreme Conflict*, 263–315; "Reading the Roberts Court: Four Advocates Discuss the Court's First Full Term under Roberts and the Emergence of Kennedy" (panel discussion), *Legal Times*, August 17, 2007, http://www.law.com/jsp/article.jsp?id=1187168522747. Of the Roberts Court, Erwin Chemerinsky writes that it "is the most conservative Court since the 1930s." He attributes this to Justices Roberts and Alito who have "voted in a conservative direction in virtually every single ideologically divided case since they came on the Court." Erwin Chemerinsky, "The Roberts Court at Age Three," *Wayne State Law Review* 54 (Fall 2008): 947, 948, 955. See also Charles

Whitebread, "The Conservative Kennedy Court—What a Difference a Single Justice Can Make: The 2006–2007 Term of the United States Supreme Court," *Whittier Law Review* 29 (2007): 1–2. For a different assessment, see Jonathan H. Adler, "Getting the Roberts Court Right: A Response to Chemerinsky," *Wayne State Law Review* 54 (Fall 2008): 983. On divisions among the justices, see Pamela S. Karlan, "The Law of Small Numbers: *Gonzales v. Carhart,* Parents Involved in Community Schools, and Some Themes from the First Full Term of the Roberts Court," *North Carolina Law Review* 86 (June 2008): 1369; Maxwell L. Stearns, "Standing at the Crossroads: The Roberts Court in Historical Perspective," *Notre Dame Law Review* 83 (2008): 875, 937–38.

[33] Steven M. Teles, *The Rise of the Conservative Legal Movement* (Princeton: Princeton University Press, 2008), 1, 4–5, 160–61.

[34] Thomas M. Keck, *The Most Activist Supreme Court in History: The Road to Modern Judicial Conservatism* (Chicago: University of Chicago Press, 2004), 61–65, 97–103, 108, 110–13; Teles, *Conservative Legal Movement,* 22–46, 60, 145–46; Alexander M. Bickel, *The Least Dangerous Branch: The Supreme Court at the Bar of Politics* (New York: Bobbs-Merrill Co., 1962), 16–23; Steven G. Calabresi and Kevin H. Rhodes, "The Structural Constitution: Unitary Executive, Plural Judiciary," *Harvard Law Review* 105 (April 1992): 1153–1216; Yoo, *The Powers of War and Peace ,* 17–29. Other originalists did not share the unitary executive thesis. Ingrid Wuerth argues that much new originalist scholarship says little about executive power. Ingrid B. Wuerth, "An Originalism for Foreign Affairs?" *St. Louis University Law Review,* 53 (2008): 8–13.

[35] Teles, *Conservative Legal Movement,* 137–42, 265–77, passim.

[36] Keck, *Most Activist Supreme Court,* 130, 135, 172; *Roe v. Wade,* 410 U.S. 113 (1973); *Planned Parenthood of Southern Pennsylvania v. Casey,* 505 U.S. 833, 876 (1992); *Stenberg v. Carhart,* 530 U.S. 914, 939 (2000) (*Carhart I*). See Reva B. Siegel, "Dignity and the Politics of Protection: Abortion Restrictions Under *Casey/Carhart,*" *Yale Law Journal* 117 (2008): 1694–1800.

[37] Partial-Birth Abortion Ban Act of 2003, 18 U.S. Code Sec. 1531; *Gonzales v. Carhart*, 550 U.S. 124, 135–40, 168 (2007) (*Carhart II*); Tony Mauro, "Kennedy Reshapes Abortion Conflict as He Refines 'Swing Vote' Role," *Legal Times*, April 23, 2007, http://www.law.com/jsp/article.jsp?id=1177059874125.

The stark language of violence in *Carhart II* contrasted with the dispassionate opinion for the Court in *District of Columbia v. Heller*, 128 S. Ct. 2783, 2822 (2008), a Second Amendment case limiting the power of government to control firearms. The context, "the problem of handgun violence in this country," was mentioned only as an afterthought at the end of Scalia's majority opinion.

[38] *Grutter v. Bollinger*, 539 U.S. 306, 310 (2003); *Parents Involved in Community Schools v. Seattle School District*, 551 U.S. 701, 746-49 (2007); *Brown v. Board of Education*, 347 U.S. 483 (1954); Adam Liptak, "The Same Words, But Differing Views," *New York Times*, June 29, 2007, http://www.nytimes.com/2007/06/29/us/29assess.html?_r=2&oref=slogin&oref=slogin; Geoffrey Stone, "The Roberts Court, Stare Decisis, and the Future of Constitutional Law," *Tulane Law Review* 82 (March 2008): 1533, 1540; Keck, *Most Activist Supreme Court*, 5–6, 143–48, 181–82, 186–90.

[39] *Heller* at 2821–22; *Lawrence v. Texas*, 539, 578–79 U.S. 558 (2003); *Bowers v. Hardwick*, 478 U.S. 186 (1986); Tushnet, *A Court Divided*, 169–76, 231–39.

[40] *United States v. Morrison*, 529 U.S. 598 (2000); *Kimel v. Florida Board of Regents*, 528 U.S. 62 (2000); *Board of Trustees of the University of Alabama v. Garrett*, 531 U.S. 356 (2001); *Nevada Department of Human Resources v. Hibbs*, 538 U.S. 721 (2003); *Franchise Tax Board of California v. Hyatt*, 538 U.S. 488 (2003); Keck, *Most Activist Supreme Court*, 148–51, 236–43; Tushnet, *A Court Divided*, 249–78; Kathleen M. Sullivan, "From States' Rights Blue to Blue States' Rights: Federalism after the Rehnquist Court," *Fordham Law Review* 75 (2005–6): 799, 800.

[41] *United States v. Lopez*, 514 U.S. 549 (1995); *City of Boerne v. Flores*, 521 U.S. 507 (1997); *Seminole Tribe of Florida v. Florida*, 517 U.S. 44 (1996); *Board of Trustees of University of Alabama v. Garrett*, 531 U.S. 356 (2001); *Federal Maritime Commission v. South*

Carolina, 535 U.S. 743 (2003); *Nevada Department of Human Resources v. Hibbs*, 538 U.S. 721 (2003); Tushnet, *A Court Divided*, 271–76; Patrick M. Garry, *An Entrenched Legacy: How the New Deal Constitutional Revolution Continues to Shape the Role of the Supreme Court* (University Park: Pennsylvania State University Press, 2008), 84–86; Christopher Banks and Jon Blakeman, "Chief Justice Roberts, Justice Alito, and New Federalism Jurisprudence," *Publius* 38, no.3 (Summer 2008): 576–601.

[42] Susan N. Herman, "Collapsing Spheres: Joint Terrorism Task-Forces, Federalism, and the War on Terror," *Williamette Law Review* 41 (2005): 941; Sidney M. Milkis and Jesse H. Rhodes, "George W. Bush, the Party System, and American Federalism," *Publius* 37, no. 3 (Summer 2007): 478, 483–84; *No Child Left Behind Act of 2001*, Public Law 107-110 (2001), *U.S. Statutes at Large* 115 (2001): 1425.

[43] Juliet Eilperin, "Rule Would Ease Mining Debris Disposal," *Washington Post*, December 3, 2008, A6, http://www.washington post.com/wp-dyn/content/article/2008/12/02/AR2008120203055 .html; David G. Savage, "Broader Medical Refusal Rule May Go Far beyond Abortion," *Los Angeles Times*, December 2, 2008, http:// www.latimes.com/news/science/la-na-conscience2-2008dec02,0, 1244120.story.

CHAPTER 4
George W. Bush and the "War on Terror"

This is the private work of the author and does not represent the views or policies of the United States Government.

[1] David Jackson, "Pondering Legacy Is Left to Others" (interview with George W. Bush), *USA Today*, January 22, 2007, http:// www.usatoday.com/news/Washington/2007-01-21-bush-qanda_x .htm (accessed December 6, 2009).

[2] George Tenet, *At the Center of the Storm: My Years at the CIA* (New York: HarperCollins, 2007), 130. Tenet used the English transliteration Usama Bin Laden in his book. For his discussion of the CIA's Blue Sky memorandum, see 130–31.

³ Richard A. Clarke, memorandum for Condoleezza Rice, January 25, 2001, http://www.gwu.edu/~nsarchiv/NSAEBB/NSAEB B147/clarke%20memo.pdf (accessed January 31, 2009).

⁴ *The 9/11 Commission Report: Final Report of the National Commission on Terrorist Attacks Upon the United States* (New York: W. W. Norton, 2004), 210–14.

⁵ Ibid., 199.

⁶ Ibid., 131–33. Curiously, Clinton did not authorize the use of lethal force against bin Laden by the Northern Alliance. Yet during the transition to the Bush administration, George Tenet told the president-elect that the CIA had all the authority it needed to kill bin Laden (ibid., 199).

⁷ Ibid, 189.

⁸ Timothy Naftali, *Blind Spot: The Secret History of American Counterterrorism* (New York: Basic Books, 2005), 288–98.

⁹ Tenet, *At the Center of the Storm*, 176.

¹⁰ Ibid., 177.

¹¹ *The 9/11 Commission Report*, 208. For a discussion of the official Pakistani reaction to 9/11, see 331–33. And for information on Bush's first post-9/11 covert action, see 333.

¹² Bradley Graham, *By His Own Rules: The Ambitions, Successes, and Ultimate Failures of Donald Rumsfeld* (New York: Public Affairs, 2009), 237–50.

¹³ Naftali, *Blind Spot*, 150–226. U.S. recognition of the threat posed by the phenomenon of international terrorism—as distinct from the challenge posed by an individual terrorist or terrorist group—varied over time. In the period 1986–91, the United States did briefly go on the offensive against international terrorism.

¹⁴ Tenet, *At the Center of the Storm*, 180.

¹⁵ *The 9/11 Commission Report*, 333–334.

¹⁶ George W. Bush, "Address to a Joint Session of Congress and the American People," September 20, 2001, *Public Papers of the Presidents of the United States: George W. Bush*, 2001, Book 2, July 1–December 31, 2001 (Washington, DC: U.S. Government Printing Office, 2003), 1140–44.

¹⁷ Tenet, *At the Center of the Storm*, 177–78.

[18] 9/11 Commission Staff, *Monograph on Terrorist Financing*, August 21, 2004, http://www.au.af.mil/au/awc/awcgate/911_commision/911_terrfin_ch2.pdf (accessed December 6, 2009).

[19] John B. Taylor, *Global Financial Warriors: The Untold Story of International Finance in the Post-9/11 World* (New York: W. W. Norton, 2007), 7.

[20] Ibid., 12–13.

[21] Ibid., 18–19.

[22] Ibid., 19–21.

[23] Barton Gellman, *Angler: The Cheney Vice Presidency* (New York: Penguin Press, 2008), 279–80.

[24] Jack Goldsmith, *The Terror Presidency: Law and Judgment Inside the Bush Administration* (New York: W. W. Norton, 2007), 177–83.

[25] In August 2008, the Department of Justice announced its conclusion that U.S. biodefense researcher Dr. Bruce E. Ivins was likely responsible for the anthrax attacks. Ivins had committed suicide on July 29, 2008, after being informed of his coming prosecution. Carrie Johnson and Joby Warrick, "FBI Elaborates on Anthrax Case," *Washington Post*, August 18, 2008, http://www.washingtonpost.com/wp-dyn/content/article/2008/08/18/AR2008081802174.html (accessed August 30, 2009).

[26] U.S. Senate Select Committee on Secret Military Assistance to Iran and the Nicaraguan Opposition, U.S. House of Representatives Select Committee to Investigate Covert Arms Transactions with Iran, *Report of the Congressional Committees Investigating the Iran-Contra Affair; With Supplemental, Minority, and Additional Views, November 1987* (Washington, DC: U.S. Government Printing Office, 1987), 431–586. For a comprehensive look at Cheney's role in the Bush White House, see Gellman, *Angler*, passim.

[27] Tenet, *At the Center of the Storm*, 187, 215; Mary Anne Weaver, "Lost at Tora Bora," *New York Times*, September 11, 2005.

[28] Tenet, *At the Center of the Storm*, 225. For information on CIA-DOD tension and the evolution of the CIA's Afghan strategy, see 224–27.

[29] Ibid., 226.

[30] Weaver, "Lost at Tora Bora."

[31] Ron Suskind, *The One Percent Solution: Deep Inside America's Pursuit of Its Enemies since 9/11* (New York: Simon and Schuster, 2006), 84–89.

[32] Tenet, *At the Center of the Storm*, 241; CIA, Inspector General, Special Review, "Counterterrorism Detention and Investigation Activities (September 2001–October 2003)," *New York Times*, May 7, 2004, http://www.nytimes.com (accessed August 30, 2009).

[33] Tenet, *At the Center of the Storm*, 241.

[34] Goldsmith, *The Terror Presidency*, 144.

[35] Tenet, *At the Center of the Storm*, 242–43.

[36] David Johnston, "At a Secret Interrogation, Dispute Flared over Tactics," *New York Times*, September 10, 2006; Suskind, *The One Percent Solution*, 117. Suskind only credits Zubaydah with the information that led to Jose Padilla's arrest at O'Hare Airport in May 2002. Tenet does not discuss Padilla's arrest in his book

[37] CIA, Inspector General, "Counterterrorism Detention and Investigation Activities," 90. On the value of what was learned using these techniques, see also Peter Bergen, "Cheney's Jihad: Why 'Enhanced Interrogation Techniques' Didn't Enhance U.S. Interests," *Foreign Policy*, August 26, 2009, http://www.foreign policy.com/articles/2009/08/26/cheneys_jihad (accessed August 30, 2009).

[38] Jane Mayer, *The Dark Side: The Inside Story of How the War on Terror Turned into a War on American Ideals* (New York: Doubleday, 2008), 155–56.

[39] Ali Soufan, "My Tortured Decision," *New York Times*, April 22, 2009.

[40] White House, *The National Security Strategy of the United States of America*, September 17, 2002, http://georgewbush-white house.archives.gov/nsc/nss/2002/index.html (accessed August 30, 2009).

[41] Naftali, *Blind Spot*, 168.

[42] Gellman, *Angler*, 226–33.

[43] Fritz Kolbe, the highest-level Allied penetration of Nazi Germany, and Oleg Penkovsky, a joint U.S.-UK source at the height of

the cold war, are just two of many examples. On the "walk in" agent who pinpointed Khalid Sheik Mohammed, see Suskind, *The One Percent Solution*, 204–205.

44 Paul Pillar, "Counterterrorism after al Qaeda," *Washington Quarterly*, Summer 2003, http://www.twq.com/04summer/docs/04 summer_pillar.pdf (accessed December 6, 2009)

45 Tenet, *At the Center of the Storm*, 246.

46 9/11 Public Discourse Project, Report on the Status of 9/11 Commission Recommendations, Part II: Reforming the Institutions of Government, October 20, 2005, http://www.9-11pdp.org/press/2005-10-20_report.pdf. See discussion of the creation of the DNI on p. 3.

47 This confrontation is well described in Gellman, *Angler*, 299–326.

48 Mayer, *The Dark Side*, 294.

49 Gellman, *Angler*, 345.

50 Philip D. Zelikow, counselor of the Department of State in 2005–7, outlined the nine elements of what he called "the new paradigm" in a public lecture sponsored by the *Houston Journal of International Law* in April 2007, after leaving the department. See Zelikow, "Legal Policy for a Twilight War," May 30, 2007, http://hnn.us/articles/39494.html (accessed August 30, 2009).

51 "National Strategy for Combating Terrorism," September 2006, 19, http://hosted.ap.org/specials/interactives/wdc/documents/wh_terro60905.pdf (accessed December 6, 2009).

52 The new military approach to counterterrorism drew on the ideas of David Kilcullen, a former lieutenant colonel in the Australian army who served as chief strategist (2005–7) to Ambassador Hank Crumpton, the U.S. coordinator for counterterrorism, and then as senior counterinsurgency adviser to General David Petraeus (2007). See Kilcullen, *The Accidental Guerrilla: Fighting Small Wars in the Midst of a Big One* (New York: Oxford University Press, 2009).

53 Associated Press, "US Deaths Down in Iraq in 2008, Up in Afghanistan," *International Herald Tribune*, December 31, 2008, http://www.Iht.com (accessed February 1, 2009).

[54] Cedric Barnes and Harun Hassan, "The Rise and Fall of Mogadishu's Islamic Courts," briefing paper, Chatham House, UK, April 2007, http://www.chathamhouse.org.uk (accessed February 1, 2009); Sarah Childress, "Al-Shabab Remains the Most Powerful Political Force in Somalia," *Wall Street Journal*, January 14, 2009.

[55] Stephanie McCrummen and Karen De Young, "US Airstrike Kills Somali Accused of Links to al Qaeda," *Washington Post*, August 2, 2008.

[56] Statement of Philip Zelikow, U.S. Senate Committee on the Judiciary, Subcommittee on Administrative Oversight and the Courts, May 13, 2009, http://judiciary.senate.gov/pdf/09-05-13 ZelikowTestimony.pdf. For the unsigned "Elements of Possible Initiative" (June 2005), which Professor Zelikow submitted as an appendix to his testimony, see http://fas.org/irp/congress/2009_hr/elements.pdf (accessed December 6, 2009).

[57] See the two May 10, 2005, memoranda and the May 30, 2005, memorandum from Special Deputy Assistant Attorney General to John A. Rizzo, Deputy General Council, CIA declassified and released in April 2009 by the Department of Justice, http://www.aclu.org (accessed August 30, 2009).

[58] For details on the players in these skirmishes, see Graham, *By His Own Rules*, 540–44, 633–36.

[59] Gellman, *Angler*, 354–57. The law did give the president the power to define what was and was not consistent with the Geneva Conventions.

[60] Somini Sengupta and Keith Bradsher, "Mumbai Terrorist Siege Over, India Says," *New York Times*, November 28, 2008.

[61] John J. Goldman, "6 Indicted in Buffalo-area Terror Case," *Los Angeles Times*, October 22, 2002; BBC News, "Airlines Terror Plot Disrupted," August 10, 2006, http://news.bbc.co.uk (accessed February 1, 2009).

[62] Council on Foreign Relations, Backgrounder, "Jemaah Islamiyah (A.K.A. Jemaah Islamiah)," June 13, 2007, http://www.cfr.org/publication/8948 (accessed February 1, 2009). Zachary Abuza, "The Demise of the Abu Sayyaf Group in Southern Philippines," *CTC Sentinel* (U.S. Military Academy), 1, no. 7 (June 2008): 10–12.

[63] Associated Press, "US Deaths Down in Iraq in 2008, Up in Afghanistan," *International Herald Tribune*, December 31, 2008, http://www.Iht.com (accessed February 1, 2009).

[64] Brookings Institution, "The Current Detainee Population of Guantanamo: An Empirical Study," December 16, 2008 (with updates as of October 21, 2009), http://www. Brookings.edu/reports/2008/1216_detaineees_wittes.aspx (accessed December 6, 2009).

CHAPTER 5
Anatomy of an Unnecessary War

[1] Michael Elliott and Jay Carney, "First Stop, Iraq," *Time*, March 31, 2003.

[2] Albert Eisele, "George Kennan Speaks Out About Iraq," *The Hill*, September 26, 2002.

[3] Quoted in Lawrence J. Korb, "A War of Choice or Necessity," *Washington Post*, December 8, 2003. See also Richard N. Haass, *War of Necessity, War of Choice: A Memoir of Two Iraq Wars* (New York: Simon and Schuster, 2009).

[4] Ron Suskind, *The Price of Loyalty: George W. Bush, the White House, and the Education of Paul O'Neill* (New York: Simon and Schuster, 2004), 85; *New York Times*, January 12, 2004.

[5] Suskind, *Price of Loyalty*, 86. Bush's election interview is quoted in Robert Draper, *Dead Certain: The Presidency of George W. Bush* (New York: Free Press, 2007), 173.

[6] This is a theme in Christian Alfonsi, *Circle in the Sand: Why We Went Back to Iraq* (New York: Doubleday, 2006).

[7] Said Wolfowitz at a congressional hearing in 1998, with reference to Saddam, "Some might say—and I think I sympathize with this view—that perhaps if we had delayed the cease-fire [in 1991] by a few more days, we might have got rid of him." Quoted in Elliott and Carney, "First Stop, Iraq." See also George Packer, *The Assassins' Gate: America in Iraq* (New York: Farrar, Straus and Giroux, 2005), 8–38.

[8] On the neoconservative ascendancy, see James Mann, *Rise of the Vulcans: The History of Bush's War Cabinet* (New York: Viking,

2004), and Jacob Heilbrunn, *They Knew They Were Right: The Rise of the Neocons* (New York: Doubleday, 2007).

⁹ Andrew Bacevich, *The New American Militarism: How Americans Are Seduced by War* (New York: Oxford University Press, 2005), 69–96, quotations at 89–90. See also Stephen Halper and Jonathan Clarke, *America Alone: The Neo-Conservatives and the Global Order* (New York: Cambridge University Press, 2004), esp. 74–156.

¹⁰ Thomas Powers, "What Tenet Knew: Unanswered Questions," *New York Review of Books*, June 27, 2007.

¹¹ George Tenet, *At the Center of the Storm: My Years at the CIA* (New York: HarperCollins, 2007), xix; Powers, "What Tenet Knew."

¹² Michael R. Gordon and Bernard E. Trainor, *Cobra II: The Inside Story of the Invasion and Occupation of Iraq* (New York: Pantheon, 2006), 16-17; James Fallows, "Blind into Baghdad," *Atlantic Monthly*, January–February 2004, 54–56. See also Stephen Kinzer, *Overthrow: America's Century of Regime Change from Hawaii to Iraq* (New York: Times Books, 2006), 289.

¹³ The text of the speech can be found in Micah Sifrey and Christopher Cerf, eds., *Iraq War Reader: History, Documents, Opinions* (New York: Simon and Schuster, 2003), 250–52. See also David Frum, *The Right Man: The Surprise Presidency of George W. Bush* (New York: Random House, 2003), 238, and Bob Woodward, *Plan of Attack* (New York: Simon and Schuster, 2004), 87–91. Former White House press secretary Scott McClellan also dates the origin of the serious war planning to November 2001. Scott McClellan, *What Happened: Inside the Bush White House and Washington's Culture of Deception* (New York: Public Affairs, 2008). On CENTCOM's planning in late 2001, see Gordon and Trainor, *Cobra II*, 19–37.

¹⁴ PBS *Frontline*, "Blair's War," transcript, http://www.pbs.org/ wgbh/pages/frontline/shows/blair/etc/cron.html (last accessed May 29, 2009). On U.S.-European differences over Iraq, see Simon Serfaty, *Architects of Delusion: Europe, America, and the Iraq War* (Philadelphia: University of Pennsylvania Press, 2008), and Philip H.

Gordon and Jeremy Shapiro, *Allies at War: America, Europe, and the Crisis over Iraq* (New York: McGraw-Hill, 2004).

[15] Alex Danchev, "I'm with You: Tony Blair and the Obligations of Alliance: Anglo-American Relations in Historical Perspective," in *Iraq and the Lessons of Vietnam: Or, How Not to Learn from the Past*, ed. Lloyd C. Gardner and Marilyn Young (New York: New Press, 2007), 48. See also David Coates and Joel Krieger, *Blair's War* (London: Polity, 2004).

[16] Manning to PM, March 14, 2002, in Mark Danner, *Secret Way to War: The Downing Street Memo and the Iraq War's Buried History* (New York: New York Review of Books, 2006), 129–32; Meyer to Manning, March 18, 2002, ibid., 133–37.

[17] Elliott and Carney, "First Stop, Iraq."

[18] John Prados, "Wise Guys, Rough Business: Iraq and the Tonkin Gulf," in Gardner and Young, *Iraq and the Lessons of Vietnam*, 111.

[19] Straw to PM, March 25, 2002, in Danner, *Secret Way to War*, 144–49. See also Bryan Burrough et al., "The Path to War," *Vanity Fair*, May 2004, 283.

[20] P. F. Ricketts, memorandum, "Iraq: Advice for the Prime Minister," March 22, 2002, in Danner, *Secret Way to War*, 139–42.

[21] Prados, "Wise Guys," 111.

[22] Rycroft memorandum of meeting, July 23, 2002, in Danner, *Secret Way to War*, 87–93.

[23] According to Richard Haass, Condoleezza Rice told him that same month that "The decision's been made. Don't waste your breath." Unless Saddam Hussein gave in to all of America's demands, she said, war was a foregone conclusion. Quoted in Nicholas Lehmann, "How It Came to War," *New Yorker*, March 31, 2003, 39. In early August, Maj. Gen. James Mattis, commander of the First Marine Division, called in his senior sergeants and top staff officers to give them, according to a draft of the official history of the division reports, "a warning order for the invasion of Iraq." Thomas Ricks, *Fiasco: The American Military Adventure in Iraq* (New York: Penguin Press, 2006), 39. See also Tenet, *At the Center of the Storm*, 309.

[24] Woodward, *Plan of Attack*, 154–55.

[25] Tenet, *At the Center of the Storm*, 318–19; Elizabeth Bumiller, *Condoleezza Rice: An American Life* (New York: Random House, 2007), 191.

[26] Ivo H. Daalder and James M. Lindsay, *America Unbound: The Bush Revolution in Foreign Policy*, 2nd ed. (Hoboken, NJ: Wiley, 2005), 135.

[27] Kinzer; "False Promises"; Todd Purdum, *A Time of Our Choosing: America's War in Iraq* (New York: Times Books, 2003), 167–68.

[28] Jim Garamone, "Rumsfeld Says Link Between Iraq, al Qaeda 'Not Debatable,'" September 27, 2002, American Forces Press Service, http://www.defenselink.mil/news/newsarticle.aspx?id=43413 (last accessed May 29, 2009). Bush quoted in Frank Rich, *The Greatest Story Ever Sold: The Decline and Fall of Truth, from 9/11 to Katrina* (New York: Penguin Press, 2006), 60–61.

[29] Brent Scowcroft, "Don't Attack Saddam," *Wall Street Journal*, August 15, 2002. See also Russ Hoyle, *Going to War: How Misinformation, Disinformation, and Arrogance Led America into Iraq* (New York: Thomas Dunne, 2008), 229–33.

[30] Military opposition to war in Iraq is a theme in Ricks, *Fiasco*. Newbold quoted on 40. See also 48.

[31] Rich, *Greatest Story*, 215.

[32] For these respective points, see Jacob Weisberg, *The Bush Tragedy* (New York: Random House, 2008), 206; McClellan, *What Happened*, 131.

[33] On the alleged assassination attempt, see Seymour M. Hersh, "Did Iraq Try to Assassinate ex-President Bush in 1993: A Case Not Closed," in Sifrey and Cerf, *Iraq War Reader*, 140–62.

[34] Notable examples of such "liberal hawks" included George Packer and Paul Berman, and the editors of the *New Republic*.

[35] Douglas Feith, *War and Decision: Inside the Pentagon at the Dawn of the War on Terrorism* (New York: Harper, 2008), 345.

[36] Quoted in David Usborne and Andrew Grice, "France and Germany Break Ranks on Iraq," *Independent* (U.K.), January 22,

2003. For de Villepin's later recollections, see Entretien avec Dominique de Villepin, "Diplomatie et action," *Politique Internationale* 102 (Winter 2004): 5–62.

[37] Elliott and Carney, "First Stop, Iraq."

[38] Colin Powell, "Presentation to the UN Security Council: A Threat to International Peace and Security," in Sifrey and Cerf, *Iraq War Reader*, 465–78; Hoyle, *Going to War*, 333. Richburg's quotation is from PBS *Frontline*, "Blair's War," transcript, http://www.pbs.org/wgbh/pages/frontline/shows/blair/etc/cron.html (last accessed on May 29, 2009).

[39] For the full text of the Bush speech, see *New York Times*, March 18, 2003.

[40] The intense U.S. pressure on friendly countries in the lead-up to the invasion is described in Heraldo Muñoz, *A Solitary War: A Diplomat's Chronicle of the Iraq War and Its Aftermath* (Golden, CO: Fulcrum, 2008).

[41] Fredrik Logevall, *Choosing War: The Lost Chance for Peace and the Escalation of War in Vietnam* (Berkeley and Los Angeles: University of California Press, 1999).

[42] Howard Kurtz, "The Post on WMDs: An Inside Story," *Washington Post*, August 12, 2004.

[43] All quotes are from Greg Mitchell, "5 Years Ago: When the Press Helped Colin Powell Sell the War," *Editor and Publisher*, February 8, 2008, http://www.editorandpublisher.com/eandp/news/article_display.jsp?vnu_content_id=1003706756 (last accessed May 30, 2009).

[44] Lincoln Chafee, *Against the Tide: How a Compliant Congress Empowered a Reckless President* (New York: Thomas Dunne, 2008), 93. See also the analysis of Congress in Ricks, *Fiasco*, 61–64, 86–90.

[45] Tom Zeller, "How Americans Link Iraq and Sept. 11," *New York Times*, March 2, 2003.

[46] Blix, quoted in Bonnie Azab Powell, "U.N. Weapons Inspector Hans Blix Faults Bush Administration for Lack of 'Critical Thinking' in Iraq," *UC Berkeley News*, March 18, 2004, http://

berkeley.edu/news/media/releases/2004/03/18_blix.shtml (last accessed on May 30, 2009). See also Hans Blix, *Disarming Iraq: The Search for Weapons of Mass Destruction* (New York: Pantheon, 2004).

[47] Quoted in Rich, *Greatest Story*, 62.

[48] Quoted in Draper, *Dead Certain*, 184.

[49] Jeffrey Goldberg, "Letter from Washington: Breaking Ranks," *New Yorker*, October 31, 2005.

CHAPTER 6
Transformative Economic Policies

[1] See Mark Smith, *The Right Talk: How Conservatives Transformed the Great Society into the Economic Society* (Princeton: Princeton University Press, 2007), 14–15, 145–49, 207. Among the many critiques of Bush-era fiscal policies are Daniel Altman, *Neoconomy: George Bush's Revolutionary Gamble with America's Future* (New York: Public Affairs, 2004), and Steven Schier, "Conclusion: George W. Bush's Prospects," in *High Risk and Big Ambition: The Presidency of George W. Bush*, ed. Steven Schier (Pittsburgh: University of Pittsburgh Press, 2004), 246–47.

[2] Robert Collins, *More: The Politics of Economic Growth in Postwar America* (New York: Oxford University Press, 2000), 154–56. See also Bruce Bartlett, *Impostor: How George W. Bush Bankrupted America and Betrayed the Reagan Legacy* (New York: Doubleday, 2006), 48–49.

[3] George Gilder, *Wealth and Poverty* (New York: Basic Books), 172.

[4] See especially Jacob Hacker and Paul Pierson, "Tax Politics and the Struggle over Activist Government," in *The Transformation of American Politics: Activist Government and the Rise of Conservatism*, ed. Theda Skocpol and Paul Pierson (Princeton: Princeton University Press, 2007), 256–80.

[5] Lou Cannon, *President Reagan: The Role of a Lifetime* (New York: Public Affairs, 2000), 93, 199–201, 235–39; W. Elliot Brown-

lee, *Federal Taxation in America: A Short History*, 2nd ed. (Washington, DC: Woodrow Wilson Center Press; Cambridge: Cambridge University Press, 2004), 147–77.

⁶ For these figures, see Cannon, *President Reagan*, 235–36; *New York Times*, March 28, 2008; and *Statistical Abstract of the United States, 2007*, 307 (henceforth cited as *SA*).

⁷ Hacker and Pierson, "Tax Politics"; Julian Zelizer, "Seizing Power: Conservatives and Congress since the 1970s," in Skocpol and Pierson, *The Transformation of American Politics*, 105–34.

⁸ James Patterson, *Restless Giant: The United States from Watergate to Bush v. Gore* (New York: Oxford University Press, 2005), 154–57, 343–44.

⁹ Allen Schick, "Bush's Budget Problem," in *The George W. Bush Presidency: An Early Assessment*, ed. Fred Greenstein (Baltimore: Johns Hopkins University Press, 2003), 78–80.

¹⁰ Brownlee, *Federal Taxation*, 221.

¹¹ Gary Mucciaroni and Paul Quirk, "Deliberations of a 'Compassionate Conservative': George W. Bush's Domestic Presidency," in *The George W. Bush Presidency: Appraisals and Prospects*, ed. Colin Campbell and Bert Rockman (Washington, DC: CQ Press, 2004), 158–90.

¹² Ibid., 165.

¹³ Ron Suskind, *The Price of Loyalty: George W. Bush, the White House, and the Education of Paul O'Neill* (New York: Free Press, 2004), 291.

¹⁴ *New York Times*, August 4, 2000. The syntax is Bush's.

¹⁵ Smith, *The Right Talk*, 146–48.

¹⁶ Alan Greenspan, *The Age of Turbulence: Adventures in a New World* (New York: Penguin Press, 2007), 214–22; Justin Fox, "The Curious Capitalist," *Time*, October 1, 2007, 56.

¹⁷ For tax policy in 2001 (and later), see Michael Tanner, *Leviathan on the Right: How Big-Government Conservatism Brought down the Republican Revolution* (Washington, D.C.: Cato Institute, 2007), 50–53; Hacker and Pierson, "Tax Policies"; and Brownlee, *Federal Taxation*, 217–28. For O'Neill's relations with Bush in 2001, see Suskind, *The Price of Loyalty*, esp. 114–25.

[18] Suskind, *The Price of Loyalty*, 171.

[19] For a defense of the cuts, see Tanner, *Leviathan on the Right*, 149.

[20] Brownlee, *Federal Taxation*, 217–18, 225–26.

[21] Ibid., 226.

[22] Most high-bracket taxpayers before 1981, of course, figured out ways (via tax shelters and the like) of avoiding these very high marginal rates.

[23] For international tax loads over time, see data released by the Organization for Economic Cooperation and Development, *New York Times*, October 19, 2007. Preliminary figures for 2006 showed that American loads ranked seventeenth among twenty industrial nations. In 1975 it had ranked thirteenth.

[24] Brownlee, *Federal Taxation*, 236–37.

[25] Altman, *Neoconomy*, 72.

[26] Roughly 40 percent of the American population—many young, low-income people, retirees, and working-class parents with large families—paid no federal income taxes.

[27] Estimates of Altman, *Neoconomy*, 75–77.

[28] Brownlee, *Federal Taxation*, 223.

[29] Mucciaroni and Quirk, "Deliberations of a 'Compassionate Conservative,'" 165.

[30] See Justin Fox, "Thanks, Rich People!" *Time*, March 19, 2007, 93.

[31] For a later evaluation of the rebates, see *New York Times*, January 19, 2008.

[32] James Livingston, History News Network (HNN), August 20, 2007; *SA, 2008*, 429.

[33] Hacker and Pierson, "Tax Politics," 257; Gerald Prante, Tax Foundation, "Fiscal Facts," October 7, 2007, http://taxfoundation.org/research/show/250.html; *SA, 2008*, 310.

[34] *SA, 2008*, 306.

[35] For the history of these struggles, see Brownlee, *Federal Taxation*, 229–31, and Altman, *Neoeconomy*, 126–322. Unemployment peaked at 6.3 percent in June 2003.

[36] For tax policies in 2002–3, see Brownlee, *Federal Taxation*,

230–42. The following paragraphs rely also on Raymond Tatalovich and John Frendreis, "The Persistent Mandate: George W. Bush and Economic Leadership," in Schier, *High Risk and Big Ambition*, 237.

[37] Suskind, *The Price of Loyalty*, 291.

[38] Cited in Brownlee, *Federal Taxation*, 236.

[39] By late 2003, 216 representatives and 42 senators had signed such pledges, which the ATR had called for. Hacker and Pierson, "Tax Politics," 268.

[40] Hacker and Pierson, "Tax Politics," 238.

[41] Ibid., 257.

[42] Ibid., 257–58. *SA, 2008*, 306, later reported these deficits (in constant 2000 dollars) as $353 billion in 2003 and $375 billion in 2004.

[43] James Pethokoukis, "The Incredible Shrinking Budget," *U.S. News & World Report*, February 19, 2007, 42–43; *SA, 2008*, 306.

[44] Paul Krugman, "Where's My Trickle?" *New York Times*, September 10, 2007. For wage figures, see *SA, 2007*, 412.

[45] Aviva Aron and Joel Friedman (for the Center on Budget and Policy Priorities), "The Capital Gains and Dividend Tax Cuts and the Economy," March 27, 2006, http://www.cbpp.org/3-27-06tax.htm.

[46] Data on middle-income taxpayers are from the Tax Policy Center, a joint venture of the Brookings Institution and the Urban Institute. See *New York Times*, August 21, 2007.

[47] *New York Times*, August 17, 2007.

[48] See Bartlett, *Impostor*; Tanner, *Leviathan*.

[49] *SA, 2008*, 306; *Providence Journal*, September 22, 2007. Figures in constant dollars. Officially measured costs for the war in Iraq totaled $500 billion during the first five years of the war ending March 2008, with an additional $100 billion or more expected at that time to be authorized to cover costs through late 2008.

[50] Tanner, *Leviathan*, 119–21.

[51] *Washington Post*, December 24, 2006, January 5, 2007; *Financial Times*, August 14, 2007.

[52] Robert Samuelson, "When Silence Isn't Golden," *Newsweek*, August 6, 2007, 37.

[53] *Business Week*, October 15, 2007, 27.

[54] *New York Times*, July 24, 2007.

[55] *New York Times*, January 8, 2008.

[56] *New York Times*, September 16, 2007.

[57] Real per capita expenditures for means-tested government transfers, however, increased during these years. See Robert Moffitt, "Four Decades of Antipoverty Policy: Past Developments and Future Directions," *Focus* (University of Wisconsin–Madison Institute for Research on Poverty) 25, no. 1 (Spring–Summer 2007): 39–44. The official poverty line for a family of four was $21,200 in 2008.

[58] James Surowiecki, "Greenback Blues," *New Yorker*, October 8, 2007, 38.

[59] See Paul Krugman, *The Conscience of a Liberal* (New York: W. W. Norton, 2007); Robert Frank, *Falling Behind: How Rising Inequality Harms the Middle Class* (Berkeley and Los Angeles: University of California Press, 2007); and Emmanuel Saez, *Pathways* (Winter 2008).

[60] CBO data in *New York Times*, December 15, 2007. See also Andrew Hacker, "They'd Rather Be Rich," *New York Review of Books*, October 11, 2007, 31–34.

[61] *New York Times*, December 15, 2007.

[62] *New York Times*, January 26, 2008. Unions represented some 35 percent of workers in the mid-1950s and 20.1 percent in 1983.

[63] Larry Bartels, "Inequalities," *New York Times Magazine*, April 27, 2008, 22; idem, *Unequal Democracy: The Political Economy of the New Gilded Age* (Princeton: Princeton University Press, 2008).

[64] For rising inequality, see Krugman, *Conscience of a Liberal*, esp. 3–152.

[65] See Claudia Goldin and Lawrence Katz, *The Race between Education and Technology* (Cambridge, MA: Harvard University Press, 2008).

[66] *New York Times*, December 15, 2007. Krugman, *Conscience of*

a Liberal, 142, estimated that CEO pay rose from forty times the average for full-time workers in the 1970s to 367 times higher in the early 2000s.

[67] *New York Times*, October 16, 2007.

[68] Hacker, "They'd Rather Be Rich." See also Greenspan, *The Age of Turbulence*, 399–408.

[69] Aron and Friedman, "Capital Gains and Dividend Tax Cuts," *New York Times*, October 31, 2007.

[70] *New York Times*, March 8, 2008; *SA, 2008*, 453.

[71] Jonathan Chait, "Captives of the Supply Side," *New Republic*, October 9, 2007.

[72] *New York Times*, January 19, February 8, 2008. For governmental actions described below, see David Leonhardt, "Washington's Invisible Hand," *New York Times Magazine*, September 28, 2008, 53; James Surowiecki, "Public Humiliation," *New Yorker*, September 29, 2008, 30; *New York Times*, November 26, 2008; and Paul Krugman, "What to Do," *New York Times Magazine*, December 18, 2008, 8–10.

CHAPTER 7
Wreaking Havoc from Within

[1] "Text of the State of the Union Address," *New York Times*, January 24, 2007.

[2] "Bush's Nomination of Abraham to Head DOE Greeted with Cheers, Jeers," *Inside FERC*, January 8, 2001, 1; "Abraham Comes with Energy Mandate," *Inside Energy*, January 8, 2001, 1; "Steward of a Department He Once Sought to Scrap," *New York Times*, August 31, 2003, 24.

[3] Charles J. DiBona to George P. Shultz, March 16, 1973; Kenneth Lay to John Rafuse, April 11, 1973; both in box 22, White House Central Files, Staff Member and Office Files, Energy Policy Office, Charles J. DiBona, Deputy-Director, Richard Nixon Presidential Library and Museum, National Archives at College Park, Maryland.

⁴ Irving Kristol, "The Politics of Appeasement," *Wall Street Journal*, February 12, 1975, 10; Gerald Ford to Donald Rumsfeld, n.d., Ford Papers, PHF, box 50.

⁵ Frank G. Zarb to Gerald Ford, "Re: National Energy Policy and Energy Policy Briefing Book, December 18, 1974"; Ken Cole, Briefing on Energy Policy, December 19, 1974, Box 50, Presidential Handwriting Files, Gerald R. Ford Presidential Library and Museum, Ann Arbor, MI (hereafter cited as Ford Library); Frank G. Zarb to Executive Committee of the Energy Resources Council, December 31, 1974, box 43, Alan Greenspan Files, Ford Library.

⁶ Michael Duval, Memorandum for the President, "Re: Energy Policy," March 4, 1975, box 6, Michael Raoul-Duval Files, Ford Library.

⁷ Harley O. Staggers and Henry M. Jackson to President Ford, September 30, 1975; Bill Van Ness and Lynn Sutcliffe, Memorandum for Senate Conferees on S. 622, the Omnibus Energy Legislation, October 1, 1975, box 12, Melvin R. Laird Papers, Ford Library; President Ford to Staggers and Jackson, October 3, 1975, box 212, L. William Seidman Files, Ford Library.

⁸ Daniel Yergin, "A Slippery Business," *New York Times*, June 19, 1977, 197.

⁹ Milton Friedman, "A Monstrosity," *Newsweek*, May 2, 1977, 20.

¹⁰ "Senate Votes Energy Bill, 94 to 4, Without Allowing Arctic Drilling," *Washington Post*, February 20, 1992, 1.

¹¹ "House Approves Vast Energy Bill," *Washington Post*, May 28, 1992, 1.

¹² "Senate Keeps Ban on Fuel Standards Study," *New York Times*, September 16, 1999, 10.

¹³ William J. Clinton, interview with Leonardo DiCaprio, March 31, 2000, *Public Papers of the Presidents: William J. Clinton* (Washington, DC: U.S. Government Printing Office, 2000), 1:761–66.

¹⁴ "Supply vs. Demand Ideas Separate Gore and Bush" *New York Times*, September 29, 2000.

¹⁵ "The Regulators: Battling to Raise the Bar on Fuel Standards," *Washington Post*, May 16, 2000, 1.

[16] "Bush, in Energy Plan, Endorses New U.S. Drilling to Curb Prices," *New York Times*, September 30, 2000, 1.

[17] "Energy Bill Focuses on Domestic Production," *Washington Post*, February 9, 2001, 20; "G.O.P. Energy Bill Is Likely to Set Off Fierce Policy Fight," *New York Times*, February 27, 1.

[18] "Cheney Promotes Increasing Supply as Energy Policy," *New York Times*, May 1, 2001, 1.

[19] Remarks on the California Energy Shortage, May 3, 2001, *Public Papers of the Presidents: George W. Bush* (Washington, DC: U.S. Government Printing Office, 2001), 1:482–84.

[20] "Bush Issues Energy Warning," *Washington Post*, May 18, 2001, 1.

[21] "Bush's Energy Bill Is Passed in House in G.O.P. Triumph," *New York Times*, August 2, 2001, 1; "Core's Split on Energy Is Costly to Democrats," *New York Times*, August 3, 2001, 20.

[22] "House Passes Bush Energy Plan," 2001, *Congressional Quarterly Almanac*, 9-7.

[23] "Democrats Present Alternative Energy Bill," *Washington Post*, December 6, 2001, 24.

[24] "The Senate's Quiet Thorn in GOP's Side." *Washington Post*, December 7, 2001, 1.

[25] "Conservation Bill Benefits Coal Industry, Critics Say," *New York Times*, July 25, 2001, 14.

[26] "Concessions to Moderate May Threaten Energy Plan," *New York Times*, July 28, 2001, 8.

[27] Remarks Following a Cabinet Meeting, October 11, 2001, *Public Papers of the Presidents: George W. Bush*, 2:1218–228.

[28] "Bush Promotes Energy Bill as Security Issue," *New York Times*, October 12, 2001.

[29] "Alaskan Takes Job as White House Energy Policy Director," *Associated Press*, January 31, 2001; "Bush Task Force on Energy Worked in Mysterious Ways," *New York Times*, May 16, 2001, 1.

[30] "Energy Task Force Works in Secret," *Washington Post*, April 16, 2001, 1.

[31] "DOE Silent on Energy Task Force Contacts," *Washington Post*, May 11, 2001, 12.

[32] E. J. Dionne, "What's Cheney Hiding?" *Washington Post*, July 20, 2001, 31.

[33] "Bush's Energy (Oil) Policy," *Time*, January 29, 2001, 48; "Enron Buffed Image to a Shine Even as It Rotted From Within," *New York Times*, February 10, 2002, 1.

[34] "Bush Advisers on Energy Report Ties to Industry," *New York Times*, June 3, 2001, 30; "No Rove Conflict, White House Says," *Washington Post*, June 30, 2001.

[35] "Top G.O.P. Donors in Energy Industry Met Cheney Panel," March 1, 2002, 1; "Energy Contacts Disclosed," *Washington Post*, March 26, 2002, 1.

[36] "White House Seeks to Restore Its Privileges," *Washington Post*, September 11, 2001, 2.

[37] "Cheney Defies GAO's Disclosure Demand," *Washington Post*, September 7, 2001, 27.

[38] "In War, It's Power to the President," *Washington Post*, November 20, 2001, 1.

[39] "Amid War, GAO Puts Legal Fight With Cheney on Hold," *Washington Post*, November 9, 2001, 35.

[40] *National Energy Policy*, Report of the National Energy Policy Development Group, May 2001 (Washington, DC: U.S. Government Printing Office, 2001), viii.

[41] "Developing Energy Bill Ignites Power Scramble," *Washington Post*, May 20, 2001, 1.

[42] "Bush View of Secrecy Is Stirring Frustration," *Washington Post*, March 3, 2002, 4.

[43] "Probe Raises Stakes on Energy Task Force Records," *Washington Post*, January 17, 2002, 7; "Enron's Influence Reached Deep into Administration," *Washington Post*, January 18, 2002, 1.

[44] "Congress Rebuffed on Energy Documents," *New York Times*, January 18, 2002, 16; "Cheney Is Set to Battle Congress to Keep His Enron Talks Secret," *New York Times*, January 28, 2002, 1.

[45] "White House Girds for Protracted Fight," *Washington Post*, February 22, 2002, 4.

[46] "Top G.O.P. Donors in Energy Industry Met Cheney Panel," *New York Times*, March 1, 2002, 1.

[47] "Judge Orders White House Papers' Release," *Washington Post*, October 18, 2002, 6.

[48] "Sierra Club Wants Scalia to Sit Out Task Force Case," *Washington Post*, February 24, 2004, 19; "Scalia Refusing to Take Himself Off Cheney Case," *New York Times*, March 19, 2004, 1.

[49] "Administration Says a 'Zone of Autonomy' Justifies Its Secrecy on Energy Task Force," *New York Times*, April 25, 2004, 16.

[50] "Top E.P.A. Official Quits, Criticizing Bush's Policies," *New York Times*, March 1, 2002, 19.

[51] "EPA Will Ease Coal Plant Rules," *Washington Post*, March 19, 2001, 1.

[52] Bruce Barcott, "Changing All the Rules," *New York Times Magazine*, April 4, 2004, 43.

[53] Ibid., 44.

[54] "Energy Giants Push to Weaken a Pollution Rule," *New York Times*, April 13, 2002, 1.

[55] Barcott, "Changing All the Rules," 66.

[56] "Vowing to Enforce the Clean Air Act, While Also Trying to Change It," *New York Times*, April 22, 2003, 21.

[57] Barcott, "Changing All the Rules," 44.

[58] *New Source Review: Report to the President*, Environmental Protection Agency, June 2002, http://www.epa.gov/NSR/documents/nsr_report_to_president.pdf.

[59] "U.S. Weighs Pollution Cases Against Big Utilities," *Washington Post*, May 16, 2002, 2.

[60] "White House Seeks a Change in Rules on Air Pollution," *New York Times*, June 14, 2002, 1.

[61] "Lawyers at EPA Say It Will Drop Pollution Cases," *New York Times*, November 6, 2003, 1; Barcott, "Changing All the Rules," 73–76.

[62] George W. Bush, Remarks on Energy Independence, February 6, 2003, *Public Papers of the Presidents: George W. Bush*, 1:132–35.

[63] "Ambitious Bush Plan Is Undone by Energy Politics," *New York Times*, August 20, 2003, 16.

[64] "Energy Bill Falls Short, Again," *Congressional Quarterly Almanac*, 2003, 9-3-9-9.

[65] George W. Bush, Remarks to the 16th Annual Energy Efficiency Forum, June 15, 2005, *Public Papers of the Presidents: George W. Bush*, 1:993–99.

[66] "Oil Majors' 1st-Quarter Earnings Shoot Up," *Washington Post*, April 29, 3005, 1; "Bush Signs Energy Bill," *Washington Post*, August 9, 2005, 3; "GOP Leaders Win on Energy Bill," *Washington Post*, October 8, 2005, 7; "Big Rise in Profit Places Oil Giants on the Defensive," *New York Times*, October 28, 2005, 1; "Energy Overhaul Includes Many Bush Priorities—But Not ANWR," *Congressional Quarterly*, 2005, 8-3-8-18.

[67] "A Breath of Fresh Air," *New York Times*, March 19, 2006.

[68] "Right in the Middle of the Revolution," *Washington Post*, September 4, 1995, 1.

[69] "Politics Keep Shifting in the Gas-Mileage Debate," *New York Times*, February 6, 2002, 1; "Debate on Fuel Economy Turns Emotional," *Washington Post*, March 10, 2002. 12; "Mileage Booster Derailed," *Washington Post*, March 14, 2002, 5; "Senate Rejects Tougher Fuel-Economy Standard," *Washington Post*, July 30, 2003, 1.

[70] "Vote on Mileage Reveals New Configuration in the Senate," *New York Times*, June 23, 2007, 11; "Crossing a Threshold on Energy Legislation," *New York Times*, December 5, 2007, 21.

[71] "House, 314-100, Passes Broad Energy Bill," *New York Times*, December 19, 2007, 24.

[72] "EPA Says 17 States Can't Set Greenhouse Gas Rules for Cars," *New York Times*, December 20, 2007, 1; "Arrogance and Warming," *New York Times*, December 21, 2007, 38; "Denial of California Bid on Emissions Should Have Been Foreseen," *New York Times*, December 21, 2007, 37.

[73] "Focus on Energy: Republicans Ramp Up Debate on Offshore Drilling," *Wall Street Journal*, June 19, 2008, 6.

[74] "Ms. Pelosi's Compromise," *New York Times*, September 16, 2008, 28.

CHAPTER 8
Ideology and Interest on the Social Policy Home Front

[1] Data from Bureau of Labor Statistics, 2008, http://www.bls.gov.

[2] See, e.g., Kevin Phillips, *American Dynasty: Aristocracy, Fortune, and the Politics of Deceit in the House of Bush* (New York: Viking, 2004); Robert Bryce, *Cronies: Oil, the Bushes, and the Rise of Texas, America's Superstate* (New York: Public Affairs, 2004); and John Anderson, *Follow the Money: How George W. Bush and the Texas Republicans Hog-Tied America* (New York: Scribner, 2007).

[3] Data from Wal-Mart Facts, http://www.walmartfacts.com.

[4] "Remarks by the Vice President to Employees of the Wal-Mart Distribution Center," May 3, 2004, http://www.whitehouse.gov/news/releases/2004/05.

[5] Laurance Zuckerman, "Bush Issues Order Preventing Strike by Airline Union," *New York Times*, March 10, 2001, A1.

[6] David Bacon, "In the Name of National Security: Bush Declares War on Unions," *American Prospect*, October 21, 2002, 15.

[7] Robert Toner, "Conservatives Savor Their Role as Insiders at the White House," *New York Times*, March 19, 2001, 1.

[8] Ronald Radosh, "A Uniquely American Life," *American Outlook* (Hudson Institute), Winter 2003.

[9] Julie Kosterlitz, "All Lined Up for Chao," *National Journal*, January 27, 2001, 270.

[10] John Judis, "Sullied Heritage: The Decline of Principled Conservative Hostility to China," *New Republic*, April 23, 2001, 19–25.

[11] U.S. Department of Labor, Employment Standards Administration Wage and Hour Division, "2007 Statistics Fact Sheet," http://www.dol.gov/esa/whd/statistics.

[12] Isaac Shapiro and Jared Bernstein, "Unhappy Anniversary: Federal Minimum Wage Remains Unchanged for Eighth Straight Year," Economic Policy Institute, September 1, 2005, http://www.epi.org/publications.

[13] John Judis, "Hidden Injuries of Class: Undermining OSHA by a Thousand Cuts," *American Prospect*, June 3, 2002, 10.

[14] Ibid., 11.

[15] Joshua Green, "Ergonomic Energy," *American Prospect*, September 10, 2001, 7.

[16] Steven Greenhouse, "Labor Department to Investigate Its Treatment of Wal-Mart," *New York Times*, February 21, 2005, A11; idem, "Labor Department Rebuked Over Pact with Wal-Mart," *New York Times*, November 1, 2005, A14.

[17] William G. Whittaker, "The Fair Labor Standards Act: A Historical Sketch of the Overtime Pay Requirements of Section 13 (a) (1), Congressional Research Service, Library of Congress, May 9, 2005, http://www.digitalcommons.elr.cornell.edu/key_workplace/ 238.

[18] Nelson Lichtenstein, "Why Working at Wal-Mart Is Different," *Connecticut Law Review* 39, no. 4 (May 2007): 1649–84.

[19] Edwin Feuler, "Laboring for Overtime," the Heritage Foundation, July 31, 2003, http://www.heritage.org.

[20] Stephanie Armour, "Companies Face More Overtime Lawsuits," *USA Today*, December 18, 2002.

[21] Steven Greenhouse, "Labor Department Revises Plans to Cut Overtime Eligibility," *New York Times*, April 21, 2004, A14.

[22] Ross Eisenbrey, "Longer Hours, Less Pay," Economic Policy Institute, July 2004, http://www.epi.org/publications.

[23] Greenhouse, "Labor Department Revises Plans to Cut Overtime Eligibility."

[24] "A New Presidency," editorial, *Wall Street Journal*, September 19, 2001, A20.

[25] Lizette Alvarez, "Bush Supports House Bill on Airport Screeners," *New York Times*, October 26, 2001, B5.

[26] Paul Krugman, "Reckonings," *New York Times*, October 10, 2001, A21.

[27] Ibid.

[28] Alvarez, "Bush Supports House Bill on Airport Screeners."

[29] Robert Pear, "Negotiators Say They're Near Accord on Legis-

lation to Strengthen Security at Airports," *New York Times*, November 15, 2001, B8.

[30] "Politics Before Safety," *Wall Street Journal*, September 4, 2002, 22.

[31] David Firestone, "Unions Lobby to Safeguard Proposed Agency's Workers," *New York Times*, September 26, 2002, A18.

[32] Ibid.

[33] Adam Clymer, "Invective and Accusations Remain Campaign Staples," *New York Times*, September 29, 2002, 1; Adriel Bettelheim, "Senate's Failure to Resolve Personnel Management Issue Stalls Homeland Security Bill," *CQ Weekly Online*, October 19, 2002, 2741; David Firestone, "Homeland Security Fight Returns to Fore," *New York Times*, October 16, 2002, A15.

[34] "Max Cleland," Sourcewatch, http://www.sourcewatch.org/index.php?title=Max_Cleland.

[35] David Firestone, "Lawmakers Move toward Compromise Curbing Worker Rights in New Department," *New York Times*, November 12, 2002, A15.

[36] Michael Luo, "Senate Passes Bill on Steps Advised by September 11 Panel," *New York Times*, March 14, 2007, A16; "Veto Victory," *Wall Street Journal*, July 18, 2007, A14.

[37] Newt Gringrich, "Medicare Bill Moves Us in the Right Direction," *St. Paul Pioneer Press*, December 5, 2003.

[38] James Robinson, "Health Savings Accounts: The Ownership Society in Health Care," *New England Journal of Medicine* 353, no. 12 (September 22, 2005): 1200.

[39] Alice O'Connor, e-mail to author, March 17, 2008.

[40] Michael Scherer, "Medicare's Hidden Bonanza," *Mother Jones*, March 1, 2004, http://www.motherjones.com.

[41] Theda Skocpol, "A Bad Senior Moment," *American Prospect*, January 1, 2004.

[42] Henry J. Kaiser Family Foundation, "Medicare Prescription Drug Plans in 2008 and Key Changes Since 2006: Summary of Findings," April 2008, http://www.kff.org/medicare/7762.cfm (accessed July 22, 2009).

[43] "Medicare Drug Program Price Rising, But It's Far Less Costly

than Expected," *Arizona Daily Star*, August 15, 2008; Joanne Landy (former executive director of Physicians for a National Health Program, New York Metro chapter), e-mail to author, July 24, 2009. Insurance companies also negotiated lower prices with drug companies than had been expected in 2003.

[44] David Rosenbaum, "Tax-Free Accounts Drew Yeas from the Wary," *New York Times*, November 23, 2003, 1.

[45] Robert Greenstein and Edwin Park, "Health Savings Accounts in Final Medicare Conference Agreement Pose Threats Both to Long-Term Fiscal Policy and to the Employer-Based Health Insurance System," Center on Budget and Policy Priorities, December 1, 2003, http://www.cbpp.org.

[46] Theo Francis and Ellen Schultz, "Health Accounts Have Benefits for Employers," *Wall Street Journal*, February 3, 2006, B1.

[47] Jason Roberson, "Wal-Mart Touts High Deductibles," *Dallas Morning News*, May 24, 2007.

[48] "President Discusses Health Care," Office of the Press Secretary, the White House, February 15, 2006, http://www.whitehouse.gov/news/releases.

[49] "False Promises: 'Consumer Driven' Health Plans," *Consumer Reports*, May 2006, 57.

[50] Robinson, "Health Savings Accounts," 1201–2.

[51] "False Promises: 'Consumer Driven' Health Plans," 57.

[52] Robert Kuttner, "Social Security and the Market," *American Prospect*, November 30, 2002, http://www.prospect.org.

[53] Joe Conason, *The Raw Deal* (New York: PoliPoint Press, 2005), 17–18.

[54] Mark Schmitt, "What We Can—and Can't—Learn from the Last Social Security Fight," *American Prospect* (Web only), February 8, 2005, http://www.prospect.org.

[55] The earned income tax credit might seem to be an exception, but it was limited to the low-income employed and served both as a conservative alternative to the minimum wage and as a de facto subsidy to employers of the working poor. Christopher Howard, "The New Politics of the Working Poor," in *Seeking the Center: Politics and Policymaking at the New Century*, ed. Martin A. Levin,

Marc K. Landy, and Martin Shapiro (Washington, DC: George-town University Press, 2001), 239–63.

[56] Kuttner, "Social Security and the Market." A decidedly "centrist" if not a neoconservative analysis of the political and ideological vulnerability of Social Security is offered by Martha Derthick in "The Evolving Old Politics of Social Security," in Levin, Landy, and Shapiro, *Seeking the Center*, 193–214.

[57] Kuttner, "Social Security and the Market."

[58] Conason, *The Raw Deal*, 46–47.

[59] Ibid., 37–38.

[60] Daniel Kadlec, "Taking the Plunge: On the Way to His Vision of an "Ownership Society," *Time*, November 22, 2004, 64.

[61] Robert Dreyfuss, "Hardball," *American Prospect*, June 18, 2001, 15.

[62] Ron Suskind, *The Price of Loyalty* (New York: Simon and Schuster, 2004), 140.

[63] Conason, *The Raw Deal*, 54–55.

[64] Ibid., 56–57.

[65] Richard Dunham, "Don't Call It Privatization!" *Business Week*, November 11, 2002, 51; "Bush's State of the Union Address," transcript, *CQ Weekly*, February 7, 2005, 313.

[66] Conason, *The Raw Deal*, 72.

[67] Paul Magnusson, "Bush's Reluctant Business Allies," *Business Week*, May 9, 2005, 69.

[68] Alan Blinder, "Social Security and the New Fiscal Policy," *American Prospect*, January 14, 2005. The trillion-dollar transition costs would have been incurred when Social Security diverted a portion of its income to private, individually controlled retirement accounts while at the same time continuing to pay retirees and near retirees their full Social Security benefits.

[69] Adreil Bettelheim, "Dependable Bush Supporters Hang Back on Social Security," *CQ Weekly*, January 17, 2005, 112.

[70] "Bush Pushes Private Accounts as Public Support Drops," *OMB Watch*, March 21, 2005, http://www.ombwatch.org.

[71] Paul Krugman, "Katrina All the Time," *New York Times*, August 31, 2007, 21.

[72] Michael Barbaro and Justin Gillis, "Wal-Mart at Forefront of Hurricane Relief," *Washington Post,* September 6, 2005, D1.

[73] Devin Leonard, "The Only Lifeline Was the Wal-Mart," *Fortune,* October 3, 2005, 76.

[74] As quoted in Philip Mattera, "Disaster Relief: How Wal-Mart Used Hurricane Katrina to Repair its Image," Corporate Research E-Letter no. 55, September–October 2005, http://www.corpresearch.org/archives/sept-oct05.

[75] Ibid., 2.

[76] John Tierney, "From FEMA to WEMA," *New York Times,* September 20, 2005, A29.

[77] Jason DeParle, "Liberal Hopes Ebb in Post-Storm Poverty Debate," *New York Times,* October 11, 2005, A1.

[78] "White House Finds in Katrina Recovery 'Opportunity' to Waive Needed Protections," *OMB Watch,* September 19, 2005, http://www.ombwatch.org.

[79] "Homeland Hijacking" *Wall Street Journal,* July 26, 2002, A10.

[80] "Katrina's Awful Wake," *Wall Street Journal,* September 1, 2005, A10.

[81] Paul Krugman, "Miserable by Design," *New York Times,* October 3, 2005, 21.

[82] Griff Witte, "Prevailing Wages to Be Paid Again on Gulf Coast," *Washington Post,* October 27, 2005, A1.

[83] Steven Greenhouse and Stephanie Rosenbloom, "Wal-Mart Settles 63 Lawsuits Over Wages," *New York Times,* December 24, 2008, C1.

CHAPTER 9
Creating Their Own Reality

[1] Ron Suskind, "Without a Doubt," *New York Times Magazine,* October 17, 2004. For one example of liberals claiming the term with pride, see the letter to the *New York Times* on April 5, 2005, from Gerald Leibowitz of Oakland Gardens, New York, who wrote, "The essay speaks for an increasingly marginalized group in

this country: the reality-based community. . . . I'm glad the author of the essay, unlike many other people, was willing to resist the widespread pressure to 'not upset' religious fundamentalists." "Confronting Foes of Reality," *New York Times*, April 5, 2005, F4.

 See http://www.journalismjobs.com/matt_labash.cfm (accessed August 12, 2009).

³ For a good statement of the inescapable need for experts, see Robert Dahl, "The Problem of Civic Competence," *Journal of Democracy* 3, no. 4 (October 1992): 45–59.

⁴ Sidney Blumenthal, *The Rise of the Counter-Establishment: From Conservative Ideology to Political Power* (New York: Times Books, 1986).

⁵ Paul Krugman, "Design for Confusion," *New York Times*, August 5, 2005, A15.

⁶ See, e.g., Joshua Micah Marshall, "The Post-Modern President," *Washington Monthly*, September 2003, 22–26; Franklin Foer, "Closing of the Presidential Mind," *New Republic*, July 5 and 12, 2004, 17–21.

⁷ Daniel Bell, *The End of Ideology: On the Exhaustion of Political Ideas in the Fifties* (Glencoe, IL: Free Press, 1960); John F. Kennedy, "Commencement Address at Yale University, June 11, 1962," *Public Papers of the President 1963*, no. 234 (Washington, DC: U.S. Government Printing Office, 1964); James Allen Smith, *Brookings at Seventy-Five* (Washington, DC: Brookings Institution, 1991), 1–4.

⁸ Walter Lippmann, *Public Opinion* (New York: Macmillan, 1922); Stewart Alsop, *The Center: People and Power in Political Washington* (New York: Harper and Row, 1968).

⁹ Michael Schudson, *Discovering the News: A Social History of Newspapers* (New York: Basic Books, 1976), 160.

¹⁰ John Patrick Diggins, *Rise and Fall of the American Left* (New York: W. W. Norton, 1992), 347.

¹¹ M. Stanton Evans, *The Liberal Establishment* (New York: Devin-Adair Co., 1965).

¹² Daniel Bell, "The Revolt Against Modernity," *Public Interest* 81 (Fall 1985), 57.

13 H. R. Haldeman, *The Haldeman Diaries: Inside the Nixon White House* (New York: G. P. Putnam's Sons, 1994), 309.

14 Alan Wolfe, "Hobbled from the Start," Salon.com, December 15, 2000.

15 Ron Rosenbaum, "Derrida, Dame Edna, and George W., Postmodernist," *New York Observer*, December 17, 2000.

16 Neil A. Lewis, "White House Ends Bar Association's Role in Screening Federal Judges," *New York Times*, March 23, 2001, A13.

17 See, e.g., "In-Your-Face Economics," *Washington Times*, February 18, 2001, B2; Donald Lambro, "Tax-Cut Foes' Analysis Flawed, Lindsey Says," *Washington Times*, March 3, 2001, A2.

18 Daniel Smith, "Political Science," *New York Times Magazine*, September 5, 2005.

19 Chris Mooney, *The Republican War on Science* (New York: Basic Books, 2005). Other notable works on the Right's politicization of science (dating to before the Bush presidency) include Mark Bowen, *Censoring Science: Inside the Political Attack on Dr. James Hansen and the Truth of Global Warming* (New York: Dutton, 1997), and Seth Shulman, *Undermining Science: Suppression and Distortion in the Bush Administration* (Berkeley and Los Angeles: University of California Press, 2007).

20 Mooney, *The Republican War on Science*, 90–95.

21 Maxwell T. and Jules Boykoff, "Balance as Bias: Science, Politics, and U.S. Democracy," *Global Environmental Change* 14 (2004): 125–36, described in Mooney, *The Republican War on Science*, 252–53.

22 Besides Smith, "Political Science," see also, e.g., Ken Silverstein, "Bush's New Political Science," *Mother Jones*, November–December 2002, and Michael Specter, "Political Science," *New Yorker*, March 13, 2006, 58–69.

23 Ron Suskind, "Why Are These Men Laughing?" *Esquire*, January 2003, 96ff.

24 In *The Price of Loyalty: George W. Bush, the White House and the Education of Paul O'Neill* (New York: Simon and Schuster, 2004), 70–76, Ron Suskind reported on a January 30, 2001, meeting at which Treasury Secretary Paul O'Neill concluded that Bush

had all but decided to invade. But Bush had also publicly hinted at doing so during the 2000 campaign. "The coalition against Saddam has fallen apart or it's unraveling, let's put it that way," he said, during his October 11 debate with Al Gore. "The sanctions are being violated. We don't know whether he's developing weapons of mass destruction. He better not be or there's going to be a consequence should I be the president." Commission on Presidential Debates, debate transcript, October 11, 2000, "The Second Gore-Bush Presidential Debate," http://www.debates.org/pages/trans2000b.html (accessed August 12, 2009). *Washington Post* reporter Bob Woodward revealed the November 2001 directive to draft invasion plans in *Plan of Attack* (New York: Simon and Schuster, 2004), 1.

[25] See, e.g., Judith Miller and Michael R. Gordon, "White House Lists Iraq Steps to Build Banned Weapons," *New York Times*, September 13, 2002, A13—an influential article that emphasized the administration position but nonetheless also included the statement that "some experts had questioned whether Iraq might not be seeking the tubes for other purposes, specifically, to build multiple-launch rocket systems." On White House second-guessing of intelligence analysts, see, e.g., Eric Schmitt and Thom Shanker, "Threats and Responses: A CIA Rival; Pentagon Sets Up Intelligence Unit," *New York Times*, October 24, 2002, A1.

[26] See, e.g., Joby Warrick, "Evidence on Iraq Challenged: Experts Question if Tubes Were Meant for Weapons Program," *Washington Post*, September 19, 2002, A18; William J. Broad, "U.N. Arms Team Taking Up Its Task, a Mixture of 'Hide and Seek' and '20 Questions,'" *New York Times*, November 19, 2002, A20.

[27] See, e.g., Walter Pincus, "Alleged Al Qaeda Ties Questioned; Experts Scrutinize Details of Accusations Against Iraqi Government," *Washington Post*, February 7, 2003, A21.

[28] Joan Didion, "The Case of Theresa Schiavo," *New York Review of Books*, June 9, 2005, 60–64, 69.

[29] See David Greenberg, "The New Politics of Supreme Court Appointments: The Unacknowledged Role of Ideology in Naming Justices," *Daedalus*, Summer 2005, 5–12.

[30] See, e.g., Elisabeth Bumiller and David D. Kirkpatrick, "Bush

Fends Off Sharp Criticism of Court Choice," *New York Times*, October 5, 2007, A1; Sheryl Gay Stolberg, "Foe of Abortion, Senator Is Cool to Court Choice," *New York Times*, October 7, 2005, A1; idem, "Bush Works to Reassure G.O.P. over Nominee for Supreme Court," *New York Times*, October 9, 2005, A1.

[31] On the EPA scandal, see, e.g., Andrew Revkin, "Bush Aide Edited Climate Reports," *New York Times*, June 8, 2005, A1, and idem, "Former Bush Aide Who Edited Reports Is Hired by Exxon," *New York Times*, June 8, 2005, A21. On the NASA scandal, see Andrew Revkin, "A Young Bush Appointee Resigns His Post at NASA," *New York Times*, February 8, 2006, A13; on the CPB scandal, see Stephen Labaton, "Ex-Chairman of Public Broadcasting Violated Laws, Inquiry Suggests," *New York Times*, November 16, 2005, A17; on the surgeon general scandal, see Gardiner Harris, "Surgeon General Sees 4-Year Term as Compromised," *New York Times*, July 11, 2007, A1.

[32] See, e.g., Brian Stelter, "MSNBC Takes Incendiary Hosts from Anchor Seats," *New York Times*, September 7, 2008.

[33] For variations on this argument, see Lee Siegel, *Against the Machine: Being Human in the Age of the Electronic Mob* (New York: Spiegel and Grau, 2008); Andrew Keen, *The Cult of the Amateur: How Today's Internet Is Killing Our Culture* (New York: Broadway Books, 2007); and Susan Jacoby, *The Age of American Unreason* (New York: Pantheon, 2008).

CHAPTER 10
Compassionate Conservatism

[1] *New York Times*, November 5, 2008.

[2] Esther Kaplan, *With God on Their Side* (New York: New Press, 2004), 1–2; David Kuo, *Tempting Faith* (New York: Free Press, 2006), 121–22.

[3] Paul Kengor, *God and George W. Bush: A Spiritual Life* (New York: HarperCollins, 2004), 61–63; Stephen Mansfield, *The Faith of George W. Bush* (New York: Penguin, 2003), 109; *New York Times*, October 22, 2000.

⁴ Kengor, *God and George W. Bush*, 63–66; *New York Times*, December 15, 1999.

⁵ David Frum, *The Right Man: An Inside Account of the Bush White House*, 2nd ed. (New York: Random House, 2005), 5–6; Lou Cannon and Carl M. Cannon, *Reagan's Disciple: George W. Bush's Troubled Quest for a Presidential Legacy* (New York: Public Affairs, 2008), 81.

⁶ Kuo, *Tempting Faith*, 126–28; Kengor, *God and George W. Bush*, 69; *Chicago Tribune*, July 23, 1999; *Los Angeles Times*, July 23, 1999.

⁷ Amy E. Black, Douglas L. Koopman, and David K. Ryden, *Of Little Faith: The Politics of George W. Bush's Faith-Based Initiatives* (Washington, DC: Georgetown University Press, 2004), 9, 75–76, 90.

⁸ Black, Koopman, and Ryden, *Of Little Faith*, 97–99.

⁹ Mark J. Rozell, "Bush and the Christian Right: The Triumph of Pragmatism," in *Religion and the Bush Presidency*, ed. Mark J. Rozell and Gleaves Whitney (New York: Palgrave, 2007), 20; Kevin Phillips, *American Theocracy: The Peril and Politics of Radical Religion, Oil and Borrowed Money in the 21st Century* (New York: Viking, 2006), 191.

¹⁰ Kuo, *Tempting Faith*, 138–41.

¹¹ *New York Times*, January 30, 2001; Black, Koopman, and Ryden, *Of Little Faith*, 190; *Washington Post*, February 26, 2001.

¹² Kuo, *Tempting Faith*, 142; *Atlanta Journal-Constitution*, February 5, 2001; Black, Koopman, and Ryden, *Of Little Faith*, 102.

¹³ *Wall Street Journal*, February 14, 2001; Frum, *Right Man*, 101–3.

¹⁴ Black, Koopman, and Ryden, *Of Little Faith*, 123, 196–97.

¹⁵ Kuo, *Tempting Faith*, 166; Black, Koopman, and Ryden, *Of Little Faith*, 205, 125; Ron Suskind, "Why Are These Men Laughing?," *Esquire*, January 2003. On the legislative struggle, see Black, Koopman, and Ryden, *Of Little Faith*, 107–84.

¹⁶ Black, Koopman, and Ryden, *Of Little Faith*, 145, 164–65; *Wall Street Journal*, August 20, 2001; Kaplan, *With God on Their Side*, 53.

[17] Kuo, *Tempting Faith*, 201–12.

[18] Michelle Goldberg, *Kingdom Coming: The Rise of Christian Nationalism* (New York: Norton, 2007), 121; Kuo, *Tempting Faith*, 212–16; Kaplan, *With God on Their Side*, 52; Amy Sullivan, "Faith Without Works," *Washington Monthly*, October 2004, 30–31.

[19] *Chicago Tribune*, January 23, 2001; *Los Angeles Times*, January 23, 2001.

[20] Kengor, *God and George W. Bush*, 94; *Chicago Tribune*, November 6, 2003; Kaplan, *With God on Their Side*, 146–47.

[21] *Wall Street Journal*, February 8, 2001; *New York Times*, May 12, 2001; *Chicago Tribune*, June 20, 2002.

[22] *New York Times*, January 30, 2003, April 30, 2003, May 22, 2003; *Wall Street Journal*, April 29, 2003.

[23] *Wall Street Journal*, May 14, 2003; Kaplan, *With God on Their Side*, 154.

[24] Frum, *Right Man*, 103; 539 U.S. 590; *Los Angeles Times*, June 26, 28, 2003.

[25] Kaplan, *With God on Their Side*, 156–61.

[26] *Los Angeles Times*, August 12, 2004; Amy Sullivan, *The Party Faithful* (New York: Scribner, 2008), 116–17; Phillips, *American Theocracy*, 211.

[27] *New York Times*, November 5, 2004; Goldberg, *Kingdom Coming*, 50–52; Rozell, "Bush and the Christian Right," 22–23.

[28] *New York Times*, November 6, 10, 2004; *Washington Post*, December 12, 2004; Goldberg, *Kingdom Coming*, 56

[29] *Los Angeles Times*, November 12, 2004, February 23, 2005; *Chicago Tribune*, March 21, 2005; *New York Times*, March 24, 2005.

[30] *New York Times*, March 23, 25, 2005; *Los Angeles Times*, March 22, 2005; *Chicago Tribune*, March 21, 2005.

[31] Sullivan, *Party Faithful*, 190–92.

[32] *New York Times Magazine*, October 28, 2007; Sullivan, *Party Faithful*, 192–93.

[33] *New York Times*, June 9, 2008; *Los Angeles Times*, August 18, 2008.

[34] *New York Times*, July 1, 24, October 28, November 7, 2008; *Chicago Tribune*, November 6, 2008.

CHAPTER 11
Minorities, Multiculturalism, and the Presidency
of George W. Bush

Robert Chase provided invaluable research assistance and shared with me his remarkable knowledge of Texas politics. A seminar at the University of Tokyo Center for Pacific and American Studies gave me an opportunity to present the earliest iteration of the ideas contained in this essay; special thanks to Jun Furuya and Ken Endo for making this presentation possible. Julian Zelizer, Larry Bartels, George Edwards, and other participants in the April 2008 Princeton Conference on the Bush Presidency provided excellent comments on an earlier version of this essay, as did my colleagues at Vanderbilt University, where I presented the arguments contained in this work as the James G. Stahlman inaugural lecture in September 2008. Robert Draper, Monte Holman, Sarah Igo, Tamar Jacoby, and Elizabeth Lunbeck offered me valuable feedback on earlier written versions of this essay. I am in debt to them all.

[1] Ralph Reed, *National Review*, July 12, 1999, 38; Don Van Natta Jr., "The 2000 Campaign: The Ad Campaign; Republicans Open a Big Drive to Appeal to Hispanic Voters," *New York Times*, January 15, 2000.

[2] Estimates of the percentage of the Hispanic vote won by Bush in 2004 vary from 35 to 45 percent, but the "standard statistic," writes a leading group of political scientists, "has become 40%." See David L. Leal, Stephen A. Nuno, Johngo Lee, and Rudolpho O. de la Garza, "Latinos, Immigration, and the 2006 Midterm Election," *PS: Political Science and Politics* 41 (April 2008): 309. See also David L. Leal, Matt A. Barreto, Jongho Lee, and Rodolfo O. de la Garza, "The Latino Vote in the 2004 Election," *PS: Political Science and Politics* 38 (January 2005): 41–49; Ruy Texeira, "44 Percent of Hispanics Voted for Bush?," http://www/alternet.org/election04/20606/, November 24, 2004; and Roberto Suro, Richard Fry, and Jeffrey Passel, "Hispanics and the 2004 Election: Pop-

ulation, Electorate and Voters." Pew Hispanic Center, A Pew Research Center Project, June 27, 2005, http://pewhispanic.org/files/reports/48.pdf.

3 Kevin Phillips, *American Dynasty: Aristocracy, Fortune, and the Politics of Deceit in the House of Bush* (New York: Viking, 2004), chap. 4.

4 Jim Rutenberg, "Texas Town, Now Divided, Forged Bush's Stand on Immigration," *New York Times*, June 24, 2007; Elisabeth Bumiller, "Behind Bush's Address Lies a Deep History," *New York Times*, May 16, 2006, http://www.nytimes.com/2006/05/16/washington/16assess.html?_r=1&oref=login&page. Serrano would later be sent to a Mexican jail for fraud.

5 Rutenberg, "Texas Town, Now Divided."

6 Jacob Weisberg, *The Bush Tragedy* (New York: Random House, 2008), 53–54.

7 Karen Olsson, "A Shrub Grows in Midland," *Texas Observer*, June 25, 1999, http://www.texasobserver.org/article.php?aid=1175.

8 Rutenberg, "Texas Town, Now Divided."

9 Weisberg, *The Bush Tragedy*, 51.

10 Rutenberg, "Texas Town, Now Divided."

11 Bumiller, "Behind Bush's Address."

12 Weisberg, *The Bush Tragedy*, 82–83.

13 Bob Geldof, "Geldof and Bush: Diary from the Road," *Time*, February 28, 2008, http://www.time.com/time/world/article/0,8599,1717934,00.html; Jemima Kiss, "*Time* magazine: Geldof confronts Bush on a number of issues," *Guardian*, February 28, 2009, http://www.guardian.co.uk/media/2008/feb/28/pressandpublishing.geo; Michael M. Rosen, "The Greatest Story Never Told," *Politico*, April 7, 2008, http://dyn.politico.com/printstory.cfm?uuid==2A4B7FB6-3048-5C12-0. Bush's interest in Africa is part of a much broader engagement on the part of evangelical Protestants in the United States with Africa, the motivation being both to relieve poverty, illness, and other forms of distress and to convert souls. We don't yet know enough about the nature of this engagement to understand the mix of humanitarian and evangelical motives that has energized this new interest and a new wave of mis-

sionaries. But it likely marks an important moment of transition in the history of American evangelicals, in particular in terms of their relationship with peoples beyond U.S. borders.

[14] Gary Gerstle, *American Crucible: Race and Nation in the Twentieth Century* (Princeton: Princeton University Press, 2001), epilogue.

[15] Ibid.

[16] Patrick Buchanan, "Text of Buchanan's Speech to the Republican Convention, on Aug. 17, 1992," Republican National Committee, http://www.qrd.org/qrd/usa/federal/1992/campaign.92/buchanan-RNC-.txt. In this speech, Buchanan also made himself the foe of other groups in the liberal multicultural coalition, such as those advocating for gay rights and feminism.

[17] Aristide R. Zolberg, *A Nation by Design: Immigration Policy in the Fashioning of America* (New York: Russell Sage Foundation and Harvard University Press, 2006), chap. 11.

[18] The intellectual architect of compassionate conservatism and an important influence on Bush was Marvin Olasky, a professor of journalism at the University of Texas at Austin whose intellectual and political journey led him from Judaism to Protestantism and from the New Left to the New Right. For an analysis of his life and work, see Michael King, "The Last Puritan," *Texas Observer*, May 14, 1999, http://texasobserver.org/article.php?aid==1079.

[19] In 1995, Hispanics formed 25 percent of the Texas population. Dave McNeely, "Texas Governor Builds Goodwill Toward Mexico," *Austin American-Statesman*, December 3, 1995, E3; Karl C. Rove, "Patterns of Partisan Change in Texas, 1970 to 1996," seminar paper, Government 340M, University of Texas at Austin (May 1997), 33–36, Governor George W. Bush Records, Senior Advisor's Office, Box 2002/151-261, Texas State Library and Archives Commission.

[20] For an interesting and complex argument for why Mexican Americans exerted more influence in politics in Texas than in California in the 1980s and 1990s, see Peter Skerry, *Mexican Americans: The Ambivalent Minority* (New York: Free Press, 1993).

[21] On Clinton's role in ending the culture wars and promoting a "soft multiculturalism," see Gerstle, *American Crucible*, epilogue.

[22] McNeely, "Texas Governor Builds Goodwill Toward Mexico"; James Garcia, "Immigration Issues Set Bush Outside GOP Fold," *Austin American-Statesman*, August, 20, 1995, D1.

[23] "Bush Assails GOP Candidate for Isolationism," *Austin American-Statesman*, August 15, 1995, B3.

[24] Garcia, "Immigration Issues Set Bush Outside GOP Fold."

[25] Ibid.; McNeely, "Texas Governor Builds Goodwill Toward Mexico"; "Bush Stands Firm on Principle," editorial, *Austin American-Statesman*, August 16, 1995, A16.

[26] George W. Bush, "Monterrey Mexico Teleconference: The Importance of Friendship and Cooperation between Texas and Mexico," Executive Office Speeches, November 6, 1995, transcript, Governor George W. Bush Records, Box 2002/151-166, Texas State Library and Archives Commission.

[27] George W. Bush, letter outlining his position on bilingual education and "English plus," Press Office Speech Files, Background Information, n.d., Governor George W. Bush Records, Box 2002/151-321, Texas State Library and Archives Commission.

[28] Tony Garza, memorandum, Press Office Speech Files, Hispanic/Mexican American Relations—Hispanic Issues, February 10, 1999, Governor George W. Bush Records, Box 2002/151-321, Texas State Library and Archives Commission.

[29] Ibid. The case in question is *Texas vs. Hopwood*, 95-1773.

[30] Quoted in Richard L. Berke, "California, Here Bush Comes, a Moderate on Immigration and Racial Quotas," *New York Times*, June 30, 1999, http://www.nytimes.com/1999/06/30/us/california-here-bush-comes-a-moderate-on-immigration-and-racial-quotas.html.

[31] Anthony Lewis, "A Simple Question Reveals Much about George W. Bush," *Austin American-Statesman*, December 1, 1999; Fred Hiatt, "Texas's Ten Percent Experiment," *Washington Post*, October 28, 2002, A19, http://aad.english.ucsb.edu/docs/fredhiatt.html; Scott Jaschik, "10 Percent Plan Survives in Texas," *Inside Higher Education*, May 29, 2007, http://www.insidehighered.

com/news/2007/05/29/percent. For a more critical appraisal of the Texas 10 percent plan, see Mark C. Long and Marta Tienda, "Winners and Losers: Changes in Texas University Admissions Post-*Hopwood*," *Education Evaluation and Policy Analysis* 30 (2008): 255–80.

[32] George W. Bush, Executive Office speech to U.S. Hispanic Chamber of Commerce, October 3, 1997, transcript, Governor George W. Bush Records, Box 2002/151-168, Texas State Library and Archives Commission.

[33] Garza, memorandum.

[34] John O'Sullivan, "Bush's Latin Beat: A Vision, But a Faulty One," *National Review*, July 23, 2001, 35–36.

[35] Garance Franke-Ruta, "Minority Report," *American Prospect*, July 2005, http://www.lexisnexis.com/us/lnacademic/results/doc view/docview.do?docLinkInd=true&risb=21_T8043322405&form at=GNBFI&sort=BOOLEAN&startDocNo=1&resultsUrlKey=29_ T8043322410&cisb=22_T8043322409&treeMax=true&treeWidth =0&csi=161341&docNo=1.

[36] O'Sullivan, "Bush's Latin Beat," 35.

[37] McNeely, "Texas Governor Builds Goodwill Toward Mexico."

[38] Christopher Hayes, "The NAFTA Superhighway," *Nation*, August 27–September 3, 2007, 13–22, esp. 14, 17.

[39] Michael Lind, *Made in Texas: George W. Bush and the Southern Takeover of American Politics* (New York: Basic Books, 2002); Phillips, *American Dynasty*, chap. 4.

[40] O'Sullivan, "Bush's Latin Beat," 35.

[41] Jena Heath, "Bush's First State Dinner: A Party and a Promise; Elegant Affair in Honor of Fox Symbolizes U.S. President's Intent to Fortify Ties with Mexico," *Austin American-Statesman*, September 6, 2001; Mike Allen, "Immigration Reform on Bush Agenda," *Washington Post*, December 24, 2003, A01.

[42] Robert Draper, *Dead Certain: The Presidency of George W. Bush* (New York: Free Press, 2007), 32–33.

[43] Draper, *Dead Certain*, 46; Weisberg, *The Bush Tragedy*, 128; Louis Dubose, "The Souls of White Folk," *Texas Observer*, August 25, 2000, http://texasobserver.org/article.php?aid=815; Z. Z.

Packer, "Sorry, Not Buying," *American Prospect*, December 2005, 46ff.; Franke-Ruta, "Minority Report."

[44] Franke-Ruta, "Minority Report."

[45] Hendrik Hertzberg, Talk of the Town, *New Yorker*, March 17, 2008, 32.

[46] Elisabeth Bumiller's *Condoleezza Rice: An American Life. A Biography* (New York: Random House, 2007) makes clear the intensity and multifaceted character of the Bush-Rice relationship.

[47] Gary Gerstle, "Pluralism and the War on Terror," *Dissent*, Spring 2003, 31–38; idem, "The Immigrant as Threat to National Security: A Historical Perspective," in *From Arrival to Incorporation: Migrants to the U.S. in a Global Age*, ed. Elliott R. Barkan, Hasia Diner, and Alan M. Kraut (New York: New York University Press, 2008), 217–45.

[48] Draper, *Dead Certain*, 147.

[49] Gerstle, "Pluralism and the War on Terror"; idem, "The Immigrant as Threat to National Security."

[50] Gary Gerstle, "America's Encounter with Immigrants," in *In Search of Progressive America*, ed. Michael Kazin (Philadelphia: University of Pennsylvania Press, 2008), 37–53.

[51] Patrick J. McGuinn, *No Child Left Behind and the Transformation of Federal Education Policy, 1965–2005* (Lawrence: University Press of Kansas, 2006), chaps. 8 and 9; Scott Franklin Abernathy, *No Child Left Behind and the Public Schools* (Ann Arbor: University of Michigan Press, 2007).

[52] These were originally the words of Michael Gerson, one of Bush's principal speechwriters. Draper, *Dead Certain*, 114.

[53] David Kuo, *Tempting Faith: An Inside Story of Political Seduction* (New York: Free Press, 2006).

[54] Thomas Frank, *The Wrecking Crew: How Conservatives Rule* (New York: Metropolitan Books, 2008).

[55] George Packer, *The Assassins' Gate: America in Iraq* (New York: Farrar, Strauss, Giroux, 2005); Thomas E. Ricks, *Fiasco: The Military Adventure in Iraq* (New York: Penguin Press, 2006); Rajiv Chandrasekaran, *Imperial Life in the Emerald City: Inside Iraq's Green Zone* (New York: Knopf, 2006); Douglas Brinkley, *The Great*

Deluge: Hurricane Katrina, New Orleans, and the Mississippi Gulf Coast (New York: Morrow, 2006).

[56] Gerstle, "America's Encounter with Immigrants."

[57] Ibid.; see also Solomon Moore, "Push on Immigration Crimes Is Said to Shift Focus," *New York Times*, January 12, 2009, http://www.nytimes.com/2009/01/12/us/12prosecute.html?scp=2&sq=immigration&st=nyt; idem, editorial, "A Sense of Who We Are," January 13, 2009, http://www.nytimes.com/2009/01/13/opinion/13tue1.html?scp=15&sq=immigration&st=nyt.

[58] Mark Hugo Lopez, "The Hispanic Vote in the 2008 election," Pew Hispanic Center, November 5 and 7, 2008, ii, http://pewhispanic.org/files/reports/98.pdf; Frank Rich, "The Palin-Whatshisname Ticket," *New York Times*, September 14, 2009, http://www.nytimes.com/2008/09/14/opinion/14rich.html?sq=Frank Rich 2008 Republican Convention&st=c; "Results of 2005 National Latino Survey: Republicans Rapidly Losing Ground Among Hispanic Voters," *U.S. Newswire*, Washington, DC, January 5, 2006, http://proquest.umi.com/pqdweb?index=141&sid=2&srchmode=1&vinst=PROD&fmt=3.

[59] Weisberg, *The Bush Tragedy*.

[60] Kuo, *Tempting Faith*.

[61] Draper, *Dead Certain*.

[62] Bush received more than a half million fewer votes than Gore did in the 2000 election, out of 100 million cast.

[63] Thomas B. Edsall, *Building Red America: The New Conservative Coalition and the Drive for Permanent Power* (New York: Basic Books, 2006), chap. 2. George W. Bush received 68 percent of the evangelical vote, significantly less than the 81 percent received by his father in 1988. See also Weisberg, *The Bush Tragedy*, 99.

[64] Edsall, *Building Red America*, chap. 3.

[65] Paul Krugman, *The Return of Depression Economics and the Crisis of 2008* (New York: W. W. Norton, 2009), chap. 1.

[66] On the gap between Bush's dreams for broad-based minority homeownership and the Bush administration's fumbling of efforts to make those dreams a reality, see "White House Philosophy Stoked Mortgage Bonfire," *New York Times*, December 21, 2008, 1, 30–31.

[67] See, e.g., Paul Alexander, *Machiavelli's Shadow: The Rise and Fall of Karl Rove* (New York: Modern Times, 2008), 11, and James Moore and Wayne Slater, *The Architect: Karl Rove and the Dream of Absolute Power* (New York: Three Rivers Press, 2006), 103–4. See also Michael Gerson, "What History Taught Karl Rove," *Washington Post*, August 17, 2007, A23. If Rove saw Bush as the second coming of McKinley, he saw himself as the second coming of McKinley's brilliant campaign manager, Marcus Alonzo Hanna. For a perceptive portrait of Hanna, see Herbert Croly, *Marcus Alonzo Hanna* (New York: Macmillan, 1912).

[68] "We can't be the party of America," Rove has said, "and get 13 percent of the African American vote." Gerson, "What History Taught Karl Rove."

CHAPTER 12
From Hubris to Despair

I am grateful to Keith Whittington, Julian Zelizer, and Gary Gerstle for their comments on an earlier draft of this essay.

[1] The best survey of modern conservatism as an intellectual project remains George Nash's *The Conservative Intellectual Movement in America Since 1945*, 2nd ed. (Wilmington, DE: Intercollegiate Studies Institute, 1998). See also Donald T. Critchlow, *The Conservative Ascendancy: How the GOP Right Made Political History* (Cambridge, MA: Harvard University Press, 2007).

[2] Peggy Noonan, *What I Saw at the Revolution: A Political Life in the Reagan Era* (New York: Random House, 1990), 149, 152.

[3] Noonan, columns of January 20, 2003, and February 19, 2004, http://www.opinionjournal.com.

[4] Noonan, column of June 1, 2007, http://www.opinionjournal .com.

[5] Michael J. Gerson, in conversation with author, May 15, 2006.

[6] Michael J. Gerson, *Heroic Conservatism: Why Republicans Need to Embrace America's Ideals (And Why They Deserve to Fail If They Don't)* (New York: HarperOne, 2007), 289 et passim.

7 Ibid., 289, 10.

8 See, e.g., Ross Douthat, "The Future of the GOP," *Slate*, November 26, 2007.

9 See chapter eleven, this volume.

10 On the Republican Right's success at presenting a "populist" image, see my *The Populist Persuasion: An American History*, rev. ed. (Ithaca, NY: Cornell University Press, 1998), 245–66.

11 And in electoral terms, George W. Bush was arguably the most successful president from any party since the mighty Franklin D. Roosevelt. No other president since FDR helped his party gain seats in both houses of Congress in his first midterm election, then won reelection while his party gained seats again, as Bush and the GOP did in 2004. However, the gains were small: eight House seats in 2002 and just three in 2004.

12 Bill Keller, "The Radical Presidency of George W. Bush: Reagan's Son," *New York Times Magazine*, January 26, 2003, http://nytimes.com.

13 Douthat, "The Future of the GOP."

14 Business firms hostile to unions and administrative regulation had long supported conservative politicians from all regions of the country. See Kim Phillips-Fein, *Invisible Hands: The Making of the Conservative Movement from the New Deal to Reagan* (New York: W. W. Norton, 2009).

15 Thomas B. Edsall, *Building Red America: The New Conservative Coalition and the Drive for Permanent Power* (New York: Basic Books, 2006), 1.

16 For a succinct summary of Reagan's legacy, see Sean Wilentz, *The Age of Reagan: A History, 1974–2008* (New York: HarperCollins, 2008), 281–87.

17 George H. W. Bush, address to joint session of Congress, September 11, 1990. Patrick Buchanan, address to the Republican National Convention, 1992.

18 Quoted in Edsall, *Building Red America*, 51.

19 Sam Tanenhaus, interview by Isaac Chotiner, March 15, 2007, http://www.tnr.com.

[20] Quoted in Rick Perlstein, *Chicago Reader*, January 24, 2008, http://www.chicagoreader.com/features/stories/rickperlstein.

[21] For an excellent survey and analysis of the activist state built since the 1950s, see Paul Pierson, "The Rise and Reconfiguation of Activist Government," in *The Transformation of American Politics: Activist Government and the Rise of Conservatism*, ed. Paul Pierson and Theda Skocpol (Princeton: Princeton University Press, 2007), 19–38.

[22] Nick Gillespie and Veronique de Rugy, "Bush the Budget Buster," *Reason*, October 19, 2005, http://www.reason.com/news/show/34112.html; Peggy Noonan, *Wall Street Journal*, March 16, 2006, online edition.

[23] Alan Wolfe, "Why Conservatives Can't Govern," *Washington Monthly*, July–August 2006, online edition.

[24] Francis Fukuyama, "After Neoconservatism," *New York Times Magazine*, February 19, 2006, http://www.nytimes.com/2006/02/19/magazine/neo.html.

[25] Ross Douthat and Reihan Salam, *Grand New Party: How Republicans Can Win the Working Class and Save the American Dream* (New York: Doubleday, 2008); David Frum, "A New Path for the GOP," *National Post*, November 5, 2008, and lecture at the Hoover Institution, Washington, DC, December 11, 2008.

[26] For an excellent summary of the results, see Ruy Teixeira, "Digging into the 2008 Exit Polls," http://takingnote.tcf.org/2008/11/digging-into-th.html.

[27] Sidney Blumenthal, *The Rise of the Counter-Establishment: From Conservative Ideology to Political Power* (New York: Times Books, 1987), 330.

[28] Tanenhaus interview by Chotiner.

INDEX

AARP, 127

abortion, 40, 230; and AIDS issue, 241; and conservatism, 291, 298; and faith-based offices, 251; Frum on, 299; Gerson on, 285; and judiciary, 44; and McCain, 249; and neoconservatives, 293; and Obama, 249; partial-birth, 55, 240; and religious groups, 54, 228, 239–40, 287; and stem-cell research, 213

Abraham, Spencer, 140, 147–48

Abrams, Elliot, 28

Abu Ghraib prison, 50, 78

Addington, David, 34, 42, 45, 46, 151

affirmative access, 263

affirmative action, 54–55, 196, 253, 263, 272, 280

Afghanistan, 287; and al Qaeda, 62, 93; and cold war lessons, 71; militia of, 74; neglect of, 87; Soviet invasion of, 145; and Tenet, 64; and William Jefferson Clinton, 63; and Yoo, 43

Afghanistan war, 77, 93; and CIA, 71–72; detainees from, 45, 49; federal spending for, 122, 124, 128; and Iraq War, 102; and Republican party, 103; success of, 87, 104, 108

AFL-CIO, 175, 178

Africa, 14, 258, 353n13

African Americans: appointment of, 2, 253, 268, 269; and culture wars, 259–60; and Hoover and Coolidge, 287; and Hurricane Katrina, 274; importance of, 267–68; and No Child Left Behind Act, 272; and Obama, 300; opportunity for, 254; political affiliation of, 252; and poverty, 129; Protestant, 233; and Republican Party, 268, 274; and William Jefferson Clinton, 262

African Union, 84

agribusiness, 127

agriculture, 170, 188, 295

Ahmed, Mahmood, 65

AIDS policy, 14, 240–42, 247–48, 249, 251, 258

Aid to Families with Dependent Children, 10

Ailes, Roger, 203

airline hijackings, 65

airline mechanics, strikes by, 172

airport screeners, 69, 179–80, 181

Ajami, Fouad, 94

Alaska, 140, 145, 147, 161

Alaska National Interest Lands Conservation Act, 147

Alito, Samuel, 53, 55, 57

Allbaugh, Joe, 220

Alliance for the Restoration of Peace and Counterterrorism, 84

al Qaeda, 14; and Afghanistan, 72, 93; and *Boumediene v. Bush*, 52; campaign against, 94; and CIA, 60, 61, 67; continued activity of, 86; decreased operational effectiveness of, 86; fear of additional attacks by, 69–70, 78; gains against, 86–87; and Hussein, 101–2, 217; initial response to attacks of, 68; and intelligence restrictions, 34; and Iraq, 76–77, 100, 107; and Iraq War, 82; leadership of, 78; and military preemption, 76; operatives of, 45; and Pakistan, 65; and Pentagon, 72; and September 11 attacks, 1, 93, 267; sleeper cells of, 70; and Taliban, 63, 93; view of before September 11 attacks, 62

Alsop, Stewart, 207

American Bar Association, 202, 203, 207, 209, 211, 218

American Center for Law and Justice, 244
American Civil Liberties Union v. National Security Agency, 314n29
American Constitution Society, 224
American Federation of Government Employees, 181
American Liberty League, 16
Americans for Tax Reform (ATR), 116, 164, 172
Americans United, 237
anarchist bombings, 270
Anderson, Terje, 242
anthrax attacks, 70, 320n25
Antiballistic Missile Defense Treaty, 61
anti-elitism, 224, 225
anti-intellectualism, 7. *See also* expertise
Antiquities Act (1906), 31
antitrust laws, 170
antiwar demonstrations, 104
appointments, 42; of administrators unsympathetic to programs, 4, 144, 159, 221; and Hurricane Katrina, 274; ideological vs. skill-based, 279; judicial, 211; of loyalists, 286; of minorities, 2, 14, 253, 268–69, 280; by Nixon, 4; of political loyalists, 11; by Reagan, 4, 159; to Supreme Court, 39–40; of unqualified personnel, 274
Arab oil embargo, 139, 141, 163, 168
Arabs, 269–71
Arctic National Wildlife Reserve (ANWR), 140, 145, 147, 148, 149, 150, 161, 162, 167, 168
Arlington Group, 243
Armitage, Richard, 65
Ashbrook, John, 24
Ashcroft, John, 81, 154, 239
Asian Americans, 300
Asian central banks, 130
Atef, Mohammed, 72
Atta, Mohammed, 69
attorney general, 24, 25, 29, 268
Aum Shinrikyo, 60
Authorization for the Use of Military Force, 42–43
automobile industry, 143, 146, 165, 166, 198, 298
Aviation Security Association, 179
axis of evil, 76, 95

Bacevich, Andrew, 92
Bacon-Davis Act, 196, 197
Baghdad, fall of, 77
Baker, James, III, 102
Ball, Robert, 189
Bank of America, 135
banks, 16, 130, 134–36, 137, 298
Banks, Christopher, 57
Barbour, Haley, 157, 158
Barnett, Martha W., 211
Barr, William, 29
Bauer, Gary, 244, 247
Bayh, Birch, 23–24
Bear Stearns, 134, 135
Bell, Daniel, 206, 208
Bennett, William, 246
Berger, Sandy, 61, 62
Berman, Paul, 296
Bernanke, Ben, 135, 222–23
Bickel, Alexander, 53, 54
Big Bang, 221
Biggs, Andrew, 191
bilingualism, 263
bin Laden, Osama, 60, 64, 86; anticipation of attack from, 63; continued activity of, 86; escape of, 72–73, 94, 103; financial assets of, 67; and Hussein, 111; and Iraq, 76; and Madrid attack, 78; and Omar, 71, 72; and Taliban, 71; use of force against, 319n6; and weapons of mass destruction, 63; and William Jefferson Clinton, 62
birth control, 58
Black, Hugo, 47
Blair, Tony, 93, 94, 112; and axis of evil speech, 95–96; and Bush, 96; and Hussein, 96; and Iraq planning, 96, 97; and justification for war, 98; and public opinion, 105; and United Nations, 97, 99
Blakeman, Jon, 57
Blix, Hans, 106, 111–12
Blue Sky memorandum, 61, 64
Blumenthal, Sidney, 202, 301
Boland, Eddie, 23, 24
Bond, Chris, 164, 165
border security, 275
Boumediene, Lakhdar, 52
Boumediene v. Bush, 52

Central Intelligence Agency (CIA) (*cont.*)
initial response to September 11 attacks, 68; interrogation by, 36, 85; and
Iraq, 90; and Iraqi weapons of mass destruction, 216; and Nixon, 209; secret
prisons of, 74; and Taliban, 63, 64; and
torture, 74, 75, 81; and Zubaydah, 74
Chafee, Lincoln, 110, 175, 181
Chambers, Whittaker, 290
Chambliss, Saxby, 182
Chao, Elaine, 173, 174
charitable contributions, 232
charities, 231–32, 234
Chavez, Linda, 173
checks and balances, 42
Cheney, Richard, 6, 23, 29, 46, 94; and Afghan war, 71; and Barbour, 158; and
containment of Iraq, 99; early attitude
toward Iraq of, 90; and energy policy,
33, 139, 140, 141, 147, 148, 149, 151–
56, 168; and energy task force, 41, 150–
56, 158; and executive power, 32, 33,
70–71, 153, 154, 155–56; and Ford, 20,
33; and Hussein, 92; influence of, 33;
and intelligence information, 218; and
Iran–Contra arms scandal, 70–71; and
Iraq, 76, 90, 99, 100; and Iraq War planning, 217; and national security strategy, 71; and Nixon, 20; and Persian Gulf
War, 145; and Powell, 100; and Reagan,
33; and retailers, 171–72; self-justifica-
tion of, 36; and tax cuts, 118, 125; and
weapons of mass destruction, 71, 100
Chicago, 267
child labor, 3, 176
China, 2–3, 20, 61, 106, 129, 173–74
Christian Coalition, 227, 228, 238
Christian colleges, 301
Christians, 227, 238, 245, 289; and conservatism, 249, 299; decrease in numbers
of, 300; and environment, 248; and
global warming, 248; and health care,
248; and media, 250; and Schiavo case,
247; and welfare programs, 248. *See
also* Catholics; evangelicalism; Protestants
Chrysler, 136
Church, Frank, 22–23, 24
Citigroup, 135
Citizens for Tax Justice, 127

civil rights, 5, 81
Civil Rights Act, 293
civil rights laws, 8, 16
civil service, 181, 182
Cizik, Richard, 248
Clarke, Richard, 62, 63, 79
class warfare, 174
Clean Air Act, 141, 145, 156–57, 158, 160,
165
Clear Skies, 160, 161
Cleland, Max, 182
Clinton, Hillary, 12, 30–31, 150–51
Clinton, William Jefferson, 2, 30, 130; and
African Americans, 262; and AIDS,
240; and balanced budget, 289; and bin
Laden, 62, 319n6; and bombing of Kosovo, 32; and centrism on domestic policy, 292; and Congress, 34; and conservatism, 30–32, 292; as damaging to
presidency, 41; and energy policy, 146,
152; and ergonomics regulations, 175;
and executive orders, 33; and executive
power, 30–32, 34; and executive privilege, 153; and federal budget, 118; foreign policy of, 61; and Hussein, 216;
impeachment of, 31, 32; and Kyoto Protocol, 213; and Lewinsky scandal, 292;
and multiculturalism, 261–62; and
New Source Review, 157; and regime
change, 92; and religious conservatives,
227–28; and Republican Congress, 9–
10; and taxes, 121; and welfare reform,
289; and Wolfowitz, 91
Clinton administration: and Afghanistan,
63; and Aum Shinrikyo, 60; and bombing attacks on Iraqi targets, 91; and
charitable choice, 231; and Federal
Emergency Management Agency, 220;
and Northern Alliance, 64; and Pakistan, 63; and Taliban, 63
Club for Growth, 185
CNN, 203
coal, 152, 153, 156–60, 161
Cohen, Richard, 109
Cohen, William, 30
Colby, William, 21
cold war: and Afghanistan, 71; and counterterrorism, 70, 71, 76, 80, 83, 87; end
of, 9; and Kennedy, 66; and Nixon, 18;
and Northern Alliance, 64; and presi-

dential power, 17; and U.S.-Pakistan relationship, 63
collective bargaining, 181, 182
Colorado, 250
Comey, James, 81, 85
commander in chief, 34, 36, 287
Commission to Strengthen Social Security, 191–92
Committee on Foreign Intelligence and Operations Advisor Group, 23
communism: and conservatism, 8; fight against, 17; hatred of, 290; international, 8; and Nixon, 20; and Reagan, 9, 300
compassionate conservatism: and campaign of 2000, 277–78; and conservative voters, 292; and election of 2000, 1; Gerson on, 285; and immigrants, 261; and Olasky, 354n18; and religion, 251; and religious and community organizations, 231, 232; and social problems, 228, 230; and war on terror, 277. *See also* conservatism
Compassion Capital Fund, 231
Concerned Women for America, 246
Congress: and AIDS policy, 241; and airport screeners, 180; and bombing of Kosovo, 32; and CAFE standards, 146; and charitable choice, 231; and Cheney energy task force, 155, 156; and CIA, 22–23; conservative control of, 10; and defense of Kuwait, 29; and domestic surveillance, 86; and economic crisis, 136, 137, 138; and election of 2008, 12; and energy policy, 140, 143, 144, 145, 148, 149, 154, 156, 161; and executive privilege, 153; expansion of social regulations by, 22; and faith-based initiative, 236–37; and fiscal policy, 116, 117; and Ford, 21, 22; and foreign policy, 21; and fuel economy, 146, 164–65; and government shutdown of 1995–96, 10; and *Hamdan v. Rumsfeld,* 50; and immigrants, 275; and interrogation, 43; and Iran–Contra arms scandal, 28; and Iraq War, 89, 105–6, 111, 287; and Iraq War planning, 109–10, 112, 216; and Lewinsky scandal, 292; and liberals, 20–21; and Military Commissions Act, 86; and military tribunals, 45; and Nixon, 18–

20; and Obama, 37; and oil industry profits, 162–63; and partial-birth abortion, 55; and Persian Gulf War, 105; and pollution controls, 160; and presidential authority, 43; and Reagan, 9, 25–26; and reform of executive branch, 21; reform of national security state by, 20–25; and regulation, 135; and Republican Party, 3, 9–10, 11, 284; and Schiavo case, 247; and science, 214; and September 11 attacks, 42–43; and Social Security, 19; and Supreme Court rulings on detainees, 49; and suspension of right to *habeas corpus,* 49; and tax policy, 120, 121, 125, 126; and Transportation Security Administration, 69; and use of force in Afghanistan, 48; and war on terror, 35; and Watergate, 6, 17; and William Jefferson Clinton, 34
Congressional Budget Office (CBO), 118, 119, 125, 126, 136
conservation, 140, 148, 149, 150, 168. *See also* environment
conservatism: antigovernment arguments of, 26; base of, 299, 300; and Bush presidency, 10–11, 14, 292–96; and business, 301, 360n14; and counter-establishment of pseudo-experts, 202–3; different factions of, 9; different views of government in, 285–86; and DiIulio, 237; disputes among adherents of, 283; and domestic surveillance, 70; and education, 272, 295; and energy policy, 139, 140, 143, 144, 168; European, 295; and evangelicalism, 299, 301; and expertise, 201, 204, 211; and faith-based initiative, 234, 236; first principles of, 298; Gerson on, 285; and governance, 7, 8, 9, 10, 293–94; history of, 7–13, 283, 288; and Hurricane Katrina, 278; and immigrants, 298; institutions of, 301; and intellectuals, 209; and judiciary, 44; leadership of, 12; and mass emotion, 302; and McCain, 249; as movement, 7–8; and multiculturalism, 259, 275; and New Deal, 293; and Nixon, 20; and Noonan, 284; and Obama, 12–13; and presidential power, 15–38; and Reagan, 8, 25–30, 32, 223, 286, 290, 291, 292, 293, 300–301; rebellion of

conservatism (*cont.*)
    activists in, 12; and religion, 227, 290;
    and Republican Party, 283, 290, 291,
    299, 301; revitalization of, 296–97; so-
    cial, 9, 120; southern, 21; and Supreme
    Court, 53–58; and tax reductions, 4;
    unity in, 297; and welfare state, 295;
    and whites, 298; and William Jefferson
    Clinton, 292. *See also* compassionate
    conservatism; neoconservatism; reli-
    gious conservatives
Constitution of the United States: Article
    II, 36, 43; Eleventh Amendment, 57;
    and nondelegation doctrine, 26; and
    president, 43; and Supreme Court, 54;
    Tenth Amendment, 56
consumers, 118, 129, 134, 136, 152
Contract with America, 31, 117
Conyers, John, 235
Coolidge, Calvin, 287
Corporation for Public Broadcasting, 221
corruption, 11, 205
Council of Economic Advisors (CEA), 21,
    141, 207
Council on Foreign Relations, 208
counterterrorism, 14; and international co-
    operation, 83; and law, 85; legitimacy
    for policy of, 78, 79; national center for,
    80; and operational coordination, 80;
    public cynicism about, 79. *See also* ter-
    rorism, war on
courts: conservative, 40, 44; and environ-
    mental legislation, 163; jurisdiction of,
    44–45; and monitoring of intelligence,
    23–24
Craig, Mark, 229
Crane, Ed, 190
creationism, 202
credit crunch, 136, 137
Critchlow, Donald, 13
cronyism, 220
Crumpton, Hank, 322n52
Cuevas, José, 256
cultural toleration, 269, 270
Culture and Family Institute, 243
culture wars, 227, 228–29, 244, 251, 259,
    261

Dar es Salaam, U.S. embassies in, 62
Daschle, Tom, 149, 162

Dean, Howard, 11–12
Dearlove, Richard, 97–98
debt. *See* federal debt
Defense Intelligence Agency, 101
deficit. *See* federal deficit
DeLay, Thomas, 10, 11, 146
democracy, 92, 94, 103, 225, 285
Democratic Party: and African Americans,
    252; and airport screeners, 180; and en-
    ergy policy, 140, 146, 148, 149, 166,
    167; and Eugene Scalia, 176; and execu-
    tive power, 28; and faith-based initia-
    tive, 237; and fiscal policy, 117; and
    Hispanics, 252; and Iran–Contra arms
    scandal, 28; and Iraq War, 105, 110; and
    midterm elections of 2006, 11; multi-
    culturalism of, 254; and Obama, 37;
    and same-sex marriage, 244; and sci-
    ence, 214; and Social Security, 193; and
    taxes, 121; and tax policy, 125
Department of Defense, 48, 85; and Af-
    ghan war, 72; and al Qaeda, 64–65;
    funding for, 2; and Geneva Conven-
    tions, 86; and Guantanamo, 74–75. *See
    also* military; U.S. Central Command
    (CENTCOM)
Department of Energy, 142, 143, 147, 151,
    158
Department of Homeland Security, 46, 79,
    80, 122, 180–81, 182, 196, 220
Department of Justice: and Cheney energy
    task force documents, 156; interroga-
    tion opinion of August 1, 2002, 74; and
    Meese, 28; and Office of Legal Council,
    42; and Office of the Vice President, 34;
    and social policy, 40; and spying pro-
    grams, 37; and Terrorist Surveillance
    Program, 81; and torture, 35, 74, 75;
    and unitary executive, 27, 32
Department of Labor, 3, 173, 174, 175, 176;
    Wage and Hour Division, 174, 178
Department of State, 85
Department of Transportation, 165
Department of Treasury, 4, 67, 68, 136
deregulation, 116–17; and Chao, 173; and
    collapse of financial markets, 14; early
    goals of, 4; economic, 7; of electricity
    markets, 148; of environmental and en-
    ergy policy, 139; and financial crisis of
    2008, 222; and Radzely, 176; and Rea-

gan, 134, 144; and Reagan Revolution, 1. *See also* regulation
derivatives, 135
desegregation, 56
detainees, 44, 81; and Geneva Conventions, 75, 85, 86; at Guantanamo, 74–75; and *habeas corpus*, 47; humane treatment of, 85; as illegal enemy combatants, 44–45; placement outside U.S. territory, 44; right to legal representation, 82; and Supreme Court, 47–52; torture of, 154. *See also* Guantánamo Bay, Cuba; illegal enemy combatants; prisoners of war; prisons, secret
Detainee Treatment Act, 49
detention: perpetual, 48–49; as subject to judicial review, 49
Detroit, 267
Dewey, John, 207, 225
DiCaprio, Leonardo, 146
Didion, Joan, 219
Diggins, John Patrick, 208
DiIulio, John J., Jr., 119, 215–16, 234, 235–36, 237
Dingell, John, 165, 167
Dionne, E. J., 151, 232
Discovery Institute, 202
Disney, 171
District of Columbia v. Heller, 56
diversity, 2, 252, 253, 264. *See also* multiculturalism
divestiture, 163, 168
Dobson, James, 243, 248, 250
Dolan, Anthony, 282
Dole, Robert, 30, 117, 233, 252, 271
domestic programs, 5–6, 169–98; funding for, 128; and Nixon, 19
domestic security czar, 68–69
Douthat, Ross, 299
Dowd, Matthew, 278
Dowd, Maureen, 230
Downing Street Memo, 98
draft, restoration of, 5
Draper, Robert, 277
DuBois, Joshua, 250
due process, 56
Duval, Michael, 142

Eagleburger, Lawrence, 102
Eagle Forum, 164

East African bombings, 60, 62
East Asia, 266
economic growth, 126–27, 129, 132, 133
Economic Policy Board (EPB), 21
economy: and business, 265; and changing demography, 3; crisis in, 58, 114, 134–38; downturn in, 121; internal debate over, 119; policy concerning, 114–38; and regulation, 8, 134–35, 169; and Republican Party, 279; role of state in, 290; and Southern states, 3; stimulation of, 119, 120, 121–22, 123, 125, 167; and stimulus legislation, 114, 136, 137. *See also* financial crisis; recession; supply-side economics
Economy Act, 16
ecumenism, 257–58
Edison Electric Institute, 157
Edsall, Thomas, 289
education, 55–56, 253; and conservatism, 295; and conservative voters, 292; cost of, 131; effect of Proposition 187 on, 260, 262; and foreign students, 271; inadequate primary, 1; and income inequality, 131; and Latinos, 287; local control of, 272; and multiculturalism, 259; national standards for, 293; and No Child Left Behind Act, 2, 57–58, 271–73, 280; and public schools, 131; and school prayer, 54; and student aid programs, 129; support of, 117
Eisenhower, Dwight D., 17, 18, 188, 207, 295, 299–300
election, of 1964, 288, 299
election, of 1988, 259
election, of 1992, 30, 260
election, of 1996, 233, 260
election, of 2000, 5, 117, 146, 286; as close and contested, 2; dispute over Florida vote in, 209–10; GB's mixed signals in, 1; legitimacy of, 2; popular vote in, 277–78; and religious issues, 232–33, 239; and Republican Party, 277–78; and Rove, 287; and Supreme Court, 40–41; and terrorism, 60–61
election, of 2004, 79, 218; and evangelicalism, 278; Hispanic voters in, 271, 274, 278; and minority vote, 252; and religious issues, 244–45, 248, 251

election, of 2008: and balance of power, 36; and conservatives, 297; and economic policy in, 133; and economy, 128; and energy policy in, 166; and foreign policy in, 87; and Hispanic voters, 276; and Latino voters, 298; and Obama, 12, 300; and religious issues, 250; and Republican Party, 296, 297

elections, 1938 midterm, 16

elections, 1982 midterm, 26

elections, 1994 midterm, 30

elections, 2002 midterm, 3, 160, 287

elections, 2006 midterm, 35, 163, 222, 284

embassies, bombings of, 60, 62

Emerick, Tom, 186

empiricism, 199, 200, 204, 206, 209

employers, 114, 123

energy: alternative, 149; and clean energy investments, 167; nonenforcement of rules on, 163; and price controls, 139; price of, 141, 142–43; renewable, 129, 140, 148, 162. *See also* fuel; oil

Energy Independence and Security Act, 165, 166

energy industry, 140, 151, 170; and Energy Policy Act, 162; and energy task force, 152; and New Source Review, 158, 159. *See also* oil industry

energy plants, 154

energy policy, 33, 139–68

Energy Policy Act (1992), 145–46

Energy Policy Act (2005), 140, 162, 168

Energy Resources Council, 21–22

energy task force, 150–56, 158

England, Gordon, 85

English Plus program, 263

Enlightenment, 199, 204, 206, 207, 208

Enron, 151–52, 154, 155, 170, 192

environment, 22; and air quality standards, 145; and arsenic levels, 33; and cap-and-trade emissions programs, 153, 160; and clean air laws, 153; and emissions standards, 165–66, 167; and energy policy, 139, 140, 143, 144, 154, 156; and evangelical Christians, 248; and Nixon, 20; nonenforcement of liberal policies on, 144; and Reagan, 26; regulations for, 4, 141, 144, 145, 146, 170;

and water quality, 2, 31; and William Jefferson Clinton, 31. *See also* conservation; global warming

environmentalists: and Abraham, 148; and Arctic National Wildlife Reserve, 147; and Clean Air Act of 1990, 145; and energy policy, 143, 153; and energy task force, 152; and global warming, 146; and New Source Review, 158

Environmental Policy Council, 221

Environmental Protection Act, 141

Environmental Protection Agency (EPA): and auto emissions, 164, 165; and California emissions standards, 165–66; cuts in staff of, 156; and greenhouse gases, 164; and Hurricane Katrina, 195–96; and New Source Review, 157, 159, 163, 164; and presidential appointments, 144, 159, 221

equal protection clause, 41

Erdogan, Recep Tayyip, 258

ergonomics, 175–76, 178

ethanol, 162, 165

Ethics & Religious Liberty Commission, 240

Ethics in Government Act, 25, 28

Ethiopia, 84–85

European Union, 266

evangelicalism: and Africa, 353n13; and conservatism, 7, 292, 299, 301; and DiIulio, 237; diversity in, 248; and ecumenism, 257; and election of 2004, 278; ethos of, 171; and expertise, 224; and Obama, 250; political support from, 229, 230; and same-sex marriage, 244; and taxes, 293. *See also* Christians

Evans, Donald, 256

Evans, Richard T., 186

Evans, Stanton, 208

executive orders: and Clinton, 31, 33; and energy policy, 153–54; and GB, 33; by Reagan, 26

executive privilege, 19, 31; and Cheney, 32, 33, 70–71, 153, 154, 155–56; and energy policy, 153; and September 11 attacks, 154. *See also* presidency; unitary executive

expertise, 199–226; denigration of, 200–201, 204, 211–26; and political choice,

202–4; post-Civil War development of, 205; and privilege, 208; professional and scientific, 200, 204; and Progressive movement, 205; as unbiased, 206–7

Exxon Mobile, 171

Fair Labor Standards Act, 177
faith-based initiative, 228, 233–39, 251, 265, 273, 277. *See also* religion
faith-based institutions, 285
faith-based organizations, 231–32
faith-based programs, 215
Falwell, Jerry, 227, 228, 237, 240, 242, 249, 251
Family and Medical Leave Act, 57
Family Health International AIDS Institute, 241
family planning groups, 33
Family Research Council, 240, 243
Fannie Mae, 135, 136
Federal Advisory Committee Act, 151
federal budget, 118
Federal Bureau of Investigation (FBI), 23, 68, 70, 75
federal debt, 116, 117, 118, 132, 134, 294
federal deficit: Clinton's reduction of, 118; and Democratic reforms, 133; and economic crisis, 134, 136–37; growth of, 116, 124; and Reagan, 294; reduction of, 115, 117; and social programs, 125; and tax policy, 114, 132; and war and reconstruction in Iraq, 126
Federal Election Commission, 228
Federal Emergency Management Agency (FEMA), 194–95, 220, 274, 279
Federal Energy Administration, 142
federalism, 56, 57
Federalist Society, 27, 53, 54, 202, 203, 224, 301
Federal Motor Carrier Safety Administration, 195
Federal Reserve Board, 21, 118, 133–34, 135, 136, 223
federal surplus, 118, 119, 124
Feinstein, Dianne, 166
feminism, 8, 353n16. *See also* women
Feulner, Edwin, 172
financial crisis, 114, 197–98, 222, 297–98, 302. *See also* economy

fiscal policy, 114
Fitton, Thomas, 156
Fleisher, Ari, 153, 155
Florida, 2, 209–10, 277
Focus on the Family, 240, 243, 250
Ford, Gerald: and Cambodia, 22; and Cheney, 33, 70, 155; and CIA, 23; and Congress, 21, 22; and conservative policymakers, 6, 20; and Economic Policy Board, 21; and energy policy, 141, 142–43, 168; and presidency, 25, 28; and Scalia, 155; and science advisor, 209; and Scowcroft, 102; and supply-side economics, 115; vetoes of, 21
Foreign Intelligence Surveillance Act (FISA), 23, 34, 69, 70
Foreign Intelligence Surveillance Act (FISA) Court, 68, 69, 86
Fortress America, 254, 260, 262
Fourth Circuit Court of Appeals, 48, 50–51
Fox, Vicente, 267
Fox News, 203, 224, 225, 301
Frachon, Alain, 95
France, 91, 95, 106–7, 111
Franks, Tommy, 71, 94–95, 99, 100
Freddie Mac, 135, 136
Freedom of Information Act, 154
Freeh, Louis, 61, 62
free trade, 171, 173, 266
Free Trade Area of the Americas, 267
Friedman, Milton, 125–26, 190, 290
Front Porch Alliance, 231
Frum, David, 230, 242, 299
fuel: alternative, 143; price of, 146, 161, 166–67; refinement and emissions standards for, 195–96; renewable, 165; synthetic, 143. *See also* energy
fuel assistance, 161
fuel economy, 140, 143, 146, 164, 165
fuel efficiency, 148, 149, 153, 165, 167
Fukuyama, Francis, 296
Fulbright, William, 15, 21

Gallo, Columba Garnica, 256
Gardez, 72
Garrison, William Lloyd, 284
Garza, Tony, 263
Gates, Bill, 122, 125
Gates, Robert, 83

gay rights, 353n16; and Catholic voters, 287; and conservatism, 286, 292, 298; and electoral strategy, 251; and evangelicalism, 278; and Frum, 299; and *Lawrence v. Texas,* 56, 242–43; and religious conservatism, 228, 242–45

Gaza, 83

General Motors, 136, 147, 171

Generation X, 190

Geneva Conventions, 35, 43, 50, 85, 86

George C. Marshall Institute, 202

German Americans, 269–70

Germany, 95, 280

Gerson, Michael, 282–83, 284–85, 302

Gingrich, Newt, 31, 117, 156, 183, 237, 298

Giuliani, Rudolph, 297

Glass-Steagall Act, 134

Global Fund to Fight AIDS, Malaria and Tuberculosis, 241

globalization, 131

global warming, 302; Democratic success with, 297; and disdain for expertise, 213–14, 221; and evangelical Christians, 248; growth in concern over, 146, 148, 149, 165. *See also* environment

Golden, Tim, 42

Golden Rule Insurance Company, 184

Goldsmith, Jack, 45, 81, 85

Goldsmith, Stephen, 231

Goldstein, Thomas, 53

Goldwater, Barry, 13, 190; and Buckley, 288; and conservatism, 289, 299–300; extremism of, 10, 188; and power, 293–94; and Reagan, 291; and Watergate Babies, 21

Gonzales, Alberto, 34, 81, 211, 222, 269

Gonzales v. Carhart (Carhart II), 55

Goodman, John, 184

Gorbachev, Mikhail, 91, 291

Gordon, Michael, 109

Gore, Albert, Jr., 2, 191, 286, 300; and dispute over Florida vote, 209, 210; and election of 2000, 41; and environment, 146, 164–65; and faith-based organizations, 231–32; and tax policy, 118; and terrorism, 61

Gorsuch, Ann, 144

Gottfried, Kurt, 212–13

Government Accountability Office (GAO), 151, 155

Graham, Phil, 182

Gramm-Leach-Bailey Act (1999), 134

Great Britain: and axis of evil speech, 95; and Iraqi weapons of mass destruction, 101; and Iraq War, 89; and Iraq War plans, 95–100, 106; and public opinion, 105; support for Iraq war by, 108; troop buildup by, 107

Great Depression, 281

Great Society, 7–8, 208, 277, 293, 298

Green, John, 244

greenhouse gas emissions, 165, 221

Greenspan, Alan, 118, 119, 125, 135, 141, 188

Greenspan Commission, 191

Group of Seven, 67–68

Grutter v. Bollinger, 55

Guantánamo Bay, Cuba: and criticism of, 87; establishment of detention facility at, 45, 74–75; and Geneva Conventions, 35; and *habeas corpus,* 47; improper treatment at, 50; and limits of war, 52; and military tribunals, 48; and Obama, 36; and secret prisons, 85. *See also* detainees

Gulf Coast, 274

Gulf of Tonkin resolution, 110

Gulf War. *See* Persian Gulf War (1991)

gun regulations, 40, 44, 54, 56

Haass, Richard, 89, 326n23

habeas corpus, 47, 48, 49, 52

Hagel, Chuck, 106, 112, 148, 182

Haggard, Ted, 248

Halliburton, 147, 170

Hamas, 83

Hamdan v. Rumsfeld, 35, 49–50, 85

Hamdi, Yasser Esam, 48–49

Hamdi v. Rumsfeld, 49, 81–82

Hanna, Marcus Alonzo, 287, 358n67

Harnage, Bobby L., 181

Hart, Jeffrey, 20

health care: consumer-driven, 183; costs of, 129; Democratic success with, 297; and evangelical Christians, 248; government-run or -mandated, 184; and Hillary Clinton, 150–51; policy for, 170; reform of, 13; support of, 117; and Wal-Mart, 176; and William Jefferson Clinton, 30–31 health insurance, 171, 183, 184; consumer-driven, 187; lack of, 129; national, 197; state-funded catastrophic, 299

health savings accounts (HSAs), 183–87

Heritage Foundation, 172, 173, 177, 195, 202, 203, 223, 225

Herman, Susan N., 57

Hernandez, Israel, 257

Hersh, Seymour, 24

Hertzberg, Hendrik, 269

Hezbollah, 60, 77, 83

Hispanics: affiliation of, 252; and attorney general appointment, 253, 268, 269; Catholic, 258; and election of 2004, 271, 274, 278; GB's comfort with, 262; immigrant, 6; and immigrants, 275; and multiculturalism, 267–68; and No Child Left Behind Act, 272; and Republican Party, 264–65, 276. See also Latinos; Mexican Americans

Hitchens, Christopher, 296

HIV/AIDS summit, 249

Holmstead, Jeffrey, 159–60

Home Depot, 171

Homeland Security Administration, 128, 180, 182

Hoover, Herbert, 287

Horowitz, Michael, 237

Horton, Willie, 259

hospitality sector, 169

hotels, 170, 177

House Energy and Commerce Committee, 167

House Intelligence Committee, 23, 24

housing, 135, 196–97

Hoyer, Steny, 193

Huckabee, Mike, 297

Hudson Institute, 237

Humphrey, Hubert, 296, 297

Hurricane Katrina, 11, 279; and conservatives, 278; and federal appointments, 274; federal response to, 14, 169, 193–97, 220, 223; and federal spending, 122; and labor standards, 179; and oil industry, 162, 163

Hussein, Saddam, 61, 93, 94; and al Qaeda, 101–2, 217; and bin Laden, 111; and Blair, 96; containment of, 91; early case against, 90; and Iran, 111; and Kuwait, 145; and neoconservatives, 92; rejec-tion of United Nations resolutions by, 97, 99; responsibility of, 112–13; and Rumsfeld, 90, 93; sanctions against, 90; as threat, 99, 104, 105, 106; and United Nations Resolution 1441, 106, 111; and weapons inspections, 97, 216; and weapons of mass destruc-tion, 76, 90, 98, 99, 100–101, 105, 111, 216, 217, 218, 223; and William Jeffer-son Clinton, 216; and Wolfowitz, 91, 93

Hybels, Bill, 248–49

Hyde, Henry, 241

illegal enemy combatants, 44–45. See also detainees

immigrants, 6, 254; and citizenship, 275; and conservatism, 298; deportation of, 276; effect of Proposition 187 on, 260, 262; Hispanic, 275; and Hispanic vote, 265; illegal, 260, 275; and income, 131; Latino, 261; legal status for undocu-mented, 286; Mexican, 257, 260, 262; Noonan on, 284; and Perot, 262; and social mobility, 132

immigration, 252–53; and business, 286; and health insurance, 129; and law, 6, 46; and reform, 277; and Republican Party, 281; restrictions on, 270–71

Immigration and Naturalization Service, 46

imports, 129

independent counsel law, 30

Independent Counsel Reauthorization Act, 28

independent prosecutor law, 25, 28–29, 32

India, 83, 86

individual retirement account, 183

inequality, of income, 114, 122, 124, 130–32. See also wages

inflation, 115, 117, 129

insurance sector, 177, 185

intellectuals, 209

intelligence: congressional oversight of, 70; coordination of foreign and domestic, 80; court monitoring of, 23–24; and humane treatment of detainees, 85; and Iraq War planning, 217–18. See also surveillance intelligence community, 79; and Hussein and al Qaeda, 101–2; and Iraqi weapons of mass destruction, 100, 101; and Iraq War, 216, 217. *See also* Central Intelligence Agency (CIA); Federal Bureau of Investigation (FBI)

Intelligence Oversight Board, 22

intelligent design, 202, 204

interest rates, 118, 127, 136

Internal Revenue Service, 228

International Longshore and Warehouse Union, 172

international nuclear freeze movement, 9

international peacekeeping missions, 2

Internet, 51, 224, 225

Internet stock market bubble, 192

interrogation, 4, 36; by CIA, 85; and Congress, 43; humane treatment in, 85; and Office of Legal Council, 43. *See also* torture

investment, 133, 134, 265

investment firms, 298

investors, 114, 115, 123–24, 266

Iran, 77, 104; and axis of evil, 73, 95; and Cheney, 94; and Hezbollah, 83; and Hussein, 111; and Reagan, 77

Iran–Contra arms scandal, 28, 32–33, 70

Iran–Contra Committee, 28

Iran–Contra hearings, 33

Iranian Revolution, 143

Iraq, 45; and al Qaeda, 76–77, 100, 107; and axis of evil, 73, 95; and Blair, 96, 97; chaos in, 219; and chemical or biological weapons, 90; and Cheney, 94; Clinton's bombing of, 91; containment of, 99, 102; control of, 79; counterinsurgency strategy in, 113; damage caused by war in, 14; death of citizens of, 89; and Great Britain, 89, 95–100, 101, 106, 108; invasion of, 77, 88–113; justification of war on, 98; and Kuwait, 29, 105, 145; and military preemption, 76; mishandling of, 87; and National Security Council, 92; nation building in, 4; and no-fly zones, 91; and Obama, 12; occupation of, 218, 219; political factions in, 113; and Powell, 90, 112; Provisional Government in, 279; and public opinion, 97; reconstruction of, 11, 274, 280;

and Rice, 96; and September 11 attacks, 92, 93, 217; Sunnis vs. Shi'ites in, 107; Sunni warlords in, 83; and Tenet, 93; terrorism in, 82, 87; tough posture toward, 2; United Nations arms and economic embargo on, 90; United Nations inspections of, 99–100; and United Nations Security Council, 91; and weapons of mass destruction, 78, 95, 97, 99, 105, 108; and Wolfowitz, 91

Iraq War, 4, 223; and Afghan war, 102; allied opposition to, 89; American causalties in, 88; American military misgivings about, 102; and Buchanan, 283; as Bush's war, 112; and choice vs. necessity, 89; and Congress, 105–6, 111, 287; and conservatism, 293, 296; cost of, 332n49; damage done by, 113; and Democrats, 105; demonstrations against, 107, 110; and federal spending, 122, 124, 128; Gerson on, 285; initiation of, 107–8; international opinion about, 106; international support for, 96, 99; and multicultural program, 277; and neoconservatives, 103, 296; and Noonan, 283–84; and oil prices, 161; permissive context for, 109; planning for, 94–100, 104, 216–18, 347n24; public opinion about, 89, 100, 104, 107, 110–11, 112, 287; and Republican Party, 103, 105, 297; selling of, 100–107; and tax policy, 126, 273; troop buildup for, 106, 107; and troop surge, 13, 83–84, 112–13, 297; and United Nations, 106–7

Islam, 269. *See also* Muslims

Islamic Court Union (ICU), 84–85

Islamic extremism, 66, 73, 86

Israel, 83, 91, 103, 291

Ivins, Bruce E., 320n25

Jackson, Robert, 311n11

Jacksonian democracy, 224

Japan, 280

Japanese, 47, 270

Japanese Americans, 269, 270

Jeffords, James, 10, 159

Jemaah Islamiyah, 87

Jesus Christ, 229–30, 257–58

Jews, 233, 238, 258, 290, 291

jobs, 119, 149
John Birch Society, 190, 288
Johnson, Lyndon, 288, 293, 296; and executive power, 16, 70; and race, 298; and research, 206; and spending, 294; and Supreme Court, 53; and Vietnam, 20–21; and Vietnam War, 277
Joint Chiefs of Staff, 80
journalists/journalism, 202, 203, 207, 212, 214, 217, 219. *See also* media
J. P. Morgan Chase, 135
judges, federal, 44
judicial appointments, 211
judicial restraint, 53
judicial review, 44, 45
Judicial Watch, 151, 155
Judis, John, 175

Kabul, 72
Kandahar, 72
Keck, Thomas, 56, 57
Keller, Bill, 287–88
Kelliher, Joseph, 158
Kemp, Jack, 115–16
Kennan, George F., 88, 102
Kennedy, Anthony, 52, 55
Kennedy, Edward, 23, 24, 272, 273
Kennedy, John F., 66, 206, 282
Kerry, John, 244, 250, 287, 293
Keynesianism, 115, 119, 121
Kilcullen, David, 322n52
Kilgore, Jerry, 284–86
King, Larry, 109
King, Martin Luther, Jr., 284
King, Peter, 149
King, Rodney, 260
Kirk, Russell, 290
Kissinger, Henry, 23, 92
Knight, Robert, 246
Knutson, Karen, 150
Koch, Fred, 190
Kohut, Andrew, 245
Korea, 64
Korematsu v. United States, 47
Kosovo, 32
Kotlikoff, Lawrence, 190
Krauthammer, Charles, 92, 296
Kristol, Irving, 141–42, 208
Krugman, Paul, 180, 197, 203, 212
Kuhn, Thomas, 157

Kuo, David, 238, 239, 277
Kurds, 90
Kuttner, Robert, 187–88
Kuwait, 29, 90, 105, 145
Kyoto Protocol, 148, 213

Labash, Matt, 202
labor, 253; and Hurricane Katrina, 195; and women, 131. *See also* workers
labor laws, 177–79, 188, 295
labor-management conflicts, 172
labor market, 194
labor policy, 170
labor standards, 174, 197
Lackawanna or Buffalo Six, 86
Lampley, Peter, 241
Land, Richard, 230, 235, 250
Latin America, 261, 266
Latinos, 2, 254; Catholic, 233; and election of 2004, 287; and election of 2008, 298; GB's comfort with, 254, 257; immigrant, 261; and Obama, 300. *See also* Hispanics; Mexican Americans
law, 39–58; and avoidance of terrorist attacks, 45–46; basic conception of, 39; and counterterrorism, 85; and environment after September 11 attacks, 46; and security, 46–47; sovereign as, 46; as tool of power, 46; and torture, 74, 75; and war, 46; and war on terror, 39, 46–47
Lawrence v. Texas, 56, 242–43
Lay, Kenneth, 141, 151–52, 154
Lázaro Cárdenas, 266–67
Leach, James, 30
League of Conservation Voters, 148
Lebanon, 77, 83
Lehman Brothers, 135, 136, 137
Leninism, 296
Leon, Richard J., 52
Lessner, Richard, 243
Levin, Carl, 30, 166
Levitte, Jean-David, 106
Lewinsky, Monica, 292
Lewis, Anthony, 264
Lewis, Bernard, 94
Lewis, Jackson, 178
Libby, Lewis, 34
liberal evangelicals, 250
liberal internationalists, 104–5

minorities, 259; affiliation of, 252; appointment of, 2, 14, 253, 268–69, 280; and No Child Left Behind Act, 272, 273; and Rove, 252, 261. *See also* African Americans; Hispanics; Latinos; Mexican Americans; race
missile defense, 61
missile shield program, 2
Mogadishu, 84
Mohammed, Khalid Sheik, 44, 77
Mondale, Walter, 133
Moore, Stephen, 185
morality, 199, 228, 245–46, 259
Moral Majority, 227, 228
Morrison, Steve, 242
Morrison v. Olson, 29
mortgages, 135, 137, 280
Moynihan, Daniel Patrick, 191
MSNBC, 224, 225
MTBE, 162
Mueller, Robert, 81
Mukasey, Michael, 222
multiculturalism, 254, 258–65, 280; collapse of program of, 276–81; and disdain for public governance, 273; and No Child Left Behind Act, 271–73; and presidential appointments, 268–69; and trade, 265–68
multilateralism, 2
Mumbai, India, 86
Murkowski, Frank, 148, 150
Musharraf, Pervez, 65
Muslims, 79, 87, 238, 258, 269–71. *See also* Islam

Nadler, Jerry, 235
Nairobi, U.S. embassies in, 60, 62
NASA, 221
National Academy of Sciences, 214
National Association of Evangelicals (NAE), 235–36, 240, 248
National Association of Manufacturers, 175
National Association of People with AIDS, 242
National Center for Policy Analysis, 184
National Commission on Terrorist Attacks Upon the United States, 46, 67, 79, 80
National Commitments Resolution, 21
National Endowment for the Arts, 259

National Endowment for the Humanities, 259
National Energy Policy Development Group, 139, 150
national forests, 31
National Guard, 194
National Intelligence Estimate, 105, 110
National Religious Broadcasters, 240
National Resources Defense Council, 151, 158
National Retail Federation, 175, 178
National Review, 288, 290
national security, 4–5; and Cheney, 71; and energy policy, 150; and federalism, 57; pre-September 11 attacks, 61–62; and Reagan, 9; and secrecy, 41; and strong presidency, 35; structure of, 79
national security advisor, office of, 268
National Security Agency, 24
National Security Council (NSC), 85, 98, 207; and Blue Sky memorandum, 64; discussions of Iraq by, 90; and Ford, 23; and Iran–Contra arms scandal, 28; and Iraq, 92; and Iraqi weapons of mass destruction, 100; and Iraq War plans, 106; and terrorist financing, 67
National Security Presidential Decision 9, 66
National Security Presidential Directive, 99
national security state, 20–25, 294
National Security Strategy, 76, 79
"National Strategy for Combating Terrorism," 83
nation building, 4, 31
Negroponte, John, 106
neoconservatism, 91–92, 104, 209; and abortion, 293; and Blair, 96; and foreign policy, 290; and Giuliani, 297; and Great Society, 8; and Iraq War, 103, 296; and Israel, 103; and Kristol, 141; origins of, 208; and Reagan, 9; rise of, 290–91; and role of government, 291. *See also* conservatism
neoliberalism, 169, 190, 266
Newbold, Gregory, 102
New Deal, 8, 13, 56, 169, 187, 197, 288, 293, 301
New Left, 16, 224, 289
New Orleans, 274, 284
New Right, 56, 224

New Source Review (NSR), 156, 157, 158, 159, 160, 163, 164, 168
New York Times, 109, 225
Nicaraguan Contras, 28
Nike, 171
9/11 Commission. *See* National Commission on Terrorist Attacks Upon the United States
Nixon, Richard, 6, 28, 37, 201, 203, 223; abuse of power by, 70; anti-intellectualism of, 209; appointments of, 4; and China, 20; and communism, 20; and Congress, 18–20; and conservatism, 17–20; covert programs of, 19; and domestic policy of, 19, 20; environmental policy of, 20; and executive privilege, 19, 153; and expertise, 211; and Ford, 22; foreign policy of, 19, 20; and Fulbright, 21; and liberalism, 18, 20; and presidential power, 16, 17–20, 22; and Project Independence, 141; and Reagan, 25; and Saturday Night Massacre, 25; and Social Security, 19, 20; Southeast Asia policy of, 19; and Soviet Union, 20; and Supreme Court, 53–54; and Watergate process, 19
No Child Left Behind (NCLB) Act, 2, 5–6, 57–58, 253–54, 271–73, 277, 280
nondelegation doctrine, 26
Noonan, Peggy, 282–84, 285, 289, 295, 298, 302
Norquist, Grover, 116, 164, 172–73
North, Oliver, 28
North American Free Trade Agreement (NAFTA), 262, 267
Northeast, 3
Northern Alliance, 63, 64, 71, 72, 75, 319n6
North Korea, 2, 73, 82–83, 94, 95, 104
Northridge earthquake, 196
Northwest Airlines, 172

Obama, Barack, 133, 167, 197, 301; and Congress, 36–37; and conservatism, 13; and economic crisis, 137; and election of 2008, 12; and energy policy, 167; and expertise, 223; and liberalism, 289; and McCain, 297; and multiculturalism, 269; and release of interrogation photographs, 37; and religious issues, 249, 250; and treatment of detainees, 37;

victory of, 296; and working class, 300; and young people, 300
O'Connor, Sandra Day, 48, 53, 55, 220
Office of Faith-Based and Community Initiatives, 119
Office of Foreign Assets Control, 67
Office of Homeland Security, 69
Office of Legal Council (OLC), 29, 42, 43, 45, 81
Office of Management and Budget (OMB), 21, 26
Office of National AIDS Policy, 240
Office of the Independent Counsel, 6, 27, 30
Office of the Independent Prosecutor, 25, 28–29
Office of the Vice President, 34
Ohio, 245
oil, 103, 144; and Carter Doctrine, 145; dependence on foreign, 139, 141–42, 144, 145, 148, 162; domestic production of, 139, 142, 144, 145, 147; and energy task force, 153; imports of, 141, 145; offshore drilling for, 167; and Persian Gulf War, 145; price controls on, 144, 168; price of, 129, 161, 166, 256; regulations on, 142–43; subsidies for, 163. *See also* energy
oil and gas sector, 3, 170
oil industry, 143, 151; and Bush family, 255, 256; and Cheney energy task force, 155; and energy task force, 152; and pipeline safety, 161; price controls on, 141; profits of, 167, 171; record profits of, 162–63. *See also* energy industry
oil lobby, 143
oil markets, 140
oil refineries legislation, 163
oil shock, of 1979, 143
Oklahoma City bombing, 220
Olasky, Marvin, 230, 354n18
Olbermann, Keith, 224
Olsen, Theodore, 156
Omar, Mullah, 64, 65, 71, 72
O'Neill, Paul, 90, 119, 125, 126, 191, 347n24
OPEC, 256
Operation Blessing, 238–39
Operation Rescue, 246
originalism, 54

overtime laws, 177–79
ownership society, 183, 185, 197, 280

Padilla, Jose, 49–50, 75, 321n36
Padilla v. Hanft, 51
Page, Frank, 248
Pakistan, 67; and al Qaeda, 62, 65; and atomic weapons, 63; intelligence service of, 63, 65, 74; military of, 63; and September 11 attacks, 65; and Taliban, 65; and William Jefferson Clinton, 63
Palestinian resistance, 291
Palin, Sarah, 12, 167, 249, 298, 300
Parents Involved in Community Schools v. Seattle School District, 56
Parsley, Rod, 245
Pashtuns, 64, 72
Paulson, Henry, 222–23
Pavone, Frank, 246
Pelosi, Nancy, 167
Penny, Tim, 191
Pentagon Papers, 19
Pepper, Claude, 189
Perkins, Frances, 173
Perkins, Tony, 240, 249
Perle, Richard, 93, 112
Permian oil fields, 254, 256, 257
Perot, Ross, 262
Persian Gulf, militarization of, 139, 144–45, 168
Persian Gulf War (1991), 76, 90, 102, 105, 140, 145, 161
Peter, Charles, 190
Petraeus, David, 83, 322n52
Pew Forum on Religion and Public Life, 248
Pew Research Center, 245
pharmaceutical makers, 185. *See also* prescription drugs
Philippines, 87
Pike, Otis, 23
Pinera, Jose, 190
Pinochet, Augusto, 190
Planned Parenthood of Southeastern Pennsylvania v. Casey, 54–55
Podhoretz, Norman, 208
Poindexter, John, 28
pollution controls, 146, 153, 156–60. *See also* environment
Popular Front for the Liberation of Palestine, 65

postmodernism, 204, 210
post-Watergate era, 41
poverty, 230, 259, 261, 268, 280; in Africa, 353n13; and aid, 189; Gerson on, 285; and Hispanic voters, 265; programs for, 231; rate of, 129
Powell, Colin, 89; appointment of, 268, 269; and Cheney, 100; and Iraq, 90; and Iraq War plans, 112; and military, 92; and Pakistan, 65; speech to United Nations, February 5, 2003, 107, 109; and United Nations inspections, 99–100
Powers, Thomas, 93
Predator, 62–63, 72, 80
prescription drugs, 127, 183, 184–85, 293, 294
presidency, 27; autonomy of, 40; and Cheney, 32, 33, 70–71, 153, 154, 155–56; congressional reform of, 21; and conservatives, 10, 15–38; and election of 2008, 12; and energy policy, 153; expanding authority of, 6–7; extraconstitutional powers and common abuses of, 21; and judicial review, 44, 53–54; post-Vietnam and Watergate restraints on, 70; power of, 15–38; public satisfaction with, 36; restraints on, 87; and support of Congress, 43; and unitary executive, 27, 29, 32, 43, 44, 49, 311n11; and war on terrorism, 42; and William Jefferson Clinton, 30–32. *See also* executive orders; executive privilege
president: authority to use armed forces, 29–30; and Constitution, 43; executive power of, 43; total control over the executive branch by, 27; war power of, 34
presidential signing statements, 35
price controls, 163
price stability, 118
Priests for Life, 246
Principals Committee, 62
prisoners of war, 85. *See also* detainees
prisons, secret, 74, 85. *See also* Guantánamo Bay, Cuba
privacy, 69, 87
professionals, 205, 207, 300. *See also* expertise
Progressive Era, 6, 8, 200, 207, 218
Progressive movement, 205, 277
Progressives, 169, 174

Project Independence, 141–43, 145
Proposition 13, mobilization behind, 115
Proposition 187, effects of, 260, 262
Protestants, 232, 233, 250. *See also* Christians
public opinion: and energy policy, 149–50, 161, 164–65; and environment vs. economy, 166; and health care, 184; about Iraq War, 89, 100, 104, 110–11, 112; and Schiavo case, 247; and Social Security reform, 192, 193
Putin, Vladimir, 258

Quayle, James Danforth, 147
Quebec, 267

race, 8, 54–55, 253; and conservatism, 290; and diversity, 2, 264; elimination of inequities of, 280; and Franklin Roosevelt, 298; and income inequality, 131; and Johnson, 298; and No Child Left Behind Act, 271, 272, 273; and Obama, 300. *See also* minorities
racism, 259
Radio Shack, 177
Radzely, Howard M., 176
Rand, Ayn, 289–90
Rasul v. Bush, 47–48, 81–82
Reagan, Ronald, 11, 197, 282, 300; and abortion, 239; anticommunism and populism of, 300; and antigovernment rhetoric, 161, 294; appointments of, 4, 159; and Arctic National Wildlife Reserve, 147; and Central America, 26; and Cheney, 33, 71; and conservatism, 8, 25–30, 32, 223, 286, 293, 300–301; and deficits, 118, 294; and deregulation, 134; election of, 289; and energy policy, 143, 144–46; and environment, 26; executive orders by, 26; and expertise, 201, 211; and federal debt, 294; and federal spending and employees, 294; and Hezbollah, 77; and Hispanics, 264–65; and income inequality, 130; and independent prosecutor law, 28–29; and independent voters, 278; Keller on, 288; and Libya, 77; and market fundamentalism, 279; and national security state, 294; and neoconservatives, 91; and Nixon, 20; and Noonan, 283; Obama

on, 13; and Office of Management and Budget, 26; personality of, 287; and policy change, 156; and presidential power, 25–30; and Project Independence, 141; and Republican Party, 297; and Robison, 229; and social programs, 294; and Social Security, 26, 188; and Soviet Union, 26, 91; and supply-side economics, 115, 116; and taxes, 116, 117, 121, 123, 131, 294; and trade unions, 172; and unity of conservatives, 291, 292; and working class, 6
Reagan Revolution, 1
recession, 116, 118–19, 133, 197, 291, 297, 301. *See also* economy
Red Scare, 270
Reed, Ralph, 238, 244
regulation, 58, 137; and economy, 8, 134–35, 169; and energy policy, 139, 144, 153, 156, 168; and Enron, 154; and environment, 4, 139, 140, 141, 143, 144, 145, 168, 170; and global warming, 213; and Hoover and Coolidge, 287; and Hurricane Katrina, 195; nonenforcement of, 140; and retailers, 171; and Union of the Americas, 266; and Wal-Mart, 176; weak, 265; in workplace, 4. *See also* deregulation
Rehnquist, William, 29, 56, 57
Rehnquist Court, 57
relativism, 199, 203–4, 209
religion, 58, 204, 219, 227–51, 257–58, 280; and Buchanan, 292; and cabinet-level offices, 234, 238; and conservatism, 290; and Hispanics, 264, 265; neoconservatives and, 290; and welfare, 253, 254. *See also* faith-based initiative
religious and community organizations, 231
religious conservatives: and election of 2000, 233; and faith-based initiative, 239; and faith-based offices, 238; and *Lawrence v. Texas,* 243; and Robison, 229; and same-sex marriage, 243–45; and Schiavo case, 246, 247, 248; and William Jefferson Clinton, 227–28. *See also* conservatism
Religious Right: and abortion, 240; and AIDS issue, 241, 242; and Cizik, 248; and conservatism, 7, 227; and conservative base, 239; and election of 2000,

232, 233; and election of 2004, 251; and faith-based initiative, 234–35, 237; and faith-based offices, 238; and McCain, 249–50; and politics, 229, 230; and social issues, 246; and stem-cell research, 213; and Weyrich, 228

Rendon, Paula, 255–56

Reno, Janet, 30

Republican coalition, 11

Republican National Committee, 244

Republican Party, 201; and Afghan war, 103; and African Americans, 252, 268, 274; and airport screeners, 179–80; big-tent strategy for, 277, 278, 281; and Buchanan, 291–92; and bureaucracies, 279; and Clear Skies, 160; coalition of, 6; and Congress, 3; and conservatism, 283, 290, 291, 299, 301; and cultural politics, 254; and disdain for public governance, 273–74, 279–80; durable majority for, 293; and economy, 279; and election of 1964, 299; and election of 2000, 277–78; and election of 2008, 296, 297; and elections of 2006, 284; and energy policy, 146, 148, 149, 150, 167; and energy task force, 152, 155; and executive power, 28; and faith-based initiative, 236–37; and fiscal policy, 114, 116; and Hispanics, 252, 264–65, 276; and immigrant policy, 275; and immigration, 281; and Iran–Contra arms scandal, 28; and Iraq War, 103, 105; and Lewinsky scandal, 292; and moral absolutism and relativism, 199; and multiculturalism, 275, 280; nativism in, 271, 281, 298; and No Child Left Behind Act, 272; permanent majority for, 252, 261, 273, 278; and poverty, 230; and prescription drugs, 184, 185; and presidency, 30; and Project Independence, 141; and Reagan, 297; and religious issues, 238, 246; and religious voters, 227; and same-sex marriage, 244; and Schiavo case, 247; and September 11 attacks, 103, 287; and Social Security, 188, 193; and South, 3; and supply-side economics, 115; and tax cuts, 117, 120; and tax policy, 126; and Wal-Mart, 171; and welfare, 253; and William Jefferson Clinton, 30, 31

Ressam, Ahmed, 60–61

restaurant sector, 169, 170

Retail Industry Leaders Association, 176

retail sector, 169–70, 171, 173, 177

Reyes family, 256

Rice, Condoleezza, 326n23; appointment of, 268, 269; and Clarke, 61–62; and counterterrorism, 85; and Iraq, 96; and Iraq War plans, 94, 112; and 9/11 Commission, 79; and rogue states, 82; and Scowcroft, 102

Rich, Frank, 103–4

Richardson, William, 161

Ricketts, Sir Peter, 97

Ricks, Thomas, 109

Ridge, Thomas, 69

Rivers, Eugene, 237

Roberts, John G., 56, 57, 221

Roberts Court, 57

Robertson, Pat, 227, 235, 238–39, 244, 249, 291

Robinson, Kenneth, 24

Robison, James, 229

Rockefeller Republicans, 291, 294–95

Roe v. Wade, 54, 239, 293

rogue states, 76, 82

Romney, Mitt, 194, 297

Rooney, J. Patrick, 184

Roosevelt, Franklin D., 63–64, 197, 269, 282; and Brain Trust, 205; courtpacking plan of, 16; electoral success of, 359n11; executive reorganization by, 16; and presidential power, 15–16; and promise of security and freedom from fear, 295; and race, 298; and Reagan, 25

Roosevelt, Theodore, 6, 15

Rosenbaum, Ron, 210

Roth, William, 115–16

Rove, Karl: and economy, 119; and election of 2000, 277–78, 287; and faith-based initiative, 233, 235, 239; and Hanna, 358n67; and Hispanic voters, 264, 265; and minorities, 252, 261; and multiculturalism, 280; and No Child Left Behind Act, 272; and religious issues, 245; and Republican coalition, 6; and same-sex marriage, 286; and Social Security, 191, 199; and tax cuts, 286; and Tomlinson, 221; and U.S. attorneys, 222; and war on terror, 103–4, 181

Rumsfeld, Donald, 20, 23; and Afghan war, 71; and al Qaeda, 101; and counterterrorism, 85; and energy policy, 141; and force levels, 99; and Hussein, 90, 92, 93, 101; and Iraq War planning, 216, 217; and military reorganization, 65; replacement of, 83

Russert, Tim, 194, 230

Russia, 61, 91, 95, 106. *See also* Soviet Union

Ryan, Paul, 185

Saddleback Church, 249

Salam, Reihan, 299

SALT II, 24

Salvation Army, 235

Samuelson, Robert, 128

sarin gas, 60

Saturday Night Massacre, 25

Saudi Arabia, 291

Savage, Charlie, 41

Scalia, Antonin, 29, 40, 49, 155, 243

Scalia, Eugene, 175–76, 177

Schaeffer, Eric, 152–53, 156

Schiavo, Terri, 219–20, 246–47, 248, 251

Schlafly, Phyllis, 164

Schlesinger, Arthur, Jr., 15–16, 19

Schneider, Bill, 109

school busing, 288

school prayer, 288

Schudson, Michael, 207

science, 129, 200, 201, 202, 207, 209, 212–14

Scott, Lee, 195

Scowcroft, Brent, 102, 113

Second Amendment, 56

Second Circuit Court of Appeals, 50

secrecy, 41, 51; and Cheney, 153; of domestic surveillance, 69, 70; and energy task force, 151–56; and torture policy, 44

Securities and Exchange Commission, 135, 279

Sekulow, Jay, 244

Senate Energy and Natural Resources Committee, 150

Senate Environment and Public Works Committee, 159

Senate filibuster, 30

Senate Intelligence Committee, 23

separation of powers, 27, 29

September 11 attacks: and al Qaeda, 1, 93; and Congress, 42–43; and conservatism, 201, 292–93; cultural toleration after, 269; and energy policy, 150, 154; and fusion of law and war, 46; galvanizing effect of, 108; institutional change after, 68; and Iraq, 92, 93; and Iraqi officials, 217; and Iraq War planning, 218; and labor standards, 179–82; and multicultural program, 277; and presidential power, 4, 34; and religious issues, 251; and Republican Party, 5, 103, 287; response to, 64, 103; and secrecy, 41; and security, 69; and time limits of war, 52; and trade with Mexico, 267; and Yoo, 42

Serrano, Jorge Díaz, 255

service sector, 3, 131, 170

sexism, 259

sexuality, 7, 213

Sharif, Nawaz, 63

Shays, Chris, 247

Shayyaf, Abu, 87

Sheldon, Lou, 247

Shibh, Ramzi Bin al-, 75

Sierra Club, 155

Singapore, 87

Sister Souljah, 262

Snow, John, 126

social mobility, 132

social policy, 40

social problems: and compassionate conservatism, 228, 230

social programs: federal support for, 129; and Reagan, 294; subversion of, 115; and tax policy, 121, 124, 125

social sciences, 206, 212

Social Security, 195, 344n68; and Congress, 19; and Eisenhower, 295; funding of, 128, 189; and Gore, 118; and Nixon, 19, 20; privatization of, 127, 183, 187–93, 197, 219, 246, 295; and Reagan, 9, 26; social rationale of, 190; solvency of, 188, 190, 192; and tax policy, 124

Social Security Administration, 191

social services, 231, 234

Society for Worldwide Interbank Financial Telecommunications, 68

sodomy. *See* gay rights; *Lawrence v. Texas*

Somalia, 84–85

Sorensen, Theodore, 282
Sosa, Lionel, 264, 265
Soufan, Ali, 75
South, 3, 18, 21
Southeast Asia, 87
Southern Baptist Convention, 240, 248, 301
Southern Company, 157, 158
Southwest, 3
Soviet Union, 9, 70, 291; and invasion of Afghanistan, 145; and neoconservatives, 91; and Nixon, 20; and Reagan, 9, 26, 91. *See also* Russia
Spain, 78
Spanish language, 263
Special Forces, 71, 73
special prosecutor, 25. *See also* Office of the Independent Prosecutor
Specter, Arlen, 175
Spellings, Margaret, 236
Spitzer, Elliot, 157
spoils system, 205, 218
sport utility vehicles, 146
stagflation, 115
Starbucks, 177
state autonomy, 56–58
state sovereign immunity, 57
Steel seizure case, 311n11
Steiwer, Frederick, 16
stem-cell research, 2, 213
Stenberg v. Carhart (Carhart I), 55
Stevens, John Paul, 50
stock market, 129, 131, 137, 192
Stone, Geoffrey, 56
Straw, Jack, 97, 99
Sullivan, Amy, 244
Sullivan, Emmet, 155
Sullivan, Kathleen, 57
Sun Belt, 3
Sunnis, 83, 107
supply-side economics: and Democrats, 133; and economic crisis, 137; and economic downturn, 119; and energy task force, 152; and growth of government, 116; impact of, 4; principles of, 114–15; and tax policy, 120, 121, 123–24, 125, 127. *See also* economy
Supreme Court, 29, 85; appointments to, 39–40; authority of, 47, 48, 49, 50; and *Bush v. Gore,* 2; and Cheney energy

task force documents, 155–56; and conservatism, 53–58; conservatives on, 287; and detainees, 47–52, 81–82; and dispute over Florida vote, 210; and election of 2000, 40–41, 61; and electronic domestic surveillance, 24; and energy policy, 164; and limits on executive power, 47
surveillance, 22–24; authority for domestic, 68; and Congress, 86; and conservatism, 70; and datamining of telephone and Internet communications, 51; domestic, 23, 24, 34, 51, 68, 69, 70, 86; doubts about programs for, 81, 82; of Muslim and Arab communities, 269; national, 6, 35; and Terrorist Surveillance Program, 81; warrants for, 23, 51, 68, 69. *See also* intelligence
Suskind, Ron, 199, 215, 321n36, 347n24

Tajikistan, 67
Tajiks, 64
Taliban, 49, 52, 72, 287; and al Qaeda, 63, 93; and bin Laden, 71; campaign against, 94; and CIA, 63, 64; collapse of, 73; documents from, 102; and Pakistan, 65; and Pentagon, 72; resurgence of, 87; success against, 104; and William Jefferson Clinton, 63
Tanenhaus, Sam, 293, 302
Tanner, Michael, 191
tax breaks: for business, 174; and energy industry, 161; and energy policy, 163
tax credit: for charitable donations, 231; child, 120, 121; earned income, 292, 343n55; and energy policy, 150, 153
tax cuts, 114–15, 116; early action on, 2; and economic crisis, 137, 138; and economic inequality, 130; and economic recovery, 127; enactment of, 293; and growth of government, 115; and investment income and accumulated wealth, 125; and Iraq War, 273; and McCain, 133; and No Child Left Behind Act, 273; public support for, 132; and Reagan, 8; and Reagan Revolution, 1; and Rove, 286; and size of government, 126; and social programs, 273; and wealthy taxpayers, 4

unemployment insurance, 188, 189, 295
Uniform Code of Military Justice, 35, 50
Union of Concerned Scientists, 213
Union of the Americas (UA), 265–66, 280
unions: actions against, 172; and Bacon-
    Davis Act, 196; and collective bargain-
    ing, 181; decline of, 8, 130, 174, 301;
    and energy task force, 152; and finan-
    cial crisis, 198; legislation concerning,
    16; marginalization of, 179; and retail
    sector, 171; and Texas business elite,
    265; and war on terror, 182
unitary executive, 27, 29, 32, 43, 44, 49,
    311n11. See also presidency
United Airlines, 172
United Automobile Workers, 198
United Nations, 98; and AIDS issue, 241;
    and arms and economic embargo on
    Iraq, 90; arms inspections by, 106; and
    Blair, 99; Hussein's rejection of resolu-
    tions of, 97; inspections of Iraq by, 99–
    100; and Iraqi disarmament, 99; and
    Iraq War, 89, 106–7; and Iraq War
    planning, 108, 216–17; and military, 31;
    Resolution 1441, 111; weapons inspec-
    tions by, 97
United Nations Security Council, 108; and
    Iraqi weapons programs, 91; Resolu-
    tion 1441, 106; and terrorist funding,
    68; and Wolfowitz, 91
United We Stand America Conference, 262
University of Texas, 263–64
USA PATRIOT Act, 42–43, 68
U.S. attorneys, 222
U.S. Central Command (CENTCOM), 71,
    72–73, 95, 97, 99. See also military
U.S. Court of Appeals for the District of
    Columbia, 25, 29
U.S.-Mexican War of 1846–48, 260
Uzbekistan, 64, 67, 72

Values Voters Summit (2007), 249
Vander, Mara, 250
Veloz, George, 256
Vietnam War, 5, 9, 70, 109, 110, 142, 277,
    288
Villepin, Dominique de, 106–7
Vitter, David, 195
voting reform, 205
Voting Rights Act, 293

wages, 127; and airport screeners, 179–80;
    and Department of Homeland Security,
    196; growth in, 170; and Hurricane Ka-
    trina, 196; manufacturing, 130; mini-
    mum, 8, 174; and overtime, 177–78; in
    service sector, 131; and Social Security
    taxes, 189; and subsidies, 299; and Wal-
    Mart, 198. See also inequality, of in-
    come
Walke, John, 158
Walker, David M., 128, 153
Wall Street Journal, 301
Wal-Mart, 3; and health insurance, 176,
    186; and Hurricane Katrina, 194–95;
    and overtime pay, 177–78; and regula-
    tion, 171–72, 175; and wages, 198
Walsh, Lawrence, 28, 30
war, 39; laws of, 46; temporal limits of, 47,
    49, 52
War Powers Act (1973), 6, 19–20, 31, 70
War Powers Resolution, 22, 30
warrants, for domestic surveillance, 23, 68,
    69
Warren, Rick, 248, 249
Warren Court, 53
Washington Post, 109
waterboarding, 35, 36, 44. See also interro-
    gation; torture
Watergate, 36, 70, 141; and Congress, 6;
    congressional reforms after, 17; and ex-
    ecutive privilege, 153; and Nixon, 19;
    and Office of the Independent Prosecu-
    tor, 25
Watergate Babies, 21
Watt, James, 144, 159
Waxman, Henry A., 151, 167
weapons of mass destruction (WMD), 59,
    70; and axis of evil, 73; and bin Laden,
    63; and homegrown terrorist groups,
    78; and Hussein, 76, 90, 98, 99, 100–
    101, 105, 111, 216, 217, 218, 223; inter-
    national controls of, 76; and Iraq, 78,
    90, 95, 99, 105, 108
Wedtech Corporation, 27–28
Weinberger, Casper, 28
Weisberg, Jacob, 104, 258, 276–77
welfare: and conservatism, 290; and evan-
    gelical Christians, 248; faith-based, 265,
    273, 277; and Hispanic voters, 265; and
    William Jefferson Clinton, 289

welfare state, 10, 56, 183, 253; and conservatism, 295; and Latin America, 266; and multiculturalism, 259; and Nixon, 20
Wendy's International, 186
Weyrich, Paul, 228
white Catholics, 227, 232, 233, 287
white Christians, 227, 289, 300
white evangelicals, 227, 233, 250, 297
White House Office of Faith-Based and Community Initiatives (WHOFBCI), 233–34, 237–38
white Protestants, 232, 233
whites, 290, 291, 298
Whitewater Development Company, 30
Whitman, Christie Todd, 158–59
Wikipedia, 224
Wilentz, Sean, 13–14
Will, George, 15, 284
Willett, Don, 233
Willow Creek Association, 248
Wilson, Bob, 24
Wilson, Pete, 260–61, 262
Wilson, Woodrow, 205, 269, 277
wiretaps, 22, 70
Wittes, Benjamin, 48
Wolfe, Alan, 210, 295
Wolfowitz, Paul, 90, 91, 93, 94, 96, 324n7

women, 131, 172, 268, 287. *See also* feminism
Woodward, Bob, 94, 109
workers: blue-collar, 131; service sector, 177; white-collar, 131. *See also* labor
working class, 6, 8, 170
workplace: health and safety in, 22, 171, 175–76, 195; and regulation, 4
World War I, 269–70, 277
World War II, 47, 269–70
Wyden, Ron, 180
Wyne, Zaahira, 48

Y2K, 60
Yom Kippur War, 256
Yoo, John, 32, 34, 42, 43, 81
Young Americans for Freedom, 288
Youngstown Sheet & Tube Co. v. Sawyer, 311n11
Yugoslavia, former, 61

Zapata Petroleum Corporation, 255
Zarb, Frank, 142
Zarqawi, Abu Musab al-, 82
Zedillo, Ernesto, 262
Zelikow, Philip, 46, 85
Zubaydah, Abu, 74, 75, 321n36